▲▲▲▲▲▲▲▲▲▲▲▲▲▲▲▲▲▲▲

COMANCHE DAWN

▼▼▼▼▼▼▼▼▼▼▼▼▼▼▼▼▼▼▼

By Mike Blakely
▲▲▲▲▲▲▲▲▲▲▲▲▲▲▲▲▲▲
from Tom Doherty Associates

The Last Chance
Shortgrass Song
Too Long at the Dance
The Snowy Range Gang
Dead Reckoning
Spanish Blood

▲▲▲▲▲▲▲▲▲▲▲▲▲▲▲▲▲▲▲▲

COMANCHE DAWN

▼▼▼▼▼▼▼▼▼▼▼▼▼▼▼▼▼▼▼▼

Mike Blakely

A Tom Doherty Associates Book ▲▲▲ New York

COMANCHE DAWN

Copyright © 1998 by Mike Blakely

This book is printed on acid-free paper.

A Forge Book
Published by Tom Doherty Associates, Inc.
175 Fifth Avenue
New York, NY 10010

Forge® is a registered trademark of Tom Doherty Associates, Inc.

Design by Basha Durand

Library of Congress Cataloging-in-Publication Data

Blakely, Mike.
    Comanche dawn / Mike Blakely.—1st ed.
       p.   cm.
    "A Tom Doherty Associates book."
    ISBN 0-312-86575-9
    1. Comanche Indians—Fiction.   I. Title.
PS3552.L3533C6   1998   98-23738
813'.54—dc21   CIP

First Edition: October 1998

Printed in the United States of America

0 9 8 7 6 5 4 3 2 1

For London

▲▲▲▲▲▲▲

Acknowledgments
▲▲▲▲▲▲▲▲▲▲▲▲▲

For helping me get started on research for this work of fiction, I thank two anthropologist-novelist-rancher friends: W. Michael Gear and Kathleen Gear. For her guidance and assistance with final research, I thank my friend and fellow novelist, Lucia St. Clair Robson. For loaning me the right book at the right time, I am grateful to Russel Buster.

For sharing his firearms, flints, black powder, and expertise pertaining thereto, I am grateful to my friend and fellow fiction writer, C. F. Eckhardt.

For making the horse a part of my life, I would like to thank my parents, Doc Blakely and Patricia Dawn Blakely. Also, I thank two friends from whom I have bought horses—Mike Siler and Marty Akins—for rare is the friend from whom one can buy a horse and remain a friend. For sharing their horses and horse stories, I thank Jack Hankins, Joe Siler, Mike Siler, Kym Bartholomew, Buddy Reid, Henry Wobbe, Sonny Andersen, and Mary Elizabeth Goldman.

For helping me understand cultures outside of my own, I thank the Comanche people, the Shoshone people, the Gathering of Nations Pow-Wow, and the many other friends and acquaintances who have taken me into their family circles to share their cultures. Special thanks to Floyd, of Taos Pueblo, for loaning me a tall horse and showing me the old trails.

For their guts and faith, I am grateful to my colleagues in New York City: Joe Vallely, Bob Gleason, and Tom Doherty.

Special thanks to the library system of the University of Texas at Austin, my alma mater.

For my own satisfaction and none of their own, as they remain above the necessity for spoken gratitude, I thank three horses I have known: Red Wing, who often kicked, bit, threw me off, fell on me, and otherwise earned my affection. Big John, who set the standard in my mind for cooperation between human and horse. And Red Man, who in learning to trust me taught me that I could still be trusted.

Introduction
▲▲▲▲▲▲▲▲▲▲▲▲▲▲▲▲▲

If you believe, as I do, that a single horse can change the life of an individual human, then perhaps you may logically conclude and appreciate that the horse as a species can and has brought about sweeping changes in various cultures throughout the course of human endeavor. Perhaps never did the horse so affect a human culture more radically than that of the Comanche people, a nation born of the horse.

Horses came to the land of the Shoshone—in and around present Wyoming—in the 1680s, when this novel begins. Some of the Shoshone people, for reasons both obvious and mysterious, so rapidly adopted the new horse culture that they broke away from their kin and drifted south, seeking more horses and better hunting grounds. These Shoshone searchers became known as Comanches. Within the span of a single generation, as early as 1705, the Comanche nation had become recognized by Europeans and Indians alike as a powerful and independent tribe. The warriors of the new nation became known as the greatest horsemen in history, possessors of the richest hunting grounds on the face of the earth—the buffalo range of the Southern Plains.

Accordingly, my research for this novel began—though I was unaware at the time that such activity would one day pass as a novelist's research—in the days of my boyhood with the land and the horse. This sometimes involved flying haphazardly off the horse and landing none-too-lightly upon the land. My resulting love and fascination for *equus caballus* and *terra firma* would later allow me a certain appreciation for and understanding of the nomadic nations of the plains.

Growing up in Texas, the term *Comanche* often seemed synonymous with *Indian*. As a nation, the Comanche people claimed and defended ownership privileges over vast stretches of prairies, woodlands, and mountainscapes ranging through present Texas, New Mexico, Oklahoma, Colorado, and Kansas. As a young Texan, I assumed that the Comanche people must have always ruled the Southern Plains. Imagine my surprise when, as an adult, I discovered the fact that the Comanche nation had not appeared in Texas until after 1700, and did not even exist as a recognized tribe until about that time. The catalyst if not indeed the primary reason for this phenomenal cultural migration seemed clear to me. The horse.

About the time that I began to research the horse-borne genesis of the Comanche nation for this novel, it so happened that horses came back into my personal life after an absence of several years. Like a Shoshone-turned-

9
▼▼▼

Comanche, I began to feel the power, beauty, mobility, nobility, and spirit of the horse in my heart and guts and soul. I felt possessed of the gifts of speed, endurance, and strength; I felt in control of things larger than myself; I felt awed by, consumed by, and tenuously linked to the very powers of the earth, the sun, and the sky. My journey into the history and culture of the greatest horsemen the world has ever known coincided with my own return to the ways of horsemanship. Without a horse to straddle, I could not have properly appreciated the Comanche, a proud nation of mounted nomads who by their own standards achieved wealth beyond their wildest dreams for a century and a half.

I am tempted here to list the written sources I drew upon in researching this novel, but find it sufficient to say that I read every book in the University of Texas library system that involved the Comanche, the Shoshone, or any number of other Plains Indian nations. I read every book I could find on the Spanish presence in New Mexico and Texas around the turn of the eighteenth century. I simply read every available source that in any way pertained to the subject of this novel, and this is in addition to interviewing anthropologists and Indian peoples and putting many miles of travel behind me in geographical research. I have judged for myself what seemed to me more accurate and likely and have used such gleanings from my research to structure a framework for this novel. The rest of the story, I believe, was given to me by the spirits.

—Mike Blakely

Author's Note
▲▲▲▲▲▲▲▲▲▲▲▲▲▲▲▲▲▲▲▲▲▲▲▲▲

In writing this novel, I used a precious few words of the Comanche/Shoshone language to lend color, feeling, and flavor. I do not profess an understanding of the language. Spelling posed a problem in translating, as the language includes certain vowel and consonant sounds not employed in English. Therefore, I have used only words that allow a reasonable phonetic spelling.

Even the Comanches' name for themselves created a problem in the writing of this book. In my research, I found this term spelled variously as *Numa, Nuhmuhnuh, Nemeni, Nimenem, Numinu, Nimma,* and *Nermernuh.* However, I have heard the word spoken by contemporary Comanche and Shoshone people, and to my ear it sounds as if it might be most accurately spelled *Noomah,* accented on the first syllable, with the *oo* sound spoken as in the English word *book.*

Though I strive in this novel to accurately render a few Comanche/Shoshone words in English, my spelling choices are my own and should not be considered authoritative. My apologies to linguists who know more than I do about these matters. I am but a simple novelist.

Glossary
▲▲▲▲▲▲

aho—*hello*
ahpoo—*father*
anah—*ouch!*
ekakuma—*bay horse*
esikuma—*horse*
hah—*yes*
ha-i'i—*oh, my!*
kiyu—*horseback*
kubetu—*hard*
kwitapuh—*excrement*
Na-vohnuh—*Apache peoples*
ohtookuma—*sorrel horse*
oo-bia—*oh!*

pinakwoo—*behind*
pogamoggan—*war club*
pookai—*hush*
puha—*power, "medicine"*
puhakut—*shaman, medicine man, medicine woman*
puku—*horse*
sohoobi—*cottonwood*
soohoo—*willow*
tecamaca—*balsam poplar*
toohooya—*horse*
tosa naboo—*paint horse*
tsah—*good*

PART I
▲▲▲▲▲▲▲▲▲▲▲

True Humans

▲▲▲▲▲

1

▼▼▼▼▼

On the day of his birth, a horse ran through his village. It made a sacred circle around the lodge at the edge of camp where his mother labored to give him life. This was not just any horse, but the very first ever seen by the Burnt Meat People of the True Humans. Among other nations, the True Humans were known as Grass Lodge People or Snake People. In seasons to come, they would be called *Shoshone*.

It happened near the end of the Moon of Hunger, during the Time When Babies Cry for Food, in the year called 1687 by the Metal Men whom, at the time, the True Humans did not yet know to exist. Wounded Bear had just walked up to the birthing lodge at the edge of camp. He had come to inquire about the child, as was the custom for grandfathers. This was the first child for his daughter, River Woman, and she gasped with pain inside the lodge, though her pride would not allow her to cry out.

"When will it be over?" Wounded Bear asked, raising his voice loud enough to be heard inside the birthing lodge.

"*Pookai!*" his wife growled from within. "Hush, old man! Our daughter will finish it when the spirits get ready!" She was an old midwife who possessed strong medicine, for though no child had been born alive to the Burnt Meat People through three winters, neither had any mother died in childbirth. This woman, Wounded Bear's wife, was named Broken Bones.

Wounded Bear shivered, clasping the edges of the woolly buffalo robe tight at his chest. He looked again at the sky, praying to the spirit who came to him in dreams and visions—the humpbacked bear who survived all wounds.

As he chanted his prayers in a low song, he noticed how the white clouds hanging still in the sky seemed to match the patches of snow on the ground, as if the patches of snow were merely clouds reflected in a still summer pool. Wounded Bear was old, and his eyes no longer saw with the keen flint edges of a young warrior, yet he could make out the red dirt between the patches of white snow. Some of the red dirt had blown onto the snow, and to Wounded Bear it looked as though the snow had been sprayed with blood bursting from the nostrils of an elk wounded in the lungs with an arrow. The elk was a beast very hard to kill with arrows, and that was why elk medicine was good. Almost as good as bear medicine, he thought.

Two or three small children took turns sobbing in the camp below, where the lodges were strung out along the steaming springs. As babies, lashed tight in their cradle boards, they had been trained by their mothers not to cry, as their mothers would place a palm over their mouths when they wept. But now they were starving and had only their tears to swallow, and not even their mothers could make them stop crying. All the meat in the camp was gone, and the mothers had no milk to give. No buffalo had strayed into these harsh hills of home for two winters, and few deer, elk, or antelope had been killed. The pemmican and dried meat had been used up. Only a few small caches of pine nuts and roots remained.

The Burnt Meat People had been eating what rabbits they could club or catch in snares. They had been eating rats and gophers that ventured early from their winter burrows, roasting them whole over coals. No one was speaking anymore of the taboos against eating the flesh of birds, and even dogs were being killed, though the families pretended not to know their neighbors were eating dog meat, for this too was forbidden. It was going to be hard to move the camp in the spring with fewer dogs to harness to the pole drags.

Wounded Bear pushed his own hunger out of his thoughts and thanked the spirit of the humpbacked bear for guiding him through his life of danger, trouble, and starvation. As always, he repeated the prayer that he might die in battle, though he was too old and his sight too poor now to follow the war trail. He did not pray for a grandson. He did not even pray that River Woman's child would live. He only asked that his daughter would survive her long ordeal of childbirth, for he loved his daughter very much. If the baby lived, how would she feed it, anyway?

It was at this moment that sunlight burst between two clouds, illuminating the village of tattered hide lodges. And it was at this same moment that the sound came—like the language of sunlight—the sound of hooves pounding the red dirt and clattering across the rock-strewn ground. They made noises like no other hooves the old man had ever heard, grinding like an avalanche of scree and thumping against the frozen red soil like the horns of rams in battle.

Wounded Bear's prayer-song caught in his throat as he squinted at the camp, his heart suddenly driving the cold from his limbs. A shape emerged— large and dark, weaving among the lodges.

Buffalo! No, the neck was too long—like an elk's—but the color was near that of a buffalo. Buffalo-elk! The animals sometimes mated that way, so he had always heard. Thus the True Humans had been created through the mating of Coyote with a *puhakut*, a medicine woman like Broken Bones.

The beast came on. Yes, buffalo-elk!

No! The tail was too long and shaggy, and the neck was shaggy, too . . . like no buffalo . . . like no elk . . . like nothing Wounded Bear had ever seen!

He longed for his bow as the beast came on toward him, and he thought he saw the feathered end of an arrow shaft already sticking out behind the ribs. Now his daughter, River Woman, screamed with pain inside the birthing lodge.

"Yes!" Broken Bones shouted. "Now it is time! Old man! What is that running out there?"

"I cannot say!" Wounded Bear admitted.

The creature dodged so near the birthing lodge that Wounded Bear felt red sand sprinkle his face, but he held his ground at the entrance.

"What is it? I must know."

"I do not know what it is!"

"Have your eyes gone completely blind, old fool?"

The creature ran headlong toward the high red bluffs that shielded the camp from winter winds and contained it as if in the palm of a great cupped hand. River Woman screamed again, in an agony of pain and fatigue, and the strange animal searched helplessly for escape along the curve of bluffs, passing behind the birthing lodge.

"What is that beast?" the midwife demanded. "The baby is coming out now! I must know!"

Wounded Bear watched the animal try a bluff and fail. "It is . . ." he said, squinting. "It is . . ."

A pack of dogs streamed from the camp, nosing the trail of the strange creature.

"Is it a buffalo? It does not sound like a buffalo. Old man? Are you out there?"

River Woman screamed again, but this time with a deliberate tone of determination. The beast was turning away from the bluffs, completing its circle around the birthing lodge, rumbling back down toward the village. It bit one of the dogs in its path on the back of the neck and tossed the yelping animal aside.

"I must know what animal that is! The baby is almost out!"

"It is a big dog!" Wounded Bear blurted. "It is the biggest dog I have ever seen! I believe it is a *shadow-dog*!"

Another camp mongrel attacked the flank of the strange creature, which kicked and screamed, and the screaming turned into the shrill cry of a baby inside the birthing lodge.

Wounded Bear realized that he was out of breath, though he had only been standing there, watching. The strange beast was running back down through the camp, followed by the dogs, fading from his dim view. He could just make out the images of warriors drawing bows and heaving lances.

Broken Bones stuck her head out between the buffalo hide of the lodge and the bear skin covering the entrance hole. Eyes glared from her wrinkled and toothless face, and cropped gray hair sprouted like dried grass from her scalp. "Where is it?"

"It ran back among the lodges," Wounded Bear answered. He smelled a faint whiff of snowberry tea from the lodge. The baby was still crying, and the old man heard his daughter, River Woman, cooing at it like a dove.

"Are you sure it was a dog? I never heard a dog scream like that. I never heard a dog run on hooves."

"It was a very strange dog. A big one. As big as an elk!"

The *puhakut* scowled. "When the moment came, you told me it was a big dog. I hope River Woman's baby does not suffer from some spirit you have offended!"

"It was a big dog, old woman! Do not speak like a witch! The spirits sent it from the Land of Shadows. It was a shadow-dog! Now, tell me about my grandchild!"

The midwife ducked inside. Her voice sounded kinder from within: "You have a close friend, old man."

Wounded Bear smiled. He began to pace along on stiff legs, weaving his way among the patches of snow, holding to the red dirt where footing was surer for an old warrior. He stalked through the camp, quiet now, after the passage of the strange beast he had named the shadow-dog.

Suddenly his old eyes caught the shape of a track in the snow, and he stooped over it to look at it closer and to feel its edges. Wounded Bear began to worry. What if Broken Bones was right? What if he had made a mistake and offended some spirit? This was like no dog track, no hoofprint, nothing he had ever seen. There was a track of a real dog beside it, which made him wonder why he had ever called the creature a big dog, or a shadow-dog, or any kind of dog. He straightened over the track and strode anxiously down through the village.

Below camp he heard the gushing of the spring called Never Freezes and saw a gathering of warriors and women. Pushing his way among them, he made out the large shape of the strange beast on the ground, still struggling against death, its legs groping helplessly for ground over which to run, its head lunging skyward in a vain attempt to rise. The arrows of several warriors stuck out of the body of the dying animal, and lance wounds ran with blood.

Wounded Bear's son-in-law, Shaggy Hump, was standing over the animal, the long buckskin fringe of his sleeves still swinging from having drawn his bow. The strange, hairy neck fell against the ground for an instant, and Shaggy

Hump shot his arrow into the spine just behind the head, stilling the animal with a final flinch.

"Where did that thing come from?" asked a younger warrior.

"It came from below." Shaggy Hump touched the bloody nose of the beast with the sole of the buffalo wood boots he wore over his moccasins. "I was waiting where Broken Bones told me to go as my wife gave birth to our child. This animal came to the spring to drink, and I stalked below it to shoot it and to drive it through the camp."

"What is it?" the young warrior asked.

"This is the animal the Raccoon-Eyed People told me about when I went to trade with them on the plains. They said it was as big as seven big dogs, but I did not believe them, for they have many strange ways."

Old Wounded Bear came closer to look at the strangely hoofed feet of the animal. "It is a big dog," he insisted.

The people laughed at the old man stooping over the dead animal.

"The biggest dog I have ever seen!" His eyes looked up to his son-in-law's face. "It is a shadow-dog."

"Why are you here, *Ahpoo?*" Shaggy Hump said, using the term of respect for his wife's father. "What has happened at the birthing lodge that Broken Bones has raised for my wife?"

"My daughter gave birth to your child at the moment this animal made a sacred circle around the lodge. Broken Bones wanted to know what kind of animal it was, and I told her it was a shadow-dog."

"Why did you tell her that, *Ahpoo?*"

"She said she must know, because the baby was coming out, and it was time to fashion the medicine. I could not see what this thing was, and so I had to tell her something. I told her it was a shadow-dog because I saw it bite like a dog."

Shaggy Hump seemed to search his heart as he walked around the dead animal. The people of his band waited for him to speak, for he was respected among them. Shaggy Hump had brought meat to camp when all others had failed, and he had shared with his neighbors, trusting that his medicine would stay strong, enabling him to kill more food. He had traveled far and brought home scalps of enemies who had attacked the Burnt Meat People. He was strong and wise, and his words made even his rivals listen.

He squatted beside the dead animal, and put his hand on it as if to enjoy its warmth. His long braids fell over his shoulders and dangled near the blood on the carcass. His smile was broad when he looked up at the people gathered around. His eyes were black and darting as they shot toward his brother, Black Horn.

"Brother, tell my wife's father again what we saw the time we traveled far to the south to find our enemies, the *Yutas*."

Black Horn stepped forward to tell the story as he had recited it in council: "We found the trail of our enemy that showed they had moved their camp. On this trail we saw the tracks of an animal with feet like this one, and the mark of poles on the ground where this animal dragged them . . ." He looked at old Wounded Bear. ". . . like a dog. Like a very big dog, for the poles were loaded heavily and cut deeply into the earth."

"What does this mean?" Wounded Bear asked.

Shaggy Hump stood, coming straight up on short, powerful legs. "It means you are a wise old warrior, *Ahpoo*. You were wise to see that this strange animal is a big dog of the Shadow Land, for our enemies have used it to pull their pole-drags as we use our dogs. The spirits have sent a shadow-dog to us on this, the same day my wife gives birth to our first child. This is a great day. Now, *Ahpoo*, will you tell me about my child?"

The dread lifted from Wounded Bear's heart, and he remembered the happy cooing of his daughter with her crying baby. "The child was born as the shadow-dog circled the lodge, and then old Broken Bones spoke to me from inside the lodge, saying, Wounded Bear—old great warrior—you have a close friend."

Shaggy Hump lifted his bow over his head, his black eyes gleaming. "I have a son!" he shouted.

Some of the men came around the dead beast on the ground to touch Shaggy Hump as if counting strokes in battle.

"My people," old Wounded Bear said, raising his hands. "Hear me! This is a good day. This is the Day of the Shadow-dog! Now, shadow-dog is a good name for this animal. It is like a dog, that is true. But it is also different— like the coyote is different from the wolf—like the lesser bear is different from the great humpbacked bear. This is a shadow-dog. It is different from a dog. It has feet with claws that have all grown together to make one solid hoof. It is the size of seven dogs in one. It has wandered over a pass from the Shadow Land and has come to serve us. It is different from a dog in many ways, and so it is not a dog at all, but a *shadow-dog*."

Wounded Bear circled the carcass and smelled the blood, which made his stomach growl. "Now, listen. Our father's fathers have told us that the dog and the wolf and the coyote are ancestors of the True Humans, from the ancient times when animals spoke and walked around like two-leggeds, and so it is not a good thing to eat a dog because it is our ancestor. But this beast is so strange that I do not think it is my ancestor. It does not come from the earth, but from the Shadow Land. I hear the spirits say that it is a very good thing to eat a *shadow-dog*."

The people laughed with relief, for they were hungry, and the beast was made of meat, whether it came from the Land of Shadows or not.

"Wounded Bear shows his wisdom again," Shaggy Hump said. "I am forbidden to eat meat until the cord dries and falls from my new son's belly, but I will find some roots or pine nuts to eat, and sing the song my spirit-protector taught me as the Burnt Meat People of the True Humans make a feast of the shadow-dog in honor of my new son!"

He began to pace very excitedly, as if he did not know what to do next. "I must wash my testicles in the cold water now, for Broken Bones is bathing the baby. I must not look upon my wife and child for thirty suns, or the spirits will cause me to bleed to death from my nose. Listen well, all you young boys, for these are things you need to know. Black Horn, my brother, go where I am forbidden and speak to Broken Bones. Tell me what she says about my son!"

And so the flint knives peeled the hide of the shadow-dog and carved warm meat from bone. The fire drills conjured smoke and flame from wood. The Burnt Meat People feasted on the animal that in times to come would be called First Horse. They declared it the best meal ever consumed by any True Humans anywhere. All night the elders told tales and sang songs and offered up blessings of tobacco smoke to the newborn son of River Woman and Shaggy Hump. In seasons ahead of this day, the Burnt Meat People would know the child as Born-on-the-Day-of-the-Shadow-Dog, and they would smile as they spoke his name, for the day of his birth held a story that would bring much joy in the telling.

2

The first moment the spirits gave him to remember began with a horse running toward him from a green and distant hill. It happened during the Moon of Geese Returning, when the True Humans killed deer and drank the mixture of warm milk and blood that ran from the slashed udders of the does. It was the time when the children played in the spring sunshine and ate curdled milk taken from the stomachs of slain fawns.

The horse of his first memories came over a faraway hill of green grass and gray sage, running toward him, becoming many horses of many different colors. The horses ran to him as he sat on a robe spread across the ground, and they shook the ground and made dirt fly onto his robe. One of the huge animals blasted him with warm, sweet-smelling breath and nudged him with a soft nose, knocking him onto his back. This pleased the horses, and they ran away, kicking more dirt at Born-on-the-Day-of-the-Shadow-Dog. But he only laughed in his little child's voice, for none of this frightened him. He rolled over to see his mother running toward him from the lodge.

As the horses galloped away from Born-on-the-Day-of-the-Shadow-Dog, River Woman reached his place on the ground and lifted him. The boy felt his arm fall comfortably over his mother's shoulder, his legs straddling her hip with familiarity. He grabbed her black hair and pulled hard, as he always liked to do. She only grabbed his wrist to keep him from pulling harder. Her voice was running like a swift river, and Born-on-the-Day-of-the-Shadow-Dog knew she was upset, but not with him. His mother never got upset with him, and so he pulled her hair with his free hand, because she liked it when he played like this.

Now the sound of another horse came, and the child looked to the green hill to see his father, Shaggy Hump, riding toward him. This would be the first time he remembered seeing a man riding a horse, and it made him so happy that he tried to slide down his mother's hip so he could go to his father, but his mother would not let him.

Shaggy Hump came to his wife and child at a trot on a bay horse and pulled the rawhide thong looped around the mount's jaw to make it stop.

"Your crazy horses came over the hill and almost stepped on your son!" River Woman said.

Shaggy Hump's smile changed to a scowl. "*Pookai*, woman!" Just as quickly, his expression became a smile again, for his son. He urged the horse forward by leaning in the direction he wanted to move and by squeezing with his knees. He grabbed Born-on-the-Day-of-the-Shadow-Dog by the wrist, wrenched the naked child away from his mother, and swung his son in front of him onto the blanketed withers of the horse.

Looking down on her, the boy could see the part in the middle of his mother's hair painted bright red—a thing he had never noticed before because he did not remember sitting so high above her. He laughed and pulled the mane of the horse.

"Look how my son holds on!" Shaggy Hump cried.

"He learned by pulling my hair," River Woman said.

"As I did!" The warrior laughed and was pleased that his wife laughed with him. "You are a great teacher of riders, River Woman."

Shaggy Hump made the horse cut and run, and his son riding in front of him squealed with joy. Born-on-the-Day-of-the-Shadow-Dog held the mane tightly and mimicked his father's use of the rawhide reins.

"Hear your father speak, my son. I was the first *Noomah* warrior of the Burnt Meat People ever to see a horse."

"*Noomah*," said Born-on-the-Day-of-the-Shadow-Dog, mimicking his father's speech. He knew this word somehow and understood its meaning. The Real People. The True Humans. Those like me.

"It happened on the day you were born," his father continued. "I killed First Horse so that the people of your camp could have a feast in your honor.

Your grandfather named the horse shadow-dog that day, but since then, the spirits have given us many other names to call the horse. *Esikuma, puku, toohooya.* Elk-dog, seven-dogs, big-dog. *Ekakuma, tosa naboo, ohtookuma.* Bay, paint, sorrel . . ."

As he listened to his father's voice, Born-on-the-Day-of-the-Shadow-Dog kicked at the withers of the horse he rode with his father. He pulled the long mane to his face, felt it tickle his lips, and smelled the good musky aroma of the beast.

"The horse comes from the south. I know this, my son. On my first ride over the hunting grounds of the plains, I came upon our enemies, the *Yutas.* I made a truce with the *Yutas* so that we might travel together to trade with the Raccoon-Eyed People far out on the plains. During this journey, the *Yutas* told me many strange stories about men with white skin and hairy faces far away to the south, who have many horses and much iron. The day you were born, everything began to change, for First Horse brought strong medicine. The spirits gave First Horse to the Burnt Meat People so that we would not starve that winter. This spirit-pony ran around the lodge where you were born, making a sacred circle. When First Horse died, his power and his soul leapt into your heart, my son."

They rode over endless green grasslands dotted with sage, across a talking brook, among the smoke-breathing lodges painted with many colors and signs. And Shaggy Hump continued to lecture his son:

"After the trading and the truce, I went with my brother, Black Horn, to the hunting grounds of the *Yutas.* There we found our enemy's camp and crept among their horses at night. We took these horses for our own. And we took the scalp of the enemy warrior who guarded them and carved his dead body so that we will know him by his scars in the Shadow Land. Now our hunters ride far and find more game to kill. We do not suffer so much from hunger, and we move quickly away from our enemies when they are stronger than we are. We are now like the antelope, as we were once like the snake."

Born-on-the-Day-of-the-Shadow-Dog leaned back and felt his skin pressing against his father's bare stomach. He listened. He did not really understand, but he would hear the same stories many times over in seasons to come, and he would learn.

"Your father is a great taker and rider of horses, Shadow Dog—a great warrior-hunter who rides far to trade and find game and count battle strokes. You will also ride far, my son. You will collect scalps like the claws of great bears. You will own ponies like our enemies own lice."

They rode and rode and rode, until Shadow Dog yawned and closed his eyes, sleeping peacefully to the good steady motion of the horse and the sound of his father's voice.

· · · ·

In seasons to come, Shaggy Hump would claim with pride that his son began training horses when his winters numbered only five. By this age, Shadow Dog had grown a good set of teeth and used them often to bite his mother. This made much fun, for his mother would yell and squirm, and he thought she liked this game, for River Woman never punished him for anything he did.

She would say, "Hear your mother! Do not bite!"

But Shadow Dog knew she did not mean it, even though she pretended to make her voice sound stern. He would say, "I bite!"

One day, Shadow Dog was taken to his aunt, Looks Away, who was the wife of Black Horn. Black Horn had captured Looks Away from the *Yutas* and had taken her as his wife, which was well, for in those days the *Yutas* knew more of horses than the True Humans, and Looks Away was able to teach Black Horn about horses.

On this day, Looks Away was tending Shadow Dog because River Woman had gone to stay in the lodge for unclean women. Shadow Dog was chasing puppies and making dust rise and blow into a paunch in which Looks Away was cooking stew. Twice, Looks Away told him to play with his puppies in some other place. The third time, she seized his wrist to make him listen, and when she did, he bit the back of her hand.

At first, it was like the game he played with his mother, for Looks Away gasped and flinched, which was fun. But then she seized his arm again, with much strength, and sank her own teeth deep enough into Shadow Dog's flesh to make him howl. She pressed her hand hard over his mouth to silence him, and said, "You will not bite!"

Like Shaggy Hump, Black Horn had horses—as many as he could keep. One of Shaggy Hump's mares had borne a foal, and Looks Away was keeping the mare staked close to the camp to prevent wolves and lions from eating the foal, who stayed close to his mother. She went to lead the mare to water that day, with the mark of Shadow Dog's teeth still in her flesh, and the mark of hers still plain in his. Shadow Dog came with her, because he loved the little foal.

As Looks Away was leading the mare, Shadow Dog played with the foal, grabbing its mane or tail, and trying to climb on its back. Looks Away was watching them play when she saw Shadow Dog kick the foal in the stomach as he tried to scramble onto its back.

Suddenly, the foal craned its thin neck and bit Shadow Dog on the back of the thigh. This made the boy flinch and yell, but he held to the foal, grabbing it now by the ear. Almost as soon as his feet were on the ground, Shadow Dog clenched the ear between his teeth and drew blood from the foal.

Grabbing the soft lower lip of the frightened foal and holding still to the ear, Shadow Dog gained control of the little animal, though it was larger than he was. He made the foal stand still, then said, "You will not bite!"

It was said that this foal never again tried to bite another True Human, even when it was grown and painted and wearing war feathers in its tail.

▲▲▲▲▲

3

▼▼▼▼▼

He saw his first enemy in the summer of his ninth year. It was during the Moon of Antlers, when all the great warriors of the deer and elk and moose tribes used their spirit powers to grow weapons from their skulls. His uncle, Black Horn, had killed a buck and given the antlers to him. These Born-on-the-Day-of-the-Shadow-Dog had lashed to the lodge poles his horse was dragging, and he held onto them as the Burnt Meat People moved north.

He was proud to be riding the horse his father had given him, while other children ran among the dogs that pulled shorter lodge poles. Because his father, Shaggy Hump, owned horses, his family could move longer lodge poles and fold more buffalo hides upon them. Most of the families of the Burnt Meat People lived in small, four-pole tipis, but the lodge of Shaggy Hump's family was the largest in the band, made of eight poles and ten skins. This caused Shadow to ride his pony with pride.

Long ago, the people of his band had shortened his name to Shadow Dog, and now just to Shadow. He knew the name would not stick his whole life, for he would one day receive a warrior's name from the spirits. But for now, Shadow liked his name. A shadow was dark and mysterious and could vanish among other shadows. It moved silently and crawled over the ground like death.

The horse he rode was the smallest Shaggy Hump had taken from the *Yutas*, and so it was easier for Shadow to climb upon. It was a stocky brown horse, with white hairs of age around its muzzle and the even temper of an old work dog. There were two things about this horse that fascinated Shadow and made him wonder beyond comprehension.

One thing was the fact that his horse, though male, had no testicles. The Burnt Meat People had once camped with the Corn People, another band of True Humans, who owned a slave with no testicles. This slave had been captured from the Northern Raiders as a boy, and the Corn People had cut the captured boy's testicles off, for the warriors of the Northern Raiders had raped many women and girls among the bands of the True Humans. All this made Shadow wonder who had cut the testicles off his horse, and why this horse had been punished by no longer being allowed to mate with mares.

The other thing that filled his heart with a yearning to understand was the scar burned onto the shoulder of his horse. From where he now rode, he could touch the scar whenever he liked and try to think of what had caused it. He knew this kind of scar was made by hot coals, for his grandfather, Wounded Bear, who now rode beside him, had scars like this upon his feet and hands.

Once, long ago, while hunting alone, Wounded Bear had been captured by the Wolf People on the plains who called themselves *Parisu*, which meant the Hunters. Their women had tied him down to stakes driven into the ground and begun to burn his hands and feet with the ends of sticks made red in the fire. But Wounded Bear's friends and brothers had come looking for him and attacked the Wolf People camp, killing all the enemy warriors there before their women could burn very many scars on him. After this battle, Wounded Bear had taken as his own captive one of the enemy women who had burned him, and he had made her into a pretty good wife. Her name was Broken Bones, and she had become a bringer of babies and a *puhakut* with powerful medicine.

The scar burned onto Shadow's horse was similar to the ones burned onto his grandfather's hands and feet, yet the pony's scar made two very straight lines that Shadow's father said surely held some manner of medicine. The design was like a long pole, with a shorter pole lain across it. When he touched it, Shadow believed he could almost feel its magic, but he could not fathom what kind of burning stick must have left such arrowlike lines upon the flesh of his horse.

As they rode on, Shadow moved his hand from the scar on his pony to the antlers of the deer his uncle had killed, the tines of which were rounded and covered with soft furlike growth that resembled the look of the bluish sage on the red hills far away.

The Burnt Meat People were crossing over high ground, the few horses and many dogs dragging lodge poles loaded with their possessions. Ahead of him, the boy watched his mother walk beside the dog that pulled the cradle board of his baby sister, Mouse. Strapped tightly to the cradle board, wrapped in buckskin and packed in moss, she watched her big brother with wide, peering, black eyes as they moved. Mouse wore a bag of crushed pine needles around her neck as a charm to assure good health.

It had been decided in council that Shaggy Hump should take two young warriors on a hunt, each riding a horse, which he would lead to the new camp, packed with meat. While Shaggy Hump was away on this hunt, Black Horn, his brother, was to lead the Burnt Meat People to their northernmost camp, at the spring called Never Freezes in the Red Canyon. They seldom came this far north in summer, for Never Freezes was dangerously close to the summer hunting grounds of the Northern Raiders. However, the Thunderbird had flown over these rough hills making much rain, bringing sweet grass that drew herds of buffalo as seldom were seen this far from the open plains. The council of the Burnt Meat People had decided that the old men would make arrows while the warriors repaired their bows, lances, war clubs, and battle axes. Then they would move north to hunt buffalo, and if the Northern Raiders wished to make war, the Burnt Meat People would be ready.

Riding beside his grandfather in the middle of the long line of travelers, Shadow held to the antlers lashed in front of him. Most of the warriors were ahead, ready to take on trouble, but a few remained behind to guard the rear of the band. As they started down the steep and ancient trail that led to the rim of the Red Canyon of the spring called Never Freezes, Wounded Bear spoke:

"Grandson, are you holding the horns of the buck your uncle gave to you?"

Wounded Bear was almost blind now, and though he could make fine arrows, he could scarcely see from one end of the arrow to the other. He wanted to make sure the boy was holding the antlers, which were lashed tight with rawhide to the lodge poles. Wounded Bear did not like this new pursuit of riding horses and rode only because he was too old to walk. In days behind him, the old ones were simply left behind to die, and so he might have been grateful for this horse to ride. But Wounded Bear was afraid his grandson, whom he loved very much, might fall off and have the loaded lodge poles dragged over him.

"Are you holding on like a hawk?" he asked.

"Yes, I am holding the horns, Grandfather."

"Good. Maybe I have told you the story about where the first deer horns came from. Even if I have told you, I am going to tell you once again, because it is a good story. Hear me, Grandson."

Shadow grabbed the antlers with both hands as his horse stepped off a small ledge that had worn away in heavy rains.

"Long ago, in the days when animals spoke words and walked about like two-leggeds, Deer was a young warrior who did not have any weapons and did not have a wise grandfather to show him how to make any. So he decided to make medicine and grow his weapons from the top of his head. His guardian spirits, who spoke to him in visions, told him he must eat green leaves and berries every night, and run from place to place to find enough food to have the medicine for growing his weapons. This was not easy to do, but after three moons had passed, the warrior had a beautiful pair of weapons on his head.

"These weapons were matched. Each one split into five branches, and they were curved like old moons. But they were still covered with fur when he grew them—like those you are holding on to, Grandson—so Deer had to polish them and make them smooth and sharp. He found many small trees that were just right for rubbing the different places in his weapons, and every day he would go from one small tree to the next and polish the different points and branches.

"After the next moon had changed, this warrior had weapons that were smooth and shining, for he had worked on them long and carefully, as you have watched your own grandfather make arrows, Shadow. The points were sharp like a lance, and the curve of each weapon was thick and heavy like a war club, so Deer went away to seek battle.

"He found his enemies and he fought many battles with the weapons on his head. His wounds became many, but his honors numbered still more, for he counted many battle strokes. He became a great warrior among his people, and every father wanted his daughter to be the wife of Deer, for a strong warrior will provide meat and shelter for a father-in-law who is not lucky enough to die young in battle.

"So Deer had many wives, and many sons and daughters. He became so powerful that his enemies would no longer fight him. Instead, they would run away and hide when they saw him coming.

"One day, Deer wanted to couple with a new young wife but she ran into the thick bushes, and it was hard to chase her around in the bushes with such large weapons on his head. So he let them fall from his head, and they landed together on the ground, but he forgot where they had fallen. He did not really care because there was no one to fight, anyway.

"But now Deer's wives were ashamed when they saw him, and to scorn him, they ran away with his rivals who still carried their weapons. Deer tried to get his wives back, but his rivals laughed at him and wounded him with their arrows and lances, and he ran like a coward.

"So Deer decided he was going to make his medicine again and grow new weapons. He prayed to his guardian spirits, but the spirits were angry because he had lost his sacred weapons and insulted them.

"And so the spirits changed Deer from a two-legged into a four-legged who would always be hunted by all tribes of people. The spirits gave him some wives but told him he would have to drop his weapons after every winter had passed, lose all his wives, and make new medicine and new weapons all summer long, every summer, as long as he lived. And even Deer's sons and grandsons would suffer for his insult. Their horns would fall off after every winter, and they would lose their wives and have to eat leaves and berries and hide from all kinds of people. And that was Deer's punishment for losing his weapons and offending his guardian spirits."

They neared the place where the trail narrowed and dropped off into the Red Canyon, and Shadow thought of Deer turning into a four-legged.

"Did you hear my story, Grandson?"

"Yes, Grandfather. That is a good story."

"Yes. It is an old story. Even older than I am."

As Shadow laughed with his grandfather, he saw his uncle, Black Horn, riding up from the trail ahead on the only horse in the band unencumbered by a pole-drag. Black Horn carried his lance in his right hand, while the rawhide thong of his stone-headed war axe remained looped around his left wrist. His bow and arrows were in his bow case and quiver, strapped upon his back. Each cheek was painted with two bright yellow stripes, with a single red stripe standing on his forehead.

Shadow checked to make sure the two lodge poles were tied securely where they crossed in front of him. He tested the buffalo-hide straps tightened around his mount's girth and running under the horse's neck. He looked over his shoulder to see that the bundle of hides for his lodge remained tightly packed.

It was an uncle's place to be stern and strict, and Black Horn took this responsibility more seriously than most. "Nephew! Let your grandfather go ahead! Do you not see the trail getting narrow?"

"Yes, *Ahpoo*," the boy said, using the term of respect for a father's brother. He lifted his reins from the deer antlers where he had draped them and slowed his horse to let Wounded Bear go ahead. His uncle fell in line after him as Shadow's little brown horse stepped stiffly down to the steepest part of the trail. Behind him, the boy heard the widely spread ends of the lodge poles dragging against both sides of the narrow red rock chasm through which the old trail ran.

He looked over his shoulder to make sure the poles would not get broken, and to judge his uncle's expression. His eye caught a mass of feathers rising above the canyon rim, followed by a face streaked with horizontal bands of red and yellow paint. From stories the elders had told, he recognized the distinctive upright shape of the headdress as that of a Northern Raider. He had heard many tales of these cruel and evil people who painted their feet black in the belief that the paint made them run faster, but this feathered and painted warrior was the first Northern Raider he had seen with his own eyes, now standing no farther away than a deer could leap, drawing a bow.

The boy gasped and then, realizing that the arrow of the enemy warrior was aiming at Black Horn, cried, *"Ahpoo!"*

By the time Black Horn caught his nephew's eye, slipped from his horse, and spotted the Northern Raider on the canyon rim, the bowstring had spoken. Black Horn drew his battle-axe back to throw as the arrow point hit him, but because Shadow had warned him, and he had begun to react, the cruel barbed war point only lodged in his upper arm. The wound seemed to give him strength to throw his axe, and it sped true, glancing off the top of the Raider's shield and smashing into the enemy's jaw with a crack that sounded like someone breaking buffalo bones to get the marrow. The axe itself bounced off the enemy and slid back into the canyon.

Shadow felt his horse lurch as he had never known, heard the enemy war cry rising. The walls of the Red Canyon seemed to spin around him as he looked for the sources of the horrible new noises that sounded like a whole war party on the rimrocks above.

Black Horn was breaking the arrow shaft from his arm, the wound gushing blood. The wounded enemy warrior on the canyon rim had stumbled back, out of view. Now the smell of blood hit Shadow, and the boy saw a red stream pouring from his horse's neck where an enemy arrow had driven deep.

Instantly figuring the path this arrow must have taken, he glanced up at the other rim of the red chasm and saw a second Raider, reaching now for the next arrow in his quiver.

Black Horn's rattling battle scream mingled with a wailing song that came from Shadow's grandfather, old Wounded Bear. Looking down the chasm, the boy saw his blind grandfather slinging his old *pogamoggan*—his war club—to ward off any foe who might come to finish him. An arrow shaft protruded from the old man's ribs, and he bled onto his leggings as he valiantly slung the club and shrieked his death song.

Shadow spotted a third Raider now, the one who had shot his grandfather, already fixing a second arrow on his string.

The little brown horse under him was trying to back up, but the lodge poles prevented it. Shadow found himself sliding from the horse, taking cover behind the body of the animal so the Raiders could not shoot him. He heard two bowstrings thump—the first sending an arrow that caused Wounded Bear to groan in the midst of his death song. The other arrow sped straight toward Shadow as he shrank behind his pony, but it glanced off the antlers lashed to his lodge poles, angling harmlessly away.

Another arrow sang, and Shadow glimpsed it as it flew from Black Horn's bow toward the enemy warrior who had shot the boy's little brown horse and had tried to shoot Shadow himself. This arrow struck the side of the Raider's head and lodged there, causing the warrior's braids to fly wildly as he vanished behind the red rock rim.

Now his mother, River Woman, was screaming, and Shadow saw the third Raider sliding into the Red Canyon with a knife to take Wounded Bear's scalp lock. The old war club missed as the Raider pounced on the old man and stabbed with his knife. The Raider tried to take the scalp, but a large red rock hit him on the shoulder.

Shadow saw the Raider turn on his mother as she picked up another rock, and he knew he must act. At his feet, he found a large rock, spotted with the blood of his own brown pony. He picked up this rock and held it over his head as he heard the hooves of Black Horn's mount clattering behind him.

He threw the large rock and it landed short but bounced, as the Raider was below him on the trail, and caught the Raider on the back of the knee, whirling him. Shadow saw the eyes of the enemy lock onto him and flash an age-old hatred, but Black Horn was coming.

The boy fell aside as he saw his uncle bounding on foot over the lodge poles and over the wounded brown pony—over everything clogged in the narrow chasm as he screamed his love of war and his hatred of enemy invaders. He had scooped up his battle-axe. Its heavy head of freshly flaked flint had been lashed with shrunken rawhide to the feathered and painted handle as fast as the horns to the head of a buffalo bull. It circled high, like the sun, then came down on the painted Raider.

The enemy raised his shield, but the axe snapped its wooden rim and stunned the warrior, who fell onto his back, continuing to slash with his knife and even reaching for an arrow from the quiver on his back.

The jagged flint edges circled overhead again and cracked the skull of the enemy, glancing and peeling back hair and skin which flopped over one ear.

"Finish this one!" Black Horn said, handing his war axe to River Woman. "And the one above, with my arrow in his head. I am going to fight the others!"

Shadow's uncle scrambled back over the dying brown pony to his own mount. The boy went toward his grandfather, lying bloody and motionless against the canyon wall, but stopped when he heard the first blow by his mother.

Looking up, he saw River Woman's eyes blaze with a fury he had never seen. She lifted the axe again and crushed the ribs of the dead Raider. She lifted it again and broke an arm. Again, into the groin of the corpse. With every blow, she grunted and screamed at once, never taking her seething glare from the corpse of the Raider who had killed her father.

In this moment, Shadow absorbed the True Humans' great and lasting hatred for all their many enemies, and it fixed itself deep in his heart, ever to dwell and harden and grow. It was a cold and pitiless ire, colored by the blood of his murdered grandfather, drummed to a fervor by the thump of River Woman's axe upon the body of the beaten Raider. It sickened Shadow's paunch, but stung his limbs with strength, and he embraced it here in the Red Canyon of his birth, and gave it shelter, and made its medicine his own.

Black Horn had mounted his horse and struggled past the screaming women and children pouring into the canyon for protection. From below in the canyon, and over the rim above, the sound of battle cries mounted as the warriors of the Burnt Meat People regrouped after the surprise attack and prepared their resistance.

The Northern Raiders, it seemed, had planned their attack well, waiting until the long line of people was half in and half out of the canyon before loosing their arrows. But the party of Raiders did not seem large, or else the entire band of Burnt Meat People might have been pinned down and slaughtered. Even in his lack of experience, Shadow surmised that the attacking force was nothing more than a small hunting party that had stumbled upon the True Humans and planned a quick ambush, hoping to get away with some scalps, or maybe a horse.

Remembering what his uncle had said, Shadow reached for the knife dropped by the Raider his mother was now preparing for an eternity of agony in the Shadow Land. The knife was made of iron, a thing Shadow had seen only once before on an arrow point for which his father had traded a horse among the Raccoon-Eyed People of the plains. He grabbed this knife of iron and scaled the canyon wall to the place where the enemy warrior had fallen with Black Horn's arrow in his head.

Here, on the canyon rim, the boy could see everything. The warrior with the arrow in his head was still, but breathing, his eyes closed, instead of open in the death stare. The brown pony below had died, and Shadow's mother had stopped beating the corpse of the enemy to wail her song of mourning and pull at her hair over the body of old Wounded Bear. Shadow's baby sister, Mouse, was still staring at him silently, the dog pulling her cradle board standing obediently, panting, the whites of his eyes showing as they rolled suspiciously in his head.

Some warriors of the Burnt Meat People were attempting to climb out of the canyon, but so many people were blocking the narrow trail that the men could not make their way to the top. The few young warriors who had been walking near the end of the moving band were now gathering on the high ground above the chasm for an attack, but none owned a horse.

Some distance away to the north, the Raider who had been hit in the jaw by Black Horn's axe was being carried away by four other Raiders, and it seemed to Shadow that these five were all that were left of the ambush party.

Black Horn was across the chasm from Shadow, mounted, his bow in one hand, his lance in the other. He had dropped his reins, for his pony had been trained to react to pressure from the rider's knees. The boy knew his uncle would not wait for the young warriors on foot, but would gallop after the Northern Raiders and kill as many as he could before falling. Black Horn was a warrior who boasted often that he would die young in battle.

Now a powerful war cry pierced the sounds of moaning and crying in the canyon, and Black Horn's mount raised red dust. The enemy Raiders, not so far away that Shadow could not see them individually, laid their wounded companion down, formed a line, and prepared their bows and arrows. To Shadow's surprise, even the warrior who had been wounded in the face with the axe pulled himself to his knees and reached for an arrow from his quiver.

The enemy warriors had been foolish to ambush a party so much larger than their own, Shadow thought. They would be ridden down by Black Horn, who could keep them busy until his friends could arrive and finish them.

Shadow could see that the Raiders had no horses. He glanced again at the warrior with the arrow stuck in his head, lying still at his feet. He gripped the iron knife tighter as he looked back across the chasm to see his uncle do battle with the horrible Northern Raiders.

When Black Horn got just inside arrow range, he veered to the left, and Shadow knew his uncle was going to circle the Raiders before dismounting to fight. He started in the east and bore south, then west, the way Father Sun circled Mother Earth. The circle, once closed, would make his medicine powerful.

The Raiders had arrows notched to bowstrings, but only watched Black Horn ride, preferring to wait for a closer shot. Their only hope was to kill him and run before the other Burnt Meat warriors arrived on foot.

The curtain of dust closed around the enemy warriors, and Black Horn paused to raise his lance and scream. Now he would dismount, Shadow thought, and charge the enemy single-handedly with the lance. That he should watch this fight filled him with more excitement than he had ever known, and the skin all over his body seemed to soak in the chilling cry that Black Horn sent rattling across the high ground. If only his father were here, that Shadow might see him go to battle as well! His grandfather and his pony were dead, and the boy of nine winters hungered for vengeance older than his own days upon the earth.

The war cry trailed away on a breeze that had sprung from the cold highlands, and now Shadow saw something he would remember as long as he lived. His uncle, seized by some new medicine, rode his horse into battle. This was not the way of his elders. The True Humans had always fought with their own feet on the ground, but Black Horn was part of the horse now, and the horse part of him, and Shadow could hardly believe how courageously he rode among the five Raiders.

Through the body of Black Horn, the spear magically took on the power of the pony. When he thrust it forward, underhanded, it went like a kingfisher plunging into the water, and its flint tip hit the same warrior who had been struck in the jaw by Black Horn's axe, driving all the way through the man and sticking in the ground behind him.

The Northern Raiders, stunned by this mounted attack, let Black Horn ride past them untouched. Now he turned and prepared to attack them with nothing but the white flint knife he had once taken from the dead body of a Crow enemy. This was glorious, for Black Horn still carried his bow and arrows, but chose to fight the enemy attackers hand to hand, for they had dishonored him by raiding the party he led. The Northern Raiders, seemingly charmed by the powers of the horse warrior, still did not send their arrows. They had expected Black Horn to dismount, Shadow thought, and the horse magic was confusing them.

What happened next seemed like something from a bad vision. Black Horn drove his pony among the enemies again, and one of the raiders reached for the reins as another raised a stick—a very long and very straight stick—putting one broad end of this stick against his shoulder. A flash of orange light like a hundred flint sparks pushed a black cloud from the stick the way a man would blow tobacco smoke from his mouth, but quicker, darker, and with more evil power than any man could muster.

Black Horn rolled backward off his war pony, and as he hit the ground, a clap of thunder came from out of nowhere, for Shadow did not yet understand that the terrible Fire Stick possessed its own thunder.

Everything seemed to hang in silence for a moment, and the warriors coming to help Black Horn lost their courage and stopping running. Shadow's heart sank into the fear of all unknown evil as he watched. His grip loosened around the handle of the iron knife and he watched helplessly as one of the Raiders rushed to finish his uncle.

But Black Horn's courage was legend, and he fought flat on his back, even in the shadow of the warrior carrying the powerful Fire Stick. A Raider descended on him with a scalping knife, but Black Horn slashed with his own knife of white flint, and the enemy warrior had to catch his own entrails as they bulged from the wound.

The young warriors of the Burnt Meat People took courage and charged again as the Raider with the Fire Stick tried to make medicine with it, going through many strange incantations. Arrows were beginning to fall among the enemy warriors, and they threw their wounded and dead over Black Horn's captured horse to flee, leaving Black Horn on the ground. The *Noomah* braves pursued them afoot until the Fire Stick warrior put the evil thing against his shoulder and made it smoke and rumble again.

It killed no one this time, but it caused the earth to blow red dust into the air very near the place where Shadow stood watching. This power frightened the boy, yet he gathered from the way the Raiders were running that the Fire Stick medicine was not all-powerful. Once used, it took some time to conjure again. Still, it caused him to fear, and his fear turned to anger as he heard the wails of mourning for this horrible day. He did not know whether his uncle was dead or yet alive, only that he had failed to rise from the ground, and this made Shadow angrier still.

The iron knife was in his hand, and he used all his weight to make it plunge into the body of the fallen Raider beside him. The body jerked as the blade cut deep, and the boy sprang away, afraid the warrior with the arrow stuck in his head might still be able to fight.

He thought it better to finish this invader with a rock, and he turned to find one large enough to crush a skull.

▲▲▲▲▲
4
▼▼▼▼▼

The medicine woman, Broken Bones, had been summoned, but had refused to come. Black Horn knew it would have been useless anyway. The evil power of the Fire Stick was greater than the old crone's magic. Broken Bones was better off with the way she had chosen, for this world had gone bad.

From where he lay in the shadow of Red Canyon's wall, Black Horn could see the old sorceress now, high above, in the fading sunlight. She stood over the crevice on the canyon rim into which the people were lowering the body of Wounded Bear, wrapped in a good buffalo robe with his *pogamoggan* and bound tightly in rawhide.

The old man had died well, swinging his war club. It was a lucky thing for an old blind man to die in battle. Black Horn felt lucky, too, for he would soon die of his battle wounds while still in his prime and never have to suffer the disgraces of old age. He would never be relegated to making bows and arrows and telling stories in winter lodges.

Yet, he worried about this wound in his belly from the Fire Stick. Would it torment him in the Land of Shadows with this same incredible pain? He had not allowed himself to be killed in the hands of his enemies, and so he should not have to worry about such a thing, but the Fire Stick was new, and its power was yet unknown.

Only his wife, Looks Away, had stayed near him, risking whatever horror the wound of the Fire Stick might still hold. Its evil magic had shot all the way through him, making a small hole where it had entered and a very large ugly wound where it had left. He had not seen the large wound on his back, of course, but he had listened to the young warriors talk fearfully about it as they carried him back to the canyon.

But this wound did not frighten Looks Away, and she had stayed with him. She had made a good wife, and he loved her. It was Looks Away who had taught him much of what he knew about horses. He had captured her on a raid against the *Yutas*. He had found her so pretty that he protected her from the other warriors and treated her with kindness. The *Yutas* had more horses than the True Humans, and Looks Away, after Black Horn made her good and took her as his wife, told him much about ways to train and handle ponies. And she told him strange tales of trading parties carrying captured *Noomah* children away to the south and returning with horses. She had been told that men with iron shirts, pale skin, and faces covered with hair would trade horses for slaves.

Now Black Horn waited for this good woman to bring water, for he was thirsty. He lay alone on a buffalo robe that felt sticky with his own blood, until Shadow came near him. He raised his chin to greet the boy, too weak to lift an arm.

"*Ahpoo*," the boy said. "They took your horse."

"Your father will follow them to get it back."

Shadow smiled. "I saw many things today that I will remember when I am a warrior like you. I saw you *ride* into battle."

Black Horn held back his smile. What had possessed him to fight astride his horse? The boy was right, strong medicine had moved him to greatness. "You were brave today, nephew. You did not run and scream like a child. But you must not seek our enemies until you have found your medicine in your vision."

"I know, *Ahpoo*."

The wailing from the top of the red bluffs became frenzied. Black Horn looked up to see the warriors throwing the rawhide lines down into the crevice, on top of the body of Wounded Bear. Broken Bones began to shriek like her coyote ancestors. She held a knife with which she cut her hair off close to her scalp. She began to slash her old arms, and her shrieking made Black Horn's ears hurt, even from this far away on the canyon floor.

She slashed through the front of her old deerskin dress, drawing thin blood from her sagging breasts. She was on her knees, facing the crevice where Wounded Bear had been lowered. Her back was to the warriors who had lowered the old man, and she was trilling a song of death that had come from her old nation, the Wolf People, with whom she had lived before Wounded Bear captured her and made her good. Her song ended, her head bowed, and she tossed the knife aside for someone else to use. Her arms dangled motionless at her side.

From the canyon floor, Black Horn watched as two warriors drew their bows. They looked odd in the evening light, colored by strange powers. Their arrows struck so close together that their points must have met in the old woman's heart. She tumbled silently into the crevice with Wounded Bear, and the shadow of the faraway mountains chilled the canyon rim.

Shadow looked at his uncle.

"She goes with him," the dying warrior said.

Shadow nodded. Never again would he speak his grandparents' names: Wounded Bear. Broken Bones. Even the thought of them upon his tongue filled him with a dread of unknown ghost things. There had once been a band of True Humans called the Snake Lodge People. They had changed this name to Crawling-on-the-Ground-Lodge People after one of their warriors, called Snake Man, had died. Shadow had been made to understand things like this, for to speak the names of the dead was to call upon terrible magic from other strange worlds.

"They were a burden to your father," Black Horn added. He saw Looks Away coming with a buffalo bladder used to hold water. She also had a piece of fur and a feather. "Go now, Shadow. Go wait for your father to return. He will hear the songs of mourning from the camp, and he will want to know right away that you and your mother are well." Black Horn managed to smile at his nephew before the boy turned away from him for the last time.

Looks Away knelt beside Black Horn and carefully poured the water into his mouth. He could not drink much.

"I brought this eagle feather to protect you from evil," Looks Away said, weaving the feather into the thin braided scalp lock falling from the top of his head. "And the fur of a weasel, also."

Black Horn sighed with relief, confident now that his step into the Shadow Land would take away the pain of the Fire Stick. He would hunt and eat in the Shadow Land. Hunt and eat.

"Looks Away, hear me. Is my brother near?"

"Shaggy Hump is coming. A runner has seen the dust from his horses in the sky."

"Good." Black Horn paused to find more breath. "You will go to my brother tonight."

"I go with you, my husband. I go to the Shadow Land." She pointed toward the bluff, now black in shadows, where Broken Bones had followed her old husband.

"No. Hear me. You will go to Shaggy Hump's lodge tonight, while River Woman mourns under the moon."

Looks Away bowed her head. "When I went to Shaggy Hump's lodge before—the time River Woman was in the lodge for unclean women—she found out that you had sent me to your brother's lodge and was very angry at me, though I was only doing what you told me to do."

Black Horn would have chuckled, except that he knew it would cause too much pain. "Were you not angry at River Woman when my brother sent her to sleep in my lodge while he was away hunting sheep? It is the way for brothers to share their wives. It is the way for wives to be angry about it at first. But it is a good way, for now you will go to live with a new husband who is no stranger to you. Shaggy Hump and River Woman will remember this day as the day many burdens were lifted from them. Now there are no old ones for them to feed, and so there will be more to eat for their children, Shadow and Mouse. In the days behind us, River Woman worked hard with all the many skins Shaggy Hump brought for her to make into robes. In the days ahead she will have the help of another wife. It will please her in time."

Looks Away put her face to the ground, and held Black Horn's hand with both of her own. "I do not want to be Shaggy Hump's wife. I want to go with you to the Shadow Land."

"The spirits do not care what you want. I have seen this day in dreams.

This is the day you go to my brother's lodge. You will serve and please my brother, and you will take special care with Shadow, and teach him well the ways of the True Humans. He was born on the day the spirits sent First Horse. His medicine will be strong, but he must be taught to use it well. He must be shown how not to offend the spirits."

Looks Away remained bowed before Black Horn, silent.

"Do you hear, woman?"

She raised her head and looked into his eyes. "Yes, my husband."

"You will do one more thing. You will teach Shadow the language of the *Yutas*. The *Yutas* have many more horses than the True Humans. Shadow may trade with them in times of truce, or steal from them in time of war. A knowledge of their language will serve him well. Do you hear your husband, woman?"

"Yes, I hear. I will teach him."

Black Horn's mouth smiled, but the smile turned to a grimace as a wave of pain twisted his insides. He waited for it to pass, then said, "You are a good wife, Looks Away."

▲▲▲▲▲▲
5
▼▼▼▼▼

Shaggy Hump sat upon his horse on the rim of Red Canyon. He had read the story of the battle in the stains of blood upon the ground. Now his brother, Black Horn, was wedged in a crevice near Wounded Bear and Broken Bones, sitting upright in his bound buffalo robe, waiting to see the sun rise in the Shadow Land. Shaggy Hump could still remember his brother's dying words:

"My brother, I have failed. I scouted ahead for the enemy, but I should have looked a second time, for the Northern Raiders crept to the canyon rim after I first scouted there. This pain of the Fire Stick is meant to punish me. Beware of the Fire Stick, my brother. It has bad medicine."

He had slipped into the World of Dreams, then into the World of Spirits, the Land of Shadows.

Now the Burnt Meat People were moving south again, away from invasion by more Northern Raiders, who were sure to come. Shaggy Hump and his hunters had returned with two butchered buffalo cows to a camp in the grips of insensible sorrow. There were no reasons to stay here longer, and many reasons to leave.

Beside him, his son, Shadow, straddled the horse his grandfather had been shot from the day before. "Look long at this place, my son. This is the place of your birth." Shaggy Hump pointed down to the canyon floor. "The birthing lodge was there when First Horse made a sacred circle around it, and then you were born. Remember this place well, because we will never return here. This place has gone bad for us, like many places we have left before. We must give this place to the ghosts, or they will follow and haunt us in terrible dreams when the moon rises."

The Burnt Meat People were out of the canyon now and moving back across the high ground. It was the same ground they had crossed yesterday, but now they were weary and deep in sorrow. River Woman carried the cradle board on her back this morning, and the baby girl, Mouse, was crying. She could not reach far enough over her shoulder to put her hand over her daughter's mouth and quiet her crying. Though Shaggy Hump had taken River Woman as his wife largely because of her beauty, she appeared ugly this morning with all her hair cut off and her eyes swollen from mourning her dead parents.

Behind her walked Looks Away, who had come to Shaggy Hump last night as Black Horn lay dying. He would never have taken a second wife as long as River Woman's parents were alive, for it would only have meant another stomach to fill. Now everything had changed in the time it took the moon to cross the sky. In time, it would be well. Looks Away was quiet, and not as strong or as fiery as River Woman, but it was good to feel a different woman under him, and she would take some of the burdens of a wife's duties from River Woman. In time, River Woman would see that this way was good.

Looks Away had mourned quietly, but Shaggy Hump knew her sorrow was real. When Black Horn died, at dawn, she had cut her hair over his resting place and stared into the crevice with vacant eyes, tears streaming.

"He was your husband," River Woman said, turning suddenly to face Looks Away. "You did not even cry out. You are no wife for a warrior! You did not even cut yourself! Coward! You should have gone with him!"

Shaggy Hump saw the angry eyes of River Woman glance his way, to make sure he had heard.

"Do not walk so close behind me!" River Woman struck Looks Away with a stick she used to guide the dogs. "You are so ugly that you make my baby cry!"

This was a bad day for both women, Shaggy Hump thought. It was well that he would not have to listen to River Woman torment Looks Away all day on the trail. He was going instead to avenge his brother and bring home his brother's horse.

"Father," Shadow said. "Do the True Humans have many enemies?"

"Yes," Shaggy Hump said. "Like the snowflakes of a long winter. They are bitter and cold against us. Where the sun rises live the Wolf People. Where it sets are the Crow and Flathead. To the north lie the camps of the White Knives and Northern Raiders, and in the south, the *Yutas*. The *Noomah* have no friends. We trade with the Raccoon-Eyed People and the Mandan, it is true, but these people will not fight our wars with us. Every way we turn, we must fight. If we do not fight, we shall die, and our families shall die before our eyes, as you have now seen, my son."

"The Northern Raiders must be our fiercest enemies," Shadow said.

Shaggy Hump thought some time before he answered, and he watched many people, dogs, and lodge poles pass. "No," he said, finally. "There is one much worse, called *Na-vohnuh.*"

"Where do these enemies live, my father?"

"I do not know. I have never seen one."

"Are they like the *Nenupee?*"

"No. The *Nenupee* are little people, standing only as tall as my knee. They come out only at night, and they shoot arrows that always kill. They are very evil, so beware of them in the night, and stay near your lodge."

"The *Na-vohnuh* are large people?"

"They stand as tall as I stand, as tall as you one day shall stand, my son. They do not have the evil medicine of the *Nenupee*, but they are cruel. In days long behind us, days of our grandfathers' grandfathers, the *Noomah* and the *Na-vohnuh* were always at war. The *Na-vohnuh* killed whole villages of True Humans to feast upon their flesh. Others they tortured slowly, keeping them alive for days."

"Where have they gone?"

"Somewhere in the south. That is all I know. The wars with the *Na-vohnuh* were long ago. No one remembers where the *Na-vohnuh* may now be found. But, there have been *puhakuts* among the True Humans, *puhakuts* with strong visions, who say we will meet the terrible *Na-vohnuh* again in war."

"How will we know the *Na-vohnuh*, Father?"

"By the way they call our kind. They call us *Idahi*. Speak this, that you may remember, my son."

"*Idahi*," Shadow said.

"Our fathers have told us to remember this name. It means Snake People in the tongue of the *Na-vohnuh*, for they would step upon us like snakes. We will know them by this name they call us and by their customs."

"What customs, Father?"

"Strange customs, my son. The warriors cut all the hair off above their ear on the bow side, and grow it very long on the arrow side. Remember this, so you will know them at a glance. They remove the eggs of lice from their clothing with their teeth, making the eggs pop between their teeth. And, so the old storytellers say, their penises are infested with maggots!"

Shadow gasped.

"When the True Humans find these *Na-vohnuh*, my son, we must drive them away from their hunting grounds. We must kill their warriors and destroy their villages. They are terrible people who cast evil spells on anyone who shows them mercy. I hope I am still alive when we find them, for I want to scalp plenty of them!"

Shadow seemed less troubled after hearing his father boast his love for battle, and the two of them watched as the last pole-drag passed, its tracks plain on the ground to either side of the paw prints of the dog that pulled it.

"You must go with your mother now, Shadow. And I must trail the Northern Raiders. When I see you again, we will have a scalp dance!"

Shadow rode away in a lope to catch up with his mother. Shaggy Hump smiled, proud of his son's riding ability. The boy moved with the loping pony like a bird clutching the branch of a tree that waved in the wind. He watched his son ride away, then turned northward to find a secluded place where he could pray to his guardian spirits to guide him into battle.

· · · ·

The moon was right when Shaggy Hump found the enemy warriors two sleeps north of the Canyon of Red Rock. It was the time of the Moon Wearing Away, when his enemies would sleep most soundly. The Raiders were packing buffalo meat back to their village on the horse they had stolen from Black Horn.

It had been easy to follow them, for their burden had made the tracks of the horse press hard against the ground. Still, Shaggy Hump had ridden carefully, dismounting before every rise to crawl ahead and look for the enemy warriors. In this way he had found the smoke of their fire just before sunset, climbing up from some timber along a stream, then turning to trail away on a high breeze, looking like a gray snake hanging over a ledge. He was among the foothills of the Mountains of Bighorn Sheep—a place Shaggy Hump had visited only once before, for it was well within the range of the Northern Raiders.

He left his horse many arrow shots away and crawled closer to get a look at the enemy, keeping his head below the tops of the sage bushes. The stream and the timber poured out of the mouth of a canyon here, making a good place to camp. He could see that the Raiders had wrapped the body of the warrior Black Horn had killed in a fresh buffalo hide. This told Shaggy Hump that the main enemy camp was near, for the warriors were taking the body home instead of burying it here. Beside the body lay the warrior Black Horn had cut across the belly with his white flint knife. The other three warriors were unhurt, and one kept the Fire Stick forever at his side.

Shaggy Hump could tell that they were young warriors who had gone out to scout and hunt and had gotten themselves into more mischief than they could handle. They were making no attempt to guard their back-trail against pursuit. They did not understand the ways of war like the True Humans—a people forever hunted. Tonight he would teach them.

After crawling back to his pony, Shaggy Hump prayed silently and used

paint of red clay and berry juice from his paint pouch to make the war marks
upon his face: two red streaks streaming snakelike, downward from his cheeks
to his jawline. Waiting for darkness to fall and the moon to rise, he crept
downwind of the enemy camp to plan his attack. The fire had burned out,
and only the moon and stars made light. He smelled the faint trace of smoke
and the aroma of horse sweat, and knew he was very near. He carried only
his knife and war club with which to kill, though he had also brought along
a single arrow with a chipped point and half a feather missing—one he did
not mind parting with.

He thought about each step he took, testing the ground gradually with
his weight in case a cracking stick from the willow and cottonwood timber
or a pair of rocks scraping together might warn the Raiders. Once, a dried leaf
crackled as he shifted on one foot for balance, and he remained still a very
long time to ensure he had not been discovered.

The spirits were making the winds gust with their breath, causing the
sounds of whistling tree branches and scuttering leaves to cover his approach,
and he moved more rapidly than he otherwise might have.

Finally, he was upon the camp and could hear the feet of the horse shifting
from time to time. He could see all three of the unwounded warriors sleeping
now. One slept near the horse, guarding it. The rawhide thong around the
animal's neck was also wrapped around this warrior's wrist. He was curled in
his robe at the roots of a *sohoobi* tree—the kind of tree that rained little tufts
of white hair in the spring. The other two warriors had gone to sleep some
ten or twelve steps away, beside the fire. Beyond them were the corpse of the
dead Raider and the wounded man, moaning in his sleep.

The wind came up, allowing three quick steps, and Shaggy Hump was
upon the rawhide thong. He grabbed it just as his scent reached the nostrils
of the horse, which pulled against the rawhide in curiosity, for the beast knew
Shaggy Hump's scent. Keeping the thong from pulling at the wrist of the
sleeping guard, Shaggy Hump began slowly sawing at the rawhide with the
iron knife his son had captured in the battle of the Red Canyon.

When at last the rawhide had been cut, Shaggy Hump tied the horse to
a stout tree, which would prevent the horse from wandering off as he went
about his duty. He chose each step carefully, until he was standing over the
sleeping guard. He raised his *pogamoggan* in one hand, taking the rawhide line
he had cut in the other.

He pulled gently on the rawhide, as if the horse were moving away. Two
coils of the rawhide slipped off of the Raider's wrist before he grabbed it, half-
asleep. Shaggy Hump slacked the tension, then pulled harder. The Raider
jerked angrily, as if to punish the horse. Shaggy Hump waited for the next
gust to roar in the tree tops, then pulled once more on the rawhide, horselike.

The enemy warrior grunted and revealed his head from within the robe.

The *pogamoggan* struck swiftly, and hard. Its thump against the skull caused the horse to shy, the hooves sounding much like the thump of the club upon the head. This was good. As the wind died, Shaggy Hump fell upon the enemy with his knife and cut his throat.

He listened as he felt the hot blood, and he could tell by a change in breathing that one of the other warriors near the ashes of the fire had woken and was listening. Shaggy Hump waited until his victim died, then waited longer. Longer. When he was sure the warrior at the fire suspected nothing and had gone back to sleep, he began taking the scalp from the warrior he had slain.

He did not take a large part of the scalp, for wrenching that much from the skull would have made much noise. He only took a small scalp lock, enough to dance around upon his return.

Tucking the trophy under the thong of his loin skins beneath his deerskin shirt, Shaggy Hump stood once more, and judged the ground between himself and the two Raiders near the fire. There were many leaves and sticks here. He would have to slide a moccasin under them gradually for each step, waiting for the wind to cover the sound of his approach.

His legs and back became stiff from the hard work of creeping upon his foes, but at last he stood between them. The moon was almost gone behind the ridge, and Shaggy Hump knew he must finish quickly, for he needed light to find footing out of this enemy camp.

He knelt, slowly, over the Raider who slept with the Fire Stick. He could only see the end of the evil thing sticking out of the buffalo robe, and he knew from the stories that this end was the one which shot embers and bad medicine. He reached for it with the hand that held his knife, though the Fire Stick was very near the face of the sleeping enemy. His club was ready in case this warrior should wake.

Holding the iron knife with his thumb and two small fingers, he reached for the end of the Fire Stick with his bowstring fingers. He touched it cautiously, felt its chill. This was iron, the thing of the white man. Once, Shaggy Hump had thought the white man a legend made up by lesser peoples. He had since decided that this white man must exist somewhere, for he kept hearing more and more strange tales—from the Raccoon-Eyed People with whom he traded, and from women captured from enemies and made into wives of the Burnt Meat People's warriors. They said the white men grew hair out all over their faces, which Shaggy Hump thought must look very ugly, for the most handsome men were those who plucked all the hair from the chins, brows, and eyelids, as he himself did. He hoped some day to see a white man, and trade something for some arrow points or knives of iron or—better still— horses.

Whether or not he wanted a Fire Stick, he was still not sure. The one against his fingertips did not seem as evil as his brother had said. It wasn't waking up or barking fire. It was not alive. Still, it must have strong magic, or the enemy warrior would not guard it so closely. If ever he found out he could master such magic without offending the spirits, Shaggy Hump would obtain his own Fire Stick, but now it was better to let this one lie.

He stood again over his enemies, who were lost so stupidly in the false peace of sleep. He tucked the iron knife under his belt. He drew the lone arrow from his quiver. He began to draw it slowly from the quiver, bit by bit.

The barbed war point had been chipped thin and flaked to a fine edge by Wounded Bear, a maker of fine arrows, though he had been almost blind. This particular point had missed its target in a fight during the last Moon of Falling Leaves and had struck a rock, breaking the tip off. Shaggy Hump had plenty of arrows, and didn't mind leaving this one here.

Once clear of the quiver, he put the sharp point of the arrow against the earth, between the heads of the two Raiders. Using his weight, he leaned upon the shaft of this arrow with a silent and grueling deliberation, pushing the point past one grain of soil, then the next, then the next. Finally the point was sunk deep enough to make the arrow shaft stand against the wind. It would greet the enemy warriors when they woke at dawn, and mock them for their youthful inability to make war.

He used even more care moving away than he had used approaching, for this was where a warrior of lesser skills would lose discipline. The moon-made shadow of the bluff was moving onto the enemy camp now, staying close against the heel of Shaggy Hump's moccasin as he withdrew, step by purposeful step. He moved no faster than this shadow, arriving at last at the tree where he had tied his dead brother's horse, now his.

He led this horse away at the same regimented pace, as if each step spanned the body of a sleeping foe whom he must not wake. He moved away so slowly that the horse cropped every blade of grass along the way as they went. Away . . . away . . . away . . . until he had gone far enough to mount, and ride back to the Burnt Meat People in victory and glory.

6

The Time of Great Change came in Shadow's fourteenth summer. It started during the Moon of Thunder, when the True Humans rolled up the bottoms of their lodge covers to let the breezes cool their resting places. Shadow was lying naked on the soft cured side of an old buffalo robe in his tipi, looking out under the rolled-up hides at the small herd of grazing horses the Burnt

Meat People owned. Beyond the horses, he could look far across the gray sage and short brown grass. A great distance to the west, he saw a purple thundercloud hanging in the sky, a curtain of blue rain slanting from it.

He wished that it might come the way of his camp, that the grass would green again and bring herds of elk, deer, or antelope—maybe even buffalo. He knew he would be taking his first hunt soon, and the things he wanted to kill for meat numbered plenty. Yet, there was no hunger now in his camp, for the roots of the yampa vine were easily dug, and much meat had been dried. Also, small animals were plentiful here and tasted good enough.

He was chewing a piece of bread made from the crushed seeds of lamb's quarters and sunflowers. His father's second wife, Looks Away, had made this bread and flavored it well with berries. Shadow loved Looks Away almost as much as his own mother, for they were both kind to him, though Looks Away sometimes scolded him.

As he ate, he listened to his father tell the story of the time he followed the Northern Raiders who had attacked the Burnt Meat People, and of how he had ridden home with the fresh scalp of the enemy who had stolen his brother's horse. Shadow remembered his uncle well, and knew his father did, also, though Black Horn's name was not mentioned in the story. To speak it might bring ghosts out with the moon.

"Do you remember the scalp dance we held when I returned, my son?" Shaggy Hump said.

"Yes, Father. It was a good one."

The warrior waved his hand modestly. "It was just a little one. Only one scalp. You have yet to see a really good scalp dance."

"Why did you not kill more Raiders that time, Father? You have said that you might have killed them all, because they slept so soundly."

"That is true, but I must do as my guardian spirits instruct me in my dreams and in the visions I seek before battle. I was told to kill only one Raider, count only one battle stroke, and take only one scalp. To have killed more would have displeased the spirits and destroyed my medicine."

Shadow inhaled through his nostrils, trying in vain to smell the faraway thundercloud. Instead, he smelled only the dung of horses, which pleased him nonetheless. "Why did you leave the arrow in the ground between the two Raiders?"

The warrior rubbed his full stomach and closed his eyes, speaking groggily now. "This, too, I was instructed to do. My markings were on the arrow shaft, so that the Northern Raiders would know who crept among them and killed their fellow warrior. This brings greater glory to the spirits who guide me and greater medicine to me."

Shadow smiled with admiration upon the resting form of his father. He was proud to be the son of Shaggy Hump, greatest war leader of the Burnt

Meat People. Shadow believed his father must even be the bravest warrior of all the True Humans of all the bands. His arms and shoulders looked like the burls of an ancient tree, his scars like battle wounds upon a great bear. He now owned enough horses to ride and ride hard every day, and still have a rested mount always ready. Shaggy Hump went almost nowhere afoot, preferring to mount a pony even to cross the camp.

"Father," Shadow said, speaking softly in case Shaggy Hump had already fallen asleep.

His father grunted.

"When I go to seek my visions, what kind of spirit do you think I might meet?"

Shaggy Hump opened his eyes, smiled, and propped himself up on one elbow. "You have no need to think about it. The spirits are wiser about such things than we are. Anyway, I think you will know very soon. It is just about time for you, my son."

Shadow's heart felt as if birds were fluttering in it, trying to escape. Soon, he would have medicine. Then, he would hunt the buffalo and the bear. Finally, he would become a warrior. Since that day at Red Canyon, the war cry of Black Horn, his uncle, had dwelled within him like an echo that never died, but only came again and again and again. Sometimes, even when that day was the most distant of his thoughts, he would suddenly hear his uncle's scream of courageous rage pass again, out of nowhere, into nothing. He would hear it so clearly that once he had even asked one of his playmates if he too had heard it. But that echo of days behind him was for his ears alone, for he was meant for great things. He had been born on the day the spirits gave First Horse to the True Humans. First Horse had made a circle of tracks around his birth lodge that was as perfect in its roundness as a full moon. This he had been told since he could remember, and Shadow yearned for the chance to fulfill the prophesies of his elders.

"What will be my new name, Father? After I seek my visions?"

"That is not for me to decide," Shaggy Hump said. "My only task is to choose your Naming Father. It is very important. I am waiting for a sign or a dream to tell me who I must choose. Your Naming Father must be a *puhakut* of great power. Greater than great!"

Shadow grinned and rolled back onto the robe, feeling a cool wind come under the hide walls from a new quarter. It was at this moment that he heard his playmate, Whip, his boyish voice squeaking as he yelled excitedly.

Crawling forward, Shadow stuck his head out underneath the hides. "Whip! What are you yelling about?"

Shaggy Hump lay back down on his cushion of robes.

"The Corn People are coming to camp with us, Shadow!"

Shadow looked back at his father, who smirked with more than a little interest, for the Burnt Meat People seldom came across other bands of True Humans across the far ranges of their hunting grounds.

"They have thirty lodges!" Whip reported.

"But how many horses?" the boy asked, knowing the question would please his father.

Whip threw himself to the ground outside the lodge of Shaggy Hump, dust flying around him. "The scout said only five."

"My father alone owns more than that."

"Yes, the Burnt Meat People have more horses. Still, the Corn People have thirty lodges, Shadow. Do you understand? They have plenty of girls!"

Shadow smiled. "When will they get here?"

"Before the sun goes behind the mountains."

"We must run to meet them!"

Shadow started to crawl out under the lodge cover, but his father called his name, stopping him.

"My son, you should go through the opening. It is bad luck to crawl under, unless you have crawled in that same way. And tie your skins on about your loins before you go. You are old enough now to wear your skins all the time, especially if you are going to meet strange girls. Look how big your pecker has grown! It looks like the pecker of a yearling! Do you want to frighten the girls of the Corn People with that thing?"

Shadow and Whip laughed like turkeys gobbling, and Shadow found his loin coverings and the thong that held them on.

7

Shadow and Whip were running with their new friend, Trotter, of the Corn People, when they chanced to jump a rabbit from some bushes near a stream called Sometimes Water. Their eyes gleamed like the eyes of their wolf ancestors as they pursued with pack hunting skills they didn't even know they possessed. Clad only in moccasins and loin skins, they tore through tangles of undergrowth in the shade of the huge *sohoobi* trees, their locks of long hair streaming behind them like the tails of black ponies.

"Ha!" Shadow shouted, spooking the harried rabbit from a moment's respite taken in the thick of a raspberry vine. Trotter descended upon the opposite side of the bramble, and the rabbit dodged, only to find Whip circling into place with a stick he had scooped from the ground at a dead run. The stick drove the rabbit onto a trail, and the boys hit their longest gait trying to keep up with the fleeing prey.

Near a place where the roots of a big tree collected the waters of the stream, making them sing, the rabbit sought protection in the hollow of a fallen tree, years in the rotting.

Whip prodded the rotten wood with the stick he had picked up, but the log was long, and the rabbit had crawled beyond his reach.

"I know a way," Shadow said. "Whip, run to the village and bring a burning coal."

Whip bolted as if a great bear had come after him. By the time he returned with a buffalo-horn fire carrier containing a smoking ember, Trotter and Shadow had plugged the opening to the hollow log with sage brush and had gathered a mound of moss and grass moist enough to smoulder. Shadow placed dry grass and sticks so that they would burn and make coals. Whip and Trotter admired his skill in constructing the pyre, applying the brand, and fanning it to a small flame.

When the coals had been mounded high enough, the boys snuffed out the open flame with moss and half-rotten grass, making smoke billow up from the coals. Shadow looked around for strange girls, then took off his loin skin and used it to fan the smoke into the opening in the end of the hollow log. He would let the smoke gather under the skins, then force the small cloud through the sage brush, into the hollow. Some of the smoke would escape and rise in a free cloud that Shadow liked to watch go up among the tree branches. He studied each puff of smoke that rose this way, until the squeal of the rabbit in the hollow log distracted him.

When the shrill screaming of the doomed rabbit began, the boys ceased their joking and looked soberly at the log, but Shadow only fanned the smoke in with increased enthusiasm. Then they could hear the animal trying to push through the sage brush blocking the entrance to the hollow, and finally, they could see it trying to push through the brush, its piercing scream of distress coming loud enough to make Trotter put a finger in one ear.

"We will have him!" Shadow said. "He sings his death song!"

Whip grinned.

Trotter lay down on his stomach to watch the rabbit struggle. He laughed. "His medicine fails him," he said.

The plaintive squeal of the rabbit weakened as the sting of smoke caused tears to streak down Shadow's face.

When Shadow was satisfied that the rabbit had suffocated, he began clawing the sage brush from the hollow. Trotter and Whip tried to push him away from either side, starting a rough wrestling match. But Shadow had seized the advantage and reached in first for the long ears. He kicked and elbowed the other boys aside and pulled the limp animal from the hollow. Taking the rabbit by the hind feet, he thumped its head against a tree several times to make sure it was dead, then raised it above his head.

"Aaa-hey!" he shouted, mimicking the cry of a warrior claiming the first stroke on a fallen enemy. Whip and Trotter scrambled and pushed each other to get at the carcass, Trotter finally touching it with a slap of his palm.

"Aaa-hey!" Trotter wailed, his voice somewhat higher than Shadow's.

As only two strokes could be claimed on a fallen foe, Whip hissed at his friends as if to make fun of them, though he had tried as hard as they to claim the honors. "It is only a rabbit!" he said. "My elder sister could count a battle stroke on a rabbit!"

"Let us go and show it to her then," Trotter said, for he had seen Whip's elder sister, and considered her as pretty as any girl the Burnt Meat People had to offer.

Whip's mood brightened. "My sister has her own lodge now, at the far end of the camp. We can run through the whole camp with our rabbit and make her cook it for us!"

By the time they neared the lodges, they had contrived the device of tossing the rabbit to one another through the air. At the edge of the camp, they avoided the tripods of lances holding the sacred buffalo-hide war shields off the ground, protected by rawhide covers. They dodged fires and darting dogs, flinging the rabbit all the way over the short, four-pole lodges of the poorer horseless warriors. They shouted as they swerved among fires and scaffolds stretching deer hides in the sun.

Spying a group of girls walking through the village, Shadow motioned with his head for Whip to run around the opposite side of them so he could fling the dead rabbit over their heads, thinking this would impress them. Trotter saw the strategy quickly and took up a third position flanking the girls, who were still so engrossed in conversation that they hadn't taken much notice of the boys.

When the carcass sailed over them, one of the Corn People girls ducked, shrieking her amusement, while the others giggled at the boys, who continued to throw the rabbit over their heads. Shadow saw that there were two girls of the Corn People in this group, and three girls he knew from his own band. Ignoring the familiar girls, he stole glimpses of the two others between his athletic capers with the dead rabbit.

One of them seemed a year or two older than the rest, and older than Shadow himself. She was attractive merely because she was nearer to maturity and exotic to Shadow, hailing as she did from another band of True Humans.

But when Shadow caught the eyes of the second Corn People girl, he was so taken by her that the rabbit hit him in the face, causing all of the girls to laugh uncontrollably. Pretending to have let this happen on purpose, he quickly grabbed the rabbit and tossed it back to Whip.

"You see that I am a Foolish One!" he said, looking at the girl who had distracted him so. "The Foolish Ones are the bravest of warriors among all the True Humans!"

The girl was his age or younger, and prettier than any girl he could have imagined. She smirked at his boast, but said nothing.

The older Corn People girl stepped boldly up to Shadow. "If you are so brave," she said, "you will give that rabbit to Teal's father, and prove that you are not afraid to mount her in your lodge!"

The girls shrieked with scandalous laughter, except for Teal herself, who gasped and struck the older girl with a sunshade she carried.

"*Pookai!*" she said. "Hush, Slope Child! You are wilder than wild!"

Whip held the rabbit at his side in dumb disbelief of Slope Child's candor, but Trotter only laughed, for he knew Slope Child and her ways.

Shadow flung aside a morsel of embarrassed surprise and framed a reply. "One dead rabbit?" he said to Slope Child. "Her father would laugh at me. I will wait until I have ten horses to present to Teal's father!"

This surprised the girls even more than Slope Child's suggestion, and seemed to embarrass and please Teal all at once that Shadow should consider her worthy of ten horses.

"Forget about Teal," Slope Child said. "You may mount me in your lodge for less than the price of the whole rabbit. I only want the fur."

The girls of the Burnt Meat People gasped in disbelief. Never had they heard a girl, or even a full-grown woman, speak so freely. All of them—boys and girls—knew of the sensual pleasures, for the nights were often quiet and the hide walls of the lodges were always thin. But among the Burnt Meat People there had always existed a certain reserve regarding intimate matters.

"Besides," Slope Child continued, "no warrior has ever owned ten horses."

"Teal's father shall," Shadow replied. "I shall own a hundred!"

The children of the Corn People laughed at this reckless boast, but Whip and the three Burnt Meat People girls only smiled.

"Come on, my friends," Shadow said. "Whip's elder sister is going to cook this rabbit for us."

"Keep the fur!" Slope Child said, as the boys broke away from the five girls.

As he left, Shadow heard one of the Burnt Meat girls say, "Shadow is the one. First Horse circled his birth lodge."

Trotter came to his side as they ran. "Do you have your own lodge yet, Shadow?"

"Yes. My mother built it for me before last winter. She said I was getting too old and hairy to sleep in the same lodge with my younger sister."

"It is good. Now Slope Child will come to your lodge in the dark. I will tell her where your lodge is if you will show me. She is a good teacher, my friend."

Shadow grinned. "I will leave the entrance uncovered for her. I know how it is done, but I have never done it. I will lie with Slope Child if she comes to my lodge, but it is Teal that I want as my wife."

Trotter laughed, but Whip said, "Shadow will have her! His words are like a circle and always come around!"

When they reached the far edge of the village, where Whip's elder sister had raised her lodge, Whip tossed the dead rabbit at her feet. "Shadow, tell my sister to roast this rabbit over the fire," he said, as boldly as a war chief bringing home a scalp.

She looked up from the rack she was building of willow limbs and rawhide to stretch and dry a beaver skin. Her face revealed her lack of enthusiasm for serving her younger brother.

"Tell my brother to skin it," she said to Shadow.

"She will skin it herself!" Whip insisted.

His sister scowled. "My brother must build the fire while I skin it. I do not have time to do everything."

Whip threw his chest forward. "She will skin it *and* build the fire. We will catch and ride some horses while she cooks our kill for us."

Whip's sister jerked a knot into the rawhide and snatched the rabbit from the ground. "Is my brother too lazy to drive a stick into the ground to roast the rabbit over the fire?"

Whip marched to the sticks piled near his sister's lodge and rifled through them, testing each one for toughness and flexibility. "Here is a good one," he announced, shaking the stick in the air.

Suddenly, he ran at his sister, striking her across the shoulders and back with the stick, hitting her again and again until she dropped the rabbit and fell to her knees. "My sister will drive it into the ground herself!" he said, throwing the stick down beside her.

The boys turned away to catch the horses they wanted to ride.

"Now your sister will roast the rabbit well," Trotter said. "You have prepared her to make a good wife for some warrior, and she is very pretty as well."

They walked several steps in silence.

"You could have struck her just once," Shadow said, "and she would have remembered the lesson. Now she will only remember the beating."

8

After riding three of Shaggy Hump's horses, they ate their rabbit, roasted whole over the open fire. They stripped the intestines between their fingers and divided them equally, wrapping the slick gut around a hand to tear off chunks with their teeth.

They had held a horse race to determine choice of heart, liver, and brains. Shadow had won easily on his father's fastest horse. He chose the heart. Whip, who had come in second, chose the brains. As the Corn People owned few horses, Trotter had ridden very little, so he had come in last in the race, but he claimed to prefer liver more than heart and brains anyway. They gnawed every morsel of meat from the bones of the rabbit, then broke the bones to suck out the delicious marrow.

"Tell my sister you want the rabbit hide, Shadow. You will need it when Slope Child visits your lodge."

Shadow laughed, but Trotter said, "I think she will go to your lodge, my friend. Slope Child is that way. She has no brother to beat her, and no mother to shame her. Not even an aunt or a sister. She does not want to be a wife of any one warrior. The young men with no wives give her gifts."

Shadow looked across the open grounds beyond the tipis and saw his father's horses looking back at him, as if they were waiting for him to come and play some more. "I will give the rabbit skin to Slope Child if she wants to come to my lodge, but I think she is foolish. A woman must have a husband, and sons. Who will take care of her when she is old and ugly?"

After they finished their meal, they borrowed some arrows from Whip's grandfather, who always made plenty of arrows for the boys. The three friends made a game of throwing the arrows at a circle they scratched in a part of the creek bank that water had worn away. They gambled the things they owned—flints and elk teeth and feathers. Shadow was winning this game, but when he looked over his shoulder he saw the horses watching him again.

"Look," he said. "The ponies want to play."

Taking the war bridles from their shoulders, the boys approached the band of horses. The animals started to break away from Trotter and Whip, so Shadow told them to stand still.

"I will teach you how to talk horse," he said. He walked toward his father's fastest horse, a big dun saying "Huh, huh," in a low tone. The animal stood still, as if charmed. He came closer, and the horse tossed his head and nickered. Then something happened that Shadow would never forget. The pony-talk changed between the horse's mouth and Shadow's ears. The spirits made the horse-sound into a word, and the word was *Noomah*.

Shadow stopped and stood like a tree, amazed that a pony had spoken to him. Affecting the tone and voice of the pony, he answered, saying, "*Noomah. Noo-oo-mah-ah.*" The big dun came to meet him. Without bothering to slip the bridle around the horse's jaw, he grabbed the mane and swung onto the dun's back. Guiding the animal with his knees, he kept the other ponies bunched so Whip and Trotter could catch their mounts. Yet, he was thinking about the way he had learned to talk to the horse he now rode. It did not seem that Whip and Trotter had heard the pony say, "*Noomah*," or heard Shadow reply the same way. It was as if the spirits wanted only him to know the language of the horse.

While the other two boys were fixing their war bridles and mounting, Shadow began leading the band of horses away. He held the mane tight as the dun changed from a lope to a gallop. The riderless horses beside him kicked their heels and tossed their heads, making Shadow smile. He could feel his own hair pulling in the wind, like the mane of the dun horse he rode.

Thundering around the big camp of the Corn People and Burnt Meat People, Shadow saw the rest of the horses—nine of them in all—grazing across the high ground above the camp. He made his pony circle them, and closed the circle tighter as they became excited. He leaned forward and hooked his heels beneath the curve of his horse's ribs. The big dun responded, leaping ahead with greater speed, snorting for breath.

As he circled the herd, he saw Whip and Trotter, and rumbled past them.

"I need my pad," Whip yelled as he passed. "This horse makes much sweat against my legs."

"Then go and get it!" Shadow shouted. "I will get on a different horse when this one sweats too much!"

As Trotter and Whip watched him, he angled into the herd, like a hawk diving on a raft of ducks. Pacing a small black, he grabbed a handful of the black's mane with one hand and placed his other hand in the middle of the black pony's back. Throwing his weight to his shoulders, his seat left the dun and he pushed off with his legs, landing behind the withers of the black horse. He still carried his bridle looped across his shoulder, and now used the reins like a quirt, whipping the black ahead of the other horses, guiding the animal with his heels and knees, as his father had taught him.

Trotter and Whip loped away to the camp to get their pads. Beyond them, Shadow saw a group of people standing, watching him as he sped around the herd. This made him bolder, and he drove the horses in a serpentine path, Mother Earth drumming under him contentedly. The black began to sweat, which made Shadow stick better to its back, yet it irritated his skin, so he angled against a red mare he knew well, and sprang to her back, now driving her through the middle of the others, forming two herds. Quickly, he had the horses together again. He pushed them toward the lodges, closer to the growing group of onlookers.

Riding by the people, he yelped in victory—"yee, yee, yee!"—as if he had stolen these horses from some enemy, and he saw his father, smiling, standing beside an old man of the Corn People. The old man was squinting to see, and his toothless mouth was open.

Next he glimpsed a face as sweet as a dew-kissed blossom and smiled at Teal as he rode by her. But before she could respond, Slope Child had stepped in front of her, staring provocatively, and then Shadow had passed.

Now he whipped the red mare ahead of the other horses, turning them sharply away from the camp. He found himself against a bay colt, and sprang to its back, realizing only as he lit that this colt belonged to some Corn People warrior, and not his father. The moment his weight settled, the colt humped his back and sprang on four stiff legs, then leapt, then ducked his head low, whirling as his rump rose.

Shadow tumbled like a war axe thrown long through the air, and he caught glimpses of the lodges, the horses, and the people. Bouncing across the back of another horse, he saw himself engulfed by horseflesh, shadows, and dust. The ground flattened him, and he heard hooves thump near his ears. A blow tore his inner thigh and another shifted hard across his chest as sunlight burst down on him like the pain that flared through his body.

His breath was gone, but his first concern was that his father would think him dead, so he rolled to hands and knees, then knelt, facing the fleeing herd. Dust caked the raw flesh across his chest and clung to the blood that trickled down his leg. A great peal of laughter came from all the people who had been watching him show off. A gasp of air came to him as Whip arrived, his mount now wearing the pad saddle.

Whip laughed and said, "You must heed what you say when you talk horse, my friend."

Shadow rose to his feet, wincing at his pain, yet proud of his wounds. "*Hah*," he wheezed. "Drive the horses back to me. I want them to smell my blood."

Trotter arrived now and helped Whip turn the horses back. Shadow spread his arms as they came to him, and he spoke to them again, saying, "*Noomah. Noo-oo-mah-ah.*" His father's dun came forward first, snuffing in the boy's direction. Shadow took this horse by the muzzle and exhaled into his nostrils, the other horses now gathering around him as if he were one of them. Taking the dun's dark mane, he sprang to its back, the horse sweat stinging the gash to his inner thigh.

He turned again to the village, the dun obeying a tug to his mane and the pressure of moccasins against his sides. Riding past the people who had come to watch, Shadow raised both arms and swept them backward, his legs clamped around the loping dun. He thrust his wounded chest forward that the people might admire the injury. When he passed his father, he saw that Shaggy Hump no longer smiled, yet neither did he scowl. Beside him, the toothless old man of the Corn People was laughing like a wheezing dog.

· · · ·

When dark came the boys played the flaming stick game. They chose straight, spearlike sticks, making one end blaze in a fire. They took turns throwing these blazing lances through the night sky, none flying farther than Shadow's, in spite of his injuries.

Later, they lay outside a lodge where many warriors had gathered. There, the boys listened to stories of battles and escapes, of great hunts for buffalo and huge humpbacked bears. There were several boys listening here, and some began to fall asleep. At last, Shadow yawned and slipped away, wending his way among the lodges to his own tipi—a comfortable little shelter of four poles and five skins. When he entered, he saw that the half-moon was shining down through the smoke hole, casting its soft light on a grassy place he had yet to cover with robes.

Shadow was tired, but he felt well. After riding today, he had bathed in the stream called Sometimes Water, getting the dirt out of the places where the horses had stepped on him. These wounds were getting sore and tender now, and he was very proud of them. He would sleep well.

He left his loin skins where they fell and lay naked upon the soft hairy side of an old, supple buffalo robe. He pulled the robe gently over his chest, careful not to irritate his wound. He was drifting quickly toward the land of dreams when he heard the faint rustling of the hide that covered the entry hole to his lodge.

Forcing his eyes open, he saw Slope Child step in and kneel beside him inside the small lodge. He started to rise, but she motioned for him to be still and quiet. She carried something in her hand—a small container made of buffalo horn.

Bending over him, she whispered, "I bring medicine for your wounds."

"They are nothing," he said, whispering back.

She gave the sign for silence, dreamlike in the moonlight that shifted down through the smoke hole. She lifted the buffalo robe from his chest. She dipped her finger into the buffalo horn container and gently, sparingly spread the medicine of herbs and bear fat on the skin that the hoof had scraped and gashed. She worked slowly, her eyes moving from the injury to Shadow's eyes. She put the horn on the ground so she would have a free hand to rest on his bare chest. Her hand was warm. She took a long time.

"Now the leg," she whispered.

Shadow tried to remain calm, but when she shifted the robe across his lower body, he felt a surge of pleasure like lightning pulsing through clouds. He kicked the robe away and was embarrassed, thinking Slope Child might make fun of him, as it was a woman's place to shame a warrior's every weakness. She said nothing, but he was afraid to look into her eyes. He just stared at the sky through the smoke hole and felt her hands go through the exquisite process of treating the wound on his inner thigh, her free hand wandering ever farther up his sound leg.

Finally, she put the medicine horn aside and lifted the deerskin dress over her hips, over her breasts. He closed his eyes, for he had been told that looking upon a woman completely naked would cause him to go blind. He wondered what to do next, but felt her straddle him, and knew he only had to lie there and learn.

Her face was just above his, for he could feel her breath upon him. "I will be gentle this time," she whispered, very softly. "When your wounds heal, I will be wild. As my friend, Teal has said, I am wilder than wild, Shadow."

9

The Na-vohnuh *had caught* him sleeping and were torturing him, galling the flesh of his chest and inner thigh with knives and hot coals. He could hear his friend, Whip, screaming outside the lodge, and Slope Child was calling his name in a voice that sounded grotesque:

"Shadow! Shadow!"

He awoke and saw his father's face looking in at him.

"There you are!" Shaggy Hump said. "Why do you sleep with the sun so high? Come!"

The waking youth looked around to make sure Slope Child was gone, then flung the robe aside. "Ah!" he cried, his wounds feeling very sore now.

"Come, my son!"

Grimacing, Shadow rose and took a hobbling step to the entrance hole.

"Where will you carry your medicine pouch?" Shaggy Hump demanded.

It took Shadow a moment to figure out what his father meant, for he didn't even own a medicine pouch, as he had yet to seek his medicine. Once he acquired it, the pouch would be carried inside his loin skins, but . . .

Suddenly he knew why his father sought him, and he hurriedly tied his skins about him before stepping outside.

They walked briskly across the camp, Shadow favoring the leg that the horse had stepped on.

"Do you wish the women to shame you and call you elder sister?" Shaggy Hump asked.

"No, my father."

"Then do not walk like a cripple. That is only a scratch!"

"Yes, my father."

They passed by his parents' lodge, where River Woman was tending to her chores.

"Give our son something to eat, woman. He will go hungry soon enough."

River Woman drew a knife from her belted sheath and cut a length of pemmican—tallow, berries, seeds, and dried meat encased in deer gut. As Shadow ate this, she went to fetch a gourd dipper filled with milk taken from the udders of an antelope Shaggy Hump had killed at dusk yesterday. He ate and drank voraciously, on his feet. His mind swam with thoughts of Slope Child last night, his vision quest to come, great hunts and battles, and Teal in his lodge of days ahead.

Looks Away came with an armload of wood. She began placing the wood stick by stick on the pile. Another woman would have thrown the whole load down at once, but Looks Away was quiet and meticulous about her work. She smiled at Shadow and spoke many wishes with just her eyes and her smile.

"Finish your food as we walk," Shaggy Hump said, pulling his son away.

They marched across the camp, until Shaggy Hump put his hand on his son's shoulder. "Do you see that lodge?"

Shadow beheld a small tipi, not much larger than his own, but painted elaborately with all manner of signs and animals and colors. The flap was open and a trail of smoke streamed from the peak. "Yes, my father."

"That is the lodge of your Naming Father. He is called Spirit Talker. He will tell you about the journey, my son, and you must listen if you wish to have good medicine. Now, go. He waits."

Shadow handed the empty gourd to his father and approached the lodge cautiously. When he looked over his shoulder, he saw his father already stalking away, so he stuck his head into the open entrance hole of the painted lodge.

"Is that you?" the gravelly voice said. "Are you the boy called Shadow?" It was the old man who had laughed at him yesterday for having gotten thrown from the colt.

"Yes, Grandfather," the boy said, respectfully.

"Before you come in, move the wind-flap poles for me. The wind has shifted and my lodge is full of smoke."

From outside, Shadow moved the poles various ways as Spirit Talker yelled, "Yes, that way . . . No, the other way . . . That is better, now . . . No, no! More to the west!" until finally the smoke hole was drawing well enough to vent the tipi.

"Now, sit," the old man said, once Shadow had entered the lodge, "and I will tell you things you need to know."

Shadow sat rigidly on a buffalo robe.

"Get comfortable. You are going to be here a long time, listening to me."

Shadow shifted and sat as naturally as his sore chest and leg would allow.

"I have heard many stories about you, young horseback. They say First Horse circled your lodge as you were born. They say you will have strong medicine because of this."

The old man paused, either to chuckle or to wheeze—Shadow could not tell which.

"What the spirits caused to happen in days behind us means nothing. The spirits sometimes change their mind." The old man sighed, threw a pinch of some kind of powder into the fire. "They are like the clouds that promise rain and bring only hail. I have spent all of my life looking for signs and talking to spirits, and still I cannot make sense of everything they bring about. So, do not think you are favored because a stray horse circled your lodge as you were born, or you will offend the spirits on your vision quest."

"I do not think I am favored, Grandfather. I only want to make my people proud."

Spirit Talker grunted. "You speak well. Now, listen well. I will tell you about my vision quest when I was a know-nothing boy like you."

Spirit Talker started in on the walking, fasting, and thirsting of the quest. He spoke of the standing, the smoking, the praying. He went on so long that Shadow thought he must be telling it at about the same pace it happened. The old man related all this sitting upright on his couch of robes, his eyes closed and his face turned up.

Then the old man began to tell of the vision he had received so long ago. It fascinated Shadow at first, but it went on too long, and began to make no sense at all. Spirit Talker spoke of birds that turned into arrows and flew far away to kill, of ancient owls that caught and ate the flesh of still-living men, of antelope that ran upside-down on the bottoms of clouds, of great lodges in the sky, of trees that sprouted and bloomed and made fruit and died in the blink of an eye, of bears who spoke the tongue of wolves who spoke the tongue of snakes who spoke the tongue of True Humans. There were councils underground where buffalo and deer and great humpbacked bears met with the grandfathers' grandfathers of the True Humans. There were worlds in the clouds, across the waters, beyond the stars. It was so confusing that after a great while, Shadow's thoughts slipped back to Slope Child in his lodge last night to Teal in his dreams of greatness to come. He began to ignore completely the old man and listen to what was going on outside the little painted lodge.

He heard the hooves of horses trotting. He heard small children laughing as they played games. He heard a woman breaking sticks with a stone axe.

Once, he heard a hawk call from high up in the sky, and glancing through the smoke hole, happened to see the hawk pass. He could not believe that anybody could go on as long as Spirit Talker without moving anything but his mouth.

". . . and when I looked again," the old man was saying, "the coyotes had turned into spirits in the shape of . . ."

The voice fell silent, and Shadow looked quickly at the old man's face, thinking maybe the *puhakut* had caught him watching for people through the open lodge entrance. But he soon realized that the old man had fallen asleep, for his mouth was open and his breathing was coming in long, slow rasps. He did not know what to do, so he lay down and went to sleep himself, until the old man's voice woke him.

". . . in the shape of jackrabbits, yet I could tell from their smiles that they were still coyotes. Then, the four bull elk in the north turned and ran away, making a cloud of red dust . . ."

Shadow sat up and listened again. As the old man went on, the sunlight moved across the floor of the painted lodge. Finally, Spirit Talker said, "then I found myself upon my robe, and I was very hungry and very thirsty, so I went back to my village to tell the old men what I had seen. They tried to tell me what it meant. But, they were wrong." He threw the strange powder on the pile of ashes, where the fire had gone out. "Do you understand what I am saying, Shadow?"

The boy waited a long time before he answered, thinking. "No," he finally said, though he feared the old man might start over. "But I wish to understand."

Spirit Talker opened his mouth wide, his laughter sounding like the roar of a fox. "The more we wish to understand, the more we learn. The more we learn, the less we understand."

There was silence in the lodge that lasted as long as a beaver could stay underwater. Then, Shadow asked a bold question:

"Grandfather, what manner of dust did you throw onto the fire?"

Spirit Talker put his fingertips in the pouch that held the powder. "Do you ask this question to make me think you want to understand things, or do you truly want to know what kind of dust it is?"

Shadow considered this question some time, thinking about how he would speak his reply. "I truly wish to know what kind of dust it was, because it smelled strange to me when it burned. I did not ask the question only to make you think I wish to understand things, but I do wish to understand, and that is why I asked the question."

"What do you wish most to understand?"

Again, he thought some time before he replied. "I wish to understand why the spirits give us things. And why they take things away."

For the first time, the old man's eyes appeared, twinkling in deep folds of aged, sun-baked flesh. "The dust is only a powder made of elk horn. The spirits do not wish me to say why I throw it on the fire. My medicine is very strong, young horseback. Its mysteries are my own to guard—a burden I must bear alone. To know of such power, such magic as you cannot imagine, is a very dangerous thing. It is like the horses you were riding yesterday."

"The horses, Grandfather?"

"Do you feel their power when you ride them?"

"As you must also, Grandfather."

"You forget, young horseback. You have known horses all your life. I am an old man upon this earth and will never ride a horse the way I saw you ride yesterday. The horse is a strange new thing to me. That is why I must ask you. I wish to learn. To understand."

Shadow gathered his legs under him, feeling very excited that the old *puhakut* should ask such a thing of him. "The power is great, Grandfather. It makes me go as fast as when I jump from the bluff into the swimming place at the Timber Camp, but the ride on the horse goes longer than the jump into the water. And it is more than the speed. It is the power!"

"Explain this power," the old man said, looking sincerely at the boy. "How does it make you feel?"

Shadow gestured vaguely. "It is like holding to the back of a great eagle as it flies low over the ground. Like riding a bull elk. It is like mastering all the wild things in the world and feeling all their great muscles between my thighs."

"Yet, these wild things you master throw you through the air and step hard upon you. They come near to crushing you, so that you might die upon the ground, without even a weapon in your hand."

"I am not afraid of them."

"But it is dangerous."

"Yes, Grandfather."

The old man threw the dust of elk horn upon the cold ashes. "So it is with spirit medicine. It makes you feel powerful. Yet, it may rub you out if you are not careful."

Shadow heard horses running, and looked through the opening to see them cavorting across a slope. "Why have the spirits given us horses, Grandfather?"

"I cannot say, young horseback. If the spirits wish you to know the answer to that question, they will tell you. You say you wish to understand, Shadow, but you must not wish to understand too much. Let the spirits understand. They are wiser than we are. They will tell you what to do if you listen. Now, go and eat well. Drink your fill of milk and water. When the sun rises, I will wait for you at the deep pool along Sometimes Water."

▲▲▲▲▲
10
▼▼▼▼

At dawn, Shadow trotted in his moccasins and loin skins to the pool on Sometimes Water, carrying his favorite buffalo robe rolled, tied, and slung over his shoulder by a rawhide thong. Father Sun was yet behind the eastern skyline, but his first rays made the tall, slender *tecamaca* trees along the stream look like huge green feathers whose tips had been dipped in crimson paint.

Following the line of trodden earth to the pool, the medicine seeker found Spirit Talker standing there, waiting for him.

"You must wash everything away in these waters that the spirits have made sacred on this morning," the old *puhakut* said.

Shadow took off his moccasins and loin skins and waded quickly into the clear, cold pool, diving headlong when he had waded thigh-deep. It felt cold, but not as cold as the streams from which he had broken ice to prove to his friends he could stay in longer than they. Coming up from the bottom of the pool, he heard Spirit Talker chanting, so he stayed in the deep middle of the pool, moving his arms and legs to stay afloat, knowing this exercise would warm him.

When the fiery gaze of Father Sun struck Spirit Walker, the *puhakut* ceased his chant and opened his eyes. "Come out. You are clean."

Shadow stood in the sun, his flesh tightening all around him, feeling cleansed, indeed, very strong, very well.

"Offer your heart to the spirits," the old man said. "*Stand* before them. Do not grovel, for that disgusts them. Tell the spirits you are getting ready to travel to a sacred place. Ask them to meet you there and grant you medicine. Do not be afraid. Fear angers the spirits the way it angers a great humpbacked bear."

"I am not afraid," Shadow said. He closed his eyes and prayed silently with the old man, feeling the crisp air dry him as the sun made him warmer.

"You are ready," Spirit Talker said.

He opened his eyes, finding the old man standing before him, still wrapped in his robe. It seemed strange to see Spirit Talker bundled up so, for Shadow was naked and felt quite warm. He was indeed ready. He had long awaited this quest. He hoped it would be as hard and as powerful as he had imagined. As he hurriedly put his moccasins and loin skins back on, he hoped the spirits would see how sincere he was and grant him good medicine.

Now Spirit Talker revealed an elk-horn pipe he had kept concealed under his buffalo robe and handed it to Shadow along with a pouch of tobacco and a wood drill for making fire. "You will need these things. Roll them in your robe for your journey."

Shadow rolled the things and tied the robe with the rawhide strap. Looping this strap over his shoulder, he stood to receive his last instructions from the *puhakut*.

"The spirits will come to you on the high bluff above the spring that feeds Sometimes Water. Go there, now, young horseback, and seek your medicine." He turned away, leaving Shadow alone.

. . . .

The medicine seeker walked until the sun was upon his shoulders, then stopped beside Sometimes Water to light his pipe. He was good with the drill, and there was much dry grass at hand to start the small fire. Stuffing the pipe with tobacco and lighting it with a burning stick, Shadow sat upon his rolled robe and prayed as he smoked.

He held his chin high as he sought contact with the spirits. Whom these spirits were, exactly, Shadow could not say. He knew of Father Sun and Mother Earth. He knew of their daughter, Sister Moon. He knew of the Thunderbird who brought rain and played the deadly lightning game with the True Humans. But there were other spirits out there as well, each waiting to share medicine with the walkers of earth. This Shadow knew. He prayed to them all at once, wondering which would accept his invitation to serve as his personal guardian spirit and shape his life with magic.

With the pipe smoked, he rose and continued the long walk to the bluff at the head of Sometimes Water. He stopped to smoke again at the spring. The water roared from the base of the bluff as Shadow had never seen. The Burnt Meat People had camped along Sometimes Water several times in his memory, but never when the water was so strong. This gave him confidence. The magic here was good. Grass stood high. Leaves were green and fruit grew everywhere. He was forbidden to eat or drink for the next four days, but the abundance made him hopeful that his father, Shaggy Hump, and his teacher, Spirit Talker, had chosen well his time and place to seek his medicine.

Halfway up the bluff, Shadow stopped to take his third smoke. He could see the haze of many campfires above his camp from here, for he was climbing high, and the day was still. The lodges were hidden in distant timber, but the thin cloud of smoke made him feel near his people. The sun was over him now, the rolling plains below him pale gray and brown in the bright light.

The climb to the top of the bluff became more difficult as the slope steepened. Shadow embraced the challenge, seeking the handholds and footholds that would lift him ever nearer his place of sacred solitude. Near the top, he found a ledge upon which to take his fourth smoke. He felt eager as he spun the drill shaft within its spirals of cured hide, for the number four was sacred. The spirits had created many four-leggeds to serve the True Humans. Four directions joined across the face of Mother Earth. Four seasons made the great circle of time. Shadow faced four most sacred days to invoke something mystic from the spirit world.

The fourth smoke seemed to give him wind to finish the climb. He scrambled over the last brink as if running a foot race, then sprinted up a gentle slope to the highest point on the bluff. Dropping his rolled robe, he turned slowly, letting his eyes sweep across the vast range.

To the east, where the bluff faced, the land rolled away in gentle folds, covered with sage and bunches of grass, dotted with dark green cedar. Between the east and the south, as he turned, his eye followed Sometimes Water, snaking away in a crooked thread of green, vanishing beyond the smoke haze of the village. Due south, the young medicine seeker noticed a thin haze of another hue hugging the horizon, wavering with distant magic. He hoped it might mean a dust cloud from a herd of buffalo. He turned farther still, now shading his brow against the late-day sun. The land rose in rugged steps to the west, broken by many dry ravines and jagged escarpments. Beyond this harsh country were the enemy highlands, the crests of which were visible though they lay several sleeps from here, even by horse. Turning north, Shadow saw the mystic regions of many strange peoples, the Mountains of Bighorn Sheep, and the Cold Dry Hills.

A tiny point of white, flashing momentarily, caught his eye on a hillock he could not have reached by sundown at a dead run. Shadow knew that signal meant antelope, for the tail of that animal could be seen flashing in the sun even when the animal itself blended into a far-distant slope. He wished he might run back to his camp to tell the hunters about the antelope he had spotted and about the dust haze he thought he detected so far away to the south. But even these matters of sustenance and survival for many became lowly cares for one who had come to seek medicine. He cast aside his thoughts of food, stood facing the south, and made his heart speak to all the unknowns.

· · · ·

At dusk, he was thirsty and hungry, but this only made him proud. He started a fire and lit his pipe, patting the smoke onto his shoulders, chest, and head as he prayed. Stars began to appear as he finished the smoke, and he stood again, facing east now. As the sky grew darker, he remembered the many stories he had been told about the evil little people called *Nenupee*—how they would shoot wanderers of the night with arrows that never missed and always killed. This high promontory also made him think about the great cannibal owls who hunted humans at night on wings that made no noise. The old men of his band had shown him the huge bones of these giant owls, turned to stone and found in ravines. Shadow had never met anyone who had actually seen one of these owls against some waning moon, but the bones proved they haunted the dark night sky.

These things made him long for the noise of his camp, but he knew to return would cause him great humiliation. The girls would laugh at him and call him elder sister. They would mock his fear. No, he would remain here and let the little people and giant owls kill him if they must. He stood straight, defying fear as the stars came out, glimmering faintly at first, like the flashing tails of spirit-antelope. Sister Moon was yet sleeping.

The sky grew blacker behind a growing nation of stars. Some of them flew long across the curve of night the instant they appeared. Shadow stood in wonder of them until his neck hurt from looking up at their numbers. Many were the nights he had lain on the ground in his camp to look up at the stars. But, here, alone and hungry, his thirst for magic even greater than his thirst for drink, he felt a far greater awe of the distant and mysterious beings of light. He prayed to them in his solitude, taking his mind away from thoughts of evil night things.

At last, he found himself shivering in the cold, weaving from exhaustion, unable to maintain his sense of balance. He lay down and wrapped himself in his robe, feeling the warmth envelope him head to foot. Though his dry mouth tasted of bitter smoke, and hunger prowled his stomach on grasshopper legs, he drifted instantly into prayerful sleep.

· · · ·

Father Sun looked over a far slope and shamed Shadow for waking so late in his robe. The seeker threw the hide from his shoulders and stood to see the great sun spirit rise. His mouth was dry and his stomach pinched, but he had known these feelings before over dry trails and hard winters. It was nothing to stand straight after his sleep, so he locked his knees and threw his chest forward. Yesterday's invitation to the spirits was now almost a taunt, for Shaggy Hump and Spirit Talker had advised him not to grovel in sight of the gods, but to greet them with confidence they would admire. Shadow's pluck bordered on arrogance.

His hunger rose like the sun, but it was his want of drink that made Shadow long for the time to pass and his guardian spirit to arrive. Occasionally, when the wind died and the world of mortals invaded his link with the Shadow Land, the seeker could hear the spring gushing from the foot of the butte. When this happened, he would force a hot chant up his dry throat and lift his arms to the Great Mystery, that he might forget his longing for so common a thing as water.

Wind spoke from the grasses and sage, birds from the limitless sky; still Shadow failed to interpret their voices. Father Sun watched the smokes, and heard the prayers, but passed over the hopeful warrior like a father of eaglets with nothing yet to feed them.

The second night had scarcely fallen before Shadow was asleep. He dreamed of rattlesnakes.

He was standing on the third day before Father Sun stalked quietly to peek over the curves of Mother Earth. His hunger was only a cold weight within him now, no longer gnawing, but his want for water made his tobacco-scorched mouth feel like rawhide. Each dry breath he drew seemed to blister his throat and prick his tongue, which felt large in his mouth.

Late in the third day, as Shadow stood bobbing on legs that refused to lock at the knees, he heard what he took to be a spirit-voice. Opening his eyes, he soon found that the sound was that of the Thunderbird, far away to the west, blasting the world of humans with bolts of fire shot from his eyes. The storm that hid and protected the great bird rose out of the distance, billowing toward Shadow's butte, coming between the seeker and the sun.

He turned from the south, to the west, thinking perhaps the Thunderbird would be the spirit to guide him through life, though he had never known or heard of a warrior with such medicine. The shadow of the great bird's cloud felt good. It refreshed the seeker and gratified his nostrils with the musky scent of summer rain.

Now the cool winds gusted down from the very wings of the Thunderbird, and the playful shafts of deadly fire cracked all around Shadow's butte, near enough that he could see things instantly blasted to dust where the shafts struck. This was a test he could not have dared hope for, and he set his teeth hard together to brace himself against fear of that unseen spirit-bird.

A large raindrop thumped hard against his brow as the seeker's hair twisted on a windflaw and his empty stomach fluttered with doubt. Would the wily Thunderbird tempt him with water? He was forbidden to drink these four days of his quest, but the smell of rain and the cool dot on his brow made him long to wet his tongue. He put his finger on the damp spot, felt a second drop hit the back of his hand, which he might have pressed against his lips.

Lighting struck a tall *tecamaca* tree on the banks of Sometimes Water below, splintering a limb—a warning from the powerful Thunderbird. Shadow began to know now what Spirit Talker meant when he spoke of the dangers and burdens of strong medicine.

The drops began to beat his head like a drum, and Shadow's eyes bulged with fear of his own failure, dread of the Thunderbird's vengeance. Was this his due for taunting the spirits? Rain was collecting on his face, trickling down. He shook his head to shed it, emptied his lungs in a single blast to turn the water from his lips. A drop cooled a crack in his lip, and the seeker closed his mouth tight, defying his tongue to lick the rain away. A magical gale spattered him with a swarm of tiny droplets, making his whole face wet.

The water hit hard now, soaking him. His long hair grew heavy. And he knew he might twist its ends over his mouth and wring out enough to swallow, but the eyes of his ancestors were upon him, and they would know his shame and punish it.

Rendered mute with his sealed mouth and his swollen tongue, the seeker could only grunt as he shook the rain from his face and snorted like a horse at the wonderful scent of his temptation. He pressed his lips together tighter, forging a grim visage of marvelous determination that would return to him in days to come—hard days of pain and sacrifice.

His whole body was wet. The wind made his own locks whip him. The wing feathers of the Thunderbird rumbled slowly through the black air of the vast mystic cloud, taunting him: *Drink! Drink! Drink, human!* Shadow shook his whole body in blatant defiance.

Now, he heard a sound that could only be the eyes of the great bird turning in their sockets. The screech from the hard beak came, instantly lost in the roar of shadow-fires. He felt the talons prick his back as heat slammed him to the ground. He slid briefly through thin mud, grit and rocks catching the flesh of his palms, chest, and face. He cowered, his ears ringing, until he realized he had kept his lips sealed against the rain. This triumph gave him courage to look behind him, where he beheld a small cedar in flames.

He heard Spirit Talker's voice: "*Stand* before the spirits! Do not grovel!"

Summoning courage of ancestors unknown, the seeker blew wind from his nostrils and stood again, returning to his high perch atop the bluff. He would not cower—in this world, or the next. Facing south again, the flames to his back, Shadow turned his wild eyes and drawn mouth to the sky. He made claws of his fingers and recklessly raked a challenge to the land of spirits.

The gods answered with hail, the first large stone thumping the top of the seeker's foot, smarting even through his hide moccasin, and making him hop. The next stone split flesh on the bone above his eye, causing him to look respectfully downward. Even still, Shadow refused to crouch. He stood upright under the icy spears that ranged down upon him without mercy. He felt ashamed for even thinking of crawling under his buffalo robe. Throwing one forearm across his eyes to protect his face, and using the free hand to cover his testicles under the flap of his loin skins, he grunted his defiance through his nostrils at the flocks of hailstones that made his limbs flinch and his skull ring.

The scourge of the Thunderbird was hard, but fleeting. The hail passed, taking the rain, leaving only the gusts of wings that had gone to hover over other heights. The seeker found himself trembling, hurting all over outside, and inside as well, where his heart had pumped courage with the force of swollen rivers. His lips remained pressed until the rain had dried from his face, but the blood still ran. This, he tasted, as no *puhakut* had forbidden him to drink his own blood. It dried in crooked scrawls that streaked his face, shoulders, and torso—war paint styled by unworldly artists.

He felt exhausted, yet charged with emotion. Never had he heard of such a quest as this, his own, and he had yet to receive his vision! The Thunderbird had challenged him, and he had withstood! The cloud was still lingering on a dark eastern horizon, tickling Mother Earth with quick, playful strokes of fire.

· · · ·

He awoke well before dawn. Kicking his warm robe away, he saw Sister Moon promising that her father would follow. He scratched at the dried blood that flaked away from his skin. The drill and the tender were still damp from yesterday's visit from the Thunderbird, so Shadow stood in the cool night without smoking.

By midmorning, the tobacco had dried, spread out in the sunshine that came down between large white clouds, well spaced. The seeker labored clumsily with the drill, feeling weak, finally getting the tinder to burst into flame. His eyesight seemed poor today, unable to see the bowl of the pipe clearly as he lit it. His mouth felt full of dirt and ashes, and the smoke from the pipe made him cough. His stomach felt twisted into a hard knot.

He was confused, and worried. This was the fourth day. He had prayed and smoked. Still, he felt no nearer to the spirits, save for his brush with the Thunderbird. He would have to go home at sundown and explain his failure to his people. Then he would have to try again—another four days. The hope given to him by the Thunderbird yesterday now seemed only a false promise designed to humble him.

Still, Shadow held to his duty, standing under the sun, facing south. He was like a hunter who would wait and watch the trail until the last light of day had faded. The south seemed sacred today, wavering under the illuminating gaze of Father Sun. It was brown in the light, gray in the shadow of the clouds.

The seeker felt the butte slam against his shoulder and found himself gasping for air. He felt weak and ashamed for having fallen. Laboriously, he pushed himself up to his knees, wondering why the butte was turning. He pulled his moccasins under him, but it was like standing on the back of a skittish horse. He looked at the sky, and saw Father Sun disappear behind a large cloud.

A curious thing happened to this cloud. It grew in size, quickly and silently, until it joined Mother Earth at the southern horizon. Now the cloud took on the color and texture of land, and became a huge world in the sky where morning was breaking, for Father Sun was coming over the edge of this new sky-world.

The horizon of the sky-world became so bright to look upon that the seeker thought he would be blinded, yet he seemed unable to close his eyes or look away. With this dazzling light, came the sound of crackling fire that quickly changed to the strain of hard hooves skittering over rocks. And as Shadow watched, he saw the silhouette of a creature emerge in the bright ball of sunlight that came around the sky-world. The creature loomed huge and grew larger than Father Sun, soothing the seeker's eyes with its shadow.

Now the rattle of hooves became so loud that it hurt Shadow's ears, and his eyes saw that the creature that had emerged from the sun was a huge deer, with antlers as large as twin trees and shoulders like hills. This giant deer had eyes that sparked, and it began to run down the cloud-slopes of the sky-world, descending on the seeker in heroic bounds, snorting whirlwinds from its nostrils. It ran hard toward Shadow, its antler points sweeping through the sky and dripping with globs of clouds like melting fat. It leapt from the sky-world onto Mother Earth and ran directly toward the butte upon which Shadow sought his vision.

The beast was powerful, but the seeker was not afraid. As the deer ran toward him, it diminished in size, until it assumed the stature of a natural deer, yet with sparks still glinting in its eyes and tiny whirlwinds still swirling from its nostrils.

"Rise!" said the deer, his voice crackling loud like popping fire and rattling hooves.

Shadow felt himself lifted to his feet, and he stood effortlessly, looking with wonder at this spirit-deer.

"I have come from the Sacred South," the deer said, his muzzle moving like the lips of a man, "where buffalo number like the drops of rain; where the spirits cause many horses to rise up from the ground; where elk and antelope and deer feed the *Na-vohnuh*, enemy of your grandfathers' grandfathers."

"What are you called?" Shadow asked, his voice a mere speck after the words of the spirit-deer.

"I am Sound-the-Sun-Makes!"

"Why do you appear as a great and powerful deer?"

"I have many forms. I take this shape so you will understand."

"Why have you come?"

"You have sought medicine, and I have heard your prayers. They sing like the good cry of an eagle and echo loudly in the canyons of the sky-world. I have come to teach you your own song."

The seeker marveled as the deer threw his head back and sang in a human voice, strong and pleasant to listen to:

"The rising sun sings.
The rising sun sings.

Hear the sound the sun makes.
Hear the sound the sun makes!"

"Remember this song always, seeker. I have ridden the clouds from the
Sacred South to bring you this song and much power."

"How shall I use this power?"

Sound-the-Sun-Makes shook his antlers, flinging cloud-droplets. He
snorted whirlwinds from his nostrils and blinked fire from his eyes. "Honor
the deer, image of your guardian spirit. Eat no food the deer eats. Eat no meat
of the deer. Tread not upon the trail of the deer. Do you understand?"

"Yes," the seeker said. "What else?"

"Keep sacred the horns of the deer. They hold great medicine for you."

"What shall I do with this medicine?"

"Seek wisdom. But beware, for power follows wisdom, and foolishness
follows power, and destruction follows foolishness."

"Sound-the-Sun-Makes, am I not to seek power?"

"Seek wisdom!" the great creature roared. "Wisdom is strength above
power."

"Shall I not use my medicine to seek power over the enemies of my
people?"

"Seek victory, quick and sure. Peace follows victory. Wisdom follows
peace. But beware, for power follows wisdom. Much power."

"But, Sound-the-Sun-Makes, is the seeker of wisdom not also then the
seeker of power?"

"Seek wisdom!" the spirit bellowed, menacing the air with his antlers.
"This is the magic of generations. Beware of the power that follows. There is
much power. Wisdom will lift you high among all your people. Power will
bring destruction of everything sacred! Know the strength of wisdom above
power!"

"If I make myself strong, sacred spirit, seek wisdom, and beware of power,
will I be great among my people?"

Sound-the-Sun-Makes ramped and pawed the sky between himself and
the seeker. "Your people are poor. They starve in the winter. They hide from
enemy slave-takers in the summer. If you fail, your weakness will make them
die, and never more shall the blood of True Humans run in men who walk
this world. But if you use your magic well, seeker, a new people will follow
you to wealth above any you could know, and you will be the greatest and
wisest of your people, for all generations, above all other peoples, on all other
lands. For this, the spirits have sent a gift to you."

The seeker raised his arms, opened his palms. "What is this gift?"

Sound-the-Sun-Makes laughed with the sound of an avalanche. He
whirled and ran back toward the sky-world whence he had come, growing
larger with each bound. Halfway home, he stopped, turned, and shook his

head fiercely, causing his antlers to fly through the air toward the spring at the base of the butte. Laughing still, he bucked and whirled, his tail growing long and shaggy, along with a mane that sprang from his neck. His great magic mended the cleft in his hooves as shaped himself into the image of a horse. This spirit-horse that Sound-the-Sun-Makes had become screamed the song of all the eagles of the earth, and leapt into the light of the sun, his scream becoming the sound of a raging fire.

And everything dissolved into a great whiteness that burst four ways at once, and lingered, and cleansed, and made new, and gave the seeker mysterious medicine that he felt streaming into him from stars, from ancestors of the days when creatures spoke, from many suns yet to rise, from the same earth that pushed green things skyward and made wild things thrive, from the good dark magic of sleep that made once-weak mortals wake strong.

11

At twilight, he woke, thinking of Sound-the-Sun-Makes ahead of all other thoughts, even his thirst. He lifted the side of his face from the butte and brushed away the pebbles embedded in his skin. He sat up and looked to the south. The haze he had seen there almost four days before was back, renewing the hope for buffalo.

Suddenly, he felt his medicine, and knew his quest was over. His breath rushed in hot, and his heart made his empty stomach hurt. Rising, he gathered his things and turned west.

The bluff was easy to descend from the west side, which was the reason Shadow had avoided climbing up this way, preferring a more difficult ascent to prove his sincerity to the spirits. But now, a most powerful spirit had answered, filling Shadow with joy and anxiety, and he only wanted to get back to his village to tell his father and Spirit Talker what he had seen in his vision. But first, to drink! His mouth felt like the sole of some old man's foot, and his whole body craved water.

Trotting down the west side of the slope, the seeker turned south and found a game trail that led to the spring at the base of the bluff. He was warm from weaving down the hill, so he did not crouch quietly at the water's edge, but walked straight in and fell forward.

Sucking the cool water in too quickly, he felt himself choking and floundered to his feet in utter dread. To die for want of air—whether by drowning or suffocation or strangulation—was to deny one's soul the way to the Shadow Land. This he knew. Finding wind again, he dropped to his knees and plunged his face back in the pool, taking three big swallows before pausing to breathe.

Instantly, he felt the cool medicine stream into his chest, and knew he would have the energy, after a brief rest, to trot back to his village. He drank until his stomach hurt, then turned downstream.

The sky was as dark as a vulture's wing, and he swung his feet carelessly through the tangles of weed, brush, and vine in the creek bottom. His toe thumped against something hard and heavy, and he felt it pull against the undergrowth when it moved. Stooping, the curious seeker saw the curve of slick bone in the dying light, and lifted a large deer antler, so freshly shed that scarcely the tooth mark of a single mouse marred it.

Gasping with excitement, he took off at a run to find better light out from under the *tecamaca* trees. He had sprinted only a few steps when something grabbed his ankle and threw him to the ground. Looking back, he found a second antler, a perfect match to the first. Holding them up to look at them against the sky, he began counting their points. He counted eight on the first antler. The same on the second. This was the sacred number four, four times over.

Shadow broke into a run, the antlers pumping magic through his fists.

12

The old men had heard of the seeker's vision, and thought long about it, searching wisdom as Shadow rested and ate. Now they had summoned the youth to join them in the big lodge of Shaggy Hump—eleven wise and powerful warriors and Spirit Talker, the old *puhakut* of the Corn People, possessor of strong medicine.

As Shadow entered the council lodge he saw the eyes of all the men turn to meet him, bright with some new respect. No longer did they look at him as a loud and playful boy. He saw an empty place in the circle on the north side, facing south, and here he sat.

The pipe was lighted without a word, and passed from Spirit Talker, on the east, to the man at his left, the pipe thus moving south in a curve as the sun moved through the great blue sky. When the pipe reached Shadow, he took a long pull and filled his lungs with the sacred cloud, sending it with a prayer to join the fire smoke on its journey through the vent above and on to the Shadow Land. His father, Shaggy Hump, was the last to smoke, sitting at Spirit Talker's right side.

When the pipe had completed the circle, Spirit Talker looked at him and said, "You have told us things about your vision, and we have all thought about it. Now it is time for you to sing the song that your guardian spirit has taught to you."

Shadow rose. Remembering the way Sound-the-Sun-Makes had sung, he angled his face upward and filled the lodge with his voice:

"The rising sun sings.
The rising sun sings.
Hear the sound the sun makes.
Hear the sound the sun makes!"

He sang this four sacred times, forcing the words from his chest on high, strong notes, as he had heard the greatest warriors sing around the drum during war dances and scalp dances.

After the song, Spirit Talker's brow gathered in folds of weathered skin, and he placed his fingertips on his chest, as if searching his heart. He took a pinch of powder from his pouch and threw it on the fire. "I did not think the song would sound that way," he said. "Tell me the story again, young horseback."

Shadow again gave the long recitation he had practiced and memorized and told and retold since returning from his quest. Twilight came as he spoke, and a good cool breeze streamed in under the raised covering of the lodge, and the men seemed to admire the words he chose.

When he had finished, he sat back down, and Spirit Talker placed his fingers on his chest again and looked all around the inside of the lodge, his age-darkened eyes seeking. "Now I am not as sure as I was before," he finally said. "The song changes my heart, the way it is sung. I must think about this carefully before speaking out."

The old man threw another pinch of dust on the fire and sat, contemplating. The fire burned down and Shaggy Hump added a few sticks. These, too, burned to ash, and Shaggy Hump added still more. When these were gone, Shaggy Hump rose silently, left the lodge, and came back with more wood. Stoking the fire again, he returned to his place in the circle.

Still, Spirit Talker meditated, his eyes closed, head bowed, his breath coming in long rasps. To Shadow, he seemed asleep, but the young warrior knew that this was part of the old man's magic.

Finally, Spirit Talker lurched with a snort and opened his eyes. "I have it now," he said. "My friends, help me rise."

Shaggy Hump and the man to Spirit Talker's left lifted him by the arms.

"On the day of this young horseback's birth, First Horse ran through the camp of the Burnt Meat People and circled his lodge, and so he has been called Born-on-the-Day-of-the-Shadow-Dog through fourteen winters, for it was thought by a wise old man that First Horse was a dog from the Shadow Land. Now we know that the horse is not a dog at all, but a gift to the True Humans that will carry the young horsebacks into a new age. From where the sun now stands, he shall no longer be known as Shadow. His name now is *Horseback*."

He gasped slightly at the sound of his name, for in the language of the *Noomah*, it was spoken as *Kiyu*, and rang with grace and strength, like the call of a hawk. He looked into the eyes of his father, who was holding his face in a visage of fierce pride.

"Horseback," the *puhakut* said, "rise."

He rose.

"Your medicine is strong. The strongest I have ever known, besides my own. You must understand that this is dangerous to you."

"I do not fear danger," Horseback said.

"It is not only you who must fear such power as is yours. It is your people. All the True Humans—even those who have crossed to the Shadow Land— even those yet to walk upon this earth. I tell you these things, Horseback, that you may know this: The sun may rise on a day that you find this medicine too powerful to control. If this day comes, you may give your medicine back to the spirits, and no word will be spoken against you, in this world or any other."

"I do not think now of that day," Horseback said.

Spirit Talker raised a finger in warning. "All your life, you have been told of the horse that circled your lodge as you were born. Many eyes have watched you grow, expecting more from you than another boy. You are proud, Horseback, and your people are proud of you. Look, your father swells with so much pride that he is like a honey ant, ready to burst!"

The warriors laughed, and even Shaggy Hump himself managed a smile.

"But now comes the time of manhood, and no longer do you prove yourself by playing with wild horses. Do not hold more magic than you can handle simply because you have greed for it in your heart. Do not take too much pride in your power."

"Grandfather, I seek wisdom, not power."

The old man smiled. "I have spoken with the others in council as you rested. I have heard their words, all true, wise, and heartfelt. Now, I will tell you what your vision means."

"I am ready to hear."

"First, you must eat no food the deer eats. Now, the deer eats wild plums, but only as high as this," the *puhakut* said, reaching one arm high and touching a lodge pole over his head. "Above this, the deer cannot reach, so you may stand on something or jump high or climb to pick the plums you wish to eat. When you take a woman into your lodge, make sure she knows this, for she must choose the right fruit for you to eat—that which is beyond reach of the deer."

"I understand."

"Eat no meat of the deer. You may kill the deer to feed your family, but you must not eat any of it yourself. You must honor the deer that you kill, thanking it in a prayer before you kill it. If you are starving and kill a deer, you may not eat this deer unless you give your medicine back to the spirits forever, or you will destroy everything sacred in the way of the True Humans. When you ride the war path, you must not kill a deer. No member of your war party may kill a deer or eat the meat of a deer. To do so will cause defeat. Besides this, you may eat whatever you want, as long as it does not go against the way of the True Humans—like eating a fish or a frog or a dog."

"I understand."

"The track of the deer is sacred. Do not step on it, or let your pony step on it, for it angers the spirits for you to act as if you should walk where they walk. When you see the track of a deer at the edge of the water, step aside and drink at another place along the bank."

"Yes, Grandfather."

"The horn of the deer is sacred, as you have seen." Spirit Talker motioned for Shaggy Hump to hand him the two antlers the seeker had found as he returned from his quest. "You must protect these horns and keep them with your weapons, safe from things that make them unclean."

"When I have enough hides, I will make a lodge just for my weapons and sacred things," Horseback said, "to keep them clean and out of the weather."

"Good. Now, when you find a small antler, you will grind it with rough stones to make a sacred dust. A woman may do this for you, unless she is in the time of unclean bleeding. You will carry the sacred dust in a pouch in your quiver and throw it on the fire in times of prayer." At this, Spirit Talker pinched another morsel of powder from his bag and flicked it at the fire in the center of the lodge.

"Now I understand," Horseback said.

"The spirit who guards and protects you—the one only you have seen and only you will know—the spirit you have spoken of, named Sound-the-Sun-Makes—this spirit speaks of the Sacred South, where many horses rise from the ground. The same spirit tells you that the horse is your gift—the gift of your people—given to you on the day of your birth by the spirits. And so, Horseback, you will seek this land of the Sacred South where horses rise from the ground, and buffalo number like drops of rain, and elk feed the ancient enemies of the True Humans. You will seek this land."

Horseback found himself looking south, through the open flap of the lodge, where the land was black under the gray sky. "What shall I do when I find this land, Grandfather?"

Spirit Talker threw another pinch of antler dust into the fire. "You will know. Seek wisdom, and you will know."

Horseback remembered a pony he had once owned—his first pony, killed on the day his uncle and grandfather died at the Canyon of Red Rock whence he would never return. He remembered the signs burned on the hide of that pony. Now somehow he knew those signs were the medicine of strange people in the Sacred South. His stomach felt full of things that fluttered and crawled, and he longed to ride hard to the south. Yet, he knew he must seek wisdom and pray about this before riding. Already, his medicine felt like a burden to him, making his thoughts swarm and hum like flying bugs.

"I have collected sacred things for your medicine pouch, Horseback." The old *puhakut* gestured toward a square piece of soft tanned deerskin at his feet. On this small skin several items lay, neatly arranged. "The tooth is from the skull of a deer. The tuft of hair from the tail of a deer. The feather is from the turkey, who sometimes walks with and watches out for the deer. This strip of fur is from a weasel, to keep evil spirits away. The pebble is one found in the track of a deer. The claw is from a great humpbacked bear and will bring you courage."

Spirit Talker motioned for Shaggy Hump to bundle the sacred items in the piece of deer skin. Taking the bundle, he sprinkled powder from his pouch upon it, then held it high and chanted a song to which only he knew the meaning, for it had no words—only sounds taught to him by his guardian spirit:

"Ya-hi-yu-niva-hu,
 Hi-yu-niva-hi-yu-niva-hu,
 Ya-hi-yu-niva-hi-na-he-ne-na,
 Hi-yu-niva-hu."

As he sang, the *puhakut* wrapped a long rawhide thong around the closed bundle and drew the edges tight together with a jerk, tying it off with a hard knot. When he had finished the task and his song, he passed the medicine pouch to the young warrior newly named Horseback.

Knowing what must be done, Horseback untied the belt that held his loin skins on, and let the skins fall between his feet. He tied the rawhide thong of the medicine pouch around his hips and let the pouch itself hang down in front and lay against his penis. Now he stooped to pick up his skins and replaced them under his loins, tying them fast with the belt. The men chuckled at the way he hiked his legs up and prodded at his groin, trying to get accustomed to the new bundle in his loin skins.

Spirit Talker sang again and threw magic powder on the fire, and Horseback saw his father's herd of horses through the open flap, faintly against the slate sky.

"I have seen a vision," Spirit Talker said. "In this vision, I am going blind, for I see like one looking through a blizzard. Yet, I know it is Horseback that

I see in this vision, and he hunts, and fights, and goes to strange places. I can not see how he does all of these things—only that he does them riding a good pony. He does *everything* astride a pony."

And Horseback felt a fire grow in his chest, making the things that fluttered and crawled in his stomach move even faster, as along his back a chill finger of wind crept, tickling the nape of his neck, making his hair stiffen upon his whole scalp, and he held his breath and swallowed hard, for he had seen Spirit Talker's very same vision in a dream just last night.

▲▲▲▲▲▲
13
▼▼▼▼▼

They found the buffalo three sleeps south of Sometimes Water, flocks of ravens having led them to the herd. Watching through the leaves of a saskatoon bush in a draw where the land dropped off to the valley of a place called Two Rivers, Shaggy Hump and Horseback plotted the strategy for the hunt.

"The wind is ours, Father," Horseback said, optimistically.

"Yes," Shaggy Hump replied, "but the ground is the buffalo's."

Horseback noticed the ripe berries on the saskatoon bush, and almost reached for one out of habit and the memory of winter hunger. Then he remembered his medicine and a pang of dread coursed his soul, thinking of how he might have eaten this food of the sacred deer, ruining the chances for a successful hunt.

He turned his concentration back to the herd, in the river valley below, moving slowly upstream along the north bank, like a shadow of speckled brown against the green lowlands flanking the river. It changed shape like a cloud as it passed.

"I have not seen a herd this large on our hunting grounds since I went on my first hunt," Shaggy Hump said. "But we must be ready. The *Yutas* may know of these buffalo and come down from the mountains to hunt them. That is a good place to camp, down there in the timber where the two rivers become one, and there have been fights there before."

"If the *Yutas* come, will we attack them?" Horseback asked.

"Do not think of these things, my son. Trust your medicine to guide you as times come for other things. Now, we are hunting, not making war."

Horseback watched a distant pack of wolves emerge and vanish along the timber at the river's edge, silver like trout rising in a brook. "Here the ground is the buffalo's," he said, putting his mind back on the hunt, "but ahead of them, a ridge reaches close to the river. If we ride far around, to the other side of that ridge, the buffalo will not see us come down close to the timber.

Then, we can crawl near with our buffalo robes over our shoulders, and shoot them with arrows."

Shaggy Hump followed the strategy with his eyes. "*Hah*, good." He put his hand on his son's shoulder. "Now we will see if your bow shoots straight, like your medicine."

"My bow shoots straighter than straight," Horseback replied, more out of confidence than bluster.

Easing back from the saskatoon bushes, they crept up the draw and over the brink of the river breaks, back to high ground, where their horses waited out of sight of the buffalo.

Shaggy Hump had trained these ponies not to run from him by catching them and tying a long strip of rawhide to one front foot. Then he would walk briskly toward them, and if they ran, he would jerk the rawhide, tripping them—time and time and time again—until they learned. Now they would not shy away from a man who approached even at a dead run. To Horseback, this way his father had of teaching horses things was medicine beyond hope of possession, yet he too was learning.

After getting thrown from the black colt in front of all the Corn People and Burnt Meat People while showing off for Teal, Horseback had given much thought to ways he could make himself stick to the back of a pony. In a dream one night, he had seen a rope wound four times, loosely, about the barrel of a pony, just behind the forelegs. Waking the next morning, he had found a rope and made four wraps with it around a gentle mare, as he had seen in his dream. Mounting the mare, he found that he could slip his knees under the four loose coils of rope, the thickness of his thighs tightening the coils and holding him fast to the back of the mare.

Soon, he was able to ride even a wild colt and stick to its back as if he possessed lion claws. Yet if the colt slipped or stumbled, he could quickly and easily remove his knees from the coils and fall away from the pony. On long rides, he could let his legs dangle comfortably, yet the moment he needed to run hard over rough country, he could slip his knees under the coils and dash away as if he and the pony had become one.

As he mounted now, in this place near the valley of the two rivers, he checked the knot in the coils he had tied around his pony. Even his father, Shaggy Hump, had admired this new way to ride and had begun to equip his mounts with the coil of rope whenever he expected hard riding ahead.

They trotted away from the river, crossed over two high rolls, and returned to the main body of the hunting party. Seven good hunters of the Corn People and the Burnt Meat People had agreed to come on Shaggy Hump's hunt, bringing their women to set up the camp and butcher the meat. Each had a horse, owned or borrowed, while Shaggy Hump and Horseback had each brought two—one for riding and one for harnessing to the pole-drags.

After hearing the scouts' plan, the other hunters loosed their horses from their lodge poles and mounted, their bow cases and quivers slung over their shoulders, hairy buffalo robes rolled and thrown across withers of their mounts. Shaggy Hump and two others also carried lances, to use in finishing wounded animals.

They circled to the finger of high land that reached for the river, and rode into the draw beyond it, still out of sight of the buffalo. The horses plunged through low brush in this draw that widened near its mouth. Here the hunters found wispy *soohoo* trees and *sohoobi* trees large enough to conceal their horses, so they dismounted and tied the animals. Carrying robes and weapons, they hastened to the tip of the finger of high land that still shielded them from the buffalo.

Horseback stayed close behind his father, hoping the buffalo had continued upstream and would be very near around the rise. In his life, he had seen few live buffalo close up, and never as close as a bow might fling an arrow. He had hunted nothing larger than rabbits with success. The thought of a whole herd of large beasts coming very soon within range made his heart pound.

Shaggy Hump motioned him forward, and the young hunter came to crouch behind a clump of birch scrub. Through the foliage, he saw the leaders of the herd, their heads down, busily grazing tall grass in the river bottom. The finger of high land seemed to point to a bulge in the stream-side timber, both of which served to funnel the herd, crowding the animals, and bringing them near.

Shaggy Hump carefully dragged his buffalo hide over his shoulders and head, and Horseback did the same. Looking back, he saw the other hunters preparing. They would ease out of the mouth of this draw, passing as buffalo themselves, until they were near enough to send a volley of flint and iron points into the big animals.

"When you shoot your arrow," Shaggy Hump whispered, "do not aim at the herd. Do not aim at a single animal. Aim for the soft flank behind the last rib. Choose a curl of hair for a target."

Horseback signed his understanding and began to crawl into view of the big beasts, trying to move like a grazing calf. He wondered if the buffalo would notice how small he was. It would be well to appear the size of the buffalo, and this gave him the idea to cover himself with a wooly robe while mounted on his horse. Hadn't he and Spirit Talker had the same vision of him hunting horseback—doing *everything* on horseback? But this was just his first hunt, and there would be time to try new things later.

For now, he continued to lumber closer to the approaching herd. A large cow raised her head, and he was close enough to see her eye shine, but she kept chewing the grass that disappeared into her mouth, then lowered her head and stepped forward for another mouthful before the last one was even gone. He could hear the sound of many beasts tearing grass away from the good rich earth of the river bottom.

They held their arrows and inched closer to the herd. The leaders of the herd grazed past Horseback and Shaggy Hump and finally came within range of the last hunters along the line. Moving cautiously, Shaggy Hump notched an arrow on his bowstring, and the other hunters followed. Horseback's heart was beating so hard that he wondered if he would have the strength to draw the bow. But he thought of Sound-the-Sun-Makes, which filled him with confidence, and he easily drew the bowstring back and touched it to his cheek.

Looking beyond the arrow's shaft and point, he found a cow that quartered away from him. He lined the arrow shaft with the animal, then remembered to aim behind the ribs. This cow happened to have a tuft of shedding hair hanging from her flank right where the arrow should hit, so the hunter chose this as his target, feeling the exact trajectory through much practice.

When he heard his father's bowstring sing, he did not even have to think to let his own slip between his fingers. All down the line, arrows flew, each hitting its mark, though two of the hunters had unknowingly chosen the same animal to shoot.

Horseback watched his own flint point arch high—too high he feared—then saw it slant down and disappear in the cow's flank just over the tuft of hair that served as his target. The wounded animal jumped straight up to a height that seemed impossible for an animal her size and came down on legs that were already running. Veering toward the river, she ran into a yearling calf, knocking it down as she fled in pain and terror.

The other wounded animals acted the same way, sending an instant scare through the herd, as a whole flock of blackbirds would suddenly move almost as one in the sky by some spirit's power. Only two of the wounded buffalo fell in view of the hunters, one of them being the cow that had been shot twice. The others scattered with the fleeing herd, making the whole valley tremble and livening the air with sounds of snapping branches down in the timber.

Flinging his robe aside, Horseback started sprinting back up the draw as the other hunters watched the herd run. There were sounds of splashing water coming faintly now through the timber.

"Where are you going?" Shaggy Hump shouted.

"To my horse!" the young hunter replied. "Maybe some will sink in the mud, where I can kill them with a lance!"

"Ride my horse! He was caught running with buffalo and will not be afraid to run with them again!"

Horseback reached the buffalo pony winded, his legs aching from the charge uphill. He grabbed his father's lance and mounted quickly, knowing the horse would do his running for him now. Excited by the familiar noise of the herd below, the horse would barely wait for the rider to swing across his back. The instant he had mounted, Horseback slipped his knees tightly under the coils of rope his father had tied around the barrel of this pony, and this too seemed to alert the horse to a hard ride.

Plunging through *soohoo* clumps and weaving around the larger *sohoobi* trees, Horseback came galloping onto the grassy bottom lands between the slopes and the river timber. He thundered beyond the hunters, who watched him pass like a thing they had never seen. He rumbled past the two dying cows on the ground and entered the shadows of the timber. Dead falls and low branches slowed him down, but the buffalo had trampled a broad path for him to follow.

Suddenly he saw a big dark mass of fur moving strangely through the trees and rode that way, finding a young bull with a broken leg flopping piteously. He thought of dismounting and rushing the bull with his spear, keeping behind trees to protect himself from the horns. But something made him lean forward over the neck of his mount, as he reined toward the crippled bull.

The animal tried to turn away, but Horseback rode hard against the side opposite the broken foreleg, knowing the young bull would not be able to push against the broken limb to wheel and hook him. The lance was firm in his grip, the shaft clamped hard between his arm and ribs. The horse acquired some magic that made him rush the bull with neck outstretched and teeth popping.

Horseback lowered the broad flint point of the lance as he galloped forward and stuck it in the bull behind the ribs. Once through the tough hide, the lance went easily into vitals. The buffalo bellowed, tried to whirl, but fell on the broken leg, his weight yanking the lance from Horseback's tight hold. The hunter veered away, then spun his mount to face the dying beast. His eyes were large, thinking of what he had done. Never had a tale been told of a warrior lancing a buffalo bull from the back of a horse. The muscles across his shoulders writhed, and power consumed him.

Sucking in much air, he loosed a joyous cry, "Ye-ye-ye-ye-ye!" so his father and the other hunters would know he ridden well.

The sound of splashing water came from lower down, so Horseback reined his mount close enough to grab the shaft of his lance, angling up from the heaving bull. He pulled and pulled at it, finally using both hands and a wrap of the horse's mane to dislodge the flint point. Finding the point unbroken, he spun his horse toward the river.

Riding out of the timber, Horseback saw one cow bogged in quicksand, then saw a stray bunch of seven animals crossing back to his side of the river, fleeing insensibly from unknown terrors. Across the river, buffalo were scattering everywhere. He remained still until the seven had come out of the water on his side of the river, then he reined his excited mount in behind them.

The beasts were tired from having swum the river, and Horseback closed on them quickly, his mount leaping obstacles in the timber as he ducked low limbs. Seldom had he ridden in thick timber, and this made the going slower. The hunter thought to himself that he had better practice this kind of riding in days to come in case he should ever have to attack or escape through thick trees.

Finally, the trees began to thin, and the buffalo burst onto the grassy bottom lands where the hunt had begun. Horseback felt sunlight hit his bare shoulders as he came out of the trees, and it felt like the voice of Sound-the-Sun-Makes, giving him strength. His father and the other hunters were watching now. His mind raced even faster than he rode, plunging across the green grassland with a wind of his own making, pulling his hair long behind him.

Suddenly, his guardian spirit gave him the idea. He veered to the right of the herd, as his hunting party remained spread out to the left, against the steep banks. He would choose an animal to lance from his horse, and at the same time frighten the other animals into the range of the bowmen.

The buffalo horse seemed crazy with the idea of catching the buffalo, his mane streaming with every galloping lunge of his head. The horned beasts were tired, their tongues hanging out as they ran. Horseback angled into the right side of the herd, choosing a lagging cow as his prey. The beasts cut to their left, but Horseback and his crazy buffalo horse stayed with them, closing fast.

The bloody flint point swooped downward as the gap closed, and Horseback leaned into the coming resistance just as the blade found its mark behind the ribs. He had learned from just the one kill of the broken-legged bull, and he reined his horse back as soon as the shaft reached deep enough to kill. The lance slipped free and the cow bellowed as she stumbled and weaved, finally falling with a cough of blood, and rolling with legs kicking air.

The rest of the buffalo scattered toward the other hunters. Horseback turned his heaving mount to watch. They were hiding behind the animals they had already killed, and when the live buffalo sped by in range of their arrows, they rose, and sent feathered shafts speeding with such expert magic that not one missed, and all six of the animals ran wounded toward the slopes, some dropping within view, some lumbering into the trees.

"Ye-ye-ye-ye!" he cried, the dripping shaft of the lance held above his head. He felt a trickle of blood run warm across his knuckles, and lowered the fist to lick the fresh blood away.

The answer came back like a nation of echoes, and he felt like a great hunter—the first of his kind. Only now did he realize that he had lived his vision—and Spirit Talker's—only now the vision of hunting horseback had come out of the fog and was plain.

But there were other still-hazy visions of other things to do on horseback. And the one nearest in the mist was battle. Horseback was ready. He was going to ride the war path soon. He would kill or die astride the gift his gods had given him.

▲▲▲▲▲
14
▼▼▼▼▼

Horseback woke happy and eager to get on with the day's work. They had butchered and feasted until dark yesterday, gorging themselves on raw brains, blood, and curdled milk, raw liver smeared with juices of gall bladder, and raw marrow raked with sticks from bones broken open. Only half of the kill had been skinned, and plenty of butchering was left to do.

The women were already working at the Two Rivers camp, making many good things for the men to eat as they woke. Coming out of the lodge he had shared with his father and mother last night, Horseback saw River Woman stripping lengths of slick buffalo intestine between her fingers to carry to the river for washing.

She smiled when she saw him. "May the sun rise now in your heart, as it rises soon over the rim of the river valley." She offered him the length of gut in her hands.

Horseback scratched his stomach and respectfully declined the raw intestine, having eaten plenty of that delicacy yesterday. Looking toward the cook fire, he saw a fresh buffalo paunch suspended by four sticks to make a cooking vessel, now bulging with water. "What are you cooking in the paunch, my mother?"

"Anything you like. Brains? Heart? Tongue? Liver?"

"Tongue," he said.

Happily, she snatched a calf tongue from a branch where it hung and plunged it into the paunch filled with water. "The stones are hot," she said. "It will not take long."

Grabbing the forked limb she had fashioned for the purpose, River Woman slipped the green forks under one of the stones in the coals. Bending the other end of the green limb over, she clamped the hot stone firmly against the fork and lifted it, smoking, from the fire. The stone was the size of a turkey egg, smooth from much use and travel. River Woman carried her best cooking stones with her from camp to camp, for they were heavy and hard and possessed the magic of holding much heat—more than ordinary stones.

Using the bent and forked stick, she dropped the stone into the paunch with the water and calf's tongue. The music of the boiling water made her smile, and she turned back to the fire to get another hot cooking stone.

Soon the tongue was boiled and Horseback was tearing at it with his teeth, holding it on a sharpened stick. His mother had added some marrow and wild onion to the water, flavoring the tongue to his liking. As he ate he saw the ponies standing in the grass, and noticed the buffalo horse he had ridden yesterday looking at him while the others grazed.

"My son," Shaggy Hump said, walking briskly back to the lodge from upstream, "we have one more cow to track. I hit her with an arrow yesterday when you ran the six strays past us. She did not bleed much, but I have found a trail."

"I will find her," Horseback said. "I know how to look for blood and tracks. If my father shot an arrow into a cow, she could not have run far."

"It was not my straightest shot, but straight enough to kill. We will find her around the next bend of the river, or the next. The wolves and coyotes scattered far after the herd yesterday. If our medicine stays strong, we will find the cow before them. And if they find her first, they will have her, for they are our ancestors, and we have already made much meat."

They fixed the war bridles around the jaws of their horses and threw the buffalo-hide pads over backs and withers, winding the coils of rope around behind the forelegs. Grabbing a handful of mane, each rider vaulted onto his pad. Returning the proud looks of the other hunters, they rode upstream, seeking the last of the wounded animals from yesterday's great hunt.

"The cow ran into the timber here," Shaggy Hump said, "between these two *sohoobi* trees. From this place, only Mother Earth can tell the story of where our meat has gone."

Horseback slid off the horse and crouched, looking for some tiny speck of blood on a blade of grass. He covered the distance between the two trees painstakingly, but failed to find the sign he sought. He heard his father chuckle.

"My son, when the hawk hunts, does it walk upon the ground? Does it slide through the grass like a snake?"

"The hawk flies."

"Yes. It looks not for the track, but the trail."

Horseback straightened and led his horse away from the place. He mounted again, and thought of himself as a hawk. He looked again at the space between the two trees, and saw what the hawk would see. A trail of grass stalks bent slightly lower than those around them showed plainly where the wounded cow had run into the timber. He had come near obliterating it with his own trail, but saw enough of it to show which way the buffalo had entered the timber. He made his horse walk beside this trail and leaned to one side as he watched the ground pass slowly under him, as if he were a soaring bird of prey.

The signs came to him like little leftover pieces of yesterday: a broken stick, a trampled vine, a tuft of hair on rough bark, the print of a dew claw in the forest litter, a speck of dried blood on a leaf. Through them, he remembered sounds he never heard, glimpsed sights he never saw. Two led toward the third, three to the fourth, four to the fifth, and so the tracks became the trail, and the signs became the story.

He remained astride his horse, looking down, plodding steadily up the river bottom, until he came to something that made him jerk his horse to a standstill. There were deer droppings here, and part of one deer track, crossing the trail of the wounded buffalo. Worrying that he might have missed other deer tracks, Horseback stopped to judge the path of the lone deer, so he would not tread on it and offend his guardian spirit. Making his pony back away from the deer trail, he found a dead limb on the ground to make the horse jump over, assuring himself that he would jump over the deer trail as he crossed it.

His search for the wounded buffalo continued until, riding down into a draw that led to the river, he heard a deep growl, and looked up from the ground. There across a small clearing, a great humpbacked bear was tearing a huge piece of meat from the loin of the dead buffalo cow. He reached for his bow as his father came up beside him.

Suddenly the bear turned its head and looked at the men. It roared once, loud and quick, then charged with its muscles shaking fur violently all across its shoulders. To his surprise, Horseback heard his father yell the war cry and felt him rush by to meet the bear with the lance he had brought to finish the cow should she still live. Shaggy Hump's mount refused to meet the great bear, shying to one side, but the bear came on, and ran onto the point of the lance. Screaming, in rage and pain, the great beast swatted at the shaft, then gathered it in with its forepaws and snapped it in its jaws.

Horseback was trying to string his bow, but had to hold his frightened horse. He had never tried to use a bow while riding a calm horse, let alone one crazed by an attack of a huge humpbacked bear. Glancing up, he saw that his father's bow was strung, and Shaggy Hump was reaching for an arrow.

The bear charged Shaggy Hump's mount again, which ran around the edge of the clearing in terror, against every effort of the rider to hold it. Plunging into the trees, Shaggy Hump was knocked aside by a limb and landed on the ground at the same moment the bear raked its claws across the rump of the horse. Kicking and squealing, the horse drove the bear away with hard hooves and made an escape.

Before he could think, Horseback was using his bow on his mount's rump to charge ahead and draw the attack of the bear away from his father. When the bear turned to him, he let his horse dodge and run back up the trail. Looking over his shoulder, he saw the bear turning back for his father again, but Shaggy Hump was drawing his bow, and his arrow sank deep into the great bear's flank.

After biting at the new wound, the bear charged Shaggy Hump again, and again Horseback had to whip his horse into the middle of the clearing to lure the bear away from his father. Horseback even held his mount back so the bear would chase him longer, for he could not stand to think about his father falling into the jaws of this ravenous beast.

The bear chased Horseback from the clearing, but still refused to leave the dead cow it had claimed, and turned back to do battle with Shaggy Hump. Shaggy Hump was climbing a tree when Horseback came back to the clearing, and this seemed to enrage the bear. Nothing Horseback could do could keep the bear from swatting at his father, and one sharp claw raked Shaggy Hump's leg, almost causing him to fall. Yet, the pain gave the hunter more strength and he scrambled higher, beyond reach of the creature so crazed with bad medicine.

Horseback took confidence, seeing his father safe in the tree, and he started to string his bow again. His hands were shaking, so he thought of his vision, of Sound-the-Sun-Makes. He felt his medicine pouch inside his loin skins, and knew it granted him protection. He hooked the bow over his thigh and under his foot and bent it to loop the bowstring on the other end. He heard his father's bow string thump, followed by the roar of the bear.

Reaching for an arrow in his own quiver, Horseback saw the bear shaking the *sohoobi* tree that held his father, biting at the trail of blood that ran down from Shaggy Hump's wounded leg. He notched the arrow, thought of his shadow-song and let the shaft fly into the bear's back.

Startled by a noise behind him, he turned to see the other hunters coming, having heard the fight all the way from the camp. Arrows flew like wasps, and the great bear attacked his own flesh where each point stung him, finally attempting to drag himself into the trees. Even before the bear had stopped crawling, Shaggy Hump was coming down from the tree. Dropping to the ground, he favored his mangled leg.

The bear tried to snap at him, but Shaggy Hump poked a hind quarter with his bow, yelling, "Aaa-hey! I claim the first honors!"

Now Horseback raced ahead to beat the others to the second battle stroke, for he deserved it more than they. The other hunters had left their horses to fight the bear afoot, so Horseback easily beat them to the dying bear. Leaning from his mount, he struck the very head of the bloody beast with his bow and yelled, "Aaa-hey! I have the second!"

The men sang like their coyote forebears over the carcass of the bear, so the women back in camp would know of their victory. Then Shaggy Hump tied a leather strap tight around his leg under the knee.

"Your leg, my father," Horseback said, as the others looked over the huge dead bear.

"Let me ride behind you, son. Your mother will know how to make the leg well. The strap will make the blood stop flowing, and the pain makes me feel proud. You fought bravely, and the great humpbacked bear is as dangerous as any of our many enemies in a close fight. You will do well in battle."

Horseback helped his father onto the horse behind him. "I will make my father and my mother proud, and all of my people. I will kill or die on my war pony."

Shaggy Hump pointed down the trail that had led him and his son to this glorious fight. "It is better to wear battle scars and count honors on living enemies, than to kill or to die. Too much killing makes our enemies crazy to enslave our women and children and to take our scalps. Dying makes our women weep and slash their breasts, for they will have no one to feed them when we are gone. But these are things for the spirits to teach. Listen to the spirits, my son, not your father."

15

With a buffalo rib held delicately in her hand, Looks Away lightly scraped at the deposit of fine white clay she had found, gathering it into the palm of her other hand. She took care to pick out all the pebbles and particles of dirt that did not gleam with the pure brilliance of snow. Satisfied that the handful of clay was pure, she poured it into a small buckskin pouch. This clay would make fine white paint for her husband. As she filled the pouch, she heard hoofbeats over the crest of the river bank, so she left the small outcropping of white clay and climbed higher up the steep bank to see what caused the commotion.

Peeking over the crest of the river bank, she saw Horseback and his two young friends stalking a tawny mare with golden mane and tail. The mare watched, head high, as they crept up from three directions, their arms spread wide as if to gather her in. This mare was the one horse in the herd who dragged a long rawhide tether, looped around her neck. She was difficult to catch, but once mounted, made a good riding horse upon which to catch the other horses.

As the young warriors closed in, the mare made a dash between Horseback and Trotter, and Horseback ran hard to leap for the rope before the mare could drag it past him. She pulled him along the ground until Trotter and Whip could help him hold on. Knowing she was caught now, the mare let Horseback put the war bridle around her jaw and scramble onto her back. He left the long tether dragging behind, in case he fell off and had to catch the mare again.

Looks Away made sure she would not be seen by the boys, for she enjoyed watching them work with the horses and did not want to interfere with their fun. She was responsible for much of what the boys had learned, and this made her heart feel light.

Looks Away had lived in the mountains as a girl, with the *Yutas*. She had known horses as long as she could remember, for the *Yutas* had owned horses many winters before the *Noomah*.

When Horseback's uncle, Black Horn, captured her and made her his wife, she brought with her much knowledge about horses that she did not even know she possessed. Looks Away's brother, a *Yuta* warrior named Bad Camper, had traveled far to the south to steal some ponies. Bad Camper had told the warriors of his band that the ponies came from strange men in the south with iron shirts and pale skin and hairy faces. It always frightened her to think of such things.

Looks Away tried not to ponder her old life in the mountains. She missed many things from that life. Her name had been Pine Cone there. Summers were cool, and winters spent in protected canyons. Food was more plentiful than it was among the *Noomah*. The hunting grounds of her people were green and there were many elk, whose whistling she missed during the Moon of Falling Leaves.

Among these happy mountain people, the *Noomah* had been regarded as savage foreigners with very dark skin, bowed legs, and broad faces. The *Yutas* called the *Noomah* by the word *Komancia*, which meant Those Who Always Want to Fight Us in the *Yuta* tongue. Looks Away had been warned as a girl that they were horrible torturers, that they ate bugs and snakes and even their own filth. Judging from the few captives she had seen as a girl, these strange people were small and squatty, shorter and more heavily muscled than other peoples she had seen. Now she noticed that this compact build seemed to make the *Noomahs* more suited to riding the horse, as their weight and bulk stayed low on the back of the animal, making them almost become a part of the horse itself.

Many things were different here among these embattled people who had captured and adopted her, but she did not dwell on the *Noomah* hardships. Here she had already served two great warrior husbands. First, Black Horn, who had died well. And now, Black Horn's brother, Shaggy Hump, who was the bravest and richest warrior of all the Burnt Meat People, and perhaps all the *Noomah* nation. And she had become a second mother to Horseback, whom she loved as much as any child she could have borne herself. Horseback was a rider with medicine, and she had brought much of the knowledge he needed to become great. Though life was hard here—harder than it had been with the *Yutas*—the spirits had acted wisely when they sent her to live with the people who call themselves the True Humans.

"Looks Away!"

The grating voice made her flinch, and she turned quickly to see River Woman scowling at her from below.

"What are you doing?"

"Gathering clay."

"For what?"

"To make a white paint for my husband."

"*Your* husband!" River Woman hissed her disapproval. "Shaggy Hump is *my* husband. Are you the one who carries his shield when we move the village?"

"No."

"But, I am. You are little more than a slave. If you were a sits-beside wife, you would know that Shaggy Hump does not like white paint. He likes yellow and red and black. I do not see that you are gathering anything, anyway. What are you looking at up there?"

"Your son. Come see."

River Woman climbed the crumbling dirt bank and crouched with Looks Away behind the brink. She saw Horseback darting back and forth on the yellow mare, trying to pull Trotter on behind him as Whip scrambled around like a four-legged. "What are they doing?"

"Can you see the circle they have made in the dirt, my sister? That is the clearing in the woods. Whip is the great humpbacked bear, and Trotter is my . . . *your* husband."

River Woman watched the boys play. "They play a new game. It will serve them well one day in battle. My son is young, but he is wise to think of such a thing."

Looks Away did not try to explain that the new game had really been her idea. She had asked Horseback what he had learned from the fight with the great bear. After thinking a while, Horseback had said that he had learned he was not the great rider the spirits wanted him to be, or else he would have prevented his father's wound.

"Show the spirits that you want to ride better," she suggested.

"How will I show them?"

"Ride as you wish you would have ridden during the fight with the great bear. The spirits watch always."

Now she felt her heart grow with pride as Horseback clasped arms with Trotter and pulled him onto the horse behind him with one smooth pass.

This was a thing she had never seen before, even during her old life among horsed warriors in the mountains.

"Look," River Woman said, pointing down the brink of the river bank. "Our eyes are not the only ones watching the young horsebacks play."

Looks Away spotted a girl of the Corn People crouching behind clumps of saskatoon bushes, her eyes glistening and her girlish mouth open in awe.

"Yes. That girl watches Horseback all the time."

"What are we to think of this girl?" River Woman said.

"There is none prettier among the Corn People. I think Horseback likes the way she looks."

"I thought he liked that other girl."

"Slope Child? No, that was only a few nights in his lodge. She showed him the way, but now she visits some other boy's lodge. Horseback likes that girl, there, much better."

"She is small, but she looks strong."

"She is very healthy. I have seen her run like a coyote and climb trees like a little skinny bear cub."

River Woman turned to face Looks Away. "What is her name?"

"Teal."

"Her hips look good for bearing warrior babies."

"Yes, I think so."

"Her father is poor, yes?"

"Among the Corn People he is a rich one, my sister."

"A rich one among the Corn People is the same as a poor one to the sits-beside wife of Shaggy Hump. You do not know that because you are not a sits-beside wife."

Looks Away did not try to argue with River Woman, for it was always futile.

"We should go together to speak to the mother of this girl, Teal, then she will know my son's father is a great warrior to have two wives, and she will want her daughter marry my son."

Looks Away remained silent. She only hoped River Woman would not offend Teal's mother, for River Woman was proud and haughty.

"Do you not agree, sister?"

Looks Away liked to hear River Woman honor her with the name of sister, but knew she only used it to get something she wanted. "I have listened to the girl's mother before. I am worried that she is greedy. If we both go to her and prove how great your husband is to have such a proud and beautiful sits-beside wife, and a second slave wife as well, then she may want too much for the girl. Teal's father has only one horse, and he may demand many more from the great Shaggy Hump."

"I shall go alone to speak to her."

"Yes. That would be better. Or send me with the words you choose me to say. I am only a plain second wife and will not excite the Corn woman's greed."

River Woman looked at the girl spying from the bushes, then looked back at her son, practicing his riding skills. "You must tell me everything she says before you promise anything."

"Of course. I will be only the ears to hear, and the mouth to speak. It is your heart that guides your son, my sister."

Just then a cry came up from the village below, and the women turned to hear through the sounds of wind in the leaves. A crier was running among the lodges, shouting excitedly.

"What is the crier shouting?" River Woman asked.

"I cannot hear, but he sounds very excited."

"Go! Take your pouch of white clay to your lodge. I will shout at Horseback and his friends."

16

The council assembled in the grassy flats near the timber that lined the river, where a long line of lodges had been raised. The men came together outside of Shaggy Hump's lodge, for it was near the center of the string of tipis, and considered an honorable place to convene.

A few old *puhakuts* filed into the lodge, forming the inside ring of the council circle. Around them gathered the elite warriors renowned for their battle scars and strokes counted. Around these, the younger men gathered. Horseback and his friends, Whip and Trotter, made up part of the outermost curve, for they had yet to ride the war trail, though they had sought visions and hunted.

Though they now stood together, the feeling had changed between Horseback and his two friends. Horseback had received a powerful vision— one that all the people of two bands were talking about. Trotter had spent four days seeking, only to receive the vision of a spirit-grouse. And Whip— poor Whip—had failed in two vision quests to receive any medicine at all. The spirits did not wish to speak to him. Horseback knew that both Whip and Trotter envied his medicine.

When the council began, Spirit Talker spoke first, for he possessed powerful magic, which gave him much wisdom. "My people," he said, waiting for those around him to quiet down. "It is well that the Corn People and the Burnt Meat People have lived and traveled and hunted together from the Fat

Moon to the Red Calf Moon. We have made a time of laughter and much meat. Now, this time is no more. Echo, tell the people what you have seen."

Horseback craned his neck to see Echo-of-the-Wolf stand as Spirit Talker sat back down. Aside from his father, Horseback admired no warrior of the Burnt Meat People more than Echo. Only a few winters older than Horseback himself, Echo had already taken scalps and captured horses. He was as vane and arrogant as any rich war chief ten winters older, and Horseback wanted to be much like him.

"One sleep after the great hunt at this place," he began, "I made a scout to the land in the south, following some of the buffalo and watching for signs of the *Yutas,* for we camp near their country. My guardian spirits, who grant me much power, instructed me to make this scout in a dream as my belly was full the first night after the great hunt.

"Riding two sleeps into the dangerous Land Between the Two Mountain Ranges, I noticed a dust cloud to the east, rising from the base of the sacred Medicine Bow mountains. I rode that way and found our enemies in camp. My guardian spirits made me brave, and I crawled near enough to listen. Like Shaggy Hump, I learn words of other nations, for I wish to travel far and trade in days to come. I listened to the *Yutas* and knew some of their talk, and watched their gestures. I began to understand.

"When the seven hunters came with Shaggy Hump to kill the many buffalo here at Two Rivers, one of these enemies saw us, for he, too, was scouting the big buffalo dust he had seen from his camp in the mountains. We were seven, and he was only one, so he did not attack us, but rode back to his village in the mountains to get more warriors. Now they ride twenty warriors strong, and they come to destroy us as we butcher our kill. They carry their weapons with them, and two of them carry Fire Sticks.

"The bad things they say make me want to fight. They say we are cowards and they will capture us without a fight and take us back to their mountains and let their women torture us. They say they will take our women away and defile them, and beat them, and if they are strong enough to survive, they will make them into slave wives. They say they will take our children and tie them up until they are trained like dogs, and they will cut the testicles from our young boys and make them into slaves to sell to other nations. These are just some of the terrible things they laugh about at their camp."

Echo stood silent for a moment, his face frozen in a scowl of hatred.

"Yet, our enemies are foolish. They do not know that the rest of our village has now come to join us. They do not know that the two bands of Burnt Meat People and Corn People have come together to make us stronger. They believe we are only seven hunters with a few women and children.

"When I left them, I rode fast, and I know that they did not find out about me, for my medicine has made me invisible to them. They are coming. They will attack us when the sun rises if we remain in this place."

Echo-of-the-Wolf sat down and men stirred with excitement all around the council circle.

Shaggy Hump rose and spoke: "Spirit Talker, our wise grandfather, what do you say about what this brave young warrior has discovered?"

"I say we must prepare now to fight or to leave this place."

"What is your counsel, Grandfather?"

"We have hunted well here at the Two Rivers, yet our women have not had time to dry the meat and make the pemmican. I like pemmican. The women put berries and tallow in the gut with the dried meat, and it tastes good after it has stayed together a while. If we leave now to avoid a fight, we must leave much good food behind. The Burnt Meat People make good pemmican. I must tell the women of the Corn People to learn from them, for the Burnt Meat People pemmican is the best I have ever eaten. But if we leave this camp, the women will have no time to make good pemmican."

"Shall we fight, Grandfather?"

"I am an old man. The only reason I want to fight is so I may go to the Shadow Land and see how the pemmican tastes there. No one would miss an old man like me. But if we choose to fight, some of the young men may die before they have had the chance to eat their share of pemmican. The spirits talk to me. They say the winter will be long and cold, and we have gathered few pine nuts. We must survive on pemmican this winter. Which is better? To die fighting for the meat we have made, or to die starving this winter because we leave our good meat behind?"

Horseback saw the eyes of his people turn from old Spirit Talker to Shaggy Hump, and his heart swelled with pride that his father would speak for both these bands of True Humans.

"With few words, Grandfather, you speak much truth. Our shame would heap upon us like enemy coals if we had to listen to our children cry for food this winter because we were too afraid to fight. We have no reason to fear, for the spirits have brought us to this place. Did not my son, Horseback, see the dust of these many buffalo from the sacred place of his vision quest? Did not our medicine make our arrows fly straighter than straight?

"We are strong together. The enemy does not know of this strength. Let them come. We will take down all the lodges except the ones brought here by the seven hunters. We will lead away all the horses except the ones brought here by the seven hunters. At dawn our enemies will attack our seven lodges, but we will be waiting for them in the timber and in the draws, and we will close around them. Then we will take scalps and count many battle strokes and let our women show these enemies the real way to torture a captive warrior if they are cowardly enough to be taken alive!"

A chorus of female voices rose outside the walls of the council lodge, saying, "Yee-yee-yee-yee."

Horseback grabbed Trotter by the arm. "We are going to know battle!" he said. But now he looked in Trotter's eyes and saw the fear.

The circle was breaking up as quickly as it had formed, and the people were moving away to prepare for battle—the women and children to their lodges, the men to their weapons. But Trotter and Whip lingered near Horseback.

"I am afraid I will not be brave," Trotter said. "My *puha* is not strong like yours, my good friend. My vision was only of a grouse who taught me to make myself invisible in the sagebrush. I am afraid I will only hide and disgrace my people. I did not even get a new name. My Naming Father said Trotter was a good enough name for a seeker who gets a grouse vision."

"I am still called Whip," the other youth added. He seemed more angry than ashamed. "The spirits would not speak to me at all."

Horseback motioned toward the woods. "Come pray with me, my friends. My Naming Father, Spirit Talker, has told me that I may share my great power with another who needs it. I will give you both some of Sound-the-Sun-Makes's *puha*, and you will be brave."

Trotter sighed with some relief. "May scalps hang thick from your shield," he said.

Whip said nothing, but he walked with the others toward the timber.

"After the fight, you may give the *puha* back to me," Horseback suggested. "To keep it long is a dangerous burden."

"Yes, I only want to borrow it," Trotter said. "If I die in battle, my shadow will send it back to you."

Whip remained silent and sullen, in contrast to the hopefulness Trotter seemed to have taken on.

"If you die," Horseback said, "you will die with courage. Sound-the-Sun-Makes has much medicine to give."

17

The Two Rivers seemed to speak louder in this time before the first bird song of the morning. Horseback listened to the waters anxiously, hoping to hear some spirit wisdom in their ceaseless conversation. His eyes kept darting to the high south bank of the valley, just visible over the *sohoobi* trees. The ridge there was dark as a buffalo hump, the sky behind it the color of slate. The stars had let their fires burn out and the Great Mystery was pulling the robe of night away from the eastern horizon. Horseback's eyes kept returning

to the south bank, though he doubted he would see the stealthy enemy warriors until they attacked the camp of seven lodges.

Waiting in this pale light before dawn, he identified the thing that worried him. There had been no war dance last night. Many times he had imagined his first journey down the war path, and always he had thought of a loud
war dance the night before, with women's voices trilling all around him as he
danced to the beat of drums and shook the buffalo rattle. But, last night, a
noisy war dance would only have alerted the enemy to the ambush that
waited.

Instead of dancing, Horseback had checked his arrows and his bow. He
had placed them ceremoniously in the quiver and bow case that were embraced by the sacred deer antlers he had found returning from his vision quest.
He had chosen his best *pogamoggan*, made of a hard piece of wood with a rock
on the end, the rock wrapped in rawhide to hold it fast to the end of the club.
He had painted his face black and thrown the sacred dust of ground deer
antlers into a small fire to beseech Sound-the-Sun-Makes for medicine. He
had taken the painted cover from his shield of hardened rawhide. The shield
itself was painted, too, with a bright red sun that made a sound represented
by yellow lightning shooting out of it. An eagle feather was tied to an antler
point strapped tight to the middle of the shield. This was his *puhahante*, which
gave the shield much magic. He had spoken to his *puhahante* last night, praying for courage. Now Horseback was confident and anxious for battle. Still,
he wished there had been a war dance.

He twisted his reins in his hands as he watched the clearing under the
belly of his horse. No one had questioned his catching the horse before dark.
He was Horseback. He possessed peculiar magic. He would count his first
battle stroke astride a pony.

This stallion, by no means beautiful, was nonetheless one of Horseback's
favorites. Smaller than average and round-bellied, his color was a common
bay. His black mane hung tangled in front of his eyes. His face was rather
ugly, due mainly to his long nose and sagging lower jaw. Much of his black
tail had been bitten off by another stud. His back was low between high
withers and widely protruding hip bones, but this swayed back tended to help
a rider stay with the horse.

This ability to keep a rider seated, coupled with the little stud's heart,
made him a good choice for battle today. Unlike some horses, this bay liked
and trusted people. Though his wind died quickly on a long trail, his spirit
was always good for a short hard run. This made him useful around the camp,
especially for catching the wilder horses in the herd. As a mount, the bay
seemed crazy to do the bidding of the rider, and would charge into any kind
of unknown. No strange sound nor sight nor smell could prevent him following the touch of reins on his neck, or heels against his ribs. He would leap

willingly into a wall of tangled brush or run right up the back of a bear if his rider so desired.

The little stud made Horseback feel good as he waited for the enemy. He knew how they would come. They would leave their horses well beyond the south bank and sneak afoot into the valley. They would cross the water below the meeting of the Two Rivers, and creep through the timber until they came to the open flood plain where the good grass grew. They would advance swiftly toward the seven lodges, divide their number among them, and leap into them screaming, expecting to find their victims asleep.

This would serve as the signal for the warriors of the True Humans to rush from the wooded draws and the timber along the north bank, close a sacred circle around the invaders, and make running cowards of those they could not kill.

In a way, he wished he could trade places with the attackers. He had always imagined his first fight at the end of some long war trail, in the land of some horrible enemy. Here, there were women and children to defend. Last night in a vision, the *puhahante* in the center of his shield had cautioned him not to endanger his people or his fellow warriors with foolish courage. Such greed for glory would risk the lives of mothers and babies, and make him a taunted fool instead of the rider-protector the spirits wished him to become in this, his first fight.

He was low in the grass, watching between the legs of his mount, his whole body tense with anxiety. A branch dragged across something behind him, and he whirled halfway round, making his horse snort and lift his head high against the reins.

"It is only me," Teal said.

"Go away!" Horseback scolded. "Your place is with the women. Now you have made my horse move and the enemy will see me."

"The enemy will not see, because I come with much magic," she whispered, coming closer to him.

"A girl knows nothing about magic," he said, admiring the way she had painted her face: yellow on her eyelids, red circles on her cheeks.

"That is true," Teal answered, "but this magic comes to me in a dream. I do not have to know anything about magic for the magic to use me as it will."

Horseback smirked. He had never spoken to Teal alone like this, and had not expected her to speak so well. "What was this dream?"

"In my dream, the spirits showed me that if you would carry the feather of the bird of the Sacred South in your quiver, it would make the arrows of our enemy go around you."

"What kind of bird wears this feather?"

"I have never seen the bird, but I have the feather. An old grandmother of the Corn People gave it to me. She said it came from some *Yuta* woman who camped in places in the south where the bird lives. I know nothing about the bird, but the feather is beautiful." Reaching behind her head, Teal removed the feather she had woven loosely into her hair. It was long and slender, dark-colored except for the pointed tip, which was white.

When he took it from her, his hand closed around her smaller hand, and he felt her warmth. "I will carry this feather in my quiver, Teal. Now, go hide with the women."

"Use your weapons well, Horseback. Do not let our enemies carry me away."

"My mother will cut off all her hair before our enemies take you away." He turned from her and tried to concentrate on the coming fight again, but her smile and her sparkling eyes possessed his thoughts. No longer did he dwell on the war dance that had not happened.

They came so soon after Teal left that Horseback had not had time to make himself anxious. They were several steps into the clearing before he even noticed them under the belly of his horse. At first he thought his own warriors were coming back to the lodges, for they strolled upright, walking casually toward the empty decoy village.

Then he noticed their height—they were taller than any of his own people and more slender. He noticed the strips of fur some had woven into the braids they wore on either side of their heads, in the *Yuta* way. One looked toward him, and Horseback felt his heart try to leap from his chest. The enemy warrior was looking at the bay horse, and Horseback feared he had been seen. But the bay had his head down, grazing, concealing the war bridle around his jaw, and the rope Horseback had woven around the pony had been stained dark to match his bay color, and was hard to see in the light of dawn. Other horses grazed not far away, so the enemy warrior thought nothing strange about this one standing in the edge of the brush. When the attacker looked back toward the lodges, Horseback knew he had not been discovered. His war paint of black had made him like the night, unseen and unknown.

He tried to count them, but they continued to emerge from the timber, and he saw no real reason to enumerate them. They seemed many more than Echo-of-the-Wolf had reported. They carried bows with arrows already notched, clubs and war axes, slender lances as straight as a stake line stretched tight by a wild horse. It was going to happen very soon now. He must ride well, for the eyes of the Great Deer were on him, and the magic of the feather from the Sacred South enveloped him.

Now something happened that Horseback had not predicted. Two of the warriors broke away from the large party that crept toward the village of seven lodges. They angled toward him to capture the horses, which they would drive south toward their own mounts as the fight started. One of the horses nickered at them as they approached, and the others raised their heads, including the bay warhorse, but the enemy still did not notice the war bridle or the rope wound around the bay's chest. The bay stood apart from the other horses, so the enemy warriors came straight toward him, in order to drive him into the rest of the herd.

Horseback's heart galled him with pain and made his chest throb. They looked like horrible butchers coming at him, and they were two to his one. The bay grumbled at them and lay his ears back, and Horseback took courage from his mount. He only hoped the terrible warriors would not notice the war bridle on his bay until the fighting had started. Like any proud *Noomah* warrior, Horseback wanted to die in battle someday—but not in his very first battle.

He no longer took time to think. His mind went away to the clouds and the talk of the Two Rivers ceased. All he could hear were the blades of grass brushing the leggings of the painted enemy warriors coming right toward him. Beyond them, the main party of invaders had come silently among the seven lodges.

Suddenly, the warrior nearest him stopped, and Horseback knew he had noticed the reins hanging from the mouth of the warhorse. Sound-the-Sun-Makes leapt the eastern horizon, into Horseback's body, and made him go crazy with strength and courage.

He sprang to the back of his war horse with the ease of a lion, and felt the ancestral war cry of wolves and eagles and rutting bull elks building in his chest. The enemy brave near him was stepping backward in surprise as the cry rose from the invaders at the empty decoy camp. Horseback released his own battle scream, and it made all four legs of the bay kick crazily for footing. He charged hard toward these strange slender thieves and murderers who had strayed too far from their own ground.

The rider's right hand held the war club. The magic shield was strapped tight to his left wrist and forearm. His left hand held both his bow and his reins.

As horse and horseman charged, the enemy brave hastily drew his bow and shot an arrow, but the magic of the feather in Horseback's quiver made the arrow sail high. His *pogamoggan* swung upward as the enemy warrior turned to run in terror. He grabbed the long black mane, for the wise warhorse was closing on the enemy and needed no touch of the reins. As the *pogamoggan* came down, the fleeing warrior looked back with fearful eyes, and the weapon struck solidly on his forehead, driving him to the ground.

To Horseback, high on the back of the bay, the fallen warrior looked suddenly small. He was in fact, just a boy, no older than Horseback himself. He glanced toward the seven lodges and saw his fellow *Noomah* warriors closing in on the surprised invaders. The other boy who had come to steal the horses was running away to join his war party. He, too, was young. Horseback could have ridden him down and clubbed him as well, but something was making him linger over the body of his first victim.

His heart felt bad. It seemed these two boys his age had been sent to gather the horses away from the most dangerous fighting at the lodges, for they had seen nothing of battle. It had been his duty to strike this invader, no matter how young and inexperienced. But now he wished he had hit the boy on the shoulder, and driven him away still living to spread his fame, as his father had once left an arrow standing between the heads of two sleeping foes who would talk forever about it. Now he feared he had not yet killed the boy, and knew that this young warrior at the feet of his prancing war horse was destined to die slowly at the hands of vengeful women, or to be castrated and enslaved.

Some brave women were emerging from the brush to watch the fight. "Do not let them take us away and defile us with their seed!" one cried.

Horseback let the war club dangle from the thong around the wrist of his arrow hand. He drew an arrow from his sacred quiver and notched it on the bowstring. Since the fight with the great bear that had wounded his father, he had practiced shooting many arrows from the back of his pony, and knew he could hit the boy on the ground. The shot was straight down and close. When the string sang, the bay horse jumped away from the prone invader, but Horseback held his place, his knees thrust tightly under the loops of rope encircling his war pony's chest. His arrow pierced the body in the grass. When the corpse failed to flinch, Horseback knew the young warrior was dead, and his heart felt glad.

A cry of "Yee-yee-yee-yee" went up among the women, for few of them had ever seen a kill made from a horse before. Horseback slid down from the bay stallion and pounced on the fallen enemy. He felt strength fill his arms as he took the scalp lock of the dead boy in his bow hand. He drew his knife and slit the skin just in front of the hairline, pulling hard. The scalp would not come off, so he made new slashes with his knife until he heard the flesh tearing away from the skull, sounding like the hoof of a horse pulling out of a mud hole. The trophy suddenly came free, and Horseback held it high.

"Ahh-hey," he screamed, in a voice that screeched so high that he scarcely recognized it as his own. Looking toward the brush, he saw many women. He saw his mother, who seemed crazed with joy as she danced in the grass with a long spear. He saw Teal standing farther back in the bushes, and heard her voice among all the others:

"Drive them away! They come to take me to their mountains and spoil my virtue!"

Suddenly the bay war horse screamed and lunged hard against the reins. Horseback barely managed to stay on his feet as his mount tried to bolt, but he hung on. An enemy warrior had lobbed an arrow in a long arch through the sky and hit the bay in the hip. Tucking the trophy scalp under his loin skin belt, Horseback grabbed the arrow and pulled, but the barbs of the war point only drove the bay to wild lunges. He heard the voice of a spirit telling him he should have painted his horse with magic signs for protection, and felt ashamed that he had not heard this voice last night.

Breaking the shaft of the enemy arrow, Horseback again sprang behind the withers of his war horse who kicked a hind leg in protest of the pain, but did not attempt to throw the rider. He wheeled the wounded horse toward the seven lodges and tried to take in the battle.

His own people had surrounded the enemy warriors and were closing in slowly, sending an occasional arrow into the village of empty lodges. At the closest point of the surround, Horseback saw Echo-of-the-Wolf standing up-right, a shield in one hand, a long-handled stone axe in the other.

"Come out and fight!" he shouted. "You hide behind the lodges like children behind the skirts of your ugly women!" He drew an arrow from his quiver and stabbed it into the ground in front of him. "I will defend the ground where my arrow stands. I am Echo-of-the-Wolf. Come let me kill you. I never retreat!"

As he loped to join the circle of the surround, Horseback saw many enemy warriors drawing their bows to shoot at Echo. Then, rounding one of the lodges, he saw an enemy brave who wore three feathers placing a strange weapon to his shoulder.

"The Fire Stick!" he shouted.

Echo had stood and laughed at the first arrows that flew by him like shadow-wasps, but now he crouched behind his shield as he heard Horseback's warning and saw the evil weapon pointing his way. Fire and thunder shot from the end of the iron stick. At the same instant, Echo rolled over backward as if kicked by an invisible horse.

A battle scream went up among the *Yutas* and they poured from the cover of the seven lodges and rushed toward the place were Echo had fallen.

Yet, Echo stirred! He rose to his knees, slipping his arm from the loops of his magical shield. The warriors of the True Humans were rushing to him, to lift and protect him, and Horseback saw Trotter reach him first, making his heart grow with pride of the power he had loaned to Trotter. As the enemy charged on, Echo hung his shield on the notch of the arrow that stood in the ground, making sure the sacred shield would not touch the ground. He let his wounded shield arm dangle at his side, but raised his axe in his good hand, inviting the enemy to come on.

It looked bad to Horseback, for the enemy warriors were running desper-ately at the braves who had stopped to gather around Echo. He saw his own father, Shaggy Hump, and Trotter, and Whip, and other men he knew. It seemed the enemy had the power, for they were charging. They would fight desperately to break out of the surround and escape. The True Humans would be swept back, as if by the raging waters of a flooded river.

He felt the voice of Sound-the-Sun-Makes hot upon his face. Leaning over the long black mane of his war horse, he swung his *pogamoggan* back and bounced it lightly off the rump of the bay, who sprang forward like a lion making a charge. He rode fast, screaming his battle cry until his throat hurt, angling hard against the near flank of the enemy charge.

One by one, the invaders faltered as they saw him come on. Each slowed, exposing the next man in the charge, and Horseback galloped among them as a hawk would dive into a flock of prairie chickens. He glimpsed faces, eyes wide, mouths open. Arrows curved away from him. One brave warrior stood with a lance for the warhorse to run upon, but the horse and rider had taken on the power of the sun, the bay baring his teeth and striking with a front hoof as Horseback leaned all the way across the mount with his shield to catch the point of the lance and fling it aside.

He leapt through the line now, and found himself behind the enemy charge as it neared the arrow and shield of Echo standing on the ground. His club reached out as he galloped on, and he knocked two warriors down and made others duck and reel away with fear.

The enemy charge bogged like buffalo in quicksand, and Echo came forward with his axe swinging. Its long handle reached beyond an enemy shield and its sharp flint edges struck the shield bearer under the ear, bringing forth a spray of blood. The *Yutas* scattered, their courage shaken, and the fights were warrior against warrior now, hand-to-hand, the enemies fleeing as they fought.

Reining in the bay, Horseback heard the thunder of the Fire Stick again, and two men locked in battle behind him fell to the ground. But the medicine of the enemy had gone bad, for the one killed wore the skins of a *Yuta*. It was Whip who rose, the intended target of the Fire Stick. He had wrestled his foe at the right moment to pull him into the path of the killing magic. Whip screamed a crazy war cry as he scalped the mountain warrior who had died by the Fire Stick of his own kinsman.

Turning his mount, Horseback saw the Fire Stick warrior between two of the seven lodges, making the peculiar incantations over his weapon. He kicked the bay's ribs and charged toward the seven lodges to stop this brave before he could instill the magic in the weapon again. He was riding hard when he heard the screams of the women, and saw that two of the *Yutas* had broken toward the horse herd and were trying to catch mounts on which to escape. He glimpsed his own mother running toward the horse thieves with her lance.

Horseback clashed with the Fire Stick warrior, running into him before he could finish the evil Fire Stick spell. But this warrior wore three kill feathers in his hair and knew much of battle. As Horseback swiped at him with the *pogamoggan*, Kill Feathers ducked in front of the bay and struck Horseback on the other side with his Fire Stick, almost knocking him from the pony.

Without a pull of the rein, the bay was turning, snapping his teeth at Kill Feathers. Horseback let his mount attack, but the warrior was quick and came around the head of the horse with an iron knife. Horseback caught the first thrust with his shield, but the second plunged into his leg, and the third into the bay's shoulder. The horse screamed, wheeled, and kicked just as Horseback's war club glanced off Kill Feathers's head and smashed into his shoulder.

The enemy staggered back and fell, but quickly rose. "Get off your horse and fight like a true warrior!" he demanded.

Horseback understood this talk, because his second mother, Looks Away, was born *Yuta*, though she had been made into a good *Noomah* wife. Looks Away had taught him *Yuta* words for many winters, for she hoped always for peace and trade between her old people and her new people.

But Horseback thought nothing of peace and trade now, for Kill Feathers had come to destroy him, and would carry Teal away if he could. As his blood ran hot down a leg seared by pain, a new rage engulfed him, and he remembered the day the Northern Raiders had attacked his people and killed his grandfather. The ancient hatreds he had inherited that day plunged like shadow-warriors into his soul, and it seemed the ground all around him shook with his anger. He felt his grip like stone around the handle of the war club. "I am Horseback!" he cried, and he ran upon the thrice-feathered warrior.

Reining wide with his bow hand, he passed beyond reach of the enemy warrior's knife and leaned far toward Kill Feathers with the heavy *pogamoggan*. The warrior tried to shield his head with an arm, but the power of the passing horse was in the blow, and Horseback felt bones break through the wooden club handle. The bay was planting hooves and turning back with snapping teeth as Horseback brought the club down again, landing it solidly among the three feathers.

A victory cry came from the direction of the river, and Horseback did not even have to look back to know that his fellow warriors had broken the enemy charge. Now the sound of screaming women pierced the victory yell, and he looked up to see his mother, River Woman, jabbing her lance at an enemy warrior who was trying to avoid the sharp blade long enough to notch an arrow on his bow.

The bay was tired, but leapt toward the women at Horseback's signal. The warhorse seemed to run very slowly and River Woman seemed very far away as Horseback rode to protect her. As he watched from the back of his pony, his mother made a deliberate advance with the spear, but the enemy warrior dropped his bow and caught the shaft with his hand. He was stronger than Horseback's mother, and Horseback feared he would wrest the weapon from her before the bay could get there.

Now Looks Away came darting from the brush nearby. Above her head she wielded a war axe, and her eyes were round and cold as snowflakes. Her lips curled back and she screamed as the warrior got the spear from River Woman.

Horseback was four leaps away. The enemy warrior twirled the shaft of the lance in his hand. River Woman was falling back as the enemy lunged and stabbed her below one breast. The bestial scream of Looks Away caught in her throat as her axe broke through the skull of the enemy warrior and Horseback's club knocked his brains onto the grass.

The young warrior jumped from the bay, who staggered, bleeding and heaving. He ran back to his mother, but Looks Away was already upon her. Looks Away screamed a denial of the wound that stained River Woman's deer skin dress with blood. Then suddenly, strangely, the Two Rivers casually took up the conversation they had dropped when the battle started.

It seemed to Horseback that this fight was a trifling thing to the Two Rivers. To him it was everything glorious and horrible, for his mother lay wounded on one hand, and he had counted his first strokes against an enemy war party on the other hand—and counted them well. Now he prayed that his medicine had not gone bad and caused his mother to get hurt. He feared he may have stepped upon the track of a deer, or eaten a morsel of food a deer might have taken, or offended his powerful spirit guardians in some other foolish way.

When he fell beside his mother, he found her covering her wound with a hand and trying to sit upright. She looked at Horseback, saying, "My son, you are wounded?"

"Only my leg, Mother. Lie back and rest."

River Woman did lie back, grimacing against the pain of her wound. "Did you see Looks Away, my son? She killed a warrior of the people she was born among to protect me. You must credit her with the first stroke, and take the second for yourself, for her axe struck before your *pogamoggan*."

"Mother, I cannot count a stroke on that warrior. It was your lance that touched him first. You must count the first stroke. Looks Away will count the second."

River Woman smiled. "Yes, my son. You are honest. Looks Away came to defend me only a moment before you did." She let her eyes meet those of the woman her husband had taken as a second wife, and she said, "Now Looks Away is truly my sister."

The victory cry rose again, and Horseback glanced back to see his friends dragging the Fire Stick warrior, Kill Feathers, still alive, from the village of seven lodges. Some beat him with their bows and others kicked him all over, but they would not kill him. Horseback himself had won that honor. He might kill the captive himself, or present him to any woman in camp who had lost a husband or son in battle with the *Yutas*, letting her decide how quickly or slowly the enemy warrior might die.

As he was thinking about this, a strange thing happened. Looks Away turned from the scene of the battle won and ran. She ran until the timber stole her shadow.

▲▲▲▲▲
18
▼▼▼▼▼

The day of his first battle was not the day for his mother to die. River Woman lay sleeping in the shade of the timber as the old *puhakut*, Spirit Talker, made prayers over her and wove magic around her. Looks Away had come back from the timber to stay with River Woman during the heat of the day, fanning her with an eagle's wing to keep her cool and drive flies away from her wound. Shaggy Hump went away up the river to pray.

The younger warriors gathered in the shade of the timber to talk about the battle. Echo-of-the-Wolf took the protective cover from his sacred shield to show where it had swallowed the evil power of the Fire Stick. Though the shield had saved him, the Fire Stick had broken his arm, which he now carried strapped in a willow splint and bound with wet rawhide.

Horseback marveled at the neat round hole punched in the face of the shield. He summoned his protective medicine and stuck his finger into the hole, jerking it out at first, then probing deeper. He could feel through the first layer of hardened buffalo hide into the fur packed tight between it and the back layer of hide. He forced his finger deeper into the hole until his finger touched something that moved. He jerked his hand back.

"What is it?" asked Whip, who was watching over Horseback's shoulder.

Horseback set his jaw. "I will find out." He probed into Echo's punctured shield again and touched the unknown thing. "It moves," he said. "It is like a stone against the back piece of hide that protects our brother, Echo."

Echo took the shield from the younger warrior and bravely felt for the thing himself. Jerking his knife from its sheath with a flourish, he bored into the rear layer of rawhide from the back of the shield until he could push a misshapen hunk of dark gray unknown matter from the hole. It landed on the ground with a thump and lay there like something dead. The warriors surrounded it.

Finally, Horseback picked it up. It felt heavy for its size, and he knew by the way it had almost penetrated the sacred shield that it was powerful. "This is the thing that kills," he said.

"Where are the things captured from the Fire Stick warrior?" Echo demanded.

The trappings of the enemy prisoner were laid out on a robe for study. There was the Fire Stick itself, which was passed around among all the warriors once Echo and Horseback had proven that they could handle it without incurring any evil. The only familiar thing about it was the small flint stone growing out of one side of it. Some of the men tried to put the thing to their shoulders the way they had seen Kill Feathers hold it, but it would render neither noise nor smoke. Trotter did worry it long enough to make a spark jump from the piece of flint, whereupon he dropped it on the robe, shaking his hands as if to fling the evil power from his fingertips.

Examining the rest of the captured paraphernalia, the warriors found a deerskin pouch filled with small round balls, dark gray and heavy like the misshapen thing cut from Echo's shield. They noticed that these heavy little balls just fit in the hole at the killing end of the Fire Stick. In this same pouch, they found strange hairless patches of tanned hide, very thin, perhaps from a rabbit skin.

The oddest thing among the possessions of the captured enemy was the buffalo horn. The hollow of its broad end was enclosed by rawhide that had been strapped on wet and allowed to shrink and dry hard. The point of the horn had been cut off flat, and the flat place now had a smooth wooden peg sticking out of it.

At length, Echo called on his courage and pulled this peg out. A dark, evil-looking powder poured from the narrow end of the horn. It burned the nostrils of those who smelled it. Thinking of his own sacred powder of ground deer horn, Horseback took a pinch of this black powder to a smoldering cook fire nearby and threw it onto the coals. The quick burst of flame that engulfed the powder made him leap back in momentary fear.

"Young brother," Echo said to Horseback, "your *pogamoggan* counted the first stroke on the Fire Stick warrior with three kill feathers. This Fire Stick belongs to you." He presented the piece to Horseback, affecting much ceremony.

"It is true," Horseback said, taking the heavy killing tool. He looked across the clearing and saw Looks Away and Spirit Talker bending over his wounded mother. "It is also true that my father and mother will celebrate my first strokes with a giveaway dance when my mother has healed. My medicine has become so strong after our battle that I do not fear giving away all my possessions, for I know my guardian spirits will provide for me. So, I am going to give this Fire Stick away now. Trotter, my friend, you have fought well on this day. I give this Fire Stick to you."

Trotter looked up from the powder-filled buffalo horn he had been study-

ing, the surprise plain on his face. He took the Fire Stick Horseback offered.
"I will master its magic and make it good. My brother, I now return to you
the *puha* you loaned to me in the sight of our spirit-sister, the Moon, last
night. It is very powerful and fills my paunch with crawling things. Now I will
find my own *puha* and make it strong in my heart."

Horseback looked at Whip. "My friend, do you wish to return the power
I loaned to you? You used it well today."

Whip snorted. "I borrowed nothing from you, Horseback. I have my own
power." He turned and walked away from the group of astonished warriors.

Just then, a cry of agony rose from the tree line, not far away, followed
by a cackle of childish laughter. The warriors turned to look at the captured
Fire Stick warrior, Kill Feathers. He had been tied all day to an overhanging
tree limb, his hands bound behind his back and hoisted up painfully high.
His head had been struck hard by Horseback's club, and he could not stay
awake, but sleeping made his weight wrench his shoulders joints and made
pain shoot through his chest, making his day one of agony.

The clutch of children gathered around him had been jabbing him with
arrows. One had touched Kill Feathers with the end of a stick he had held in
a fire, causing him to cry out.

It was the duty of all True Humans to seek revenge against any enemy
warrior who tried to kill a *Noomah* brave, and especially one who attacked a
Noomah village full of mothers and babies. Kill Feathers knew he had risked
such vengeance in coming here to make war, and now his suffering was just
beginning. The boy jabbed the hot coal into the small of Kill Feather's back,
making him cry out again.

Kill Feathers suddenly yelled something in the *Yuta* tongue, lifting his
head to reveal a face covered with blood.

"What did he say?" Trotter asked Horseback, knowing that Horseback
had learned much of the enemy language from Looks Away.

"He said, 'I howl at this mockery. You send your children to torture me.
Bring someone fierce.'"

Echo made a rare chuckle. "He is still acting brave. Wait until he begs
to die. Horseback, it is your duty to decide what must be done with this
captured enemy. Perhaps your mother will heal quickly enough to kill him
very slowly. Let the wound in your leg and the pain it brings you help you
decide his fate."

Horseback swallowed some bad shadow pressing up from his chest. "My
father has taught me not to decide these things. I will listen for the voices of
the spirits to tell me what I must do with the captive."

The warriors seemed to hum their approval of the words spoken by
Horseback. Trotter had been studying the wound on Horseback's leg, and
now poked it with his finger, making his friend flinch.

"It grows very red," Trotter said.

"My father's wife, Looks Away, will heal it," he replied. "She will pack it with grass and smear bear fat on it. She knows many ways to heal."

"I think it will make a fine scar," Trotter said.

"A flint knife raises an uglier scar than an iron knife like the one the enemy stuck you with," Echo said. "But that scar is better than none at all."

"You can make some girl tattoo the scar," Trotter suggested, his brow raising where he had plucked all the hair from over his eyes.

"No," Horseback said, wondering about Teal for the first time since the battle, and whether or not he might find her in the dark somewhere tonight. "I will not flaunt the loneliness of a single scar."

· · · ·

That evening, at sunset, River Woman woke. Her chest was so racked with pain that she could only whisper, and Looks Away had to place her ear over River Woman's mouth to hear her speak.

"She wants to know why she cannot hear a great scalp dance." Looks Away said.

And so the lodges were brought out of hiding and set up in a sacred circle. Five enemy scalps were placed on spare lodge poles set in the ground. The old men began to cajole the young unmarried women, saying, "Now these young warriors have protected you! You know how to reward them!"

Hearing the crier tell that his mother had woken, Horseback trotted to her place in the timber to see her. He found that she had gone back to sleep. Shaggy Hump was there, with Spirit Talker.

"My son, your mother is strong. Spirit Talker is letting her borrow much magic."

"How long will she rest?"

"Only the spirits know. Why do you wonder such things?"

Horseback sat on the ground beside his father. "What must I do with the *Yuta*?"

"He is your captive. I cannot say what you must do. Listen for the shadow-voices."

"Perhaps he will die there, tied to that tree."

Shaggy Hump said nothing.

Spirit Talker had been sitting near River Woman's head, slumped over as if asleep. Suddenly, the old man lurched and began chanting without opening his eyes.

"Before she went back to sleep your mother told me that we must have a giveaway dance tonight to celebrate your first battle strokes counted. Your medicine was strong today. We must give away everything to show the spirits our faith and keep our medicine strong."

"Must we give my mother's lodge away? She may need it if a storm comes."

"We give away *everything*," Shaggy Hump said, sternly. "Our *puha* will provide anything we need."

They sat without talking, listening to Spirit Talker's chant and River Woman's shallow breathing.

"You must go to my second wife," Shaggy Hump said. "Your wound looks bad. You should have Looks Away heal it."

Horseback rose, glad to have something to do other than watch his mother lie in pain. "Yes, Father. Where has she gone?"

"She went up the bank of the river. She worries about her sister."

Horseback limped up the bank of the river, stopping only briefly to look at his wounded bay horse, tied at a quiet place in a draw. The bay's head hung low and his eyes looked dull and watery. He had been thrown down, and the arrow head cut out of his rump as many warriors held his legs and head to keep him from thrashing. Now he was still able to stand, and this was a good sign to Horseback, though the warrior also noticed that the knife wound between the stallion's ribs oozed a bloody fluid. He hoped the bay would live, for the pony had proven useful in battle on this day.

Reaching the top of the river bank, Horseback swept his eyes across the sage, growing dim now in the twilight. He searched for a long moment before he located a human form moving away beyond the horses. Looks Away was far from camp, heading over a rise, stopping briefly against the sky before she disappeared behind the hill.

Curious, Horseback ran to the ponies and caught one that his father had trained not to run away when approached. He didn't have his war bridle with him, so he took off his loin skins. He threw the skins over the back of the pony for a pad, and tied one end of his belt to the lower jaw of the pony, so he could make the pony stop. This pony knew how to turn in response to leg pressure, so Horseback did not need two reins. Mounted, he overtook Looks Away quickly and called her by name.

"I am going away," she said, without stopping in her brisk walk.

"Where?"

"I do not know."

"Why?"

"Because of the warrior you have captured. I cannot bear to see him tortured and killed."

Walking the horse beside her, Horseback thought for the first time how it must feel for Looks Away to see a warrior of her own blood suffer at the hands of her adoptive people. "His fate is my decision. I will make him die quickly in the morning sunlight with my arrow. I will not let him be strangled or killed at night. That way, his spirit will fly to the Shadow Land."

"His name is Bad Camper," Looks Away said. Her eyes looked up to Horseback, full of tears. "He is my brother."

▲▲▲▲▲
19
▼▼▼▼▼

None of the Corn People, nor the Burnt Meat People, could remember such a giveaway dance. First, Shaggy Hump presented his weapons to young warriors who had fought well against the invaders. He gave his best horses to leading warriors like Echo. He gave his older, easier-to-handle horses to aging men so their wives could more easily move their lodges. He gave the small lodge in which he had kept his weapons to a young warrior of the Corn People who had just taken a wife and yet had no lodge. He gave the large lodge of ten poles and twelve skins to Spirit Talker, so that the old *puhakut* might tell stories on long winter days and pass the pipe among many warriors. He gave Looks Away's small lodge to a poor crippled girl of the Corn People whom no one would take as a wife. He gave his seven spare lodge poles to families who had mended old broken and rotting poles with rawhide. He gave his water bags to hunters he had seen ride or walk farther than others to bring home meat.

He gathered the young wives and tossed the cooking vessels and utensils of River Woman and Looks Away among them, letting them scramble for them, providing fine entertainment. Then he gathered all the young horsebacks and tossed pad saddles and bridles and cords of twisted rawhide or yucca fibers among them. This amused the women, seeing the warriors kick and push one another to get at items they wanted, even pulling on two ends of the same rope, like two dogs fighting over a length of gut.

Then Shaggy Hump started giving away all the food his wives had prepared to the poorest and hungriest of the True Humans. Meat, marrow, berries, and seeds; pemmican stuffed into sections of scrubbed intestine. Yampa roots in parfleche bags. Tallow stored in paunches. Buffalo tongues and cactus fruits dried and enriched under the sacred gaze of Father Sun.

He gave away everything—paint, flint, rawhide, tanned deerskin, sinew for making bowstrings—everything but the clothes he wore and his sacred shield, for the shield would have burdened some taker with powerful magic.

Horseback had little to give, but he added his warhorse and its trappings, his weapons, and the good robe he slept on. He kept only his shield and the quiver embraced by deer antlers with the feather inside from the bird of the south. Then, he gave his moccasins to a barefoot old man who would not last as long as the moccasins themselves. Shaggy Hump was moved by this gift, and also gave away his moccasins and the leggings he wore, leaving himself and his son with only their loin skins, their feathers, their shields, and their quivers.

A scalp dance began, and women's voices trilled. Old men told stories of bygone battle strokes. Cook fires were stoked and feasting began. Shaggy Hump was given a piece of meat, but before he would eat it, he held it to the dark night sky and cut off a chunk to bury in the ground in homage to the spirits. The enemy scalps dried and stiffened in the breeze, high on poles surrounding the dancing ground.

"My father," Horseback said, at the height of the celebration, "have you ever seen a scalp dance like this one?"

Shaggy Hump thought for several long moments, his face drawn and serious. He would have enjoyed this more with River Woman. "No, my son. Never have I seen so many scalps on the poles. I hear no women mourning dead husbands or sons. We have seen a great victory on this day. And we yet have a captive."

Horseback smiled. His father was going to be surprised at what he would do with this captive.

As they feasted on pieces of hump that had been suspended above the fires on sticks jammed into the ground at a slant, Horseback kept his eyes moving for a glimpse of Teal. He saw Trotter moving away into the dark with Slope Child and felt a measure of regret that he had not secured her for himself, for she had made him feel good several nights in his lodge that was now given away. But she had made many a young warrior feel good, and so Horseback also felt a measure of relief that Trotter had taken her on this night. She was no longer a mystery to him. Teal was.

Anyway, his mood was not completely given over to celebration, though it was his duty to join the dance and feast. Not until he knew whether his mother would survive could he give Teal the attention he wanted to give to her. She was different from Slope Child. He felt a longing for Slope Child in his loins. His lust for Teal came from his heart, and it welled up in him in pangs that tormented and pleasured him all at once.

Perhaps she was waiting for him in the dark somewhere. Perhaps she was wise not to show herself at all, knowing that Horseback should be more concerned with his wounded mother than his own pleasures. When it came to Teal, it was difficult to know what to do. He would wait for guidance from the spirits.

He felt eyes upon him and looked toward the timber to see Bad Camper staring at him. This warrior was brave. His head had been thumped soundly with Horseback's *pogamoggan*, yet he continued to keep his feet under him, and his head raised, though his arms had been hoisted up high behind his back. He had to be battling much pain now, yet he still possessed the fight to glare at the warrior whom he knew had the right to decide how he would be tortured.

Horseback walked toward Bad Camper and sat near him on the ground.

He watched the scalp dance, listened to the good cadence of rattles and drums. He thought of letting the captive down from the tree so he could rest, but decided against it. His people deserved to see this invader suffer.

· · · ·

As the light of the waking sun began to lift the robe of stars away from the sky, the people tired of the scalp dance and went to their lodges. Horseback was left alone with Bad Camper. He borrowed a horse from Echo's string, borrowed a lance from a friend's stack of weapons. He used the lance to cut the rope holding Bad Camper's arms up behind him. When he cut the rope, Bad Camper fell face-forward in exhaustion.

Prodding the captive with the butt of the lance, Horseback made him rise, which he did with difficulty, for his wrists were still bound tightly behind him. Horseback made him march toward the river. There was a sandbar there where the river was easy to cross on foot, and he forced Bad Camper to the south bank, knowing that the captive intentionally fell into the water to refresh himself and drink. Horseback was alert. The captive was likely to try to kill him to affect his escape.

Going up the south bank, Horseback would not walk his mount behind Bad Camper for fear the captive would jump down on him. He walked to one side, making his own trail. At the top of the bank, Bad Camper suddenly broke into a sprint, jumping clumps of sage and running as fast as he could go with his hands tied behind his back. Horseback loped along behind, remaining alert with his weapon. They ran until Bad Camper realized he could not outrun the horse, and he wheeled on his captor, snarling like a snared badger.

Horseback remained a safe distance away, laughing.

"Come kill me!" Bad Camper finally said. "My hands are bound! You have the only weapon! If I must die this day, may my killer prove his skill with the lance! Are you a girl or a warrior?"

Horseback took no glory in the fear he saw behind Bad Camper's mask of courage. He knew it was a more powerful thing to face a sound enemy in battle than to torment this beaten foe. "If this was your day to die, you would be screaming at the coals heaped upon your pecker," he replied. "Today you will return to your people and tell them how we danced under the scalps of your slain brothers."

The desperate fear flew from Bad Camper's eyes, and his face became laughable with surprise. "Why? Why do you release me?"

"It gives me more power than you can understand because you are less than a True Human. Now, go, before the spirits decide I should let the women slice and burn your flesh before your own eyes. Go back to your mountains and tell your people that you were defeated in battle by a *Noomah* warrior."

Bad Camper took a few cautious steps backward, then stopped. "What will I tell them when they ask me the name of this warrior?"

He rested the shaft of the lance across his thighs and sat tall. "I am Horseback."

▲▲▲▲▲
20
▼▼▼▼▼

River Woman's wound did not heal easily. She lay in a trance through many suns. Though Spirit Talker wrapped her in a sacred robe and made long prayers over her, she would flinch as if fighting evil shadow things and call out in tongues grotesque and unintelligible. Sweat would drench her, and Looks Away, who kept her clean and wrapped in dry skins, feared she would shrink up and die, for she would swallow very little of the water, milk, or blood poured into her mouth. Her skin felt as hot as a stone under the summer sun.

As soon as the buffalo meat had been dried, pounded, and made into pemmican, the council decided to move the great camp-together north, for the *Yutas* were sure to return with more warriors, seeking vengeance if the True Humans did not retreat deeper into their own country.

River Woman had to be moved on a pony drag. Not until the people reached the canyon of the River of Bighorn Sheep, did the evil spirits leap out of River Woman's soul. Spirit Talker said that he saw them leap out, and they looked like flames in the form of little people, running down into the ground. Spirit Talker had powerful medicine that allowed him to see such things.

When River Woman woke, she asked for food. She was given a stew made of boiled meat, flavored with wild onions and lily bulbs. She said nothing for a day, then began to speak of her vision.

In the strange world of her vision, River Woman was taken up into a cloud. She had to fight evil beasts in this cloud, which was so dark that she never knew the demons were upon her until they had bitten her. River Woman could not say how long she battled these cloud-beasts, but it seemed like four suns.

When the fighting was over, she fell out of the dark cloud and found herself flying over a beautiful country. "There are mountains there where all kinds of four-leggeds run," she said, "and trees grow tall. There are many lodge poles standing as straight as the stars that fly. There are plains where no sage grows, only grass. Much grass. There are rivers flowing from the mountains, onto the plains, giving water to many deer, antelope, and elk. But, especially *buffalo*. Oh, you have never seen so many buffalo! The herds were like great clouds that come in the spring.

"But there is danger from many strange people there," she continued. "Along the rivers on the plains, our ancient enemies, the *Na-vohnuh* are living. They make peace with strange white men and make war with all others. There are people who live in lodges made of mud. There are white men who wear shirts of iron and carry Fire Sticks. There are women and children who are also white. There is much killing and war—much slavery among all the people there. But there is trade, as well, for it is a rich country—not like our country at all.

"And . . ." she said, pausing for effect, "there are *horses*." She looked at Horseback. "My son, if you want to see more horses than your father has seen of antelope and buffalo and bears, you must find this country. The horses there have many colors and travel in herds like elk. The hair from their manes and tails would make a rope as long as this river!" She made a motion toward the River of Bighorn Sheep.

"When I came back to our country, I believe I was flying north, for the sun passed from my right to my left. I saw myself lying on the pole drag behind the pony, and I was very sad. Then I fell into my own body and woke up here."

River Woman would never be the same after this vision. Never again did she boast of being Shaggy Hump's sits-beside wife. Never again did she carry Shaggy Hump's shield when the True Humans moved. Never again did she lie with Shaggy Hump, except to stay warm in winter. She continued to work and serve the True Humans, and her husband, and especially her son, but she would not laugh, nor watch games, nor listen to the men in council, nor gossip with other women. When she was not working, she spent all of her time praying and chanting and courting dangerous powers. In seasons to come, some would call her a sorceress. But she was only a woman with a vision.

21

With his sixteenth summer behind him, Horseback's band, the Burnt Meat People, decided in council to break camp and move away from the Corn People. When the Corn People heard of the Burnt Meat People holding a council without them, they knew the reason and quickly called their own council, their peace chiefs deciding to break the bond with the Burnt Meat People, pretending they knew nothing of the Burnt Meat People's decision. This was well for both bands, as neither would take offense to the other's wanting to break away.

The two bands had camped, traveled, hunted, and fought well through the moons of summer, and so they had remained together longer than two bands might. Now several young men of the Burnt Meat People had found wives among the Corn People, and young warriors of the Corn People had taken Burnt Meat People wives. It was time to go different ways and remember the summer of the great victory over the *Yutas,* when Horseback counted his first battle strokes and set the captive, Bad Camper, free. Few understood this release of the captive, but none spoke against Horseback, for even in his youth, he was known to possess medicine of such remarkable power that he could charm wild horses.

After the councils, Spirit Talker moved the lodge Shaggy Hump had given him to the Burnt Meat People's side of the camp-together. No one questioned why he would stay with the Burnt Meat People, for he was the naming father of Horseback, who would need Spirit Talker's advice to shape his medicine.

On the last evening of the great camp-together between the Corn People and the Burnt Meat People, Horseback found himself sitting against the warmth of a boulder overlooking the River of Big Horn Sheep, just downstream from the lodges. The horses grazed here in a narrow floodplain lush with grass, its rich green texture so inviting against the hard rock of the river valley that he could taste and smell the color, as if he were himself a grazing horse.

Some of these horses would go with the Corn People tomorrow, for Horseback and his father had given many mounts to Corn People warriors in the great giveaway celebration. Even now, Horseback's feet were sore from walking without moccasins the many sleeps from Two Rivers to this place on the River of Bighorn Sheep.

He heard a pebble roll behind him and twisted his neck to see Teal coming to him with her water bag. Her eyes met his only briefly before she sat beside him, making herself invisible to the camp behind the large boulder. Though Father Sun had gone beyond the canyon walls, his warmth was still with this boulder, and it felt good, as a cool wind was streaming down from the mountains.

"The Corn People go west tomorrow," she said.

"I know."

"Trotter has promised to return to the Burnt Meat People to take your sister, Mouse, for his wife when it is her time to serve a husband."

"*Hah.* Trotter is my brother. He gave two horses to my father as his promise to return for Mouse, and now I will ride with my father to the mountains to cut lodge poles and trade them for more horses."

"It is dangerous in those mountains. The Northern Raiders live there."

"My medicine is strong. I do not fear the Northern Raiders."

They sat in silence and watched a young colt run around his mother.

"Echo-of-the-Wolf tried to take me," Teal said. "He offered my father all three of his horses. My father wanted to take them, but I begged him not to."

Horseback looked at Teal's face. He had not heard this about Echo. "I will go to your father tonight," he said. "I will promise to bring one hundred horses in the spring."

"You should promise ten," Teal said.

"Do not doubt me. I have good power. I will get one hundred horses."

"I do not doubt you, Horseback. But my father will doubt you if you promise one hundred horses. He will give me to someone else. Promise ten, and he will believe you. Then you may give one hundred if you wish and that will only make my father prouder."

Horseback saw that this was wise, so he did not argue. He sat watching the horses. Shifting, as if to sweep a pebble out from under his thigh, he moved closer to Teal, and remained closer to her even after sweeping the imaginary pebble aside.

"My father and I have been talking," he said, watching a colt drink from a pool at the edge of the river. "After we get our lodge poles from the mountains of the Northern Raiders and trade for more horses, we want to go to the south to find the strange country my mother has seen in her vision."

"Everyone is talking about it," Teal said. "Why do you want to go there? It is so far away."

"It is my duty, according to the vision my spirits showed me on my quest. I cannot explain it to you, for this vision is too powerful for a girl to know about. The magic would destroy you, Teal."

Teal sighed. "If you do not come for me in the spring, my father will give me to another warrior. It is time that I took a husband. My father and my mother wish for a young warrior to bring much meat to them."

"If I do not come for you, Teal, you will see me in the Shadow Land, for it will mean that I have died bravely. Death is the only thing that will keep me away from you." He felt well upon saying this and looked at Teal's face. Her beauty only grew with each passing day, and he could not imagine how wonderful she was going to look to him by the time he came to claim her.

Teal let her eyes rise from the ground below and search, as if looking for something, until the magic powers that streamed from her soul and gave her sight joined with the powers of Horseback, linking the throbs of their hearts through the air. They shifted, moving closer together, shoulders now touching. Horseback felt as if he were spinning, so he looked back down to the valley of horses.

"Why do you watch the horses here?" Teal asked. "You watch them all the time."

"They teach me how to talk horse."

She looked at him and smiled. "They do not speak."

"They speak in many ways."

"Tell me."

Horseback looked over the herd for a moment, until he saw two young studs tossing their heads as they came together. "See those two warrior horses," he said. "The spotted horse has three winters and much power among the young horses. The brown horse has only two winters, but he wants to fight and be a war chief. Now the brown is saying, 'I will hurt you and make you run, and have all the mares! You are spotted like a molting ptarmigan, and no more brave!'

"And the spotted horse is answering now, with his ears back on his neck, saying, 'You are brown like the dirt you will join when I step upon you! Do not come near me, or my hooves will take hair from your hide!' "

The brown stud reared and menaced the spotted horse with forehooves and bared teeth. But the spotted horse quickly wheeled and kicked the brown in the stomach just ahead of the tender flank.

"There!" Horseback said. "That is how to talk horse! Now, when I am trying to ride a horse and he bites me or strikes with his hooves, I kick him hard in the stomach that way and he knows that I am more powerful."

The young brown stud was running away from the spotted champion.

"Do they only speak of battle?" Teal asked.

"They speak of many things—as people do." He looked over the herd and found two mares standing together, each nibbling on the withers of the other. "Do you see those two?" Horseback said, leaning harder against Teal, so that she might follow the way he showed with his arm and finger pointing. "The one nearer to us is saying, 'Sister, I have missed you all day. I am glad to see you. You make my heart glad.' And the other one is now answering, 'Sister, it is I who have missed you more. When we are together, my heart is like a cloud in the sky.'

"Now, Teal, when I wish to tell a horse that he is good, I use my hand and fingers upon the shoulder of that horse, the way those two sisters are talking to each other there."

Teal smiled, for it pleased her to hear Horseback talk. She made her eyes sparkle starlike at his for an instant, then looked back across the river. The sunlight was gone from the canyon rim to the east, and the sky had turned the color of a blue heron.

"There," she said, now feeling warmer against Horseback than the boulder behind him. "Those two . . ."

Horseback looked and saw a stallion, a five-year-old who had made good colts, walking toward a fine young filly who waited, head high, ears perked forward. As the stallion slowed, she made the last few steps with him, the two of them coming together, muzzles touching.

"What are *they* saying, Horseback?"

Horseback watched, then he translated as well and as truthfully as he knew how. "The stallion breathes these words into the nostrils of the mare: 'When I see you, I want to come near to you. Only my duty takes me away from you. When I breathe in the sweet smell of your breath, I think of all the grasslands we might run over, and all the little four-legged children who might follow us.'

"And the filly breathes these words into the nostrils of the stallion: 'Now your spirit lives within me, and my spirit lives within you, for we have taken breath, one from the other. And now we will know each other's heart, and suffer each other's pain, and live each other's joy.'

"Now, Teal, when I want to know the spirit of a horse, and I want that horse to know my spirit, I shall breathe in the air from his body, and he shall breathe mine."

She leaned away from Horseback and shifted to face him. "I believe you know well the talk of horses, except for the things the filly was saying to the stallion."

"Do you know better?"

"Only because I am more like her."

"Then what does she say now to the stallion?"

Teal moved close to Horseback, her eyes not daring to look into his. She put her hand on his shoulder and sensed that he had not expected her to come so close. She saw no harm in causing him this little surprise. She eased closer, her arm resting on his shoulder, and her thigh against his thigh. The long slender fringes of her deerskin sleeve brushed the bare skin of his chest, making his muscles like rocks. Her mouth came nearer to his, until she could feel the moist warmth of his breath.

"The young filly says, 'Stallion, you shall have me when it is time. Until then, let your heart beat with mine, and know that the love I keep for you is like the love of the river for the rain, and the love of the cloud for the wind.'"

Horseback breathed these words into his lungs as Teal spoke them and felt the fires inside flare as he consumed her spirit. He touched his fingertips to her ribs and found she shied from his touch for a moment. Then he flattened his palm against her and felt his fingers bend around the soft firmness of her back. The sweet scent of her breath drew his lips closer to hers, and they were about to touch when a familiar voice called from far away.

"Daughter! Elder daughter!"

Teal gasped and pulled away from Horseback, but happened to catch his hand and she peeked over the boulder that shielded them from the village. She knew her mother was angry when she called her elder daughter, for Teal had no brothers or sisters.

"I must go," she said. "My mother waits for water." Reluctantly, she let her hand slip from the young warrior's grasp and went quiet as a cat back toward the lodges.

Horseback felt the way he had felt when the hail storm struck him during his vision quest. He released a sigh he had held since Teal left, then he lay his face down on the rocks and stared across the canyon at nothing.

▲▲▲▲▲
22
▼▼▼▼▼

He saw his first white man during the Moon of Scarlet Plums, as he and his father gathered lodge poles in the mountains of the Northern Raiders.

The country where they cut the lodge poles was a dangerous place, but the pines were straight and tall and slender. He worked as quietly as he could with his father, taking his turns at watch without ever letting sleep cloud his eyes. He was on watch when he first saw the white man riding a horse. It was so far away that Horseback could barely make out the color of the horse, let alone the rider, yet he could sense something strange in the manner of this man. He only glimpsed the strange rider angling down a mountain face on a trail that showed itself but briefly in a gap between two nearer slopes. The moment the rider disappeared behind the near mountain, Horseback jumped astride his mount and rode to his father.

"My son, what have you seen?" Shaggy Hump asked. The lodge poles behind him numbered as many as the two ponies could drag back to the Burnt Meat People. The edge of the stone axe in his hand had been flaked and flaked again until the flint head was light and chipped away back to the rawhide straps that bound it tightly to the pine handle. "This is the last pole. I am almost finished chopping it."

"I saw one rider, too far away to hear your axe, for not even I could hear it where I watched, and the rider was far beyond me."

Shaggy Hump's eyes were combing the slopes around him. "I will chop lightly and quickly and get this tree down. When the Northern Raiders find this place in times to come, I do not wish them to think they frightened us away before we could finish stealing their trees."

Quickly, he made the last calculated strokes with the axe and let the pine sapling fall. He trimmed the branches away, each with no more than three blows, then turned to his son. "Now, show me the place where the rider passed."

"This way, Father."

Horseback led Shaggy Hump to the lookout place and pointed to the trail, far away. "I felt something strange about that rider."

"Strange?" Shaggy Hump said.

"He was like a bird that passes so quickly that you cannot see what kind of bird it is."

Shaggy Hump thought about this, and said, "The spirits are trying to show you something, my son. I am going closer to see this strange rider. Are you coming?"

"Yes."

They rode in such places that the Raiders would not be able to follow their trail back to the cut lodge poles should they be discovered. They rode watchfully and quietly, arriving finally at the trail where Horseback had seen the strange rider pass. They looked at the hoofprints on the trail, then sank back into the cover of pines and scrub oak flanking the trail, listening to the sounds of the mountains around them, searching for any sight or sound or smell that might warn or inform them, for they were in a strange and dangerous country.

But, it was a good country, cool and green, with plenty of waters singing, with tracks and droppings of much game everywhere, with lodge poles growing like quills on the back of a porcupine. Horseback thought of the day when the True Humans would claim such a rich country.

He knew it was true that there were other peoples poorer than the True Humans. He had heard of a nation to the west called Diggers, whose people spoke the *Noomah* language and were so poor that they would surround grasshoppers as if they were antelope, then smash the grasshoppers into a paste and eat them. So, his country was not so poor, though the antelope and buffalo ranged far and were hard to kill. When he claimed Teal and began to make sons and daughters, Horseback wanted his children to play in a country with plenty of meat and skins from four-leggeds to make big lodges and warm clothes. He would pray for the spirits to give him the power to make this happen.

"Father," he hissed in a rough whisper. "I must not ride behind you. You have taken to a deer trail where I am forbidden pass."

Shaggy Hump leaned to one side to look at the tracks on the trail below him. He grunted. "It is good that you live in a country where few deer pass, my son."

At length, they came to an open grassland surrounded by low wooded crests and saw a string of lodges lining a stream. Seven enemy horses grazed in the open park, including one sandy-colored mare dragging a rope to make her easier to catch.

"What do you see?" Shaggy Hump asked his son, as they looked on, far back in the shadows.

Horseback studied the camp. "The horses wear no war paint. No elk or deer hides hang fresh. They do not come to make war, or to hunt."

"What, then? Listen to the spirits."

Horseback listened for some time. "The strange rider I saw on the trail has led us to this place. He comes from another nation. I believe these Northern Raiders have come here to trade with the strange rider."

"Now you are listening well, my son, for that rider's horse made deep tracks. He carries many things to trade. He comes from a strange land, yet rides the trail unafraid. Yes, he comes to trade. Now, let us go closer and see this strange rider and count our enemies. Do you remember the story I have told you about the time I snuck into the camp of the Northern Raiders, took a scalp, and left my arrow between two other warriors?"

"Yes, Father."

"We must creep ahead quietly, as I crept that night. If we fail, we will surely die fighting on this day."

They left their horses far enough away that a nicker would not be heard. They went ahead on foot, slipping through tall timber that grew dense along the stream. Rushing water covered any noise their footsteps might have made. They came downwind so no dogs or horses would scent them, and Horseback smelled a faint wisp of tobacco smoke, ensuring him that the spirits had spoken wisely of the trade.

Voices came from the camp, and at last the two *Noomah* stalkers moved far enough up the stream to reveal a circle of Northern Raider warriors flanked by lodges. As soon as he saw them, Horseback crouched low, like a grouse hiding from a hawk overhead. His eyes widened. One of the men across the circle had a pale face half covered with long dark hair that was shaggy like that of a buffalo, instead of straight like the hair of a human. Horseback was afraid, for this was the rider he had seen, and the rider was grotesque, as if part animal.

The white man's shirt was made of fine deerskin, quilled with many colors and adorned with long fringes. The strange rider's chest and arms filled this shirt like the muscle of a buffalo filled its own hide. Across his lap, the strange rider let a Fire Stick rest as he took the pipe from the Northern Raider next to him. Though his clothes were like those of the nations Horseback had seen, the white man's appearance was bizarre. The pale features of his face seemed swollen, and hair grew right out of his jaw and chin like some terrible disease. The pipe stem disappeared into his mouth, which looked like the den of an old bank beaver with roots hanging down in front of it.

"Father," Horseback whispered. "Is that a man?"

"That is a white man, my son. He makes our enemies his allies."

Upon his head, the white man wore a headdress of red fox hide, with the face of the fox looking forward over his own face. After passing the pipe, the white man removed the red fox headdress to scratch his head. Horseback was astonished to see that the white man had no hair upon his pate. Not even a topknot. He had heard stories of Wolf People shaving part of the hair from their heads, but never all of it.

Horseback and Shaggy Hump watched as this strange, hairy-faced white man rose and began to place rawhide parfleche bags in the circle before him. He untied the thongs binding these bundles and folded back the flaps. The first revealed iron arrow points that he held up to show the Northern Raiders. Next he displayed axe heads, then knives. When he held these things high, Horseback noticed that he grew dark hair out of the backs of his hands.

For the women, the white man had brought tiny colored pebbles with holes growing through them so that they could be strung like drilled elk teeth. He held up a string of these. He opened the next bundle and presented a handle affixed to a thing that was like a small dark pool, and the women had a wonderful time looking at their own reflections in the surface of the thing. He had many of these things to trade.

After he had presented all his wares, the warriors began offering skins of beaver, buffalo, and deer. The bargaining promised to last into the night.

"Father, what should we do?" Horseback's whisper blended with the rush of white water.

"How do the spirits speak to your heart?"

He looked beyond the circle of traders and the angled lines of the lodges and saw the herd grazing in the open park. "The spirits tell me we should steal their horses."

"I hear the same voices, my son."

Slowly, they crept backward, keeping their eyes just high enough in the bushes to watch the enemy. Having pulled beyond sight of the Northern Raiders, they trotted to the place where they had left their horses and mounted. Horseback thought of Sound-the-Sun-Makes and prayed for courage and strength. Through his loin skins, he grabbed the medicine bundle.

"You are the better rider," Shaggy Hump said. "You will circle the herd and start it toward our camp where we cut the lodge poles. I will stand guard between you and the enemy village. They are foolish to leave all their horses together. They will not be able to follow us if we steal them all. They should have left their best ones staked in their village."

Horseback thumped the cord of twisted buffalo sinew he had strung tight to the ends of his bow.

"Are you ready?"

Horseback leaned over the neck of his mount, letting the horse feel his excitement. He had spent many days riding quietly in this strange land, and now he was going to get to run hard and vent his war cry. His mount sensed this and began to shift about on his feet.

"We are ready," Horseback said.

Shaggy Hump smiled. "Your medicine is good, my son. Your pony hears you when you speak." He kicked his mount in the ribs and turned toward the enemy camp.

When they reached the open park, they held their mounts to a trot. Horseback felt strange moving into the open like this, after so many days of sneaking around in the timber. Now they rode as if they were in their own country. He felt wind pulling at his hair, and he could tell his mount liked the same feeling through his mane. The pony saw the strange horses in the enemy herd and wanted to run and join them, but Horseback held him to a trot.

He glanced at his father beside him, sitting his stallion proudly, hair streaming, eyes blazing. They were almost within range of a long arrow shot when one of the animals of the enemy herd noticed them, singing out high in the language of horses.

Together, the two invaders lunged forward to a gallop, shoving their knees under the coils of rope looped about the barrels of their mounts. Four-leggeds began to stir in the park, and two-leggeds in the village. Knowing now that he had been discovered, Horseback sang a battle cry that matched the timbre of the horse-song and felt his mount stretch longer in his charge. It was good to feel this animal take joy and courage from his magical cry. Shaggy Hump veered away to guard against the coming attack, and Horseback thought only of making a sacred circle around the horses of the Northern Raiders, soon to be his own.

Mother Earth was his drum, and the hooves of his horse were the fingers he used to play upon her surface. His cry charmed the horses and drew them together, making them easier to circle.

"The Fire Stick! My son! The Fire Stick!" Shaggy Hump warned.

Completing the circle around the captured herd, Horseback looked toward the village. He saw Shaggy Hump standing on the ground, holding his reins. He watched his father's arrow fly long toward the enemy lodges. The terrible enemy warriors had gathered there around the strange white man with the hairy face. And now Horseback saw the Fire Stick against the shoulder of the white man.

Shaggy Hump's arrow flew over the white man's head and stuck in a lodge pole behind the bunch of warriors. Shaggy Hump pulled his horse in front of him as a shield, and the Fire Stick came alive, puffing smoke like a bull elk whistling out his hot breath on a cold morning.

As the cloud of black smoke came, Shaggy Hump's horse screamed and fell, thrashing the air with hooves as blood spouted from his shoulder. The enemy warriors yelled and began to charge from their village. Their women came right behind them, urging them on with trilling voices.

Horseback leaned forward and raced to his father. He had practiced shooting his bow from the back of a running horse, but now everything was happening so fast that he drew the string without choosing a single enemy warrior as his target. He let the arrow fly hastily, and it landed short of the oncoming attack.

His father's next arrow flew truer, but found the shield of a Northern Raider, instead of vitals. He took the next moment to remove the war bridle from his dying stallion, for his son was coming fast.

An arrow thumped the carcass of the stallion, and others passed Shaggy Hump like bees. He turned away from the attack to watch his son ride to his rescue. He had seen the boys practice pulling one another onto their horses, and knew how it was done, though he had not tried it himself.

Horseback reached for his father and ignored the arrows that brushed by him. He clasped his fist tight above his father's elbow and used his weight to pull Shaggy Hump on behind him. Having sprung at the right moment, Shaggy Hump landed astride the rump of the horse, quickly scooting up behind his son. He cawed like a crow and smiled over his shoulder at his enemies, though their arrows seemed to swarm. Beyond them, he could see the white man preparing the Fire Stick for more magic.

Soon they were beyond arrow shot, riding toward the horses, which had bunched ever closer for protection, too curious to run from the two strange riders. Horseback rode directly into this herd, and leapt upon the sandy colored mare that dragged the rope. Quickly, he grabbed the rope around her neck and slid off. Standing on the ground, he let the mare pull against the rope as he motioned to his father for the war bridle.

Shaggy Hump tossed the bridle he had taken from his dead stallion, and slid up behind the withers of the pony, taking the reins Horseback had dropped. As his son charmed the horse at the end of the rope, Shaggy Hump rode around the captured herd to keep them from scattering. The Northern Raiders were coming swiftly on foot, picking up their arrows as they ran.

Grunting at the captured mare to calm her, Horseback worked his way up the rope until he could touch her head. He stroked her a few times, gently, though she tried to pull away. He said, "Noomah. Noo-oo-oo-mah-ah . . ." He used a firm and steady hand, and the mare ceased to fight. Quickly, he hitched the horse-hide bridle around the lower jaw of the captured mare and mounted. She was a beautiful animal the color of fine river sand, with a dark stripe down her back and another across her shoulders. Her ears stood straight, like two young pines reaching for the same sun, and her eyes were large and round and black.

Coiling the rope to keep her from stepping on it as they made their escape, Horseback heard a strange voice shouting from the enemy village. Glancing, he saw the hairy-faced white man waving his arms at the Northern Raiders, warning them aside, for the enemy warriors had moved in between the horse takers and the Fire Stick.

"Ride low, my son!" Shaggy Hump said, starting the stolen herd toward their own camp of cut lodge poles. "Keep our enemies between us and the white man!"

Horseback tied the coiled rope into the sandy mare's mane and swatted her rump with his bow to make her run. Looking over his shoulder, he tried to keep the enemy warriors between himself and the Fire Stick, yet he had to weave to herd the horses. He saw his father lying along the neck of the horse he rode, and thought this was a good idea, making a smaller target of himself for the Fire Stick, which he knew would soon lick with its evil tongue of black smoke.

Falling against the neck of the sandy mare, Horseback found the coil of rope he had tied into the mane pressing against his bow arm. The lower curve of the coil was just right for his elbow to settle into, so he let this coil of rope bear his weight, and found he could use the neck of the horse as his shield by resting his elbow in this circle of rope.

All the wild sounds of this ride suddenly died away, and Horseback could feel the spirits talking in his head, though he could not quite understand their words. They were trying to tell him something, give him something, make him wiser. His thoughts came like water from a mountain cascade.

The growl of the Fire Stick came, and one of the horses in the herd fell with a shattered leg. The spirit voices faded in Horseback's head. Now that the Fire Stick had missed him and his father, he knew he was going to escape with stolen horses, and stolen lodge poles, and much glory.

Shaggy Hump moved in front of the herd and made the six surviving horses stop at the edge of the trees. He began filling the air with laughter and cries of victory. The Northern Raiders had ceased in their pursuit, for they were tired of running and knew they could not catch horsemen.

"Where is the magic black paint for your feet," Shaggy Hump said, "so that you may catch me with the speed of an elk?"

"Father," said Horseback, "they do not understand the tongue of the True Humans."

"They hear the laughter in my voice, and it speaks more than all the words of all the nations." He shouted again at the enemy warriors: "I leave you with much horse meat to feed your white man while I take the live horses to ride in my own country!"

"We must go," Horseback replied, "before the hairy-faced man fills the Fire Stick with more medicine."

Shaggy Hump gestured his approval, but before he could start the horses, a shrill voice spoke from the line of Raiders who had stopped in the middle of the park. One of the women had caught up to the warriors and was cajoling the horse takers in their own language.

"Your Snake People will curse your name, horse taker! All the warriors of my great nation will hunt you down, and burn the lodges of your village, and scalp your sons, and rape your wives and daughters! You are the most evil of enemies of my people, for you killed my husband's brother seven winters ago, and left your arrow in the ground to boast of it. Now you leave your arrow again in the shield of my husband. You leave your tracks upon the soil of our country, and our warriors will follow them forever, and you will know peace never again."

Horseback looked at his father, and saw the surprise on Shaggy Hump's face.

Shaggy Hump shouted: "You speak the tongue of the True Humans, ugly woman. Who are you?"

"I was born a child of the *Noomah*, but my people captured me and brought me to this better life, and this finer country. Now I hate you and your ways. I hate your language, and speak it only to torture you with knowledge of your own days to come. You will die a most painful death, horse taker, and your soul will live in an agony of pain forever!"

Horseback was watching the white man, far away at the edge of the village. He had seen enough of Fire Sticks to know when the killing spell was almost finished. Now the ugly hairy-faced man was pulling the medicine stick from the mouth of the evil weapon. "My father, she makes us stay too long. The Fire Stick!"

"My name is Shaggy Hump, woman. Tell your warriors to come die in my country! As for you, I will not speak of you to the *Noomah*, for you have ceased to exist. You are nothing!"

They moved their stolen herd into the timber and drove the animals toward the lodge poles they had cut, two ridges distant. The horses would be tired when they arrived and would stand while the horse takers burdened them with many lodge poles. Then they would drive the new horses mercilessly back into the country of the True Humans before the Northern Raiders could get more mounts and follow.

The killing power of the Fire Stick rattled through the limbs behind them, followed by the growl of the Fire Stick itself, muffled by distance. But they were safe inside the protection of the forest.

"Father, what did she mean?"

Shaggy Hump's face turned to look at him, drawn with more worry than Horseback had ever seen before in his eyes. "You remember the story I have told of how I avenged my brother. I rode into the country of the Northern Raiders, killed one of their warriors, and left my arrow between two others that the spirits would not let me kill. The one I killed and scalped must have been the brother of a great warrior, for they remember the markings of my arrow, and now they have found me again."

"Is this not why we mark our arrows, Father? So our enemies will know us?"

"The markings bring medicine from our guardian spirits. If our enemies know us by the markings, it is as the spirits wish."

"Then you are great in the eyes of our enemy."

"Yes, my son. I am great, for they have chosen me."

"What does it mean to be chosen?"

"I am more than a man to them now. More than a warrior. To take my scalp would mean great medicine for one of their warriors. The things that woman said to me are true. They will destroy my family and my whole village to avenge the warrior I killed."

Horseback weaved among the trees on the sandy mare, keeping the stolen horses herded together and moving in the right direction. When he came close enough to his father again, he said, "You could have killed all three of their warriors. Why do they hate you so much for letting two of them live?"

"They do not hate me. They fear me. I stood over them like a shadow, like a breath of wind that never touches the ground, like a spirit-warrior. I pushed my arrow into the ground while they slept like helpless babies in cradle boards. Now they dream of me when they sleep and wake up covered with sweat, even on the coldest of nights. Do you hate the great humpbacked bear, my son?"

"No."

"Is it not a great thing to battle and kill the humpbacked bear and win glory?"

"It is a great thing, Father."

"So it is. I am chosen. We must move away from this country of Northern Raiders. I am not afraid to die, but I do not wish our enemies to rub out our whole band of Burnt Meat People. We must move to the south." '

"Yes," Horseback said. "Far to the south."

23

As his seventeenth winter came near, he began to have powerful dreams. It started during the Moon of Falling Leaves, when the groves of aspens on the faraway mountains turned the color of tanagers; when the sacred deer battled one another with their antlers; when the cranes and the geese and the ducks made noisy lines in the sky; when the antelope danced before the early blasts of cold air and were good to touch as they lay dead on the ground, for they wore much fat under their hides.

It was in this good part of the circle of time, before the harsh days of winter, in the country of the True Humans, that Horseback began to see visions in his dreams.

In one of the first dreams, he was attacking a war party of Northern Raiders who had come to rub out the Burnt Meat People. Riding with the speed of a falcon, he made a sacred ring around his enemies. All the while, the Northern Raiders shot arrows at him. The arrows flew around him in such numbers that he ducked his head behind the neck of his horse, using the horse as his shield. He leaned so far that he began to fall, and he feared he would land on the ground and be killed by his enemies. Then the dream made a horsehair rope appear, looping under the neck of his mount. As he fell, Horseback slipped his arm into this loop almost up to the elbow, and found he could ride at full speed hanging on the side of his warhorse.

When he woke after having this dream, Horseback began making a rope of corded rawhide made from the hide of a dead pony. He started with two strips of hide, each as thin as a quill shaft. He would twist one strip away from himself with his fingers, then turn it toward himself with his wrist. Holding it there, he would then twist and turn the second strip, adding new strips of rawhide all the while, making a cord of the two twisted strips. When this cord was long enough, he doubled it, again twisting and turning, making the cord twice as thick, with four bundles now making up the cord. Doubling the cord again, he finally finished a rope of eight strands, as long as he was tall.

Horseback looped this rope under the neck of the sandy-colored mare he had captured, weaving each end of the rope into the mane of the mare. The Burnt Meat People watched as he rode around the camp, hanging from the side of his horse, his forearm resting in the loop he had made. Only one leg slung over the back of the mare remained exposed to his imaginary enemies.

Spirit Talker, the old *puhakut*, told the other young warriors that they should fashion like slings under the necks of their warhorses. "Horseback's medicine grows strong," he said. "Watch him well."

When Looks Away saw what Horseback had done, she went to River Woman and said, "Do you see what your son has made, my sister?"

"I saw it in the dream," River Woman replied.

"What dream, my sister?"

"The dream my son had."

River Woman spoke strangely like this all the time now. It was said that she never came all the way home after battling the demons in her trance-world. This sometimes happened to warriors who had seen much battle, as it had happened to River Woman.

The next dream vision Horseback had was very strange. He spoke of it to Spirit Talker:

"I rode over much land, Grandfather, and my horse had much speed and could leap over great canyons and rivers. I saw many strange lands. In one place, the land was so flat that it looked like the surface of a lake with no shores. It was covered with nothing but grass that rippled like water. While I rode over this land, I came to a place where buffalo were coming up from the ground, like water from a spring."

Spirit Talker threw a pinch of sacred powder into the fire.

"What does it mean to have a vision like this?"

"I do not know. Maybe it means you are hungry." This was all Spirit Talker had to say about the dream.

Then, Horseback saw another vision in his dreams and came to Spirit Talker to tell him about it:

"I came out of a cloud over some mountains with lodge poles and much timber. Across the mountains I saw people living in lodges made of dirt. I went into one of the dirt lodges, and it was very dark. While I was in the lodge, I heard horses running outside. I heard so many horses that it took them all day to run by the lodge."

"Did you see the horses?"

"I only heard them, Grandfather."

"Then it could have been just a few horses running by many times." Spirit Talker would say nothing more about this vision.

Horseback continued to dream and came to Spirit Talker to tell him of yet another vision:

"Grandfather, I was in a strange place. I was looking into a pool of clear water. There were leaves of some strange tree floating on the top of the water. I saw many deer tracks at the edge of the pool. The water was so clear that I could see fish swimming in it. It was so still that I could see the sky, and limbs of a strange tree reflected in the surface, but when I bent over the water to get a drink, I could not see my own image."

Spirit Talker seemed thoughtful for some time. "I once had a dream that I was walking along and looked down to notice that I cast no shadow."

Horseback straightened, hopefully. "What did that mean, Grandfather?"

"The sun was behind a cloud."

Spirit Talker would offer no further interpretations of Horseback's many visions. Finally Horseback dreamed of white men with hairy faces, iron shirts, and Fire Sticks. They tended many beautiful horses. There were only a few white men, and many horses. In this dream, night came, and the moon rose full. Horseback found himself running with the horses, as if he were one of them. The sun rose on his right and set on his left many times before he came to his own country and found the village of the Corn People, and gave the many horses to Teal's father.

He did not ask Spirit Talker to interpret this dream. He knew he was to search out the source of horses to the south. He told his father that he was going to raise a party to travel into the distant country of the Sacred South.

"I will follow you, my son," Shaggy Hump said.

When Spirit Talker heard, he came to Horseback and said, "Now you have found the meaning of your own visions, young Horseback. I do not understand why you have been called to travel so many sleeps from your own country, for your spirit power is more than I can understand." Then he came very close to Horseback and spoke in a low voice, saying, "Always remember, if the visions grow too powerful, if the magic makes too much danger, you may give it back to the spirits, and no one will speak out against you. Do not let your gift destroy you, young Horseback."

Others heard about Horseback's search, but few trusted his visions enough to ride with him on the trail south. Most of the men with wives and children said they must stay with their families through the winter. One young married man named Bear Heart, who had elder brothers to take care of his wife, said he would go south with Horseback, for he wanted many horses. Echo-of-the-Wolf and Whip also agreed to follow Horseback.

They prayed the whole night before they left, except for Whip, who still had not received a vision and did not believe in praying. The women prepared a small lodge for the searchers, packing it on a pony drag. Before dawn Shaggy Hump went to Looks Away's lodge, and Bear Heart went with his wife into his lodge. But when the dark robe of night began to roll away from the east, all of Horseback's followers were ready to ride.

They took very little pemmican, for they expected to move onto better hunting grounds, and wanted the people in the camp to have the pemmican for the winter. They left their barbed war points at home, carrying only hunting points in their quivers, hoping to avoid battle with the many strange nations to the south. When they left, the whole band of the Burnt Meat People came out to sing prayers to them as they turned south, except for River Woman, who was chanting strangely in the lodge she shared with no one. Then, when the riders were almost too far away to hear, she came running out of her lodge, shouting, "My son! My son!"

Horseback held his party of searchers back long enough for his mother to catch up to him. "Mother, why do you keep us from leaving? Father Sun looks upon us."

"My son," she replied, placing one hand on his leg and one hand on the mare he rode. "It is well that you let Bad Camper go free. I know he is the brother of my sister. You have done well, my son." She turned and walked back toward the lodges.

Shaggy Hump smiled, for he found a certain charm to River Woman's crazy talk, though others accused her of sorcery. The other searchers looked southward, wanting to ride. Only Horseback made sense of what his mother had said, and he took it as a powerful sign. A good sign. Horseback loved his mother very much.

▲▲▲▲▲
24
▼▼▼▼▼

Sound-the-Sun-Makes blessed and protected Horseback's party of searchers
many sleeps to the south. They traveled far each day, stopping to rest and let
their horses graze only as Father Sun began his return to earth in his great
leap across the sky. For the first few nights they made no fires, eating only the
dried meat and pemmican they had brought with them. The night sky stayed
full of stars, so the searchers left the hides for their small lodge folded and
lashed to the pole-drag, choosing to sleep under the open sky, trusting their
medicine to keep the giant cannibal owl from plucking them from their robes.

The Thunderbird flew over on the fourth day, making the riders wet and
cold. But the rain softened the ground, which made traveling easier on the
feet of the horses. On the evening after the rainstorm had passed, Horseback
began unpacking the lodge at that night's camp.

"We will not need the lodge, my son," Shaggy Hump said.

"The Thunderbird may return," Horseback replied. "His cloud hangs over
us still."

"Spider tells me no rain will fall this night."

"Does my father know the talk of spiders?"

Shaggy Hump took Horseback to a place along the bank of the nearby
stream where a spider was building a new web between two bushes. "When
the web is thicker than a hair from the tail of a horse, rain will come soon.
If the web is thinner than the hair, the Thunderbird will fly over another
country."

"My father knows much that I do not," Horseback said. He left the lodge
skins packed on the pole-drag and slept dry under the cloudy sky, rolled in
his buffalo robe.

As they rode southward on their search, Horseback drank in the sights
of this new land. The sage had given way to grass as he left the country of
the *Noomah*, and the grass had grown thicker and taller with every day he led
his party south. Small herds of buffalo had become common, and antelope
were more numerous than he had ever imagined. Large bands of elk congre-
gated in the valleys of streams. Through stands of timber, lesser bears ambled,
ranging in color from that of the night sky to that of sand along a cutbank.

The searchers kept the mountains in sight to the west, the vast plains
under them rolling away to the east, carved by creeks and rivers. The mountains were their landmarks, but the mountains also harbored the *Yutas*. These
plains were often used as hunting grounds by the *Yutas* and by other fierce

peoples, such as the Wolf People, who lived far to the east, but sometimes wandered all the way to the great mountains to hunt and wage war and take captives. Horseback's father was his guide on this part of the journey, for Shaggy Hump had made this long dangerous trip once before, to trade with the Raccoon-Eyed People far out on the plains.

On the fifth day, Echo rode up one of the streams they crossed and killed a fine young elk cow. That night, they made a small fire and cooked some of the meat. The searchers were eating plenty, and good grass was keeping the horses strong.

Through seven suns they encountered no people. Shaggy Hump knew how to avoid the likely campsites of his enemies. Horseback listened to the advice of his father on these matters and hoped the tracks of his party's little pole-drag would not arouse suspicion. The True Humans had no allies, and so they had to travel cautiously and make ready to run or fight.

On the eighth day, they awoke to find the Great Mountains dusted with the first snow of the coming winter. Traveling under the rising sun, they soon came to a streambed that held water in pools where their horses could drink.

"My son," Shaggy Hump said, letting his pony drink next to Horseback's, "when we leave this place, I will ride behind you. The land to the south of this stream is as mysterious to me as the Shadow Land. Now there is nothing to guide us but your vision, and the power of your medicine, for no True Human has ever searched this far south. In the old times, before First Horse came and circled your birth lodge, our people could not think of traveling this far. Your children will know a way much different from the way my grandfathers knew."

"The way will be better," Horseback replied. "This is why I have had my vision."

They had drifted far from the mountains, so Horseback decided to ride up the stream of pools, as it would lead them to the south and west, closer to their landmarks. The shadows of their horses were beginning to fall behind them when Echo noticed a smudge of smoke in the sky not far ahead. Riding carefully on, they peered over the scrubby willows at each bend in the stream until they located a large camp of hunters at a place where water trickled from pool to pool in the sandy bed of the stream.

The searchers looked upon the strangers' camp for a good while. The camp was larger than that of any band of True Humans Horseback had ever seen—even larger than the village of the Corn People and the Burnt Meat People during the great camp-together. He counted forty-two lodges in view, with others yet unseen around the bend in the valley of the stream. The lodges were small, made of buffalo hides draped over four poles, the hides dyed red and white. Only a few horses stood near camp, and they looked poor.

Horseback noticed several fresh buffalo hides spread on the ground, their fleshy sides still pinkish with blood. Butchered meat stood in piles on one hide, ready to pack onto several nearby pole-drags that were small enough for dogs to pull. Near the edge of the camp, five of the hunters were using pointed sticks as skewers to hold meat over a small fire. They laughed much as they roasted their kill.

"My father," Horseback said, "what kind of people are they?"

"I do not know, but I see that they possess things that I saw in the villages of the Raccoon-Eyed People the time I went there to trade. See the blue blanket the nearest one wears across his shoulders? They use many-colored blankets the way we use our hides and buffalo robes. They make the blankets from the wool of sheep and from the hair of the cotton plant. That is what I have been told. They say the blankets are warm and the wool ones will turn water away. I do not know why they like it more than a good deerskin or buffalo robe."

"The color of the blanket is good," Horseback replied. "Like the sky. But I have seen blankets that our warriors have captured from enemies. They come apart in little pieces."

"*Hah*. Now, see the woman cooking at her fire beside the fourth lodge? She uses a bowl made of iron. The iron bowl carries the magic of heat from the fire, so she does not have to drop hot stones into her stew."

Horseback looked over the camp for some time as the strange people moved about. The five hunters began to eat the meat they had roasted. "We could easily take the horses of these hunters," he said in a whisper, "but the horses are poor and would only slow us down."

"They number greater than our small party," Shaggy Hump said. "To fight so many for such poor horses would be foolish."

Horseback glanced at Echo, who was scowling at the strange camp through green willow leaves. "Yet, if we sneak away, they will find our tracks where we have looked upon them, and they will think us cowards. We must show ourselves and make talk with them. If they try to take our horses from us, we must fight until we have all escaped or died."

"This is a good place to die," Echo said, "and a good time. The sun is shining and the air is like the wind from the wings of a great eagle. I hope they will try to take my horse."

Mounting their ponies, the searchers rode onto the brink of the stream bank, into view of the strange hunters. Several of the hunters ran out of the camp on foot to challenge Horseback and his riders, but since the searchers wore no paint and left their bows unstrung in their quivers, they were invited into the camp with gestures.

The strangers gave Horseback's riders some buffalo meat, and Horseback gifted them, in turn, with the hide of the elk Echo had killed a few days before. This pleased the strange hunters very much, and they began trying to make talk with the mounted searchers. There was a short talk among the hunters, and one of them ran away to the main part of the village, for what reason the searchers did not know.

Horseback touched the blue blanket one man wore as he tried to make sense of the many signs these strangers made with their hands. He had heard of this hand talk, but had seen little of it. He knew how to make very few of the signs, yet he found them easy to understand when the strangers repeated them slowly. He felt he should learn more of this talk, as he had heard that many nations of the plains used it.

Soon, Horseback and Shaggy Hump had learned that the strange hunters came from a nation of people called *Tiwa*. They knew much about the hairy-faced white men, whom they called Metal Men. These *Tiwa* hunters lived in a village just one sleep south, called Tachichichi.

The visitors roasted and ate meat as the sign talk went haltingly along. Finally, the runner who had left for the main part of the village returned with another warrior, a young man who urged the *Noomah* searchers to speak, so that he might hear their language.

"I am Horseback. I come in peace with my friends. We are searching."

The young *Tiwa* warrior frowned, for he did not understand.

Then Horseback repeated the same words in the *Yuta* tongue he had learned from Looks Away.

Now the *Tiwa* smiled and answered in the language of the *Yutas*: "I am Speaks Twice. You are welcome in my camp." As he spoke, he made corresponding signs in the hand talk.

"Why do you know the *Yuta* tongue?" Horseback asked, fearing that he may have stumbled into a camp of *Yuta* allies, and as such, enemies to himself and his searchers.

"At Tachichichi, we trade with many nations," Speaks Twice replied, "so it is good to know many tongues." Again, he made talk with his hands as well as his voice. "How far away is your country?"

"It lies north of the *Yuta* lands."

"I have heard others speak of your nation," Speaks Twice said. "They call you Snake People."

Horseback had known for a long time that many other nations referred to the True Humans as Snake People. He could not understand why the true two-leggeds would be named for no-leggeds, especially when the *Noomah* avoided snakes, according to the wisdom of their grandfathers' grandfathers. He thought maybe it was a joke among all the inferior nations, because they could not understand the importance of the snake taboo to the True Humans. Horseback did not understand the wisdom of the taboo either, for it was ancient and mysterious wisdom, and therefore the most powerful and un-questionable of all wisdoms.

"Our enemies call us Snake People," Horseback explained. "In our country, we have many enemies."

Speaks Twice took a moment to translate to his friends. "We have only one enemy. The Wolf People who come across the plains from the east to attack our villages."

"The *Yutas* are your allies?" Horseback inquired.

"No. We have no need of allies. The *Tiwa* people trade under truce with all nations of people, except the Wolf People. We do not take the war trail with other nations. We are traders, planters, and hunters. Even the Metal Men are at peace with us, though once we were at war."

Horseback took a bite from a piece of buffalo that he had removed from the flames to cool. He grunted his appreciation for the meat. He liked this *Tiwa* warrior named Speaks Twice who spoke with his hands as well as his tongue. He felt he might learn much of the hand talk by making conversation with him. "Are all the warriors of your village here in this camp?" he asked, looking across the many lodges of the *Tiwa* hunting camp.

When Speaks Twice translated this to his friends, the hunters laughed.

"If Tachichichi were the size of my hand," Speaks Twice said, "this camp would make only my little finger."

"I would like to see that many people in one place."

"I will take you to Tachichichi." Speaks Twice pointed south. "It stands one sleep south, near the banks of the River of Arrowheads."

"I have heard talk of this river," Shaggy Hump said to his son. "Warriors of many nations find flint at a place along the banks of the river."

Among these strange people, Horseback felt as if he wanted to dance, or sing the song Sound-the-Sun-Makes had given him. The spirits were trying to tell him things that he could not quite understand—much like the hand talk of Speaks Twice. He thought of Teal, and the moments he had stolen with her alone. He wanted to tell her of the things he was finding here in the south. He longed to show her these places.

The halting talk between *Tiwa* and *Noomah* went on as searchers and hunters feasted on buffalo meat. Speaks Twice did not know all of the *Yuta* words, but he was skilled at the hand signs, and he easily learned new words Horseback taught to him in their awkward attempts to communicate. Speaks Twice seemed about the same age as Horseback. He was taller than any of the *Noomah* riders, the features of his face straight and long. He seemed strong and quick, though his muscles did not bunch and ripple like those across the shoulders and arms and legs of the burly *Noomah*.

"You ride near the hunting grounds of your enemies, the *Yutas*," Speaks Twice said. "Your party is small. Why do you undertake this danger?"

"I have received a vision telling me to seek the country of Metal Men and get horses. Do the Metal Men have many horses?"

Speaks Twice translated this very slowly, as if making time to consider his reply. "Yes, the Metal Men keep many, many horses of many different colors," he finally said. "But the chiefs of the Metal Men forbid all trade in horses."

"You have horses," Horseback said, pointing at the poor mounts grazing near the *Tiwa* camp.

Speaks Twice smiled. "There are ways to get horses, though my people do not need many."

"What ways?"

"Some trade with other nations who steal horses from the Metal Men. Some battle with enemies who have large herds. And then, some of the Metal Men disobey their chiefs and trade in horses, though it is forbidden."

"What do they take in trade for these horses?"

Young Speaks Twice seemed uncomfortable with this question. "I have never seen this trading take place. I cannot know in my own heart what my eyes have not seen. Why do you want so many horses? The ones you ride now look good."

Horseback chewed a piece of meat. "In my country, the four-leggeds that make meat do not number as they do here. We must ride far to find enough to eat. We are surrounded by enemies, and our numbers are few. The horses help us move our villages when our enemies come in great numbers."

While this talk was going on, Shaggy Hump had been studying the red-and-white lodges of the *Tiwa* hunters. "Your lodges," he asked through his son, "do your women make them?"

Speaks Twice turned his hand over in front of him to make the sign meaning *no*. "In Tachichichi, we live in great lodges made of earth, and stone, and timbers. We use the hide lodges only when we hunt. We trade for these lodges."

"With whom?"

"The people from the plains who come to trade at Tachichichi."

"What do these people call themselves?" Shaggy Hump inquired.

"*Inday*," Speaks Twice said.

At mention of the lost *Noomah* enemy, Shaggy Hump sprang from his crouching position near the fire and drew his knife. Horseback and the other searchers joined him quickly, for all had heard the stories from their grandfathers of the cruel and treacherous *Inday*, most ancient of all *Noomah* enemies.

Almost as quickly, the *Tiwa* hunters sprang and formed a defensive half-circle, reaching for the weapons they had on hand, one brandishing the pointed stick upon which he had roasted his chunk of buffalo meat.

"Stop!" Speaks Twice shouted. "We only trade with the *Inday*. That is all. Sometimes they camp at our village. We do not go with them on the war trail. Our village, Tachichichi, is a place of peace for all nations who wish to trade. Many peoples come there under truce, even if they make war with one another when they leave Tachichichi. So it is with the *Inday*."

Horseback took his hand from the handle of his flint knife, noticing now that all the knives, lances, and arrow points of the *Tiwas* were made of iron. Other *Tiwa* warriors were coming with more iron blades, having seen the strangers spring and reach for their weapons. It would be foolish to fight these people, he thought. Horseback did not fear the *Tiwa*. He did not fear death or battle. He feared only that he would fail Sound-the-Sun-Makes in achieving his great vision, which yet stood shrouded in his heart by a blizzard of ignorance. To die here in battle, however bravely, would mean the end of his great quest, the end of the hazy thing that Sound-the-Sun-Makes wanted him to achieve.

And there was yet another reason in his heart that made Horseback want peace with the *Tiwas*. Never in the memories of his elders had the True Humans known peace with any nation. Never before had he been greeted and allowed to enter the camp of another people, to feast and exchange gifts. Horseback did not need allies, but he liked the feeling of feasting with friends. Yet, he dared not trust these *Tiwas*, for he could feel the spirits moving in his stomach, warning him not to trust what he did not know.

"Listen to Speaks Twice," he finally said. "Let no blood stain this place of peace. I see no enemy of my people here. To trade with a nation under truce is not the same as taking that nation as an ally. Sometimes there must be trade, even between enemies."

Horseback's warriors sheathed their weapons. Whip went to the fire and picked up the piece of buffalo meat he had dropped. Brushing away the dirt and ashes, he began to gnaw on it again. The talk between Speaks Twice and Horseback resumed, though they spoke no more of the *Inday*. Instead, they spoke of the *Yutas*.

"You must pass through the hunting grounds of the *Yutas* if you wish to ride straight to the villages of the Metal Men," Speaks Twice warned.

"I will ride straight," Horseback boasted. "Straighter than straight."

"The *Yutas* are powerful."

"I do not fear them."

When Speaks Twice translated this in the *Tiwa* language, the *Tiwa* warriors all laughed. Many of them had now gathered around. Horseback only laughed with them, for he liked the *Tiwas*. They laughed much and made graceful conversation with the sign talk. They possessed many beautiful and useful things they had acquired through trade with other nations. He found more iron in this camp than he had ever seen before in all his winters put together.

The *Tiwas* were handsome people, in a lesser way. They were tall compared to *Noomah* people. Horseback saw one of them riding a pony, and thought how odd the warrior looked, so tall above the back of the mount. The rider's broad shoulders made him seem off balance. His long legs stuck out, away from the horse, unlike the short, bowed legs of the *Noomah* warriors, which held a horse like a palm cupped around a gourd dipper.

He was glad the spirits had made his people to fit astride their ponies. He was happy that the spirits had sent First Horse on the day of his birth. He was proud to have made this trip into the Sacred South, though it was dangerous and fraught with uncertainties.

Horseback asked many questions about the Metal Men, and Speaks Twice began to answer:

"The Metal Men first came to our old villages in the south many generations ago, bringing much iron, and many horses and other animals. They came in peace and spoke of the Great Spirit, but soon began taking our corn and other things that they did not own. Some took *Tiwa* girls and defiled them.

"They call us *Pueblo*. It is their name for the kind of village we live in. They call our allies to the south by the same name—those who speak the *Towa* and *Tewa* tongues, and those who speak *Keresan* and *Zuni* and *Tompiro*. At Picuris and Cochiti and Nambe and many other villages. They call us all by the name of *Pueblo*, because of our lodges, but we are not related to all those peoples. The Metal Men do not understand this.

"Twenty-five summers ago, the *Tiwa* nation and its allies made war against the Metal Men and drove them far away to the south. Many warriors died in this war, for the Metal Men fought bravely with many weapons of iron, but the victory was won by the *Tiwa* and our allies."

"Did they fight with Fire Sticks?" Horseback asked.

When Speaks Twice translated the question, his fellow warriors laughed. "My brothers laugh because you say 'Fire Stick' like the old men used to say. The weapon is called a *gun*. Sometimes *musket* or *escopeta*. The Metal Men have many guns, but not much powder."

"Powder?" Horseback answered.

"The powder that makes the gun kill."

"The black medicine dust."

Again, Speaks Twice translated, bringing howls of laughter from his friends. "Gun powder. The Metal Men have little of it, so they fight mostly with bows and lances and swords."

"Swords?" Horseback asked.

Speaks Twice stared for a long moment, but did not translate any more of Horseback's ignorance for his friends' enjoyment. Horseback felt that Speaks Twice honored him by not making him the object of more ridicule, but imagined that Speaks Twice would only make the translations later.

After explaining the thing called a sword, Speaks Twice told more about the war with the Metal Men. "They wore shirts of thick leather. Some wore shirts of iron. They were hard to kill, and fought bravely. Still, my people defeated them and drove them to a place far away in the south, whence they had come.

"When they fled, the Metal Men left many horses behind. Some of my people traded some of these horses to the *Yutas*, and some to other nations. Other horses ran away and went wild like their elk ancestors."

Shaggy Hump spoke, pausing after each sentence to let his son translate: "The first horse the spirits gave to my people came on the day my son was born." He gestured with pride toward Horseback. "It made a sacred circle around his birth lodge. We were hungry that winter, and so we killed First Horse and ate it. We did not know then that the horse was as good to ride as it was to eat. Since First Horse came to bring medicine to my son, the *Noomah* people have become richer."

"It is true," Horseback added. "We will ride to greatness on the backs of many ponies. The spirits have told me in visions and dreams that I must seek the hairy-faces that you call Metal Men and get horses. Tell me more about the Metal Men, Speaks Twice. Tell me what happened after your people and your allies drove the Metal Men away in the big war."

Speaks Twice began making signs to match his words, and his movements were like those of a good dance. "The Metal Men stayed away twelve winters. When they returned they brought many weapons, many soldiers, and many families with women and children. There were too many of them. I was a child when they came back, thirteen winters ago. The Metal Men attacked my village and took me and my mother captive. They took many women and children captive. They would not give us back to our families until the village surrendered to them. The village surrendered, but the Metal Men made some of us work for them, like slaves. Some of us did not want to live there with the Metal Men, so we fled to the plains where we made our new village called Tachichichi. The Metal Men have come to Tachichichi in the past, but they do not stay. They come to bring us back to the old villages in the south. When they come, some of our people go with them, to make them happy. But they will only return, one by one to Tachichichi. In this way, we avoid war with the Metal Men."

Horseback had been translating all of the his talk in the *Yuta* tongue so his brothers would understand. Now Echo-of-the-Wolf spoke, and urged Horseback to translate his words:

"Your people should make war on the Metal Men again. Take their horses. Make slaves of their women and children. Kill the warriors who stand and fight, and drive the rest away to the south. You have said that this was done before."

"The Metal Men number too many," Speaks Twice explained. "Some of our people have gone south with the white medicine men who wear the black robes. They saw a single village far to the south that held more white people than all the people of all the other nations of all the earth. They number like the blades of grass on the plains. No nation of warriors can melt all the snows of winter."

Many buffalo chips and sticks of wood were added to the fire as Horseback learned what he could about the white men, asking next how far away the country of the Metal Men lay.

"Ten sleeps," Speaks Twice said, and he began to fashion a map of dirt and ashes raked out of the fire.

As Speaks Twice and his friends conferred on the making of the map, Shaggy Hump leaned closer to his son and spoke very low. "They do not know how to travel as we do. We will reach the place of the hairy faces in five sleeps if these *Tiwas* take ten."

The map took shape on the ground, the *Tiwa* warriors arguing about the twists and bends in the rivers, the contours of certain mountain ranges, and the distances between villages. When it was finally finished, the map gave Horseback a thunderbird's view of the whole *Tiwa* world.

Speaks Twice had mapped the plains by brushing the dirt smooth with a bunch of buffalo grass. These plains swept far away to the east and evaporated into the unknown country of other strange nations. Far out on the north-eastern plains of the map, Speaks Twice pointed out a village of the Raccoon-Eyed People.

"They call this village Quivira," he said.

"That is the place I went to trade many winters ago," Shaggy Hump added.

Indicating a vast sweep of plains surrounding Quivira, Speaks Twice said, "This is the country of our enemies, the Wolf People. Sometimes they come far across the plains to the west to make war with us."

The plains on the map were marred only by the courses of streams carved with a pointed stick. Speaks Twice drilled a small dot to mark the place where the *Tiwas* and *Noomahs* now held council, and Horseback could see that the stream along which this camp stood was a mere tributary compared to the larger rivers on the map. This camp was near the northern edges of the map, giving Horseback the impression that this was about as far north as the *Tiwa* ever ventured.

All along the western extremes of the map, ranges of mountains rose abruptly from the plains, forming an undulating wall of steep slopes that stretched many sleeps north and south. A large river ran from the heart of the mountains, flowing south, then turning east to divide the plains.

"This is the River of Arrowheads," Speaks Twice claimed. He made a mark with his finger along its southern bank, far out onto the plains. "Here is our village of Tachichichi."

Well west of the village, a pair of mountain peaks stood apart from the other ranges, as if they had drifted slightly out onto the plains. Their contours and proximity to each other made them resemble the ample bosom of some young woman.

"These two mountains are called the Breasts of Mother Earth," Speaks Twice explained. "The straightest trail to the Metal Men passes to the south of them, through the country of the *Yutas*."

The *Tiwa* mapmaker's finger moved south from the Breasts of Mother Earth, crossing the first range of mountains at a pass, and coming to the banks of a very large river. This river flowed southward through a canyon gouged deep with a stick. On a level plain between the canyon and the west slopes of the mountains, he indicated a village situated on a small tributary.

"This is the village of my birth," Speaks Twice said. "It is called Taos. It is now the northernmost dwelling of Metal Men." He pointed to another village, farther south along the same big river. "This village is called Picuris. Taos and Picuris are the two old villages of the *Tiwa* nation."

Now Speaks Twice indicated a group of villages farther south along the great river, some on the west bank, some on the east. "These are the villages of our allies, the *Tewas*. South of them, the Metal Men have a very large village they call Santa Fe. Here live the soldiers with thick leather shirts, the medicine men with black robes, and many families. They make things of metal, and grow corn and beans and squash. Many of our allies work for them like slaves. Their lodges are large, and filled with things to sit on and sleep on and eat on, all made of wood carved in strange designs with metal tools. They keep many animals. Chickens, goats, and sheep; but not like the wild ones you know. Their animals are weak and ugly and slow."

"And horses?" Horseback inquired.

"Yes. Many, many horses of all colors."

"That is where I must search."

While Horseback studied the map, Speaks Twice conferred with his fellow hunters in the language of the *Tiwas*. Finally, he spoke to Horseback in the *Yuta* tongue:

"I will ride with you if you wish. I know the trail to Taos like a river knows her own course. Then, if you want to see many Metal Men and their women and children and horses, I will take you to Santa Fe. But you must go in peace, as you have come here."

"I go in peace. You will ride with my party if you wish. You will guide us, while I lead."

Speaks Twice held his right hand, palm down, in front of the left side of his chest. Sweeping the hand away, level with his heart, he smiled. The sign meant *good.* "First we will take our meat back to Tachichichi for our women to dry for the coming winter. Then, I will guide your party of searchers to the country of many horses before the snows begin to fill the mountain passes."

"Will there be *Na-vohnuh* at Tachichichi?" Shaggy Hump asked.

"*Na-vohnuh?*" Speaks Twice answered, a quizzical look on his face.

"Our ancient enemies. Those you call *Inday.*"

Speaks Twice paused before answering. "My village is a place of truce among all nations. If the *Inday* camp there when we arrive, they will honor the truce. Will you?"

The *Noomah* searchers looked at Horseback, who found himself lacking in wisdom. Even his own father looked to him, for this was his journey, the quest for his vision. What was he to say about this matter of the *Na-vohnuh?* His father had told him many times of the *puhakuts* who had prophesied the return of the wars with the *Na-vohnuh.* These enemies had brought so many unspeakable horrors upon the True Humans in ancient times that they could never escape vengeance. The thought of observing a truce with them was cowardly.

He looked toward the sun, hoping for wisdom from his guardian spirit. He stood and listened long, until his eyes were blinded by the glare. Then he heard something in his heart that filled him with courage.

"From the center of Tachichichi," he said, the defiance plain in his tone, "as far as my arrow flies in any direction, we will honor your truce with all nations. Beyond the place where my arrow falls, our enemies must beg the mercy of our spirit-protectors."

Before Speaks Twice could reply, or make the translations to his kinsmen, Horseback turned quickly toward his mount. His followers went with him.

25

Never had Speaks Twice seen such riding. As his *Tiwa* hunting party plodded slowly southward to Tachichichi, Horseback and the *Noomah* riders seemed to swarm everywhere on their mounts, riding to every distant ridge to look beyond, then returning to the single file of footmen, dogs, and ponies comprising the hunting party.

The *Tiwa* hunters traveled afoot, saving their horses for the work of pulling the pole-drags that carried their meat, hides, and hunting lodges. Their few horses could not pull all the meat and hides, so many dogs had been harnessed to small pole-drags to carry the remainder of the kill.

As he walked along beside one of the pole-drags, Speaks Twice saw Horseback coming toward him at a lope.

"How tall does the grass grow at Tachichichi?" Horseback asked, coming to a jolting halt on his mount.

Speaks Twice held his hand against the ribs of the pony pulling his lodge, measuring the height of the grass around his village as near as he remembered.

Horseback made the sign meaning good. "My mount will be hungry." He patted the pony on the neck, making a loud slapping sound. Then he jammed his knees under the coils of rope that surrounded the barrel of his mare and dashed away again, galloping toward two of his warrior friends on a distant rise.

These Snake People who called themselves *Noomah* made Speaks Twice uneasy. Circling all the time like bees, it was impossible to keep them all accounted for. And the riding! Speaks Twice had seen many warriors ride. The Wolf People were frightening when they appeared on horseback, but they did not swarm like these Snake People. The *Inday* rode without fear of speed or danger, yet seemed out of place mounted, compared to Horseback and his searchers. The *Yutas* were fine riders, accustomed to plunging down impossible slopes in their mountain country, but never with the ease and abandon of the *Noomah* riders Speaks Twice had seen today leaping gullies and bounding down washed-out dirt banks.

The Metal Men possessed great riding skills, even though they encumbered their mounts with saddles and bridles made heavy with iron and silver. In the village the Metal Men called Santa Fe, Speaks Twice had once seen these riders play a game with a rooster buried up to its neck in the dirt. The object of the game was to gallop by the rooster, lean from the saddle, grab the rooster by the head, and pull it from the dirt. One of the riders had accomplished this feat at full speed. Until today, this was the finest riding Speaks Twice had ever seen.

When Horseback rode, he seemed like a part of the mount he straddled. The other Snake People rode almost as well. Standing on foot, these strange warriors looked awkward, short and bandy-legged. But on the backs of horses, they became as wild and powerful and agile as elk.

As he lamented his own lack of speed, Speaks Twice suddenly realized that the *Noomah* riders were nowhere in sight. He looked all around, but saw none of them. Surmounting a grassy rise, he heard the rumble of hooves, and beheld the riders chasing a lone buffalo cow they had scared out of some draw, her tongue lolling out of her mouth as she ran.

Speaks Twice could not imagine what the warriors intended with this cow so badly spooked, unless they just enjoyed chasing her. Then, as he watched in wonder, he saw Horseback reach for an arrow from the quiver on his back. The rider's bow was strung. Somehow, he made his mount close in on the crazed cow without holding his reins. He drew the bow, and the arrow sped true.

The rider named Whip moved in for a second shot, and the cow began to stumble. Now the fierce looking warrior called Echo-of-the-Wolf closed with his lance, using the weight of his horse to drive the flint blade deep into the vitals of the buffalo. The cow fell, and Speaks Twice realized that his whole *Tiwa* party had stopped to watch the spectacle—even the dogs and ponies with their pole-drags.

. These people were wild. They made him nervous, yet he admired them. They were not Snake People at all. They were Horse People. He was glad he had befriended them, yet he was concerned about what might happen once they reached Tachichichi. Speaks Twice knew that some *Inday* people would likely be camping there. He prayed that the truce would hold. He did not wish to make enemies of a nation of people who could shoot arrows from the backs of galloping horses.

Speaks Twice made sure Horseback rode beside him as they surmounted the last roll in the prairie before Tachichichi came into view. Before he reached the top of the rise, he began to watch Horseback's face, knowing the *Noomah* searcher would spot the village before him from higher up on his mount.

The reins tightened as the young *Noomah* warrior's eyes widened. "The dirt rises so high above the ground," Horseback said. "Are the lodges in the dirt?"

Speaks Twice laughed. Coming over the rise on foot, he tried to look at the spectacle the way Horseback would. What if he had never seen a lodge made of anything but buffalo hide? This village of a hundred families might indeed make his own eyebrows rise. He laughed again, realizing that Horseback had no eyebrows, having plucked out all the hair from his face—even his eyelashes. This aversion to facial hair was going to make the hairy-faced Metal Men seem particularly grotesque to the *Noomah* riders.

Turning his attention toward the *Tiwa* village, Speaks Twice noticed that the River of Arrowheads was running lower since he and his party had left to hunt buffalo. This would make the crossing to Tachichichi an easy one. Beyond the river, he checked over the fields where the corn, beans, and squash had been harvested before the hunt. A few horses browsed through the fields, being tended by an old man and a couple of boys. Beyond the fields stood the walls of Tachichichi, rising straight up from the ground, like the face of a sheer bluff. The village consisted of twelve adobe structures, formed around a square. To his relief, Speaks Twice saw no *Inday* lodges erected near the village. This was the time of year when the *Inday* left their fields near the river and moved their lodges out onto the plains to hunt. Speaks Twice hoped he could guide the *Noomah* on their way south before any *Inday* warriors returned.

He glanced again at Horseback and tried to imagine what the stranger was thinking of this place. The other *Noomah* riders had stopped beside him, and they were all staring in silence at the sight of the *Tiwa* town.

"Where are the doors to the lodges?" Horseback asked.

"We climb up the ladders from the outside, then go down into the lodges through holes on top. That is why each level is smaller than the level under it, so there is room for the entrance holes."

"They go in through the smoke hole," Shaggy Hump said, and the *Noomah* searchers proved that they too could laugh at strangers with strange ways.

Just then, a woman emerged from one of the holes on the second level of the pueblo across the river. She walked a few steps and disappeared into another hole.

"I see now," Horseback said. "It is like a village of prairie dogs."

Speaks Twice chuckled, but did not translate for his fellow hunters, whom he thought might be offended. "When our enemies attack, we pull up the ladders around the lower level. We are safe inside. We have much food and water hidden there. You see many ladders around the village now. That is how I know all is well with my home place."

"What has happened to the ground between the river and the lodges?" Horseback asked.

"That is where we grow the corn and beans," Speaks Twice explained. "And the squash."

"How do your people make the ground look like a herd of buffalo has crossed over it?"

"We use sticks." Speaks Twice made a digging motion with his hands.

"In my country we use sticks to dig for yampa roots."

"It is the same with us, only we dig to plant seeds, not to get roots. Then, we pull all the grass away from the plants we grow, so the grass will not grow over them and weaken them."

Many smoke trails rose from the chimneys, making Speaks Twice anxious to get home and eat something other than buffalo meat. "We should ride across to the village now," he said.

"Yes. We will need time to raise our lodge. I do not wish to sleep inside your village. It is strange to me. My lodge is round, like a sacred circle. Your village is not round."

"It is straight," Speaks Twice answered. "Straight is good."

As Horseback started riding slowly down into the breaks of the big river, he took his bow from his quiver. Wrapping one leg around the bow, he bent the elm wood enough to get the loose end of the buffalo sinew bow string around the other tip of the bow.

"There are no *Inday* warriors at my village," Speaks Twice said. "Why must you string your bow?"

"Your warriors will be ready for us. We must be ready for them, as well. We come in peace, but we are always ready to fight."

"Why do you say my warriors will be ready for you, my friend?"

"I know that you sent a runner ahead from the hunting camp, where we met, to this village you call Tachichichi. Echo found the runner's tracks away from our own trail."

Speaks Twice kicked at a dog that was veering out of single file. "The runner was only sent to prepare our people for your arrival. We will have a feast in your honor and cook many things you have not had before. Have you ever eaten a squash?"

"No," Horseback answered. "What manner of animal is that?"

Speaks Twice translated Horseback's remark to his fellow hunters, and they all burst out in laughter.

▲▲▲▲▲
26
▼▼▼▼▼

Arriving at the north bank of the River of Arrowheads, the *Noomah* warriors stopped to shoot their arrows, one at a time, across to the south bank. The river was wide, but each warrior's arrow made a group so tight that he might collect them with no more than a few steps taken among them.

"Why do you send your arrows before you?" Speaks Twice asked.

"That river looks deep in the middle. We do not wish to get the feathers on the shaft wet, for water makes them no good."

Once they had crossed and gathered their arrows, the *Noomah* searchers turned their horses loose to graze. The animals were tired and hungry, and would not wander far from the grass in the valley. Horseback let his mare drag a rope to make her easier to catch.

Speaks Twice showed the visitors through a narrow strip of ground winding between the two largest pueblos, like a pass through a small canyon. The sun was low in the western sky, and the passage was all in shadow. Horseback had unstrung his bow. The friendly reception and the good smells of cooking food had convinced him that the *Tiwa* runner had been sent ahead only to have the feast prepared. He ran his hand lightly over the mud-plastered wall as he walked.

Leading the way up one of the ladders, Speaks Twice ascended to the first level of the pueblo, stopping to smile down at the cautious way the *Noomahs* climbed up behind him. Reaching the roof, Horseback rushed to the corner and looked over the place where he had left the horses. Seeing them grazing, he turned back to Speaks Twice, and the tour continued.

The *Tiwa* host ushered the visitors down another ladder, through one of the small holes at their feet, and into one of the rooms. The strangers felt the walls, looked suspiciously into dark corners. Horseback seemed concerned about the heavy timbers over his head. They went back out into daylight and ascended to the second, then the third level of the pueblo.

"Your people have made your lodges like a hill," Horseback said. "Does this not anger the spirits? It is only for the Great Spirit to make hills."

Speaks Twice only laughed. "Our spirits are not angry, my friend. We make our lodges to honor the Spirit World."

"The lodges of the *Noomah* make a circle. It is like the circle of the seasons. Like the sun, the moon. Like the place where the ground touches the sky all the way around Mother Earth. It is a good way to live."

Speaks Twice placed his hand on an adobe wall. "My lodge is warm and quiet when the winter winds sound like a wolf," he replied. "It is cool and dark when the heat of summer makes the grass die and curl. Its walls stand strong against the war points and muskets of the Wolf People. Our straight lodges fit together better than round lodges. That is why they are straight. The spirits make many straight things, like the pine trees in the mountains, and the stars that fly across the sky. I know that straight is good." The *Tiwa* translator punctuated his spoken words with severe gestures of the hand talk.

Horseback was looking far out over the plains, turning slowly to take in everything from this high vantage atop the pueblo. "My lodge drags behind my pony." Before Speaks Twice could respond, he scrambled down the ladder.

· · · ·

After the feast of buffalo meat, corn gruel, roasted squash, and beans, Speaks Twice was roused from his room in the pueblo by the voice of the village caller. The news he heard reaching faintly through the entrance hole in the ceiling made him spring suddenly from his soft robe, where he had lain down for some sleep. A band of *Inday* warriors was coming to camp and trade at Tachichichi.

By the time he rushed up the ladder, the *Inday* were almost upon the south walls of the village. He counted. There were six mounted warriors. Fifteen more warriors on foot walked behind the mounted men. The women numbered twenty-four. Old people and children came along behind. A long line of dogs dragged the short poles and hides of the red-and-white *Inday* lodges. For some reason Speaks Twice did not understand, the *Inday* used horses only for riding. They did not let their horses drag their lodges as did the *Yutas* and the *Noomah*.

He looked up to the third level of the pueblo, above his own lodge on the second level, and saw Whirlpool, the war chief of Tachichichi, standing with two of the elders on the roof.

"Go speak to them," Whirlpool said to Speaks Twice. "Choose your words well."

Rushing to the north wall, the translator saw the *Noomah* warriors languishing near their single lodge. The size of this lodge had surprised Speaks Twice when he saw it raised yesterday. It was much larger than the red-and-white *Inday* lodges pulled by dogs, and larger even than the *Yuta* lodges he had seen, yet Horseback claimed it was a rather small one. It was good that the *Noomah* were staying close to their lodge, still unaware of the approach of their ancient enemy from the opposite side of the pueblo. Hoping he could keep the two parties from violence, Speaks Twice climbed quickly down the ladder to have a talk with the *Inday*.

By the time he reached the top of the ladder that led to the ground, the *Noomah* horses had caught scent of the new *Inday* arrivals and stampeded up the river, as if they knew the ancient enemy of their masters had arrived. Horseback and his riders went to catch them. Horseback's mare dragged a rope, making her easy to catch. She was well trained and had not run away with the others. Horseback caught her and rode hard to get around the other ponies, while Speaks Twice went to remind the *Inday* that Tachichichi was a place of truce among all nations.

He did not know much of the language of the *Inday* yet, but the leader of the band was a chief called Battle Scar who communicated well with the hand talk.

Speaks Twice signed: "Welcome, my friends. I invite you to raise your lodges here, on the south side of my village, where the sun warms the village walls like the warmth of my heart for my good friends."

Battle Scar raised a hand in greeting. He smiled, changing the shape of the scar on his cheek which had given him name. He pointed up the river. "Who are those people who catch the horses?"

Speaks Twice thought better of naming the visitors Snake People, for the *Inday* might remember them by that name. "Horse People," he signed. "They come in peace from the north."

"As we come in peace, my friend." Battle Scar made his scar bend with a treacherous smile. "We bring captive children of the Wolf People to trade."

Speaks Twice had expected this, for Battle Scar's band made many slave raids. There had always existed some trade in captive women and children across the plains. The *Inday* raided the Wolf People to take captives to sell to the *Tiwa*—and to the Metal Men. The Wolf People, in turn, raided *Inday* camps, and sometimes the villages of the *Tiwa* and other straight-lodge dwellers, taking their women and children far east to sell to other white soldiers who were always at war with the Metal Men. These other whites were called Flower Men, for the sign they carried on their banner. Even the *Yutas* traded in a few slaves from other nations.

It was useful to have some Wolf People captives in Tachichichi. Some would be adopted into the *Tiwa* nation and grow old in the pueblo. When Metal Men came to demand that some of the Tiwas return to the old pueblos of the south to work in the shops and fields, Wolf People slaves could often be passed off as *Tiwa*, satisfying the Metal Men for a while, for few of the Metal Men could distinguish among all the many peoples of the plains.

Speaks Twice signed his approval. "We have much corn and iron things from the Metal Men. The elders will trade with you when the new sun rises."

The Inday chief seemed pleased. "We will take our horses to water."

Speaks Twice turned toward the pueblo, then stopped, turned back to Battle Scar, as if an afterthought had just occurred to him. "The Horse People camping on the north side of our village have many enemies. They may be seeking revenge on the Wolf People. A wise owner of slaves will keep his Wolf People captives away from the Horse People, for the Horse People may want to kill them. Their hearts are full of hate for their enemies. They will leave soon, and your people will not have to worry about them bothering your slaves."

Speaks Twice turned quickly away. He hoped he had not overstated the warning, which would only make the *Inday* curious. As far as he knew, everything he had said to Battle Scar was true. None of Horseback's searchers had spoken of the Wolf People, but Speaks Twice thought it possible they could be bitter enemies, since the Snake People—whom he had now named the Horse People—claimed no allies. He had not lied. He only wished to keep the two peoples apart until he could get rid of the *Noomah*.

That night, Speaks Twice was summoned to the underground kiva by Whirlpool. Because he was skilled at speaking many languages and making the signs of the hand talk, Speaks Twice had often appeared before the elders in the kiva. This time, however, he was more nervous than usual. Though he had not been in charge of the hunting party that had found the Horse People, it was Speaks Twice who had talked to them and invited them to Tachichichi. Should anything go wrong, his reputation would suffer.

After purifying themselves with smoke and praying, the elders asked Speaks Twice to stand and tell all he had learned of the Horse People. The young translator spoke well. He spoke honestly, expressing his worries about violence between *Noomah* and *Inday*. After he spoke, Whirlpool thought for a long time. The kiva remained silent. Finally, the chief of Tachichichi spoke:

"Young warrior, you have spoken with a good heart. You have done as you should have done. These Horse People would have come to Tachichichi even if you had not invited them. Now, you have brought them in friendship. They will remember.

"I have had dreams of these people coming. You have only done as the spirits would have you do. Now, here is what I want you to do next, as the spirits have shown me in my dreams and visions:

"When the sun rises, you will take the Horse People from this village.

Take them to the Metal Men, as they wish. Take them by the trail that leads south of the Breasts of Mother Earth. Take them straight, so they do not become suspicious, but do not hurry along. While you are leading the Horse People, a fast rider will take another trail to the Metal Men, to warn them of these new Horse People from the north. I do not wish the Metal Men to think these Horse People are our allies.

"The dreams I have had are fearful dreams. They show a nation of people coming down the plains, killing buffalo, killing any enemy who stands before them. In my dreams, these people ride horses. All of them ride. Even the old women, even the young mothers with cradle boards. In one dream I saw nothing but horses. Horses, and horses, and horses. And the horses shot arrows from their eyes, and the arrows pierced the walls of our lodge.

"This dream was a warning. We must not let these Horse People become our enemies, yet we must make the Metal Men understand that the Horse People are not our allies. We will be like the tree that grows upon the banks of the river. We must grow far enough away from the river that the rising waters do not tear us away downstream. Yet we must not take root too far out on the plains, where the droughts and the prairie fires will consume us.

"Speaks Twice, as you guide the Horse People to the villages of the Metal Men, Coyote Man will ride on another trail to summon the Metal Men warriors and Black Robes. I will tell Coyote Man what to say. I will pray tonight, so the spirits will tell me what Coyote Man should say to the Metal Men. I will tell Coyote Man to speak to the Raccoon-Eyed Flower Man who lives among the Metal Men. He will help us deal with these new Horse People. The Raccoon-Eyed Flower Man knows much about all the nations of the world.

"This is what shall be done. You will guide the Horse People. Coyote Man will ride to warn the Metal Men."

Speaks Twice looked briefly into the eyes of his chief to show that he had understood. As he rose to leave, he thought of how wise his chief was to have chosen Coyote Man for the ride to the Metal Men. Coyote Man was *Inday* by blood, but had married a *Tiwa* woman and was now a *Tiwa* warrior. With the *Inday*, he had learned much about riding horses, and he would go quickly to the Metal Men while Speaks Twice led the *Noomah* at a slower pace.

He breathed a sigh of relief as he left the kiva, feeling as though his chief and the *Tiwa* spirits had taken much worry from his heart. Now he knew what part he must accomplish, and he no longer felt as if all the worry over the Horse People was his own. They numbered only five, after all. It was true that they rode like no people Speaks Twice had ever seen, that each seemed to take on the strength and pride and fearlessness of the horse he straddled. But they numbered only five searchers from a poor country surrounded by enemies. How fearsome could a nation of such people be?

It was dark when he left the kiva. He reached the roof of the first level of the pueblo and stopped to watch the stars glisten like sparks of sunlight on rippling waters. He had much work to do and a long journey ahead of him, but the strength of the kiva had followed him out into the open air, and he knew he could do his duty.

Speaks Twice decided to look down on the camp of the Horse People before he went to his own lodge to sleep. Walking to the north wall, he focused on the flames of the *Noomah* campfire. His heart leapt suddenly like a live animal in his chest, for several *Inday* braves were standing on one side of the fire, while Horseback and his warriors stood on the other. Horseback was trying to calm his men, especially the eldest one, his father, Shaggy Hump. Speaks Twice could just make out Horseback's words:

"My father, I gave my word to the *Tiwas*. We will not fight at this place. Wait until tomorrow, and we will meet our enemy out on the plains, in the light of day, with our horses under us."

The *Inday* warriors, still confused and unaware of why Shaggy Hump wanted to fight, made questioning gestures.

Shaggy Hump placed his hand on his chest, and drew himself up with pride, making himself look taller, broader. "*Noomah!*" He said, with all the anger and hatred of his ancestors burning within him.

Instantly, when the word was spoken, Speaks Twice saw the six *Inday* warriors reach for their knives. He saw Horseback reach into the fire for a flaming cottonwood branch.

"Stop!" Speaks Twice yelled in his own *Tiwa* tongue, quickly realizing that neither *Inday* nor *Noomah* would understand him. The Horse People camp had gone suddenly wild, made fantastic by Horseback swinging the burning tree limb between the *Inday* and *Noomah* warriors, trying desperately to keep them apart.

Speaks Twice ran for the nearest ladder leading to the ground. "My brothers!" he shouted, hoping some *Tiwa* warriors would hear. "Bring weapons!" He landed on the fifth step of the ladder, then crouched, grabbed one pole, and swung to the ground, as he had done in play since he was a small boy.

He found himself hurtling toward the fight at the Horse People camp. Coming around the corner of the pueblo, he saw that one of the *Inday* warriors had flanked Horseback's frantic offensive with the flaming branch, and was locked in hand-to-hand battle with the Horse People warrior called Bear Heart. As Speaks Twice rushed crazily in between the two parties, joining Horseback in keeping them separated, he heard other *Tiwa* warriors shouting as they scrambled down the ladders.

Just as he thought he might avoid serious trouble, he heard a gasp of pain behind him and turned to see Bear Heart holding his hand over a bloody spot on his stomach. But even as he held his wound, Bear Heart swung a war club across the face of the *Inday*, dashing his enemy's head aside like a shinny ball in the game the women played with sticks.

Both warriors stumbled back and fell away from each other. The kinsmen of each fallen man came quickly to protect him, and this only, Speaks Twice later would realize, prevented the fight from becoming bloodier still.

More *Tiwa* braves had joined Speaks Twice now, and the *Inday* were forced to drag their fallen man back to the south side of the pueblo. A guard of *Tiwa* protectors was stationed around the *Noomah*, preventing the *Inday* from attacking the smaller *Noomah* force before dawn.

The elders in the kiva were informed, and it was decided that Battle Scar and his band would be forever banished from Tachichichi for violating the truce. Horseback, because he attempted to forestall the fighting, would retain his rights to camp and trade at Tachichichi, but would be warned about controlling the hatreds of his men.

Alienating Battle Scar, a strong *Inday* war chief, was a dangerous move, yet could not be avoided. The truce was all that protected Tachichichi from more powerful and warlike nations. A sufficient number of warriors resided in Tachichichi to resist a possible attack by Battle Scar's band. The elders could only hope that Battle Scar would not recruit more warriors from other *Inday* bands and return to seek revenge.

When Speaks Twice went to the *Noomah* camp to tell what the elders had decided, Horseback listened patiently, then thought for some time before he responded:

"If we leave for the villages of the Metal Men tomorrow, will the people of your village take care of Bear Heart?" Here Horseback raised his voice loud enough for Bear Heart to hear inside the large hide lodge. "He is lying on his robe like some one's elder sister, too weak from his little wound to ride with us."

Whip laughed.

"Yes," Speaks Twice answered. "The healers will care for him."

"Then we will leave this place when Father Sun looks upon us with a new face."

Speaks Twice rose from his place near the fire.

"But, first," Horseback continued. "There will be battle with the *Inday*."

"We should attack now," Echo growled.

"No," Horseback snapped in reply. "The spirits forbid it. One or more of us may die when we attack the *Inday*, for they number greater than we do. Our elders have taught us that warriors killed in the darkness of night do not reach the Shadow Land. You may not know this, Speaks Twice, for you are not a True Human, but it is the truth. I will not attack in darkness and leave the spirits of my slain brothers lost forever.

"I have given my word that no *Noomah* warriors who follow me will break the truce of Tachichichi. But, you must remember what I said at the buffalo camp, Speaks Twice. Beyond the place where my arrow falls, our enemies must beg the mercy of our spirit-protectors."

Speaks Twice said nothing in reply. He turned and made his way through the *Tiwa* guard. He would go once again before the council assembled in the kiva. He would inform the elders that they would watch a fight in the morning.

▲▲▲▲▲
27
▼▼▼▼▼

Dawn sliced across the vast eastern plains like a flint knife, thrusting the rough edges of orange and yellow and white up through the dark valley of the River of Arrowhead. Long, wiggling shadows retreated into the large band of *Inday* slavers and the small party of *Noomah* searchers, as each made ready to leave Tachichichi.

Father Sun stood just one fist above the eastern horizon when the *Inday* began to move south. Speaks Twice watched from the roof of the second level of the pueblo, which commanded a fine view of what was soon to be the field of battle. Whirlpool called the *Tiwa* guard into the pueblo, and the force of warriors who had kept *Inday* and *Noomah* apart all night ascended ladders to watch the coming fight from the safety of the sun-baked mud walls. They also carried the wounded *Noomah* warrior, Bear Heart, up the ladder to safety.

Before leaving Tachichichi, Battle Scar approached the wall under Speaks Twice, Whirlpool, and the elders. He led a skinny woman by the arm, her face cast down. He began to speak, using *Inday* words and hand signs.

"What does Battle Scar say?" Whirlpool asked of Speaks Twice. "My old eyes are poor. I cannot see the signs."

"He says this," the translator answered, now speaking for Battle Scar. " 'I bring a gift to the people of Tachichichi. This woman was captured as a girl by the Wolf People from a *Tiwa* hunting expedition on the plains. She was a slave among the Wolf People. Now I have captured her from the Wolf People in a raid one moon ago. I return her to the people of her own blood.' "

"This is well," Whirlpool said. "Battle Scar wishes to make amends for the attack last night."

Then suddenly, with the quickness of a snake striking, Battle Scar grabbed the woman by the hair with one hand as the other drew and slashed with his knife, cutting the throat of the poor returned captive before she could react. She fell dead in a pool of her own blood.

The men on the roof of the pueblo gasped and leaned over the walls as Battle Scar shouted up at them.

"What does he shout now?" Whirlpool said, his anger and disgust making him tremble.

"Battle Scar says, 'Now she is back.' "

Battle Scar stalked away to join his band, and the *Inday* procession began to draw slowly away from Tachichichi.

"Shall we attack them?" Speaks Twice asked his chief.

"No," Whirlpool said. "The slave woman may not have been *Tiwa*. Battle Scar taunts us with this killing because we have forbidden him to return here. Let us hope the Horse People punish him."

A clatter of hooves rose from the crooked passageway between two of the pueblo structures, and Speaks Twice saw Horseback emerge on the south side of the village. His three remaining followers came out of the narrow passage behind him. Their faces had been blackened with war paint. Horseback reached into his quiver for an arrow.

"Watch," Speaks Twice said. "They shoot arrows from the backs of their ponies."

The war chief grunted. "Last night, they did not look very fierce, standing on the ground in their little camp. But now they look terrible on their ponies, with their faces painted black."

Horseback drew his bow and angled his arrow high. It flew, arched long through the air, passed over the entire *Inday* band, and pierced the ground in front of the lead *Inday* warriors.

Battle Scar rode to Horseback's arrow, dismounted, and pulled the arrow from the ground. Breaking it over his knee, he threw the two pieces aside, and began to jeer at the *Noomah* warriors waiting back at the pueblo. The other *Inday* warriors joined in the taunting, their voices like those of a pack of coyotes. They formed a rear guard behind their women and children, daring the *Noomah* braves to fight.

"Now we will see how much courage these Horse People have brought with them from the north," said one of the elders.

Whirlpool narrowed his eyes against a gust carrying particles of stinging sand over the edge of the pueblo roof. "Courage is a thing that changes like a thunderstorm, for it is made of two parts. As the storm is made of wind and water, courage is made of pride and wisdom. The wind is like pride. It howls and lashes with anger. It can tear the limbs from a great tree, yet it cannot last for long.

"Water is like wisdom. Water draws its strength into a valley, and roars with fury. A small stream will go around hill. A large river will wash it away.

"Now we will see if these Horse People possess courage made more of wind or water. Speaks Twice, you know them better than the elders. What does your heart tell you of the Horse People's courage?"

Speaks Twice watched the *Inday* draw slowly away, even their women and children jeering now. Even the old ones were taunting the *Noomah* by waving sticks and throwing dirt in the air.

"Their courage is plenty windy," Speaks Twice said. "Yet, the young leader, Horseback, knows the strength of water. His warriors amount to nothing more than a small stream, and he knows this. Their arrows do not even carry war points, only hunting points. If Horseback's warriors attack, they will ride like whirlwinds from the four points of the sky. They will make much noise, and raise much sand, but they can cause little harm against so large a band of *Inday*."

The last of the *Inday* people passed south of the place where Horseback's arrow had fallen. Horseback rode under the gathering of *Tiwa* onlookers on the roof, looked down on the body of the murdered slave woman, then shouted up to Speaks Twice:

"Now I have kept my word. Our enemies have gone beyond the place where my arrow falls. The *Na-vohnuh* no longer hide under your truce, like a chicken under its mother's wing. I have prayed to the spirits all through the night. I have lighted my pipe and sent my prayers up to the Shadow Land on sacred clouds of smoke. The spirits have told me what must be done.

"We are going to attack the *Inday* now. The spirits have told me that my warriors must take only one scalp as vengeance for the wound of our brother, Bear Heart, and the violation of our sacred camp last night in the dark by our most ancient of enemies. We go now to take our scalp."

He turned his horse toward the *Inday*, and his searchers followed him.

"How will they ever get a scalp from such a large party of *Inday*?" said one of the elders.

"Their courage is all wind," said another. "The Wolf People are ready for them. The Wolf People outnumber them. The Wolf People have iron arrow points and guns. The Horse People have no advantage."

Speaks Twice said, "You have not yet seen them ride," but he spoke under his breath, for he did not wish to offend his elders.

The *Noomah* rode within range of the *Inday*. An *Inday* warrior drew a bow. Another raised a gun to his shoulder. But the *Noomah* warriors scattered, seemingly into chaos. Horseback rode east, into the sun, followed by Whip. Shaggy Hump and Echo rode west, but soon curled back toward the pueblo and fell into the tracks of Horseback and Whip. They thundered around the front of the *Inday* band, causing panic among the warriors who had all gathered behind their women and children in a defensive stance.

A warrior aimed an arrow at Horseback, but Shaggy Hump veered in toward the bowman with a war cry. He drew the attention of the *Inday* bowman, then veered away again, and Horseback continued to circle the enemy band. He galloped his horse among a group of frightened boys and struck three with his bow.

Whip peeled away from the circle and rode back toward the pueblo, only to fall into the circle again behind Shaggy Hump and Echo. The riding continued, the Horse People traveling like antelopes, like hawks. Horseback completed the circle, then stopped to notch an arrow and let a shrill war cry rattle up his throat.

His warriors joined him for a moment, then all four were riding again, circling, darting in toward the Inday, who scrambled to cover all sides of their band at once. The Inday warriors with horses had dismounted and turned their ponies into the middle of the band where some old men were holding them.

Horseback found a lone warrior on one side of the enemy band and rode straight toward him, somehow urging even more speed from his mount. Other Inday warriors began to move to this lone man's aid until the other three Horse People warriors angled in, shooting arrows from their ponies.

The Inday defense froze for a mere moment—all the time Horseback needed to overtake the warrior he had singled out. He rode his pony directly toward the warrior. The Inday waited with his bow strung, expecting Horseback to leap from the animal and fight. Instead, Horseback made his pony run over the enemy warrior. The Inday stabbed the horse in the shoulder with his arrow, but not deeply.

The pony wheeled with incredible quickness, and Horseback used his pogamoggan on the warrior, knocking him onto his rear. As the Inday warrior tried to get up, Horseback grabbed him by the hair that grew out of one side of his head, then gathered a shock of his mount's mane with the same hand and began to pull the warrior farther away from his kinsmen.

Echo had thrown the Inday band into turmoil by riding into the midst of it, stampeding the Inday horses, beating the old men holding them with the shaft of his lance. Whip and Shaggy Hump were still circling, darting near to shoot arrows, keeping the Inday resistance scattered.

From the roof of the pueblo, Speaks Twice saw Echo drive the captured ponies from the Inday band, joining Horseback, followed soon by Whip and Shaggy Hump. A woman in the Inday band began wailing, and Speaks Twice presumed this woman to be the wife of the warrior Horseback was dragging away.

Speaks Twice watched in awe as Horseback's war pony dragged the warrior away, his legs and arms writhing under the blows of Horseback's club. Echo galloped by at full speed and, in view of the Inday band, ran his lance through the warrior's stomach, leaving the weapon halfway through the enemy. The wailing reached a hideous crescendo as Horseback dragged the victim still farther away.

Speaks Twice felt his whole body seize with tension as he watched. It was Whip who rode by the dying warrior next, slashing with a knife even as

Horseback continued to belabor the head and face of the *Inday* warrior with his club. The warrior's legs dragged now, but his arms still groped, trying to ward off the merciless blows.

Now Horseback stopped, let his war club dangle from his wrist. He drew his flint knife and made a slash across the forehead of the *Inday* warrior, releasing a curtain of blood. A musket fired from the *Inday* band, but the invisible ball hummed harmlessly past the *Noomahs* and kicked dust into the air beyond. Horseback's mount lurched forward between his heels and jerked the scalp away from the writhing warrior's skull. The horseman hacked with his knife as the scalp peeled away, freeing the places that clung. When enough scalp had come free, Horseback made a final swipe with his jagged blade, and the *Inday* warrior fell facedown.

Speaks Twice watched in mute horror as the scalped man attempted to stand, in spite of the blood in his eyes and the lance shaft piercing his body. Shaggy Hump shot an arrow into the dying *Inday*, pinning him to the ground. He shot another arrow, and another, until the shafts rose from the warrior's body like porcupine quills.

The wind whipped stinging sand over the roof of the pueblo again, and Speaks Twice smelled a foul dust in his nostrils, felt it in his lungs. He glanced at the elders, their mouths open as they stared over the field of battle. The wailing streamed from the *Inday* band, mingling with the scalp yells of the *Noomah*. The scalp was on the end of Shaggy Hump's lance now, flying high. Whip was making his pony ride over and over the body of the dead *Inday* warrior.

"My fathers," Speaks Twice said, his voice shaking. "I must go now. I must ride with the Horse People. I must take them to the Metal Men."

Silence gripped the elders. Finally, Whirlwind turned to Speaks Twice. "Take the sacred road. The spirits will protect you. Be wise, Speaks Twice. Do not anger these Horse People against us."

28

Four sleeps from Tachichichi, two great mountains rose up from the plains, like sacred lodges large enough for the dwelling of the thunderbirds. The *Tiwas* called these peaks the Breasts of Mother Earth.

Looking upon the two snowy summits from the beautiful rolling grasslands under the hooves of his pony, Horseback became suddenly consumed with joy. He would rather die today than live fifty winters in the harsh hills of home having never seen these new places. The things he felt here made him believe that Sound-the-Sun-Makes was speaking to him, telling him to gather many horses and weapons, and lead his people to these rich lands of buffalo and grass and rivers and mountains and endless places to ride.

The Breasts of Mother Earth were unmistakable and gave Horseback much confidence that his trail to the villages of the white people was the right one. He remembered every river, every mountain range, and every pass from the map the *Tiwas* had made for him back at the buffalo hunting camp, and he knew he was only two or three sleeps from the Metal Men if the searchers continued to travel well. He also knew that he was about to cross into the country of the *Yutas*, and that he could easily encounter large warrior bands of these enemies of the True Humans.

Horseback felt glad that Speaks Twice had come with his party of searchers. The *Tiwa* were not at war with the *Yutas*, and Speaks Twice could help prevent a fight. Also, Speaks Twice would make the Metal Men know that he and his searchers had come in peace.

Now, riding close to Horseback as he looked at the Breasts of Mother Earth, Speaks Twice made signs warning of *Yutas*. For these past four suns on the trail, Speaks Twice had spent much time teaching Horseback many hand signs. This slowed the pace of the searchers, but Horseback thought it important to be able to communicate on these strange plains should he lose his interpreter for any reason.

Speaks Twice gave a warning in the language of hand signs: "The plains around the Breasts of Mother Earth are favored hunting grounds of the *Yutas*." Horseback acknowledged the warning, yet brushed it aside as if it meant nothing.

"My father," he said, as Shaggy Hump rode up to his side. "We have ridden long in the sight of Father Sun. Now we must move like spirit-deer in the shadow of tall trees."

His own talk sounded good to him, for he had thought through each word on the long day's ride.

As Father Sun buried his warm face between the Breasts of Mother Earth, Horseback's party came over a roll in the grassy plains and beheld a line of dark green timber tumbling down from the slopes. Knowing they might easily have been sighted by lookouts in the mountains, they made their horses trot, hoping to gain the cover of the trees undetected.

With the timber still as far away as a turkey could travel in one flight, a motion of some kind caught Horseback's eye where the timber began at the base of the southernmost mountain. He jerked back on his reins to halt his party as a line of mounted *Yuta* warriors, eleven strong, streamed from the trees and galloped toward a point halfway between Horseback's party, and the timber.

"Our enemies!" he said, feeling Echo, Whip, Shaggy Hump, and Speaks

Twice stop even with him on each hand. He watched the tails of the *Yuta* horses stream like black smoke whipped in the wind, hurrying to cut him off from the cover of timber. "They ride well," he said.

Shaggy Hump looked at him, a puzzled expression on his face. "My son, you should watch the ground before you as you ride with the sun at your back. Even your shadow rides better than our enemies."

This filled Horseback with confidence as he watched the *Yutas* rein their ponies to a stop on the plains between his searchers and the line of trees. He felt spirits in his stomach and in his heart. He began to hear the voice of Sound-the-Sun-Makes, and felt upon his face and bare chest the fire of Father Sun, sinking low now between the Breasts of Mother Earth.

"I will make talk with them," Speaks Twice offered.

But suddenly Horseback's voice burst loose in a wild spirit-song, and his mount flinched, leaping toward the party of *Yutas*. Leaving his bow unstrung in his quiver, Horseback rode on with his shield on one arm and his lance cradled in the other. He noticed that the ground here sounded different under a charge—better than the ground of his home country.

As he watched over the lunging head of his pony, he saw the *Yutas* slip from their mounts and thought how foolish these enemies were—like the *Inday*—to remove themselves from the power of their four-leggeds. He charged directly at the *Yutas* until he moved within the range of their arrows, then swerved to his left, beginning the circle he would ride around them. Hurtling in a curve cut through the waving grass, he skirted the shadow of the southern breast of the earth, and felt his mount taking on his great joy of moving like an antelope over new ground.

The defiant song of his spirit-protectors screamed up his throat again, lending the pony an even greater speed, when an arrow flew like a shooting star from the gathering of *Yutas*. Though Horseback knew in an instant that this arrow would fall well behind him, he flung himself to the side of his pony away from the enemy and slipped his arm into the loop slung under the neck and woven into the mane.

As the arrow passed behind him, he clung to the hot neck of the mare, his leg slung over her back, his lance lying across her withers. He had moved onto the western curve of the sacred circle. He felt the sun upon his shoulders, and heard the voice of Sound-the-Sun-Makes behind him: a great crackling and rumbling of fire, a roaring of wind and medicine-smoke, a thundering of storm and avalanche and all that was powerful. It was at this moment that Horseback chanced to look under the neck of the mare and saw her shadow. He saw nothing of himself in the image that lunged and changed fantastically across the grass and the ground. His spirit had leapt into the heart of the beast that carried him, and he was, himself, horse, as well as Horseback.

Pulling himself up by the mane of his mount, he let his soul leap from the body of the pony. He rode high, watching the *Yutas* for more arrows. He beheld, spread upon the plains to the east, a sight so glorious that it almost looked like a vision.

He had ridden into the valley of the shadow of the Breasts of Mother Earth. As he made the northern curve of his sacred circle, heading east, the dark shade of the two mountains stretched far to the eastern horizon and forever beyond. Horseback's own shadow was long now before him, like that of a giant spirit-warrior. He raised his arms and screamed his battle song as the enemy passed by to his right. Ahead, his own party of searchers waited in the orange light for his return and the closing of the sacred circle.

His enemies, his friends, the plains, the grass, himself, his shadow, his horse—they all stood in a swath of rich reddish-yellow light as Father Sun kissed Mother Earth between her breasts. And now the circle closed, and Horseback was powerful, and everyone under the gaze of Father Sun knew this, including the *Yutas*. A warrior rode out from the party of enemies, as Horseback rejoined the searchers.

"One comes to talk," Shaggy Hump said.

Horseback left the searchers once again to meet this warrior halfway between the two parties. Approaching the *Yuta* rider, he counted three kill feathers whipping behind the warrior's head.

Bad Camper rode close enough that Horseback might have struck with his lance. Instead, he raised a hand in friendship and addressed Bad Camper, saying, "Brother of my father's second wife." But he said this in his own tongue, so that Bad Camper would not understand.

"You have ridden far from your own country," Bad Camper replied.

"As I must. I obey my great vision. We wish to cross your country. We wear no paint on our faces. Our horses wear no feathers in their tails. Our arrow points carry no barbs."

Bad Camper studied Horseback for a long moment, then glanced at the party of searchers. "I know what you seek. I have been to that place to trade. The white men will not trade their ponies."

"I know little of white men. I have seen only one. He was ugly, his face covered with hair and his head bald. If they trade, that is good. If they do not, it is like wind through the grass to me. I only go there to obey my vision."

The sun plunged beyond the west, leaving both warriors in the shadow of the earth. The air was growing cool so quickly that they could feel it. This was a poor time to fight.

"Do you carry a good lodge on the pole-drag behind that pony?" Bad Camper asked.

"Yes."

"We must raise it in a sacred manner. I have tobacco. We will smoke a truce, and you will cross my country with me to the villages of the white men."

When Bad Camper turned back to his party, Horseback let his mouth spread wide in a smile. He felt his power growing stronger. Sound-the-Sun-Makes had surely blessed this journey. Scarcely now could he hear the voice of his naming father, Spirit Talker, warning of destruction that great medicine could bring.

PART II

▲▲▲▲▲▲▲▲▲▲▲▲

Metal Men

New Mexico, 1705

▲▲▲▲▲

29

▼▼▼▼▼

Jean L'Archeveque emerged from his bedroom, struggling with the silk scarf and the silver pin he used to fix it under his chin. It was not his everyday garb. He preferred his flared riding pants, cotton shirt, and leather jacket to all this silk and puffery.

Entering the *sala*, he found the Pueblo servant girl, Tia, dusting the copper candlesticks with a strip of fleece. She looked at him, smiled, and laid the fleece aside to help him with the scarf. She was a willing servant. Especially in bed, he thought, remembering last night.

"You look like a king," Tia said.

"I feel like a fool. Look at these ridiculous sleeves." He shook the huge billows of cloth on either arm as Tia pinned the scarf for him. "A man could store a month's provisions in there."

She laughed dutifully. "Where are you going, so fancy?"

"I dine at the *Casas Reales* tonight, with *Capitán* Lujan, Fray Ugarte, and Governor Del Bosque himself."

"It is my pleasure to serve such an important master," Tia said, playfully smoothing the spotless white blouse Jean L'Archeveque saved for important occasions.

He smiled at her briefly, but only with one side of his mouth. "Are the boys in bed?"

"Yes."

"Did they say their prayers?"

"They didn't want to, but I made them."

"I hope they prayed for their father's soul, for I am tempted by such a wicked servant girl." He led Tia to the door that opened out into the *placita*, and gave her rear a swat with his palm as he sent her outside. "Have Paniagua saddle the stallion."

"Whatever you wish," she said, dancing away across the *placita*, her eyes glinting back at him.

A small tarnished mirror hung beside the door, suspended from a peg sticking out of the adobe wall. He peered into it to see what kind of job Tia had done with the scarf. "You damn Frenchmen are all alike," he said to himself, exaggerating his acquired Spanish accent. "Lascivious rascals." He chuckled as he fluffed the silk. Then he found his own eyes in the mirror, and his smile slipped away like the cold plunge of an avalanche down a mountainside.

He didn't often notice the tattoos after all these years, but sometimes they startled him when he looked at his own reflection, for he might not even have thought of them in weeks. The lines like black bloodstains dripping from the corners of his mouth might have been hidden by a beard, but nothing could conceal the dark mask around his eyes. He knew that when he blinked, the tattooed eyelids flashed like dark and empty sockets, handy for scattering pesky children or striking fear into the hearts of superstitious peons. Still, there were times when he wished he could just wash his face and see nothing but clean flesh.

The tattoos also tended to have a negative effect on Jean's matrimonial aspirations. There were not many eligible women at this remote outpost of civilization to begin with, and although Jean L'Archeveque increasingly became a man of substance in the so-called Kingdom of New Mexico, not many young brides-to-be cared to spend enough time with the tattooed widower to begin to see beyond his bizarre countenance.

In the mirror, over his shoulder, he saw the portrait of his late wife hanging on the *sala* wall. Some of the superstitious peons and Indian servants were afraid of this portrait, especially Paniagua, the stable man, who said, "The eyes, they follow me when I go across the room. The soul, she lives in that wall!"

But Jean knew the poor fool was wrong. Maria was gone, body and soul. Her laughter, her temper, her warmth, her impatience, her scent, her caress, her lust for love and life. Gone, gone, gone. He was still in love with her, though she had been five years in the grave. She was gone now longer than they had been married, for they had shared only three years together. Their two sons looked less like her every day, for they were growing up, looking more like tough little boys and therefore less like their sweet Spanish mother. With Maria, Jean had never thought about his tattoos.

He considered it likely that he might never find another woman to marry, certainly he would not have another like Maria. Not that he lacked for female companionship. There was Tia, after all, and a couple of prostitutes he visited in Santa Fe now and then, and the occasional serving wench of some friend or trading partner. Women of the lower classes were often attracted by the tattoos. As for matrimonial prospects of proper social standing however, the outlook remained one of gloom.

He placed his knuckles on the rough pine table carved by an *Indio* novice at the mission and leaned closer to the old mirror, making his eyelids droop sleepily. "Damn tattoos," he muttered. But now Jean L'Archeveque remembered his dinner with the governor and drew upon his French bearing to bolster his spirits. "Stop whining," he said, chastising himself. "Count yourself lucky. You have two handsome sons, a fine hacienda. You had no choice about the tattoos. You have survived where a hundred others did not."

This last was an understatement, for the death toll of the La Salle expedition had been 135 when Jean lost count. He had been a mere youth of thirteen when he first met the great world explorer, the Sieur de La Salle, on the West Indies island of Espanola, at the port of Petit-Goave. The Sieur de La Salle had anchored there, Jean's home village, to make final preparations for his next expedition onto the wild continent of the New World. Oh, the stories told about the world explorer in the old pirate town of Petit-Goave. Jean and his young friends would follow the great man around the docks and the stores and warehouses, fascinated just to be in his presence.

La Salle let it be known in Petit-Goave that his purpose was to sail past Spain's Cuba, into the Gulf of Mexico, and thence to the mouth of the Colbert River, which he sometimes called the Messipe, after the name he had learned from savages. To young Jean's amazement, it was told that La Salle had once floated all the way down this great wild river from Canada to the Gulf of Mexico. From Canada! A place so far away in young Jean's imagination that it had made his thoughts swirl like hurricane winds. The idea that La Salle had sailed to Petit-Goave from France was not so mind-boggling, for this was commonly done. But, Canada!

Once he sailed to the mouth of the Messipe with this new expedition, La Salle intended to establish a fort and forge a new French colony, taking possession of the mainland for the crown of France. Anyone joining the colony would enjoy the ownership of immeasurable tracts of land, the protection of French soldiers, the full support of the crown, and the blessing of the Jesuit brotherhood. And though La Salle himself did not promise it, there were rumors of riches on the mainland: gold and silver, pearls and furs. Bursting with a boyish desire for adventure, young Jean L'Archeveque had joined the expedition.

The 180 colonists—most of them illiterate French peasants—sailed on four ships: the *La Belle*, the *Amiable*, the *St. François*, and the *Joly*. They carried horses, seeds for crops, tools, weapons, and kegs of gun powder. From the beginning, disaster seemed to descend upon them like a gull on fish bait. The Sieur de La Salle would not admit it, but he could not find the mouth of the Messipe. Goupil, mapmaker for the expedition, explained this to Jean with a length of hemp line, the end of which had become frayed.

"The mouth of such a great river is like this rope unbraiding," Goupil said, schooling Jean in the shade of the mainsail, "and so it issues into the sea in many tiny threads, any one of which resembles no more than a brook to a passing vessel."

Finally, the expedition sailed into an uncharted bay and began building Fort St. Louis on the banks of some small river, obviously not the great Messipe Jean had heard so much about. While the planting and building continued, La Salle took the ablest men back out to sea on the *La Belle* to search for the big river. The *Joly* sailed for France with a skeleton crew. A storm ran the *Amiable* aground, though her timbers were salvaged to use in building the fort. Pirates stole the *St. François*. Now, unless La Salle returned with the bark called *La Belle*, the colonists would be stranded.

More ill fortune beset the colony. Two men drowned—one trying to retrieve a skiff that had drifted into the bay, the other getting tangled while gathering in fishing nets. Another was killed and eaten by a huge alligator. Some children, friends and playmates of Jean, were carried away by painted savages within site of the fort. Some hunters were murdered by natives shooting arrows from ambush. Another was gored to death by a wounded buffalo. Then the fever struck, and the death toll began to mount in earnest.

Oh, the misery. Jean had not seen the likes of it before or since, and prayed every night that he never would. Even here, almost twenty years later, in his comfortable hacienda situated in the high, healthy climate of Santa Fe, in the Kingdom of New Mexico, he could still hear the moaning of the sick and smell the stench of death along that dank, mosquito-ridden coastline of brackish water and slime pits.

They died daily—men, women, and children—while others fell sick, taking to their beds. Whole families perished, member by member. A man strong enough one day to pack a hundred pounds of buffalo meat on his back would awake the next day unable to stand, vomiting blood, moaning in agony. A few—very few—survived the high fever and recovered. Most died within days.

One day, a lone member of the *La Belle* crew returned to Fort St. Louis: a peculiar little man named Minime, La Salle's personal valet. To the distress of the colonists, Minime reported that the *La Belle* had run aground. Many of the horses had drowned. The Sieur de La Salle and his men had gone overland to the northeast, still searching for the Messipe. Minime had become separated from the party and had wandered back after many days of harrowing travel. Goupil, the mapmaker, suspected that Minime had deserted, but the valet claimed to have become lost accidentally, returning to the fort under great peril.

Minime was a rude little buffoon whom Goupil despised. Minime's childishness repulsed even Jean, who was hardly more than a child himself. Constantly twitching and jerking and making grotesque faces, Minime considered himself quite the jester, and unfortunately, many of the colonists encouraged his rude foolishness.

In Goupil's presence, Minime was forever convulsing and twisting, his eyes rolling horribly back and eyelids fluttering, choking and spitting froth, writhing on the ground like a dying snake. Jean could tell the fool did this only to antagonize Goupil. One day, he asked the mapmaker why Minime always acted the fool in his presence.

"I once suffered from the falling sickness," Goupil said. "I would have fits. Minime witnessed my suffering more than once on our previous voyages with the Sieur de La Salle. He mocks me, though I am cured now. A surgeon in Paris opened my skull and removed part of my brain. I haven't had a fit since, but Minime continues to torment me. He calls me 'Sieur Hole-in-the-Head.'"

During the voyage from Petit-Goave, Jean had seen the Sieur de La Salle beat his valet for such displays, but afterward Minime would only laugh, then hop about crying, "Ouch! Oh, mercy! Ouch, ouch!" in the most convincing manner, as if still enduring the beating, though the Sieur de La Salle had already gone away. Then he would laugh again and go on with his mocking.

Once, Jean saw Minime strut up to Goupil, shouting, "Sieur Hole-in-the-Head, I have completed my inventory of the storehouse!" This at the very top of his lungs.

"Don't scream," said Goupil, maintaining his composure in the face of the fool.

"I won't!" screamed Minime. "I will not!" His voice became maniacal. "I will not scream!"

Goupil's dignity in the face of such mockery made Jean admire him. He was a good man, a hard worker. The mapmaker schooled Jean in reading and writing, and tried to ease the suffering of others in the fort. Aside from Father Membre, Jean admired Goupil more than any other personage in the colony.

But it was still Father Membre who had earned Jean's highest admiration for solitary devotion to duty after the death of Father Desmanville. As the fever continued to consume the bodies of the afflicted, Father Membre stayed with them day and night, bathing them, feeding the few who could eat, praying over them, comforting in any way he could. They were friends: Goupil, the mapmaker; Membre, the priest; and Jean L'Archeveque, the young adventurer. The two older men served as the youth's mentors in the terrible surrounds of Fort St. Louis. Their influence stayed with Jean even now, almost twenty years later.

Despite the efforts of Goupil and Membre, the cemetery outside the log palisades of the fort began to grow. Daily, friends and relatives of the departed would go to the graveyard to wail and mourn. Their piteous cries served only to depress Jean all the more. He did not understand the convulsing when it began, but Goupil explained it to him.

"It started with Fleury," Goupil said. "Fleury had the fever. He threw himself on the grave of Father Desmanville, hoping for a miracle. Strange to say, he rose and began to improve. In a few days, he had recovered. Hearing this, others began to fall on the grave to rub themselves in the dirt. They grovel in the dirt daily, and their writhings become more and more extreme. Minime mocks them, vicious scoundrel that he is!"

Goupil termed them "convulsionaries." Every evening, Jean would watch them squirm in the dirt of the cemetery as Minime mimicked their antics. Then, one day, as Minime mocked and chided the convulsionaries, a seizure struck him. At first, Jean thought the buffoon was only tormenting Goupil again, as the mapmaker also looked on from the fort palisades. But the twitching and choking went on longer than any of Minime's former travesties. The dumbstruck convulsionaries gathered around as Minime's contortions continued in the dirt of the cemetery. His whole body would arch so violently that he would lift completely from the ground. Those gathered around him began to kneel and pray. Some began to convulse with Minime, so desperate were they for miracles.

After almost an hour, Minime's convulsions stopped. Recovering, he seemed strangely subdued and frightened. The incident only swelled the ranks of the convulsionaries, for many colonists considered Minime's fit an act of God. Minime emerged as a leader among the convulsionaries, and their ceremonies became more violent. They began whipping and beating each other, to "triumph with Christ through suffering," they chanted.

During the height of this convulsionary fervor, the Sieur de La Salle returned with only nineteen of the fifty men who had sailed with him on the ill-fated La Belle. Eleven had died of disease. Several had drowned in the bay. One had been eaten by an alligator while crossing a river. The others had become lost, or had deserted, or had been murdered by savages.

After sleeping a whole day, La Salle awoke and took charge of the fort. Once he had witnessed their antics, he banned the convulsionaries from further assembly and had a fence built around the graveyard to keep them out. Then he put the colonists to work cutting and hauling timbers to be used in building a new storehouse.

The commander's return seemed to give new purpose to the colony at first. A few days after his return, however, Goupil said to Jean, "My young friend, I am afraid for us all. The Sieur de La Salle has changed. I feared this before, but since his return I am sure. His mind is touched. One day he is the leader I followed down the great Messipe on the last voyage. The next day he is mad."

"I haven't seen him in two days," Jean answered. "He keeps himself in his quarters. I was afraid he had taken the fever."

"It is not the fever. It is the madness. Do you know what he does in there, Jean? While all around him is death and decay, while the sick moan, plagued by boils and lice? While our clothes fall away from us in tatters? While savages howl about us in the night? Do you know what he does?"

"No," Jean said.

"He is writing a play. A *play!*"

Jean thought perhaps it was Goupil who had gone mad, until the next day, when the Sieur de La Salle emerged from his quarters and announced that the new storehouse would be a playhouse instead.

Rehearsals began. La Salle assigned roles in the play he had authored to members of the colony. The Sieur de La Sablonniere, being the only member of the colony with theatrical experience, took the lead roll of Jason. There was a witch in the play, to be portrayed by La Salle's valet, Minime. Minime was made to wear a woman's dress for this role and would prance about effeminately behind La Salle's back, disrupting rehearsals.

One day, Jean was watching as the playwright caught his valet in this foolishness and began to beat him with a length of cane such as the troupe was using to construct the backdrop of the stage. As he flogged Minime mercilessly, the valet began to shout, "More! More! Yes! Harder! Good!" in the manner of the banned convulsionaries. La Salle was so enraged that he thrashed Minime until the cane was bloody.

On another day, Jean went to the smokehouse to add green wood to the fire and heard strange noises when he entered. Peering around a rack hung with buffalo carcasses curing for the winter, he saw a bald man named Henri Casaubon chastising a young woman named Madeleine with blows from a whip. Jean knew the man as a convulsionary, but never Madeleine, whom Jean considered a follower of Father Membre. Now her breasts and buttocks were bare, and she asked for more abuse as the man pinched the nipples of her breasts and whipped her buttocks. Then, as Jean watched from hiding, the bald man dropped his trousers and mounted the woman as if they both were dogs.

Bursting out of the smokehouse, he ran headlong into the dark, out beyond the protective palisades of the fort, though he knew painted savages might very well be waiting to capture or kill him there. He hid himself in a shadow, so confused and afraid of what he had seen that he could not think of telling it to anyone, not even Goupil nor Father Membre.

He could still hear the moans of the dying from where he hid. Then suddenly, the howl of natives arose from the woods, in their way of mimicking wolves and owls, and Jean knew he must remain hidden until dawn, or be captured. He could smell the rank air of the shallow graves in the cemetery. He was lost, never to know civilization again. The boats were all sunk. His commander had gone mad. The colonists—all of them as far as he knew— were secretly engaging in perverse mockeries of the Christian faith. The horror of the place called Fort St. Louis fell in on young Jean that night. But the worst was yet to come.

On New Year's Day, 1687, La Salle's troupe of actors performed his play. After all these years, Jean could not remember the title of the play, nor the plot, if indeed it had possessed one. He remembered only two characters: Jason, played by the Sieur de La Sablonniere, and the witch, played by Minime. The morning of the play, the Sieur de La Sablonniere awoke very ill with a high fever. La Salle insisted that he must perform anyway, though the man could barely stand.

Only one scene from the play remained in Jean's mind through all his trials since that day. In it, the witch, played by Minime, was to cut the throat of Jason, played by the ailing Sieur de La Sablonniere. Then, the witch was to bring Jason back to life by pouring a magical potion on his wound. This murder of Jason was to be performed with the backs of the actors to the audience. Otherwise, the spectators would notice the lack of blood from the neck wound, diminishing the dramatic effect.

When the witch appeared, many of the audience members around Jean gasped, or drew back in fear, so successful was Minime in his portrayal. Few of the colonists had ever seen a play, other than the kind performed by rank street actors. Jean noticed that in contrast to Minime's spirited performance, the Sieur de La Sablonniere was so weak from the fever that his lines could barely be heard.

And so the audience sat in transfixion as Minime's witch stalked up behind the protagonist, grabbed him, and brandished the knife. One colonist bolted from his seat in fear that the whole thing was real, that Sablonniere would be sacrificed since he was probably dying anyway. Now Minime turned Sablonniere away from the audience and feigned the stroke of the knife across Jason's throat with such a convincing flourish that women screamed and men gasped. Sablonniere found his task of collapsing on stage so natural in his weakened state that he appeared truly dead. Minime tossed the knife aside and reached for his next prop, a bowl of the magical elixir. This he poured across the hidden wound of Jason and performed sundry witchlike incantations over the corpse.

When Sablonniere stirred, Jean L'Archeveque heard commotion and felt nervous movement all around him. The poor sickened actor was so weak from fever that his resurrection seemed most convincing. He drew himself laboriously to his feet, and staggered with his head bowed forward. One superstitious woman ran from the playhouse at this moment, another began to sob in fear. About half the members of the audience rose from the seats and seemed on the verge of bolting.

La Salle, who had been sitting in the front row with his script, prompting the amateur thespians, turned his back on the stage to admonish those in the crowd who would interrupt the performance with their silly superstitious outbursts. It was at this moment, with months of fear and despair poised to fall off the shoulders of the beleaguered colonists, that the treacherous Minime strayed from La Salle's script. He shrieked—utterly screaming his lungs out—and began to twitch on stage. All through the audience, screams and convulsionary antics erupted with the suddenness of a lightning bolt. The bald man, Henri Casaubon, whom Jean had seen mount Madeleine in the smokehouse, leapt from the audience to the stage, and people were jostled against one another.

Feeling a sudden instinctive dread, Jean tried to escape the playhouse, but everyone was moving at once. Someone convulsing on the floor grabbed Jean's leg as he tried to step over. He caught glimpses as the room seemed to spin around him: Minime twisting profanely on stage, his mouth frothing; the Sieur de La Sablonniere pulling Minime's knife from a wound in his stomach where it had been plunged by Henri Casaubon; La Salle falling forward as someone struck him on the back of the head with a playhouse stool.

Then Jean saw Goupil. Poor Goupil, the kind mapmaker, whose right arm was curling strangely around on itself, whose mouth was gobbling at something nonexistent, whose neck was twisting piteously, whose eyes were rolling back as he fell across the prone body of a convulsionary. Poor Goupil, who had thought himself cured of the terrible falling sickness now awakened by this horrid spectacle in this strange land of death and misery.

Jean kicked himself free. He saw Father Membre trying to help Goupil, but someone knocked the priest down with a pole. Jean fought his way through the madness—women baring their breasts, lifting their skirts, begging for whippings; men grinning as they used pieces of cane from the backdrop to flog those who convulsed at their feet; stools and theatrical props flying everywhere across the playhouse. Jean struck the crazed convulsionaries aside and reached Father Membre, pulling him to his feet.

"We must help Goupil," the father said, his face all bloody. "He swallows his tongue in the clutches of his fits."

Together, they reached Goupil and dragged him aside. Membre knew how to help the mapmaker, prying his jaws apart with a stick and forcing his hand in Goupil's mouth to keep the tongue from blocking Goupil's windpipe. Jean stood guard with a leg broken from a stool as Membre tended the fallen mapmaker.

Six colonists deserted the fort that day, preferring to trust their luck to the mercies of savages. The Sieur de La Sablonniere died a few days later, of his wound, or the fever, or both. Somehow, La Salle escaped assassination in the playhouse. Oddly, he made no mention of the thwarted theatrical production after the disaster, made no attempt to punish any malefactor's behavior. Instead, he announced his intention to make a new overland trek. He would take half of the surviving fifty colonists, leaving the weakest members at the fort. He would strike out to the northeast. His destination: Canada.

Canada! The very idea made Jean L'Archeveque's head ache. La Salle had not even been able to find the Messipe to the northeast, much less follow it for league after league through hundreds of nations of savages to the far-off and fabled outposts of Canada! Yet, when Jean was ordered to join the overland expedition, he secretly rejoiced. He would prefer even death in the wilderness to life in this twisted aberration of civilized society called Fort St. Louis, on the coast of the Gulf of Mexico, in the land the Spanish called Tejas, after one of the nations of savages who lived there.

The day of departure from Fort St. Louis was a day of heart wrenching sadness, for Jean and Goupil had to leave their friend, Father Membre. He was to stay behind to care for the sick and dying at the fort while the healthiest colonists made the journey with La Salle.

Goupil embraced the priest and said, "We will send relief by sea the moment we reach Canada."

Membre smiled sadly. "You mustn't make such grand promises, my friend. Send only your prayers. That is all I ask of you, and all I can promise in return. Go in faith."

What followed were two months of marching through landscapes of open plains, woods, marshes, hills, and swamps; crossing countless flooded rivers; hacking through canebrakes and thickets of underbrush. Rain chilled the men day and night, and turned the whole wild world to mud.

Jean, like the others, possessed only bits and pieces of clothing. His pants were from his home in Petit-Goave, now patched liberally on the knees and seat with deer skin. His shirt was fashioned from salvaged sailcloth. His shoes were raw buffalo hide, which he was obliged to keep forever wet if he did not want them to harden around his feet like iron.

There were days when the rain fell too unrelentingly to allow travel. On such days, Jean would shiver under the shelter of a raw buffalo hide. He would sit there and watch the horses steam—the only two horses left to La Salle's great expedition.

On good days, the party would make as many as twelve leagues, though seven was closer to the average. Some days were pleasantly passed over oak-studded plains teeming with buffalo, antelope, and deer. But spells of warm and dry weather seldom lasted more than a few days.

The Frenchmen encountered many villages of savages as they journeyed slowly northeast. Most treated the sojourners with astonishment and reverence, literally embracing them as they entered the villages. The cottages of these people resembled ovens to Jean, each made of poles stuck in the ground and bent inward to form a dome, then covered with buffalo hides.

Often, the savages mistook their pale-skinned visitors for gods or spirits.

They would bring their sick and wounded to the Frenchmen and the Sieur de La Salle would have his men do what they could for the ailing natives.

They came upon one village that the Sieur de La Salle had visited on his previous journey only to find the inhabitants nearly decimated by the fever. The suffering and dying was like that of Fort St. Louis, and cast Jean into a somber frame of mind.

Goupil shared the mood. "So many heathens ushered into eternity with souls unfit to enter the kingdom of heaven," he said looking back on the village the day the party left. "The thought fills my heart with anguish."

"What will happen to their souls?" Jean asked.

"They will drift forever in oblivion, if indeed they do not roast eternally in the fires of perdition. Poor, wretched, savage heathens."

Next, they came to a village of people they named Weepers, for the people sobbed with joy when the Frenchmen arrived, as if they had been awaited for generations. Only after their eyes had run dry of tears did the Weepers present a wounded man who had been shot with an arrow in battle, asking that the travelers cure him. The Sieur de La Salle, who had some surgical instruments with him, cut and probed in the man's chest and finally extracted the flint arrowhead. When the warrior recovered, the Frenchmen found many other sick or lame Weepers desiring cures.

The Sieur de La Salle had insisted upon bringing the worst troublemakers of the colony with him on this search for far-off Canada, to prevent them from further corrupting Fort St. Louis in his absence. Chief among them were Henri Casaubon, the bald convulsionary who had escaped punishment for stabbing Sablonniere during the play, and Minime, the valet. These two convinced the gullible savages that they were healers of great power. They would blow upon the sick or wounded or make the sign of the cross over them to cure them. Oddly enough, these useless procedures greatly impressed the savages to the point that some actually believed they had been cured, and they would follow the posturing healers around the village, begging cures.

"The heresy!" Goupil hissed. "They make the sign of the cross! Look at Minime and Casaubon, painted like savages!"

"Why does the Sieur de La Salle let them go on with such a charade?" Jean asked. "They should be stopped."

"Yes, they should be, my young friend, but the Sieur de La Salle has lost his will to lead. He punishes anyone only when he himself feels morose or angry. He sits all day and converses in signs with the Weepers, asking time and time again about his wretched River Messipe, of which they know nothing, while Minime and Casaubon gain more and more followers among the savages."

"Goupil," Jean said, lowering his voice, "Minime and Casaubon have more followers among the savages than the Sieur de La Salle has among Frenchmen."

"Yes, my young friend. I am aware of the danger. Even among Frenchmen, there are many malcontents who follow Minime and Casaubon. Only the officers and a few others remain loyal to La Salle. I fear for us all."

Many of the Weepers followed the explorers on to the next village. With the false healers leading them, the Weepers demanded payment from the village in exchange for cures, and took such payment by force from the lodges of the inhabitants, virtually sacking the village. Now, the inhabitants of this village followed the crusade on to the next, to plunder it in turn, thus recouping their losses. In this manner, the ranks of savages swelled, and each village encountered was ransacked, while La Salle looked on helplessly.

After a month of such travel, the Frenchmen came upon a village whose chief was none other than the Sieur d'Autray, who had deserted the year before. Jean was appalled to see that d'Autray had gone so mad among these savages that he had forgotten he had ever been a Christian. He could not speak French, nor did he recognize any of his former friends. His face and arms were streaked with horrible tattoos. The power he wielded over the natives, however, was absolute, and this impressed Jean.

"He has taken that squaw as his wife!" Goupil hissed in disgust. "She hasn't the shame to cover her breasts! The flirtatious manner of these wretched heathen women makes me ill. Who can say why d'Autray would risk his immortal soul for such a life? Neither shall you make marriages with heathens or bow down to their gods!"

After leaving d'Autray's village, three men deserted, and Jean believed these three had left to take up wives among the savages and become chiefs, as d'Autray had. Then one morning, the Frenchmen awoke to find all of the savage followers of Minime and Casaubon gone, though the two healers themselves remained in camp. This had astonished Jean at the time, but now, looking back on it, he realized that the natives had sensed the division among the Frenchmen and knew only violence could follow.

By this time, Jean and Goupil had begun to think of the members of the expedition in terms of two rival parties: La Salle's "Loyals" and the "Malcontents" of Minime and Casaubon.

"I suppose we are Loyals," Jean said.

"No. We must remain neutral as long as possible. If forced to choose, I must serve La Salle, as I have these twenty years."

"Then, so will I."

"No, boy. If we come to violence, you must run and hide in the forest. Wait and see which party emerges the victor. If the Loyals win, rejoin the party. If the Malcontents gain power, you must trust your luck among the savages. Perhaps you can return to Father Membre at Fort St. Louis. Perhaps you can find the outposts that the Spaniards maintain in the west."

"But, we are at war with the Spaniards."

"We are at war with ourselves!" Goupil snapped. "I am sorry," he said, rubbing his head as he glanced around. "You are young. The Spaniards will have mercy on you. Tell them how we have suffered, and they will have pity on you."

Goupil made Jean promise he would do this.

For two more weeks the Frenchmen trudged northeast. They came to a village of natives who laughed at La Salle when he asked about the River Messipe. The weather warmed, green buds and grasses began to sprout, but mosquitos tormented the men day and night. La Salle seldom spoke to the men, and morale sank ever deeper. The division between Loyals and Malcontents worsened.

Coming to a large and beautiful valley carved by a river of red water, the explorers camped for a few days. Jean was surprised to learn that La Salle had been to this place on his expedition of the previous year, naming it the River of Canoes. He had cached some beans and corn in a hollow tree a few leagues away. Accordingly, the explorer sent a party to retrieve the goods. The party included Jean and Goupil along with three known Malcontents: Minime, Casaubon, and a German named Hein.

"La Salle is testing us," Goupil whispered. "He sends us out with these Malcontents to determine whether or not we will remain loyal."

Arriving at the hollow tree, the men found that the cache of beans and grain had spoiled, for La Salle had failed to cover it sufficiently. Minime laughed at this, and mocked the absent La Salle, strutting about effeminately, pursing his lips and saying, "You complainers and whiners will be surprised when you see the cache of food that I, the Great La Salle, have left in yon hollow tree!" Turning to the mapmaker, the valet continued: "You, Sieur Hole-in-the-Head, get thee hither and fetch it!"

The Malconents laughed, but just then the German named Hein spotted some buffalo trailing into the valley. Hein, Casaubon, and Minime went upstream to shoot them, succeeding in killing three. Jean's spirits lifted as he and Goupil helped butcher the buffalo and roast the meat. But then, at this hopeful moment, an ill wind began to blow.

Sieur Moranget arrived from La Salle's main camp, riding the only horse left to the Frenchmen. Moranget, who was La Salle's nephew, began to accuse the buffalo hunters of trying to hoard the meat and keep it from the others at La Salle's camp. He was followed soon by the Loyals, Saget and Tesier, who arrived on foot. There was already bad blood between La Salle's nephew, Moranget, and the Malcontent, Casaubon. Jean didn't know what was behind it until that day in the valley of the River of Canoes, when Casaubon let his temper get the better of him.

"Shut your mouth, you bastard!" Casaubon shouted at the officer. "Minime, do you know what this stupid bastard did on the expedition last year?

He sent my brother back to the fort alone when he became ill. Alone! My brother was murdered by savages, but the real murderer sits there on that horse!"

"You insolent pile of shit!" Moranget shouted from the saddle. "I will see you flogged for such insult. My uncle will deal severely with you."

"Your uncle may kiss my ass, you stupid bastard!"

Later, Goupil pulled Jean aside and said in a hushed voice, "My friend, if they come to murder, remember your promise to me. You must take to the forest. If the Malcontents gain power, secure aid among the savages. Find your way back to Fort St. Louis, or to the Spanish outposts. Speak French to yourself every day. Do not make marriages with heathens. Do not end up like d'Autray, a tattooed savage."

"Save yourself and come with me," Jean begged.

"No. I must remain loyal to La Salle. If it comes to mutiny, and I am unable to save him, I will save myself, but I cannot go with you. I am old. The Spaniards would hang me as a spy, and perhaps you as well for being in my company."

"Then we will both return to Fort St. Louis."

"And wait for what? All of France has forgotten about that wretched fort. I must try to reach Canada and send aid for Father Membre—and you if you go there."

"Then I will go to Canada with you."

"No! Canada is seven hundred leagues. It is probably impossible to reach, but I must try. Your best chance is with the Spaniards in the west."

Through his decades on the wild continent, Jean L'Archeveque had heard many memorable sounds. Like the first bull elk he heard bugling in an echoey mountain basin, the first grass fire he heard popping and roaring across the tallgrass prairies, and the first Apache war cry he heard knifing through the fog of a riverbank. But the sound that awoke him that night long ago on the River of Canoes was the most unforgettable and horrible memory his ears had ever gathered in.

It was a thud like the stamping of a horse hoof, a crunch like someone breaking buffalo bones to get the marrow, a squish like a rawhide moccasin plunging into a mud hole. The sound came once, twice, then several more times, from more than one place, some nearer, some farther away. Rising in the dark of night and scrambling through underbrush to identify the strange sound, young Jean caught a glimpse of Minime standing with an axe in his hand, looking down. At Minime's feet lay the body of La Salle's nephew, Moranget, his head crushed in and bloody, brains and gore oozing onto the dirt. A quick glance around camp revealed the dead bodies of the other Loyals, Tesier and Saget, their heads also crushed by axes. Casaubon and the German Malcontent, Hein, were joining Minime, and celebrating their atrocity. Each carried a bloody axe.

Jean grabbed his bundle of possessions and fled into the timber along the river. That next day, he went hungry and watched from the timber. He saw the mutineers force Goupil to drag the corpses somewhere. He saw Casaubon leave for La Salle's camp, then return. He saw some sort of preparations being made by the excited murderers.

He was watching some eagles in the sky, attracted, no doubt, by the carrion smell of the buffalo kill, when he heard the shot. An eagle cartwheeled from the sky, its wing shattered. Glancing downstream, whence he had heard the shot, Jean saw La Salle coming on foot, black smoke still streaming from the muzzle of his musket. The jaunty explorer was virtually strutting, watching the eagle fall as he unknowingly approached the camp of the murderous Malcontents.

Jean spied Minime at the edge of the camp, gesturing idiotically to La Salle in one of his provocative mimes, twitching like a marionette at the mercy of some demented puppeteer. Near Minime, he saw another Malcontent—which he could not tell—crouching in some bushes, aiming a musket toward La Salle.

Now, farther down the river bank, between Minime and La Salle, Jean saw his friend Goupil step from some bushes where only Jean and La Salle could see him. Realizing that Goupil was risking his life in order to warn La Salle, Jean made up his mind to join the mapmaker in aiding La Salle and the Loyals.

Goupil cupped his hands around his mouth to shout, but the sound of the river overwhelmed any cry he might have made. Jean gathered himself to leap from the timber and wave at La Salle, but noticed that Goupil seemed suddenly paralyzed, staring at the ground. Was he grinning? The mapmaker's head twisted, and Jean saw his face, horribly distorted like that of a hanged man.

A shot erupted from the camp of the Malcontents. La Salle's head jerked back, and the explorer collapsed about the same time as Goupil—one dead, the other in the grips of the falling sickness.

Looking back on it, it seemed that the fit actually saved Goupil's life here, for if the Malcontents had seen him trying to warn La Salle, they certainly would have murdered the mapmaker, too. It was years before Jean heard what had become of Goupil after that murderous incident on the River of Canoes. First, came his life with the Raccoon-Eyed People.

He fled upstream after the murder of La Salle, and saw places no white man had ever seen before him. He came to a village of neat thatched huts, some of which stood on platforms head-high off the ground. It was a frightening thing to walk into this village alone, for Jean thought he might be tortured or eaten.

The first warriors who saw him walking into the village shouted and threw dirt in the air, which later Jean would learn was an invitation to do battle.

He made no menacing moves, trying to behave with the elan he had seen La Salle exhibit in entering the villages of strange natives.

At length he was approached, touched, embraced, and adorned with necklaces of shells and claws. The contents of his pack were of high interest to the Raccoon-Eyed People, particularly his strike-a-light, which shot sparks when struck by a flint.

He was given a place to sleep in one of the huts, on a bed of buffalo robes behind a curtain of deerskin. He ate with the people of this hut, learned from them. He was treated as a member of this family and seemed to be held in highest veneration by everyone in the village. Apparently, the Raccoon-Eyed People felt that to touch Jean's pale skin assured good luck. He was given a name and made to understand that the name meant stranger.

He tried to ask about the Spaniards in the west, but the Raccoon-Eyed People did not understand. When summer came, and Jean had been among these people for months, and had been happier with them than he had been since leaving Petit-Goave, he began to think he would live among them the rest of his life and never see another European. As everyone his age and older in this village was tattooed—men and women—Jean asked if he might earn his own tattoos.

An elaborate ceremony followed, lasting several days. Jean was lectured by elder warriors and medicine men, though he understood very little of the language of the Raccoon-Eyed People. There were dances and feasts. He was made to sweat and fast. He was given a red bean of some sort that made him sick and gave him fantastic visions of wild animals who spoke to him in a mixture of French and Indian dialects. The spirit-animals told him that the Great Creator of the Raccoon-Eyed People was the same as his God, and that God did not begrudge him praying to native spirits, so long as his prayers were for good and in opposition to evil. When Jean asked the spirits about his friends, Father Membre and Goupil, the spirits told him that he must trust the Great Creator to watch over them, for he would not see them again until the afterlife.

He awoke from this vision feeling very refreshed and relieved, though weak. Never again would he think of another nation of human beings as savages, as his friend Goupil had so often referred to these non-Christians. The vision he had received during his trance would forever change his idea of life, and whatever lay beyond. He was taken to a shaman who began the process of tattooing, which lasted for days and was accompanied by much prayer and smoke and chanting. The shaman would prick his skin with sharpened pieces of bone and rub powdered charcoal into the tiny wounds, eventually creating the raccoonlike mask that identified the people of this nation.

Soon, Jean understood that he was considered a medicine man himself, as sick or injured people began to come to him, seeking cures. He treated them with a combination of techniques he had seen La Salle and Minime use. La Salle had been something of an accomplished wilderness surgeon and physician. Minime, on the other hand, had used superstition to induce cures in his patients, blowing on them or making the sign of the cross over them, but such nonsensical treatments had only produced wonderful effects because of the natives' confidence in magic. By combining what little he knew of cures and treatments with the charlatan flourishes that so impressed the natives, Jean gradually became a noted healer.

The culture of the Raccoon-Eyed People was confusing, and indeed made Jean feel that he lived up to his name of Stranger. It seemed that everyone in the village was everyone else's brother or sister or mother or father. Sometimes a person would claim two or more mothers, and would refer to some of them as "greater mother" or "lesser mother." At length, Jean figured out that the people considered their cousins as brothers or sisters. Their mothers' sisters were also considered mothers. The fathers' brothers were considered fathers. A mother's older sister was called "greater mother" and her younger sister, "lesser mother."

He never did get the theology of the Raccoon-Eyed People completely figured out, and doubted that any of them did either. There was a great creator called Man-Never-Known-on-Earth who was invoked in prayers often sent up on clouds of smoke. The North Star was a fearsome spirit called the Light-Which-Stands-Still. There were goddesses of water and moonlight. The wind was sometimes a spirit unto itself, but sometimes merely the breath of the goddess, Mother Earth. It seemed to Jean that every living and nonliving thing or power or mystery was a god or goddess or spirit of some kind, benevolent or evil.

For all the mysteries of the Raccoon-Eyed Peoples' faith, however, Jean found their earthly existence simple and enjoyable. The men occasionally went off to do battle with enemies. Jean was never asked to join a war party, nor was he ridiculed for not participating, but he thought he might go some time as a healer and spiritual leader. Men of his village were seldom killed in battle, but wounds were common enough and desired by most of the warriors. When their husbands were away at war, wives would walk around in tattered dresses, refusing to bathe. But when their husbands returned, these women were treated to lavish ceremonial baths by other women and dressed in finery.

Every now and then a war party would bring back a scalp or two, or a horse the warriors had captured. The horses usually came from enemies in the south and west. Once, a warrior came riding home on a horse with a Spanish brand, and Jean wondered how far this horse could possibly have traveled. Moments like these—vague brushes with the civilizations of the Old World— prevented him from forgetting the ways he had left behind, and he would go off alone somewhere and whisper to himself in French all day.

The few horses the Raccoon-Eyed People captured in battle were helpful in hauling buffalo meat, which supplemented the crops of corn, beans, squash, pumpkins, and melons. They seeded these crops in holes poked into the ground with sticks. They pulled weeds and grass away from the plants they grew and enjoyed rich harvests.

The women and girls did all this work, and Jean was never made to do anything. He asked one of the elderly men to make him a bow and some arrows, however, and asked some warriors his age to teach him how to shoot. After mastering the basics of archery, Jean spent much of his time hunting small game. The first time he brought a dead deer home to the people of his hut, they carried on as if he had slain enough meat for a year, and a great feast commenced that lasted three days, and entirely depleted the village's reserve of meat.

By this time, Jean had long since learned that the huts which stood on stilts were occupied by unmarried girls. The girls entered through a ladder that led to the floor. At night, the mothers of the girls would remove the ladders, so boys could not get at the girls. The women of the Raccoon-Eyed People prided themselves on their chastity, even if the younger girls did not. And some of the girls most certainly did not.

It was no great feat for a young warrior to crawl into one of the huts on stilts in the middle of the night, even without a ladder. It was no more difficult for a nimble girl to drop out of her hut on the way to some prearranged tryst. One such girl, named Starlight, persuaded Jean to join her in such a meeting on the second night of the great feast brought on by his first deer kill.

The idea of meeting Starlight terrified Jean, especially after the perverse and confusing scenes he had witnessed at Fort St. Louis, but his heart and loins urged him to make the rendezvous. Starlight was waiting for him in the moon shadows by the river. She was so gentle and warm and soft and willing that Jean felt his eagerness for her overwhelm his dread. Her hands were like spirit-creatures that roamed his body and gave pleasure. Her mouth was soft and wet and warm. Her bare breasts pressed against him like goddesses unto themselves. Her thighs and hips and all her mysterious inner reaches took him away from the whole bizarre world, if only for a time.

Afterward, he spoke to her romantically in French as they lay naked on the robe she had brought, and Starlight giggled girlishly at Stranger's gibberish. Soon after this night, Starlight was married to one of the most promising young warriors in the village and would not speak to Jean, nor even look at him. At times likes these, Jean was painfully aware of his own whiteness, no matter how thoroughly the Raccoon-Eyed People had adopted him.

One day a council was held, and Jean sat in the circle with the others to hear the elders speak. He was understanding more of the language now, and gathered rather quickly that the council had been called in order to arrange a trading expedition to the north. The destination was a place called Quivira.

Quivira! The name rang in Jean's memory like the knell of hope. In his old home, the pirate town of Petit-Goave, he had known turncoats from several nations. Many were Spaniards who had deserted the Spanish Armada to become freebooters. These Spaniards delighted in telling legends of the fabled land of Quivira.

Only a couple of priests, they claimed, had been to Quivira, but the tales of riches these priests had brought back to Mexico City exceeded anything the conquistadors had ever encountered, even among the Aztecs or the Incas. The Quivirans possessed ingots of gold and silver that they used as skipping stones upon the waters of a vast inland sea. Their children played games with pearls. Rivulets of quicksilver ran like springs of fresh water. Jewels and gem-stones were swept aside like so much rubble.

Excited more by the prospect of finding Spanish explorers than treasures, Jean joined the trading expedition and traveled north to Quivira. After eigh-teen days of walking across wooded hills and beautiful open plains, his party approached a village that looked much like the one he had left, except that it was surrounded by many hide tents of other nations. When they arrived, Jean's people were greeted with great fanfare by many tattooed Raccoon-Eyed People.

"Is this Quivira?" Jean asked a friend.

"Yes. It is the richest place under the sun!"

Jean found no gold nor silver nor jewels, but there was much food in Quivira: fresh meat, dried meat, corn, beans, squash, grapes, plums, pumpkins, wild roots, seeds, honey, tallow, bear fat. And trade goods! Robes, furs, and hides of buffalo, elk, deer, sheep, pronghorn, bear, mink, beaver, otter, rabbit. There were more horses than Jean had seen in one place since entering the wilderness. There were seashells and elk teeth and bear claws, buffalo horns and deer antlers, ropes made of rawhide or corded plant fibers, mats made of pumpkin fibers, pipes made of red stone. Tobacco. Medicinal herbs. Lodge poles so green that they still oozed sap.

Traders from strange nations mingled. Jean was able to group some of them by their tattoos or their paint or the way they braided their hair or wore their skins. The commotion of all these people was unlike anything he had ever seen. A dozen different languages drifted among the lodges, and every-where men gesticulated in the hand talk that allowed traders of different nations to communicate.

Though many warriors went about armed, and some eyed others suspi-ciously, it was obvious that Quivira was a place of truce. Jean witnessed several instances of captives being sold as slaves or ransomed back to their rightful peoples. Most had been reduced to skin and bones, and many had sores, bruises, and burns on their bodies from being mistreated. Jean's heart sank at the condition of these unfortunates, but the natives around him showed little pity for the captives. Even when they had been ransomed back to the nations of their birth, the former slaves were not embraced by their people, but rather were scorned as if the shame was theirs for having submitted to capture.

There were no Franciscan priests, and no conquistadors in Quivira. As Jean began to focus on the trade goods, however, he found hints of Europeans. A few iron arrow points, an iron knife, glass trade beads, a mirror, a leather bridle with a Spanish bit. Then he saw the Spanish flintlock in the arms of a warrior from a nation of mountain people known as *Yutas*.

The third day of the trade fair, a band of the fierce *Inday* people arrived from the southwest and brought news that made the whole village of Quivira hum with excitement. Metal Men had been spotted, seven sleeps to the southwest.

Just seven sleeps away! Jean knew these Metal Men must be Spaniards. Suddenly he wanted nothing more than to be among his own kind, and was willing to risk his life to find the expedition the *Inday* had run across.

He traded his strike-a-light and his bow and arrows for pemmican, dried meat, and a water container made from the bladder of a buffalo. He slipped away from Quivira in the moonlight, following the back trail of the *Inday* who had seen the Metal Men. The trail was easy enough to see, for the tall grass was yet pushed down where the *Inday* dogs had pulled their pole-drags.

By the third day of travel, however, Jean had lost the trail, as it seemed the grass had risen again where it had been pressed down a few days before. Now he simply wandered southwestward. He traveled at night, so he would not be seen by strange people, and so that he could keep the Light-Which-Stands-Still over his right shoulder. He ran out of food. He came to a flat country devoid of streams where he might fill his water vessel. Finally, he stumbled upon a trail made by horses with shod hooves. He tried to follow the trail, but it was old, and he was exhausted.

Realizing that he was in danger of thirsting to death, Jean fell down in the sparse shade of a thorny bush and lapsed into fearful dreams. The next thing he remembered was the pain of something lashing his face. He awoke to find himself bouncing along on a travois. The whip he had felt was the tail of the horse who pulled the travois. He covered his face with his hand and focused his eyes on the scowling face of a friar clothed in a tattered black robe.

"What are you?" the friar said in Spanish.

Having grown up in Petit-Goave, Jean was conversant in Spanish as well as French. He understood, but he did not answer. He pretended to go back to sleep so he could think about his response. He feared the Franciscans and the Holy Office of the Inquisition would take issue with his heathen tattoos.

Later, when he opened his eyes again, the friar asked the same question: "What are you?"

"Water," he said in Spanish.

The friar gave him water and it felt good running down his throat.

"What manner of man are you? Tell me!"

"I am a child of God," Jean replied, using his first language, French.

The return to civilization was slow, but uneventful compared to his former travails. He was taken to El Paso del Norte, then to the City of Mexico, where he was questioned. The Inquisition authorities tried in vain to get Jean to admit to some heresy, and he claimed the *Indios* had forced him to submit to the tattooing, which, Jean said, had no religious significance whatsoever. He sang the praises of Father Membre, denounced heathen witchcraft, and recited his Hail Marys flawlessly. These were Franciscan friars here on New Spain's northern frontier. Jean did not trust them as he had Father Membre and the Jesuit brothers.

The viceroy and various military authorities questioned him at length, wanting to know all about the French menace in the east. When they learned that Jean had been with La Salle at Fort St. Louis, the Spanish officers shook their heads solemnly and informed him that a Spanish expedition had been dispatched to oust La Salle, but had found only the aftermath of a great massacre where the Fort had stood. This was how Jean learned of the death of Father Membre.

Next, he sailed across the Atlantic as a prisoner-of-war to convene with officers of the Royal Court and the Council of the Indies. He was grilled about his knowledge of inland America, its terrain, its riches, its natives. Finally, he was given the opportunity to swear allegiance to the Spanish Crown, and he readily accepted, knowing his former countrymen would surely hang him for cooperating with the Spanish.

From his Spanish captors, Jean had learned the fate of his friend, Goupil, the mapmaker. That intrepid frontiersman had actually managed to walk all the way to Quebec! It seemed that after the murder of La Salle, Henri Casaubon murdered the treacherous valet, Minime, in his sleep, over a leadership squabble among the Malcontents. Then Casaubon murdered the German, Hein.

Terrified by the libertinism that had swept over the remnants of the expedition, Goupil had fled, fearing he might be murdered next. He had walked northeastward, sometimes alone, sometimes in the company of native guides. It was told to Jean that Goupil's adventures on this great journey—recorded in his diary—were as harrowing and as fascinating as the travels of Marco Polo.

A few of La Salle's Loyals also managed to make their way back to Quebec, and, desiring a scapegoat upon whom to lay blame for the failures of the expedition, singled out Goupil. He was hanged for conspiring in the murder of La Salle, when Jean knew him to be wholly innocent. Hanged! One of the most intrepid explorers and mapmakers ever to venture into the wilderness of the New World.

This, more than any other factor, convinced Jean that he could never again be French. Of course, his tattoos and the stares they attracted from civilized folk helped him decide that his place was on the frontiers of New Spain, where tattooed natives were not considered so freakish. A plan began to form in his mind. He knew he could move with ease among the Raccoon-Eyed People of the plains, known as *Jumanos* to the Spaniards. If he could forge links with other nations through the *Jumanos*, he could establish himself as a plains trader on the frontier and perhaps earn enough to survive.

Besides this, Jean found himself longing for the wilderness. He missed the sensation of peering across far slopes without a village in sight, while great herds of buffalo surged across the grasslands like rivers, their shores teeming with bunches of elk, deer, and pronghorn. At night, wild wolves would moan and coyotes would sing, lions would scream like the tortured souls of wanton women, and birds of the darkness would echo one another's calls.

He pledged his loyalty to the King of Spain and sailed back to Mexico. In the year of 1693, at the seasoned age of twenty, Jean L'Archeveque joined the Spanish effort to recolonize New Mexico. The various nations collectively called Pueblos by the Spaniards had revolted and succeeded in driving the Metal Men out thirteen years before. Jean rode northward out of El Paso del Norte, a militiaman with the reconquest. The trail was tough, but the Pueblos had been weakened by infighting and put up no resistance at first. When the Spanish force pushed into the foothills of the Sangre de Cristo Mountains, Jean began to absorb a sensation peculiar to him. It was the feeling that he belonged.

The day he rode into the reconquered Spanish capital called La Villa Real de la Santa Fe de San Francisco, he knew he was home. The cool pine-scented air, the timbered mountains, the sage, the adobe walls—all felt somehow familiar though he had never been near the place before. Santa Fe seemed to embrace both civilization and the wilderness at once, as Jean himself had learned to do.

Some of these northern Pueblo peoples resisted the return of the Spaniards, but after a few campaigns, the new colonists subdued the *Indios* and reconquered the Kingdom of New Mexico. Jean became a merchant, a trader, and a freighter. He found that his tattoos and his experiences among the natives indeed allowed him to trade successfully with the wild nations termed vaguely *Norteños* by Spanish authorities.

As he established himself as a landowner and a man of wealth, he made the fortuitous acquaintance of Maria. Newly widowed, she was able to see beyond Jean's gaudy facial markings, and soon fell in love with him. They were married, blessed with sons, and then, the fever. The wretched fever. Maria was gone after only three years of happiness.

Still, Santa Fe remained Jean's refuge. In a way, he was a man without a nation—a Frenchmen among Spaniards, a Raccoon-Eye among Pueblos. He was a white man shunned for his tattoos, an *Indio* scorned for his whiteness. He was a Christian who had seen heathen visions. But in another way, he was all that Santa Fe had become: partly civilized, partly wild; a product of the plains, the mountains, the desert; the result of strange cultures clashing, yet tenuously coexisting. Here, they would not even call him Jean L'Archeveque, having Hispanicized his name to Juan Archebeque.

But Jean knew who he was, and he knew he was home.

▲▲▲▲▲▲

30

▼▼▼▼▼

When Jean reached the stable, he found that Paniagua had saddled his best stallion and was holding the reins for him to mount. The stallion, a noble chestnut of eight years, bore the features of hot Arab blood—the flaring nostrils, the arched neck, and the pointed ears. The stable man, upon hearing that his employer would dine at the *Casas Reales*, had chosen the fine polished saddle with fire-breathing lions and tangled vines carved and dyed into the sprawling leather skirts. He had bridled the stallion with the fancy headstall decorated with silver conchos all the way down to where it looped around the rings of the spade bit.

Paniagua was from Picuris, making him a *Tiwa*. He had supposedly converted to Catholicism and apparently enjoyed living among the Spaniards and working for Jean. He had even taken a Christian name of sorts, calling himself Paniagua. Jean was not sure whether this name stemmed from *pan y agua*, Spanish for bread and water, or from *paniaguado*, which was a Spanish term for a favored servant. Either way, the name probably did not mean much to the stable man. Jean knew Paniagua still worshiped the *Tiwa* gods and attended secret ceremonies in the kivas of the *Tiwa* pueblos. Not that it bothered him. Jean's heart possessed a touch of heathenism, as well.

He slipped his boot into the iron stirrup covered with the ornate leather tapadero whose tips reached lustily for the ground. "I will be late, Paniagua. Don't concern yourself with my return. I'll take care of the stallion myself."

"Thank you, señor," said Paniagua, as he handed the reins up to the rider.

Jean held the stallion to a fast walk as he left his hacienda. Santa Fe lay two leagues to the northwest, on the road from Pecos. After the first league, he let the steed lope, passing a herd of sheep in the cool twilight, a field of oats whose irrigation laterals glistened like ropes of silver, a pumpkin patch dotted with big orange *calabazas*. It was almost dark when he cantered among the torch lights of the adobe outpost of Santa Fe, letting the stallion walk the rest of the way to the plaza.

Shadows had engulfed the sprawling walls of the *Casas Reales* by the time the rider arrived. Jean considered the collection of adobes, almost a century old, more venerable than any building the Spaniards had managed to erect and maintain in the Kingdom of New Mexico. Yet, compared to some of the *Indio* buildings—most notably the two fine and ancient ones at Taos—the *Casas Reales* were mere parvenus. As he rode up to the gate and dismounted, he could see that several fires were burning inside the walls where the soldiers quartered, for the flames silhouetted the weeds and grasses growing on the dirt roof of the governor's residence on the southeast corner.

A guard recognized him and let him enter. A stable boy took his mount. Jean proceeded through the garden to the rudely appointed hall where he had often dined with the governor and other important functionaries. He was always invited as a militia captain and member of the *cabildo*—the citizens' council—but everyone knew that his true value to the colony was as a trader and negotiator among the *Indios* and an expert in French affairs.

"Welcome, *Capitán* Archebeque!" said Governor Del Bosque as Jean entered the hall through an arched doorway in an adobe wall as thick as a horse was broad.

"Good evening, *Capitán-General*," he replied, addressing the governor by his military title. He vigorously shook the hand of Antonio Del Bosque, for he considered the governor a wise man, a good friend, an intrepid politician, and a capable administrator.

Passing the governor, he let his iron spurs ring against the tile floor, and glanced across the room to see with whom he would dine tonight.

Beside the governor stood Captain Lorenzo Lujan, commander of the Santa Fe *presidio*—a good soldier, tough as a badger, but still just a soldier. "*Capitán*," Jean said, shaking the officer's hand.

"*Señor*," Lujan returned. He refused to address Jean by his rank of captain in the militia, for Jean was not a regular soldier and didn't deserve a military title in Lujan's opinion.

Across the dining room table stood Fray Gabrielle Ugarte, father-custodian over all the missions in New Mexico and the friar who had discovered Jean in the wilderness a dozen years ago.

"Hello, Padre," Jean said, with a smile.

"Juan," the priest replied, with a somber bow of his head. No typical friar, Ugarte possessed the will of a lion and the physical strength of a bull. Many of the Franciscans in New Mexico had been sent here almost as punishment for lack of ambition or some other perceived shortcoming. Fray Ugarte had *requested* this assignment. His only cause was to save souls from perdition: to reduce heathen savages to Christianity. He hungered always for the next expedition into the wild. He seemed to like danger, and he did not care if he had to capture, whip, chain, or starve a barbarian in order to effect a conversion.

Sitting at the table, enjoying a large gulp of wine, was the *alcalde-mayor* of Santa Fe, a likeable civilian appointee named Manuel Durazno, who had no authority, and knew it, and furthermore did not care. Durazno had once been an employee of Governor Del Bosque, but had been appointed *alcalde-mayor* and ordered to take over most of the functions of the civilian *cabildo*, which Del Bosque thought had grown far too powerful.

"Please, remain seated, Manuel," Jean said, jokingly, seeing that the *alcalde-mayor* had no intention of getting up.

"If you insist, my friend." Durazno replenished his clay cup from the chipped glass bottle, many times refilled and recorked in this land where even glassware had to be hoarded like gold.

A mestizo servant girl was lighting candles on a wrought-iron chandelier that had been lowered to a height just above the dining table. After touching flame to the last wick, she went to the wall and pulled on the rope that raised the chandelier high overhead. The rope ran through a hand-forged iron pulley bolted to a *viga*—a peeled pine timber that spanned the breadth of the ceiling. The candles on the chandelier and a few others around the dining hall were all the light the men would have. Luxuries like oil lamps seldom reached the northern frontier, and then were snatched up by high officials for personal use in their homes and bed chambers.

Fray Ugarte recited a brief blessing, and servants began to enter with platters of corn tortillas, beans, squash, tomatoes, chiles, and various meats including lamb, chicken, and tamales made of venison and pork. As they feasted, the men talked about the caravan that had recently arrived from the south—the first major shipment of goods in three years. With it, much correspondence had arrived for the colonists in Santa Fe, some of the letters dating as far back as five years.

"I was informed that my brother's ship was lost at sea," said Captain Lujan. "He is presumed dead, of course. Father, will you remember him at vespers this week?"

"Yes, of course. When was the ship lost? How long ago?"

"Two years. His name was Gregorio."

"My condolences," Jean said, though it didn't seem to him that Lujan was very badly upset over the loss of his blood kin.

As the conversation flowed, the men began to share the tidbits of good news they had received in their letters. Fray Ugarte's uncle had been granted the title of Hidalgo by King Felipe.

"Hidalgo!" said Alcalde Durazno, enviously. "Did he inherit the title or purchase it?"

"Neither," the priest said, a prideful smile on his face. "He won the title for a most extraordinary accomplishment. He sired seven sons in a row!"

"Bravo!" shouted Durazno.

Jean smiled and pounded his fist on the table with the other men, but his mind was on his own two sons fast asleep at his hacienda and their departed mother, whom he missed so much. Jean had received no correspondence from Spain, so he could only listen to the others share their stories.

From the open doors of a large *trastero* at the end of the dining hall, the servant girl brought forth coffee cups baked in local kilns by mission novices. The *trastero*, made of pine from the mountains, was carved and gaily colored with mineral paints the *Indios* used. As the girl approached the table with the cups, Jean glanced at her and caught her ogling his facial tattoos curiously.

"I received the final inventory of the caravan that arrived from the Land Outside," the governor announced as a second servant poured coffee. A third servant placed a silver dish on the table, five pieces of chocolate spaced evenly upon it. "As you see, we received chocolates!"

The men laughed at the irony.

"I would rather have powder," Captain Lujan stated.

"There was powder. Not much, I'm afraid. But plenty of lead for making balls."

"Flints?"

"No flints."

"I can get flints from the *Tiwas* at Tachichichi," Jean offered. "I have established a trading house there, as you may have heard."

"Linen for making patches?" Lujan asked, ignoring Jean.

"No linen. Not even scraps. We will have to continue to make our patches from skins. But we did receive a bolt of silk!"

Again, the sardonic laughter.

"Paper and ink?" Jean asked.

"Of course not," the governor replied, "but we received a dozen fine quill pens. Oh, and fifty new prayer books for the missions."

"Are there fifty literate Christians in all of New Mexico?" Fray Ugarte said, and his laughter erupted so suddenly that it startled the mestizo girl.

The governor went on with the inventory: three kegs of nails, but no saws with which to make lumber. A used loom and some carding tools for making cloth, but no needles nor thread. Hammers, axes, plows—that was good. But no iron cart tires. A few kettles and knives, such as the *Indios* liked to get in trade. Locks and keys, but no chain.

"We will improvise," Jean replied. "One never knows what the office of the viceroy will send. It seems no one is in charge down there. The right hand knows not what the left hand does."

"*Salúd!*" Durazno said, as if Jean had just made a toast.

"I am more interested in what our caravan will send south, governor. Is the inventory complete?"

"Yes, Juan, and we have done well. Better than the caravan of three years ago, and twice as rich as the one three years before that. Thanks mostly to you, we have greatly increased our trade among the *Norteños*. Over one thousand deerskins have been baled. We have already loaded three hundred fanegas of piñon nuts, and almost five hundred buffalo robes. The haciendas and missions have produced well, also. Six hundred pairs of wool socks, fifty cowhides, two hundred oxen, seventy mules, and a large herd of surplus sheep. Your hacienda is now first in the breeding of mules, my friend, and third in overall production, according to the assessor's office. Thanks to you, and a few others, we will send quite a caravan south."

"How many slaves?" Jean said.

A tense silence fell abruptly into the middle of the conversation.

"What do you mean, Juan?" Governor Del Bosque said. "You know slavery is illegal."

"They are *genizaros*, not slaves," Fray Ugarte blurted. "They have been converted."

Jean smiled. "I only meant that they were slaves before—among the *Indios*, though I doubt many were made to work as hard among the so-called savages as they will be made to work among Spaniards."

"There is nothing wrong with hard work," Ugarte insisted.

"True, but without pay?"

"They will be paid."

"None of them will ever earn more than a peso, and even then, the overseer who hands them the coin will be holding a whip in his other hand. They spend all their earnings on vile drink anyway, and I don't even blame them. It is their only escape. Those poor devils will be worked to death in fields and mines. Most will look back fondly on their days as slaves among the *Indios*."

"What are we to do?" said Captain Lujan. "Tell the savages we won't ransom them anymore? And see them tortured to death before our very eyes?"

"We should continue to ransom them, of course, but we must become better negotiators. We must take the profit out of the slave trade until it dries up. It is a matter of simple economics."

"How do you propose to do this?" Governor Del Bosque said, a curious smirk on his face.

"First we must recognize that the trade in *Indio* slaves is our fault. The *Tiwa* elders tell me that in old days, slavery indeed existed, but the slaves were eventually adopted into the nations of their captors. But now the Apache make regular slave raids on the *Pani*, and sell the women and children to Spaniards here. The *Pani*, meanwhile, are raiding the Apache rancherias and selling their captives to the French across the plains."

"It is the fault of the French," Lujan said, without offering to explain his observation.

"Get to the part about negotiations," the governor said, trying to keep the debate on track.

"We must simply offer less for the slaves, and at the same time, offer more for other trade items—buffalo robes and beaver pelts, deerskins and wild honey. We must make it understood that we have enough slaves, and we will pay but little for them. At the same time, we must convince the *Indios* that we will trade items of much higher value for robes, skins, and furs."

Alcalde Durazno snorted. "That would be fine, if we had anything of value to a barbarian."

"We have *escopetas*."

Lujan straightened in his chair. "You would trade guns to our enemies?"

"The old *escopetas* are as worthless to them as they are to us with this shortage of powder. Even your own soldiers won't use them, *Capitán*. They prefer the bows and arrows captured from the *Indios*."

"Even if it were legal," Governor Del Bosque said, "we have only so many *escopetas* to trade."

"A valid point, governor. That is why our primary item of trade must be something we can renew—mules and geldings."

"You would arm *and* mount our enemies!" Lujan growled.

"They are already armed and mounted. They have horses, and their horses will breed more horses. But mules and geldings will not. First, we must get the mares and stallions from them by offering two mules or geldings for each mare or stallion—three if necessary. Since they cannot breed up their herds without stallions and mares, they will be dependent on us for their mounts, which we will trade to them for hides and furs and honey, but not for slaves."

"Indeed," Lujan said, a jeer in his tone.

"The Apaches and *Yutas* are raiding the settlements for mounts, anyway. Why not legalize the trade in mounts in a way that gives us the advantage."

"We already have the advantage," Lujan insisted. "The savages are either too stupid or too clumsy or too cowardly to fight from the backs of their horses."

"It is curious," Jean admitted, "that the *Indios* have not yet adopted our cavalry tactics. They use their horses only as transportation, preferring to fight on foot. But this only means that they are slow to change, not that they are not slow to learn. I have seen some marvelous riders among the *Norteños*, especially the Apaches and the *Yutas*. When they start to fight from the backs of their horses, they will be a devastating force. That is why we must take control of how many mounts they possess, before it is too late."

"Your idea seems to have some merit," Del Bosque said. "Unfortunately, the Crown forbids the trade of mounts to the *Indios* whether they are mules or geldings or jackasses. Besides that, mules and horses represent a good part of our export economy to New Spain. We cannot afford to trade all of them to the *Indios*."

"We would continue to send the best animals south, or sell them to *Capitán* Lujan's soldiers," Jean said, though he could tell by now that his whole proposal, which he had thought out carefully for some time, was futile. He added one other observation: "We are a long way from the Crown."

The governor looked at Fray Ugarte, who had remained silent during Jean's discourse. "Padre, what say you about these issues of slaves and horses?"

Slowly, almost ceremoniously, the friar placed his cup on a glazed saucer. "The slave trade is the work of God. We should encourage the savages to continue it. The more slaves we ransom, the more souls we save."

Jean scoffed. "Encourage the *Indios* to enslave one another? Even when the slaves are mistreated? Some are beaten or burned—occasionally to death."

"Better for one to suffer and die that ten may know eternal life."

"The ratio is more like ten deaths for one salvation, *Padre*."

"You think too much of worldly things, Juan. It is better for ten to die violently that one may know the grace of God, than for all eleven to die peacefully in their sleep of old age, in ignorance and sin, their souls fated to drift in oblivion."

Jean sighed, sensing the uselessness in arguing with the Franciscan. "If they are going to be ransomed, at least they could be set free instead of marched south to die in mines and fields."

"There is no work for them here," Governor Del Bosque said. "They must be taken south where there is work."

Jean shook his head. "Set them free and give them land to colonize on the northern frontier. Give them weapons to fight with, and let them serve as a line of first defense against the Apaches who enslaved them in the first place."

"If set free," Fray Ugarte argued, "they would either revert to their heathen ways among their own people, or they would linger around here, falling into temptation."

"They would become misfits and thieves," Captain Lujan said.

"Then they would make good soldiers," Jean mumbled.

Alcalde Durazno burst into laughter, until he caught Lujan's angry glare.

"At least they have God on their side," Jean said, failing to hide the sarcasm in his voice, "for, as Fray Ugarte assures us, the friars have splashed them with holy water, which I am sure lends great comfort to their hearts as the whip lashes their backs."

"Careful, Juan," Governor Del Bosque warned.

Jean frowned. He knew the governor was right. To criticize the clergy too severely was to tempt the powers of the Holy Office of the Inquisition. "I'm sorry, Father. I mean no disrespect. I understand the need to save souls, but is conversion a matter of the heart, or a matter of the skin sprinkled with holy water?"

Jean found himself locked in Fray Ugarte's powerful glare, until a glob of molten wax fell from the chandelier and thumped onto the back of Ugarte's hand, making him flinch. By reflex, the priest started to fling the hot wax off the back of his hand, but caught himself. As if in some ritual of penance, he watched the wax congeal, the heat reddening his sun-browned skin.

"Sorry, Father," said Governor Del Bosque. "I must send that chandelier back to the forge and have the *herrero* fix that problem."

Father Ugarte pulled the solid lump of wax from his hand, tearing hairs out by the root.

"And as for you, Juan," the governor continued, "I know you mean well, but we cannot solve all the problems of the world this evening. However, there is one issue you can help us to decide."

Jean raised the brows above his tattooed eyes.

"I have discussed it with Fray Ugarte and *Capitán* Lujan, and we are at an impasse. We need your council."

Jean shifted, making his chair squeak. "I'm listening."

"A messenger arrived from Tachichichi this morning, having ridden his horse to exhaustion. He told a peculiar story. He claims a large invasion force of Frenchmen and *Pani* allies is now marching on Tachichichi from across the plains. The Pueblos at Tachichichi are requesting Spanish troops."

Jean stroked his chin, the tips of his fingers seeming to paint the tattooed lines that descended from the corners of his mouth. "And what do you say of this, *Capitán?*"

Lujan waited until the mestizo girl had refilled is cup with strong black coffee, as though he were too dull to watch her and answer Jean at the same time. "I say the report is preposterous and should be ignored. The Pueblos at Tachichichi are fugitives. They are probably laying a trap for us."

Jean grunted. "Padre?"

"No matter what their motive, any time the Tachichichis request our presence, we should go there and bring back *genizaros.*"

Jean spooned sugar into his coffee cup, measuring the rare treat carefully. He took his time thinking about his response, enjoying the fact that these Spanish officials *needed* his advice—he a Frenchman with heathen tattoos.

"Well?" Governor Del Bosque finally said.

"I both agree and disagree with *Capitán* Lujan," he said.

"What is that supposed to mean?" replied the soldier in an irritable tone of voice.

"I agree that the report is preposterous. It is not the way of Frenchmen to send a large force into the wilderness."

"That's exactly what happened with La Salle's Fort St. Louis," Del Bosque argued. "You have told me about it yourself."

"And it was a miserable failure—one reason it is no longer the French policy. The French have realized more success sending independent *couriers de bois* to live and trade among the *Indios*. So, I agree that the report of a large invasion force is quite preposterous. However, I disagree that the report should be ignored. If the Tachichichis made up the story, they did so for a reason. Obviously, they want us there. We should find out why."

"So they can overwhelm and massacre us," Lujan suggested. "Or lure the soldiers away so that they can attack Santa Fe."

Jean nodded. Despite Lujan's narrowness of mind, the man understood military strategy. "Perhaps. On the other hand, they may simply need protection from their enemies, the *Pani*. They could have fabricated the part about Frenchmen simply to get our attention."

"So you agree that we should mount an expedition immediately?" Ugarte said, hopefully.

"Not necessarily. How many regular soldiers have you at the presidio, *Capitán?*"

"Only eighty-three. To march on Tachichichi would mean exposing Santa Fe."

"I agree. Militia and Pueblo scouts might triple the size of your force, but we are still short-handed compared to the hundreds of warriors the Tachichichis might muster if this turned out to be another uprising." He turned to the priest. "No, *Padre*, it is not a good idea to mount an expedition until we know what we are up against at Tachichichi. I have a better idea. I will find out what is going on. I am trusted at Tachichichi. If I have to, I will ride all the way there myself."

Lujan scoffed at the offer. "Tachichichi is eighteen days march. We might have been overwhelmed by that time."

"Tachichichi is eighteen days for a company of soldiers," Jean said, "but only seven days for me."

Lujan snorted.

"At any rate, the trip will probably not be necessary. I will speak to the *Tiwa* messenger who arrived this morning. He will probably tell me all I need to know. Where has he gone?"

"*¿Quién sabe?*" Del Bosque grumbled. "He has disappeared."

Jean nodded knowingly. "He will find me."

"How do you know that?" Lujan said.

"I know. If they need help at Tachichichi, they will come to me." Jean reached for a cube of chocolate on the silver dish. He studied it from various angles, thinking about nibbling on it. Instead, he decided he would rather devour it all at once, letting the experience hit him like a blast of wind whipping over a mountaintop. He tossed the confection into his mouth, leaned back in his chair, and closed his eyes. As the sweet, rich chocolate melted in his mouth, he could feel the stares of his dinner companions suspiciously regarding his painted flesh.

31

When Jean returned to his hacienda, he found Paniagua waiting in the stable, a candle burning. The stable man had a peculiar look on his face.

"What is it, Paniagua? I told you not to wait for my return."

Without pointing, Paniagua glanced toward the door to his quarters. The door was ajar, and the light of the fireplace flickered through the crack. Jean guessed what it meant. The messenger from Tachichichi had indeed sought him out.

"May I?" Jean said, though he didn't need Paniagua's permission to enter his stable man's quarters.

Paniagua merely led the stallion away.

Jean crossed the tiny *placita*, pausing in the middle of the open square to look up at the countless stars visible over the high adobe walls. The normal nightly chill had crept out of the mountains, so he proceeded quickly to the door of Paniagua's room. Peering inside, he saw a young *Indio* man wearing a mix of traditional *Tiwa* and Apache dress—deer-hide moccasins and leggings, white cotton shirt under a woolen blanket. He recognized the young warrior, having traded with him at Tachichichi.

"Welcome, Coyote Man," he said, in Spanish. "You have had a hard trip."

Coyote Man glanced toward Jean, but did not meet his eyes. "Only for the horse."

Jean chuckled. "Under how many suns did you ride?"

Coyote Man held up six fingers, the sixth being the thumb of his left hand, the tip of which touched the tip of his right thumb, in the *Indio* way of enumerating in signs.

"You must carry much wisdom to ride so swiftly."

"The spirits order it."

Jean crossed Paniagua's tiny room, to a chair made of leather stretched over a frame of crisscrossed pieces of cedar wood. It squeaked like a saddle as he sat in it. "One must obey the spirits," Jean said to Coyote Man. "Tell me, what wisdom of the spirit world do you bring?"

"There have been visions among the elders in our village."

"What kind of visions?"

"Fearful visions of a new nation."

"What nation?"

"A nation of Horse People."

Jean sat silently for a few moments, thinking about this. He believed every vision a valid message from the spirit world. It was only in the interpretation of the vision that mortal men sometimes failed. The *Indios* were much better at receiving and interpreting visions because they were closer to the spirit world than white men, but Jean was trying to overcome his lack of spiritual sophistication. Of course, he could never speak of these things among his Spanish friends, who might accuse him of practicing sorcery. Even now there was the risk that Coyote Man had been recruited by some enemy of Jean's—perhaps a rival trader—to report to the Holy Office of the Inquisition. Such were the risks of a frontiersman in the Kingdom of New Mexico.

"What do the visions of the elders tell us about these Horse People?"

"They are coming from the north."

"When will they arrive?" Jean asked.

Coyote Man seemed to be staring at nothing on the wall, but Jean understood that it was considered impolite to look into the eyes of a respected person.

"The first have arrived already at Tachichichi," the messenger answered. "They are coming here."

"Why do they come here?"

"They seek horses."

Jean felt a pang of dread in his chest, but could not say why. "How many are they?"

"Four warriors."

"Only four?"

"They are like twenty."

Jean pondered what Coyote Man might mean. Were they fierce? Large? Strong? Why had Coyote Man ridden a horse nearly to death to bring this news? Why were the elders at Tachichichi inventing fanciful stories to lure Spanish troops onto the plains? What was going on out there?

As if to answer all of Jean's questions, Coyote Man said, "They *ride*. Their leader is a very young warrior, and he rides even better than the others, who are like riders of the spirit world. His mount feels what is in his heart, and obeys him. This warrior scalps his enemies without touching the ground with his own moccasins."

Jean considered what this might mean. Coyote Man had married into and adopted the ways of the *Tiwa*, but he was *Inday* by birth and by blood. Coyote Man was himself one of the better riders among the *Inday* horsemen Jean had seen. Jean had heard how Coyote Man had earned his name: He had found a coyote far from cover on the plains, and had chased this coyote until it was tired enough that Coyote Man could lean from his horse and pick up the animal by the tail. For Coyote Man to feel awed by another's riding ability spoke of something remarkable.

"The elders have seen this riding in their visions?" Jean asked.

Coyote man thumbed his chest with his fist, the thumb extended upward, then he made his first two fingers point forward in front of his eyes. More emphatically than any words he could have spoken, the messenger had said, "I have seen this riding with my own eyes."

"Battle Scar's people came to Tachichichi," he added. "They had a little fight with five Horse People warriors camped there, wounding one of them. The next morning, the other four Horse People warriors attacked Battle Scar's whole band. They stole all of Battle Scar's horses, and killed one warrior, all of the Horse People warriors escaping without a wound. I saw the young Horse People leader scalp the *Inday* warrior without getting off his horse. He made the horse pull the scalp."

Jean listened to the pine wood pop in the fireplace. He had dreamt of horses himself lately. They were coming. A new nation. It was exciting in a way. But, for some reason he felt a hint of incredible dread. How would he prepare himself for the arrival of the Horse People? "What is the name of the young leader?" he asked.

Coyote Man lay down on a pallet Paniagua had made for him. He looked tired. "He is called Horseback."

32

Horseback felt the pony pitch forward, and absorbed the jolt of the animal landing hard on its knees. The coils of twisted horsehide rope looping over his knees and around the pony's chest prevented him from sliding over the mount's neck and head. The tough little yellow stud slid on his knees down the steep mountain trail, but lowered his hind end, scraping hide from his hocks, to keep himself from tumbling forward. As the trail leveled out, the stud sprang quickly from his knees, tossed his head, and released a blast of air that rattled his nostrils.

"Wait," Horseback ordered, halting the party strung out single file on the narrow trail. Slipping his knees out from under the coils of rope, he grabbed a handful of tawny mane and hung from the side of his pony's neck to check the animal's knees for damage. Seeing little blood, he pulled himself back upright. Next, he reversed himself on the bear hide he used for a saddle, facing backward. He lay on his stomach across the pony's rump and peered over each hip to check the hocks for cuts. A good deal of hair had come off, but the hide was only scraped.

Horseback wouldn't have tried crawling all over just any pony this way, but the yellow stud had earned his trust. Captured from Battle Scar's band, this little stallion had at first seemed listless and cowed, having been beaten too often by some *Na-vohnuh* rider. Soon, however, the stallion had assumed the haughty spirit of his new master, Horseback. Pony and rider had spent much time together, breathed air from each other's lungs.

The stud was small, but quick and strong. His color was almost as bright as that of the meadowlark's breast, except for his mane, tail, and feet, which were reddish brown, like the dirt of the *Noomah* homeland. A dark line of the same color ran right down the center of the pony's back, straight as a tight bowstring. Horseback felt that the line possessed *puha* that pulled at the medicine bundle in his loin skins and helped him remain seated.

Of all his new ponies, he liked this yellow line–back stud the most. The entire captured herd belonged to Horseback now, for he led this party of searchers and protected it with his spirit-powers. Yet, the other *Noomah* riders trusted that Horseback would distribute the spoils evenly among them, should they manage to return alive to the country of the True Humans. This was the way of the elders, and it was good.

Satisfied that the yellow stud was uninjured from the slide down the steep trail, Horseback swung back around on his bear skin, ready to move on.

"You will have time to play on your ponies soon," Bad Camper said, two mounts ahead of Horseback. He was guiding the party of mixed nations, followed by the *Tiwa* interpreter, Speaks Twice.

"We are near the Metal Men?" Horseback asked.

Bad Camper did not answer. He simply turned to face the trail ahead and started the line of riders moving down the slope again. They had ridden two suns among tall trees and mountains. Now, the trail dropped off to the west, snaking around smaller piñon pines, opening up wide views of a huge valley. The trail was beaten deep into the mountainside, the limbs of the piñon pines gnarled where many travelers had kept them broken back from the path. Horseback sensed that much trade had been carried out on this trail for many generations.

At a place where the trail widened and curved sharply to the south, Bad Camper reined his mount aside to an overlook that afforded a splendid view of the valley to the west. Speaks Twice followed, signaling behind in the hand talk he had been teaching to Horseback: "Come see."

Horseback rode the yellow stud in between Bad Camper and Speaks Twice, watching the east floor of the valley move into view as he approached the rocky precipice. Stopping near the rim of the overlook, a neck ahead of the other two riders, he leaned slightly to one side to see around the stud's head.

The sight astounded him. Far below stood a village larger than any he had ever beheld—a city. It was made of the kind of lodges he had seen at Tachichichi, but covered twenty times as much ground.

"What is that place?" he asked.

"The city of the Metal Men," Speaks Twice said. "They call it Santa Fe."

Horseback could see that the Metal Men believed in the power of lines over circles. Their lodges were straight, the paths between them straight and long and very wide. Beyond the city were more lines and other strange things upon the land. There were patches where the sage was gone and the earth was broken up, and the sun shone on water that webbed these places. The water was coming from little brooks that were straight like the paths of the Metal Men between their lodges.

On other patches of land, Horseback saw strange animals: little pale ones that resembled maggots from this distant overlook; larger black ones that looked like unhealthy buffalos. Then he saw a small herd of horses standing in a trap made of lodge poles stack upon each other. "Where are all the horses?" he asked. "I see only one small herd."

Bad Camper chuckled, as if to ridicule the searcher's ignorance. "The Metal Men keep them well guarded in special places. They build lodges for the best horses and keep them inside."

"Inside? What do they eat?"

"Snake People." Bad Camper burst into laughter.

Horseback frowned and looked toward Speaks Twice.

"The Metal Men feed them dried grass that they cut and stack up in the horse lodges. Also grain from a plant they grow called oats."

As the rest of the *Yuta* riders and the loose horses filed down the trail, Horseback's searchers reined aside to the overlook. They peered with silent wonder out over Santa Fe.

"When will we see Metal Men?" Horseback asked.

Bad Camper pointed. "We will raise our lodges on the stream above Santa Fe. The water is foul below, for the Metal Men have filthy ways. When our camp is made and our horses under guard, I will take you to meet the Metal Men."

"Why must we leave the horses guarded at our camp?" Horseback asked. He was not aware that they had ridden into enemy country.

"The Metal Men may try to steal them," Bad Camper said.

"They steal horses?" Shaggy Hump asked.

Speaks Twice answered: "Horses, land, women, children. They steal everything. Their god tells them to do this."

"We come here only as seekers, under a sacred truce," Horseback said.

Bad Camper grunted his amusement. "No truce is sacred to the Metal Men. In their city, they hold one thing sacred: metal that is shiny, heavy, and cold. Sometimes yellow, sometimes white. They believe it has the power of gods to make things happen. They form it into circles and use it to trade." He reined his mount back onto the trail, as if he had grown ill from looking too long at Santa Fe.

The old trail led the travelers to a meadow flanking the mountain stream that supplied Santa Fe. Here, the warriors began raising lodges, and Horseback prepared to ride to Santa Fe. He caught his least-favorite mount to ride, an old white mare. Should the Metal Men indeed succeed in stealing his pony as he entered the city, he did not intend for them to have his best one. As he threw the bearskin pad on the mare and wound the horsehide coils around it, Bad Camper approached.

"Listen, Snake warrior, and I will teach you a word in the language of Metal Men. It means a camp-together for the purpose of trading."

"They say that much with one word?"

"It is the way with their language. They have many words that they use seldom. They believe this great number of words gives them wisdom."

"Wisdom comes from the heart, not from the tongue," Horseback said.

Bad Camper nodded. "Now, listen. It is said in this way: *rescate*."

Horseback raised his head, like a pony who had heard something new and strange. "Say it again. Slowly."

"Res-CA-te."

Horseback let the sound of the strange word echo in his ears, then he spoke it: *"Rescate."*

"You speak it well," Bad Camper said, sounding a bit surprised. "The Metal Men will ask you why you have come to their city. When they do, speak the word, and they will know you have come to trade."

Horseback turned back to the saddle, repeating the word: *"Rescate . . . rescate . . . rescate."*

He mounted the old white mare and rode around the camp. His eyes searched the ground habitually for deer tracks, for he was ever mindful of honoring his guardian spirit and wished to avoid defiling the trails of the sacred deer. Though he found no deer tracks, he did see the sign of a single horse—hoofprints and dung. Hanging from the side of his mount, he reached down and scooped up a handful of dung, finding it warm to the touch. He was going to need much *puha* to ride into this city of strangers, for the Metal Men had placed a scout here, and they would be ready.

A few of the *Yuta* warriors stayed behind to guard the horses, as the rest of the party rode toward the city. As they traveled on the trail beside the river, Horseback noticed that the water became calm. He expected to find a beaver dam ahead, making the water still. Instead, he found a great mass of rocks and earth blocking the river, forcing the water to flow south of the river bed into a brook that ran as straight as an arrow. He stopped to puzzle over the sight.

"The Metal Men make dams, like beavers," Bad Camper said.

Horseback had often seen women scratching little ditches around lodges to channel rain water away, but he could not imagine digging a ditch as deep and long and straight as the one that took water from this stream. "Why do they bleed this river?" he asked. "Her waters flow away like life from a wound that doesn't heal."

"They make the water flow over the ground where they grow plants to eat," Bad Camper explained. "They call this the *acequia madre*. It means the mother ditch."

"They force the water to go where it doesn't want to go," Horseback said. "Do they know nothing about the spirits in the water? This will make the spirits angry, and a flood will come."

"There have been floods before," Bad Camper said. "They do not learn."

"The Black Robes don't believe in water spirits," Speaks Twice added. "They are afraid to talk about any spirits or gods, except for their one Great Spirit."

"Their Great Spirit must be a very jealous god," Horseback said.

"The Black Robes say their god is the same as the Great Creator to whom we pray. If it is true, the Great Creator does not speak the same way to the Metal Men as to us."

"The Metal Men do not *hear* the same way," Bad Camper said.

The party rode on along the north bank of the river until the trail widened and veered toward Santa Fe. As they came to the edge of the city, Horseback saw a sight that startled him. Two sickly looking buffalo, of the kind he had seen from the overlook, were pulling a thing like no pole-drag ever strapped to a pony. It seemed to ride on two sacred circles, like the hoop targets the *Noomah* bowmen rolled along the ground and shot at for practice. It made very little dust rise from the wide trail, for it rolled, unlike the butt ends of a pole-drag, which scraped the ground. This rolling buffalo-drag was heaped with dried grass. It made a horrible moaning sound as it moved down the wide path that led to the city. A man walking beside the buffalo goaded them with a stick. As the party rode past the buffalo-drag, Horseback's pony shied away from the sound, and the hairy-faced Metal Man, in turn, drew away from the travelers, not having seen them until they passed.

"What is that noise?" Horseback asked.

"It is made by the wooden circles rubbing on the thick wooden pole around which they turn," Bad Camper explained.

"What have they done to those buffalo?"

"Those are cattle." Bad Camper glanced at Horseback's face. "You have much to learn."

Horseback was looking back at the hairy-faced man. The strange man wore cotton clothes. His ugly moccasins were just plain leather, devoid of any dye or colorful quill work. He wore a strange headdress with a sun shade attached to it, making a circle all around his head. He did not look the least bit fierce, and in fact seemed afraid of the travelers.

As they rode deeper into the city, Horseback sensed people scurrying from lodge to lodge ahead of him, as if the arrival of the travelers caused great excitement. At last they came to a square in the middle of the city where no lodges had been raised making Horseback think the square must be sacred.

Six light-skinned, hairy-faced men came out of a lodge on the north side of the square. Horseback knew they were warriors by the weapons they held—lances and guns. One wore the weapon called a *sword*—the first Horseback had seen—and appeared to be a greater warrior than the others.

Then one of the Black Robes he had heard about came out of the lodge—a large man with huge shoulders and eyes that seemed to hold great powers. The Black Robe grew no hair from his face, and the hair on his head grew in a sacred ring, the top of his head being bald. The Black Robe was followed by a hairy-face whose clothes were finer than those of other Metal Men he had seen, making Horseback think he must be a chief. This chief's moccasins were shiny black, his leggings green as pine needles, with rows of shiny metal circles down the outside of each leg. He wore a brilliant red belt tied around his waist, and a shirt as white as a mountain goat. A strange little Metal Man walked behind the chief, acting like a slave. The slave carried a feather and some kind of square thing that unfolded in his hand. Soon, Horseback realized that the feather was magic, for when the chief spoke, the slave touched the tip of the feather on the surface of the square thing he held on his arm, and the tip of the magic feather made a mark like a trail of dark blood.

All around him, Horseback felt the dirt lodges tower, and he wondered if he could escape should the Metal Men attack. He thought of his guardian spirit, Sound-the-Sun-Makes. Had he ridden his pony upon the trail of a deer in the mountains? He looked at his father, and found Shaggy Hump's face tense. His guides, however—Bad Camper and Speaks Twice—seemed at ease, so Horseback attempted to behave as they did.

Just when Bad Camper raised his hand in a sign of greeting, another man stepped from the shadows of the large square lodge. Horseback knew who he was immediately. The man's hairless face wore the tattoos of the Raccoon-Eyed People, yet his skin was light and his clothes like those of the Metal Men. This was the Raccoon-Eyed Flower Man Horseback had heard about in Tachichichi, the great trader who possessed both wisdom and power. Horseback could not say why, but the presence of this man gave him a feeling of peace in the middle of this dreamlike world of strangers and strange ways. Immediately he could tell that Raccoon-Eyes knew what was good and powerful, for he was looking first at the ponies.

▲▲▲▲▲
33
▼▼▼▼▼

Jean had remained in the shadows of the *Casas Reales* to form his initial impression of the Horse People. Captain Lujan had simply walked out into the street with his soldiers, followed by Fray Ugarte and Governor Del Bosque. Del Bosque had summoned a scribe to accompany him with a tablet and quill pen to record any intelligence gleaned from the *Norteños*. These Spaniards were inordinate recorders, yet all of them thought this just another visit by *Yutas*, and didn't yet realize that a new people had appeared.

Jean was the only white man who understood what was going on, a distinction that carried with it an ominous responsibility. He had spoken much with Coyote Man about the new nation coming down from the north, yet many mysteries still swirled in his head. Why were the Horse People now riding with *Yutas* when they were said to have no allies among the nations? How many of these Horse People lived to the far north? How many warriors could they mount? Most important, what power, what magic, what medicine did they possess?

It was said that the Horse People had broken away from a nation known as *Shoshoni*, or Snake People, yet it was not clear to Jean whether the Horse People had indeed broken away from the Snake People, or were simply destined to do so, according to the visions of the *Tiwa* elders.

No one knew much about these Snake People. They kept to themselves, completely surrounded by enemies, forced onto bad hunting grounds, bereft of allies, distrustful of all other nations. What would happen, Jean wondered, if such a people came into possession of a new tool and suddenly saw a chance to break free from a life of retreat and poverty. What if the tool were also a weapon, and the weapon, wealth?

The riders had pulled up in the street and made a line, all the horses standing abreast. A silence had ensued, and the people of these diverse nations—strangers brought together by forces none could fully comprehend—all simply stared at one another. The silence seemed to last a long time, and even the horses stood with their heads high and their ears forward.

Then Jean stepped out of the shadows, studying the horses first, then the weapons and the men. The ponies were small and rather poor, the weapons primitive—bows, knives, lances, war clubs. Most of the riders were *Yuta*, their dress and equipage familiar to him. He recognized two individuals: Bad Camper, of the *Yuta* nation, and Speaks Twice, the *Tiwa* translator from Tachichichi. He identified only four warriors whose dress he had never seen, and knew these four had to be the Horse People. In their eyes he saw the look of the lost. They were far from home.

Jean doubted the Spaniards would notice any difference in the *Indios* at all. Indeed, their outward appearance would seem much like that of any other *Norteño* to an uninterested European eye. But Jean noticed many distinctions among these people:

All four Horse warriors wore earrings of shell or bone. One especially fierce looking brave had four earrings along the curve of each ear. They all wore their hair greased, parted in the middle, and braided on either side. A loose lock of hair remained at the front of the head and fell over the brow. The oldest warrior of the four wore a black feather in this scalp lock. The younger three wore yellow feathers there. The more mature warrior also had tattoos on his chest, and a scar on his shoulder accentuated by tattoos. They all went bare-chested today, though the wind was brisk, leading Jean to believe that they indeed came from somewhere far to the north, where they were accustomed to cool weather. Their leggings, though chafed and dusty from their long journey, were dyed a uniform blue.

In physical build, Jean found the Horse People shorter and more muscular than their companions. The longer legs of the *Yuta* riders seemed to hang listlessly along the flanks of their horses, while those of the Horse People warriors clutched their mounts the way an eagle claw would grasp a fawn.

Each pony of the Horse People wore two strange pieces of equipage. A loop of braided rawhide hung under the neck of each pony, woven in at the mane. Another rope wound loosely around the barrel of each mount, just behind the forelegs. One of the riders had his knees slipped under the coils of rope, making its purpose clear. None used more than a bear hide for a saddle.

Jean only glanced at the faces of the men, not wishing to offend them with a long stare into their eyes, as though to discover their powers. Still, he looked long enough to realize that none of the Horse warriors grew any facial hair. The eyebrows and even the eyelashes had been plucked out.

Jean broke the silence as he spoke to Bad Camper in Spanish: "Welcome, my friend. I hope you have come to trade, for we have new things from the Land Outside."

Bad Camper nodded. "We ride under many suns to bring the skins you like—beaver, fox, mink, and otter."

Jean smiled. "I hope you bring buffalo robes and deerskins."

"A few buffalo. Many deer," Bad Camper replied.

"Flints?"

"Yes."

Governor Del Bosque spoke. "What about the yellow metal we asked you to look for. Have you found any?"

Without looking toward the governor, Bad Camper said, "No."

"We will prepare a feast for your arrival at my hacienda," Jean said. "After we eat, we will smoke. Then, we will trade."

"Who are these warriors with the blue *pantalones?*" Captain Lujan suddenly said.

The observation impressed Jean, but then Lujan was a soldier, and soldiers knew of uniforms.

"We call them Comanche," Bad Camper said.

Governor Del Bosque nudged his scribe, who dipped his quill into the small ink well and began writing.

"It means our enemies in the *Yuta* tongue," Jean explained. "It is not the name these warriors would call themselves."

"No matter," Del Bosque said. "As long as we record them."

Jean considered pressing the issue for the sake of accuracy, but knew it was useless. Neither the governor nor the crown cared what heathens called themselves. The Spaniards had adopted the word *apache* to refer to certain *Inday* bands only because a *Zuni* elder had so named them, *apache* being a *Zuni* term meaning those against us.

It was too late to make sense of it all for the Spaniards. Some of the erroneous labels had been in use a hundred years. At least these so-called Comanches had been set apart with a name unto themselves, though it be an inaccurate one. It was not lost on Jean that even the term *Indio* was a misnomer left over from the bygone days of Columbus.

Jean spoke to Bad Camper in the *Yuta* tongue, for he did not want the Spaniards to know as much as he: "My friend, who is the leader of these people you call Comanche?"

"This one," Bad Camper said, indicating the young warrior beside him.

"Does he speak the *Yuta* tongue?"

"Yes."

Jean turned to face the young warrior on the white mare. "What are your people called?"

The young warrior lifted his chin high with pride, and said, "*Noomah.*"

Jean tried to speak the name, but the young warrior corrected him, making him speak the name three times before approving.

"*Noomah,*" Jean said with a nod. This would have been difficult for the Spaniards to pronounce and spell. The warrior had made the first vowel sound by spreading his lips, almost in a smile, making a sound that differed from the Spanish *u* sound. Perhaps Comanche was the better term to use after all. "Some of the nations know your tribe as Snake People," he said. "Is this the meaning of *Noomah?*"

The warrior stiffened on the back of his pony. He raised his right hand and signed his response. "No Snake. True Humans."

Lines creased the Frenchman's tattoos as he smiled. He laid his palm on his chest. "Jean," he said, then signed, *"What is your name?"*

"Kiyu." Upon stating his name, the *Noomah* warrior made a sign Jean had never before seen. He made the first two fingers of his right hand straddle his left hand as the legs of a rider would straddle a horse. He made the sign with emphasis, as if his name were a powerful thing.

"What is he saying, Juan?" the governor demanded.

"This young one is the leader of these warriors you have written down as Comanche. His name is *Kiyu.* It means . . ." Jean paused, considering the proper translation from the *Noomah* tongue to the Spanish language. "It means *Acaballo,*" he said, applying his best Castilian accent to the name.

Del Bosque nodded as he spoke to the scribe. "Write him as down as Acaballo, chief of the Comanche."

The scribe recorded the name with the magic feather.

"Ask him his purpose for coming here," Governor Del Bosque ordered.

"Why have you come to this place?" Jean asked, in the *Yuta* language.

"Rescate," Horseback said.

"The ransom," Fray Ugarte blurted. "He wishes to be bought from these other heathens."

"I don't think so," Jean said.

"He said he came here for the *rescate,*" the priest insisted.

"Many of the *Norteños* use the word ransom to mean trade, thinking it is one and the same."

"Nonsense," Ugarte insisted. "This heathen speaks for himself. He is here for salvation, and therefore God demands that we grant it!"

"He has come to trade—nothing more. Listen, I will test him out." Jean turned to Horseback and spoke in *Yuta.* "What do the Metal Men have that you want?"

Horseback simply smiled, leaned forward, and patted his white mare ostentatiously on the neck.

Jean looked at Bad Camper and detected a hint of a smile. He continued to speak in the *Yuta* tongue so the Spaniards would not understand: "Go now. Come to my lodge at sunset for a great feast."

Bad Camper let the hidden smile break full across his face. He turned his pony around and left at a trot, followed by his warriors, the *Noomah* riders, and the *Tiwa* translator, Speaks Twice.

"What was that?" Captain Lujan demanded. "Why did they leave?"

"Relax, *Capitán.* I was only inviting them to come to my hacienda to trade tonight. You may all come, of course. I will negotiate a peace with these *Noomah,* whom you have written down as Comanches."

"You must arrange the ransom of that one called Acaballo," Ugarte insisted.

"He did not come here to be ransomed, Father. Does he look like a captive to you?"

"You said yourself that the *Yuta* called him an enemy."

"Enemies sometimes travel together. The *Indios* employ the truce just as Spain and France do, when the need arises. I think our friend Bad Camper plays the coyote with Horseback. He takes advantage of Horseback's ignorance. He wants us to believe that Horseback wishes to be ransomed, but Horseback is not a slave. Does a slave carry a war club? He told me that he came here to trade for horses."

"Then you should have told him he came to the wrong place," the captain said.

"I will explain it more diplomatically tonight, after food and gifts have been proffered. It is important to handle these Comanches delicately. Do you remember the messenger who arrived a few days ago from Tachichichi?"

"Yes, what of it?" the governor replied.

"I have spoken to him. He convinced me that these Comanches are the reason the *Tiwa* elders wanted Spanish protection at their *ranchería.*"

"*Ridículo!*" Lujan said. "Their weapons are primitive, their horses are poor. And there are only four of them!"

"There were five at Tachichichi. One was wounded in a scuffle with Battle Scar's *Apaches* and could not travel. And of course they would not have ridden their best horses into our city."

Governor Del Bosque shook his head. "Even so, Juan. Are we to believe that five warriors have thrown an entire *ranchería* the size of Tachichichi into a state of panic?"

"The *Tiwa* elders have had visions."

"Heresy," Ugarte snapped.

"Even if we do not believe in their visions, Father, *they* do—wholeheartedly. Their visions warn of a powerful nation of Horse People from the north."

The governor chuckled. "Still, Juan . . ."

"These Comanches are said to be very good horsemen."

Captain Lujan began laughing, and his soldiers joined him. "Is this the intelligence you have gathered? Are we to believe that those four scrawny warriors on their sorry mounts will overwhelm the entire northern *frontera?*"

"Yes, beware," Father Ugarte added, a rare smile on his face. "The four riders of the apocalypse!"

The soldiers burst into obligatory laughter.

"It is only a scouting party," Jean replied, "but those four riders put on quite an exhibition at Tachichichi. The four of them attacked Battle Scar's entire band and exacted revenge for their kinsman wounded in the scuffle the night before. I am told that they stormed into the middle of Battle Scar's band, stole all the Apache horses, and scalped one of the warriors alive without ever dismounting."

"Nothing but fantastic gossip spread by the same *Norteños* who claimed only a few days ago that a huge invasion force of *Pani* and French was coming across the plains!" Captain Lujan spit in the street to punctuate his disgust. "Governor, may I dismiss my men, now that the horrible Comanche threat has retreated?"

"Go ahead, *Capitán*." Governor Del Bosque answered, a weary tone to his voice. Ever the politician, he shrugged apologetically at Jean when the captain turned his back.

After the soldiers and the friar left the street, Del Bosque spoke to Jean with a tone of confidentiality. "We come into contact with new nations of heathens from time to time," he said, a hopeful glint in his eye. "Why must these Comanches be treated with any greater degree of diplomacy? Are they rich?"

Jean shook his head. "It is said that the Snake People are poor."

"Then why must we be so cautious with them?"

Jean paused, watching the riders disappear around a corner. "Because they are tired of being poor."

34

In seasons to come, under the great council lodges, during the Moon of Blinding Snow, the elders would tell of the searchers' first journey south, the fighting and the glory, the wealth of buffalo and horses, the blessings of spirit-protectors. They would tell of Horseback in the city of the Metal Men.

"There," a wise elder would say, "Horseback learned as quickly as the colt who stands and walks and nurses his mother in the short time the sun takes to dry his soft coat of curly hair."

Raccoon-Eyes came to Horseback that first night in the strange land, after the feast and the presentation of gifts. It was inside the walls of the square lodge owned by Raccoon-Eyes. Horseback did not like the walls around him, but the gates stood open, and there were ladders like those at Tachichichi leading to the roof of the lodge. He saw many ways to escape, and he watched them closely, in case the Metal Men tried to close the gates and take down the ladders, making him a prisoner.

Raccoon-Eyes spoke to him in the *Yuta* tongue, and with the hand talk. "Last night I had a dream," Raccoon-Eyes began. "I found a great wealth of good things out on the plains. There were robes, weapons, skins, furs, and many sacred objects. I found tobacco, fresh meat, sweet water, paints, and feathers. Tall lodge poles, wood stacked high, vessels filled with fruits and pine nuts and good roots. When I tried to gather all this wealth in for myself, it shifted shape, and became a pony who ran about me in a circle, and shot arrows with his eyes."

Horseback smiled. He was admiring his braids in the looking glass given to him by Raccoon-Eyes—a thing as wonderful as a pool of still water. "I, too, dream of ponies."

"I know you have ridden far," Raccoon-Eyes said. "But I cannot make a trade to you for horses. It is forbidden."

"I came for horses." He struck a few sparks on the fire-making thing that the Metal Men called a *chispa*. It sparked even better than the flint stone on Trotter's musket. "I must take many horses back to my country."

"Where will you get them?"

"From the *Na-vohnuh*. Those who call themselves *Inday*. They are evil things. Not even human. In ancient times, there was a great war between the *Noomah* and the *Na-vohnuh*. The *Na-vohnuh* tried to kill all of the True Humans, but my grandfathers' grandfathers escaped into a bad country. There, the *Noomah* have lived for generation upon generation. We have become like our wolf ancestors. We have learned to fight and survive. Now it is time to hunt down our enemies as though they were rabbits, and tear them to pieces. We will have horses."

Raccoon-Eyes paused out of respect for the power of Horseback's words. "Will you make a sacred peace with the Metal Men?"

Horseback looked beyond Raccoon-Eyes and saw the suspicious glares of the Black Robe, and the hairy-faced war chief. The wealthy peace chief looked on, too, but with trust for Raccoon-Eyes. "I will smoke with the peace chief," he said. "The one who wears the red cloth around his waist."

Jean nodded. "It is good, my friend."

After Horseback passed the pipe with the peace chief of the Metal Men, Raccoon-Eyes invited him to come as often as he wished to his square lodge, and learn the ways of the Metal Men. Horseback's heart told him to trust this Raccoon-Eye white man, and he began to learn many things—so many things that when he went back to the lodge of the searchers at night at the camp on the river, his head swam with images, and his heart ached with questions.

"I must learn many things here," he said to himself. "Teal's father will respect my knowledge as much as my ability to offer the gift of ten horses."

Horseback's name in the language of the Metal Men was Acaballo but Raccoon-Eyes called him *Kiyu*, as a True Human would. "Come, *Kiyu*, my friend," he said the first day. "I will show you all about the Metal Men's ways with horses."

Horseback learned that the whites strapped much iron and other heavy things upon their horses, taking from them much speed and many tracks. They forced large pieces of iron into the mouths of their horses. The saddles used by the Metal Men were beautiful, but heavy and rigid, locking onto the withers of the horses where they were strapped down tight. The foot pieces called stirrups were made of iron, while the rest of the saddle must have taken half of a hide from one of the lesser buffalo the whites called cattle. The leather from these cattle was not as fine as buffalo hide, yet the Metal Men knew how to paint, carve, and polish it. Raccoon-Eyes let Horseback ride upon one of these saddles one day.

"How do you like it?" Raccoon-Eyes asked.

"I can not feel the heart of the pony between my legs through all that wood and leather."

Later, Raccoon-Eyes took Horseback to a place where slaves were making saddles. They started with a piece of wood that the Metal Men called a tree. They covered this tree with wet rawhide, stitched on. When the rawhide dried, it shrank around the tree, making a strong saddle. To this tree, the slaves fixed the leather pieces with tiny iron thorns.

Horseback picked up one of the saddle trees and said, "It is not heavy this way. Too much leather makes it heavy. You should ride your saddle like this."

Raccoon-Eyes's brows raised when he heard this. He told a slave to fit the saddle tree with light iron stirrups, a leather cinch strap to hold it onto the horse, and also a sheep skin to make the seat soft. He threw a blanket over a horse, and strapped the saddle tree on over the blanket.

"Yes," Horseback said, after riding the padded saddle tree. "It is better than your heavy saddles. I am closer to the heart of the pony." He leaned to one side, then the other, noting the way the saddle stayed locked onto the withers of the horse. "This would be a good saddle for a woman."

Raccoon-Eyes laughed. "I give this saddle to you as a gift from the nation of Metal Men. Perhaps you will present it to one of your *Noomah* women."

Horseback smiled as he dismounted and removed the saddle carefully from the pony.

The next day they rode to a place called a forge where slaves from many nations made things of iron. Here, the strong *puha* of fire spirits caused powerful things to happen. It changed hard cold iron to a thing that glowed, smoked, and moved like a living being trying to escape. The slaves would pour it into shapes, and beseech the iron to change like water to ice. Once cool, it possessed a heft and a hardness greater than any stone.

In the forge, the Metal Men made wonderful things. Weapons that never broke, flaked, nor chipped. Tools that dug and cut and chopped and scooped and bored and raked and scraped and pounded. Handles that pulled and pushed and twisted and lifted.

Sometimes the slaves in the forge would offer shapes of iron to the fire spirits, making the shapes smoke and glow and yield just enough to be pounded into new shapes between a cold hammer of iron and a cold hunk of sacred metal called an anvil. This work made ringing noises that hurt Horseback's ears.

Other times, the slaves would plunge a red-hot piece of iron into water, then heat the iron again, then plunge it back into the water.

"This makes the iron very hard," Raccoon-Eyes claimed.

"The spirits work the same way with *Noomah* warriors," Horseback replied. "When I was a small boy, my father would take me from my warm robes beside the fire in our lodge. He would carry me out into the coldest day of winter and throw me down into a hole broken through ice. This made me hard, like iron."

One day, Horseback helped Raccoon-Eyes take all his horses to the forge. There a slave heated and pounded iron that came in the shape of a river bend. This slave made these pieces fit the hooves of the horses, and drove iron thorns into the hooves to hold the pieces in place. Raccoon-Eyes called these curved pieces of iron pony-moccasins.

"A pony that needs iron moccasins," Horseback said, "is better to eat than to ride. When my pony has a sore foot, I wrap it in wet rawhide. That is the only moccasin my pony needs."

Besides the fine horses and the cattle, the Metal Men kept other strange animals. One was a lesser pony called a burro that was neither graceful nor good to ride. Horseback thought this race of ponies must have displeased the gods in ancient times and become malformed forever.

When a male burro mated with a true horse, the offspring was called a mule. This kind of animal was strong and useful to the Metal Men, but not as fast or as good to ride as a true horse. Also, the mules would not produce colts. Horseback understood this to mean that the gods did not approve of the mating between the two races. However, he thought a mule would make a fine feast for many families. The Metal Men packed many things on the backs of mules, without the use of a pole-drag. Horseback watched the way they did this, and learned.

Another strange animal of the Metal Men was a kind of sheep, but it scarcely resembled the wild sheep Horseback had seen in the high-mountain country of the Northern Raiders. Raccoon-Eyes explained how the curly hair of the sheep could be cut from the animal during the Moon of Shedding Buffalo.

"With much labor," Raccoon-Eyes said, "this sheep hair is made into warm clothes, and robes, and blankets that are almost as warm as a buffalo robe."

"You should kill these sheep and skin them," Horseback replied, "then eat their meat. The robes last longer when the hair stays on the hide. I have seen good robes passed down for generations."

"True," Raccoon-Eyes said, "but the Metal Men have a saying that they believe is wise: 'Shear a sheep many times; skin a sheep but once.' "

Horseback thought about this and said, "The spirits give us lambs so we will have more sheep for skinning when the circle of seasons comes around again. A robe made from sheep skin lasts longer than a blanket. It is also warmer and will shed rain. Why is a blanket better?"

"A blanket can be washed."

"The wind and rain will cleanse a robe. If the spirits wrap the sheep in his own hide, why should I not wrap myself in the same hide? Am I wiser than the spirits?"

"No," Raccoon-Eyes replied, with a big smile bending the tattooed lines around his mouth, "but I think you are wiser than Metal Men when it comes to the matter of sheep."

Horseback nodded. "It is only because my heart is closer to the Great Mystery. The Metal Men have learned many things, but their hearts are far from the voices of spirits. Speaks Twice tells me that the Metal Men believe in only one god."

"Speaks Twice tells the truth. The Metal Men worship the Great Creator, but do not know lesser gods."

"How can this be? When the pony-moccasins fall red hot into the water, can they not see and hear the power of the fire spirits meeting with the water spirits?"

"They think it means nothing."

"Everything means something."

"That is true," Raccoon-Eyes said.

"You are white, but you have lived among the Raccoon-Eyed People. You know the power of visions and spirits."

Raccoon-Eyes looked away, as if he had heard something in the mountains. "I know what I know," he said.

"You should teach the Metal Men what you have learned."

Raccoon-Eyes shook his head. "They would burn me alive for practicing sorcery. They are afraid that the Great Creator will be jealous of lesser gods and spirits, and will punish anyone who worships them."

"Will the Black Robe speak to me about these things?"

"He is very powerful," Raccoon-Eyes warned. "Many of the Metal Men fear his power and will do whatever he says."

"Will he speak to me?"

"Yes, but he does not understand your way, and he is afraid that the Great Creator will punish him if he tries to understand."

"How will the Creator punish him?"

"By making him burn forever in the Shadow Land. This is what the Black Robe believes."

"I want to speak to him."

Raccoon-Eyes sighed. "Listen, my friend. The Black Robe wants one thing with you. He wants you to know about the son of the Great Creator, who walked the earth, like a human, a long time ago."

"Is it true?"

"In my heart, I believe it is true."

"Then I want to know about this."

"I will tell you about it. It is dangerous if the Black Robe tells you."

Horseback thought of how old Spirit Talker had warned him about the danger associated with great *puha*. "What will happen if I listen to the Black Robe?"

Raccoon-Eyes made graceful moves with his hands as he supplemented his *Yuta* vocabulary with signs. "The Black Robe hears the voice of the Great Creator telling him to make all people believe in the son of God who walked on earth. He believes this is more important than anything. More important than my life, or yours, or even his own. To him, the soul of one who believes his way is more important than all the souls of all others who believe all the other ways, even though the others number like blades of grass."

Horseback narrowed his eyes at the white man. "You make him sound evil. Is he not a holy man?"

Raccoon-Eyes shrugged. "The brightest light makes the darkest shadow."

Horseback said nothing more about the matter. His heart told him to trust Raccoon-Eyes. He would stay away from the Black Robe. He would listen to Raccoon-Eyes tell the story of the son of God who walked on earth, but he would trust first in his own spirit-guide. He would purify himself with cedar smoke in his lodge and pray to Sound-the-Sun-Makes for protection from shadows made dark by bright lights.

. . . .

The next day, Raccoon-Eyes took Horseback to the sacred lodge of the Black Robes. This lodge had a large metal noisemaker with a tongue in it that made it ring loudly. Inside were many strange things: a vessel of water said to be sacred; paintings and carved wooden likenesses of white holy people from long ago; an altar where the Black Robes made people kneel before the Great Creator, which Horseback knew would only anger and disgust the spirits.

On the far wall of the holy lodge hung a large carving in the shape of a man who was bleeding from many places. This man was stretched across the sacred symbol of the Metal Men: the cross. Blood came from places where his hands and feet had been pierced by spikes that held him to the cross, and from a wound in his side where he had been stabbed. Thorns circled his head, and these, too, made him bleed. The carving made Horseback fear evil spirits, for the body of the man seemed misshapen, rudely carved from pine branches. He was familiar with hide paintings depicting warriors, but this was different. All the features of the face had been painted on, including eyes that looked sadly upward. The crimson streaks of blood seemed to glisten as if still wet. Yet the body on the cross looked as twisted and unnatural and as ill-proportioned as a grass doll carried by a *Noomah* girl.

"Why do the Black Robes hang such a thing in a sacred place?" Horseback asked.

"It is supposed to look like the son of the Great Creator who walked on earth. His name was Jesus." Raccoon-Eyes made the sacred sign across his face and chest. "It is not a very good carving. Jesus did not look like that. He was a natural human, like you or like me."

"You and I are very different."

"We are both human."

"I am a True Human."

Raccoon-Eyes nodded. "So was Jesus."

Horseback studied the carving. "Was Jesus not half god?"

"He was all human, yet all God."

"How did he show that he was god?"

Raccoon-Eyes thought about this for some time, using the curious habit the white people had of scratching their heads while thinking, as if wisdom came from their heads instead of their hearts. "He had powerful magic to cure sick people and heal lame people. He made things appear and disappear. He was God."

"Why does a god endure such torture? Why does he not call on his powers and destroy those who torture him?"

"He wanted to prove his courage to those who would worship him."

Horseback's heart beat strong to think of a god brave enough to lay aside his powers and live among people. "Did he fight well before he was captured and tortured?"

"He did not fight at all."

Horseback shot a curious glance at Raccoon-Eyes. "If he knew he was going to be tortured, he should have fought. He should have made his enemies kill him swiftly on the battlefield rather than die slowly on the cross. When I ride the war path against my enemies, I know I will be tortured if I am captured. That is why I fight so fiercely. That is why my brothers will ride into certain death to keep me from being taken alive. They know I will do the same for them, for if we are captured, our enemies will make us suffer tortures much worse than Jesus on his cross."

Raccoon-Eyes folded his arms across his chest and looked at the carving on the wall. "Like you, Jesus did not fear death, for he was God. Yet he was human, and he feared torture. Still, he endured it, proving that his courage was great. The Black Robes say Jesus died this way to wash away the sins of all humans—even those who came after his time, like you and like me. The Black Robes say that if you believe this, you will go to a good place in the next life, and if you do not believe, you will go to a bad place."

"Do you believe this?" Horseback said.

Raccoon-Eyes sighed, then spoke in a voice almost as soft as a whisper: "I believe what I believe. I say only as much as I must. The Black Robes are powerful."

Horseback looked for a long time upon the likeness of the god-man on the cross. Finally, he turned toward the door of the sacred lodge, saying, "The Great Creator of the True Humans would have counted many strokes upon his enemies before enduring such torture."

35

While Horseback learned from Raccoon-Eyes and Speaks Twice, the others—Shaggy Hump, Whip, and Echo—hunted in the mountains for deer, elk, bear, and lesser game. The hunting was hard near the city of the Metal Men, yet over the mountains, meat abounded. Also, there were signs of *Na-vohnuh* camps.

"My son," Shaggy Hump said one evening, as Horseback returned from the square lodge of Raccoon-Eyes, "I have found the trail of a *Na-vohnuh* band over the mountains. It is only four suns old and shows the tracks of sixteen horses. Echo and Whip wish to go with me to steal the horses."

"Will you take scalps?" Horseback said.

"I have prayed, and the spirits tell me this band of *Na-vohnuh* is not for killing, but for providing the horses for us. I wish to kill many *Na-vohnuh* in days to come, but I do not wish to displease the spirits."

"The spirits are wise. We are only four warriors. Go. I will stay here with Raccoon-Eyes. He is going to show me how the Metal Men catch the cattle by throwing a snare made from rope."

The next day, Horseback woke alone in the lodge of the searchers, for the others had left in the night to steal ponies. He rode through a light snow to the square lodge and found Raccoon-Eyes waiting there with three horsemen.

"The riders are dark-skinned," he said, "but they dress like whites."

"They are *Indio* by blood," Raccoon-Eyes explained, "yet their grandfathers lived among the Metal Men far to the south, and they know the ways of the whites. You will like them. They ride well."

Horseback looked at them suspiciously. "I will see."

The *Indio* riders used the heavy saddles of the Metal Men, and this made Horseback doubt that they could show him anything he did not know about riding. He noticed that each of the riders, including Raccoon-Eyes, had a large coil of rope tied to his saddle. He had studied this kind of rope before, and had even watched a slave making a length of it. It consisted of rawhide strips woven expertly into a strong cord about as big around as a finger. Horseback wanted to trade for such a rope, for it would be good to trail behind a buffalo pony.

To hold his horses and cattle, Raccoon-Eyes's slaves had made a trap of straight tree trunks that were too big around to serve as lodge poles. Inside this trap he saw six cows. Taking down the lighter poles that closed the trap, the five riders stood their mounts in the opening so the cattle would not escape the trap. Then one of the *Indio* riders took the coil of rope from his saddle. As if by magic, he formed a noose in the end of the rawhide rope. It reminded Horseback of how his father once tricked him when he was a boy by making things appear from nowhere in his empty hands.

As Horseback tried to catch the rider at this sleight-of-hand trick, the others let one of the cows out of the trap. The beast loped away, then began to trot aimlessly, as if uncertain where it should go. These beasts the Metal Men kept were stupid animals who had no spirits in their hearts to guide them.

Suddenly, the rider with the noose in his rope galled his horse with the iron things the Metal Men wore on their heels like the weapons of turkey gobblers. They had to wear these spurs, as they were called, to make their horses run, after strapping all that heavy wood and leather and iron onto them. The horse lunged into a gallop, lay his ears back, and angled directly toward the cow that had been released from the trap.

Now Horseback saw the rider whirl the noose above his head like a *Noomah* boy playing with a bull-roarer. The cow turned away, but the horse gave chase and closed quickly on the slower animal. When the rider came near, he lashed out with his noose, making it fly ahead of him and settle around the head and neck of the cow. Now he wrapped the end of his rope around the part of the Spanish saddle the Metal Men called a pommel. He flicked the slack around the hocks of the cow and angled sharply away, jerking the snared beast to the ground.

Horseback smiled as he watched the *Indio* rider jump from his mount and tie three legs of the stunned cow together, leaving her writhing on the ground. Before he could ask any questions, Raccoon-Eyes had chased another cow from the trap and another *Indio* rider was whirling a noose. This rider made his loop touch the ground just in front of the cow, and when the cow stepped into the noose with her front legs, the rider jerked the rope, tripping the cow hard to the ground.

A third cow ran from the trap. Raccoon-Eyes and the third *Indio* rider gave chase. The *Indio* caught the cow by the neck. Raccoon-Eyes rode in behind the cow, threw his noose, and caught her by the back feet. The two riders pulled the cow in two directions until she fell on the ground.

After the cow had been tied down like the others, Raccoon-Eyes shouted at Horseback: "Release the rest of the cows from the trap, *Kiyu!*"

Horseback rode his pony around the inside of the trap until the four remaining cows ran out. Each of the riders chased one of the cows, yet none whirled his noose as Horseback had expected. Raccoon-Eyes rode the fastest horse and closed in on the nearest cow. Riding to the left side of the cow, he leaned to his right and grabbed the tail of the cow. He threw his leg, stirrup and all, forward and over the tail he held in his hand. Using the strength of his leg and arm together to hold the tail, he suddenly angled his horse to the left and pulled the cow off balance, releasing her tail as she tumbled to the ground.

Horseback laughed at the silly-looking animal lying stunned on the ground. The three *Indio* riders caught the cows they chased about the same time, and made three more clouds of dust rise as they jerked the cows off their feet. He laughed out loud at the trick the men had played on the stupid beasts.

Riding out to meet Raccoon-Eyes, Horseback said, "That is a good game, my friend, but why not kill these beasts with a lance? That is also a good game that makes much meat. Why tie them on the ground?"

"The Metal Men have different ways. They live in one lodge and keep their cows nearby to make calves, so they do not always have to hunt. The owners catch the cows with the nooses so they can mark them with a hot iron that burns their own symbol on the cow." He pointed to the brand on the hip of the cow. "When they want one for meat, they bring it to a pen, and kill it by cutting its throat."

Horseback nodded and put his fingertips on his chest, searching his heart for questions. "They own cows, as I own horses?"

"Yes."

Horseback grunted at the strangeness of this thought, then pointed at Raccoon-Eyes's coil of rawhide rope. "The noose is good. I would like to learn to throw it. Can it catch an enemy?"

"It has been used that way before. Also as a game to catch lions, wolves, coyotes, and bears—even the great humpbacked bears."

"Buffalo?" Horseback asked.

"It has been done, but it is a dangerous game. The Metal Men send large hunting parties out onto the plains to the east, in the country of the *Inday*. They kill the buffalo with lances, as your hunters do. It is better to kill the buffalo with the lance than to rope it."

"Can the noose catch wild horses?"

Raccoon-Eyes smiled. "If the pony you ride is fast."

"I ride fast ponies. Slow ponies move my lodge and make meat for my fire. Will you teach me?"

"Of course, my friend. It is forbidden for me to trade horses to you, but I can teach you how to catch them with . . ." he lifted his coil of rawhide before him ". . . *la reata.*"

"*La reata,*" Horseback repeated. He reached for the roll of snakelike line as Raccoon-Eyes handed it to him.

In the days that followed, Horseback learned to make the noose, whirl it, throw it, and catch with it. Without a Spanish saddle, he had no pommel around which to wrap his *reata*, so Raccoon-Eyes showed him how to tie the home end of the rope to his own mount's tail. The tail was strong and would hold any horse or cow of equal or lesser size.

"You can even catch an animal larger than your mount if you choke it to weaken it," Raccoon-Eyes said. "But it is dangerous for your horse to be tied to the rope. When I wrap my rope around the pommel of my saddle, I can just as easily unwrap it if I need to get free."

"My horse is not afraid to be tied to the rope. My horse shares my spirit power when I ride."

At first, Horseback's mounts feared the noose whirling above their heads, but he sat on them and whirled the rope as Father Sun crossed over him and the horses pranced under him. He made the rope sing through the air until his arm was tired and sore. The horses learned not to fear the rope.

After learning to rope cattle, Horseback asked Raccoon-Eyes if he could try roping a colt, two winters old, in the big pasture of the hacienda. Raccoon-Eyes nodded. This time, Horseback did not tie his rope to the tail of his mount, for he wanted to try another way.

He threw many times at the colt and missed. His mount was tired, but Horseback kept chasing the colt until he finally caught it. Before the slack could straighten from the *reata*, he sprang from his pony. With his moccasins on the ground, he fought the lunges of the frightened colt. He held the rope until the sun sank from the sky, finally laying his hand on the colt at dark. He spoke to the colt, saying, "*Noomah. Noo-oo-oo-mah-ah.*"

His heart told him that this was the way to catch wild horses. He had heard from Raccoon-Eyes, Speaks Twice, and Bad Camper that wild horses ran among the buffalo on flat lands to the east, in the country of the *Na-vohnuh*. Horseback began to dream of riding into that country, of hunting buffalo, catching horses, and killing *Na-vohnuh*.

As he trained his ponies, Horseback rode much in the hills over the city of Santa Fe. One day, when Raccoon-Eyes rode with him, they came over a crest, and Horseback slowed his pace to peer cautiously over the rise and down into the next *arroyo*. He was looking for deer sign, for enemies, for meat.

Instead, he saw a bird that was strange to him, stalking among the low sage bushes.

This bird was the size of a very young turkey, but conformed differently. It was not like the fat chickens the Metal Men kept, nor was it like the wild chickens from *Noomah* country. It was not like a grouse of the plains or a ptarmigan of the high mountains. When it moved, it carried its head and tail low. When it stopped it raised both head and tail alertly, giving Horseback the impression that it was both hunter and hunted. Whatever it was, it looked like a good piece of meat, so he strung his bow.

Slipping from his pony to stalk closer on silent moccasins, he moved easily within range before the bird knew he was there. When the strange winged one stepped from behind a large rock, Horseback loosed his arrow, hitting the bird at the base of the neck. It flopped on the ground until he walked up to it and found its eyes wide and dull in the stare of death.

Smiling, he spread the wings to look at the feathers, as Raccoon-Eyes rode up beside him, leading Horseback's pony.

"Good shot," Raccoon-Eyes said. "Do you know this bird?"

"No," Horseback replied, surprised now to find a hidden sheen to the feathers that had before looked so dull.

"It is the bird of the chaparral. Some call it road runner."

Suddenly, Horseback noticed the wing feathers, white-tipped and elegant. He gasped and sprang from his crouch, backing away with fear. He stumbled backward, and startled the horses.

"What is it?" Raccoon-Eyes asked.

"The sacred one!" Horseback cried. He clawed at his quiver and reached inside. Carefully, he removed the feather Teal had given him. Comparing it to the feathers of the bird on the ground, he knew he was right. "The Sacred Bird of the South!"

"No," Raccoon-Eyes argued. "It is only a chaparral bird. I would not have let you kill it if it was sacred."

Horseback shook his head in anguish and shame. "I have offended the spirits. The protection of the sacred feather is lost!"

Raccoon-Eyes was silent for a while, then he said, "We must perform the ceremony of the Black Robes. We will bury the sacred bird and raise a cross over it. Those who believe in the cross are forgiven. So says the son of the Great Creator who walked on earth."

Horseback was unsure, but he trusted Raccoon-Eyes, who knew more about the Sacred South than he did. They dug a hole in the ground using Raccoon-Eyes's iron knife. They placed the Sacred Bird of the South in the hole and covered it with dirt. Raccoon-Eyes made a cross of two branches cut from a piñon pine and lashed together with leather strips from his saddle strings. Over the grave of the dead bird, the tattooed white man made much sing-song talk with his eyes closed. Finally, he touched the points of the cross upon his face and chest, then opened his eyes.

"It is done," Raccoon-Eyes said. "You are forgiven."

Horseback stood and searched his heart. "I believe I am forgiven. The spirits will not punish me. Yet, I have offended the spirit of the Sacred Bird of the South, and no longer will arrows go around me. I must be careful now, for only my shield protects me."

· · · ·

One day, Raccoon-Eyes invited Horseback to the city of the Metal Men to witness the preparations being made for a great journey. Just outside of the walls of Santa Fe, herds of burros, mules, cattle, sheep, and goats were being held by *Indio* slaves.

"Much meat," Horseback said. "My people will wonder if I have gone crazy when I tell them about this." Then he became silent and thought of his faraway country. He was longing to go home now. He did not yearn for a cold winter with little meat, but he wanted to see his mother again, and his father's second wife, Looks Away. He wondered about his friend Trotter, of the Corn People. But mostly, he thought of Teal with the reflections of sunset glowing in her eyes, her warm body near his own, her voice speaking to him of the ways of horses.

As they rode into the city, Horseback could hear a commotion, almost like the hum of a beehive. Everywhere, white people and *Indio* slaves carried tools and burdens and led animals toward the sacred square in the middle of the city.

"The way of Metal Men is a strange way," Horseback remarked as they neared the plaza. "The warriors are not warriors at all. They work beside the women and the slaves."

"In your country, my friend, a man must prove himself in battle. Yes?"

"If he wants to be respected."

"Here, among the Metal Men, a man must prove himself by winning the coins of yellow metal and shiny white metal. It means as much or more than counting strokes in battle. The ones you call slaves, are slaves only to the metal, not to other men. Among the Metal Men, slaves are forbidden. The workers are given food and a lodge and sometimes coins when they work. The Metal Men believe that they are not slaves if they are given these things."

"They work like slaves," Horseback replied. "They do not ride horses or carry weapons. In my country they would be called slaves. It is strange. The slaves here seem to number more than the Metal Men. Why do they not rise and fight?"

"They have risen before. Once, all the *Indios* rose and drove the Metal

Men away. For twelve winters the *Indios* held this land. But the Metal Men came back. I came with them when they returned."

"Why did the *Indios* let the Metal Men return?"

"Some fought, but their ways had been changed, and they were weak. The Metal Men had corrupted them, and they had become like the sheep or goats—once strong and wild, now weak and confused, unable to survive without their masters."

"I will not be corrupted by Metal Men. I will live like the horse. When the horse leaves the villages of people, it runs free again, and survives."

They rounded the corner and beheld a line of large carts being loaded with all manner of goods, some strange, some familiar. Horseback had seen cattle lashed by the horns to these carts, but now the carts stood like lodge poles without ponies to drag them. The cattle would be brought to the carts later, as the drivers of the carts prepared to leave.

"Governor Del Bosque is preparing this trading party to go far to the south, where the Metal Men gather in larger cities."

"Larger than Santa Fe?"

"Much larger."

Horseback found this hard to believe, the way his own people would find his stories of Santa Fe hard to believe. As he rode around the east side of the sacred square, he watched the people swarming around the carts. "It is the work of women to load these cattle-drags. Why do men do most of the work?"

"The women are busy cooking and looking after children."

"Among the True Humans, women can cook and look after children, and at the same time gather wood and take down lodges and load pony-drags and butcher meat and make fine robes and moccasins. These women of the Metal Men are weak."

"They are taught to be weak. The Metal Men believe there is honor in providing for and protecting weak women."

Horseback laughed. "Weak women make a weak nation."

Raccoon-Eyes nodded. "If I ever have a daughter, I will teach her to be strong."

"As will I," Horseback agreed.

As they weaved their way among the workers, Horseback noticed the Black Robe moving from one cart to the next, making the sacred sign of the cross over each one. He still did not understand why the thing that had killed the holy god-man named Jesus would now be a sacred symbol to the Metal Men, but it was so.

"He is blessing the carts," Raccoon-Eyes said, having noticed the look of curiosity on Horseback's face.

Horseback saw the Black Robe suddenly turn his head and look at him, and Horseback looked quickly away, afraid of the *puha* of the holy man.

Governor Del Bosque shouted at Raccoon-Eyes and came from the door of his large lodge to talk. Raccoon-Eyes got off his horse to listen. The governor bowed to Horseback, and Horseback nodded in return. He liked this peace chief, and he could sense that Raccoon-Eyes trusted him. The servant with the magic feather stood behind the governor, making the strange markings that were said to speak, which Horseback did not believe, for he had never heard the markings say anything, neither with his ears nor his heart.

As Raccoon-Eyes spoke with the peace chief in Spanish, Horseback made cautious glances toward the Black Robe. The power of the strange holy man made him uneasy. Raccoon-Eyes had told him many strange things about the Black Robes. They were forbidden to couple with women. To do so would make them as weak as a warrior who had coupled with a woman in the time of unclean bleeding. It was a bad thing to kill a Black Robe. Raccoon-Eyes claimed that to kill one was to make all the others more powerful, for they honored their dead. Some sought death, but not in battle. They wanted to die like the son of the Great Creator who walked on earth. They wanted to be tortured to death.

All these strange things made Horseback long for his own country, and he gave thanks for the warmth of Sound-the-Sun-Makes beaming down on him over the dirt walls of the lodges. This place was noisy and smelly. He was tired of Metal Men and their slaves who were not really slaves. He wanted to go back to the True Humans. He would miss this fine country of the south, but perhaps his spirit-guide would tell him to return here someday.

He had more than ten horses, and his fellow searchers had gone to steal still more from the *Na-vohnuh*. Teal had been wise to convince him to promise ten ponies instead of a hundred to her father. Now Horseback could return in honor with great tales of this strange land, and he could trade the ten ponies for Teal, and still have some to give to Shaggy Hump, Whip, and Echo. But not to Bear Heart, for he was lying like a wounded woman in Tachichichi.

Yes, it was time to go back to the hard country of the *Noomah* and take Teal as his wife. His heart was already going that way. Beyond the thought of his homecoming and his coupling with Teal, Horseback did not know what the spirits held in store for him. He did not know now that in days to come he would look back on this time as the Season of Ignorance. The Moon of Knowing Nothing. For this was the time before his Great Vision. He did not know how much he had yet to endure.

▲▲▲▲▲
36
▼▼▼▼▼

Fray Gabrielle Ugarte caught the wooden cross that hung around his neck, preventing it from swinging as he strode briskly up the street to the *Casas Reales*. Santa Fe was alive with joyous sounds tonight. The teamsters and herdsmen had gathered around fires in the plaza to laugh and sing and tell stories. The great journey to the south would begin tomorrow. South, to the heart of New Spain, to the City of Mexico. South, to the Land Outside. To civilization.

Ugarte preferred to suffer here on the frontier. It was God's plan for him to suffer.

The whole plaza smelled like roasting meat as he crossed to the *Casas Reales*, his black robe lunging on his shanks with each step. He enjoyed the hush of the *campesinos* that enveloped him as he strode among them, the reverent bows and murmured greetings. It was difficult to resist abusing the power of the robe, but Father Ugarte managed. He knew that he could look across this plaza and find something that smacked of heresy if he wished. He could inform the Holy Office of the Inquisition and have some soul whipped or tortured or burned alive. In the Land Outside, he had known brothers of the robe to become crazed with such power, and to live as demons addicted to the odor of burning flesh and the sound of dying screams.

He had seen harmless Christian peasants accused, imprisoned, and tortured over the most trifling matters. One unfortunate man he remembered had been caught bathing on Friday, a Jewish custom, and as such, a crime according to the Inquisition. Another had been accused by an enemy of "primping" on Saturday in violation of the Law of Moses, which demanded the day be spent in religious service. Married people had been cast into dungeons for the crime of sleeping in separate rooms. On the frontier, Christians who sought relief from illness through *Indio* healers had been charged with sorcery and whipped.

Fray Ugarte could have been an Inquisitor himself, but had heard his true calling among the savages. He had risen to Father Custodian of the Kingdom of New Mexico, head man among all the missions of the colony. He had always restricted his inherent authority to prescribe corporal discipline to the occasional flogging, and then only for backsliding novices, or heathen savages who corrupted his converts. Never had he ordered the flogging of a proper Christian subject, and for this he was liked and respected.

Yet, he knew he was feared, for he was a man of considerable power, unquestionable convictions, and unconquerable faith. And, no matter how he may have succeeded in distancing himself from Spain, he was still the northern frontier's link to the Holy Office of the Inquisition, a source of horror that struck dread into the hearts of even the most pious believers.

As he approached the tiny portal in the protective wall of the *Casas Reales*—which served as *presidio* and governmental headquarters to the kingdom and also contained the governor's residence—he caught sight of Captain Lorenzo Lujan, the presidial commander, engaged in debate with one of the teamsters. Ugarte stopped to watch. Gestures were made. Money changed hands. Ugarte smiled. It was customary for the captain of the presidio to extort payment from the *aviadores* whose goods he would protect on the journey south. This only reminded the friar that he must extort his own portion from *Capitán* Lujan for the coffers of the mission treasury. Such was the nature of all enterprise on the frontier, as the Crown appropriated scant funds for operations.

As he ducked to enter the tiny portal in the high wall of the *Casas Reales*, the soldier languishing there straightened and lowered his eyes reverently. "Father, the governor awaits your arrival. Please allow me to escort you."

"Thank you," Ugarte replied, lending a smile to the soldier.

They walked quickly through the garden, crossing to the door of Governor Del Bosque's study. The soldier knocked three times on the pine planks and announced the arrival of the friar in a voice loud enough to be heard inside.

Candlelight illuminated the governor's smile as the door opened. "That will be all, corporal," he said. "Father, come inside. I have some good wine from Spain."

The two men exchanged pleasantries and talked for several minutes about the triennial trading expedition soon to leave Santa Fe. Finally, a silence fell between them as each took a long slow sip of the precious wine, savoring the rare body and bouquet.

"I come to you with a concern," Ugarte began.

"Oh?"

"I fear for the spiritual well-being of a certain subject of ours."

"Someone I know?"

"Yes, someone you know well. Someone upon whom you must rely." The friar swirled his remaining portion of red wine in the bottom of the blown glassware vessel. "I have served our Lord on this savage frontier for many years now, governor, and experience has taught one peculiar lesson regarding heathens and Christians.

"A good Christian in this land is all too easily seduced by the heresies and sorceries of the savages. I have known even the most devout friars to take up residence among the savages and condemn their own immortal souls to eternal damnation. I have known Christians who have been carried off by savages and within the span of a year have completely forgotten how to speak a civilized tongue or recite a simple rosary. It is puzzling the effect these *bárbaros* wield over the hearts, minds, and souls of good Christian folk."

Governor Del Bosque nodded solemnly. "The seduction of the wild. I have seen it also."

"On the other hand, a savage blessed with salvation remains faithful only on the most precarious of terms. I know very well that many of our *genízaros* continue to practice their old heathen rituals in secret, right here in the city of Santa Fe. The *ranchería* of Tachichichi is nothing more than a den of such backsliders worshiping false gods upon heathen altars."

Del Bosque sighed. "Yes, a novice among white men reverts easily to his heathen ways, while a white man among *Indios* all too often turns irretrievably savage."

Father Ugarte finished his glass of wine and smacked his lips thankfully. "There are exceptions—men with faith enough to reject the false religions of the savages. The Frenchman, for example, Juan Archebeque."

"Ah, yes, Juan."

"He spent two years among the *Jumanos*. His facial tattoos bear witness to the fact that he must have completed the tribal rituals of those barbaric people. Yet, he sought a return to civilization and Christian ways. I was with the expedition onto the plains that found him almost dead of thirst, governor. He had heard of our exploring party and deserted the *Jumanos* at peril of his life to find us."

"Yes, for all he knew he might have been garroted as a French spy. He must have relished Christian companionship to take such a risk."

"I have watched him since his return to civilization. He has made remarkable strides. Not even the death of his wife has shaken his faith. In fact, I think he is stronger because of her passing. His sons are good Christian boys. His hacienda is orderly and productive. He attends mass regularly. He often travels alone among the *Norteños*, yet has resisted the temptation to revert to heathen rituals."

"Yes, his example is most encouraging."

"Still, I fear for his soul."

"Juan? Why, Gabrielle?"

"He has befriended that savage called Acaballo, the chief of the Comanches."

"Yes, so I have seen, but Juan forges many friendships among the savages. It is only for trade purposes. And, I believe, for the purpose of gradually introducing the savages to Christianity."

"So I thought, too, governor. But, this is something different."

"How do you know, Father? Have you seen or heard something?"

"I would not raise my concerns to you had I not. A few days ago, I was in the belfry of the Mission San Miguel chapel and I saw Juan and the Comanche, Acaballo, riding toward the chapel gates. Juan had not come to confession for some time, and I assumed, perhaps too optimistically, that this was the reason for his visit. So, I descended to the confessional to await his arrival. No sooner had I concealed myself in the confessional than I heard the chapel door open. Peeking through a crack, I saw Juan enter alone. He looked about the chapel—as if to make sure no one was present—then he went back out to bring Acaballo into the chapel with him.

"I remained silent in the confessional as Juan and the Comanche walked to the altar. They were speaking in that *Yuta* tongue, so I could not understand their words, but Juan's voice carried the unmistakable tone of a man struggling with doubt."

Governor Del Bosque's face went blank as his whole body seemed to freeze. "What are you suggesting, Father?"

Ugarte raised his callused palm to comfort the governor. "Relax. Hear me. I know Juan wants to do the right thing. He was trying to tell *Acaballo* about Jesus Christ, Our Savior. That much was obvious. Yet, at the same time, he was engaging in religious debate with that heathen. *Debate*, governor. The savage had manipulated him into a defensive posture."

Del Bosque shook his head. "But, if you couldn't understand their words, Father, how can you be certain?"

"The tone of voice was unmistakable, and in addition, they conversed through the hand signs of the *Norteños*, and you know how suggestive and representative that language can be. I am certain. I was in the confessional, after all, and I trust completely in the intuition God grants me on these matters. In the end, Acaballo turned and walked out, rejecting Juan's arguments. Juan stood alone for some time, in doubt, before he left. He made the cross, but he was shaken, governor."

"It is well that you came to me, Gabrielle," the governor said, engaging his diplomatic guiles. "I will handle this matter before it becomes any more serious."

"But, there is more, Antonio. After the incident in the mission chapel, I put one of my Apache *genizaros* to following Juan and the Comanche—stealthily, so he would not be detected. He witnessed something very bizarre in the foothills. Juan and Acaballo went hunting. The Comanche killed a chaparral bird with an arrow. Then, he and Juan buried it in a mock Christian ceremony. They erected a cross over the grave of the bird! This is dangerous, governor, for the Holy Office of the Inquisition would certainly judge such action as heresy."

"You don't intend . . ."

"No. Not yet. Even though I place myself in peril by not reporting these facts to the Inquisitor in Mexico City. But, I fear for our Christian friend, Antonio. He spent two years with the *Jumanos*, and before that, he lived with Jesuits and heretical Huguenots at La Salle's ill-fated fort on the *Tejas* coast. I have heard about some of the fantastic perversions that occurred there!"

Governor Del Bosque kneaded his brow so forcefully that he reddened the pale skin. "I will speak with him, Father. I will warn him quite adamantly."

Ugarte shook his finger. "I am afraid we will frighten him back into the wilderness if you do that. He travels so often among the *Norteños*, that he could easily slip away and be lost forever."

"But he has such a fine hacienda, and two sons!"

"I am afraid we will lose the boys, too. They are very small, but already he teaches them to ride. I fear we may lose them all."

"What can I do, Father? Juan is useful to the colony. I believe he wants to be a good Christian. You yourself have said he wants to do the right thing. If he is experiencing doubt—as even Christ did in the garden—then I wish to reassure him, to bolster his faith."

Father Ugarte nodded. "As do I, my friend. That is why I came to you instead of writing to Mexico City, because I believe you will handle this matter with more care than the bishop or the Inquisitor. I am confident that God gives us the wisdom to deal with this challenge."

Shifting uneasily in his chair, the governor said, "What shall I do?"

"It is very simple. We must remove this heathen influence from Juan's life."

Governor Del Bosque got up and reached for the wine bottle, turning his back on the friar. Ugarte knew this subject would strain his good working relationship with the governor, so he remained silent now as Del Bosque contemplated the issue. He considered the governor a capable administrator, and a crafty politician. Together, the two men had managed to work together, a feat some other governors and father custodians had found impossible to achieve, to the point of bloodshed and imprisonments. They usually kept their noses out of each other's business, but occasionally Father Ugarte found need to press a particular issue. On these rare occasions, Governor Del Bosque knew enough to grit his teeth and let the friar meddle.

"What do you have in mind?" the governor grumbled, turning to face the friar.

"Send the Frenchman off on some errand that precludes his taking the Comanche with him. Meanwhile, I will have *Capitán* Lujan help me in subduing the savage. The trade caravan will leave soon. I think it is best that we baptize Acaballo and send him south as a *genízaro*. You remember what he said to us the day he arrived. He said he had come here for the *rescate*."

Del Bosque rubbed his stomach with his fingertips, as if it were burning with the pressures of his station. "Juan claims that the *Yuta* only tricked him into saying that."

"No matter. The *rescate* is the best thing for him."

"What if Acaballo refuses to be reduced?"

"The savages understand savage ways. Leave the reduction of the Comanche to me and *Capitán* Lujan. And to God, of course."

Governor Del Bosque paced across his study for some time, clearly uncomfortable with the entire arrangement. Finally, he looked at the friar. "It is almost time to gather the *ciboleros* for the annual buffalo hunt. This year, I am going to send Juan out onto the plains to treat with Apaches over hunting grounds. Perhaps this will spare the *cibolero* expedition the usual attack. It is said that the Apaches and the Comanches are bitter enemies. Juan will not take Acaballo with him into Apache country."

Father Ugarte resisted his urge to gloat. Instead he donned a smile of gratitude and bowed his head humbly. "This gives me hope for the soul of our French brother in Christ." He clasped Del Bosque's hand between both of his own. "And if Juan Archebeque is correct in his wild predictions about this new nation of Comanche horsemen, then it is important that we make an example of Acaballo. We will send a message to the Comanches. This is Christian domain. Walk here only by the grace of Jesus Christ."

37

Horseback sat upon the rawhide-covered saddle tree given to him by Raccoon-Eyes, trying to figure out why a man would let such a thing come between himself and his pony. The sheepskin pad felt good, and the high cantle lifted him upward as his line-back dun pony climbed the steep mountainside. But he felt uneasy about the large pommel situated in front of his groin. It might prevent him from sliding forward if his mount came to a sudden stop, or had to descend a steep embankment, but then again, it might crush both his testicles in a fall, preventing any chance of making warrior sons with Teal.

Coming to a high, level roll in the terrain, he made a loop in the *reata* Raccoon-Eyes had given him, his pony immediately becoming nervous about the snakelike noose shaking and whirling in the rider's hand. This made Horseback smile, in spite of his uneasiness, for he loved the feeling of four powerful hooves dancing beneath him.

He felt alone today. The *Noomah* were far away in the poor country to the north. Teal was somewhere with the Corn People. Bear Heart was healing like a hurt dog at the village of Tachichichi. Shaggy Hump, Echo, and Whip were over the mountains stealing horses from the *Na-vohnuh*. Bad Camper had gone back to *Yuta* country. Speaks Twice had returned to Tachichichi. And now, Raccoon-Eyes had gone away on some mysterious errand. The only friend Horseback had left in this strange country of Metal Men was Paniagua, the *Tiwa* slave who was not a slave, who tended Raccoon-Eyes's horses.

He made the noose whirl above his head as the dark riders of the south had taught him. The rope made a song in the air, and the song made his pony want to run away.

"Listen," Horseback said to the pony. "This song is good. You will like this song in time."

As he watched the rope pass over his head, the beauty of the tall aspen trees made him smile, and he forgot his uneasiness for a moment. The leaves had turned golden, and they fluttered in the breeze like sunlight on water. He was high in the mountains, and the trees were tall, the white trunks rising about him like the bare ribs of some huge carcass. It was cool up here, and his flesh tightened over his muscle as he whirled the rope and reined in the nervous pony.

The conversation he had had with Raccoon-Eyes came back to him again, like the mystery of an echo.

"You must go back to your country," Raccoon-Eyes had warned.

"Why?"

"Something is going to happen."

"What?"

"I do not know. Something bad. The peace chief sends me away, and I fear you will be in danger. You must go away for a while."

"I cannot go," Horseback had replied. "I must wait until my father and my friends come back to our camp."

Raccoon-Eyes had frowned and said, "Do not sleep at your camp. Sleep in the timber. Stay away from your lodge at night. Keep your ponies ready to move. As soon as your friends return, leave the country of the Metal Men. Most important, beware of the Black Robe and the soldiers."

As Horseback remembered the warning words of Raccoon-Eyes, he shook the rope all over the body of his pony. He ran the loop up the side of the dun's neck, then flipped it around the back of his rump. This made the dun lunge and tremble and sweat. Horseback laughed, easing for a moment the bad feeling in his heart, as if he were giving all his worry to the pony through his rope.

Now he swung the loop over his head again and urged the pony into a slow lope. He watched the beauty of the aspen grove pass overhead as the rope song played. His people were going to be glad about the things he had learned here in the Sacred South.

A noise intruded on the good rope song, and Horseback felt it the instant he heard it—felt it through the body and the legs of his pony—a hind hoof striking something hard, something that rang with a single dull musical note.

Reining the pony around quickly in the tall grass, Horseback leaned to one side to see what the hoof had kicked. He grabbed the pommel and swooped low to see it close. The grass parted, and the curve of a deer antler rose from the ground like a snake throwing a hump in his back. In terror, Horseback tried to draw away, but his nervous pony felt him flinch and shied quickly to the right. As Horseback felt the strange saddle pull out from under his right leg, he heard the *reata* he held whir across the pommel, the strange noise causing the pony to bolt from the hallowed ground of the sacred deer.

He landed in the grass beside the deer antler, and to his horror, found it freshly broken where his pony had kicked it. He scrambled to his feet as he heard his mount running away. His shoulder hurt from the impact with the ground, and he heard the laughter of vengeful spirits in a wicked wind that whistled through branches. He wanted to pick up the broken antler and put it back together, but he knew it was too late. To touch it now would only further defile it, for his *puha* had been instantly tainted in a moment of carelessness.

"*Oo-bia!*" he cried out in anguish as his heart suddenly swelled with a very bad feeling. Father Sun looked around a cloud, his gaze hot and angry on Horseback's bare shoulders. He could not even bring himself to look up, fearing Father Sun would strike him blind for this wanton disrespect.

He backed away from the broken deer antler, and ran the way his pony had gone, back down the mountain toward Santa Fe. He felt as though he would be sick. His heart made bad blood go all through his body, down into his limbs. He had been too occupied with matters of humans to watch the ground for spirit signs. This was worse than stepping on the track of a deer. Worse than eating the food a deer would eat. He had broken the weapon of a warrior buck. This was as bad as letting an unclean woman carry his shield.

Now Horseback knew real fear. His weapons would be as useless as if they, too, were broken. Killing the Sacred Bird of the South had been foolish, but Raccoon-Eyes had helped him atone, and his powers had recovered. But now he had violated the trust of his very own spirit-guide, and he would certainly suffer.

He heard Spirit Talker's voice far across the many sleeps and remembered his warning: "*Hold sacred the horns of the deer.*" Spirit Talker had tried to warn him about the dangerous burdens of powerful medicine. Raccoon-Eyes had cautioned him about the dark shadow made by the bright shining light. And still, he had let this thing happen. Tears filled his eyes as he cursed himself for his own stupidity. Already, he was weak. He doubted he could even string his bow, much less draw it. If he should die now—whether killed by enemies or animals or fever or injury—he would suffer evermore in the Shadow Land. The elders said this was a hard fate. Harder than hard.

The hoofbeats of the pony had faded, and Horseback found himself afoot, alone. Not even his spirit-guide would walk with him now, for Sound-the-

Sun-Makes was angry, and was even at this moment deciding how to punish the lowly human who had insulted him.

His heart beat furiously with fear, and he fell to his knees, tears blurring his vision. How had he been so stupid? It was his first duty to honor his spirit-guide, and he had been seduced by human games, whirling a rope above his head. He was ashamed, weak, unworthy of his vision. He was vulnerable, helpless. Any enemy who came to him now would easily overpower him, and take him away for enemy women to torture slowly through days of agony. This was probably what the spirits had in store for him. It was just punishment.

He longed to speak to Spirit Talker now, or even his own father, Shaggy Hump. Perhaps one of them would know a means of redemption. What would they say? Whatever it was, it would begin with sweats an purification by cedar smoke. Yes, there was some hope. He would go back to his camp and build a sweat lodge. He would fast and sweat, then sit in his lodge and purify himself with smoke that would carry his prayers of humiliation up to the Great Creator. Perhaps he would be granted a vision that would tell him what he must do to make amends for the terrible affront of the broken antler.

Yes, he would try to be pure and strong again. He rose and began stumbling downhill. This was simply horrible. He was afraid. How could he have been so stupid? Never had he felt so weak and vulnerable. He did not know how his spirit-guide would punish him for this, but the punishment would be severe.

He tried not to think about the vengeance of the Shadow Land because the spirits would only exceed whatever punishment he imagined. If he thought of sickness, the spirits would cripple him. But then, having thought of being crippled, the spirits would make him crazy as well. Crazy and crippled. He would be scorned and laughed at by his own people, and all his afflictions would follow him into the everlasting life of the Shadow Land. While his friends were getting fat on buffalo meat and killing enemies, he would be wandering, crippled and crazy in the Shadow Land.

It was better not to even think of the punishment. Instead he would concentrate on his insolence, and try to figure out how he could keep it from ever happening again. He was almost glad that he was not riding a horse at this moment. He was not worthy of riding. The horse would probably kill him.

"Oh, Sound-the-Sun Makes!" he moaned. "Oh, great spirit-protector. Forgive me this disrespect. Punish me well, Great One. Make me to suffer!"

38

Captain Lujan burned his fingertips on the pinched end of the cornhusk he had used to roll his *cigarillo*. He put the end of the smoke in his mouth and inhaled until he felt the heat of fire on his lips, the he spat the remaining bit of tobacco and corn husk on the ground. When he spoke, his words came out as smoke.

"Here comes the *padre*," he said to the three soldiers lounging in the shade of a tall willow on the riverbank. "Look at him. I have led *entradas* into the interior with Padre Ugarte as chaplain. He can pace a man on a walking horse all day long and never fall a step behind. He is a tough bastard."

The soldiers rose, dusted themselves off, straightened their leather jackets, picked up their lances and rawhide bucklers. They stood looking down the road to Santa Fe until the friar came close enough to speak.

"I was beginning to think I would have to handle this matter without you, *Capitán*."

Lujan smiled. "I was simply waiting for the most advantageous opportunity, *Padre*."

"If you had waited any longer, there would be no opportunity at all. The expedition leaves at dawn tomorrow."

"The timing is lucky. I believe the Comanche will be easy to take."

Ugarte shaded his eyes with his hand so he could judge the look on Lujan's face. "Why do you think that?"

"I have employed two Apache scouts to watch him. The Apaches hate the Comanches. There was a fight between Acaballo's Comanches and Battle Scar's Apaches at Tachichichi, and now there is bad blood. The scouts tell me that they are ancient enemies with these Comanches, though they have lived far apart for generations."

Father Ugarte mopped his wool sleeve across his brow. "Enough *Indio* nonsense. Tell me about the Comanche."

"It is very strange, and for us, very lucky. Acaballo's men are all away on a hunt. He is alone. More important, the scouts tell me he has been going through some kind of purification ritual. He hasn't cooked anything in two days, so we may assume he is fasting. He has made a crude steam tent at the Comanche camp, and he has been sweating for two days. Now he is in his lodge. The scouts smelled cedar smoke and heard strange songs and chants."

Fray Ugarte's teeth gnashed with anger. "It is time to punish that heretical savage. The idea of such a heathen living among us—even entering my church. It makes me feel the anger of our Lord God in my very Christian heart."

Lujan gestured toward the horses, and began walking that way. "Have the preparations been made?"

Ugarte swallowed his rage and nodded. "You will act as the agent. One of the trading expedition *aviadores* has agreed to purchase the *genizaro* contract once we have reduced the savage. The *aviador* has connections in the copper mines of Chihuahua. He will advance to you a commission on the Comanche's earnings. Of course, the Mission San Miguel would appreciate any generous contribution the *capitán* would care to make."

"Your mission will receive its rightful share, *Padre*. This little incident will benefit everyone involved."

"Yes. Especially Juan Archebeque, and of course the Comanche himself. The seduction of barbaric sorcery is strong, *Capitán*. We must deal with it severely."

"And so we will, *Padre*. I have chosen three good soldiers. Each is skilled with the *reata*."

The soldiers mounted and proceeded up the road that flanked the river, the friar keeping pace with their fast walk. Soon, the Comanche camp was in sight around a gentle bend in the road. There, the two Apache spies met the party.

"*Capitán*," one of them said, "the Snake man is back in the sweat lodge. No clothes. No weapons. His lance and shield stand outside his lodge. Bow and arrows and war club inside the lodge."

Lujan smiled. "This is lucky."

"It is not luck," Ugarte argued. "The grace of God goes with us."

"Of course," Lujan answered. He turned to his men. "Prepare your nooses. Garcia, you get between the sweat lodge and the Comanche's horses. The rest of us will cut him off from his weapons. If he wants to fight, make him do so with his bare hands. If we get two nooses on him, he is ours. But remember, he is worth no money dead."

"Wait," Father Ugarte said. "In case you have to kill him in order to protect yourselves." He turned to the Comanche camp, murmured a prayer, and made the sign of the cross in the air.

· · · ·

Horseback felt weak and hungry, yet he knew he had not even begun to atone. He felt impure, unable to call on the spirit powers that had served him so well before his careless act of insolence. The fasting and sweating and purification of cedar smoke had only served to prove his sincerity. His punishment and, hopefully, his return to power were yet to come.

He threw another dipper of water upon the rocks he had heated in his lodge while praying and patting himself with cedar smoke. The fire spirits and water spirits made a battle cloud of steam rise in the tiny makeshift sweat lodge constructed of buffalo robes draped over bent willow boughs whose ends had been stuck into the ground. He put the gourd dipper aside and clutched the sacred medicine bundle he usually wore inside his loin skins. Now he was naked, as he had come into the world. The medicine bundle was the only vestige of spirit power left to him.

Outside, he heard his horses nickering, and wondered if his father and his friends were returning. It shamed him to think of them finding him in such a weakened state, all his *puha* drained from him by the vengeful spirits.

Something dropped on the ground outside. A whirring sound, the drumming of hooves. Sunlight burst down on him as the sweat lodge fell apart all around him. Cool air braced him. As he rose in alarm, he could see horsemen between him and his weapons. A noose hit him, tightened before he could lift it over his shoulders. He got one arm out above the noose, but the tightening loop cinched his other arm against his left side. He saw the Black Robe coming down the road as the rope pulled him over the hot rocks of his sweat lodge, scorching his bare feet.

Fear grew like a cold chunk of ice in his stomach, and though he knew his spirit powers and his body were both weak, he found himself hurtling toward the soldier who had thrown the rope on him. He felt like a snared animal whose fear made him fight with ferocity. He ran at the soldier, heard himself snarling, felt his right hand gripping the sacred medicine bundle. The soldier lowered his lance tip to ward off the attack, at the same time moving his pony farther away to keep the loop tight. Horseback reached for the enemy lance and summoned the antelope spirits to make him run faster, but the spirits did not hear. He was reaching for the weapon when the second noose fell around his shoulders.

He almost flung the noose away, but it tightened around his neck and began to choke him. Now his fear burst from his heart like a swarm of bees. They were going to strangle him! The soul could not escape from a True Human killed by strangulation. He would drift nowhere, as nothing, for eternity!

The Black Robe was near now, and Horseback could feel the evil darkness of his shadow. The pain of the tightening nooses shot through him and he realized how hopeless his plight had become. If he did not fight to the death, he would be tortured, for that was the way with captives. If he did fight, he would be strangled, and his soul would never know the Shadow Land.

"Fool!" he croaked, chiding himself. You should have seen the sacred deer antler. Now you will know the wrath of many gods.

The Black Robe was in front of him, speaking to him, pointing to the ground at Horseback's feet. He understood that the Black Robe wanted him to kneel, but he would not. Again and again the Black Robe ordered him to kneel, growing angrier each time.

Finally the Black Robe stalked around him and ducked the tight rope that ran from Horseback's neck to the soldier's saddle. He saw the evil holy man wield his staff, heard the air sing, felt the stinging blow on the back of his knees. He kicked ineffectually at the Black Robe and heard the laughter of the soldier who had roped his neck. He swiveled his eyes far enough to recognize this soldier—the warrior leader who gave orders to the others. Even under all his fear, an anger smoldered.

The Black Robe's staff struck him again behind the knees. Then again, and again. Then the ropes began to tighten, and Horseback knew his soul was being buried deep inside his body, never to escape. His powers of vision failed. All he saw was darkness. All he heard was the angry rumble of Sound-the-Sun-Makes. He knew his punishment had just begun.

Cool air tore into his chest, and light flooded him. He felt the pain on the back of his legs where the Black Robe had beaten him, more pain where his knees had hit the rocky ground. Vaguely, he remembered the sensation of his medicine bundle slipping from his hand, and now he knew he was completely powerless.

He heard the Black Robe murmur something. The noose around his neck loosened enough to let a breath of air slip into his lungs. Looking up, Horseback saw the evil holy man making the sign of the cross—the thing that had killed the son of God who walked on earth. He tried to get up, but the Black Robe struck him hard over the head with his staff. Blood ran into one of His eyes. He heard laughter and watched the Black Robe go to the place where the sweat lodge had been. The sacred-evil one picked up the gourd dipper. He filled the dipper at the edge of the river and came back to stand over Horseback.

The power of Sound-the-Sun-Makes was behind the Black Robe, and Horseback felt the chill of the evil shadow. Water poured over his head, thinning the blood that had blinded one eye. In a burst of escaping fury, Horseback sprang, reached with his free hand, and seized the Black Robe by the throat. Instantly, the ropes tightened, but his hand was like an eagle talon. He would fight to the death! He pulled the evil holy man toward him and wrapped both legs around his black garment, feeling his fingers gouge deep into the flesh of the *puhakut* of the Metal Men.

The Black Robe was a big man, and strong, but Horseback held on. The ropes tightened, cutting off his air, making his bones stretch and pop. Still, he tore at the throat of the white man. His chest began to burn as his soul sought escape. The sky darkened, his grip weakened. He felt the big white man slip away. Soon, pain slammed into his head like a huge beesting. Again and again.

Air came back into his lungs, but Horseback was unable to move. He felt the soldiers taking the ropes from him, fixing them now to his hands and feet. He rested, tried to feel something beyond the horrible pain that swarmed about him. He felt his hands stretched two ways, as his feet pulled another. His mouth was full of dirt. He heard the angry voice of the Black Robe.

Twisting his neck, Horseback saw the big *puhakut* standing over him. He heard the rope song, felt the blistering sear of pain on his back. He heard the song again, and again, until the sound of his own screams joined it. The only thing he could see in the blur of pain and blood and sweat was his medicine bundle lying dusty on the ground in front of him. He could not reach it.

The pain was more horrible than anything he could have imagined. The gods were indeed angry with him. He could not have foreseen such punishment, such torture. He was coming apart, like a rabbit skin pulled too quickly from the rabbit. All the world was pain. Pain. Darkness.

Dragging across the ground. Cold river water. Searing pain. Angry, angry spirits. Torture. Darkness. Darkness. Darkness.

▲▲▲▲▲
39
▼▼▼▼▼

In seasons to come, children and grandchildren and even grandchildren's children would hear the story of the Great Vision. And so it was told by the elders:

In his sleep, Horseback felt a great heat bearing down upon his back. The rays of Sound-the-Sun-Makes pierced his flesh like porcupine quills and lifted him. Higher, higher. He opened his eyes and saw Santa Fe, the city of the Metal Men, falling farther below him. Icy winds whistled around his naked body like blasts from the wings of the Thunderbird. His own hair, in which he took such pride for its length and sheen, whipped him like a quirt would whip a pony.

He rose as high as the mountain peaks to the east of the city, yet he was not afraid. It felt good to fly. He was like a hawk, tracing sacred circles in the sky. He shivered with chills and groaned with waves of pain, but the flying was good. He was safe here, away from Metal Men, and *Na-vohnuh*, and deer antlers lying hidden in the grass.

Now he circled and saw his own camp beside the river. He swooped low to look closer. His father and his warrior friends had returned. There were many horses in camp. They were calling for him, looking at his blood on the ground near the ruined sweat lodge. His father was worried. Turning on a blast of wind, Horseback saw Paniagua coming from the lodge of Raccoon-

Eyes, and knew Paniagua would tell the others what the Black Robe and the soldiers had done.

A strong southern breeze lifted him away before he could call to his father. He was carried higher than the clouds, and the scorching rays of Sound-the-Sun-Makes fell unshadowed on his back. He flew northward like a spirit-eagle, and mountain peaks that stuck up above the clouds moved by as quickly as stones passed at a gallop on a fleet young pony.

The clouds cleared away below him, and there in a valley of brown grass, beside a stream of rushing water, Horseback saw a camp. Diving like a falcon, he came low enough to recognize horses he had seen Bad Camper ride. Songs came from the camp. Warriors danced, surrounded by women and children. He saw Bad Camper dancing and he smiled, remembering that Bad Camper was the brother of his father's second wife, Looks Away. He felt no hatred of these dancing *Yutas* and wondered why he should fight them.

The rays of Father Sun pulled up at the flesh of his back again, and Horseback rose, pushed northward by the southerly breeze. He sped on like a shooting star. The country changed below him, the trees and grass of the mountains giving way to rocks and sage of the bad lands. These were the hunting grounds of the *Noomah*, the harsh lands that had made him strong, and tough, and hungry. He angled to the east and saw a camp in the distance, near the stream called Sometimes Water. From far away he recognized the lodges of the Burnt Meat People, and his heart rushed to think of his family and friends.

He shot forward with the speed of an arrow and heard a terrible sound that turned his heart to ice. All the women in the camp were wailing. He flew low, and found his sister, Mouse, kneeling, crying, cutting off all her hair. He circled the camp, and found Looks Away, crouching beyond the limits of the camp, apart from the others. She was weeping. Facing the wind now, he hovered, like a red-tailed hawk watching a rat below, and he found his mother, River Woman. She screamed as she slashed her arms and breasts with a jagged flint knife. Blood poured from the wounds in sheets, and her horrible screams turned to a pitiable wail.

Glancing aside, Horseback saw two bodies lying upon burial robes. Quickly, he flew that way, and saw the lifeless face of Red Pipe, two winters younger than himself. Red Pipe had been afraid to ride horses, but was a good young foot-warrior. There were many wounds on his chest and stomach. His scalp was gone. The women covered him with the burial robe.

Lying next to the body of Red Pipe, was that of old Spirit Talker, scalped, his throat cut, one wound to his rib cage. The women paid little attention to this corpse, for though Spirit Talker was wise and powerful, he was old and weak and not missed as much as a rising warrior who might have fed and protected the people for many winters to come. The old man was left uncovered by the wailing women for a long time, as Horseback looked down on him and felt very sad.

He thought a tear would fall from his eye and land upon the body of Spirit Talker, but just then a powerful blast of wind lifted him violently in the air, twisting his whole body and making his joints hurt all over. He found himself hurtling northward on a crazy wind, into the good mountain country of the Northern Raiders. The wind took him to a camp in the foothills, with many lodges, and more ponies than Horseback ever thought the Northern Raiders would possess.

He cringed with hatred when he realized that his enemies were holding a scalp dance, their women trilling with joy even as the women of the Burnt Meat People were wailing with sorrow. He saw two scalps on poles, and knew they were the scalps of Spirit Talker and Red Pipe. They were feasting and singing and dancing, and Horseback hated them.

He heard a battle cry, and flew through the darkening sky to hover over the warrior who had made it. There were other warriors here, laughing and smoking. Then he saw the backside of a naked warrior, and realized there was a woman under the warrior. Horseback's breath seemed to sull in his chest, and he did not want to look closer, but the winds forced him lower, and he saw the eyes of Whip's sister, White Bird, staring up him, looking right through him as he floated above her. She was bloody and bruised, and the warriors were waiting to defile her, one at a time.

His rage grew within him, but he was weak, and could only float, like a leaf on the wind. He tried to cry out in anger, but his breath was stuck inside, and his whole chest hurt. The sun's rays scorched his back again and pulled him away . . . away to the south and east . . . back into the *Noomah* country . . .

Not very far from the camp of the Northern Raiders—maybe three sleeps for a war party—Horseback spied the camp of the Corn People on a stream called Lightning River, far out in the open sage and grass plains. His heart began to pound, for he knew he would see Teal in the camp. He passed over warriors hunting buffalo, hiding under wolf skins to sneak within arrow range of the herd. The Corn People still hunted in this old way, for they possessed few horses and did not care much about riding.

It was good to see the Corn People warriors hunting, and now, closer to the camp, he saw women digging up yampa roots with their sticks, and this, too, made him feel good. Yet, Horseback knew they were in danger, for the war party of the Northern Raiders was only three sleeps away in the foothills. The breeze was gentle here, and Horseback floated lazily as he searched for Teal.

Now he heard a sweet song drifting upward and passed over a swale to find Teal alone, singing, digging up roots. Her slender arms writhed with muscles and made Horseback want to hold her. He saw his birdlike shadow fall on her, and called out, but his voice came out like the cry of a hawk. She looked up, but the sun blinded her, and she could not see that it was Horseback. Horseback tried to pull in his wings and dive down to her, but the talons of Sound-the-Sun-Makes pulled viciously at his back and Horseback knew he should not have called out to her, for he did not yet deserve to hold her and know the pleasures of her flesh. He had much to do. He was yet weak. His power was just now coming back to him. He rose in the air, and Teal became a tiny speck down in the grassy swale.

The crazy wind returned and wrenched Horseback away, causing pain to crawl around under his skin from head to toe. The pain made him groan, and he remembered that he was still being punished for the bad thing he had done. He sped above the clouds again, heading south. The great mountains passed to his right, and below he could see herds of buffalo dotting the fine grassy plains. Among the buffalo moved elk, antelope, wolves, coyotes, and deer. Horseback sang the Song of the Sun in homage to the deer he saw below, for he knew he must revere his spirit-guide animal now more than ever before.

Passing over grass-covered plains that went on and on, he recognized the earthen village of Tachichichi where his friend Speaks Twice lived, and where Bear Heart lay wounded. Now he began to see camps of *Na-vohnuh*, recognizable by the red-and-white lodges. His hatred flared again, and he wished he had the strength at this moment to attack these ancient enemies of the True Humans, but he was weak and was barely able to ride on the crazy wind. He looked a long way across the great plains, and saw that the *Na-vohnuh* held all of the good grass, and the best hunting grounds Horseback could ever have imagined.

Suddenly, he saw something strange appear below. It looked like a herd of buffalo, but it faded, then vanished, then appeared again, as if viewed through a mist. Something circled this herd of buffalo, and when Horseback looked closer, he could see spirit-warriors who wore the feathers and blue leggings of the True Humans. He watched them with fascination as they rode horses that were finer than any he had ever known. They swarmed around the misty buffalo and killed many, many of them. Now Horseback saw more misty warriors joining the hunt, and they carried scalps on their belts and feathers in their hair. They were coming from the north. Many, many warriors, all misty and hard to watch. They kept coming and coming, and they made camps that wavered like the spirit visions that appeared in the bad lands under the hot summer sun. And for each warrior there were twenty misty horses. Horseback wondered why they were not real. He wondered why they looked like dream-people. It was strange.

As he watched the nation of mist people, a roar like that of a huge prairie fire came from above, the flames making the flesh of his back crackle like fat thrown into the fire. Horseback's mouth opened to scream, but no noise came out. He tumbled in flight, and when he stopped, he saw the angry red eyes of Sound-the-Sun-Makes, the Great Deer, boring his soul with rays of pure power.

"You have been careless!" the spirit said, his voice coming out like a roar. He shook his head in anger, making flames lash about his neck like the mane of a spirit-pony.

"Yes," Horseback said. "I must atone."

"It is not I who punishes you. It is the shadow of evil made dark by my bright flame. You have suffered enough. Give back the power I gave to you in your vision quest, and you will suffer no more."

"Give back my *puha?*" Horseback asked.

"And you will suffer no more."

"I want to keep my medicine."

"You do not deserve to keep it. You have been careless with it. This time, you alone suffer. Next time, your whole nation may suffer."

"I have learned, Sound-the-Sun-Makes. I will not be careless again."

"Give back your power, and you will return to your own country. You will live long and have sons. You will survive the winters and eat things of the earth. You will escape your enemies."

"And if I choose to keep my power?"

"You will flirt with the shadow again."

"What will happen?"

"You have seen the nation of Horse People in the mist of seasons to come. This is your nation, Horseback, if you honor your spirit-guide. All the greatness and all the blessings of the Shadow Land will go with you. *If* you honor your protector."

Horseback felt the lure of greatness swell in his heart. "I will honor my spirit-guide, Sound-the-Sun-Makes. I will serve the new Horse Nation. I know now what happens to those who are careless with power."

Sound-the-Sun-Makes laughed, a great ball of fire roaring from his mouth and engulfing Horseback's battered body. "You know nothing! You have experienced a morsel of retribution, like a drop that falls into a great river of suffering. You have not heard the screams of dying babies or seen the rotten souls of strangled warriors. Medicine like the fires of the sun goes toward the making of a great nation from a poor one. The fires of the sun make a very dark shadow. Such a shadow possesses as much power as the sun that makes it. Will you flirt with the shadow, Horseback?"

"I will honor you, Sound-the-Sun-Makes. I will beware of the shadow. I will not grow careless again in my duties to you."

Sound-the-Sun-Makes ramped and pawed the sky, he shook his great head and flung his weapons far away, beyond the ends of the earth. He shifted to the shape of a horse and ran back toward Father Sun, leaping into the great fire. From this fire, Horseback heard the voice:

"So be it."

Suddenly, he felt very tired of flying, and Father Sun was passing beyond the unknown land in the west. Horseback shivered with chills, and felt his muscles burning with fatigue. The nation of misty True Humans vanished, and he passed over the mountains, over Santa Fe. In the twilight he saw the Metal Men's road that went south. The long string of carts stood on that road not far south of Santa Fe, and many cook fires lit the camp of the traders. Horseback began to groan, because he did not want to go back to the camp of the Metal Men. It had been good to fly, to feel safe in the air. But now the cold winds from the wings of the Thunderbird were pushing him down to the camp of the Metal Men. He saw soldiers, and traders, and slaves, and slaves-who-were-not-slaves, and women, and horses, and mules, and cattle, and sheep. He saw one of the Black Robes moving through the camp like an evil shadow. He smelled food cooking, and felt his stomach cramp violently.

All the good air fell out from under him and he dropped from high above. He tried to scream, but his voice would not come. He landed hard on one of the carts, and felt all the breath knocked out of his lungs. He was hurting badly, and he shivered uncontrollably. His mouth was dry. His head throbbed with pain. He lay on a bundle of hides in the cart, and he could hear the Metal Men talking all around him. Horseback felt very bad. He closed his eyes, and everything went dark.

40

Horseback felt himself being dragged from the oxcart. Scabs ripped open on his back, while his sore muscles and joints stabbed him with pain. He groaned. A hand pressed over his mouth, and a whisper penetrated the fever that confused his thoughts. The words came in the *Noomah* tongue:

"Keep quiet, elder sister."

He felt the agony of being pulled onto someone's back, and he was lifted, carried away. He heard the snores of Metal Men. He made his eyes open, and in the sparse light of a half-moon, he saw a dead ox driver lying with his throat cut, a black pool of blood glistening beautifully in the moonlight. Silently, he was moved away from the camp of the white traders, sensing that he rode upon his father's back while Whip and Echo guarded the retreat. He sighed with relief, and his heart felt good, though the rest of him felt very bad.

Waking again, he smelled horses, and felt the warm sweaty coat of a pony slide under him. He let his arms and legs dangle across either side of the mount, and clinched some mane between his teeth to keep himself from sliding off as the pony began to move.

The next time he awoke, he found himself in a new camp, hidden among pine trees. He tasted broth and swallowed, his stomach instantly convulsing. His head no longer ached, but his back still felt sore.

He heard his father's voice. "Drink, my son. Your sweats have passed. You need food. Paniagua brought medicine for your back, and you are better. You must eat."

Horseback found himself lying on his side, his father holding his head up so he could drink the broth. He took another swallow.

"Shaggy Hump," someone said, "shall I make a cradle board for your son?" The disgust in the voice was plain.

Taking another drink of the broth, Horseback opened his eyes and, to his surprise, saw Bear Heart sitting with Whip and Echo. All three of them slumped dejectedly, ashamed to be camping with one as weak as himself. It was Bear Heart's voice that had suggested the making of the cradle board.

He tried his voice, and it croaked, but he summoned his strength, and spoke: "Bear Heart, the last time I saw you, our enemies had made your guts spill out."

Bear Heart's temper flared, and he slapped himself in the stomach to prove he had healed. "You will not find the scars of a slave on my back, elder sister."

Horseback growled. "You will see my slave scars as I rush before you to steal your strokes counted in battle."

Shaggy Hump chuckled. "My son is coming back."

Horseback drank more of the broth, then asked, "My father, how many ponies have you taken from the *Na-vohnuh?*"

Shaggy Hump held the ladle of stew to Horseback's lips. "We took seven ponies, but it was no great feat. There was a bad spirit in that *Na-vohnuh* camp, my son, and we were afraid to enter it. All of our enemies were moaning and dying from the Metal Men's sickness. Paniagua tells us this white sickness has killed many people. It is good that we stayed away from it."

Horseback propped himself up on one elbow and took the buffalo horn ladle from his father. Drinking from it, he found a tender piece of meat to chew. "Listen, my father. I have had a great vision. I must get stronger, soon. I have seen things both wonderful and terrible."

He drank a second ladle full of the stew. Then, a third. But even this made him tired, and he soon lay back down. Before he went to sleep, he glanced at Whip, Echo, and Bear Heart, and found them sitting taller now.

. . . .

When Horseback woke again, he was starving. He ate greedily, forcing himself to stand as he ate, though Whip and Shaggy Hump had to hold him up to keep him from falling over. After eating, he walked, leaning on the trees around the camp to steady himself. He went to see the horses, grazing in a nearby meadow. He had Bear Heart and Echo help him onto one of the horses, and he rode slowly around the meadow, making a sacred circle, feeling his power come back. While he was riding, he watched carefully for deer tracks, deer dung, and most especially, deer antlers.

The medicine Paniagua had given him was good. It came from a plant Horseback did not know. The plant, wherever it came from, possessed strong *puha*. There was some of the medicine left over, so he wrapped it carefully in rabbit fur and put it in a safe place in one of his parfleche bags.

For two days, Horseback ate, walked, rode, slept, and thought about his vision. The third day he looked at his weapons. The foolish Metal Men had been too busy torturing him to think about destroying them. His father had found them along with his medicine bundle, and had taken care of them. His shield and his *pogamoggan* were sound. His lance was sharp, his arrows straight, his bowstring strong. He purified himself and his weapons with cedar smoke, then called his warriors to the sacred fire.

"I want to tell you about my great vision," Horseback began. "In my vision, I flew like a hawk. I saw things that made me laugh, things that made my heart bad, and things that made me want to punish my enemies. I heard my mother weep. I cannot yet say all the things I saw in this great vision, but I know a way that I can prove to you that the vision was real."

"How, my son?" said Shaggy Hump as he stuffed the bowl of his elk-antler pipe with tobacco.

"Soon, we must return to the country of the True Humans. When we arrive at the camp of the Burnt Meat People, my Naming Father, Spirit Talker, will be dead. If this is so, then you will know that I have seen his death and other things in my great vision."

Echo laughed. "Spirit Talker has been one sleep from the Shadow Land since I was hunting rabbits with a stick."

The men laughed. Horseback thought about this, and smiled. The smile melted from his face when he thought about what he must say next. "When we return, young Red Pipe will be dead, also. If it is so, will you believe in my great vision?"

The warriors looked at each other worriedly, and glanced suspiciously at Horseback, as one would regard a sorcerer.

"If it is so, I will believe in your vision," Echo said. "If it is not so, your medicine has gone bad, and no one will ever believe you again."

Horseback nodded solemnly. "In my vision, my spirit-guide—the Great

Deer called Sound-the-Sun-Makes—warned me. My medicine will be strong, but it will be dangerous. Those who follow me will tread upon the trail of evil things and risk their souls for the good of all True Humans."

"Why would any warrior flirt with such dangerous medicine?" Bear Heart asked.

"Because," Horseback answered, "the glory for those who survive will be greater than any ever known by a *Noomah* warrior. A new nation will rise. There will be fresh meat, even on the coldest day of winter. We will raise lodges taller than any ever seen, for every warrior will have enough ponies to drag many poles and hides. We will conquer much country, with good water, grass, tall trees for lodge poles, and much fruit for our women to make into sweet things. We will have so many horses that we will need much country with much grass, and we will have it. The buffalo and elk and many other good things to eat will number like all the stars of all the night skies since the days of our grandfathers' grandfathers. Our lodges will fill with children. We will own more horses than any nation of people ever to walk upon the earth."

The men sat silently, wondering why Horseback would make such crazy talk.

"Fresh meat on the coldest day?" Whip said.

Horseback nodded. "My vision is great, but dangerous."

"How must a warrior ride to follow the path of your vision, my son?"

"I will tell you. The vision begins here, with the smoke of this sacred fire. From here, I will ride to the party of traders the Metal Men send south. They move slowly. I will catch them within one sleep. I will attack these men who held me captive and tortured me. I will take the scalp of anyone who tries to stop me. I will use my *pogamoggan* to count strokes on anyone who comes within reach. I will take every horse and every mule in the party of traders, and they will be mine. I will scream my war cry so loud that it will echo in the nightmares of the Metal Men who tortured me."

"I like the sound of this talk," Echo-of-the-Wolf said.

"There is more. I will take my horses and scalps northward, toward the land of the *Noomah*. On the way I will raid the *ranchos* of the Metal Men. I will take every horse I see, except for the horses of Raccoon-Eyes. I will go around his *rancho*. Raccoon-Eyes warned me about the Black Robe and the soldiers, but I was too foolish to listen. I will protect his lodge as I would my own. Raccoon-Eyes is not one of the Metal Men. He comes from another nation."

"And then will you go home?" Whip said. "Back to the country of the True Humans?"

"Yes. I will go northward with many horses through the country of the *Yuta.*"

"Through the country of our enemies?"

"Bad Camper will help us get through to our own country. I will give him many mules, but keep all the horses. When we reach our own country, we will find the camp of the Corn People. I will trade ten horses to Teal's father, and she will be mine."

Whip smiled. "And then we will go home to the Burnt Meat People. They will sing with joy when we arrive with all our things."

"No," Horseback said. "This is not according to my vision. Those who ride with me and use the protection of my spirit-medicine will ride to the country of the Northern Raiders. There we will count many strokes in battle, take scalps, and steal many horses. We must not let the Northern Raiders have horses. The horses are a gift to the True Humans from the Great Creator. Our enemies will raise their horses for us to take. Horses are power. Power makes the *Noomah* strong. Anyone who chooses to ride with Horseback will attack the Northern Raiders before going home to the Burnt Meat People."

"Why, my son? Why must we raid our enemies before we go home to our women? Why not rest one moon, then attack the Northern Raiders?"

"Because this is not what my vision tells me I must do. You will know why, my father, if you make the raid with me. You will be angry, and you will fight like the great bear that scarred you that time near the camp of Two Rivers."

Silence fell over the mountain camp of the *Noomah* searchers. A wisp of sacred cedar smoke carried the council talk up to the spirits.

"When I was wounded at Tachichichi," Bear Heart said, "and lying around like a woman, I had a vision of my own. My spirit-guide spoke to me in this vision. He said I must join Horseback again in the country of the Metal Men. My spirit-guide told me I must do this, or else give back my *puha* and live among the *Tiwa* at Tachichichi the rest of my days. I am a proud *Noomah* warrior. I will not live among the *Tiwa*. I want to keep my medicine. I am not afraid to die, for I have seen the trail up to the Shadow Land in my sleep at Tachichichi, and I know it will be a good place for a brave warrior to go. I believe in Horseback's vision."

Horseback took the elk-antler pipe from his father. He pulled a flaming pine stick from the fire and touched it to the tobacco his father had packed into the bowl. He drew deep and felt the sweet, powerful smoke purify his lungs. Bear Heart sat on his left side. Horseback passed the pipe to Bear Heart.

This was the way of the elders. He who chose to ride with Horseback would smoke the sacred tobacco. He who doubted Horseback's medicine would pass the pipe on without smoking. No man would speak against the warrior who did not smoke, for no man could know another's *puha*.

Bear Heart smoked, and passed the pipe to Whip. Whip smoked and passed the pipe to Echo. Echo smoked and passed the pipe to Shaggy Hump. Shaggy Hump smoked and returned the pipe to Horseback. Horseback smoked again, exhaled, patted the smoke from his mouth onto his chest and shoulders.

When the tobacco was gone, Horseback said, "Tonight we will make a war dance. We will leave our lodge poles and our little lodge here. It has served us well, but we have no time to drag it now. We must move fast for many sleeps. Then, when we are home, in our own country, I will tell you the rest of my great vision, for I have kept the most wonderful part hidden away from you, as if behind a cloud of mist."

41

The herd appeared out of nowhere ahead of the trade caravan—twenty to thirty horses milling in confusion. From their midst a horseman rose, face painted black. The rider carried a shield, a lance, a war club. Across his back he wore a quiver holding arrows and bow. A single feather angled from his topknot.

Captain Lujan raised his hand to halt the carts. "Dragoons!" he shouted. "Come forward!" He looked toward the caravan's herd of horses, traveling parallel to the carts some distance to the west. Some of these Spanish ponies began calling to the *Indio* horses ahead, their voices coming out in stirring musical screams. Three regular dragoons and several mounted militiamen came forward from their positions in the caravan.

"What is it, *Capitán?*" asked the first soldier to arrive. "Apaches?"

"No," Lujan answered. "Comanches."

"Comanches?"

"I have been expecting them since they killed that freighter and rescued Acaballo. I knew they would come back."

"Is that him—Acaballo—ahead with the horses?"

"It cannot be him. After the whipping he got, he will not ride for weeks. It is a wonder he survived at all."

"Then there will only be three of them."

"Yes. Acaballo's father, and the two others." Lujan chuckled. "Now we will see what kind of riders these Comanches really are. Valverde, take your two dragoons and guard the herd of mules and horses."

"*Sí, Capitán!*" Valverde thundered away toward the caravan's horse herd with the two regular soldiers.

Lujan drew his sword, the ring of fine Toledo steel bracing both him and his mount. "You three militiamen, come with me to attack that lone rider ahead. The rest of you stay with the caravan to guard the flanks and rear. Santiago!"

The three militiamen answered the traditional yell of the cavalry charge, and galled their mounts with huge iron spurs, charging past the leading oxcarts. As they closed on the single rider ahead, they saw him disappear in his herd of milling horses. Suddenly, the *Indio* horses were on the move, angling toward the Spanish herd. Lujan searched the cloud of dust, but could not see a rider rising above the back of a single horse.

"Where did he go?" shouted one of the militiamen. "I don't see him!"

"We frightened him away!" another sang.

"No matter," Lujan shouted. "Drive the horses in with ours."

Circling the captured herd, Lujan still could not see the painted Comanche anywhere among the horses. The two herds rumbled the ground as they moved closer together, raising a plume of dust that drifted toward the caravan on the southerly breeze.

"This is too easy!" Lujan shouted. "Something is wrong. As soon as we get these two herds together, you militiamen go back to the caravan to guard the carts!"

From somewhere behind the caravan, a high human scream knifed through the dusty air and pierced the noise of the horse herds. Lujan looked back toward the carts, and saw four mounted *Indio* warriors storming into the rear of the caravan, scattering men, women, and animals. One of the raiders slowed down just long enough to drive his lance into an ox, then all four began weaving among the people and carts.

"Four riders!" a militiaman shouted. "There should only be three!"

Suddenly, a fifth rider materialized from the herd of horses, rising from nowhere between Lujan and one of the militiamen. The black-painted face scowled through the dust. "Look!" the captain shouted, his warning coming too late. The war club swung down on the unsuspecting militiaman who was watching in horror as the raiders plundered the caravan.

The club cracked against the skull, and the warrior screamed a battle cry that chilled the captain's bones. Lujan saw long lines of scabs crossing the back of the rider, who quickly dropped from view again, vanishing behind veils of dust and flowing manes of horses.

"*¡Dios mío!*" Lujan cried. How could Acaballo have recovered so quickly? He found himself woefully out of position, on the far side of the two herds as they came together. Horses began to fight. The roar of *escopetas* erupted from the caravan, but Lujan knew there was no one there to direct the fire. He rode around the windward side of the herd to avoid the dust, hoping to rally the guards at the caravan.

"Dragoons, come with me! Militiamen, hold the herd!"

This time, Lujan saw Acaballo rising from the off side of the horse nearest to him and realized that this Comanche warrior could somehow cling to the flanks of his mount like a spider, and then rise to the back of the pony in one swift, fluid motion. The war club carried the momentum of the rider's weight as he swung over the back of the horse and stuck with the force of the horse as it angled toward him. Lujan parried in time to catch the blow with his hilt, but he felt his two smallest fingers splinter under the impact of the hard wood.

Screaming in pain and rage, the captain wheeled his mount in a practiced maneuver that reversed his position and allowed him to swing his sword back-handed with all his arm strength. His eyes followed the thrust in time to see the sharp steel edge split Acaballo's painted shield, releasing a few tufts of buffalo hair stuffed between the layers of rawhide. The blow seemed to knock the Comanche rider from his mount, but then he was gone, and Lujan realized that he had simply ridden away again, clinging to the side of his horse.

He tasted the hot blood on his hand and looked back toward the caravan. The Comanches had scattered everyone along the whole line of carts. Fright-ened freighters were hiding among the sage and cactus. *Genizaros* were run-ning to escape in the hills. Half the oxen had died with their heads still in the ox bows. Lujan saw one of the Comanches ride down a girl who fled. Grabbing her by the hair, the raider pulled her kicking and screaming across his thighs and rode away with her, beating her into submission with his club. He saw another Comanche dragging a dead man by the hair until the hair came off like the bloody pelt of an animal.

The dragoons had followed orders to return to the carts, but they were too late, coming in behind the raiders. Everything at the caravan was dust and blood, moans and screams. Lujan galloped that way, watching warily for Acaballo to rise up again from the edge of the horse herd. As he approached the caravan, he saw the four Comanche attackers circle to the west, two riding to Acaballo's aid at the horse herd, the other two curling back to attack the freighters once again.

"*Escopetas!*" the captain shouted. "Who has a loaded weapon?"

No one answered. The two circling Comanches neared. Screams at the herd of fighting horses told him a stampede was coming. Lujan sheathed his sword and drew his horse pistol from the saddle scabbard. Hoping the prime charge had remained fast in the frizzen pan through all the chaos, he cocked the hammer and aimed at a returning warrior. It was the older one, who was said to be the father of Acaballo.

Taking aim, Lujan saw the old warrior drop behind the neck of his mount, and this time saw the arm thrust through the loop woven into the pony's mane, and the heel hooked over the hip bone. These were horsemen! He fired with the enemy horse just a couple of hoofbeats away. The horse took the ball in the shoulder and rolled, sprawling the warrior in a snarl of his own weaponry.

Lujan dropped his pistol on the ground and drew his sword, charging the downed warrior. To his astonishment, he found the man attacking him on foot! The Comanche lance thrust toward him, piercing Lujan's mount in the flanks behind his stirrup. He smelled the vile odor of guts and knew his horse was useless. Another warrior—Lujan could not tell which one—passed between him and the father of Acaballo. The stampede was near. He slipped from his dying horse and looked back just once to see the animal stepping on its own entrails.

Lujan found himself running toward the Comanche he had unhorsed, but now the stampeding ponies were all around him. He dodged the first few, then got knocked to the ground. A hoof came down full force on his shoulder, and slipped off. He sprang, felt himself knocked down again. He lost his sword, covered his head, and cringed at the thought of dying like this.

The sounds all around him were horrible. How could five warriors cause such chaos? What kind of killers were these *Norteños*, these Comanches?

The stampede passed and Lujan rose. He looked for his sword, but the dirt gummed his eyes. He made out the shape of a dragoon riding to his aid until an arrow shaft appeared in the hardened leather armor the soldier wore. The soldier grabbed the shaft, and pulled the arrow out, but then fell from his horse, motionless.

Lujan started running toward the saddled horse the dragoon had fallen from, but an arrow caught him in the thigh. As he fell, he looked to see where the arrow had come from, and saw the blackened face of Acaballo riding him down. Lujan drew his knife as he rose, but Acaballo used his horse to send the captain staggering. The Comanche circled, whipping Lujan fiercely with his bow as he tried to rise and fight.

Lujan heard the war cry: "Ay-yee!" and slashed viciously at nothing with his knife. He felt the club knock his iron helmet away from his head with a metallic knell. He hit the ground, then felt the knife pulled from his hand. He felt his own blade slash down his back, and he screamed in pain as he felt the cold air on his sweaty skin. Acaballo was pulling his leather armor and his shirt away from him. He heard his dragoons shouting, and hoped for salvation.

A whir of something sang through the air, and Lujan felt the doubled rope whip his back. It sang again, and again, and again, as he screamed and tried to rise. Pulling himself to all fours in spite of his dizziness, he tried to rush Acaballo, but missed and staggered. He saw more Comanches circling, horses everywhere.

He heard the strange tongue of the warriors, felt a fist in his hair. He rose to his feet, smelled a sweaty horse against him. The knife traced a small circle against his skull as he screamed in anguish. The ground moved out from under his feet, rocks banged his ankles, cactus spines pierced his shins. The fist pulled at his hair. Pain. Screams. Thunder in his own skull. Powder blasts.

Lujan hit the ground, felt the hot gush of blood from his torn scalp. The Comanches were riding away, horses stampeding everywhere. The rumbling lingered . . . dwindled . . . faded . . . He hoped they wouldn't come back. Please, God, do not let them come back . . .

▲▲▲▲▲
42
▼▼▼▼▼

In later generations, even after the circle of seasons had turned many times and the souls of the fighting men had gone to the Shadow Land, the elders would talk still of the first, great, long-ago fight with Metal Men. His grandsons' grandsons would not call the leader of this fight by name, for this would be after Horseback's time, and to speak of departed warriors would summon evils from the Shadow Land. But those old enough to remember would know it was Horseback, and hear his name whispered in their memories. And even the younger ones, who would never hear the name spoken, would picture this warrior-leader in their hearts, and they would know that the leader of the first fight with the Metal Men was the same great man who had been born on the day of First Horse, who had searched for the source of ponies in the south, who had led a new nation into glory and wealth.

After Horseback carried away a piece of the scalp of the Metal Men's soldier-captain, he led his party northward, through the *ranchos* and villages of the Metal Men, taking more horses wherever he found them.

Whip had taken a slave girl captive and begged for time to stop. "It will not take much time for me to make her good," he said.

"No," Horseback insisted. "Not until we reach the country of the *Yutas* and give them mules in exchange for safe passage to our own country."

"Very well," Whip replied, eagerly eyeing the girl whose feet he had tied under the belly of the horse she rode. "I would have shared her with you, but now I will make her good all by myself."

"Remember whose power protects us," Horseback said, angrily. "All that we take belongs to me. That is the way. All the horses and even that girl slave you grabbed belong to me until I give them away."

"My son speaks the truth," Shaggy Hump said, frowning at Whip. "If you go against the way, you destroy the *puha* that protects us all."

"Very well," Whip repeated. "If I cannot stop to make her good, I will content myself with beating her, for I can beat a slave girl at a full gallop." He angled toward the captive and started beating her across the back with the shaft of his lance.

"Enough!" Horseback said. "I take the girl slave for my own."

"You cannot tell me not to beat a slave," Whip said. "I respect your spirit-powers, my friend, but I am not afraid of you. We have played rough games together all our lives, and I have won as many times as you." He made his lance shaft glance off the head of the tied captive.

"I do not claim the girl for myself," Horseback said, "but to give her to Echo. He will decide what to do with her, who will beat her, and who will make her good. Tell me you are not afraid of Echo, for he rides close enough to hear you say it!"

Smiling, Echo rode in between Whip and the captive girl. "I will make her good," he said. "When we are in the *Yuta* country under protection of a truce. If you are lucky, I will let you watch me while I make her good."

Bear Heart and Shaggy Hump laughed at Whip, who quirted his horse and rode angrily away.

They drove the horses and mules beyond the *Tiwa* village of Taos, the northernmost outpost of Metal Men. They found a few more ponies to take here, and kept riding hard to the north, into the country of the *Yutas*. They rode the poorest horses on this return, and when one of the poor horses would stumble and refuse to run, they would kill it and take the best things to eat from it, then move northward again, away from the evil Metal Men.

It was told in later times that Horseback knew his way on this return to his own country because he had flown over these mountains like a bird in his vision. In this way, he found the camp of the *Yuta* leader, Bad Camper, and gave many mules in exchange for a place to rest, and safe passage to the country of the *Noomah*.

It was at this camp that Echo made the captive girl slave good. She did not resist him, for Echo did not beat her as Whip had. After he had lain with her and made her good with pure *Noomah* seed, Echo let her eat and gave her fresh water to drink. He told Whip to stay away from her, for she had been given to him by Horseback, in accordance with the way, and to violate the way would endanger the spirit-powers of the party.

Whip was very angry that the girl slave he had captured had been taken from him before he could make her good, and he refused to speak to his companions through many suns.

On the journey through *Yuta* country, the girl slave proved useful, making food for the men, lighting fires, and gathering wood. She told Echo with signs that she had been born to a *Keresan* mother in one of the missions of the Metal Men. She had never known her father, but knew he was white. The Metal Men scorned her because her mother was not married. Her mother's people rejected her because she was half-white. Having passed sixteen winters, she had come of age, and so the Black Robes had sent her south with the caravan, though they had not told her what would become of her in the south. She told Echo that she was happy to be away from the Metal Men, who hated her, and that she would serve him in any way he wished.

Horseback let his men rest two sleeps at Bad Camper's village, then rode northward again, pushing his ponies through *Yuta* country. Bad Camper rode with him to ensure no other band of *Yutas* would attack the party of returning

Noomahs. In generations to come, this would be spoken of as the beginning of the time of peace between the new Horse Nation of True Humans and the *Yutas.* It was said that the peace came about because of warrior respect between Horseback and Bad Camper, and it would last as long as both men lived. On the way north, Bad Camper showed the True Humans the way through mountain passes, along cold streams of rushing water, and through good hunting grounds for elk, pronghorn, bear, and deer.

But this country frightened Horseback, for he had to watch constantly for the sacred trail of the deer, so abundant in the mountain fastnesses of the *Yuta.* He told Bad Camper that he would be happy to reach his own country, where he would find fewer sacred trails to avoid. "I offended my spirit-guide in the land of the Metal Men," he admitted, pointing over his shoulder to the scars now healing well on his back. "You see how my punishment left scars to remind me. When the new nation goes out, it will find a place with few deer to disturb."

"It is good that you say this, Snake man. My country has many deer. You will stay out of my country if you know the best thing for yourself and your new nation."

Crossing downstream from the camp called Two Rivers, the *Noomah* searchers stopped to rest, for now they were safe in their own country. Horseback gave a fine pony to Bad Camper before the crossing, for the *Yuta* leader would not cross this river, saying he wished to return to his own village in the southern mountains before the Moon of Long Nights brought much snow.

At this camp, Whip came to Horseback, and spoke to him for the first time since the girl slave had been taken from him.

"My friend," Whip said. "I have been thinking about the story of your vision. We must find the Corn People so that you can trade your ponies to Teal's father. Then, we must go fight with the Northern Raiders before we go back to our village of the Burnt Meat People."

"I know this, my friend. Why do you tell me what I must do to fulfill my own vision?"

"You have given the girl slave to Echo. You will have Teal to take back to the Burnt Meat People. Your father has two wives already, and Bear Heart has a wife waiting for him to return, as well. I want to take a girl from the Northern Raiders and make her good with my seed. I want a woman in my lodge when we return from this long journey."

"Very well, my friend. If we take a girl from the Northern Raiders, I will give her to you. But, I warn you. My vision tells me that when we fight the Northern Raiders, your hatred for our enemies will make you go to battle like a Crazy-Dog-Wishing-to-Die. I will not let you keep any Northern Raider girls until your anger has blown away like the ashes of a fire. You do not have to beat a captive woman without reason to make her good with your seed. If she fears you, she will not know how to raise brave sons. If you want to follow me, Whip, your sons must be as brave as you."

After resting two sleeps, Horseback led his men to the northeast. They traveled far under each sun, moving from river to river, until they found the Corn People drying buffalo meat at camp on the Lightning River where it cut across the plains. They saw the village from a distance, and Horseback stopped his men long enough to choose the finest pony from his herd. He would ride this good pony into the camp of the Corn People, and the True Humans would see him carrying the shield that had been sliced open in battle with strange hairy white men far to the south.

"My son, I have counted the horses," Shaggy Hump said with a smile, as they spotted the village in the distance. "You have one hundred and one. Never have I dreamed of one warrior owning so many. I am proud my son owns more horses than any True Human before him."

Horseback smiled over the withers of his good pony as he prepared to mount. "When I told Teal I would bring her father one hundred horses, she told me I must promise only ten. I do not think she believed I would ever have one hundred. But now I see that it is wise to have promised only ten. Her father will see that I have one hundred, and that will make him feel good about giving his daughter to me, yet I will only have to give him ten. I will have plenty of horses to attack the Northern Raiders and to give to the brave warriors who have followed me. Teal was wise."

"She will be a good wife for you. Looks Away likes her. River Woman does not like her yet, but she will, my son. Teal will bear good grandsons for me. I will teach them how to hunt, how to ride, and how to use their weapons. I will not let them see my hair turn white or my teeth fall out. No brave warrior dies old."

"Do not speak of dying on this day, my father. This is a good day for a scalp dance."

"And for a feast. I am hungrier than hungry."

Horseback smiled and thought of Teal. He swung onto his bear-skin pad and waved at his friends who were holding the herd of horses. Out here on the grass and sage plains, no deer trails would cross his path, requiring his homage, so he urged his mount forward at a lope. When Teal saw him, he would be riding in triumph.

▲▲▲▲▲

43

▼▼▼▼▼

She was thinking of him the moment he appeared.

Strips of fresh buffalo meat lay draped over Teal's arm as she carried the heavy red meat to the drying rack. Suddenly the camp of the Corn People began to stir around her and hooves rumbled the ground. Her heart pounded, thinking Northern Raiders had come to carry her away to a life of wretched slavery.

Instead, she saw Horseback, which only made her heart pound harder. He rode a beautiful pony. Scalps dangled from his belt. Behind him, a huge herd of horses came over the rise of the riverbank, clouding the air with dust. Never had Teal seen so many horses in one place, and she felt laughter burst from her lungs as tears sprang in her eyes. Teal was a good daughter. She ran first to the drying rack to hang her buffalo meat.

It was not unusual that Horseback should appear as she thought of him, for Teal thought about Horseback all the time. He had been gone on his great search through many suns, and she worried that he might not ever come back, that she might not ever know what had happened to him.

But here he was. Horseback! See how he rode! She counted the warriors who rode with him. She knew from the stories that he had left with four warriors. Look! There were still four! And so many horses, and so many strange things! Horseback's medicine was strong! A woman rode with Echo! A captive? A wife? She realized quickly that Horseback could have claimed this woman, but he had let Echo have her! This was good!

She stood by the drying rack and watched him as his eyes searched for her. He had not seen her yet, but his gaze was darting like the blasts from the eyes of the Thunderbird. When at last he found her, his eyes struck her like lightning and made mysterious powers swarm inside her, all through her body, down the back of her neck, around the nipples of her breasts, through her belly, high between her thighs. She bit her lower lip and wondered how she looked to him, her hair loose and blowing, her hands painted with buffalo blood, her moccasins dusty. Maybe it was better this way, for now when he saw her next, she would look much finer, wearing the golden wedding dress her mother had helped her make from a perfect antelope skin, knowing Horseback would disapprove of her using the hide of a deer, which was sacred to him.

He rode by her with a most serious and prideful scowl. Behind him, all his horses and warriors were lining up on the riverbank, the ponies wanting to drink at the river, yet fearing the lodges of the Corn People. "Teal," he said. "Where is your father?"

Her heart beat so furiously that it pounded all the breath from her lungs. She pointed with a tilt of her head and managed to draw in a breath. "Resting in his lodge."

When Horseback rode away toward her father's lodge, Teal found herself surrounded by excited girls.

"He has come for you!" said her friend Little Cloud. "Look at all the horses!"

Grass-in-the-Wind grabbed her arm. "He has taken scalps! He has strange things on his pony!"

Slope Child spoke to her from behind. "Yes, he has gone far, and now he has come back to take you to his lodge, Teal. The warrior in his loin skins is too big for you. I know this, but you do not. You do not know how to please him. Before spring, he will want a second wife who knows what to do."

Little Cloud stepped between Teal and Slope Child. "Do not listen to this wild one who couples like a bleeding she-dog. You do not have to know what to do. The wisdom is in your heart. The winged ones know how to build their nests when the time comes. This is what my grandmother says."

Slope Child laughed. "I have never heard your grandfather moan with pleasure in his lodge."

Teal smiled, refusing to let Slope Child intimidate her. "Elder friend, you are wilder than wild. Why don't you get a husband?"

Slope Child smiled. "I will be a wife someday, but I wish to be a second or third wife who doesn't have so much work to do. My husband will have many brothers, so when he goes away, I will still have men in my lodge to lie with me."

The girls gasped and giggled at Slope Child's brazen ways. Teal liked hearing what Slope Child had said, for Horseback had no brothers at all.

"Go now," said Grass-in-the-Wind to Teal. "Go bathe in the pool around the riverbend, and make yourself ready for your wedding. We will listen to the talk in the village and come to tell you what we have learned."

. . . .

Teal expected to be married to Horseback before the sun had set, but strange things began to happen. She heard about it while bathing. Girls came running to tell her the news.

"Horseback has given many wonderful gifts to your father!" said Little Cloud.

"What kind of gifts?"

"Ten horses!"

"And strange iron tools from the south," Grass-in-the-Wind added.

"Horseback told your father that hairy white people made the tools. There is one that cuts like two knives bound together. Another that makes fire when struck."

Slope Child came swishing to the pool, her skirt held high on her thighs, as if she had really been running fast. "Listen, bride," she said, "you are not to be married today."

Teal splashed water, turning quickly in the pool. "Why do you say this?"

"Horseback has not returned to the Burnt Meat People yet. He came here first, to give the gifts to your father."

"I will marry him now and go with him to the Burnt Meat People. We will return later to our own village. My husband will provide for my mother and father here, with the Corn People. It is the way."

Slope Child shook her head. "Horseback has had a vision."

"What kind of vision?"

"He will not tell anyone what he saw, but his vision has told him he must attack the Northern Raiders before he can marry you. Tonight we will hold a scalp dance to celebrate his victory over hairy-faced white men in the south. The next night, we will hold a war dance, to prepare our warriors for battle. Then Horseback is going to attack the Northern Raiders. He says his vision tells him they are camped only three sleeps away for a warrior who rides horses."

Teal looked at Little Cloud and Grass-in-the-Wind as if she did not believe Slope Child.

"It is true," said Little Cloud, "and it is a revenge fight."

"Revenge?" Teal said. "For what? The Northern Raiders have not attacked our village for three winters. The elders have chosen our camping places wisely."

Little Cloud held her upturned hands wide apart. "Horseback has said that it is a revenge fight according to his vision."

"He says he flew in his vision," added Grass-in-the-Wind, "and saw you gathering roots."

Teal felt her flesh gather with spirit-powers, tightening all over her body. She began wading out of the pool.

"Are you alright, my friend?" said Grass-in-the-Wind.

"One day when I was gathering roots, I had a strange thought about Horseback. I was sad. I felt that he was dying. Then I heard a hawk and looked straight up. I could not look at the hawk because he flew just under Father Sun."

"Was it Horseback in the shape of a hawk?"

"I believe so."

Teal wrung out her shiny black hair, then pressed water from her flesh with her palms, first from her arms, then her body, and finally her legs. The other girls admired her grace, the fullness of her high breasts, the smoothness of her skin as she stood drying in the cool breeze.

"Now I am clean for the scalp dance," she said. "It is good that Horseback goes to attack our enemy. It is good that he has had a great vision, for it will protect him. I am going to dance well at the scalp dance, and at the war dance on the next night. If my husband is wounded when he returns, I will take care of him."

"If he returns alive," Slope Child said. "Horseback is very brave. He will seek danger."

"Hush!" said Grass-in-the-Wind. "Teal is not afraid. She makes prayers to the spirits!"

"So does Slope Child," said one of the other girls. "She prays to the spirits that make all peckers stiff with lust!"

The girls gasped at the suggestion, then laughed. Even Slope Child laughed. Teal laughed, too, hiding the bad feeling she felt in her heart. She had hoped to be married to Horseback by the time the moon rose. Now she would have to wait, and dance, and pray, and wait some more.

Still, she felt excited. Horseback had come to her first, even before going to see his own mother. She knew that life as the wife of a great warrior would require courage, and she did not intend to show any lack of courage now. She was not even a wife yet, but she was prepared to serve her husband-to-be. Besides, in the chaos of two nights of dancing, she knew opportunities would arise to meet Horseback in secret. She was ready.

Horseback was the one. The Corn People girls all talked about him since meeting him during the great camp-together. He had been born on the day of First Horse. He had special powers over the hearts of horses. He had traveled to the land of hairy-faced white people. Now he had seen a Great Vision. Teal barely knew him, and already, she loved him very much.

. . . .

The camp of the Corn People went crazy with dancing through two nights. The first night, Teal had no chance to be with Horseback, for he danced under the scalps hung high on the scalp poles, and he danced well, and he danced all night long. He slept all the next day, for he seemed very tired from his long journey.

On the second night, Horseback bathed in cold water, purified himself with smoke, painted his face black with war paint, and went to the lodge of the elders with the other men. There he listened to the old warriors tell stories of great victories and strokes counted in battle. When the more experienced warriors had spoken, Horseback had the chance to tell what had happened at the fight with Metal Men in the far south. His talk held the attention of the men more so than that of any other speakers, for although Horseback was a warrior of very little experience, he was known to possess great medicine. Teal only heard some of the story, for she had to listen through the hides of the lodge, like the other women.

After the telling of stories, there was dancing. Again, Horseback danced well, never looking up for Teal. The drums sounded like spirit-thunder, and the trained voices of singers stirred the souls of all True Humans with loud wails and high piercing yells. As dawn neared, the warriors who would accompany Horseback went to their women, for soon they would have to gather their weapons and mount their war ponies.

Horseback found Teal between the dancing circle and the lodge of her father. He looked fierce and powerful painted for battle. He wore a headpiece of buffalo horns and carried a new shield that had been given to him by the Corn People, to replace the sacred shield the Metal Man had damaged in the far south. A single yellow feather protruded from his scalp lock.

"My woman," he said. "Pray for me while I am gone. I will bring back scalps." He strode closer to her, his fierce eyes gleaming bright from the black paint on his face, searching her all over, as if passing judgement on a fine horse.

She took two small steps toward him—cautious steps to show him she wanted to be nearer, yet did not want to interfere with his preparations to fight. When they came together, she pressed herself hard against him, feeling her own heart beat furiously. "My warrior, I have something to tell you."

"What is it?" he said, his hand slipping around the back of her neck.

"I have been riding horses. When I go to dig roots, and no one sees, I catch my father's horse—the one that drags the rope. This horse teaches me to ride. I no longer fall off. My father does not know about this, but it is true."

"This is good, woman. When I take you for my wife, we will ride together. You will see."

His lips were on her cheek now, so Teal turned her face toward him and felt his lips on hers. She leaned harder against him and felt the spirit-mysteries swarm over and through her again. Then he was gone.

44

Two warriors from the Corn People joined Horseback's revenge raid. One was Teal's father, High Feather, who was known as a great foot-warrior, but was learning the ways of the young horsebacks. The other was Horseback's friend Trotter, who was promised to marry his little sister, Mouse, when the Moon of Green Grass returned. Trotter was the best horseman among the

Corn People and wanted to prove himself to his future father-in-law, Shaggy Hump.

High Feather rode the Spanish saddle tree covered with sheepskin. He had seen this strange saddle and admired it, so Horseback had given it to him. Now, after a day of riding, High Feather praised the saddle, though Horseback could see that the hard riding had made him sore.

"If I do not return from this battle," High Feather told Horseback, "you must give this saddle to my daughter when you take her into your lodge. It will keep her from falling off. She thinks I do not know, but she has been riding my horse."

The second day, they passed from a rough sage country onto high rolling plains covered with fine grass, brown now after the time of frost. When the sun started down, they found themselves among ponderosa pines, and knew they had crossed into the country of the Northern Raiders.

"My son," Shaggy Hump said as twilight gathered around their tired ponies. "You are leading us to the lodge pole camp of the Northern Raiders, though I know you have never been there. I raided this camp many winters ago, before you were born. How do you know where to find it?"

"I have seen the way in my vision," Horseback said. "Ride ahead, my father, and watch for signs of the sacred deer. When darkness comes and the giant cannibal owl rises into the sky, we will camp. I do not want to stumble across any sacred deer trails in the dark."

Shaggy Hump nodded. "We have passed from the country of antelope, into the country of the deer nation. I will watch the trail for you, my son. Your power protects us. We must all honor it."

Horseback slept soundly that night, for he wanted to search his dreams for spirit-guidance. When he awoke, he could only remember one dream. In the dream, Whip's sister, White Bird, was saying, "Help me, Horseback. Help me, friend of my younger brother." She was only standing there in the dream, as she might stand in her own camp of the Burnt Meat People, yet Horseback awoke with his heart beating furiously, and his body covered with sweat.

The warriors did not speak that day until the smokes of the Northern Raiders' camp were seen in the sky. They gathered around Horseback as he put his war bridle on his battle pony, which he had spared from riding until now.

"This fight is for revenge," Horseback said. "Only I know the reason for this revenge, but you will know soon. Trust my vision. We have cause to hate and kill our enemies." He swung onto his pony, who started to prance and snort. "Stay out of Whip's way. He will be angry. Do not race Whip for strokes counted in battle. There will be plenty of strokes for all of us, for this is a big enemy camp. Fight on the backs of your ponies. My vision says we must use the spirit-power of our horses to defeat our enemies. When you see me chase the horses of our enemies through their camp, you will know the time has come to finish the battle and go back to our own country."

The True Humans looked at each other, drawing courage from the black face paint worn by all, and from the tattooed scars of the old ones. Their weapons and shields looked good, dancing with feathers and scalp locks.

High Feather spoke. "I am an old warrior. I wish to die in a good fight before my hair goes white, like the head of the great eagle. Maybe today I will die, and while you shiver this winter in your lodges, you will think of me running without shirt or leggings, hunting elk in the Shadow Land."

Horseback shook the shield given to him by the Corn People. He leaned on his war pony, and the whole party ran toward the enemy camp at a gallop.

The Northern Raiders of the lodge pole camp did not see the *Noomah* warriors until they had galloped almost into the village. Horseback screamed his shrill war cry, and the seven True Humans scattered, weaving through the camp like swallows racing through the air. Their war clubs swung at enemy warriors running for their weapons, but only Echo-of-the-Wolf counted a stroke, as he had trained his pony to get him close.

Horseback rode all the way through the camp without taking a swing at his enemies, yet he liked the way they ran from him. He remembered his grandfather dying in the Red Canyon, his mother stoning the Northern Raider warrior to death. He remembered his vision, the bodies of Red Pipe and Spirit Talker. His eyes swept angrily through the camp as an arrow flew past him, tearing the flesh on his shoulder.

Finding the source of this arrow, he saw a warrior drawing a bow for a second shot. High Feather appeared behind the enemy bowman, distracting him with a war cry and a swipe of his club, and Horseback charged. The enemy bowman wore a scalp on his belt, and Horseback knew it belonged to young Red Pipe. He threw himself to the side of his pony as the arrow sailed over him. He swung over the top of the pony and felt his war club shatter the skull of the enemy who wore Red Pipe's scalp. Holding the mane of his pony in one hand, he reached low to grab the hair of the enemy so he could drag him aside and take his scalp.

The other *Noomah* warriors had already left three dead in the camp. Enemy screams mingled with glorious *Noomah* war cries, yet through the noise Horseback heard a shrill voice speaking in the tongue of True Humans.

"Help me, Horseback! Help me, friend of my younger brother!"

When his eyes found her, White Bird was using a length of fire wood to fight off an enemy warrior's knife. White Bird fought well, but she was weak and thin from her captivity.

Now Whip came between two lodges, his eyes as wild as the scream of rage that escaped his lips. He rode his horse over the enemy warrior, then turned, drawing his bow before the stunned enemy could rise.

"You defile my father's blood with your seed!" he shouted. He pinned the warrior to the ground with an arrow, slipped from his horse, and gave the reins to his sister. Cutting the belt of the dying man's loin skins, he grabbed the evil penis of his enemy and cut it off, throwing it aside. Horseback circled protectively, and he happened to see Trotter breaking off the shaft of an arrow that had pierced his thigh.

Now Whip had the scalp of his sister's despoiler, and he tucked it under his belt as he mounted. "Take my sister on your pony, Horseback. I am going to catch an enemy woman and make her good!"

The *Noomah* warriors continued to swarm, but the Northern Raiders had gathered women and children protectively at the north end of camp and had started to fight their way back into their own village. Horseback knew the time had come to take the enemy horses and retreat with scalps and war wounds. He pulled White Bird on behind him and circled toward the small herd of enemy horses that had drawn near the camp to see the strange ponies.

He passed Bear Heart, who had loosened his loin skins to urinate on an abandoned enemy shield in sight of the Northern Raiders. He laughed as arrows arched through the sky, missing him.

Looking back, Horseback saw Shaggy Hump and High Feather going from lodge to lodge, using their lance blades to pull the bear-skin entrance covers aside so they could look inside. White Bird held tightly to him as he circled the enemy horses and drove them toward camp.

As his warriors drew toward him, he heard a shout, and saw Whip riding at a gallop all along the front line of the enemy. Arrows sang around him like wasps, his shield catching two. Suddenly, he angled into the surprised enemy warriors and scattered a bunch of women and children who had gathered behind their men for protection. The enemy bowmen would not shoot at him here, for fear of hitting one of their own. Whip chased a young girl who ran faster than the others. She dodged, but he leaned far to one side, grabbing her by the hair and pulling her away through a tangle of low pine branches.

Shaggy Hump and High Feather circled back to cover the retreat of Whip with his captive. As High Feather whirled his pony, an arrow angled in behind his shield and pierced his side, hurting him so badly that he fell from his mount. As the Northern Raiders rushed to count the first strokes, Trotter and Echo turned back to protect High Feather. Riding one to either side, they ignored the weapons of the enemy as they swooped downward to grab the arms of High Feather in a maneuver they had practiced often around their own camps. Lifting the old warrior between them, they bore him beyond the reach of enemy scalping knives, yet High Feather left a trail of blood on the ground.

Horseback chose this moment to stampede the captured horses south-ward. His *puha* had empowered his party, but with the fall of High Feather, the spirits were telling him to withdraw with the ponies and escape further bloodletting.

Echo pulled High Feather onto the rump of his mount, and they retreated in a rain of arrows. Shaggy Hump and Trotter rode to either side to hold the wounded man on the back of the horse, and the whole *Noomah* raiding party moved southward. Already they could hear the wails of women, and Horseback knew that one woman who shrieked especially loud must have been the mother of the girl Whip had taken. The shrill, mournful yells sounded as sweet as morning birdsong to Horseback, and a dizzying swirl of power engulfed his whole heart and mind.

He cried, "Ye-ye-ye-ye-ye!" in a piercing victory yell that echoed through the voices of his warriors.

Passing over the first ridge, Horseback pulled up to look over his war party. Every man had taken a scalp. Never had he heard of such a victory. Even High Feather, though he was badly wounded, had a fresh patch of hair tucked under his belt. They had rescued Whip's sister, and Whip had caught the girl he wanted to make good with his seed. This was medicine beyond anything ever told at the council fires.

Bear Heart was changing to another horse, for the one he rode had been wounded in the hind quarter and was bleeding to death.

"Get down," Horseback said to White Bird, and she slid to the ground.

He cut three poor horses out of the herd and White Bird caught one wearing a rope around its neck. Bear Heart caught another, and helped High Feather onto it, though the old warrior could barely sit up straight. Whip gestured for his captive girl to catch the third horse, and she obeyed, much fear showing in her face.

"My father," Horseback said, "will Teal's father live?"

"The spirits know. The arrow is deep inside him, and we must move. He fought well. The brave never die old."

"Before we move," Whip blurted, "I must know." He rode his pony up next to the girl he had captured, grabbed her hair, and put a knife to her throat. "Am I going to keep this girl and make her good? If I do not keep her, she dies here, and she will never be good."

"My friend, you will have the girl," Horseback replied. "You fought well and caught her by yourself. But you will not have her until we are safe in our own country. Even then, we will have much ground to cover, and she will ride better if she is not bruised and hurting from your blows."

Whip grinned and returned his knife to its sheath. The Northern Raider girl seemed to understand. She knew she would live. She knew she would belong to the warrior who had caught her. And she knew that if she tried to escape, she would be punished.

"I will watch her for my brother," White Bird said, a vicious edge to her voice. "This one never struck me in that camp, but neither did she ever give me food."

Horseback chuckled. "Your sister has done well, Whip. See how bruised and skinny she is. She has not honored our enemies. Now we will take her home."

"My sister should not have let herself get caught. She should have fought until they killed her."

"She is only a woman. She has done well."

"We have all done well," Shaggy Hump said. "Lead us home, my son."

As they started away, High Feather began to sing the song that his spirit-protector had taught him in his vision many winters before. It was a good death song, and it made the younger men ride livelier upon their ponies. Somewhere beyond the foothills, upon the high, grassy plains that looked out over the sage country of the True Humans, High Feather's death song ended, and his soul flew to the Shadow Land.

45

Teal wrapped her arms around Horseback's waist and worked her cool hands under his antelope skin shirt to warm her fingers. She flattened her palms against the rigid muscles of his stomach. "Do you know what the Corn People say about you, my husband?"

They rode double on a docile mare, beyond sight of the lodge poles of the Corn People's camp on the River of Lightning. The mourning period following the death of High Feather had ended, and Horseback had taken Teal into a new lodge. The first snows of winter had fallen and melted, and now the two lovers would enjoy each other's warmth through the cold moons.

"I know what they say," Horseback replied. "They say it is well that I have married Teal and come to live with the Corn People to hunt meat for Teal's mother, now that Teal's father has passed to the Shadow Land."

"Yes, they say that," she replied, pulling herself closer against him as a cold blast of north wind lifted the mare's mane. "But they say something more."

"What do the Corn People say, wife?"

"They say my husband does *everything* on his pony."

He reined the mare to a stop. "Everything?"

"Yes. This morning when you rode your pony to our lodge and took the piece of meat roasting over the fire, my friend Little Cloud said, 'Look how Teal's husband eats the meal she cooks for him. He does everything on his pony!'"

"Everything?" Horseback repeated, looking over his shoulder at his wife.

"That is what they say. Two suns ago, my friend, Grass-in-the-Wind said, 'Teal, your husband is strange. Look in the shade of that willow. He *sleeps* upon the back of his pony!' "

Horseback chuckled. "I may need to sleep horseback on the war trail in days to come. I prepare myself, according to my visions. But there are many things I have not tried on the back of my pony."

"Like what, my husband?"

"I have not coupled with my wife."

Teal put her lips against Horseback's ear and laughed low in her throat. "Not even Slope Child has coupled with a man on the back of a pony." She slipped her hand under the flap of his loin skins and squeezed. "Is that your medicine bundle, my husband, or the tall warrior in your loin skins?"

"If it grows, it is not my medicine bundle." Horseback knotted the reins and tied them into the mane of the mare. He slipped his knees tightly under the coils of rope that wound around the mare's barrel. He twisted far to his right and wrapped his right arm around the curve of Teal's left hip. He grabbed her right leg at the knee and pulled her over his right thigh, leaning to his left to maintain his balance on the pony. She squealed in surprise but he continued to swing her around his right side until she sat in front of him on the mare, facing him, her thighs on top of his.

"How do you love your husband?" he said, reaching under her skirt as he worked it over her hips and untied the soft hide belt of her loin skins.

Teal's heart was pounding from the way he had so suddenly and skillfully moved her around to face him. She wrapped her legs around him and crossed her feet behind him on the back of the mare. "I love my husband the way a storm loves the tall aspen tree, and surrounds it with rain and wind to make it move and grow."

She reached for his waist and untied his belt, releasing the tall warrior she knew so well from their nights alone in their lodge. He brushed his lips across hers and pulled her closer with his hands cupped hard around her hips.

When she settled onto the tall warrior, Teal sighed, and Horseback made the mare walk. The motion of the walking pony eased him farther inside with each step. They closed their eyes and rocked to the cadence of hoofbeats as the mare plodded obediently across the rolling sagebrush prairies. Wind cooled the bare flesh of their thighs.

They rode on, and Teal began to make sounds in Horseback's ear. She liked the feeling of the cool wind, so she lifted her dress higher, until she felt the breeze caress her breasts. She rested her elbows on Horseback's shoulders, pulled his face against her breasts and threw her head back. The pony was walking faster now, ambling aimlessly through the sage. Horseback's arms were around Teal's waist, pulling her hard against him.

Teal held each breath as long as she could to prolong the ecstasy she felt approaching. When she knew by the strength of her husband's embrace that his release was near, her legs locked around him and clenched tightly as waves of pleasure surged between them, and their gasps sounded like mighty blasts of wind moaning in the mountains. She held on until her legs and arms grew tired, then she relaxed and enjoyed the continued gait of the mare.

Finally, she drew back and looked at Horseback's face. *"Ha-i'i!"* She sighed. "Now you have made me good."

He chuckled quietly. "You are *Noomah.* You were born good."

"Yes. But now you have made me good for the new nation. The Horse Nation of your Great Vision."

Horseback smiled. "Perhaps the nation of my vision has now been conceived on the back of this pony."

"Perhaps this time," Teal replied. "Perhaps next time. But next time will be different."

"Different?"

Her eyes glistened and she smiled cunningly. "Next time we will make the pony trot."

PART III

▲▲▲▲▲▲▲▲▲▲▲▲▲▲▲

Nation
in the Mist

▲▲▲▲▲

46

▼▼▼▼▼

"On the day of my birth," he said to the ten ponies surrounding him, "First Horse circled my lodge—a gift from the Shadow Land, but only for the brave."

When he gestured with his hands, the ponies tossed their heads in mock alarm, as Horseback knew some of the elders would when he gave the same talk at the council.

"Those who master the ways of the four-legged spirit-gift will die with stomachs full of buffalo meat and other good things. Those who do not will die with empty stomachs, or stomachs only half-full of bad things like snakes and grasshoppers and—"

The sound of hoofbeats interrupted his rehearsal and made him look beyond his listeners to see who approached. It was his wife, Teal, her hair bouncing in rhythm to the lope. Horseback smiled. She rode well on the Spanish saddle he had brought back from the Land of the Metal Men five winters ago. This saddle had made other women so envious that many had copied it, shrinking rawhide over frames of wood, elk antler, or buffalo bone.

Beyond Teal, Horseback could see the lodges of a great village strewn out along the banks of Icy-Water Creek, on the eastern slopes of the mountains called Medicine Bow by the *Yutas*. Once, the True Humans had been afraid to camp long at this good place, for it was on the fringes of *Yuta* country. But now, the *Noomah-Yuta* war was like a hibernating bear. For the past five winters, fighting between the two nations had dwindled away to nothing and trade had increased. The *Yutas*, who once had seemed so eager to raid for *Noomah* slaves, now preferred to trade for captives the *Noomah* had taken in horseback attacks on the Northern Raiders and the Crows. It was told throughout the nation of True Humans how a young warrior named Horseback had ridden right through *Yuta* country five winters ago, winning the respect of a *Yuta* leader called Bad Camper, and how Horseback and Bad Camper had agreed not to make war on each other's camps. Now there was peace in the south of the *Noomah* country, as long as the *Noomahs* did not invade the *Yuta* hunting grounds.

Horseback knew he could abide with this condition. There were better hunting grounds than the *Yutas'* to invade. The best hunting grounds lay far to the east and south—on the buffalo plains, in the country of the Wolf People and the *Na-vohnuh.*

It was the spring that followed Horseback's twenty-second winter, in the year that the Metal Men called by the number 1710, during the Moon of Flowers, when the True Humans watched the skies for birds returning from the south, when wobbly legged colts rooted at their mothers' udders for milk, when the hunters bleated fawnlike to lure does within arrow range, when the children devoured raw brains and marrow blended together and served on squares of rawhide. A great camp-together had risen in this good country near the plains, including the lodges of the Burnt Meat People, the Corn People, and a band called the Wild Sage People.

Neither the Corn People nor the Burnt Meat People had heard much about the Wild Sage band for twelve winters, for they had been living in the western extremes of *Noomah* country for a long time. Now they had come south and east to investigate strange things they had heard about horses and hairy-faced white men and a warrior named Horseback who had traveled far to the south and knew the hearts of ponies.

The winter had left much snow slowly melting in the high country, feeding the streams. Rains had come, and grass was high, allowing the horsebacks to remain camped longer in one place. The three bands raised more than one hundred lodges along Icy-Water Creek. None of the elders in the village could remember seeing so many lodges in one place.

The people hunted and feasted. They worried little about war, here on the fringes of *Yuta* country, far from the villages of the Crow or the Northern Raiders. There seemed to be two horses for every lodge, for although some warriors owned no horses at all, many of the Corn People and Burnt Meat People warriors owned several apiece. Horseback, who owned more ponies than any warrior ever known, claimed one for every day of the moon.

The hunters had made enough meat that men, women, boys, and girls spent their days and nights playing games, dancing, and gambling. The women chose teams to play shinny, each team trying to knock the stuffed rabbit skin ball into the other team's goal with their sticks. They played hard, the younger girls possessed of great speed.

The men threw colored sticks on hides staked to the ground, and wagered ponies and robes and lodge poles and slave wives on which colors would turn up. And every day, horse races began with the sun overhead and lasted until dark.

The races made the *Noomah* boys ride well, and trained the ponies for battle. One race was ten arrow shots in length and would make the ponies return wearing coats of sweat. In another race, the riders would start at a line scraped on the ground and ride toward a single tree, two arrow flights away. As they neared the tree, the riders would clash, pushing and pulling one another from their ponies at full gallop, for the winner would be the first rider to touch the tree.

Horseback devised a third kind of race. He stretched two rawhide straps waist-high above the ground, the second strap only three paces from the first. The riders had to jump the first strap, landing between the two without touching the second, then jump back out the way they had come to return to the starting place. Horseback was never beaten at this race, for he knew how to make his pony run fast, then spring high, then stop and turn, then jump again.

In another race, the riders tied a pole between two trees, chest-high to a rider. The racers ran two at a time, and the winner was the first to bring his pony to a full stop and touch the pole. The two riders would gallop toward the pole at full speed, each warrior wanting the other to be the first to pull rein. Many times, they waited too late, and ran their ponies under the pole, which knocked them to the ground. The elders from the Old Men's Smoke Lodge loved to laugh at the boys unhorsed in this race, but the game taught the young riders how to stop their ponies short.

There were many good horse-warriors at this great camp-together, yet there were many good foot-warriors as well. The foot-warriors played their own games and gambled at their own contests of skill. Holding their arrows together with their bow, they would first shoot an arrow high into the sky above their heads, then fling more arrows and keep flinging them until the first arrow had come back to earth. The winner was the warrior who could make the most arrows fly before the first fell to earth.

It was a good time, yet some of the elders were not happy. They did not like the changes brought about by so many horses. The young horsebacks were beginning to talk louder around the camp at Icy-Water Creek, and the elders did not like their talk. Horseback knew a great council would convene to decide the future.

"Where is Sandhill?" he said, as his wife came near.

Teal rode up to him, pushing through the ring of horses that had come to listen to her husband's speech. "Your son is with my mother. She teaches him about Wolf and Coyote."

"*Tsah*. Now, why have you ridden out here so swiftly? I am in council with my ponies."

"I have heard talk in the village. Some of the young horsebacks want to move the camp to find more grass. The elders do not want to move because there is much food here. There will be a council to decide it, my husband, just as you have prophesied."

"My speech is ready."

"There is more talk. Some of the young warriors want to move far to the south—all the way to the River of Arrowheads. They want to see the places my husband has spoken of. And to make war on the *Na-vohnuh.*"

Horseback's eyes darted with excitement as he reached for the reins of the horse he had ridden out of camp. "My wife listens well. For five winters I have waited for this day, and this council. I know the elders will not agree to move, but maybe the time comes for the new nation of my vision to break away from the old. Perhaps the spirits have shaped this camp-together so the new nation will take horse-warriors from the Corn People, the Burnt Meat People, and the Wild Sage People, yet leave each band with their foot-warriors who follow the ways of the elders." He mounted in one familiar, fluid movement.

"My husband thinks too much of days to come. Let the spirits decide."

"The spirits have decided."

Approaching the village, Horseback saw his son, Sandhill, coming from the lodge of his mother-in-law. The boy raised his arms, a signal to his father. Smiling with pride, Horseback loped past one side of his son, reached low, grabbed the boy's arm and swung him up behind him on the pony.

"Look, my mother!" Sandhill said, riding with his hands in the air, holding nothing. "Ye-ye-ye-ye!"

"*Tsah!*" Teal shouted. "Good!"

"I am going to take our son to stay with Looks Away while I prepare for the council," Horseback said. He could feel the excitement in the camp, and knew the men were finding their finest skins, combing their hair with brushes made from porcupine tails, and weaving fresh feathers into their scalp locks.

At his father's lodge, he swung Sandhill down from the pad saddle and left his pony standing. "Go to your grandfather," he ordered, seeing Shaggy Hump emerge from his lodge.

Looks Away came out behind Shaggy Hump, smiling at Sandhill.

"*Aho*, Mother," Horseback said, using the term of respect even though Looks Away was not his blood mother.

"*Aho*, my son." She took Sandhill from her husband and tickled the boy under the chin. Looks Away seemed happy camping here, this close to the *Yuta* country of her birth. Even now it was known only to Horseback and Looks Away that she was the sister of Bad Camper, and the real reason for the truce between the two nations. Not even Bad Camper knew his sister had become the wife of Shaggy Hump, or that she had convinced Horseback to release him from torture five winters ago.

"My son," Shaggy Hump said, "Are your words straight for the council?"

"Straighter than straight."

"Good. You will be called to speak. Let the spirits use your tongue. Your words will be like shadow-talk."

River Woman's lodge rose next to the lodge of Shaggy Hump, and as they passed her lodge, her voice came from inside, saying, "My son!" Then she leapt through the entry hole of the lodge, dashing the wolf-skin cover aside. She stepped in front of Horseback and said, "My son, you must watch for signs of the sacred deer."

"Yes, mother. I will watch. As the sun is my witness."

His mother's hair was streaked with gray now, and she had begun to walk hunched over. Shaggy Hump had not lain with her in his lodge for many winters, for since her wound and her vision, River Woman did nothing but pray. Some of the Burnt Meat People claimed she practiced sorcery, but none brought this charge to the council out of fear and respect for Shaggy Hump, who was still a great warrior.

"I know your dreams," River Woman said. "I see your vision. I walk behind you."

"Good, my mother. *Tsah*."

As Horseback and his father walked on toward the lodge that had been raised for the council, they passed the Northern Raider girl called Dipper, whom Whip had captured five winters ago. Upon her cheek she wore a fresh bruise that Whip had given her. She was called Dipper after the bird of the mountains who walked underwater, for she spent much time in streams, cooling her bruises and washing away blood from her face.

Since taking this girl from the Northern Raiders, Whip had made her good with his seed. She had given him a daughter, but he would not stop beating her, as if she were still a slave. Horseback no longer spoke much to Whip, for Whip had stayed with the Burnt Meat People, while Horseback had joined the Corn People in order to care for Teal's mother. He did not see Whip often, but he did not like the way Whip beat his woman for no reason at all.

Dipper saw Horseback looking at her and turned her face in shame, concentrating on the new moccasins she was sewing for her husband. Horseback wondered if things would be different for her in the new nation of his vision.

As he continued toward the council site, he and Shaggy Hump were joined by Echo-of-the-Wolf, who rode his horse right through camp, for he had joined the order of the Foolish Ones, and did crazy things no other True Human would think of doing. He even rode upwind of cooking fires, let his shadow fall on cooking meat, and violated many other lesser taboos. No longer would Echo carry his weapons into battle, for the Foolish Ones carried only a quirt and a buffalo-scrotum rattle with which they struck their enemies. Now he was riding his special Foolish pony, and many young boys trotted along behind him to see what peculiar thing he might do.

"*Kiyu!*" he shouted. "When will you join the order of the Foolish Ones with me? Are you not foolish enough yet?"

"When the nation of my vision moves south, my friend. I have told you."

"Hurry. I do not wish to be foolish forever."

It was best with Foolish Ones to work in twos. The only way out of the order came with death, or with the death of one's partner in foolishness. Echo had only recently declared himself a Foolish One and had rejected all other partners, saying only Horseback was foolish enough to ride with him. It was an honor for Horseback. Few warriors in the three bands camped together had won as many battle strokes and scalps as Echo.

As they strolled on toward the council lodge, Echo darted forward on his Foolish horse, looking for something crazy to do. He moved a lodge pole to close the smoke flaps on someone's lodge, then rode away. He left behind a cluster of boys laughing at an old man who had to come out of his lodge naked to escape the smoke.

"It is strange how well Echo performs his mischief," Shaggy Hump said. "He never did anything crazy before he became a Foolish One."

"It is good. Now all those young boys will want to join the order so that they can get away with nonsense like that. Boys like to have fun."

The women had raised a special lodge for the council, using the longest poles available to make the lodge larger than any other in camp. It was so large that they covered it only part of the way up with robes and hides gathered from many families. After the council, it would be taken apart and its pieces returned to those who owned them.

Horseback's lodge was near the council lodge, so he went there to make himself ready. For a long time, he judged his reflection in the looking glass Raccoon-Eyes had given him five winters before in the Sacred South. It was the only mirror in camp, and perhaps the only one in the whole *Noomah* nation. Horseback was very proud of it.

Much time passed before all the men had gathered, so those who came first stood talking about many things, clustering in two groups: horse-warriors and foot-warriors. The men who were the most vain took a long time to appear, for they had to make their braids fall just right, and preen the feathers they wore in their hair like meticulous cranes. Whip was the most vain of all. It was said that he would pick up the hair cut off by mourning women and weave this into his own braids, to make his hair look longer.

Finally, the elders entered the lodge singing the council song. They circled like the sun just around the inside of the hide walls. They were followed by the active warriors with the most experience, causing the circle of councilors to spiral toward the center of the lodge. The young warriors entered last, all the while singing and shuffling the council dance, until all the men were inside the lodge, elders at the center, youths around the edges of the circle.

The pipe was lighted and passed. All the men smoked, while outside, women kept their ears turned toward the lodge, hoping to hear some of the talk of the men when it began.

An elder peace chief of the Wild Sage People spoke first. His name was Blue Butte, and he had counted his first battle stroke many winters before First Horse appeared to the Burnt Meat People. Blue Butte spoke of the old ways of the True Humans, the pole-drags fitted for dogs, the smaller camps where the people stayed longer, moving only when they needed to find more food or escape from enemies.

"Now we move because the ponies of the young horsebacks need more grass," Blue Butte said. "There is more fighting with the nations to the north, and the young warriors who survive take too many captive women of bad blood into their lodges. The horses make our young men powerful, but it happens too quickly. Power and danger take the same path, and sometimes one must move aside for the other. All the young men want to do now is raid and fight and move and get more ponies. It is not good to become so rich with ponies. The ponies burden more than they serve. I need only one pony to pull my lodge. That is enough. One pony does not eat much grass. I am too old to ride ten sleeps for a fight. I will defend my village with my moccasins on the ground, so I can feel the heart of Mother Earth. The spirits tell me to do this in my visions. If we began eating all the horses around this camp, we would have enough meat to last until next winter! I have spoken."

The other elders spoke in turn, as the sun sank behind the Medicine Bow mountains. Each agreed with Blue Butte. Too many horses. Too much moving. Too much fighting for no reason. Too many captive women making wives for young *Noomah* men.

"It is good to have a few ponies," said old Turtle Rattler, elder councilor of the Corn People, "but they should be used like big dogs, to move good lodges, not to ride off on a raid for the sole purpose of stealing more ponies."

In time, it was Shaggy Hump's turn to speak, and he rose, looking around at all the councilors. "It was the way of the spirits that I should discover First Horse on the day of my son's birth. My son knows the heart of the horse, for the spirit of First Horse leapt into his body as he was born. He knows the reason for the horse. He knows the mystic powers of great spirit-ponies. We will hear him talk straight before the moon passes over the mountains. I have spoken."

The brevity of Shaggy Hump's oration so stunned the council that for a long moment—a moment that lasted longer than the speech itself—no one moved. Finally, the next warrior in turn rose. It was Bear Heart. He stood silently for a while, thinking about what he had planned to say. The other councilors waited patiently as he thought. A great horned owl began to hoot nearby, and it hooted a hundred times before Bear Heart decided what he would say.

"My friend, Shaggy Hump, is wise. I will let Horseback speak."

Echo rose next, though it was not his turn, and said, "I will not have Horseback speak for me!" But because he was wearing the paint of a Foolish One, the other councilors understood that he meant just the opposite.

One by one, the younger warriors swallowed the long talks they had rehearsed. The ones who held to the old ways of their grandfathers said the elders had already spoken for them. The young horsebacks said *Kiyu* would do their talking.

When finally he rose, Horseback's heart was good. From where he now stood, he could see two trails. The first trail would change the hearts of the elders and cause them to move the camp, making the people of the Icy-Water camp-together the first people of the Horse Nation. Should he fail in changing the hearts of the elders, the second path would lead him south with his new followers. They would break away from the camp-together and go to conquer new hunting grounds.

Horseback did not know which of these paths would be better for the Horse Nation of his Great Vision, but he trusted that his spirit-guide, Sound-the-Sun-Makes, knew well.

"I have listened to my elders," he began, "and I grow wiser by their words. My elders have seen things I have not, and done things I never will.

"Yet, I have seen things my elders have not seen, and done things they will not do. I have been far to the south, across the River of Arrowheads, where no *Noomah* warrior ever went before. I have seen hairy-faced white warriors called Metal Men. I have seen them make spirits sing in iron. I have seen them pull pole-drags upon sacred hoops that roll on the ground. I have seen their Fire Sticks and their strange beasts and the shiny yellow metal they worship. This is not all I have seen.

"In the south, I have seen rich grasslands with buffalo that number like pine needles in a great forest that takes one hundred sleeps to cross. Antelope run like flocks of ducks flying in the autumn sky. A blind man could hunt the elk and the lesser bear in the river timber, for he must only listen to hear them pass. There is more meat than my elders have ever seen and plenty of fruit and other good things for our women to gather.

"Also, I have seen a great vision. When my medicine went bad and the dark shadow of my protector fell on me, the Metal Men captured me to torture to death. My father and my friends rescued me from this shame. You have seen the torture scars on my back. My wife has begun to tattoo these scars so no one will forget about the danger of the Metal Men. When I was sick from my torture, the spirits gave me a Great Vision. In this vision, I saw a new Horse Nation moving south from the land of the True Humans. The nation will move upon the backs of ponies. It was a nation in the mist of tomorrow, yet I know that it will come out into the sun."

Horseback stood long enough to let his breath catch up to his words, thinking about what he planned to say next.

"My elders speak of the old times. I remember some of these old times. I remember hiding from the Northern Raiders. Now, our warriors attack the Northern Raiders and take scalps, and slaves, and ponies. We must continue to take the ponies of our enemies, for the ponies make us strong in battle, and will make our enemies strong if we let them keep the ponies.

"Blue Butte has spoken of his bravery in battle. He will stand with his moccasins on the ground to feel the power of Mother Earth. That is good. But I feel the power of my pony between my legs, and my pony feels the power of Mother Earth through four legs. The way of the horsebacks is also good.

"When I was a boy, I remember starving through the Time When Babies Cry for Food. We have not known times that bad since our ponies began to number as many as our lodges, for now we can search more country, find more food, and move more quickly to make meat. The pony is better than the dog. The dog eats meat. The pony makes meat. Our ponies have made us richer, but still our land is poor. It is a good and sacred land, washed in the blood of our grandfathers, but it is a poor land. The land to the south is rich. There, we will not have to move our camp so much to find grass for our ponies, for the grass grows like hair on a dog. And we will have no need to move often. There is food everywhere."

Horseback thought it well that he could smell meat roasting on the cook fires just as he spoke of food. The men had been in council long enough to grow hungry.

"The wisdom of the ancient ones, great-grandfathers of our great-grandfathers, lives on in the lodges of our storytellers. By this sacred passing of truths from one generation to the next, we have held many things in our hearts that our ancestors learned before us.

"The keepers of this wisdom remember that in ancient times, a war arose between the *Noomah* and the *Na-vohnuh*. Our ancestors fought bravely, but the *Na-vohnuh* numbered ten to our ancestors' one. To escape destruction to the last warrior, our ancestors moved the True Humans to this country . . . this poor country . . . this hard country. It is a sacred country, for it has preserved the seed of the *Noomah*. Sometimes the spirits bless this country with rain and meat, and it is good for a while. But then it is poor again. The *Na-vohnuh* pushed our ancestors into this country to become surrounded by enemies: Crows, Northern Raiders, *Yutas*, and Wolf People. But now we have ponies. Ponies!

"By the light of Father Sun, Sister Moon, and all the star-spirits, it is true what the *puhakuts* have prophesied from ancient times, that the *Noomah* and the *Na-vohnuh* would one day meet again to make war, for I have drawn *Na-vohnuh* blood myself on the River of Arrowheads. As the storytellers have said, they are horrible people, stinking of *kwitapuh* and crawling with vermin. They hold the good lands in the south. They number many, but they are weaker than our horsebacks, for they do not know the hearts of their ponies. In my great vision, I see a horse nation of True Humans avenging the souls or our ancestors. We will chase the *Na-vohnuh* out of the good country in the south, and win wealth beyond the hopes of the richest warrior.

"I have seen great visions. I have survived the dangerous shadow of bright powerful medicine. I have prayed for wisdom and courage.

"The grass is all gone from this camp at Icy-Water. Those who have horses must move to keep them fed. The new trail goes south. We have made peace with the *Yutas* and will go along the borders of their country for safety. We will fight any nation that rises in our path. We will honor and avenge the True Humans who have gone before us to the Shadow Land, and conquer a good country for those not yet born."

He changed his weight from one foot to the other, and thought in silence for a long moment to make sure he had not forgotten to say something.

"On the day of my birth," he continued, "First Horse circled my lodge—a gift from the Shadow Land, but only for the brave! Those who master the ways of the four-legged spirit-gift will die with stomachs full of buffalo meat and other good things. Those who do not . . ."

Suddenly, Horseback heard the warnings of spirit-talk in his heart. It was not wise to say, as he had planned, that the foot-warriors would die with empty stomachs, or stomachs only half-full of bad things like snakes and grasshoppers. This would insult the foot-warriors and make him a prophet of bad things to come.

"Wait," he said, putting his hand over his heart. "I must listen."

He sat down to hear the voices of the spirits. The moon appeared above the hides covering the lower part of the lodge poles, and still Horseback did not speak. A branch in the council fire crumbled to coals, then turned to ash. A wolf howled seven times in the mountains. The moon moved across the open top of the council lodge. Still Horseback remained silent, and all the councilors waited.

Finally, he rose to speak again. "Those who master the ways of the four-legged spirit-gift will die with stomachs full of buffalo meat and other good things. But, those True Humans who choose not to go with the Horse Nation will remain sacred in the heart of the Great Creator, and when the Horse Nation goes out, there will be more food in this country for those who remain behind, for many will go out. It is good. The spirits have decided what will happen. I have spoken."

The elders lighted the pipe again, and passed it. Blue Butte took some time rising to his feet, for he was old, and his joints pained him. "We have called this council to speak about moving our camp. Many have said we should stay. Some have said we must move. We have not made one choice. Maybe this camp-together is too large. It is good to see so many friends, but it is also good to follow different paths. Long ago the spirits made many bands of True Humans for many reasons. Maybe now, the spirits have made a band of horse-warriors who will make a new path under the hooves of their ponies.

"Listen, all of you young horsebacks. Your young leader, *Kiyu*, has power, but he misinterprets his vision. It is not a new nation he sees riding south. It is a nation of brothers, as our ancestors, Wolf and Coyote, were brothers, yet they are now different. You were born *Noomah*, my grandsons, and so you will remain as long as your blood runs and your hearts beat.

"We have not chosen to stay or to move, but until we meet again in council, we will stay here. Not because we have agreed to stay, but because we have not agreed to move. This is the way of the council. It is also the way for those who do not agree with the council of one band to go out to another band. The wisdom of our ancestors makes a place for every man. If the young horsebacks go to seek a place for their own band, that is good. Perhaps next time a great camp-together meets in this sacred place, and the people smoke and speak, they will agree. Now, we are hungry. Let us all fill our stomachs, as *Kiyu* has prophesied. This is the way of the council. I have spoken."

The men filed out of the lodge, and immediately women began to take it apart. Horseback could see that some of the people were sad. It was plain that the horsebacks would ride out and make a new brother nation. This was good, but it made some people sad who would have to see their friends ride away.

Echo came to Horseback, but walked around behind him to speak, in a foolish way. "We must kill a bull and make your rattle from the scrotum. Now, my friend, you are going to be a Foolish One."

Horseback turned around and found himself looking at the back of Echo's head. "*Hah.* I only hope I am wise enough to become as foolish as you."

That night, the people held a dance. The drums and the songs and the leaping shadows made Horseback happy. During the height of the favorite dance of the Burnt Meat People, Whip whirled into the brightest light of the fire, trying to dance harder than all the other warriors, for he was vain. He tossed one long braid over his shoulder as he whirled, and the end of the braid flew off and landed on the ground. The people laughed like crazy. Whip picked up his tresses and stalked away to his lodge.

▲▲▲▲▲
47
▼▼▼▼▼

"They are horrible two-leggeds," Shaggy Hump said. "I cannot call them people, just two-leggeds."

"Do they torture?" Whip asked.

They rode eastward across the vast rolling grasslands, beyond sight of the big mountains of *Yuta* country—six horse-warriors, all painted and armed with killing tools, except for the Foolish Ones, who only carried their rattles and quirts for counting battle strokes. The day was warm, and their topknot feathers jerked like nervous birds in the wind.

"*Oobia, hah!*" Shaggy Hump replied. "How the Wolf People love to torture! There was a Wolf woman among the Wild Sage People many winters ago. She has since died, but she was of Wolf People blood, though a *Noomah* warrior had captured her and made her good. She knew the ways of torturing like the Wolf People."

"Who did she torture? How?" Whip asked, leaning anxiously toward the older warrior.

"It happened only once, for you know it is hard to catch an enemy alive for torture. But, once, the Wild Sage People found three Crow warriors hunting in our country. Two were killed, and the third was hit in the head with a *pogamoggan*. While this wounded Crow floated under the pass to the Shadow Land, the *Noomah* warriors tied him up, *tsah!* Then they brought him back to the camp for the Wolf woman to torture."

"What torture did she use?" Whip prodded.

"She staked the Crow warrior out, arms and legs, tight, like this." Shaggy Hump spread his arms and legs, making his pony take a nervous leap forward. "The Wild Sage People had been attacked by the Crow two winters before, and the Wolf woman's son killed. She was very angry. So, first, she heaped coals on that Crow's hands and feet and listened until he could scream no longer. Then she cut off a hand, above the burn, to make it hurt again, and heaped more coals to stop the blood so the Crow would not bleed to death. Bleeding to death would go too fast. They say that Crow started screaming again. Then, the other hand, same way. Then a foot. Then, another foot."

Trotter put his hand over his ears. "*Anah!* I do not want to hear it!"

Shaggy Hump grabbed Trotter's wrist and pulled his hand away from his ear. "Hear it! Now you know why I will not leave you on the battlefield today, floating under the pass to the Shadow Land. I will die in the fight before I let

▼▼▼

them catch you and torture you. And you will do the same for me. That is the way. That Wolf woman with the Wild Sage People kept cutting and burning until that Crow had no arms or legs, and still he lived. Do you wish to go to the Shadow Land like that?"

"No," Trotter said.

"Then you will fight like crazy. The Wolf People are horrible. They shave almost all the hair off their heads. Ugly! If you see one with a hand painted on his chest, watch out. That one has killed hand to hand. They are dangerous."

"More dangerous than the Northern Raiders we have been killing?" Whip asked.

"Like a great humpbacked bear is more dangerous than a lesser bear! They have a warrior society called the Tied Penises. They guard the retreats. They tie a cord to their penises and stake the cord to the ground so they will not abandon the ground they guard. These Wolf People fight! That is why we stayed off of the plains in the old days."

"Now we have ponies!" Whip said, brandishing his lance.

"Yes. Use them well. Remember Horseback's vision. The spirits say we must kill only those who come out to fight. We will take back all the horses they stole from us. Even if we find a village, we must take no captives. You listen, Whip. No captive girls this time to make good, or sell to the *Yutas*. If you take one, our medicine will go bad. Take only the scalps of those who come out to fight us."

"What if they will not come out to fight?" Whip asked.

"Then we will take no scalps. Those Wolf People scalps are not much good anyway."

"No scalps?" Whip said, a complaint in his tone.

"That is what the spirits have said in my son's vision. Is it so, my son?"

Shaggy Hump looked into the eyes of his son, for Horseback had been riding backward on his pony the whole time, facing those who followed him.

"No, my father, it is not so!" he said, but he was a Foolish One now, and meant the opposite of what he said when he wore his Foolish paint and rode his Foolish pony.

"If someone gets killed," Shaggy Hump said, "that is all right. It is good to die on a day like this. But if I die, do not let the Wolf People keep my body. They will cut it all up and send me to the Shadow Land to live forever with my guts hanging out and my eyes burned away."

"*Hah*, we know the way," said Trotter, respectfully.

"Good. Those Wolf People are horrible. We should stay away from them, but my son says we cannot let them take our horses like that. The tracks show only three warriors. Maybe we will catch them before they reach their village."

"They were stupid not to take all of our ponies," Whip said. "They will regret leaving ponies behind so we could follow them."

"Perhaps they wish us to follow," said Bear Heart.

Shaggy Hump nodded. "*Hah*, be ready. Trust my son's medicine."

"Do not worry about deer tracks ahead," Horseback said. "This is the country of the antelope nation."

Shaggy Hump caught Trotter's eye and pointed forward with a nod of his head.

"I will watch for deer sign anyway," Trotter said. "We must honor the deer *puha* that protects us."

As Trotter urged his pony past Horseback, the Foolish One reached out with his buffalo scrotum rattle and jabbed Trotter's pony in the flank. The mount began to kick and wheel, finally tossing Trotter into the grass.

The warriors gathered around the unhorsed rider and laughed, making strange lines appear in their war paint.

"My son, you are a good Foolish One!"

"Your words make me angry, my father." His grin showed white teeth in the middle of a face painted half-black, half-red, with streaks of each color running into the other.

. . . .

His first fight as a Foolish One came far out on the plains, where the land of tall grass began. Horseback's party overtook the Wolf People warriors as they cooked horse meat over a fire of dried buffalo dung. There were only three enemy warriors, as the tracks had suggested, but Horseback sent Bear Heart to circle the Wolf People, to make sure a larger camp did not lie beyond the next hill.

Bear Heart returned without having been seen by the enemy warriors. "There are only three. No village beyond. They are on the open prairie. No timber or even a creek bank to hide behind. They do not expect us to catch up to them so quickly."

"How many horses?" Shaggy Hump asked.

"Three of their own, and eleven of ours."

"They stole twelve," Whip said.

"One died. That is why they have stopped here. To butcher the dead pony."

"Which pony died?" Trotter asked, for he had lost two of his mounts in the theft.

"The red horse with high white leggings on the back feet."

"*Kwitapuh!*" Whip said. "That was my horse!"

"They have three horses of their own," Shaggy Hump said. "When we take them, perhaps my son will give you one to replace the red pony that died."

"I must have the best of the three as my replacement. That red horse with white leggings was a good pony."

Echo frowned. "*Hah*, a very good pony. For the vultures." He pointed to the sky.

"That pony was good!" Whip said, glaring at Echo. "And stolen on the watch of a Foolish One!"

"*Pookai!*" Shaggy Hump snapped, cutting in front of Whip. "Are you going to watch your brothers fight from a distance?"

"I will ride before anyone!"

"Then you will probably die in the fight and will have no need to replace your stolen pony that the vultures say is good. Anyway, the horses we take belong to my son, for it is his *puha* that guides and protects us. If you live, and if the spirits tell my son to give you a horse, he will."

"If I live, I will remind your son that his father said so."

Shaggy Hump turned to the rest of the young men. Since Horseback had become a Foolish One, Shaggy Hump had done much of his speaking for him, as it was too confusing for the warriors to think in opposites like a Foolish One.

"Remember my son's dream," he said. "Kill only if the Wolf People warriors come out to get us. It is good enough to leave them afoot, a long way from their village. We will be far away by the time they get back to their village."

Whip sniffed derisively, but would not argue with Shaggy Hump.

Horseback shook his Foolish rattle. "The Wolf People are good, but their ponies are very bad." He turned his mount, and led the party over the low, grassy hill.

When Horseback loosed his battle cry, the three enemy warriors mounted their ponies to flee, but they had made the mistake of leaving their bridles on tired mounts. The horses of the *Noomah* riders were tired as well, but they were warm and drew spirit power from the war cries of their riders.

Quickly, the Wolf warriors gave up hope of keeping all the stolen horses and rode away on the three they had bridled. The True Humans surrounded and held the herd of eleven, as the two Foolish Ones in the war party galloped ahead to count strokes on the Wolf People. The men with the herd sat upon their horses and watched anxiously as the chase reached far across the sward.

Horseback and Echo overtook the slowest rider, one to either side. As Horseback belabored the fleeing Wolf warrior with his rattle, Echo reached for the war bridle of the pony. Catching the reins, he angled away. Horseback caught the tuft of hair growing from the back of the warrior's otherwise shaved head and pulled the other direction, unhorsing the rider.

Once on the ground, the enemy warrior drew a knife to confront the two Foolish Ones, but they had no trouble dodging his thrusts as they rode around him yelling, "Ye-ye-ye-ye-ye-ye!" Their twin cries streamed thinly across the prairie as they dishonored the enemy horse thief with repeated blows.

"Look!" Whip cried. "The other two Wolf warriors have stopped. One has a Fire Stick!"

The onlookers could tell by the way the Wolf warrior put the butt of the gun on the ground that he had not yet poured in the magic powder, or dropped in the little heavy ball.

The Foolish Ones rode headlong toward the two enemy warriors, oblivious to the danger of the gun.

"They must hurry," Bear Heart said, "before the Fire Stick is ready!"

"I am going to help the Foolish Ones," Shaggy Hump said. "If the Wolf warriors kill my son, I will not let them cut him to pieces!"

"I am going, too!" Whip shouted.

The two *Noomah* horsemen thundered away, leaving only Bear Heart and Trotter to hold the captured herd.

The Fire Stick warrior put the gun to his shoulder. Smoke streamed from the breech, but no thunder erupted.

"My son's medicine is good!" Shaggy Hump shouted as he abandoned his charge. "The Fire Stick will not roar!" He stopped to watch the fight again from a distance.

Before the Wolf warrior could prime his gun with more powder in the frizzen pan, Horseback and Echo were upon him. The third Wolf warrior got off his horse, strung his bow, and tried to notch an arrow, but Horseback struck him with his rattle, then reached for his pony's bridle.

At the same time, Echo clashed with the Fire Stick warrior, knocking him over with the shoulder of his pony as the warrior tried to raise the gun again. The Foolish One then wheeled quickly, swooped low, and yanked the gun from the grasp of the Wolf warrior, crying, "Ye-ye-ye-ye-ye!"

"That is a big honor!" Shaggy Hump said to Whip as they watched from their position between the herd of ponies and the fight. "Echo takes the weapon from his enemy's hand."

"Yet, the enemy lives," Whip added.

Horseback answered the victory yell as he took the other warrior's pony, and both Foolish Ones rode back toward Shaggy Hump and Whip. The four horsemen came together where the first enemy had been unhorsed. This young Wolf warrior was running away as fast as his feet would carry him. He circled wide to join his two friends as the True Humans laughed at his cowardice.

"They will not fight us now," Shaggy Hump said. "We are four with horses. They are three afoot. We have taken all the ponies. It is over."

"Maybe they will fight one of us," Whip said. "I must have a scalp!" He rode away from the other three *Noomah* braves and stopped alone on a rise in the plains.

"Come out and fight, Wolf boys!" he shouted, gesturing with his lance.

Echo scowled. "Whip is very wise," he growled. "Those greasy Wolf warrior scalps are good to hang on a shield."

"He thinks only of his own prowess," Shaggy Hump said. "He does not care about our *puha*."

"Come out and get me!" Whip screamed, his voice reaching an idiotic pitch. "Fight me! I want your scalps! Your fathers copulate with she-dogs! Your war cries sound like horse farts! Why do you not tie your penises to the ground now?"

Horseback chuckled. "Our enemies understand every word of Whip's insults. Look how angry he makes them."

"They are not going to come out and fight," Shaggy Hump said. "It is time to go. We are far from the safety of our camp."

They trotted away from the battle ground, leaving Whip to rant at the enemy warriors who would not come out and fight.

· · · ·

After two sleeps, the horse-takers approached their camp on the fringes of *Yuta* country. Before entering the camp, they dismounted and rubbed their ponies with grass to make them look sleek and beautiful. Then they returned in glory, shouting victory yells. A great celebration commenced, and when the warriors told of their exploits, Whip spoke longer than any.

"I was angry and wanted to fight because the pony the Wolf warriors killed was a good pony," he said. "I know this pony was good, because it belonged to me. It was my fastest pony, and the Wolf warriors cooked it. Only a very good pony can replace this lost one, and that is why I was so angry at our enemies. I begged them to come out and fight me, but they would not. Our spirit-guides forbade us to kill any warriors who would not come out to fight. I do not know why the spirits would protect our enemies, but Shaggy Hump told us that Horseback, the Foolish One, had shadow dreams that forbade us to kill. I have no scalps to replace my lost pony. That pony was fast! I miss that pony. I won many races with that pony. As Father Sun is my witness, that was the best pony I ever rode! How will I ride as fast as an antelope now that our enemies have killed my finest pony? I have spoken."

Whip's speech tainted the celebration, for everyone in the band heard the greed in his words.

As leader of the party of pony-takers, it was Horseback's duty to speak last and divide the spoils of the raid as he saw fit. He made his talk quietly to his father, for he did not wish for his words to be mistaken for the Foolish talk he often used, for he still wore his paint. When Shaggy Hump understood his son's wishes, he addressed the circle of people.

"My son, Horseback, the Foolish One, has searched his heart for the wisdom of spirits. My son says this: The spirits are pleased with our raid on the Wolf People. Our shadow-guides tested us on this raid, telling us we must not kill any Wolf warrior who did not come out to fight. The spirits are pleased that we honored their wishes, though we wanted to kill. Our *puha* remains strong.

"Now it is time to divide the things taken on the raid. Echo, the Foolish One, took a Fire Stick from one of the Wolf warriors. As a Foolish One he is forbidden to use a weapon, so the spirits have said that Trotter should own the Fire Stick, for he knows how to use that weapon well."

Trotter could not keep the smile of surprise from branching across his face as men touched him to share his good fortune.

"Now, the ponies," Shaggy Hump said. "My son has listened to the spirits. The spirits have heard a sacred oath sworn to Father Sun, here before this circle of True Humans. The oath proves that the red pony with the high white leggings—the pony butchered by the Wolf People—this pony was the fastest pony that ever lived."

Shaggy Hump's talk cast a spell of utter silence over the people, and they all looked toward Whip, yet refused to meet eyes with him.

"The spirits have decided that no one pony can replace the red horse with high white leggings, so Whip must take all fourteen ponies from the Wolf people raid. My son has spoken."

Whip stood still for a long shameful moment amid the silence. The muscles in his face writhed as his eyes rose to glare at Horseback. No man could have missed the anger of all those who had lost ponies to the Wolf People thieves, only to see Whip claim them now. Yet, the anger of the people fell not upon Horseback, but upon Whip, for no man could say that Horseback had acted unwisely.

In days to come, it would be said that Whip's heart went bad at this moment. The elders would tell their grandchildren that Whip could have announced a great giveaway. He could have shed his shame by giving away all his ponies and other things, trusting that his spirit-power would return him to wealth. But Whip did not believe in spirit-power. He chose to harden his heart at this moment. He would never give the ponies back to their rightful owners. He tossed his head in mock pride and stalked away from the circle.

The Foolish One Echo spoke: "This is good. Whip deserves this gift from the spirits."

The people began to go back to their lodges, and Teal noticed that Whip's wife, Dipper, ran away sobbing. She caught up to Dipper and grabbed her by the arm.

"Why do you cry?" Teal asked.

"I am afraid," Dipper said. "He beats me. He is very angry now. He is going to hurt me bad this time." Her eyes were filled with the same kind of humiliation that had filled Whip's eyes at the circle. "How am I going to care for my daughter, if I am broken up?"

Teal pursed her lips and looked toward her husband. Were the spirits wise to endanger Dipper this way? Dipper was just a captive made-good wife, but her daughter carried real *Noomah* blood. It was true that Whip was bad about beating his wife. A man had the right to beat his wife, and even his sister, but Whip used the right too often, sometimes for no reason.

Five winters ago, after Whip's sister, White Bird, had been rescued from her captivity with the Northern Raiders, she had started to grow large with a child—the child of some Northern Raider defiler. Noticing her pregnancy, Whip had beaten her mercilessly with a pole for bringing Northern Raider seed to the Burnt Meat People camp. In shame, White Bird had snuck away from camp, where she had pounded her own belly with stones, trying to rid herself of the child her brother hated. The Burnt Meat People had found her dead in a dry gully, the ground under her stained with her own blood.

Now the name of White Bird was never spoken among the True Humans who knew the story, and Whip had only his wife to beat. It was known that Whip gave his dead sister her beatings through his wife, Dipper, for sometimes he called his wife elder sister when he beat her.

"Stop crying," Teal ordered. "You will hide in my lodge. Your husband will have to use his anger on one of his horses. I will speak to my husband about the beatings. You are good now. You have borne a *Noomah* child. My husband will make your husband stop beating you."

Making sure that Whip had left the camp, Teal pulled Dipper away by the arm, leading her quickly to her hiding place.

48

His band of True Humans came to be known by his name. In the *Noomah* nation, they were called Horseback People. In the summer that the Metal Men called by the number 1711, the Horseback People made a large camp on the River of Arrowheads, a morning's ride upstream from the earthen village of Tachichichi.

The day the women raised the first lodge poles of the camp, all the True Humans in the new band of Horseback People yet hailed from one of three old bands: the Burnt Meat People, the Wild Sage People, and the Corn People. But by the time the Moon of Heat rose full, True Humans of many other bands had come to join the Horseback People. They came from the Root Diggers, the Downstream People, the Head-of-the-Stream People, the Liver

Eaters, and the Bend-in-the-River People. They came from the No Meat People, the Steep Climbers, the Undercut Bank People, and the Hill Wearing Away People. They came in small parties, in ones and twos, in family groups that spanned three generations.

Two poor warriors of a band called Grasshopper Eaters came all the way from their poor lands in the western extremes of *Noomah* country. These people spoke the same language as the True Humans and practiced the same customs, but they were very poor and knew little contact with the other bands. The two Grasshopper Eaters who came to Horseback's camp wore holey skins and were covered with fleas and lice. They owned one spear between them and had almost starved to death on their long journey, living mostly on roots, seeds, grubs, bird eggs, and rancid meat they had stolen from vultures and wolves.

Horseback fed these two men, but told them they could not live in his camp until they had rid themselves of vermin. He told them to shave their heads and to purify themselves with steam and cedar smoke. When they had done this, he led them to a place where an abundance of a certain weed grew, tall and rangy, topped with tiny red blossoms.

"Pull many of these plants," he said to the Grasshopper Eaters, "and rub them on your bodies, especially your heads."

"Oo-bia!" said the Grasshopper Eater called Crooked Teeth. "This plant stinks!"

"It drives the fleas and lice away," Horseback replied. "It is good. Now, go to my mother, River Woman, and she will give you a powder made from the crushed seeds of another plant. When your hair grows back, you will sprinkle this on your heads to ward off the return of fleas and lice. When you are wealthy in times to come, you will bring my mother a pony."

When they were free of biting bugs, Horseback gave each of the men tanned skins for making new clothes, and good buffalo hides for making their lodges.

"Those Grasshopper Eaters will not have women to make their lodges or their pole-drags," Teal said. "No father wants his daughter to marry a Grass-hopper Eater." It was a good point, for even now, Teal was wrapping a length of wet rawhide around a new pole-drag she was making to move Horseback's lodge. The Grasshopper Eaters would need good wives in order to ascend in social standing.

Horseback smiled and brushed her comment aside, as if swatting at a fly. "They will capture their women, or trade for them." He wore no Foolish paint today and spoke like any other natural *Noomah* warrior.

"Where?"

"Maybe in trade with the Raccoon-Eyed People, or in war with the Wolf People."

"We are far from their country," Teal argued.

"Soon we will ride farther than any other people ever dreamed. Our horses are getting fat here in this land of much grass. The nearest village of Raccoon-Eyed People lies only seven sleeps away on the plains for a rider who knows how to travel. As for the Wolf People, Speaks Twice tells me they come sometimes to attack Tachichichi. If they bring women, some of the young men may capture slave wives."

"I do not wish to have any Wolf women in my camp," Teal said. She used her teeth to pull the strip of wet rawhide snug where she had bound two poles.

"Even a Wolf woman can be made good."

"Maybe the Grasshopper Eaters will get women from the *Yutas*."

"My wife speaks wisely. Now that we are at peace with the *Yutas*, our boys may find women among them without raiding. My father's second wife is *Yuta* by blood, and she is a good woman."

"Do the Metal Men have women?" Teal asked.

Horseback's bare eyebrows rose. Now he could see his wife thinking far ahead. Their son, Sandhill, was only four winters old, but one day would need a bride. "Their women are not as beautiful as my wife, but a woman of the Metal Men could serve a Grasshopper Eater well enough."

"Will my husband raid the Metal Men?"

"I will trade with some, like my friend, Raccoon-Eyes. I will raid others for horses. My dreams tell me my camp will need many horses. Many, many horses. Plenty of horses."

"Will my husband take scalps from the Metal Men?"

"Their scalps do not prove much, for they would rather hide in their lodges than fight. Except for the soldiers. They like to fight. Their scalps are worthy."

Teal glanced up from her pole-drag and began to giggle. "Look, my husband. The two Grasshopper Eaters are coming. They have no hair upon their heads! They are spotted all over from flea bites!"

"Quiet, woman. They come seeking honor."

Horseback greeted the two men with shaved heads and looked approvingly at the new loin skins they had fashioned.

"We come to thank our host for giving us food and good tanned hides," said the one called Crooked Teeth.

"We wish to learn about the ponies now," said the other, a man called Crazy Eyes, for his eyes seemed to watch two different things at once.

"Go watch the ponies I have given to you," Horseback suggested.

The two Grasshopper Eaters looked at each other, then glanced at Teal, who was giggling as she worked on her pole-drag.

"We do not know which horses to watch. The gift is a great one. Any horse is more horse than either of us has ever owned, but we do not know which horses our good host gives to us."

"Go watch the horses." Horseback said. "My mother, River Woman, will loan you tools to make moccasins. While you work on your moccasins, you will watch the horses. You will work and watch. When you finish your moccasins, you will wear them and you will follow the horses wherever they go. Watch them. When your hair has grown out of your heads long enough to make braids, then you will know which horse I have given to each of you."

"How will we know this?" Crazy Eyes said. "We know nothing of horses."

"You will know. When you are able to lay your hand upon your pony, I will teach you the things you need to know to ride. Now, go. Ask my mother for the tools for making your moccasins. She has prepared the powder made of sacred plants that will drive away the tiny bugs that bite. My mother knows the shadow secrets of all the plants. She finds new things growing in this good country, and her visions teach her their uses. Do not be afraid of her. She says strange things, but her heart is good."

When the two Grasshopper Eaters turned away, Teal burst into laughter, unable to contain her amusement any longer. "Spotted bald men go to watch the horses," she sang after them. "The horses will run away in fear!"

"Quiet, woman," Horseback said, though he too chuckled.

"They know nothing. How are they going to know which pony to claim?"

"How does a man know which woman to claim as his wife?" Horseback said. "The spirits tell him, and it is good."

As he drank in the beauty of Teal's smile, Horseback heard the crack of a stick, and the muffled cry of a woman. Looking across the camp, he saw Whip standing over Dipper, a broken stick in his hand. Dipper held one hand over the back of her head and used the other arm to shield her stomach, as if she expected Whip to kick her now that he had broken the stick over her head.

"Now you will learn!" Whip shouted.

Sure enough, he kicked her, but the gasp came from the lips of Teal. "She carries a child," Teal said.

Whip stalked around the place where Dipper lay, jabbing her with the splintered end of the stick and taunting her with fake kicks. He laughed at her all the while, his long braids dangling menacingly, his eyes like cracks in a dark bank of clouds. Again, he kicked her, causing her to cry out and clutch her knees to her stomach.

The Foolish One emerged from Horseback, and he stalked toward Whip. He shouted, "*Hah!*" as though he approved, yet he knew everyone near would see the Foolish One in his bearing and his walk. "It is good to beat a wife that way! What terrible thing has she done, my friend, that she should be beaten like a dog? Has she coupled with another warrior? Has she touched your sacred shield during her time of unclean bleeding? She must be a very bad woman to deserve such a beating, my friend. Tell me, how has this woman dishonored you?"

Whip's face showed his anger at the interference of the Foolish One. "I will not say what my wife has done! I do not need to say!"

"It is so bad my friend cannot speak it!" Horseback yelled. "I must ask the woman, herself!" Dropping to the dirt, Horseback grabbed Dipper by the hair and turned her face to his. "Tell me, woman, what thing you have done!"

Her small voice came out with a sob: "I let my shadow fall on the meat that I was cooking for my husband!"

"*Oo-bia!*" Horseback shouted, drawing away from Dipper as if she were diseased. "This is a very bad woman! Is it not a taboo to let one's shadow fall on cooking meat? Such a careless person must be pushed roughly away, so the shadow does not taint the meat. But, the way my friend punishes his wife, I believe she must have stood with her shadow on the meat a long time, on purpose."

"I saw Dipper cooking," a voice said.

Horseback looked and saw Bear Heart, a man known for truthfulness. "Tell us why my friend beats his wife so!" Horseback said.

"I cannot say. I did not see her shadow fall on the meat."

"She lies!" Whip shouted. "The beating has nothing to do with her shadow. She is a wicked slave wife. She makes spells against me. I beat a witch. She practices Northern Raider sorcery!"

"Winters have passed since you made her good," Horseback argued. "Is her witchcraft even stronger than your seed?"

Some women ducked behind lodges and hooted at Whip like knowing owls who see everything.

Horseback pointed at the sky. "Let Father Sun witness your oath, my friend, for he who swears falsely to Father Sun is struck down, and so you will prove your right to beat this woman!"

Whip dropped the broken stick he had been holding, and took two steps back. "I do not have to swear. She should be the one to swear!"

Without hesitation, Dipper lifted her face and palms to the sun. "As Father Sun is my witness, I am not a witch. I am only a woman!"

The people looked on for a long moment of silence, and knew Dipper spoke the truth, for she would not have sworn falsely for fear of sure death.

"*Hah!*" Horseback shouted. "She is good. My friend has beaten the evil witchcraft out of her! Now there is no more reason to beat her!"

Whip sneered. He kicked dirt at his wife and stalked away.

As the onlookers went back to their own concerns, Teal hurried to her husband's side.

"He will beat her again," she said. "It gets worse for her every time."

The look of foolishness fell away from Horseback's face, and he became serious. "There is only one way I can protect her."

"I know the way," she said, looking at the ground.

"Does my wife wish me to protect this woman?"

Teal looked at him and sighed, a look of frustration and helplessness in her eyes. "She should not be beaten to death with a *Noomah* child in her belly, but I cannot tell my husband to protect her. He must want to."

Horseback looked across the river and saw the high, grassy bank above the greenery of the timber. He saw a stallion nipping at his mares there, and felt better. He slipped his hand around the back of Teal's neck, and pulled her closer. "Always, you carry my shield. I could love no wife more than I love you, my sits-beside woman."

Teal put her hand on his bare chest. "I will speak to Dipper. She will know what to do."

49

Jean L'Archeveque held the tallow candle as the governor's scribe lit the oil lamp with its flame. It was quite a rare pleasure to sit under the steady glow of a lamp, as opposed to the flickers of a candle flame that made shadows lurch all around the room. Even bear oil was precious in Santa Fe, and only to be used when necessary. But Captain-General Antonio Del Bosque had insisted on this late-night meeting at the *Casas Reales*, and so Jean had come to burn precious oil and discuss the problems of the kingdom.

"It gives me no end of consternation," Del Bosque said. "The viceroy has become obsessed with the *Indios*. In the old days, I could refer to them as savages, or *Norteños*, or what-have-you, and get along well enough. Now, the viceroy—his highness, the Duque de Albuquerque—insists that I produce a map demarcating the range of each group of savages, using their particular names. He requires a lengthy *noticia* describing their ways of subsistence, types of shelter, and all other manner of ridiculous detail. It is so confusing to me that I am going to place the entire affair in your hands, Juan. You will help my scribe make the map and prepare the *noticia*."

Jean shrugged and rubbed his stomach, feeling stuffed after the feast in the dining hall. He wondered what fee he might command for this assignment, but thought better of asking just now. "How far does the viceroy want the map to extend?"

"To the very ends of Spanish influence among the savages. I must satisfy his curiosity once and for all, so I can get on with the important affairs of this colony. The viceroy has no concept of our hardships here in this remote outpost. No concept at all, my friend."

Juan stepped across the governor's cramped office and took the quill pen from the scribe. He dipped it into the inkwell and began tracing a crooked line onto a piece of parchment spread across the governor's cluttered desk. He wondered why Antonio Del Bosque had not requested this information long ago. "Let us begin on our own Rio Grande," he said, labeling the line he had drawn with that name. "Now, the first problem is with the Pueblos. They are not one nation, but several. They are *Tewa, Tiwa, Tompiro, Keresan, Zuni* . . ."

"*Basta!*" the governor cried, waving a hand. "Do not complicate, Juan. Simplify. The viceroy does not have to know everything you know. It is more than he can understand."

"But, the Pueblo nations all speak different languages," Jean argued.

"I don't care if they debate in Latin. They all live in the same kind of houses, and so we will continue to call them all Pueblos."

Jean sighed. "Very well. The mapmakers know where the villages lie."

"*Sí, sí*. Get to the Apache problem, the one that vexes me with its complications."

Jean sketched an oblong territory east of the Rio Grande, and another circle west of the river, but north of the Pueblo villages. "*Apache* is not really the proper name, for it is merely a *Zuni* word meaning enemy. The French call them *Padouca*. They call themselves *Inday*."

"With God's blessing, they will one day call themselves Christians, and their heathen names can be removed from the pages of history. Until then, they will be referred to as Apaches."

Jean frowned, but he did not argue. "The confusion is in the number of bands. They are like little cities, except that they move around to hunt after they harvest their crops. Most of them are also misnamed—the Pharaohans, the Mescaleros, the Lipanes. To add more confusion, they sometimes make war on each other, as one village might attack another in the old feudal days of Spain. Then there are the Navajos, here, across the river." He pointed to the separate territory he had sketched to the west of the Rio Grande. "They speak the *Inday* language, though they live independent of the others."

"The Navajo will remain Navajo," Del Bosque ordered. "We will continue to consider them a nation unto themselves. This is no time to arouse the curiosity of the viceroy by changing our names for these *bárbaros*. With the Apaches, simply write down the name of each band in its recognized territory. I don't care if they are misnamed or not. You will have the mapmaker write Apache in capital letters, and the band names in lower case."

"Very well," Jean said. He carefully wrote each band name in its appropriate place on the map. He stepped back and looked at his creation for a moment, deciding not to add other nations he had encountered far to the east with La Salle—the *Tejas*, the *Caddoes*, the *Carancahuas*. These peoples lived beyond Spanish influence.

He brushed the plume of the quill pen absentmindedly against his cheek as he studied his rough map, then drew in a large territory north of the *Navajo* lands. "This is the mountain domain of the *Yutas*, with whom we are well acquainted. And far to the north of their mountains, hundreds of leagues from here, lies the country of the Snake People, sometimes called Shoshone. They call themselves *Noomah*."

"Label them Snakes," Del Bosque said. "The office of the viceroy will enjoy a certain familiarity with the term." He chuckled and nudged the scribe, who also felt obligated to laugh.

Jean made the entry, then motioned vaguely to an area north of the Snakes. "I have heard of nations beyond the Snakes. The Blackfeet. The Crow. Here, to their northeast, the Snakes tell of a people they call Kiowa, meaning Mouse People. The Kiowa are allied with two nations lately arrived from the east and supplied with French guns. These two are called the Throat Cutters, or Lakota, and the Finger Choppers, or Cheyenne."

"Have any Spaniards had contact with these *Indios?*" Del Bosque asked.

"No."

"Then we will not bother the good viceroy with their existence. Continue, Jean. What about the plains tribes?"

"To the east of the Snakes lies the land of the Wolf People, who live in villages of large earthen houses. The French call them *Pani*. They call themselves *Parisu* or *Chahiksichahik*."

"Label them *Pani*. It is a term we have used before."

Jean dipped the split quill point into the ink well again and carefully wrote the label on the parchment. "Now, south of the *Pani* lie the villages of grass houses inhabited by the Raccoon-Eyed People, among whom I spent two years. The French call them Painted *Pani*, or sometimes Wichita, which is the name of one of their villages. They have been called *Jumanos* in Spanish records."

"Very well. We will continue to call them *Jumanos*. Tell me, Juan. Are there really any riches at Quivira as the old legends suggested? Is it not indeed one of the seven cities of gold?" His eyes sparkled with hopeful fascination. "Tell the truth, my friend."

"The truth is, you would be lucky to find a copper ingot there. But they do have fine gardens of corn, pumpkins, and squash. And excellent plums."

Del Bosque chuckled knowingly, as if he understood some hidden meaning in what Jean had said. "I know many expeditions there have turned up no gold. But, they could hide it in tunnels under their grass huts, no?"

Jean shook his head. "I have seen Quivira without a white man within three hundred leagues. There is no gold there, Antonio."

"Do you forget that you, yourself, are a white man? Maybe they tattooed your face like theirs, but do they forget you are white? Do you think they would show you the gold? Think of it, Juan, there could be riches there, yet."

Jean smirked and said, "I suppose all things are possible, no matter how unlikely." He turned back to the map, shaking his head. Now he drew the meandering line of a river that started in *Yuta* country. It flowed due south, then turned abruptly to the east, slithering across the vastness of the plains. He labeled its serpentine course Rio Napestle.

"The *Indios* call this the River of Arrowheads," he added. "The French call it the Arkansas. There is a French post many hundreds of leagues downstream where this river empties into the great Colbert, or Messipe."

"We will retain the term Rio Napestle. So it has been identified for many years. What savages live along its course?"

"Here," Jean said, "far to the east, even beyond the *Jumanos* of Quivira, live the Osage. They are powerful. Some of them are seven feet tall and can run almost as fast as horses for short distances."

Del Bosque snorted. "Please, Juan, do not attempt to entertain me with ridiculous heathen legends. Have these Osages had any contact with Spaniards?"

"No, but they are supplied with French guns."

Del Bosque stared at the map and rubbed his chin. "Then we will exclude them from the map. If the viceroy learns of their existence, he may order an expedition into their country. I simply cannot spare the men or materiel for that. And don't mention any of these distant nations to Father Ugarte. He will begin his own campaign for an expedition to reduce them to Christianity. Those Franciscans all dream of martyrdom, but that doesn't mean they have to take any of us poor sinners with them."

"I rarely engage in conversation with the padre," Jean replied.

"Good. Now, is that all?"

"There is one more nation on the Rio Napestle." He placed the point of the pen at a location upstream of Tachichichi. "Do you remember the Comanches?"

Slowly, Del Bosque's expression darkened. "Six years ago. The attack on the caravan of *carretas*."

"Yes."

"They took a captive girl with them as I recall—the daughter of a whore—and she was never heard from again, though Father Ugarte walked all the way to the *Yuta* country looking for her. The Comanches stole all the horses and mules they wanted on their way back through the colony. Their leader—what was his name? Acaballo? He cut away a piece of *Capitán* Lujan's scalp in the battle of *carretas*."

Jean nodded. "I saw the *capitán* without his helmet on a few days ago. I barely noticed the wound."

"Yes, the scalp has grown back nicely." The governor stared at the map for a few seconds. "Why do you mention those wicked *bárbaros* now, Juan?"

Jean tapped the parchment with the point of the pen. "My informants tell me they have returned."

Del Bosque stood silent for a long moment, then snorted. "There were only five of them here six years ago. They were very lucky with that raid on the *carretas*. *Capitán* Lujan might have killed them all had he been more prepared. I think he learned much from that defeat. He has become a terror to all Apache raiders since that day."

"He will not find terrorizing Comanches as easy," Jean said. "I have learned more about these people. They are really Snake People." He pointed to the Snake lands on the map, far to the north of the *Yutas*. "They have broken away from their brothers to seek horses, buffalo, and trade. This time, a whole village has come south. They have come to stay."

"How many warriors?"

"I have heard their camp has fifty or sixty lodges. That could mean one hundred fifty warriors, or more."

The governor laughed in relief. "Is that all! Juan, you worry about strange things."

"We must not underestimate them. One mounted Comanche is equal to ten foot-warriors, or three of our own mounted soldiers. They are marvelous horsemen. In addition, they are now allied with the *Yutas*."

"You know the royal policy, Juan. We cannot align ourselves with every warrior nation on the frontier. We treat only with the most powerful, and that is the Apaches. As long as we maintain relations with the Apaches, they will shield us from the others."

"But, Antonio, you know as well as I do that the *Apaches* have become increasingly belligerent. They steal and kill and take captives wherever they wish, among the Pueblos and even among the Spanish settlements."

"And Captain Lujan punishes those who raid."

"Lujan has only eighty soldiers. He cannot handle the increasing *Apache* raids. Besides that, I have evidence that he often punishes the first bunch of *Apaches* he encounters, whether they are guilty of raiding or not. This only leads to increased hostility."

"So, what do you recommend, Juan?"

"That we make peace with the new Comanche-*Yuta* alliance."

Del Bosque held his chin and shook his head. "We cannot afford to ally ourselves with too many *Indios*. We make peace with the most powerful nation, and promote warfare among all the others. We must keep them fighting among themselves, Juan. If they ever unite against us, this outpost will be finished, and you and I will find ourselves roasting over some heathen's fire."

"In this case we can make peace with both the Apaches and the Comanches without ever having to fear them uniting against us. They hate each other like English and Turks. There was a war between the two tribes generations ago, and both still remember."

Del Bosque rubbed his face and groaned. "Juan, I asked you to come here to simplify this issue, and you are only making it more complicated. I do not understand your obsession with these Comanches."

"It is simple," Jean insisted. "The Comanche-*Yuta* alliance is on the verge of becoming more powerful than the Apache nation. We must eventually break our alliance with the Apaches and align ourselves with the Comanches. We might as well start preparing for that eventuality."

Del Bosque's eyes flared in the oil light. "Are you mad? The Apaches can muster thousands of warriors. You have said yourself that the Comanches have fewer than two hundred. And the *Yutas* have never been as fierce as the Apaches."

"More Comanches arrive almost daily from the Snake lands. There will soon be more than one band. I assure you, Antonio, one hundred Comanche warriors can patrol the entire New Mexican frontier for us. You must remember that the Apache bands do not cooperate. In fact, they fight among themselves. No one band of Apaches will be able to repel the Comanche hoard that is coming."

Del Bosque looked at his scribe. "Can you imagine my writing to the viceroy and telling him that I am breaking ties with thousands of Apaches in order to forge a treaty with a handful of Comanches? The same Comanches who all but destroyed our trade caravan six years ago?"

The scribe smiled sheepishly and glanced with uncertainty at Jean.

"There is going to be a great Comanche and Apache war," Jean said, "and the Comanches will win. With their *Yuta* allies and with their new arrivals from the Snake country, they will wage the bloodiest mounted war you have ever seen. As long as Santa Fe is allied with the Apaches, the Comanches will raid us as well, and *Capitán* Lujan will pluck his beard in his inability to catch these riders."

Del Bosque looked at his scribe again and pointed his thumb at Jean. "This plan comes from the same gentleman who once suggested we give the *Norteños* all the mules and geldings they wanted."

Jean sat down on a wicker chair made of corded yucca fibers. "Let me share a story with you, governor. My informants at Tachichichi have kept close watch on the Comanches. Not long ago, they noted that the young Comanche leader, Acaballo, passed through their *ranchería* on the first day of the full moon. Two days after the full moon, a group of *Tiwa* hunters from Taos encountered Acaballo not far north of their pueblo. They spoke to him. They described him and his mount perfectly."

"What is the point of this story, Juan?"

"Acaballo covered more than forty leagues in those two days, riding the same horse. That is the way the Comanches travel. Twenty leagues a day without changing horses!"

Del Bosque brushed the intelligence aside with a flick of his fingers. "Pueblo informants cannot be trusted. They have no concept of time. No clocks, no calendars. They were mistaken. No one can ride from Tachichichi to Taos in two days."

"Acaballo can. He and his warriors. They are hungry people, Antonio. They have been starved for generations. Their warriors are small of stature, but that only makes them stick better to the backs of their horses. They are muscular and tougher than rawhide. They ride like nothing the world has ever seen. Arabs and Mongols would gape at them in disbelief. They are the very embodiment of the Thessalian centaur!"

Finally, Governor Del Bosque seemed to sense some possibility of truth behind Jean's adamance. "I cannot make decisions such as these based on hearsay." He turned to his scribe. "Roberto, prepare a letter to the viceroy. Tell him that I have commissioned the renowned frontiersman, Juan Archebeque, at . . ." he paused and looked at the vigas overhead ". . . fifty-four pesos, three reales, and nine granos—you know the viceroy is suspicious of even numbers. Tell the viceroy that Juan will investigate the *Indio* situation along the Rio Napestle. Make it sound important, with plenty of flowery phrases. Date it and sign it, May God guard Your Excellency many years, your most obedient servant, Don Antonio Del Bosque, etcetera, etcetera."

"As you wish, governor," the scribe said, collecting his tools. "Will there be anything else tonight?"

"No, that is all. I will sign the letter tomorrow. Juan, you will stay and have a glass of brandy with me."

When the scribe left, Del Bosque watched him walk quite a way through the torch-lit garden before he closed the pine door. He poured the brandy in silence, handed Jean a glass, and sat facing him across the desk. "Juan," he began, "you have prospered since I became governor."

Jean gulped half his brandy and narrowed his eyes at the governor. "I have been fortunate. Your trust has benefited me."

"I know it was hard for you after Maria died. You with two sons to raise alone. I have always done everything I could to help you in your business ventures." He raised his glass and half whispered. "To the point of overlooking certain rules and royal decrees, my friend."

Now Jean knew something strange was happening. Never had the governor spoken to him in such terms. "I am grateful for all you have done, Antonio."

There was a long silence as the governor watched the brandy swirl in his glass. "I need your help, Juan. I am in trouble."

"What kind of trouble?"

"The worst kind. Financial trouble." He sighed. "I have made loans to certain family members in New Spain. Bad loans. I am in debt. I have no way to pay, and worse still . . ." He rubbed his brow with trembling fingers. "I have invested the funds of this colony in my attempts to recoup my losses. I have made bad investments."

Jean gulped the rest of his brandy and got up to refill his glass. "How much money have you taken from the colonial funds?"

Del Bosque looked at the floor. "About three thousand pesos."

"Three thousand. How did you divert that much?"

"In the form of deductions assessed from the salaries of the soldiers."

Jean took several deep breaths to consider that substantial amount. "Does anyone know you have used government funds?"

"Not yet, but there is going to be an audit of my records before winter."

"How do you know that?"

Del Bosque smirked and looked Jean in the eye. "Your informants are among the *Indios*. Mine are in the government."

Jean nodded. "Three thousand pesos. I would give it to you if I had it, but I don't. I can't make that much money in three years of trading and farming. How am I going to help you?"

"You mentioned something to me once. One of your wild ideas. You said the profits for this colony would be incredible if we could but trade with the Frenchmen across the plains. Do you remember?"

He nodded. "It is still true. We have things the French need—gold and horses. They have things we need—gun powder, guns, iron tools, textiles . . . things we cannot seem to get from Mexico City. But trade with the French is forbidden by the crown. You told me that years ago."

"Were it not forbidden, how would it work?"

Jean began to pace, feeling somewhat trapped, yet excited by the conversation. "I would hire *Indio* traders to move the horses and other goods across the plains, and bring back the French goods. I would sell the French goods here or in New Spain. The guns would be in particular demand among the colonists."

"And the profits?"

"Very high. We would triple or quadruple our investment. The *Indios* will work for a small part of the horses and guns. But such a trade would break all manner of laws. It would be very risky, not only legally, but bodily."

Del Bosque reached under his desk and produced a pair of saddlebags. They were well-used bags of sturdy but ordinary manufacture. He used both hands to lift the sagging bags onto the desk top, and they rattled with the timbre of hard metal when he set them down.

"What is that?" Jean said.

"A thousand pesos in gold. All I could possibly take from what is left in the treasury without bankrupting the colony. If we can triple it before winter, I can avoid prosecution for misuse of funds. Then, I can begin to settle my debts with next spring's trading expedition."

Jean looked at the saddlebags, a storm of excitement building in his stomach. Just the thought of trading with Frenchmen was enough to make him crave the adventure.

"Beginning with the spring expedition," Del Bosque continued, "we will divide the profits two to one, in your favor. I will be getting out of debt while you are getting rich, my friend."

Yes, and while I am taking all the risk, Jean thought. But he knew he would have to pay off the governor to allow the continuation of the illegal trade. That was the Spanish way. The way of the *mordida*.

"Juan, will you help me? I have nowhere else to turn."

Jean threw the brandy back, and felt its heat engulf his lungs. "You have been a good friend, Antonio." He reached for the saddlebags.

50

Hair grew long from the heads of the Grasshopper Eaters, and each chose his pony. Crazy Eyes seemed to use his peculiar gaze to charm a brown colt. This colt was two winters old and had never been ridden. His mane and tail were dark, connected with a perfect dark stripe that ran down his back. Across his withers, he wore another dark stripe that crossed the one running from mane to tail.

Crooked Teeth chose a yellow mare that would soon foal. "I will return the foal to you when it is weaned," he promised.

Horseback smiled. "You have chosen well. Keep the foal."

Crooked Teeth was soon riding his mare, but Crazy Eyes had to ask for help from Horseback to train the young line-back colt. Each day, as they worked with the colt, boys from the camp would come to watch and learn. Even Sandhill would watch for a while, before running back to the camp to be with Teal. Horseback was happy that his son loved horses.

"Crazy Eyes, what have you learned while you watched the horses and your hair grew?" Horseback asked the Grasshopper Eater who wanted to join the Horseback People.

Crazy Eyes looked at two different things for a while, then said, "I have learned much about horses, but I cannot say what I have learned."

"You must learn to speak what is in your heart, so that you may teach your sons. I believe the spirits were wise to choose this pony for you, Crazy

Eyes. The dark lines on this colt have strong power. The line that runs down the back will hold you on the pony's back if your heart is good and strong."

"And the line across the withers?" Crazy Eyes asked. "Does it hold power, too?"

"This is a magic line, my friend. All horses have this spirit-line, but with most it is invisible. The spirits have revealed the magic line on this colt so that you may learn about horses."

"What power does the line have? Is it different from the line down his back?"

"Very different. I will show you." Horseback took the colt's lead rope from Crazy Eyes and approached the pony from the front. The colt raised his head and backed away a few steps. "If I stand in front of the line, the horse wants to go backward," he said.

Now he handed the rope back to Crazy Eyes and moved around the colt until he stood behind the dark line that ran across the withers. Approaching from this angle, the colt moved forward, toward Crazy Eyes. "Stand behind the line, and the pony wants to go forward," he said. "The line goes through the heart. When you ride a pony and you want it to back up, wrap your legs around in front of the line and the pony will learn to back up. When you want your pony to go forward, touch him with your heels behind the line, and he will go forward. That is the power of this line."

Crazy Eyes smiled. "My pony shows the magic line. I have chosen well, *hah?*"

"*Hah.* Very well. But the warrior who chooses ponies well must learn to ride well. You have much to do."

The next day, as Horseback helped train the colt, the young pony shied from Crazy Eyes when he reached to touch his head.

"The hand strikes," Horseback explained, holding his palm flat and his fingers outstretched. "The hand grabs and holds. The horse knows this. But a single finger will charm the wild spirit in this pony."

He curled all but one finger against his palm and approached the colt slowly. The colt watched the finger Horseback extended toward him, seemingly more curious than afraid. His nostrils quivered as the finger eased closer to his head. Finally, Horseback touched him between the eyes with the single digit, then slowly spread his other fingers and rubbed him on the forehead. The colt nodded his head in appreciation and leaned into the palm that rubbed him now between the eyes.

"Begin with one finger," Horseback said, "then slowly move your hands over every part of the pony. You must touch him everywhere. Go slowly. He may kick at you when you touch his flank. Stay out of the way, and he will get tired of kicking after a while. Touch him everywhere and do not hurt or frighten him. Then he will trust and serve you."

Crazy Eyes looked somewhat disappointed. "When will I ride him?"

"When he trusts you. You have much work to do before you ride this pony."

After two days, Crazy Eyes was able to touch the line-back colt all over. He could walk behind the colt without getting kicked. The colt would stand sleepily while Crazy Eyes moved a hand gently under his belly or between his hind legs.

"Now breathe from the nostrils of your pony," Horseback said. "His breath is warm and sweet and carries his spirit. You will breathe in his spirit, and he, yours. You will know his heart."

"Breathe from his nostrils? Will he not bite?" Holding the lead rope, Crazy Eyes turned away from his colt to cast his crooked glance at Horseback. When he turned, the colt promptly bit him on the shoulder. *"Anah!"* he cried.

Horseback burst into laughter, along with all the young boys who were watching, trying to learn.

"I will not breathe from her nostrils!" Crazy Eyes found blood on the tips of his fingers where he had grabbed the bitten place on his shoulder.

"This is good!" Horseback said. "He treats you like a pony. But you must know how to talk the pony talk. It is a sign of disrespect for one pony to turn its back on the other. That is why he bit you."

"I must turn my back on my pony to lead him," Crazy Eyes argued. "Will he bite me every time I turn?"

"You must earn the right to turn away from him. Next time he bites you, bite him back. *Kubetu!*" he growled, gritting his teeth.

"Next time?" Crazy Eyes said, uncertainly. "Will he bite my nose off if I breathe from his nostrils?"

"Come, elder sister. Will a pony bite kill you? Do you wish to ride with the Horseback People?"

Crazy Eyes drew himself taller and held his chin high. "*Hah!* I am not afraid of pony teeth!"

"Breathe from the nostrils of your pony, and his soul will be yours—his power, his spirit."

Crazy Eyes approached his colt cautiously. He put his hands on the round jaws and eased his nostrils closer to the colt's. The first time he felt the blast from the pony's lungs, he pulled back, causing the colt to flinch. Soon, however, he was nose-to-nose with the colt again, seeking its spirit. The exchange of breath seemed to charm both man and horse for a moment. Then the line-back colt's head turned and his mouth opened. Yellowed teeth parted and reached for the side of the warrior's head.

The Grasshopper Eater was quicker. In an instant he had the soft nose of the colt between his own teeth. He bit so hard that the colt reared, lifting Crazy Eyes's new moccasins from the ground before he released his hold.

The onlookers fell about the grass and laughed as the trainer calmed the pony on the end of his lead rope.

"Good!" Horseback said. "Now he knows you will bite something bigger than a grasshopper. He begins to respect you, my friend."

Crazy Eyes's grin glistened with pony blood.

The next day, Horseback gave Crazy Eyes a war bridle to use on his pony. They looped the length of corded rawhide, twice the length of an eagle's wingspan, around the lower jaw of the colt and gave him some time to grow accustomed to the feel of the thing in his mouth. When he stopped trying to push it out with his tongue, they began leading him around with it, teaching him to stop when he felt the rawhide tighten around his jaw.

The first time Crazy Eyes climbed onto the back of the line-back colt, he darted so quickly away that Crazy Eyes landed on his rear in the grass.

"Come," Horseback said. "This one has the quickness of a heron. Let him plunge into the river."

Gathering around the colt, the cluster of onlookers urged him into the water until he stood knee deep. He drank as Crazy Eyes gathered in a handful of dark mane with the same hand that held the reins. When he sprang from the water to throw himself across the colt's back, the colt tried to dodge, but the power of the river prevented him from moving quick enough to get out from under the rider.

Soon, Crazy Eyes was astride the dark line that coursed the colt's back. He smiled until he felt the pony rolling.

"Slip off!" Horseback said. "He will lie down!"

Crazy Eyes came off one side as the colt sank and rolled toward him.

"Now, back on!" Horseback said.

Crazy Eyes mounted again as the colt found footing in the mud. The colt turned for the bank, but the rider tightened the war bridle and pulled hard with one rein.

"Good!" Horseback said. "Make him walk. Make him turn. Use the power of the river!"

The sun moved three fists across the sky before Crazy Eyes let his colt come out of the water. Now he rode at a walk across the grassy riverbank and made the pony turn with hard pulls on the reins.

Horseback said nothing now, for Crazy Eyes had found the heart of his pony. After the river water had dried from the colt, and he began to tire and make sweat that turned as white as the tufts of a *sohoobi* tree in spring, Crazy Eyes dismounted to let him rest. He rubbed the colt with grass all over, making his coat look sleek and shiny and good.

Placing his palm on the flanks of the colt where the rays of Father Sun struck most directly, the Grasshopper Eater smiled, and said, "He is warm. He feels good." Crazy Eyes placed his cheek against the flanks of the pony to warm his face. His eyes grew wide.

Horseback chuckled. "What do you hear with your ear pressed against the flanks of your pony, my friend?"

"I hear a great heartbeat, strong and steady."

"What else?"

Crazy Eyes listened a long time. "A sound."

"What is this sound?"

"It is a spirit-sound. It rumbles like the cloud-lodge of the Thunderbird, and roars like the winds of a storm in a canyon. It sounds far away, but it is near, for my pony possesses it within his own hide."

Horseback eased around the opposite flank of the colt so he, too, could listen, though he knew the sound well. "You hear the power and feel the warmth of the fires of the sun, my friend. This is your pony. This is your gift from the spirits. Honor it. Use it. Consume it. Ride it to glory. When it is gone, get another."

As the colt lowered his head and began to graze, the two pony-warriors listened, one to each side, their ears pressed against the ribs of the animal.

51

Jean L'Archeveque climbed up the ladder of his cubicle and looked out over the village of Tachichichi. The red face of the sun clung hopelessly to the eastern horizon, lending its glow to the earthen walls of the town. He wondered how low the same sun now shone on Paris. Was it noon in the pirate town of Petit-Goave? Did the cannibal coast of Fort St. Louis still reek of death and slime pits?

Jean had seen much of the world in his thirty-nine years. He missed France, and Petit-Goave, where the language of his people drifted through the taverns and streets, lilting from the lips of women like the songs of warblers, growling from the throats of men like the threats of grackles. But a man who wore the Raccoon-Eyed tattoos of the wilderness on his face belonged on the frontier.

Scanning the grounds, he found Speaks Twice mounted and waiting. The translator had even gone so far as to saddle Jean's horse for him, seemingly anxious to meet with his friends upstream.

Jean, too, looked forward to seeing the Comanches again, especially Horseback. Six winters had passed since these first Comanches rode into Santa Fe with Bad Camper, the *Yuta* chief. Six winters had passed since Padre Ugarte and *Capitán* Lujan had attempted to beat Horseback into slave captivity. Six winters had passed since Horseback's little band of mounted warriors had stormed through the governor's trade caravan, and through the entire frontier kingdom of Nuevo Mexico, taking every pony they cared to own.

Often Jean had wondered how Horseback had fared in the Snake lands far to the north. Somehow, he had known the young rider would return. Jean lowered the ladder to the ground outside the little rock-and-adobe room that served as his lodge and trading post. He made his way down the steps and walked briskly across the plaza to join Speaks Twice. He said nothing as he mounted, but smiled and nodded westward. Speaks Twice returned the smile, and they rode.

· · · ·

Their shadows darkened the grass below the bellies of their horses when Jean first noticed the tall hide lodges ahead in the valley of the Rio Napestle. He reined in his mount to observe the surprising size of the camp. Even the lodges themselves were larger than he had expected. He had always heard that the Snake People were poor. Even Horseback, who would naturally shed the most favorable light upon his own people, had described the *Noomah* as surrounded by enemies, forced onto poor hunting grounds, and constantly in search of food.

Were the people of Horseback's band still Snakes? Had they not broken away from their brethren hundreds of leagues to the north? Yes, they still spoke the Snake tongue, and held fast to the Snake customs. But Jean had seen poor *Indios*, and this camp spoke of wealth. Little things told of a rise from Snake poverty. The lazy camp dogs lounged in the shade of river timber instead of prowling hungrily through the valley. Most of the lodges were painted with bright designs, belying leisure time for artistic endeavors. Sacred shields and weapons stood in neat clusters, hanging from tripods of lances bedecked with feathers and furs. The drying racks sagged with the weight of meat. Many square frames stretched the upright skins of deer, antelope, and bear, while buffalo and elk hides lay staked to the ground like leaves scattered under a maple tree.

Then there were the horses. Fat. Sleek. Few showed a rib. There were more foals here than would be found in a camp of starving people. Jean tried to number the ponies, but lost count at ninety when the herd wandered around a bend in the valley.

These people were not poor. These people were no longer Snakes. They were Horseback People. They were Comanche. The *Tiwa* prophesies had come true. A new nation of riders had risen beyond the mountains and migrated south, seeking wealth and land and especially—yes, most especially—horses.

But with new power, came danger. Jean knew from his travels that the most dangerous people and the most dangerous persons were those who had suffered, then decided to suffer no longer.

He thought of Minime Duhaut, the buffoon from La Salle's ill-fated Fort

St. Louis. La Salle had caught the little sneak-thief stealing from his own bed chambers in Paris. He had beaten Minime and impressed him into years of service on the frontier. But all the beatings in the world could not reform the likes of Minime Duhaut. Small of stature, he had been beaten all his life and had become immune to the pain of even the cruelest blows. And when Minime discovered a peculiar vehicle upon which to rise above the oppression he had suffered his whole life—the Cult of the Convulsionaries of Fort St. Louis—he had seized his chance at revenge, destroyed Fort St. Louis, and murdered the great explorer, La Salle.

Jean saw more nobility and honor in Horseback's *Comanches* than Minime Duhaut had ever dreamed of mustering, yet the danger in their rise from oppression existed as surely as Minime's act of retribution. Revenge was a prime motivator in the codes of the simplest civilizations. Thanks to the stupidity of Fray Ugarte and *Capitán* Lujan, Horseback already had reason to hate the Spaniards.

Then there was the problem of the *Inday*. This was strange. A war lain fallow for generations. Jean had heard of it from both the *Inday* and the *Noomah*. At some time lost in the recesses of antiquity, these two people had made bloody war upon each other. Both nations spoke of this in terms of legendary tribal memories from some distant land far to the north and west. By both accounts, the *Inday* had virtually exterminated the *Noomah*—the source of *Noomah* suffering and *Inday* power.

How long ago this war had occurred was something Jean had been unable to determine. The *Zuni*, who call the *Inday* "Apache," claimed the *Inday* had come to the Pueblo country no fewer than a dozen generations ago. If this were true, the ancient *Inday-Noomah* war must have taken place hundreds of years ago. It was remarkable that a hatred could exist so long between two people separated by many generations and many ranges of mountains. But to a society faced forever with a struggle for survival, the threat of extermination could live a thousand years in the stories of old men and in the bloodlines of warrior sons.

No clash with the *Inday* had occurred since Horseback's *Comanches* had moved south to stay, but Jean knew it would come. War was on the horizon, and no amount of diplomacy could avert it. True, Horseback had made peace with the *Yutas*, but the *Noomah-Yuta* war had never been one of extermination. The *Inday* and the Comanche were bound to fight.

The question was one of which nation to take on as an ally. The Spaniards were already on poor terms with the *Inday*. Yet, relations with the Comanches had begun just as poorly. The *Inday* had been weakened by European fevers, yet strengthened by modern weapons given to them by French traders to the east. They were much more numerous than these new Comanches, all of whom lived in this single camp on the River of Arrowheads for all Jean knew.

But in their semipermanent farming villages, the *Inday* would present easy targets for the horsemen of the Comanche nation.

The Comanches were unpredictable. They were no longer starving, but they still remembered hunger. When it came to the warriors, each grown man possessed two memories: his own recollection of personal battles with enemies, and a tribal recall of an ancient *Inday* holocaust. They neither expected nor preferred to die old.

Most important, Jean had seen Horseback ride. He had heard stories from *Tiwa* warriors and Spanish soldiers of how a single Comanche warrior could kill and scalp an enemy without ever breaking the stride of a full gallop. They could shoot arrows from the backs of ponies, even while hanging alongside the flanks of the beast, using the mount as a living shield.

It was odd, but not even Horseback himself seemed to know what manner of horseman he was. It was said that Horseback had been born on the day the Snake People discovered their first horse. If this was true, Horseback belonged to only the second generation of *Noomah* horsemen. How he had learned in his short lifetime to ride better than all the horsemen the world had ever known was a mystery Jean sought to unravel.

Jean L'Archeveque, meanwhile, found himself in the middle. A Frenchman on Spanish soil. A white man with a red man's tattoos. Perhaps today's meeting with Horseback would help him determine the future for the Spanish frontier. Jean thought it well that he had learned to adapt to many cultures. He did not know which one might survive here.

"Look," Speaks Twice said. "We have been sighted." His right hand alone made the signs as his tongue spoke perfect Spanish.

Jean saw several warriors catching mounts, and knew he must react quickly to avoid trouble. Was Horseback even in camp? He could take no chances.

"Come," he said to Speaks Twice, curling the heels of his moccasins against the flanks of his mount. He rode to the brink of the riverbank, where everyone in the camp could see him. A few warriors were already riding his way, for they kept their best mounts staked in camp should they need to mount quickly.

Raising the musket he carried across his thighs, he lifted the frizzen and checked the pan to make sure his charge of priming powder remained. Finding the pan half-empty, he quickly used his teeth to pull the stopper from his buffalo-horn powder flask, and refilled the pan.

Speaks Twice's concern showed on his face. "Will you shoot at them?"

"Of course not." He latched the serpentine back against the tension of its spring, put the musket butt to his shoulder, and aimed vaguely southward. Just before the *Comanches* came within arrow range, he pulled the trigger. The serpentine sprung forward, striking the flint against the steel frizzen.

Sparks shot down into the frizzen pan holding the priming charge. The powder flared with a wizard's burst of flame and smoke, a split second later setting off the main charge in the breech. The musket bucked to the roar of escaping lead and flame, and the mounts under Jean and Speaks Twice darted suddenly, only to be gathered in with taut reins.

The Comanche horsemen scattered at the sound of the musket shot, some of their ponies ramping in fear of the explosion. Jean grinned, slid the long weapon into its fringed scabbard, drew the two flintlock pistols from his saddle holsters, and cocked them. He clenched his reins in his teeth, angled both pistol barrels high at arm's length, and pulled the triggers. The one in his right hand fired, but he had to cock the left pistol two more times before it would spark enough to set off its charge.

"Is that Horseback?" he asked, returning the pistols to their holsters.

"Yes," Speaks Twice answered. "On the near horse. The bay with black mane."

Jean raised his hand and drew in a breath. "Horseback, my friend!" he shouted in the *Yuta* tongue. "My guns have spoken my greeting! I come in friendship!"

The Comanche riders leaped their mounts forward. In an instant Jean found himself surrounded by warriors singing joyous yelps. He recognized Horseback first, though he had matured, his chest and shoulders broader than before, his eyes filled with more suspicion, his face struck with confidence. Horseback sent a rider back to camp—to prepare a greeting, Jean supposed—then rode close enough to clasp hands with the tattooed visitor.

"Raccoon-Eyes, *mi amigo*."

Jean's brows peaked in surprise.

"Speaks Twice teaches me the tongue," Horseback added, his Spanish accent passable, though learned secondhand.

Jean grinned and glanced at the other faces. He recognized Shaggy Hump, a little more grizzled but plenty sound. Bear Heart sat smiling on a prancing red pony. Echo-of-the-Wolf seemed strangely amused. Then there was Whip. Something had happened to him. His scowl was the same one Jean remembered, but now his eyes looked hollow, almost like those of a dead deer laid upon the ground.

Wild yells of "ye-ye-ye-ye!" accompanied Jean into the camp, and he could see immediate preparations being made for a lavish feast. Dogs came running into camp, barking, as women went scrambling for stacks of wood to stoke larger fires. The excitement made his pony prance.

The day had warmed during the ride from Tachichichi to the Comanche camp, so Horseback invited Raccoon-Eyes into his lodge for a smoke. Before he stepped in, Jean removed his flat-brimmed Spanish hat, letting the breeze briefly cool his brow. Inside the lodge, the robe-covered ground yet retained the overnight cool, and no fire burned in the center ring of rocks. The shade of the hide lodge felt good in contrast to the glare of the white summer sun. It was a large lodge—larger than any tipi Jean had ever entered. Some twenty hides must have been used to cover the tall lodge poles. As he waited for the others to enter, he counted twenty-four poles—more than he had ever seen used.

Jean was in no hurry to sit down, as he had been riding for hours. He waited for the circle of powerful warriors to form, then sat when they did, the thick buffalo robe under him pleasant after the hard leather of the saddle he had straddled all morning.

A young warrior brought fire to the door of the lodge in the form of a stick with a glowing ember on one end. This was passed to Horseback, who used it to light the tobacco he had stuffed into the red stone pipe. Horseback began to chant. Jean did not know the Snake words, and Speaks Twice did not offer to translate, but Jean felt the power of prayers offered to the spirits on smoke that rose to the opening above.

When the pipe had completed the circle, Horseback sighed with satisfaction, and glanced briefly at Jean. "Raccoon-Eyes," he said, "you travel far from the city of the Metal Men." He spoke in the *Yuta* tongue, knowing Jean would understand, yet he used hand signs as well, layering talk on talk.

Jean nodded. "I am a trader. I must travel far to bring my friends the things they need."

Horseback chuckled. "My friend, have you come here to bring us what we need?"

Jean thought about this, trying to be careful. "I have come to visit friends. I do not see that you need anything. Your camp is rich."

Horseback translated to the approval of the Comanche warriors, then said, "You know what we need, my friend. More True Humans join us with every moon, traveling far from our old country. Most of them come on foot, yet they want to ride."

The pipe circled to Jean again, so he paused to draw smoke up the long, elegant stem. "The pony trade is forbidden in the country of the Metal Men."

Echo began to chuckle, soon joined by other laughing Comanche warriors. Jean pretended to fight back a smile. He had seen ponies in Horseback's herd wearing Spanish brands. When the Comanches needed horses badly enough, they took them.

Shaggy Hump spoke: "Our enemies, the *Inday*, have plenty of horses, and they do not know how to use them. Soon, we will begin to take their horses, and their scalps."

Jean frowned. "Yes, they have many ponies, for they have many villages, and many camps. Horseback, my friend, I must tell you about things the *Inday* have said to nations I trade with. The *Inday* know about your camp. The chief called Battle Scar remembers your attack on his band, six winters ago. The *Inday* have been smoking, and dancing, and trading for weapons. They say they will find your camp and destroy it."

Horseback thrust his hand into the air. "Our war with the *Na-vohnuh*—the *Inday* as you call them—is to you *no importante*," he said, finding use for some of the Spanish he had learned from Speaks Twice. "It is the war of our grandfathers' grandfathers, and it cannot be stopped now that we have found the horrible *Na-vohnuh* again."

Jean nodded. "I warn you only as a friend. I did not come to talk of war, but of trade."

"I want to hear this talk," Horseback replied. "You know we need ponies. We need more than our mares can provide. But why do we talk of this trade, when you say that the Metal Men forbid the trade of ponies?"

"I am not one of the Metal Men. The people of my blood are enemies to the Metal Men. I know a way to get the horses you need."

Silence swirled through the lodge like the dust in the narrow ray of sun that streaked down through the smoke hole.

"Tell me."

Jean nodded. "I am born of the blood of a nation called France, in the old country of hairy white men, far across the great waters. To the south of France is the nation called Spain—the old country of the Metal Men. France has been at war with Spain many times over the generations. Here, in this country, the Metal Men of Spain hold the Big River to the west of the southern plains."

"The Rio Grande," Horseback said.

Jean nodded. He was impressed. Speaks Twice evidently had been schooling him on geography as well as language. "Across the plains to the east, in the land of timber, my kinsmen from France live among the nations, and trade weapons to them, and iron, and pots, and many good things. My people are called Flower Men, for the sign of the blooming flower on their banner."

Horseback gestured his understanding. "I have heard of the Flower Men living among the nations. The first white hairy man I ever saw was one of these Flower Men. A bald one with hair on the backs of his hands. He traded things to our enemies, the Northern Raiders—those who paint their feet black."

"Yes," Shaggy Hump added, "and we took the horses of the Northern Raiders and the Flower Man in that camp! That was a fine raid, my son. Yes?"

"Finer than fine, my father."

The men laughed, including Jean, who understood the humor in taking things from enemies.

"Now," Jean said, "hear what I have to say about the Flower Men. They are different from the Metal Men. They do not take country away from the nations. They do not wish to conquer, only to make allies, and trade. They are not forbidden to trade anything to the nations. They have many things in the land of timber that the Metal Men need along the Rio Grande. And the Metal Men have many things that the Flower Men want."

Horseback held one of his long braids in his hand, stroking it as if it were a pet. "How many sleeps are the Flower Men from this place?" he said, his head turning to one side like that of a curious dog.

"For good riders with ponies such as yours, twenty sleeps. The grass grows taller to the east."

"Will you guide us to this land of the Flower Men?"

Jean shook his head with sincere sadness. "It is dangerous for me to take you all the way there, my friend. Many winters ago, one of my countrymen, a great leader, was killed by men in his own camp. I was in that camp. My countrymen believe that I helped to murder the great one. I did not, but they will not believe me. If I go back to the Flower Men, I will be killed."

"You should go back to the Flower Men and swear an oath under the eyes of Father Sun, then your people will believe you."

Again, Jean shook his head. "The Flower Men do not understand such a sacred oath, for they do not know the power of Father Sun as your *Noomah* people do, and as I do."

Horseback sat silent for some time, thinking, as the pipe came to him. He took more tobacco from his pouch and refilled the pipe, lighting it from the stick that Bear Heart had kept burning by blowing on it. "It is a strange country to us. Who will guide us, if you will not?"

"I will take you as far as the villages of the Raccoon-Eyed People, among whom I lived for two winters. If we do not find a Flower Man there, one of the Raccoon-Eyed men will take you farther east. It will be dangerous, of course. There are many nations at war to the east. Some of them hate the Flower Men for trading weapons to their enemies."

"We are *Noomah*," Horseback said. "We seek danger. Brave men die young."

Jean nodded his admiration. "I, too, seek danger. But, I do not wish to die with a rope around my neck, trapping my soul in my body." He almost regretted saying this, for he could feel the dread of this evil thing pass among the men in the lodge. "This is how the Flower Men will kill me, if I go back."

"What do the Flower Men wish to gain in trade from the nations?" Horseback asked next. He said it almost casually, yet Jean knew he understood the importance of the question.

Jean shrugged. "Hides. Furs. Meat."

"These things they can get from any nation. What of slaves?"

Jean let his face serve warning. "That is a bad trade to begin. The slave trade almost destroyed the Metal Men. It makes enemies, as you know."

"If you wish to trade with the Flower Men, what will you offer that no other nation can?"

"The Flower Men want what the Metal Men own," Jean said. Slowly, he reached into his shirt and began to pull out a fine chain of gold, forged with heavy links. "They want the yellow metal, and the white metal. These metals are sacred to all white men."

Horseback seemed unimpressed with the chain, and even less moved by the attached cross that came last from Jean's shirt. "Then why do the Metal Men not take this sacred metal across the plains to the Flower Men?"

"It is forbidden. France and Spain are no longer at war, but Metal Men and Flower Men are still enemies. Each nation has a great chief, and each is suspicious of the other. The great chiefs forbid this trade."

"And you, Raccoon-Eyes, cannot take the metal across the plains, because the Flower Men—your own people—will kill you."

"This is my fear. But your people can take the metal for me," Jean said. "It is dangerous, but your people do not fear danger. There is something else the Flower Men want. Horses. If your warriors take the horses and the sacred metal across the plains, and bring back the things the Metal Men need, you will keep a portion of the horses—let us say one in ten. It is a way to get horses without raiding the Metal Men or fighting the soldiers."

Jean could see Horseback glancing about the lodge, judging the expressions of his fellow warriors.

"If my people take the shiny metal across the plains to the Flower Men for you, what will the Flower Men give in exchange for the metal? What will we bring back to you, Raccoon-Eyes?"

Jean admired the way Horseback rooted out details. "They have cloth the Spaniards need to make their clothes and to unravel so the Pueblo nations can make fine blankets from the fiber."

"Do you risk forbidden trade only for cloth and blankets, Raccoon-Eyes?"

Jean smiled and bowed his head in acquiescence. "The Flower Men have the magic powder for the guns. They have iron and copper for making pots and weapons. They have better guns than the Metal Men. Also, they have much honey from the nations of the timber."

"Will the Metal Men know of this trade?" Horseback asked.

"I am forbidden to trade with the Flower Men. The Metal Men will not know about this trade, but they will be glad to have the things you bring back from the Flower Men."

"The rich chief in Santa Fe and the Black Robes and the soldiers will question where you get these good things," Horseback said.

Jean smiled, impressed with the *Comanche's* understanding of power in the Spanish outposts. "A few pieces of the sacred yellow metal will silence their questions."

"The great chiefs of the Metal Men and the Flower Men forbid this trade." Horseback said. "Do you not fear them?"

"The great chiefs are far away, beyond water so wide that it takes two moons to cross. They do not understand how we must trade to survive."

Horseback narrowed his eyes. "My friend, you speak like a man who serves no nation. You are neither Metal Man, nor Flower Man, nor Raccoon-Eyed Man."

Jean smirked. "Perhaps I serve all those nations."

"That is the same as serving none. He who lives everywhere, lives no-where—like the buffalo, wandering."

The truth in Horseback's words made Jean's heart sink. There had been a time, with Maria, when he thought he had become an adopted Spaniard, and it had felt good. Now Maria was many years dead, and he knew he was no nation's man. He was a rogue bull, searching aimlessly.

Still, a rogue bull was defiant, so Jean lifted his chin. "And, you, Horse-back? Where is your country? The old *Noomah* land? Or here?"

Horseback angled his face upward and drew in a prideful breath. "My country is here, given to me by the spirits. I have seen this country in my great vision. It has mountains and timber, rivers and plains, grass and buffalo. It touches strange places in the south and east, still misty in my vision. Now, the *Na-vohnuh* hold this country. They are our most ancient of enemies. My path is as plain as a trail of blood in the snow. I must take this country from the *Na-vohnuh* to avenge my ancestors and feed my grandchildren's grand-children. I will die here. The Great Creator, and all the spirits, and my own shadow-guide have chosen the way for me. I will need ponies to bring my vision out of the mist. Many ponies. Let us say, three in ten."

Jean chuckled, bending he tattoos on his face. "So be it. For every seven ponies you take to the Flower Men, you will have three to keep in your camp. Will you speak about this in the council lodge?"

"Yes, my friend. But first, we will have a feast. I smell good things cooking. Let us fill our bellies."

Jean rose with the rest of the men, his head spinning from standing so quickly. He felt the shoulders of warriors against his own, heard the good sound of the *Noomah* tongue, smelled the mingling of sweat and tobacco smoke. He was hungry. This was a good place to be right now. He smiled.

52

"It is called Quivira," Jean said. "This place has tormented the Metal Men for generations. Long ago, someone told the Metal Men that the Raccoon-Eyed People in Quivira held much of the shiny yellow metal. The Metal Men have come here many times, never finding any sacred metal. Still, some of them believe Quivira to be a city of gold. This is the way the metal makes them think crazy."

They straddled good ponies on the broad bank of the river, looking down on the ancient plains village of the Raccoon-Eyed People. They were fifteen sleeps from the camp of Horseback's people on the River of Arrowheads. On the pole-drags lashed to three of the ponies were a number of hides, and Governor Del Bosque's small cache of gold, all tightly bound in rawhide to protect from the weather. A modest trading expedition, Jean had to admit, but one that would hopefully lead to larger caravans in the future.

Horseback's *Comanche* council had agreed to try this trade expedition to the east, eight warriors volunteering to make the trip. Among them were all the searchers from the first Comanche expedition five years ago; two new horsemen from a distant Snake band called the Grasshopper Eaters; Speaks Twice; and Horseback's brother-in-law, Trotter.

Jean looked at Horseback and had to chuckle, for the young rider was sitting backward on his light pad saddle, peering studiously out at Quivira over the rump of his horse, the whole aspect of which struck Jean as comical. This trip had provided Jean's first experience with the warrior society of the Foolish Ones. Both Horseback and Echo-of-the-Wolf had kept the entire band entertained and alert for pranks for fifteen days.

In spite of the foolishness of riding his horse backward and turning his mount around to look over Quivira, Jean could see that Horseback was carefully studying what must have been a strange sight to him—a village of Raccoon-Eyed People.

In a way, Jean was coming home. The Raccoon-Eyed People had taken him in from the wilderness after the murder of La Salle. He would never forget their kindness. It stirred him to look out over the fields of squash, beans, corn, and pumpkins—the women now running from these fields to the village, having seen the strange party on the rise. The grass-thatched lodges looked like the firm breasts of young women from this distance. He smiled when he saw the raised platforms built to house the young girls. He remembered Starlight, who had taught him his first lessons of lovemaking many winters ago in a Raccoon-Eyed village far to the south.

The people of that village had brought Jean to Quivira to attend a trade fair when he was still just seventeen years old. This was the first time he had been back since, and he felt years of fatigue overwhelm him as he looked down on the fields and huts. The village seemed smaller now, and Jean instinctively felt the sorrow of mothers who had lost little ones to the diseases of white men, the fear of wives who had lost husbands, the bewilderment of babies who had lost mothers. He wondered if there was anyone alive who would still remember the tattooed white boy called Stranger.

"*Vámanos,*" he said, trying to keep Horseback's ear tuned toward learning Spanish.

As he descended the steep brink of the stream bank, he saw to his amusement that Horseback was actually backing his pony down the bank, still sitting backward on the mount. Never had he seen a pony willing to back blindly down such a steep decline, yet Jean noticed slack in Horseback's reins, and had to wonder how the rider signaled the pony to back up. Horseback seemed to lend his very heart and will to the pony, who backpedaled as quickly as the other mounts rode forward.

All the while, Horseback said, in Spanish, "Forward, forward, forward!"

With a yelp, the rider finally wheeled his pony around to face Quivira, at the same time spinning himself on the pad saddle so effortlessly that he never lost sight of the Raccoon-Eyed village. Now he rode like the other riders, yet insisted on shouting, "Back!" to his horse in Spanish. "Back up! Go back!"

"Stay behind me," Jean ordered, and he nudged his mount to a lope to ride ahead of the others. Raccoon-Eyed warriors were running toward the fields, their weapons ready. Jean raised a hand in a sign of friendship as he approached. When he rode near enough for his tattoos to be seen, the men of Quivira lowered their weapons and began to sing a song of greeting to him.

Jean smiled, enjoying the familiar sound of the Raccoon-Eyed tongue. Now there would be a feast, he knew, and much storytelling and celebration. He hoped to forge a trust between the Quivirans and the rising *Comanche* nation. Any trouble between the two would mean the end of his scheme to use the Comanches in establishing a black-market trade with the French across the plains.

He smirked at his own audacity. Imagine, linking the Spanish and French frontiers through an illegal trade carried out by these upstart Comanches, about whom he knew virtually nothing. If it worked, he would amass as much wealth as anyone in the Kingdom of New Mexico. If it failed, he would likely end up dead or in Spanish chains.

As he led his men among the singing Quivirans, Jean saw a strange man step from one of the grass-thatched lodges. A white man, with a red stocking cap only half covering a head that seemed completely bald. The man had a dirty red sash belted around his solid, mulelike girth. The worn hilt of a cutlass protruded from a scabbard slung on a leather strap that crossed his ample chest. Riding closer, Jean saw a glint he did not like in the man's eyes, though his eyes were hard to see, since they squinted as if the sun hurt them.

A pang of dread dropped like a chunk of snow into Jean's stomach, for he recognized this man. Henri Casaubon, the accomplice of Minime Duhaut in the murder of La Salle. Henri Casaubon, leader of Convulsionaries and Malcontents. The moment he recognized Casaubon, Jean remembered that horrible and confusing night when he, as a mere lad, saw the ugly Convulsionary humping the comely Madeleine like an animal in a Fort St. Louis storehouse on the cannibal coast of *Tejas*.

A tall warrior followed Casaubon from the lodge, and Jean immediately recognized the markings and garb of the Osage nation. The warrior held an iron battle axe festooned with beads and feathers. Jean knew that most Osage people were tall, but this one was almost equal to two Comanches. It was strange to see him here, for Osage and Raccoon-Eyed People hated each other. The Osage stood directly behind Casaubon at all times, on guard. His head was shaved in typical style, except for a ridge of hair left standing along his crown, like the roached mane of a horse. Behind, the hair grew long enough to form two braids that fell over his shoulder.

Henri Casaubon smiled and straightened his stocking cap as Jean dismounted. Two teeth were missing from the top row. "Hello, *mon ami*," he said.

Jean had heard rumors of Casaubon over the years since the murder of La Salle. It was said that Casaubon had become a French *courier de bois* who had courted much trade among the nations, mostly in slaves for the French outposts and the sugar plantations on the islands of the Caribbean. He was known as Bald Man among the nations. His trade was illegal, for the market of the independent *couriers de bois* had been outlawed for decades, under penalty of death. France awarded monopolies only to recognized traders, but Casaubon had survived by keeping his operations constantly on the move up and down the plains. His presence now in Quivira did not bode well for Jean's trade with French merchants in the east.

Jean did not answer Casaubon's greeting, except to raise his chin a little. He turned to Speaks Twice, and in the *Tiwa* tongue he knew Casaubon would not understand, said, "Tell the Comanches to stay away from the Bald Man and the tall Osage guard."

As the warriors of the trade expedition removed the pole-drags from the ponies and turned their mounts out to graze, a bank of ashen clouds began to form in the west. By the time the feasting had begun, a cool wind was whipping the dried grass on the lodges, bearing the sweet scent of rain.

"Behold," said Night Hunter, the head elder in Quivira, "our friends bring us rain for our gardens. The sun has passed behind a robe of clouds as dark as charcoal."

"*Hah*," Horseback replied, waiting for the translations to go through Raccoon-Eyes, "the Thunderbird follows us to bring the gift of rain."

Rain began to fall during the feast, and the guests had to crowd into Night Hunter's lodge—the largest in the village. Inside, robes and blankets hung to partition off the beds of various family members and provide scant privacy. But these hanging robes were tied aside now to open the lodge for the gathering of visitors. The grass house had an open doorway facing east. When rain began to splatter in through this opening, Night Hunter got up and placed over the opening a cover made of a willow frame thatched with bundles of grass.

Jean sat on a thick, soft buffalo robe rolled under him to make a comfortable couch. He leaned against one of the heavy upright posts that supported the roof framing. He ate a stew of meat and squash and many other good things from a clay crock of French design.

Thunder rolled overhead during the feast, and the Comanches enjoyed many cooked vegetables some of them had never before tasted. Rain was still rattling the dried grass roof, dripping through here and there, as the conversation began. Pipes were filled and lighted, passed among the Comanches, Jean, Speaks Twice, Night Hunter, and Henri Casaubon. The tall Osage guard had gone to Casaubon's lodge when the storm started, prompting Jean to reason that Casaubon must have some store of trade goods in his lodge whose value made them worthy of guarding.

The presence of Casaubon in Night Hunter's lodge prevented Jean from explaining as freely as he would have liked the nature of his proposed trade between French and Spaniards across the Great Plains. Secretly, Jean had already warned all the men in his party against mentioning the small cache of gold they carried, for fear Casaubon would steal it. This gold was hidden between layers of buffalo robes, covered with rawhide, lashed to a pole-drag that was now standing out in the rain.

After the first smoke, Casaubon got up, covered himself with a buffalo robe, and removed the thatched cover that fit in the doorway to keep rain from splashing in. He stepped outside into the heavy downpour, not even bothering to replace the door cover. Speaks Twice got up to cover the hole. Jean was hoping Casaubon would retire to his own lodge. He took advantage of the bald man's absence to provide Night Hunter with more details about the trade he hoped to forge to the east.

This talk only seemed to worry Night Hunter, who replied, "We trade with Bald Man. Speak to him."

After several minutes, Casaubon came back in and flung his soaked buffalo robe aside to reveal a jug, which he offered to Jean. Jean let his eyes show mock fear of the trader's jug, and refused to drink. He did not intend to drink after the likes of Henri Casaubon. More important, he did not intend to be the one to introduce the Comanches to the white man's spirits.

Seeing Jean's refusal to drink, Night Hunter also declined, but only to honor his tattooed guest. The Raccoon-Eyed elder seemed so disappointed, in fact, that he went to his willow-frame bed and lay down. The Comanches, too, began to stretch out on robes, their bellies full, their muscles tired, and the rain lulling them to sleep.

Speaks Twice got up and walked to the door Casaubon had again left uncovered. He urinated into the rain, replaced the door cover, then collapsed on a pile of robes nearby. Jean had noticed that Speaks Twice lavished a great deal of attention on doors, and supposed that the *Tiwa* translator must have missed the security of a pueblo with the ladders pulled up to turn back intruders.

Other than Henri Casaubon, and Jean himself, Horseback was the last to lie down. Without speaking, he pulled a soft buffalo robe over his head, leaving the conversation to the two Frenchmen. The liquor seemed to be taking the sparkle from Casaubon's squinted eyes.

"You are French," the bald man said.

Jean answered in his native tongue. "Born French." He sighed. "I belong to no nation now."

"What is your Christian name?"

"Jean."

The bald one turned the jug up, making the drink slosh with musical notes. "Are you sure you won't take a drink? This is my own good brandy from Arkansas post, not the wretched trade whiskey I bring for the savages."

Jean shook his head. "Not with these Comanches."

Casaubon sniffed and nodded. "Yes. One must watch his scalp among drunken savages, no?" He laughed hoarsely as he wrapped his meaty fist around the hilt of his cutlass, still slung in its scabbard across one shoulder. "This trade with the Spaniards, it is rich?"

Jean shrugged. "So far, it is worthless."

"Bah! Hides!" Casaubon growled. "The French forts can get hides from any savages. The good trade is in slaves, *mon ami.* Slaves!"

"I have seen too much trouble with the slave trade across the plains. The Spaniards forbid it now, though it still exists to a certain extent. The Spaniards call them converts and send them to work in the mines and guano pits. They pay them a pittance, but they are slaves."

Casaubon stared blankly, then took another drink. "I have sold Spanish slaves—little boys and girls!" He laughed again, his throat like a caldron of gravel. "The *Padouca*—Apache as your Spaniards call them—capture them around Santa Fe, and bring them to me on the Arkansas River—the River of Arrowheads—the Rio Napestle. The savages take anything for them—powder, guns, whiskey. And then—listen to this, *mon ami*—then, while the *Padouca* are away from their camps to bring slaves here, the *Pani*—the Wolf People—they raid the *Padouca* camps and take women and children. These the *Pani* keep for me in the camps to the north. The slaves are no trouble when I get them. Almost starved and beaten to death. It is good business, heh?"

Jean said nothing. Darkness, gloom, and fatigue began to close in on him, and he longed for his hacienda in Santa Fe and a tender embrace from Tia, his willing servant girl. He wished now that he had come alone, ahead of the Comanches, to discover Casaubon here. Then, he could have gone to one of the more southerly villages of the Raccoon-Eyed people—perhaps to the one called Wichita. But he had had no way of knowing Casaubon would turn up here.

"There is gold in Santa Fe, *non?*"

"Some," Jean replied. "But it comes from New Spain. There are no good mines in New Mexico, as the Spaniards hoped there might be."

"If you want to trade hides, bah! But if you want to trade in slaves or gold, *mon ami*, you need—what shall we say—an agent to the east of the plains. I know the savages from the Ousconsin River to the mouth of the Messipe—from the Blackfeet to the *Tejas*. You send the gold and the slaves. I will send good muskets, powder, whiskey, cloth. Hey, do you want me to send you a real French girl? I know where to get one or two."

Jean slid off the rolled buffalo hide and feigned a yawn, though Casaubon's talk was making him more wary than tired. "No girls. No slaves. This whole trip has been wasted. I am going back to Santa Fe. Forget this trade, Casaubon. It is no good."

Jean pulled his hat over his eyes, but kept the bald man in view under the brim. The fire in the center of the lodge had burned down to a few flickers, but he could still see the whiskey glistening on the slave trader's lips after he took another swig. He followed Casaubon's eyes: touching upon each of the sleeping *Comanches*, drifting to the door, finally settling on Jean himself.

Casaubon took another drink and smiled. He looked for a long time at Jean, grinning all the while. He knew he was being watched from under the hat brim, and Jean knew that he knew. It unnerved Jean to the point that he decided he had better not fall asleep.

Finally, he sighed, pushed his hat back on his head, and sat up. He said nothing. He thought about his pistols, out of reach now in his saddle holsters just inside the door. The powder was probably too damp, anyway. He wanted to reach for the knife on his belt scabbard to make sure it was ready, but he resisted.

Pretending to rub his brow as if his head ached, he covered his eyes and glanced across the floor of the lodge to look for a weapon equal to Casaubon's cutlass. He saw none. All the *Comanche* lances had been bound in tripods outside, the shields hung from them in their protective rawhide cases. There was not even a good-sized stick left in the fire.

Then he happened to glance at the place where Horseback lay. Under the cover of the heavy buffalo robe, he saw the faint glisten of two open eyes, though Horseback's chest was rising and falling heavily, as if in sleep. Relief washed his dread away from him like the rain cleansing the thatched roof of the Quiviran lodge. Horseback was awake and watching.

Jean knew very well that Horseback, as a Foolish One, carried only his buffalo scrotum rattle with him as a weapon. Still, the thought of Horseback remaining awake filled him with courage. The young *Comanche* would be of little help to him against the cutlass of Henri Casaubon, yet the mere fact that the proud young warrior was watching made Jean feel more bold. He would not behave as a coward in the eyes of the fearless pony warrior.

"I know who you are," Casaubon suddenly said.

Jean removed his hand from his brow, a new confidence willing him to lock eyes with the slaver. "Do you?"

"*Oui, mon ami.* I recall. Fort St. Louis, on the Spanish Main. The slime pits. You remember me, *non?* You remember the day of death for the great lunatic, Rene Robert Cavelier, Sieur de La Salle." He rasped in laughter again and took a drink of whiskey. "I was in Quebec in 1688 when your friend Goupil, the mapmaker, was hanged." He looked at the dark smoke hole in the thatched roof. "Good God, that was twenty-three years ago!" He shook his head and took another swallow of whiskey. "Your name is in La Salle's diary, *mon ami.* And in the diary of your friend, Goupil, the hanged murderer."

"Goupil was no murderer."

"Bah! Who will believe you, Jean L'Archeveque, accomplice of the mapmaker, he who consorts with savages and Spaniards, a tattooed traitor?"

Jean grunted. He leaned back against the heavy post and crossed his arms over his chest. "I am no traitor. I am no murderer. I live among Spaniards because Frenchmen do not want to listen to the truth. It was Minime, the valet, who murdered La Salle—Minime and his followers. And you were one of them, Henri Casaubon. You would have murdered me, too, had I not fled to the Raccoon-Eyed People, who treated me as a brother and a son. I live as I must, not as I choose."

Hacking laughter rattled from deep within Casaubon's chest. He coughed, spat toward Night Hunter's bed, and put the whiskey jug to his lips again. "We are a long way from the nearest French fort, *non?*"

"What matter is that to me?"

"What matter, you say? A hangman's rope waits for you there, L'Archeveque, and a bounty of gold for me. I suppose I might have some trouble getting you there, *non?* More than the slaves—women and children—who are starved and beaten. I would have to keep you bound and guarded all the while. A difficult proposition, *non?* And you with your friends. How do you call them? Comanches?"

Jean shifted on his roll of hides. Now he indeed reached for his knife, and felt it pull smoothly from the sheath when he tested it. "You would attempt to take a brother of the Raccoon-Eyed People from their own village?"

"You are their brother, *oui.* But here is their master." He held the jug before him at arm's length, grinned, and stuck his tongue hideously into one of the gaps in his row of discolored teeth. "Now, listen, traitor. It is known everywhere across the kingdoms of France and Spain that Jean L'Archeveque wears the tattoos of a savage on his face. Charles the Second, that bastard king of Spain, boasted of your capture in 1688, when you were taken across the ocean to report as his spy."

"I am aware of my infamy, Casaubon. Why do you remind me?"

The slaver pulled the red wool cap from his bald head and tucked it into the waist of his trousers, as if preparing for a fight. "Your heathen tattoos betray you." He reached for the hilt of his cutlass. "I have taken heads with one blow. I have a keg of trade whiskey in my lodge where yours would fit. Nothing rots in that swill. I need not take you alive to the forts, *mon ami.* All I need to collect his majesty's bounty for a traitor is your tattooed head."

A certain realization struck Jean. To complete the plans for his illegal trade between the French and Spanish frontiers, he would have to kill Henri Casaubon. Perhaps within the next minute. He prepared to spring from his sitting position if need be. His heart was pounding furiously. "Your head is probably worth more than mine. You are the most infamous *courier de bois* on the continent, Henri Casaubon. If you wish to take my head, then come and get it. You will be hanged as soon as you arrive with it at Arkansas post, or Creve Coeur, on the Seignelay."

Casaubon removed his hand from his sword hilt and laughed at the ceiling, a voiceless burst of whiskey breath grating up his throat. "You know me well, *mon ami.* Yet, there are ways. I could sell your head to some legal trader, but it wouldn't be worth as much. I will make a bargain with you, L'Archeveque. Work with me in this trade for Spanish gold, and I will let you keep your head."

"I have already told you that there is but little gold in Santa Fe. The trade I wish to begin here is for my friends, the Comanches. I only want to keep them from raiding the *ranchos* around Santa Fe."

The ugly smile slid from Casaubon's face. "You are a liar as well as a traitor. Do you think I am so stupid? Earlier today, when your Comanches untied the ponies from the travois, I was watching. You had them stack two of the travois on top of the other one. What were you trying to protect in that bundle of hides on the lower travois?"

Jean sniffed as if in ridicule, but he knew now he had been observed paying too much attention to the one pony-drag. "I merely wanted to keep the best furs above the mud. A fool could see that a storm was coming."

"You lie well, L'Archeveque. But I see through your lies. Earlier, when I went into the rain to fetch my jug of brandy, I visited your stack of three travois." He pulled his cutlass from its sheath and jabbed at the air between himself and Jean. "I pushed my blade in between the layers of hides and felt the metal of your cache, *mon ami*."

Jean's anger began to boil as he watched Casaubon reach into the front of his shirt and slowly pull a chain of gold into view. At the end of the chain came the golden crucifix Jean had flaunted to Horseback on the River of Arrowheads.

"You see, I already have your gold, traitor. You might as well take what whiskey and guns I offer in trade. I will throw in a young French whore girl as a token of my good faith. If you decline, I will be forced to take your gold— and your pickled head—back to Creve Coeur."

Jean reached his right hand around the back of his right hip, where his knife hilt jutted above the sheath. It was a plain knife, but good, made of tempered steel with an ivory handle. He kept it honed and serviceable at all times, but it was no match for a cutlass. He would have to move quickly to avoid Casaubon's first blow, and hope he had truly seen Horseback's open eyes gleaming under the cover of the buffalo robe.

Jean wrapped his grip around the knife hilt and said, "You are a thief, Casaubon, and as such you deserve no quarter. If you do not take that gold chain from your neck, you will not leave this lodge alive."

"Too late for that," Casaubon said. "My Osage guard has already ridden off into the night with the rest of your gold cache. This I cannot return, no matter how fiercely you threaten me. I love the treason, but hate the traitor. The die is cast. *Iacta alea est*."

The suddenness with which Casaubon moved startled Jean, and made every muscle in his body convulse. He saw the blade of the cutlass sweep back for the blow, and he instinctively curled himself into a ball and rolled forward, under the path of the sword. Somersaulting, he saw the blur of Horseback's buffalo robe flying as if by magic into the air. He heard the cutlass strike the post he had been leaning against—a muffled ring of metal and a sharp thud of wood. He felt his shoulders hit hard, then drew the knife as he rolled to his feet. He whirled to his right and slashed backhanded with the blade.

He felt the tip of the knife rake a long wound across Casaubon's shoulder, saw the slaver's head jerk with the pain, as a turtle would retreat into its shell.

Casaubon released his right hand from the sword hilt and pulled with his left to dislodge the blade from the heavy post, but now Horseback was upon him, grinning, striking with the only weapon a Foolish One would carry into battle. The blunt stub of the buffalo scrotum rattle jabbed Casaubon in the eye, driving his head back until his ugly grimace faced the ceiling. His mouth opened, and his groan of agony seemed to roll into the thunder above.

Blankets and robes began to toss about the dim lodge like waves sloshing in a barrel, yet no voice called out, as every man had enemies to awaken.

Casaubon grabbed Horseback by the throat as he fell backward, and began to snap his gapped teeth viciously at the Foolish One's face. Horseback landed on top of the slaver, then used his weight to roll to one side, exposing the bald man's vitals to attack from his white friend, Raccoon-Eyes.

Jean saw his opening and jumped onto the two men, driving his sharp knife deep between Casaubon's ribs, where a hunter would drive an arrow into a buffalo. Casaubon's head lolled back, blood flowing from his eye. His mouth gaped, and would have screamed, but Echo-of-the-Wolf had landed on the dying slaver and stuffed the corner of a blanket into his mouth.

As Jean scrambled away from the horrible bloody pile, he saw Night Hunter bolt for the thatched door. The Raccoon-Eyed elder screamed a warning cry that was half-lost in a peal of thunder, then Speaks Twice drove a knife into the elder's chest, lifting him from the ground as he clamped his palm over Night Hunter's mouth. Speaks Twice slammed the Quiviran chief to the ground, withdrew his knife, stabbed again. Night Hunter squirmed under him, and blood flowed from the hand Speaks Twice used to muffle the elder's cries. Grimacing at the pain of his bitten hand, the translator managed to hold on until death clouded Night Hunter's eyes.

"He would have called the others," Speaks Twice explained, in Spanish, to Jean. "The Raccoon-Eyed People would avenge the killing of the bald one."

Jean sheathed his knife and shook his head. He realized that he was panting for breath, and every muscle in his body felt near to paralysis. Then he heard the voice calling from the next lodge, barely audible through the rainstorm and the thatched walls. His breath caught in his throat as he strained to hear.

"Elder!" the voice cried. "Do you call?"

Jean looked down at the bleeding body of Night Hunter. "Tell the Foolish Ones to laugh," he said to Speaks Twice. A sick feeling began to grow in the pit of stomach. "Tell them!"

Speaks Twice gave the order with signs, his hand bleeding badly from Night Hunter's bite. Horseback began to chuckle, jabbing Echo. They laughed together, and cajoled their Comanche brothers into joining them. The laughter quickly died, and all listened through the patter of rain.

Jean barely heard the chuckle from the neighboring lodge. Then faintly, so faintly, he heard the words in the Raccoon-Eyed tongue: "They drink Bald Man's fire water."

Jean raised his hands, as if conducting an orchestra, and the Foolish Ones made more laughter roll. But Jean could not even try to join the Comanches.

He looked at Speaks Twice, and saw his same feelings of unavoidable remorse and shame in the translator's face. He knew Speaks Twice would not take Night Hunter's scalp. They lifted the Quiviran elder and carried him to his bed. Jean crossed the dead man's arms over his chest, and signaled for an end to the ridiculous laughter. He covered Night Hunter with a good robe, and wiped the blood from his hands on a French trade blanket.

Horseback took the gold chain from Casaubon's neck and handed it to Jean as he approached. "The yellow metal made the bald one go crazy."

Jean nodded. "The yellow metal, and the fire water," he said in a low voice. He took the chain with the cross, and considered for a moment tossing it into the ashes of the dying fire. But the craziness was in him, too, and he knew he must keep the gold. "We must sneak away before dawn. I must go after the Osage guard who took the rest of the yellow metal. I do not expect you to come with me. This trade has gone bad."

"You should forget the yellow metal," Horseback replied. "Let the tall Osage have it. Yet, if you must go after it, I will ride with you. It is true the trade has gone bad, but my medicine stays strong. I want to see the country of the Osage in the east. I may want it for my own country."

Jean frowned, but he knew he could not change Horseback's faith in his spirit powers. He kicked a bloody robe on top of Casaubon to cover the ugly sight. "You saved my life from the bald one. You are welcome to ride with me."

Horseback glanced at the pool of blood where Night Hunter had died. "Now you are an enemy to your own nation of Raccoon-Eyed People," he said. "You were rich with the Metal Men. You should have stayed with them."

Jean shook his head. "You do not understand. The Metal Men let me stay there only as long as I make them rich, too. I am a slave to their god of yellow metal."

Horseback rubbed his throat where the bald man had attempted to strangle him. "When you have no nation left, Raccoon-Eyes, come to my camp. I will give you a pony, and a good lodge, and a lance to hunt the buffalo. You will have a good woman, and plenty of good country to ride over. Then you will know the meaning of wealth."

Jean could not help smiling. He felt the horrors of bloody death begin to slip behind him, and knew he would have the will to go ahead. Horseback was a good friend—and wise.

53

Horseback rode between his friends, Raccoon-Eyes and Speaks Twice. Their ponies traveled eastward at a long walk that verged on a trot, but felt much smoother. Behind these three leaders rode Echo-of-the-Wolf, Shaggy Hump, and the Grasshopper Eater called Crazy Eyes.

"This country is no good," Horseback said, trying to make Raccoon-Eyes's heart lighter. "The grass is too tall. It rains too much. Everything looks so green that my eyes hurt. The buffalo are always getting in the way."

Raccoon-Eyes smirked. "Do not grow too fond of this country, Foolish One. It belongs to the Osage. They are fierce, and they number many."

"I do not want to know about the Osage," Horseback said, comically cupping his hand behind his ear.

The tattooed white man rolled his eyes. He had been in a poor humor since the trouble at Quivira, and he was not in the mood for the antics of a Foolish One. "You remember the bald man's Osage guard at Quivira," he said. "He was tall, but some of their warriors are even taller. They fight well. They run like antelope-men. I have never seen it, but I am told that they can catch ponies by the tail and throw them down."

Horseback laughed. "Now who speaks more foolishly? You or I?"

"It is true," Raccoon-Eyes insisted. "Keep your pony fresh."

Horseback whirled to face the rear of his mount, holding his reins behind his back. He signaled with one heel and a tug of one rein, and the pony turned around and began to walk backward, keeping pace with the other mounts.

"What are you doing?" Raccoon-Eyes said, sounding irritated.

"I am going to back my pony until he gets fresh again."

Raccoon-Eyes cracked a smile for the first time since leaving Quivira in the dark and rain. "Tell me, Foolish One. How do you make your pony walk backward with a loose rein?"

Horseback whirled his pony back around and spoke in his normal voice so the white man would know he meant no foolishness. "Start with a tight rein. That is the signal to back up. When the pony starts back, you must loosen the rein and feel joy in your heart. Let the pony feel this joy, and he will be happy to walk backward. He will go that way as long as you feel joy."

"You must make the pony part of yourself?" Jean said, following with the sign that meant he was asking a question.

"That is only half."

"What is the other half?"

"You must make yourself part of the pony. Feel what the pony feels. If he gets tired of walking backward, you must get tired of it, too. You must know that if you fail to serve as the pony's eyes, and he steps on something that hurts him, you have hurt yourself, for he will no longer serve you. Unless you are only going to cook and eat that pony at the end of the ride, you must make yourself a part of him."

Raccoon-Eyes thought about that in silence as they rode on, and Horseback simply admired the land. Never had he dreamed of a country so rich. His moccasins were lost in the seedy tops of grasses that the horses tried constantly to crop as they walked. Across distant hillsides, he could see small herds of buffalo. Trees stood on some of the ridges and in the low crevices between hills. The day was cloudy and warm, and the air strangely sticky. A breeze from the south made the tall grasses ripple like the waters of a great lake.

The trail of the tall Osage guard was plain before them, a line of bent-over grass stretching eastward, almost arrow-straight. They had snuck out of Quivira in the night, leaving their three pole-drags loaded with hides and furs. They had taken all the ponies of the Quivirans. Raccoon-Eyes said it made his heart feel bad, but it had to be done to keep the warriors of Quivira from chasing them down. Bear Heart, Trotter, and the Grasshopper Eater called Crooked Teeth had taken all the captured horses westward. Raccoon-Eyes and the others were to catch and kill the *Osage* guard, recover the stolen yellow metal, and turn westward to cath up with the captured horses.

Unlike Raccoon-Eyes, Horseback felt good. He had agreed to this trade expedition to get horses, and he was getting more than he had imagined, since stealing the horses from Quivira. He was not afraid of the Quivirans, but they had many more warriors than his small party. It was a good idea to take their horses. Besides, their horses were fat.

It was true that things had gone bad at the village of grass houses last night. The death of Night Hunter and the theft of the horses would likely make enemies of the Comanches and the Raccoon-Eyed People, though it had been the *Tiwa*, Speaks Twice, who had actually killed the Raccoon-Eyed elder. None of this worried Horseback. He was accustomed to having enemies. He felt bad for Raccoon-Eyes, whose trade had gone all wrong, but he was seeing plenty of new country and enjoying much foolishness. As long as his medicine remained strong, he rode with confidence and thought about the many stories he would tell Teal and Sandhill when he returned to his camp on the River of Arrowheads.

Looking up, he saw Whip riding back to the party, having gone ahead to scout. Whip had been worthless during the whole trip, and Horseback had begun to think he had come along merely to make things difficult. Last night's fight with the bald Flower Man had not been Whip's fault, of course, but every other little nuisance could be traced to him. The mere fact that he had volunteered to ride ahead as scout made Horseback uneasy, though he had said nothing, thinking it would be good to get rid of Whip for a while.

When he rejoined the other riders, Whip's pony was winded and white with frothy sweat. "I have found the pony of the tall Osage guard," he said. "The Osage rode it to death. He has gone on afoot."

"How far?" Raccoon-Eyes asked.

Whip pointed. "The dead pony lies over the second ridge. The Osage cannot be far beyond."

Horseback noticed dark stains on Whips hands when he pointed. "Why do you have blood on your hands?" he asked.

"I made meat. I wish to eat something better than horse meat after we get the yellow metal back from the Osage."

"What meat? Where?"

"Let us catch the Osage. Then we will worry about the meat."

Raccoon-Eyes seemed to agree. He urged his pony forward, and the party began to lope. Over the first ridge, Horseback saw the side trail where Whip had ventured into some timber to kill his meat. He had probably spotted a fat cow or a buffalo calf through the trees and used the timber as cover to get close enough for an arrow shot.

The grasslands rolled on, dotted with stands of timber. They rode near one stand, and Horseback noticed strange things about one of the trees. The bark was rough like the scab of a bad wound. The large coarse leaves had soft hairs underneath.

"What is that tree?" he asked. "I have never seen it before."

"Slippery elm," Raccoon-Eyes answered, offering a glance at the tree. "The nations of the timber country make good medicine from its bark. Tea for coughs and poultices for wounds."

Over the second ridge, they found the dead pony. Two coyotes were already sneaking toward it. Approaching the carcass, they found that the Osage had cut the horse's belly open to eat the raw liver.

"This Osage knows how to use a pony," Shaggy Hump said. "It is better to count ribs than tracks."

"He is afoot now," said Whip. "We will catch him easily."

Raccoon-Eyes shook his head. "It is never easy to catch an Osage, even on foot. He will step long and go all day. You have never seen a man run like an Osage can run."

Whip scowled, as if he did not like being counseled by an elder who was not even a True Human.

The coyotes had withdrawn beyond arrow range, for they were wise ancestors of the *Noomah*. They sat on their haunches and watched the mounted men. "Look," Horseback said, tilting his head at the coyotes. "Our ancestors are hungry. When they finish eating this pony, they will go to the meat Whip has made, and we will only gnaw bones and howl after we kill the Osage."

"They will not get the meat I made," Whip said. "I hung it high in a tree."

Horseback frowned. He knew Whip could not have lifted even a buffalo calf into a tree. The calves had grown too large. He had not had time or the tools to quarter the animal. "What kind of meat did you make?" Horseback asked. "I have seen no antelope in this country."

Whip smiled and lifted his chin in pride. "I made the meat of a young buck deer, not too heavy to lift into the fork of a tree for one as strong as I."

The sun blazed suddenly through a hole in the clouds, scorching Horseback's shoulders, and he heard a far-off echo of warning from the Great Deer, Sound-the-Sun-Makes. "Fool!" he said. "You kill the sacred deer! My *puha*! Our protector is angry!"

"*Our* protector? You are the only one forbidden to eat the meat of a deer."

"Those who follow me on the war path must honor my medicine. You have broken the taboo!"

"Do you think I follow you on the trail of this trade for ponies? I follow Raccoon-Eyes. I do not worry about your *puha*."

"My spirit-guide has protected us," Horseback insisted. "Now you have dishonored him."

"Your spirit-guide has not spoken to me. Do you think everything is yours? This country? This nation of Horse People? This trading party? Since you were a boy, they have told you: 'born on the day of First Horse, born on the day of First Horse . . .' Now you think the spirits made the pony for you, and no one else. Everything is not yours, Foolish One. I follow Raccoon-Eyes."

Horseback felt his anger rise. "Raccoon-Eyes is my friend, but he is not a True Human. It is my *puha* that has protected us, and now you have destroyed it."

"I have only destroyed your pride. You think I follow you? I would not follow you to make dog meat." He turned to Speaks Twice. "*Tiwa*, ask the Raccoon-Eyed man which god he serves on this trail!"

Speaks Twice asked, and the eyes of the party turned on Raccoon-Eyes. Horseback watched the tattooed face, and saw the look of worry go to a look of shame. Raccoon-Eyes could only stare at his pony's mane. Finally, he spoke:

"I serve the god of yellow metal. I expect no one to follow me."

Raccoon-Eyes reined his mount away and began to trail the Osage. Whip went with him. Speaks Twice followed close behind.

"My son," said Shaggy Hump, "what will you do?"

"It does not matter. Any trail I take, my spirit-guide will punish me. Whip has summoned the shadows made dark by the great light."

"Then we should go the way Whip goes. If something goes bad, let us all witness it together. Let Whip see it."

They followed the foot trail of the Osage in silence, each mount in a trot. Horseback looked back on the carcass of the dead pony to see the coyotes closing in on it. The trail of each pony lay plain in the grass. It was impossible to hide a fresh trail in this grass. Anyone who hunted him could find him, and he was a stranger here. He felt as if cast suddenly naked into a strange land. He longed for the short-grass country of his camp on the River of Arrowheads, or even the rocky sage country of the old *Noomah* lands.

"There are many strange things here," he said to Raccoon-Eyes. "When we kill the Osage, I hope we will turn around and ride west."

"You will," Raccoon-Eyes said. "I will go on alone to complete the trade with the Flower Men. You will ride hard. All the warriors of Quivira will be looking for you."

"We have their ponies."

"They will send runners to other Raccoon-Eyed villages. They will get ponies."

The trail of the Osage was a mere rift in the sea of grass, but it was easy to follow. It led over one hill, then the next, then the next. The hills were low, their summits far apart, but the trail just went on and on. Horseback had no idea what might lie in wait over the next rise.

As the party mounted that rise, Horseback began to feel bad. He was indeed a Foolish One. He carried only his buffalo scrotum rattle. Whip had killed a deer. Fool! Whip knew nothing about the power of a spirit-protector. He did not understand medicine as great as that of Sound-the-Sun-Makes. Whip had never spoken of great visions. He thought all his power lay in his hands and his weapons. He had killed a deer! Horseback could feel his *puha* seeping out of him like blood from a wounded man. He was weak, and the hill hid something horrible.

He reined his horse to one side, unwilling to draw the wrath of Sound-the-Sun-Makes down on anyone but himself, for it was coming. Whip had killed a sacred deer. Horseback felt sick. He noticed the other warriors spreading out, stringing their bows. They could all feel it. No one spoke. He remembered the fury of his spirit-guide in the land of the Metal Men, six winters past. *Oh, Teal, I am afraid! Oh, Great Deer, have mercy. My power has darkened.*

Coming over the rise, Horseback could see much timber to the east. In the distance, he saw a smoke. There was a camp near. Probably Osage. He watched the trail of the yellow metal thief: grass bending eastward toward the smoke. As he came higher over the hill, he saw the Osage running. Raccoon-Eyes was right! The Osage covered ground in long strides, like a two-legged antelope! It was going to be hard to catch him before he got into the timber, but it could be done.

The moment Horseback started down the eastern slope of the hill, he noticed something peculiar. There were other trails of bent grass on this side of the hill. These trails led up from the distant Osage camp. The grass of these trails bent westward. These trails led nowhere. They simply stopped.

He drew in a breath and yelped a warning call, but it was too late. As the reins of his Comanche brothers tightened, seven tall warriors rose from the grass. They towered like giants! They sprang from the grass silently and ran straight toward the Comanches, their long arms swinging, their knees coming all the way out of the tall grass. The Comanche horses bolted in fear.

Horseback looked for Echo, his fellow Foolish One. Echo's pony was dodging away from one Osage giant, while another ran to catch the pony's reins. The giants ran fast! The hearts of the ponies were telling them to run downhill, so they could go faster, but this carried them into the Osages. The Comanche riders were trying to tell their ponies to run away uphill, so they could escape the attack and swarm around the enemy. But this only confused the ponies, and made them slower. The attack was happening too fast. Raccoon-Eyes's prophesy was coming true. The Osage runners were closing on the ponies!

Horseback gathered his courage, and made his pony feel his heart. He screamed a battle cry and rushed to the aid of his fellow Foolish One. Echo was bearing down on one Osage, unaware of the other who closed in on him from behind. The other Comanches were dodging aside, or breaking downhill, through the Osage line. Raccoon-Eyes rode low as an Osage arrow sped over him. He headed downhill at a gallop, bound for the thief of his yellow metal. Horseback rode toward Echo, glancing over his shoulder once to make sure none of the giant antelope-men was about to catch his pony.

"*Pinakwoo!*" he warned. "Behind you!" But Echo did not hear as he screamed a battle cry and shook his Foolish rattle at the Osage ahead of him. The giant behind caught the pony by the tail and pulled to one side. Echo kicked himself away from the falling pony. He hit the ground, bounced to his feet, and turned on the Osage behind him, but the other struck him in the back of the head with an iron axe.

Blood gushed from the wound as the Osage vanished in the grass to take the scalp. Horseback screamed so loud his throat felt as if it would tear apart. He made his pony ride over the Osage in the grass, knocking him to one side. He wheeled, saw his father tangled in battle with the giant who had caught Echo's horse. Horseback knew he had to protect his fellow Foolish One's body to prevent him from going mutilated to the Shadow Land.

My pony is my weapon, he thought. He dropped his rattle, for he was no longer a Foolish One. Oh, Sound-the-Sun-Makes, let my pony feel my heart one time more before I am to be punished.

The pony leapt and snorted, striking with its front hooves like a deer fighting off a wolf. The Osage reached a long arm toward his reins, just as Whip's lance pierced his chest.

The battle swarmed in the favor of Comanches now, as the survivors escaped the initial foot speed of the Osages and began to use their weapons on this new enemy nation of giant antelope-men. Horseback reached low for the arm of Echo, and felt the weight of death. Whip brought his pony stomping to the dead Foolish One's other side, and together they lifted and dragged him to safety as Horseback heard Raccoon-Eyes's single gunshot from the timber.

As they paused so Horseback could muscle the body of Echo across his thighs, he heard an ominous song whistle in the air and felt the sun burst through the clouds again. Something hit him hard in the chest, knocking him back onto the rump of his pony. Opening his eyes he saw an arrow shaft protruding from his breast bone, the barbed war head completely hidden in his own chest. As he sat up, he noticed the angle of the arrow shaft. It had come from above. From Sound-the-Sun-Makes. Immediately, he broke the shaft off, causing pain to stab all through his body.

The Osages were running on foot back toward their village. Echo's pony was stumbling, a lance wound bleeding heavily. In his pain and shame, Horseback thought it well that someone had prevented the capture of the pony by killing it. He could see Shaggy Hump, Speaks Twice, and Crazy Eyes coming together, and each man seemed to be favoring a wound. Far down the hill, at the edge of the timber, Raccoon-Eyes was getting back on his pony with his bundle of yellow metal. The body of the tall Osage metal thief lay at his feet.

When the riders all came together, they looked first at the dead body of Echo, laid across the thighs of Horseback. Then they looked at one another's wounds. The arrow wound in Horseback's chest only trickled blood, and he tried to ignore it, though it sent waves of pain through him with every little movement he made. He knew he would have to live with the arrow head imbedded in his breast bone until he was safely out of the country of the Osage and Raccoon-Eyed People.

Shaggy Hump held an ugly gash on his upper arm, though blood flowed heavily between his fingers. Speaks Twice seemed sleepy and was bleeding from his nose, which looked crooked and swollen. The Grasshopper Eater, Crazy Eyes looked the worst. His wound was from an arrow that had passed all the way through his stomach. No one spoke for a long moment, then Crazy Eyes began to sing the death song his spirit-guide had given him in his vision quest, not so many winters ago. It wailed like the voice of a tortured wolf mixed with the howl of a great wind in a canyon.

Horseback looked at Whip and scowled. He knew, even if Whip did not, that the killing of the deer had caused all this death and pain. Why had Whip himself not been wounded? It was he who had killed the deer and angered Sound-the-Sun-Makes, yet he had fought well, killed an enemy warrior, helped to protect the body of Echo. Then a pain racked Horseback as his pony pranced, and he understood. Whip's power came with darkness.

It is light that makes me powerful. It is the shadow made darker by the brightest light that gives Whip his power. The great hot power of the blinding sun lends the shadow form, distinct and dark, making it stronger. Never again shall we ride the same war path again. His power weakens me. Our paths must part.

Raccoon-Eyes joined the survivors, having ridden around the tall enemy foot soldiers. "The Osage will bring more warriors," he said, tying his recovered metal down behind his saddle. "We must ride hard."

54

His mother named him Noomah. So she called him the moment he found his four legs under him and began to root for her milk. He had felt forever hungry since that day. First for the milk of his mother. Now for grass.

He had left his mother two winters ago, when his father drove him from the herd of mares and foals. Noomah's father was stern and had made him run in terror of his popping teeth and slashing hooves. He had tried to return several times, but his father would punish him more severely with each return, and Noomah learned to respect the power of pain his father wielded.

Noomah lived in the land between the river and the mountains. He feared the river. It made much noise and felt boggy under his hooves, as if it would suck him down and hold him for the flesh-eaters to devour. He stayed away from it except in dry times when it was the only place to drink, and then he would pick his way cautiously to the water's edge, testing each step, avoiding the fearful piles of driftwood that surely concealed unimaginable horrors.

The mountains, too, made Noomah uneasy, their steep slopes choked with trees and underbrush that prevented him from running. In the timber, he could not smell the stinking odor of the flesh-eaters until they were almost upon him.

So he lived in the sage and grass country between the mountains and the river, where he could run from danger. Noomah loved to run. Sometimes he did not wait for danger. He would pretend that the aroma of rain was the odor of a flesh-eater, and he would bolt across the flat country and kick his hooves at imaginary fangs. When he came to a place where the land dropped out from under him, into a draw or creek bed, he would lower his head as he slowed his pace just slightly, and he would choose his footing well as he plunged down dirt banks almost as straight up and down as the great trees in the mountains. He learned to climb rocky inclines with his hooves rattling a song on the stones. He learned to hurtle fearlessly across the rough ground, adjusting his footing instantly as a burrow or a snag passed under him, his legs churning, then gathering, then flailing four wild ways to keep solid ground under him as they drove his great weight and muscle into the wind.

For a long time, Noomah searched for his mother in this country. Then the memory of her grew dim, and he ceased to crave the taste of her milk. He joined a herd of young stallions, and they practiced the ways of war for the Time That Would Come. Noomah never questioned the mystery of the Time That Would Come. He simply knew he must learn to fight. Soon, he was able to fight better than the others, and proved it often, for there were many challengers. He knew he would not stay forever in the band with his young rivals. The Time That Would Come was calling him—calling them all.

Noomah heard other calls, as well. Most came from the Ancestors of Long Ago. They said, "Run . . . Kick . . . Fear . . . Fight . . . Live!" On the grasslands, these ghost voices would call to him when he smelled an odd odor, glimpsed a new sight, or heard a strange sound. Then he would run as if a nation of flesh-eating killers held his tail, and he would not stop until sweat foamed between his legs and hot pain filled his lungs.

In the summer he was the color of shadows and light that fell together on the ground, and this was good because Noomah liked to stand in the shade of the trees that fringed the banks of drinking places, where he melted from sight like a ghost horse. In the winter, his coat matched the pattern of patchy snow on the dark earth, and this was also good, for he would paw for dried grass in places where snow and earth mingled.

This coat of Noomah's helped him hide from the two-leggeds, for they could not smell things on the wind, and relied mostly on their eyes. The two-leggeds were slow, but they would sometimes rise from the earth on the backs of horses, lending strange powers to the four-leggeds they rode. Noomah had known the presence of two-leggeds since the days of suckling his mother's milk. He feared them. They were strange. They made sounds unlike any other in the land between the river and the mountains—shaking-singing-rattling-squeaking-thumping-croaking-whistling sounds.

Noomah especially feared the sight of a two-legged upon a horse. Any other horse he would fight. But a horse with a two-legged on its back would cause Noomah to run head high and eyes wide. The two-leggeds reeked with the odor of death and filth.

Still, Noomah would sometimes wander near the places where the two-leggeds gathered, for they kept horses there, and the scent of mares crazed him so that he forgot his fears of the odor of two-leggeds and ventured near. The Time That Would Come seemed to call him there. Then, some two-legged would rise from the earth and remind him of his fear with the terrible sounds and smells.

One day, the Time That Would Come arrived in the land between the river and the mountains. The scent of a filly came to Noomah on the sage flats, and crazed him beyond all reason. He charged into the wind until he found a herd led by an old gray stallion. This gray warrior flew at Noomah with all his hard weapons, but the young stallion was strong and quick and fired by ancient powers. He drove his hooves into the skull of the old one and ripped the gray coat with his teeth until the smell of blood hung everywhere on the wind.

The old gray one's mares scattered as he limped away, and many young stallions rose from the earth to fight for them. Wild, violent clashes went on for days all across the land, until Noomah found himself in possession of four females. One was the filly whose scent had crazed him into battling the old gray one, for he had pursued her relentlessly and fought off all challengers who wished to possess her.

Now the voices of the Ancestors of Long Ago told him what to do. He mounted the filly and felt his loins explode with pleasure such as he did not know to exist in the hard world of snow and heat, rock and cactus, hunger and fear. From here forward, the Time was no long a mystery to him, and he would marshal his herd with rapacious vigilance, and seek forever to bring more mares into his possession.

One day, while guarding his females, many two-leggeds came, riding the backs of horses. There were so many that all Noomah could do was run, driving his herd before him. He ran toward strange places, and the two-leggeds followed. Other horses joined him, and they all ran together until Noomah's insides burned and his feet ached from pounding over rocky places. The mares from different bands became mixed, and stallions would clash and fight as they ran.

The flight from the two-leggeds carried the running horses into a tall barrier of dead limbs and things that looked to Noomah like the fearful stinking piles of driftwood along the river. He was afraid to approach, so he ran along the barrier, keeping between it and the two-leggeds on horses. Somehow, the barrier coiled around him like a huge swirl of wind, and Noomah was caught in it with all the strange horses.

The stallions continued to fight, and Noomah had to prove that he feared none of them. He was tired from the long flight from the two-leggeds, but so were the others, and he fought off each challenger with sharp kicks and bared teeth, though sometimes two and three at a time came to fight. The whole terrible place smelled like sweat and blood and dirt, and made Noomah go crazy with anger and fear.

When the fighting finally died down, he began looking for a way out of the circle of dead brush that stood between him and his home of open sage and grasslands. Dust clogged his nostrils and throat, and he snorted his anger. He rose and fought the barrier of dead branches that looked like the strange piles of drifted wood along the river. He stood high with his hooves flailing, and heard branches snapping as pieces of wood flew. He saw the light of the open sage flats in a hole he had beaten into the barrier and leapt through it.

In a moment Noomah was free and running. He heard the ancient voices singing: *"Flee! Flee-ee-ee-ee!"* He felt his heart pounding in time with his hooves as the sounds of the trapped herd fell behind him. But the two-leggeds came, and one threw a snakelike thing at him that caught him around the throat and choked him. Noomah fought, but the noose made him fall deep into a land of pain and black nothingness.

When he felt air in his lungs again, he rose from the ground to find a rope wrapped all about his head and stuck into the ground. He could not get away. He could not run. His fear was like a nation of biting flies that crawled all over him and made his skin twitch and tremble. He pulled against the rope until his head was sore and bleeding.

The darkness came. Then light. Then darkness. Then light. Noomah's throat felt like a spider's hole in the ground. His fear left, replaced by weakness. He thought of water, only of water, but none came under the circle of earth he could reach.

Finally, one of the two-leggeds approached. Noomah was too weak to fear. He let the two-legged pull the rope that held his head. The rope pulled, and he followed, for it hurt his head when he fought against it. The two-legged brought him to water, but not enough to give him strength. Only enough to make him live. Noomah liked the water, but he did not like the two-legged. He longed for his strength.

The days that followed were bad. The two-leggeds kept him tied in the sun, taking him once a day to water, once to graze for a short while. Noomah felt himself wasting away. He needed grass. He had to follow the two-leggeds who led him, but he hated them.

His life with the two-leggeds got worse. They would come at him three and four at a time. They would strap some bad squeaking thing around him tightly, and one of them would climb onto his back. It was like having a flesh-eater upon him, and Noomah would twist out from under the horrible beast. Then a pain would seize him across the nose and his lungs would burn for air. Sharp things would gall his ribs and two-leggeds would pull at his ears, making pain shoot all through his sore head. Always, the shaking-singing-rattling-squeaking-thumping-croaking-whistling sounds followed the two-leggeds.

Noomah learned to avoid the pain. Soon, he was standing still and letting the two-leggeds climb onto him. He would carry his rider until he was almost too weak to stand. Then the two leggeds would let him have grass and water.

The days got better. The two-leggeds took him to a place with good grass and water. He got stronger. To avoid the pain the two-leggeds knew how to inflict, he continued to let them crawl onto his back. He feared them less, but hated them more. Sometimes he would let his hatred go and kick or bite one of the stinking two-leggeds, but they always hurt him worse. He needed grass and water, and for that reason only did Noomah let the two-leggeds ride him.

He grew stronger, but the two-leggeds only rode him harder. Now one of them in particular came to make him suffer. This one grew shaking-singing things from its heels that gouged Noomah's side and made him run. This most horrible of two-leggeds would force a hard cold thing between his teeth. It would wrench his jaw with such pain that Noomah had to obey. This most horrible of two-leggeds carried a thing that struck like a tail caked with mud and gravel, and it too made Noomah run. Now he lived inside a circle of dead trees stacked one on the other, too high for him to jump.

Or so he feared. There was one low place in the circle. Noomah would stand and watch this place while he waited for torture, grass, and water. The place whispered to him, saying, *"Escape . . . Run!"*

One day near sundown the most horrible of two-leggeds came to the circle of dead trees. Others came with him. They made the loud bursts of sound from their mouths that Noomah feared, for often they came to beat him when they made this sound. Then Most Horrible forced the hard cold thing between Noomah's teeth and tightened the squeaking thing on his back. But this time, the thing was not as tight as usual, and Noomah began to feel voices call.

There was something wrong with Most Horrible. His breath smelled sweet, and his movements were like that of a stumbling foal. When he climbed onto the squeaking thing, Noomah could feel him swaying from one side to the other. The two-leggeds perched on the barrier of dead trees made the loud noises that he hated. Noomah began to snort, for he was worried and confused. He began to look around the top of the stacked-up trees for the low spot that had whispered to him.

Suddenly, the squeaking thing slipped around Noomah's chest, and Most Horrible fell to the ground. Straps slipped back on Noomah's flanks and made him kick. He felt his hooves coming down on the flesh of Most Horrible, whom he was dragging through the circle of dirt behind him. Two-leggeds poured over the rails like wolves leaping a deadfall, and Noomah fled in terror, kicking at the squeaking thing and dragging the body of Most Horrible.

They reached for him, but he heard the voices screaming, saying, *"Fight! Kick! Bite! Flee! Live!"* He kicked and stomped and felt his hoof crush the skull of Most Horrible. The squeaking thing slipped over Noomah's hips, and he felt speed gather behind him. He saw the low place and charged through the two-leggeds to fly over the rails. He ran, dodging, and felt his freedom.

He stepped on something that wrenched his head down, but it broke, and he shook the painful hard thing from between his teeth.

Noomah ran all night. He found water and grass. He felt strong. He snorted his hatred of two-leggeds. He wished he could return to smell the blood of Most Horrible, but he still feared the other two-leggeds.

And they came after him. They chased him on horses and made sharp cracking noises, loud as thunder, that caused pain to sear the flesh across one of his shoulders. So Noomah ran. He sought the timber of the mountains he had once feared. He ran through places the two-leggeds could not ride. He ran until the slopes pitched easily down before him, and then he began to walk.

The two-leggeds were gone. Noomah was free. He would not go back to the land between the mountains and the river. He would follow these slopes downward.

When daylight came, he looked out from a high place. He could see something vast and pleasing far in the distance, where the warm light rose. It called to him. Noomah walked that way. He wanted to go to that pleasing place and run. Noomah loved to run.

55

The call of a distant killdeer woke Teal in her lodge. She kept her eyes closed but listened. She knew two things by the call. First, dawn had begun to break; second, Mother Killdeer had a baby in trouble.

Mother Killdeer was a wise bird. She would lure enemies away from her young by feigning injury to a wing, and by calling in such plaintive tones that even the trickster, coyote, would be fooled.

The desperate calls of the killdeer made Teal think of her own child, and she sleepily opened her eyes just enough to look upon Sandhill. He lay nearby in the pale light that fell in through the smoke hole. Teal smiled at his sweet face half covered by the soft, tanned calf hide.

Closing her eyes again, she listened to the sounds outside. She heard the rolling snorts and stamping hooves of horses, the squawks of crows who had begun to gather around the growing bone piles outside this camp, the melodic notes of warblers fluting in the *sohoobi* trees along the riverbank. Two camp dogs were growling, and it sounded as if they were pulling on opposite ends of a gut.

Teal wanted to sleep again, but thoughts of things she must do kept her awake. Her own mare—the one who pulled the pole-drag that carried her things—would surely foal any day. This mare had been tied near her lodge for protection from wolves whenever the foal came. She would have to be moved to new grass, which was becoming hard to find around this camp. And that was just the beginning.

She needed to make two new rawhide parfleches to replace old ones that had begun to crack and split. She had been thinking about what kind of designs to paint on these new carrying cases. She would need paints, and would have to trade something to River Woman, who always had the best paint powders in many bright hues, made from all kinds of mosses, roots, and berries. River Woman would let her have the paints for almost nothing, however, for she too wanted her son's parfleches to bespeak his wealth and pride.

Yesterday, Teal had finished stitching the new covering for the extra lodge she and Sandhill sometimes slept in when Horseback wanted to be alone with his prayers and visions. But there was still the old covering to deal with. She would cut away the cowhide from the top of the old lodge cover, where smoke and grease from many fires had bestowed upon the hide a magic that would make rainwater gather itself into beads and roll away. This hide she would clean and cut to make a robe that would protect her husband from cold rains when he was caught far from his lodge in stormy weather. She would surprise Horseback with this garment when he returned, and he would be happy with her. The Thunderbird liked this good country of the south along the River of Arrowheads, more than the *Noomah* lands she had once wandered across with her band of Corn People. Horseback would use the rain shield often.

Trotter and Bear Heart and the Grasshopper Eater called Crooked Teeth had returned to the camp of the Horseback People two suns ago and told of the killings that had happened at Quivira. Yet, they had come back with many stolen ponies, making the people happy. Trotter had explained that the rest of the party had gone after the tall Osage warrior who had stolen Raccoon-Eyes's sacred metal. Surely, Horseback and Shaggy Hump and Raccoon-Eyes and the others would return within a few suns.

All this made Teal sigh, for she knew she would not get back to sleep now, thinking of all the things she wanted to get done before her husband returned. Suddenly, her eyes flew open and she sat upright, tossing the soft robe away. This was the day! Twenty-eight suns had crossed over since the last time! Now she remembered. She would not make parfleches today, or rain garments, or even a meal for Sandhill. The bleeding would begin today and she would be unclean. She would go and stay with others in the lodge for unclean women, away from the rest of the camp.

A big smile crossed her face. Happily, she pulled on her moccasins, and threw a plain old antelope-skin dress over her head. She crawled to Sandhill's bed, yanked the warm robe away from him and shook him. "Wake up, my son. Wake up, now! Today makes twenty-eight suns. It is always twenty-eight."

She pulled the naked boy out of the lodge and he stumbled along groggily, rubbing his eyes with his one free hand. She went straight to the lodge of her husband's sister, Mouse. Stopping before the doorway to the lodge, she said, "Sister, I am here. Your nephew comes to stay in your lodge."

In a moment, the bear-skin covering flew aside, and Mouse looked out, bare-breasted from sleeping under the robes with her husband, Trotter. She smirked at Teal. "You wake early."

Teal took Sandhill's face in her hand to make sure he was listening. "Be good in your uncle's lodge, or *Tso'apittse*, the giant made of rock, will come from the mountains and take your head in his pitchy hands and carry you home for his children to eat!"

Mouse took the boy by the hand and pulled him into the lodge.

Turning away, Teal said, "Do not forget to move my mare to grass."

Closing the doorway to the lodge, Mouse replied, "Do not forget to keep away from my husband's shield and weapons."

"I am not unclean yet, but it will begin today."

Skipping back to her lodge, Teal gathered some things to eat, a wooden bowl, a buffalo-horn spoon, her back rest, and a new pouch she was decorating with dyed and flattened porcupine quills. Inside the pouch was her awl and some thread made of tendons separated from the back of an elk carcass, and also four dried buffalo bladder containers holding four different sizes of quills. The pouch would give her something of her own to work on while she spent a few days in the lodge for unclean women. She would not make anything for her husband while she was unclean, for her bleeding might taint his power.

When she left, she secured the door flap of her lodge with a wooden pin, in case rain fell while she was away. Then she trotted happily out of camp.

The lodge for unclean women stood downstream from the camp, around a grove of *sohoobi* trees that kept it out of sight. As she approached, she smelled the aroma of tallow melting. She smiled hungrily. Already, there was giggling in the lodge, though Father Sun had not begun to show himself.

The woman at the cook fire looked up from an iron pan and smiled. "Looks Away, the wife of your husband's son is here," she announced.

It was Slope Child's voice that replied from inside the lodge: "Even one so pure becomes unclean."

Laughter erupted inside the lodge. Looks Away stepped out, eyes cast low, not wanting to take part in making fun of Teal.

Teal touched Looks Away as she passed her, then she marched close to the lodge and spoke loudly: "Is that the mother of Coyote's child?"

The women gasped, then burst into laughter again.

Slope Child had never married, but had a daughter. She would not say who the father of the girl was, and most women agreed that it was because she did not know who the father was herself. Among the *Noomah*, such a baby was known as Coyote's child. When she came to the lodge for unclean women, Slope Child had to pay someone to look after her daughter. This did not seem to bother Slope Child. She always had plenty of things to pay with, even though she had no husband.

"Perhaps it is Coyote's daughter," Slope Child answered. This was a scandalous thing to say, for the elders often told the story of how Coyote tricked his own daughters into coupling with him. Slope Child seemed to enjoy shocking the women by saying such things.

"When you leave this lodge," Teal said, knowing Slope Child would go back to camp on this day, "I know a place where you can gather much stone seed."

The women howled with laughter, for Slope Child was said to take stone seed to prevent getting pregnant. Slope Child stepped out of the lodge and glared at Teal. Finally, she smiled, and said, "Do not trifle with me, pure one. Is this true about the stone seed?"

The women laughed, and even Looks Away smiled, though she covered her mouth with her hand.

Teal set her back rest on the ground, and sat down to lean against it. She began eating a piece of boiled breadroot that she had brought along with her. The woman at the fire was adding honey and water to the melted tallow to make a fine sauce. She offered some to Teal, that she might dip her breadroot in the good sauce. Unclean women were forbidden to consume meat, but they could still eat well.

"Where did you get that iron vessel?" Teal asked, enjoying the sweet sauce.

"My husband traded two good robes for it at Tachichichi. The *Tiwas* there have many metal things."

Teal ate until she was full, then began to work on her new pouch. Slope Child was gathering her things and preparing to go back to the camp.

"You leave early," Teal said.

Slope Child smiled wantonly. "I would rather be among men now. I have stayed long enough among women."

As Slope Child turned, a sound like that of a lightning bolt erupted from upstream, but no clouds hung in the sky. A scream and a chorus of war cries followed, like the songs of geese in the sky. Hooves rumbled across the valley, and two more guns fired.

Teal sprang from the ground and sprinted beyond the timber shielding the women's lodge from camp. She saw the camp's herd of horses stampeding her way. Looking into the camp, she saw strange warriors running on foot among the lodges, shooting arrows into the doorways that were open.

The women who came up behind Teal began to scream and cry, but she thought only of Sandhill, and ran immediately toward the camp. The horses were galloping her way, so she waved the quilled pouch that was still in her hands, turning part of the stampede into the camp. As hundreds of hooves shook the ground to either side of her, she saw a mounted warrior driving the ponies. She recognized his appearance from the stories she had heard in the winter lodges of the elders. The warrior's hair grew long on the right side of his head, but was folded over and up, with the end tied to the top of the long lock. His hair was cut short above his left ear, giving him an evil lopsided look. He rode near enough for Teal to notice the red stripe painted across his eyes and the bridge of his nose, but he would not come near her, seeing that she had come from the unclean women's lodge.

She saw another enemy warrior driving the horses, then another. They were *Na-vohnuh*, the most ancient of all *Noomah* foes. A born hatred gripped her heart like a hand just pulled from icy water. She kept swinging her pouch over her head to keep the horses from running over her, and followed about twenty ponies into the camp.

The *Noomah* warriors were rallying now, and even women were stepping from the lodges with weapons. Everything had gone suddenly crazy in a camp so peaceful just before dawn. She caught glimpses of *Na-vohnuhs* darting among the lodges. They had come from upstream, against the wind, and had run on foot all the way through the camp to the downstream side. Many of the warriors of Teal's camp were now pursuing them, or trying to catch the horses that Teal had so luckily driven among the lodges. She kept weaving through the ponies and frightened people to get to the lodge of Trotter and Mouse.

She picked up a warrior's lance from a tripod that had been knocked over by horses, and ran toward the lodge where she had left Sandhill. She saw Bear Heart on a pony that dragged a rope, and knew now that he would help other men catch mounts, drive the *Na-vohnuh* foot-warriors from the valley, and maybe even recapture the ponies that had been stolen. It was well that she had divided the horse herd and frightened some of them into the camp, yet Teal could not feel any relief from her terror until she knew her son was well.

When she came to the lodge, she saw an enemy warrior trying to get in. She ran at him with her lance, and he looked at her, piercing her with his evil glaring eyes. Teal was afraid, but she ran ahead anyway. Then a *pogamoggan* swung through the entrance to the lodge, bashing the warrior on the side of his head and knocking him back. As he hit the ground, Teal drove her lance into him, possessing the presence to turn the edges of the flat flint blade upright so they would slip between the ribs of the attacker when she stabbed him.

The enemy warrior screamed and grabbed the lance shaft, trying to get up, but Mouse sprang through the entrance and smashed his face in with the war club. Sandhill came to the entrance and looked out at the dying enemy warrior bleeding at his feet outside the lodge. He stared, but said nothing. Teal stepped in front of him, to shield him from arrows.

"Where is my mother?" Mouse screamed, glancing around the camp.

Trotter rode bareback to the lodge on a pony, and motioned for the war club in Mouse's hand.

"Find my mother!" Mouse shouted.

Trotter took the *pogamoggan* and wheeled his pony, looking for his mother-in-law. Then Teal herself spotted River Woman, standing outside her lodge, singing a death song, an arrow sticking out of her back. As Trotter rode to her, a great war cry rose, and a long line of enemy foot-warriors appeared on the river bank upstream.

The first assault had been a ruse by the bravest enemy warriors to decoy most of the Comanches downstream. Now the main enemy body was descending on the upstream side of camp. Yet, Teal knew that the horses she had frightened into the camp would give the *Noomah* men power and quickness. They would come at a gallop and clash with the enemy, she hoped before the horrible *Na-vohnuh* reached her son.

Shoving Mouse back into her lodge, she said, "Get your baby." She pulled Sandhill out of the lodge. When Mouse came out with her baby in his cradle board, Teal said, "Take them to the riverbank, away from the enemy. Hide in the bushes." She pulled the lance from the dead *Na-vohnuh* and handed it to Mouse.

Sprinting toward the enemy attack, Teal reached her own lodge, wishing now that she hadn't closed the flap with the wooden peg. She pulled the peg out, flung the flap aside, and dived inside to retrieve her bow case and quiver full of hunting arrows. She strung the bow inside, shaking as she listened to River Woman's death song and the screams of the attackers. When she stepped out of her lodge she saw Trotter pulling River Woman onto his pony, the strap of his *pogamoggan* looped around his wrist. It made Teal proud to see Trotter protecting his mother-in-law, as every *Noomah* warrior was sworn to do.

Teal notched an arrow and looked for a target. They were already near enough to shoot. She aimed at a *Na-vohnuh* raider headed for Trotter, and saw her arrow speed into the enemy warrior's hip, crumpling him instantly. Trotter whirled his mount to take on the next warrior, who ran upon him and stabbed his pony with a knife as Trotter knocked his shield away with the club. An enemy arrow hit the already wounded pony in the neck, and Trotter's second blow crunched the skull of the *Na-vohnuh*.

Teal drew the bow again and saw her second arrow go all the way through the next attacker. As she groped for a third arrow, she saw Trotter take River Woman away, the pony leaving a solid line of blood on the ground. Beyond Trotter, the enemy foot-warriors had invaded the camp and were leaping into lodges, screaming battle cries.

Teal turned away from the attack. She saw *Noomah* horsemen coming like hawks that dived on mice. Suddenly, the horse-warriors and the foot-warriors collided all around her, and the battle screams made her skin crawl as she dodged the chaos of gnashing weapons. She looked for Mouse and the children now, and saw her husband's sister holding off a warrior with her lance.

Sandhill was standing behind Mouse, holding the cradle board with the baby, looking bewildered and afraid. Teal drew her bow, saw her arrow drop low, into the ankle of the enemy, spinning him, and giving Mouse a chance to stick the blade of the lance into his guts.

Mouse dropped the lance, and turned to take the cradle board from Sandhill. She grabbed for the boy's wrist, but he had seen his mother, and was running toward Teal. An enemy foot-warrior broke through the line of horsemen and scooped Sandhill up like a puppy before Teal's very eyes. She would not shoot with her son in the warrior's arms. She feared she could not catch the enemy raider, and if she could, was not sure she could kill him, for he was muscular and scarred from many battles. He was grizzled, one particular scar raised in an ugly welt across his face. Teal knew this warrior as Battle Scar, the *Na-vohnuh* chief.

A black craziness tried to possess her, until she remembered Mother Killdeer. She dropped her bow and quiver, holding only one arrow. Lifting her antelope skin dress she stabbed herself high on her thigh. The hunting point came back out easily, and with it came the blood, and a searing pain. She gritted her teeth and snapped the arrow shaft one fist behind the point. Keeping the killing end of the arrow in her hand, she jabbed the broken stob of the back portion of the shaft into the wound she had made, so the feathered end stuck out of the wound.

Now she screamed in hideous pain and saw the horrible eyes of Battle Scar look at her. She pulled her dress higher to show the curve of her hip, and limped piteously toward an abandoned lodge, as if to hide there. She shook her hair across her face, and through the dark tresses saw Battle Scar drop Sandhill, and run for her, drawing his knife. She gripped the forward shaft of the broken arrow in her hand, and crawled into the entryway of the lodge, dragging her bleeding leg behind her, like Mother Killdeer luring Coyote away from her chicks.

She fell into the lodge and saw the shadow of the evil one follow her. She turned, saw his loin skins fall away as he descended on her with a leer and an iron knife. She slashed suddenly at the bowels of her attacker, saw the pain a surprise in his face as he reached across his belly to hold his own entrails in. She scrambled out from under him with the quickness of a frightened ground squirrel, rolling away from his knife hand. She sprang to her feet and ran right over his back to get out of the lodge.

Mouse had collected Sandhill again, so Teal pulled the arrow shaft out of her wound and ran to help her sister-in-law. Her leg throbbed with pain and gushed blood. The enemy foot-warriors had been pushed all the way back to the edge of camp now, and had begun to run back upstream, away from the ferocity of the horsebacks. Teal saw Battle Scar crawl from the lodge, holding his guts in. He was too badly hurt to do anything but skulk away, hiding from the *Noomah* horsemen as he retreated. She wished for her bow and arrows, but could not find them now.

The sounds of the battle faded, leaving the death song of River Woman to pierce the dusty air. The *Noomah* horsemen broke off pursuit under Bear Heart's leadership and circled the camp, preparing for another attack. Blood stained the ground in pools and trails all through camp, and young warriors began to compare wounds, but it seemed only River Woman was dying. She stood facing the rising sun, her arms held high, her voice climbing in pitch.

The *Na-vohnuh* raiders stopped on the highest part of the riverbank and began shouting down at the camp. They threw dirt into the air and taunted the Comanches. The attackers had managed to drag all their dead warriors away with them, leaving the Comanches no one to scalp, and some of the young men wanted to ride after the raiders.

"No!" Bear Heart shouted. He rode in front of the younger men, his face bloody from a scalp wound, his expression like that of a snarling wolf. "We will stay to protect our women and children. Listen to the death song of River Woman. Let her pain into your own hearts and hold it there. Let her pain turn to anger in your hearts. Let it swirl like a whirlwind and hold it there. Release it only when we go to take our revenge on our enemies. When we take our revenge, Horseback and Shaggy Hump must ride with us, for one is the husband, and one is the son of River Woman. Then we will take our scalps. Then we will count our blows in battle. Then we will reclaim our horses. Now we will guard our camp and mourn our dead and let our anger grow like a thundercloud."

The True Humans began to gather around River Woman, who stood singing, the arrow still protruding from her back. Blood ran down the back of her legs and pooled at her feet. No one touched her, for it was known that she possessed strange power. Her song chanted meaningless sounds. Then it came in real *Noomah* words, saying,

> "Hear the sound the sun makes,
> Hear the sound the sun makes.
> The Great Deer sees a nation.
> A nation in the mist
> A nation in the mist."

Teal stood touching Mouse, and Mouse had tears streaming from her eyes, though she made no sound. Both women held their children.

"Yesterday, my mother gave me her best awl," Mouse said.

"She gave me a fine hide scraper," Teal replied, "all wrapped with new golden rawhide."

. . . .

River Woman lingered the rest of the day, singing on her knees. Mouse and Teal knelt to either side of her. She died the moment the shadows of the mountains fell upon her. The camp mourned her death. Teal and Mouse cut their hair off and scratched themselves across the legs and breasts with the points of knives.

The next day, the body of River Woman was taken to an outcropping of rock near the river, where a crack in the rock made a good burial place. She was wrapped in a good robe and lowered into the crack. Her daughter and her daughter-in-law lowered rocks onto her to cover her. Teal sprinkled the crushed leaves of sweet sage over her.

At the camp, women began preparing to move. The ghost of River Woman would surely haunt this place if they stayed. No one would speak her name again, for to do so would summon her specter down from the Shadow Land and remind those who loved her of the way she died. Those who wished to speak of her would call her Horseback's mother, or Shaggy Hump's first wife.

Teal was still mourning and packing her parfleches at dusk the day after the battle, when she realized that her time of bleeding had not come. This could mean only one thing, for her time came at twenty-eight days, as sure as the rising of the moon or the circling of the stars. She was going to have another child. She hoped she would give Horseback another son.

If only the *Na-vohnuh* had not come. She could have surprised Horseback with her news when he returned, and he would have rejoiced with her. Now she would have to tell him that his mother had died, and though she had protected Sandhill, she had failed to protect her mother-in-law. Mother Killdeer had wakened her with a warning, and Teal had not listened. She felt foolish and ashamed. Perhaps River Woman was laughing now on her way to the Shadow Land, but Teal was weeping on earth.

56

In winters to come, through the days that followed the time of his walk on earth, the elders who had witnessed it would tell the younger generations about Horseback's return to his camp on the River of Arrowheads. The Great One was wounded with an arrow in his chest, they would say, and his mother had been killed by *Na-vohnuh* raiders while he was away. For two moons, the old woman had been teaching her daughter all she knew about healing with plants and prayers. She had seen her death in a vision, but had told no one about it.

The Great One had allowed no one to remove the arrow from his chest, knowing that his mother would treat the wound better than any other. But when he returned to his camp, he heard the wails of mourners and learned that his mother had been killed.

And the wailing became louder with the Great One's return, for he brought news of two more deaths, and the dead ones were not gray-haired women, but strong young men. One of the slain warriors was a man from a distant band called the Grasshopper Eaters. The other had been a Foolish One at the time of his death. This one left a wife, who had been taken from the Metal Men six winters before. When she heard of her husband's death, this woman began to slash her legs and breasts with a knife, for she had loved her husband. She mourned so long and piteously that the women who heard her wept, and the men looked at the ground in pity.

These were the dark days of the New Nation. The Great One grew weak from his grief and his wound. He slipped away to float under the pass to the Shadow Land. His sister could not treat his wound in the ways she had learned from her mother, for such familiarity between a brother and a sister was a bad thing. The Great One's father had to carve the war point out of his chest while warriors held his arms and legs. The Great One hovered under the pass, wasting away, as those who loved him prayed for him—for the nation.

The people of the Great One's camp wanted to move away from the bad place where three deaths had been mourned. His wife and his father put him on a pole-drag and moved him to a new camp, upstream. The new camp was on a small creek that flowed from the south into the River of Arrowheads. This new camp was nearer to the *Yutas*, who were allies of the True Humans in those days.

But the Great One had a dark rival in this camp. The rival had a wife whom he loved to beat. He had captured this woman from the Northern Raiders, and made her good, yet he still beat her like a slave wife. The wife of the Great One tried to hide this poor woman, but the dark rival would find her and beat her. This rival had returned from the *Osage* fight without wounds, and with battle blows to his credit. He claimed great power because of this, yet some said he had caused the downfall of the Great One by killing a deer, which was the Great One's spirit-guide.

While the Great One lay wasting away, the dark rival began to harangue the True Humans. He boasted of his *puha* and said the people should follow him into the *Na-vohnuh* lands to recover stolen ponies and take enemy scalps. Many of the True Humans agreed with the dark rival, for his power seemed strong. While the Great One wasted away, twenty lodges moved southward with the dark rival who liked to beat his wife. It was a bad day, with much weeping among women who had to part with friends, and some arguing among warriors who had chosen to follow different leaders.

Yes, it was a bad day, but the thing that happened was good. The Great One and his dark rival could not have continued to live in the same camp. One weakened the other's power.

When the dark rival moved out of the Great One's camp, with twenty lodges, a new beginning was made. Now there were two bands of Comanches in the country of the Sacred South. More would come. Through this division, the nation would grow strong. The spirits move in ways mysterious to those who walk on earth.

· · · ·

Horseback heard a sweet voice singing and opened his eyes. Beside him, he saw Teal's outline against the light that streamed in through the smoke hole. Even this light hurt his eyes. He squinted and noticed something twisting above his head, suspended from a lodge pole on a thin cord. When his eyes focused, he could see that the thing was a tail feather from a flicker. This was a good curative charm. He smelled stew.

"I am hungry," he said.

Teal stopped abruptly in the middle of her song. She looked down at him, smiled, and left the lodge.

Horseback saw his father move into view above him. "You should eat, my son. You look like someone's frail sister lying there."

Trotter looked down at him, grinning. "I hope the elder sisters of our enemies do not come to torture you, my friend, for you cannot defend yourself. Not even against girls."

"He cannot even keep himself clean," Bear Heart said, his head blocking the light from the smoke hole. "When he soils himself, his wife must clean him like a baby."

"Perhaps she should make him a great big cradle board," Trotter added, and the men laughed.

"Get out of my husband's lodge," Teal said, her voice stern. "He is going to eat, and he doesn't want to listen to you."

Horseback ate, then slept. When he woke, he made himself sit up. He sat there a long time, then told Teal to help him stand. He felt dizzy, but his wife helped him step out of the lodge. Looking around, he found himself in strange surroundings, though he recognized some of the tallest mountain peaks and knew where he was.

"Have you found any dogwood trees growing around this camp?" he asked Teal.

"Yes," Teal said, "in a place down the creek."

"Take me there."

Horseback found a good, straight dogwood branch and told his wife to cut it for him. For three days—while he ate and rested and regained his strength—he scraped and smoothed the dogwood stem into an arrow shaft. Teal followed him everywhere, making sure he had stew or pemmican to eat, for he was always hungry. She carried a water vessel with her to slake his thirst. She carried a heavy buffalo robe for him to rest on when he got tired, and a lighter calf robe to cover him when he felt chilled.

When he slept, Horseback would leave his arrow shaft suspended on forked sticks near the fire to cure it properly. When he woke, he would check the shaft for straightness. Finding a curved spot, he would rub grease onto the spot, heat it, then bend it straight.

"Bring me a good piece of the sacred white flint so that I may make a point," he told Teal as he worked on the dogwood shaft. "And boil some rawhide and buffalo hooves for glue so I can stick the point to the shaft before I bind it with strips of sinew. Do these things for me, and do not let your shadow fall on the things as you work on them."

"Yes, my husband," was all Teal said. She did not question. She boiled the bits of rawhide and buffalo hooves in an iron vessel until she had made more than enough glue. This she collected on a straight green stick and let cool. ·

After the third day, Horseback walked out to look at the few ponies his camp had left since the *Na-vohnuh* raid and the split with Whip's followers. He looked carefully at each pony. At last he frowned, walked back to camp, and began to flake a fine, sharp point of the white flint Teal had brought for him.

The fourth day, his father came to him as he painted black rings around the dogwood arrow shaft. "My son, the people in this camp are wondering about you. They call you elder sister. Some of them want to go away and join Whip."

"Whip!" he answered, a snarl in his voice. "Whip wants to ruin me!"

Shaggy Hump sat silent for a long time, and watched his son paint the black rings around the arrow shaft with the tip of a kingfisher feather. Finally he spoke: "My son, Whip did a bad thing. He should not have killed that deer in the country of the Osage. He knows that you pay homage to the deer as your spirit-protector. But Whip has never had a vision like yours. He does not understand. It is not all Whip's fault that your power left you. It is your fault as well, my son."

Horseback looked up from his work. "I have honored the deer!"

Shaggy Hump chuckled. "You watch for deer trails, so that you do not tread on them. You refrain from eating the meat of the deer, or the food a deer would also eat. These things are good, my son, but there is more to medicine than the things you do in the sight of other men. The real power in your medicine lies in what the spirits see in your heart."

Horseback sat for a long time, thinking about this. The paint dried on the end of his feather brush, and he had to wet it with his mouth. "Tell me how I have failed, my father. You are wise. I do not understand."

Shaggy Hump smiled. "Sometimes it is easier to know how to hunt a herd of buffalo if you watch it for a while from a distant hill. When you get too close to the herd, you think too much of eating fresh brains and liver, and you cannot see how the herd moves. I have watched you from a distance, my son, and that is why I seem wise to you."

Shaggy Hump paused, and appeared to be listening, or smelling the breeze.

"Six winters ago, my son, you had a great vision. Your spirit-protector revealed to you a nation in the mist. Since that time, you have sought to serve the spirits, and create this nation of horse people."

"Yes," Horseback said. "That is true. I am called to do this thing."

"But do you seek this vision with your heart, or with your weapons?"

"I must use my weapons."

"You must use your weapons as the spirits tell you to use them. Did the spirits tell you to seek battle with Wolf People because they stole three skinny ponies? We were lucky, and we got the ponies back, but your trouble with Whip deepened on that chase. Did the spirits tell you to follow Raccoon-Eyes? I know he is your friend, but he is not a True Human, and he does not understand our ways, or your vision. Did the spirits tell you to seek battle with the Osage, or to serve the gods of the yellow metal? Does the horse nation of your vision take up the lands the Osage now hold? Why did you follow Raccoon-Eyes there?"

"To get more ponies," Horseback said, rather defensively.

"Did the spirits tell you to do this?"

Horseback thought about his father's question. He sat silent for a long time. He listened to the wind in the *sohoobi* trees. He heard the chatter of a kingfisher, and felt the power of the feather in his hand. He looked toward a bend in the creek and saw the kingfisher dive into the water after a fish.

"No, my father," he finally said. "The spirits have not told me to get ponies. I wanted them for myself. I wanted my people to think of me as wealthy."

"You have shadow-wealth, my son. You need not seek the wealth of earthly things. Trust the spirits to provide your ponies. It is not good to have too much of one thing. Do you remember the story of Rolling Rock?"

Horseback thought about the old days, listening to his grandfather tell stories in the winter lodges. "I do not remember it all, my father. Tell me again."

"Well, it is not winter, but I will tell this story now anyway. I think you need to hear it, and perhaps I need to tell it.

"In the ancient times, all the animals were humans. Wolf and Coyote were brothers. Wolf had a beautiful earring made of a shell that made many colors in the sunlight. Coyote wanted an earring like his brother, so he asked Wolf where to get one.

" 'They are on the mountain,' Wolf said, 'under that big rock. You will find many to choose from. You must take only one. Do not take more.'

"So Coyote went up on the mountain, and found the earrings under the big rock. He put one on his ear. He liked it. He picked another one, and another, until he had earrings all over both ears. Coyote began to dance, and he liked the way the earrings rattled when he danced. He said, 'If I take just one, like my brother said, they will not rattle. I will take them all.'

"So Coyote left the mountain, but when he looked back, he saw the big rock rolling after him. Coyote got scared. He ran across the flats with Rolling Rock chasing him. He climbed the next hill, but Rolling Rock came right up the hill after him. Coyote said, 'No rock can roll sideways.' So he ran around the side of the hill, but Rolling Rock followed him. Coyote said, 'No rock can roll through timber.' So he ran through the timber, but the rock came right through the trees.

"Coyote asked his friend, Bear, to stop Rolling Rock. The rock ran over Bear and killed him. He asked Snake for help, but Rolling Rock killed Snake. He asked Eagle. Same thing. Finally, Coyote asked Night Hawk, and Night Hawk jumped high in the sky and dove down on the rock, smashing it to powder.

"Night Hawk said, 'You should not have taken all the earrings. Because you were greedy, Rolling Rock has killed your friends. Now you must wear those earrings so their shaking will remind you of how greedy you have been. Go straight now, and stop trying to have more things than everybody else.'

"This is a true story, my son. You will know it is true when you see the night hawk diving on bugs, the way Night Hawk dived down on Rolling Rock to smash him."

The unfinished dogwood arrow shaft lay across Horseback's thighs. "I have killed my friends," he said. "I have been foolish, like Coyote."

"Your friends followed their own hearts. They died bravely in battle. Do not worry about them. They are hunting in the Shadow Land. Worry about yourself."

"Where do I begin?"

"In your heart. Listen to the spirits. When you had your great vision, what did your protector tell you must be done to create the new nation of horse people?"

The answer was so plain, that Horseback felt foolish for having forgotten it. "I must avenge the souls of my ancestors killed in battle. I must make war with the *Na-vohnuh,* our most ancient and terrible of all enemies."

Shaggy Hump smiled. "You see how the spirits have reminded you. They have sent the *Na-vohnuh* to attack your camp in your absence."

Horseback nodded. "The spirits are wise, but sometimes wisdom is cruel."

"The greatest power has the cruelest dark side. You know The Way, my son. You may give your power back to the spirits, and no man will speak against you."

Horseback moistened the feather and began to paint his arrow shaft again. "I cannot give my power back now. These people have followed me here. I will lead them to the new country of the Horse Nation, or through the Pass to the Shadow Land."

"*Tsah,*" Shaggy Hump said. "Now, tell me, my son, why do you make this arrow? If you want a better brush to paint with, I have one in my lodge. That is just a feather."

"It is part of my new vision."

"Another vision?" Shaggy Hump sat up straight on his robe. "Tell me."

"Sound-the-Sun-Makes came to me while I slept, wounded. He was very angry. His fires burned me. He told me I must make an arrow of dogwood. The point is to be of white flint, like our ancestors used. The sinew binding the point to the shaft must be red, to remind me of the blood of my ancestors. I must paint black rings around the shaft with the feather of a kingfisher. This will make my wounds heal as the water closes up after a kingfisher dives in. Each ring I paint will represent the soul of an ancestor I must avenge. The feathers on my arrow must be from the tail of a hawk."

"Hawk feathers are no good for making arrows, my son. Blood ruins them. You should use vulture or owl feathers. I have some fine turkey feathers I will give to you."

"Sound-the-Sun-Makes told me I must use hawk feathers to give my war pony quickness. This is a sacred arrow. It will never draw blood. I must sacrifice this arrow to the sun, in the sight of four brave men."

"And then, you will have your *puha* back?"

"No. There is more. After I sacrifice the arrow, I am forbidden to eat meat, and I am forbidden to ride until Medicine-Coat comes."

Shaggy Hump smirked. "Who is Medicine-Coat?"

"My warhorse."

"How will you know him?"

"Sound-the-Sun-Makes told me I will know him."

Shaggy Hump nodded. "Then you must believe."

"I do, my father. I believe." Carefully, he painted another ring around his sacrificial arrow.

When Horseback was ready for the glue, he came to Teal's fire. He softened the glue in hot water and stuck the end of his arrow shaft into the mass of glue. He had made a notch there to receive the white flint point he had flaked.

"The glue is good," he said, feeling the point stick firmly to the arrow shaft.

"When it cools, I will place the glue stick in your bow case," Teal said, "so you will have it to mend things."

"I must mend my heart, first. I must mend my medicine. I could not do these things without you, Teal. You are a good woman, my sits-beside wife. You make me strong." He twisted a length of sinew between his fingers and prepared to wrap it around the tip of the arrow shaft and the base of the white flint point.

▲▲▲▲▲
57
▼▼▼▼▼

Horseback climbed the first mountain to the west with his sacred arrow in his quiver. The climb on foot made him tired, and he knew this was part of his penance. This would remind him not to displease his spirit-guide in the future, for he did not like to walk.

Four brave men came with him: Shaggy Hump, Bear Heart, Trotter, and Crazy Eyes, who had distinguished himself during the *Na-vohnuh* raid by stabbing an enemy warrior though wounded himself with three arrows sticking out of him. Coming within easy bow range of the mountain top, Horseback stood under the sun all day, chanting, praying, and smoking his sacred pipe. When the sun touched the mountain top and began to sink beyond, he notched his sacred arrow and drew his bow. He let the arrow fly, and the four brave men all agreed that Father Sun swallowed it with fire.

Returning to camp, Horseback began to assess his weapons while he waited for the arrival of Medicine-Coat. He killed the kingfisher that lived near his camp, piercing it with an arrow as it came up from the water with a fish. He sang many prayers over the dead bird as its plumage dried. He skinned the bird carefully, instructing Teal to tan its thin hide with buffalo brains. When Teal had preserved the kingfisher skin, Horseback told her to fill it with sage and grass to which he added a pinch of the sacred antler dust his Naming Father had given him many winters ago. Then he told Teal to sew the skin up, making the bird look almost alive again. He attached this sacred kingfisher *puhante* to the center of his shield.

Horseback began to crave the pleasure of a ride, but knew he must await the arrival of Medicine-Coat, or anger Sound-the-Sun-Makes. For days, he watched the ponies, followed them, walked among them, spoke to them, smelled their sweet breath. None became Medicine-Coat.

Waking one morning, he gently picked up little Sandhill while the boy slept, carried him to the creek, and threw him into a little pool. Horseback laughed as the boy came out of the cold water, coughing and shuttering with surprise.

"My son!" he said. "This is a good day to wake up early. Come, you are going to ride today! You are Comanche—the one your ally calls his enemy."

He warmed the boy in his arms and had Teal feed him a mixture of milk and blood collected from the slashed utters of a buffalo cow Shaggy Hump had killed the day before. Then Horseback took Sandhill to the pony herd and chose a gelding. It was not the wildest pony in the herd. Neither was it the laziest. As he wove a short length of rawhide rope into the gelding's mane at the withers, Shaggy Hump wandered out of the camp to watch.

"Climb onto your pony," Horseback said to Sandhill. "Use the rawhide rope to pull yourself up."

Sandhill clawed at the rope that hung down from the mane. The boy kicked and grunted, as his father and grandfather laughed. The gelding stood still through the entire travail, until finally Horseback boosted the boy onto the back of the pony.

"You must learn to climb up by yourself," he said, handing the reins to the boy, "unless you want to stay in camp with the women and girls while the men go hunting."

Sandhill only smiled and kicked his legs wildly at the flanks of the pony. He had ridden many times with his father. He knew how to handle the reins and send signals to his mount. The pony trotted away, veering this way and that to the wild pulls Sandhill made on the reins.

"Not that way!" Horseback shouted. "Come back here!" When Sandhill returned to him, he said, "Where are you going? Your pony darts around like a squirrel. You must know in your heart where you go, then make your pony feel your heart. See that cactus? Ride there. Keep the way in your heart so your pony can feel it. Go straight."

"Straighter than straight!" Shaggy Hump added.

Sandhill rode to the cactus and back, making the pony trot in a near perfect line. Returning to his father, he tried to hang onto the side of his mount like a warrior using his pony for a shield, but his leg slipped over the back of the pony and he landed flat on his back in the dirt. Horseback and Shaggy Hump laughed at him as he rose and gasped for breath.

"Why did you fall off?" Horseback asked.

"I was trying to use my pony for a shield, like the warriors," Sandhill said.

"It is easier after your pony sweats, then his coat sticks to your leggings better. You must ride hard first. Now, get back on and make that pony sweat. You will learn."

Sandhill turned and looked at the pony, standing several steps away. He clenched his fists and gathered himself for the challenge. He backed up two steps, then hurled himself at the gelding, leaping to grab the rawhide rope higher than the time before. Kicking and clawing, he groped for a fistful of mane, found it, pulled himself higher, got an elbow over the withers. Horseback and Shaggy Hump almost doubled over in their valiant efforts to restrain their laughter. After three attempts, the boy threw a leg over the back of the pony and lay there, catching his breath.

"Now you mount like an elder sister, but that is better than a younger sister. You will learn. Ride, my son!"

Sandhill spent most of the day on his pony as Horseback shouted encouragement and advice. When the pony was sweating, the boy indeed rode like a warrior for a short distance, clutching the mane with one hand, and keeping one leg fast across the back of the gelding, before falling off again, this time onto a yucca plant that pierced his skin in three places that he fancied as arrow wounds.

It was near sundown when Horseback saw dust over the southern river-bank and ran for his weapons. The dust turned out to be that of a single rider who came trotting into camp all bruised and swollen. It was Whip's woman, Dipper.

"He was going to kill me," she said. "The people in that camp believe I am a witch. They were going to let him beat me to death. I got away in the night after he went to look for *Na-vohnuh* camps."

Horseback took her gently by the arm. "Go with Teal. You will live in my lodge now. But remember that Teal carries my shield."

Dipper pursed her swollen lips together in relief that almost turned to tears. "Yes, Teal carries your shield. I will obey your sits-beside wife."

Teal came to take Dipper away with her, an odd strained look of pride and jealousy on her face.

"Wait," Horseback commanded. He knew it would be easier to go through this just once. He had been thinking of this since the death of his fellow Foolish One, Echo-of-the-Wolf. Echo's wife, Sunshade, had been mourning, surviving by virtue of the generosity of the camp since Echo's death. No blood brother survived Echo. It was up to Horseback, his Foolish Brother, to see that Sunshade was cared for. He might have given her more time to mourn before taking her as a wife, but he did not wish to rouse Teal's jealousy more than once.

"Sunshade," he said, seeing her in the gathering of people who had come to witness the arrival of Dipper, "you will go with Teal also. You will serve her. When you have mourned the loss of your dead husband for one great circle of seasons, then I will lie with you." He spoke loudly now, so the people of his camp would hear. "Now I have three wives. I am richer than rich, yet

I must not lie with any woman until my power is good. I await only my war pony, Medicine-Coat, to bring back my *puha*. Then I will hunt buffalo and my wives will make many robes. Each wife will have her own lodge."

He paused to look over the remnants of his camp. "We must prepare our weapons. When my war pony comes, I will ride south to avenge my ancestors. For those who follow me, there will be a great war with the *Na-vohnuh*. The victor in this war will win all this country of the big buffalo herds. I am ready to die here. The spirits have shown me a nation in the mist. I have spoken."

He glanced at Teal, who was glaring angrily at him. He understood. She had served him well, and now he was taking two new wives at once. He would keep a safe distance from her for a few days, and she would see that he was right. There was no one else to take care of these two women.

Choosing not to wallow in Teal's anger, he looked out beyond the edge of camp, and saw Sandhill, still riding his pony. This made Horseback smile.

· · · ·

Whip did not appear for two more suns. When he arrived, Horseback met him beyond the lodges of the camp, no weapons in his hand. Whip carried his lance, his shield, and his bow and arrows.

"I have been waiting for you, my brother," Horseback said. He knew Whip would understand his use of the term brother, for brothers shared wives, and he had taken Whip's.

"You live," Whip said. "I remember you lying wounded, like a weak woman."

"I am strong now."

"You do not ride."

"I await a pony from the Shadow Land."

Whip scoffed. "I come for my slave."

"I have taken her into my lodge. How many ponies do you want for her?"

"I want to cut off her nose for coupling with another warrior."

"She has coupled with no one, and she will not until you have been paid for her."

"If I wish, I will take her back to my camp and beat her. My people want to burn her."

"If they burn her, she will be gone, and you will be no richer. If you sell her, she will still be gone, but you will have more ponies."

Whip glared, yet obviously saw the logic in Horseback's words. Perhaps the long ride from his camp had taken some of his anger, Horseback thought.

"Ten ponies," Whip said.

"I am rich in wives, but poor in ponies. I have only six to offer."

"Six ponies and five robes."

"Six ponies, two robes, and two lodge poles."

"*Tsah*. It is good. A pony for each winter that witch tried to destroy me. You will regret taking her into your lodge, my brother. She is bad."

"I will make her good. Go get your ponies from the herd. You know which ones are mine. I will tell my wives to pack two good robes on the lodge poles." He turned back to his camp.

"Now I am more horsed than Horseback," Whip said, the boast obvious in his voice.

Horseback stopped and turned back to his friend of boyhood days. "I will have horses again. My *puha* is coming back. Things change, my brother. Things always change."

Whip's arrogant countenance slowly gave way to a look of deep sadness. "*Hah*. It is true."

Horseback turned away from Whip for the last time. Change was something upon which they could agree. Never would they speak again.

58

Danger lurked everywhere, like lightning poised to strike from the clouds. Around each bend. Over every rise. Under all the cutaway banks along the streams where Noomah would drink. Lions waited on limbs in the trees. Wolves darted from brush and timber. Great humpbacked bears lumbered across hillsides, themselves moving hillsides of muscle and stinking fur.

For days, Noomah wandered. He found grass. Sweet grass. Tender shoots. He ate, and ate, and ate. He grew strong and quick again. He felt good, for the scents and sounds of the horrible two-leggeds were far behind him.

He stayed away from timber and brush and held to the sage and grass country where he could see far and run fast. The scent of stinking meat-eaters drifted to him often, and he learned to hold his head high and look into the wind for the hunters. Often, an indeterminable sound or motion provided all the encouragement Noomah needed to bolt and run.

It was well, for sometimes meat-eaters would chase him when he bolted. Wolves that came low to the ground, quick as swooping birds. Lions that bounded in great leaps, down from trees or over boulders. Once, he came to drink and blundered into a great she-bear with two cubs. She rose from the willows and came so suddenly and swiftly at Noomah that he felt her terrible claws rake hair from his rump as he turned to flee. He ran so far that his feet ached and his lungs burned, but he learned to approach his drinking places with the wind in his nostrils.

He moved down the streams that had led him out of the mountains. He liked the land below. Here, he could see far across grass and sage. One day he watched some strange dark thing in the distance. He watched a long time. It moved like a huge cloud shadow across a distant hillside. Noomah knew this thing was a herd. The voices told him that a herd meant protection from killers and meat-eaters.

As he wandered toward the herd, Noomah found a group of bull elk, their antlers waving above their heads like falling trees. They looked at him a long time, then turned to trot away. He followed. After many days, he came closer to the elk. Closer and closer, until they knew his scent. Finally, he moved among them. Now their eyes and ears and noses were his. He learned their call. They whistled to warn him. Among them, Noomah could lower his head and fill his mouth with fresh grass. The elk would make feints at him with their antlers, but this only made him dodge playfully and kick his hind hooves. The elk did not know how to fight.

The buffalo knew. Noomah came among the buffalo with his friends, the elk. The buffalo numbered many and made the air smell strange with dust and the scent of chewed grass. The buffalo ate much grass, and this made Noomah lay his ears back against his neck in anger. The bulls were large and quick and possessed of dangerous horns. Noomah had to dodge their heads when they came at him, but he was quicker still, and faster. Noomah liked to wander among the elk, but he did not like the buffalo. He would run at them sometimes, flailing his hooves and popping his teeth, and the cows would run and Noomah would chase them with his ears laid back and his head low. They wanted his grass. This made him angry.

One day a scent made his heart pound and his loins flare with desire. He darted across the plains until he found the scent again, and he drew much wind into his lungs, making the scent stronger. He saw the mare upon a distant hill, and charged after her. She ran. He chased her. He had seen no horses since his escape from the two-leggeds, and the sight and smell of a mare made him crave her pleasures.

The mare ran to a herd of horses, and Noomah plunged among them with violent joy and reckless cravings, until they scattered—and then he saw the two-legged. Noomah flinched as if bitten by something. He tore sod from the ground in his wild flight. He kept his distance from the two-legged, yet could not bring himself to leave the herd of mares.

For a long time, he studied the two-legged who wandered with the herd. Circling downwind, he caught the scent of the two-legged. It smelled only vaguely of meat-eater stench. This two-legged was like none Noomah had known. It moved silently, lacking the shaking-singing-rattling-squeaking sounds of the two-leggeds he had known before. The horses tolerated the two-legged, as the elk had tolerated Noomah himself. The two-legged moved among the horses even at night.

The horses remained near a place where many two-leggeds lived, but Noomah would only watch this place from a distance, for it was strange. There was much commotion at this place, and strange smells, so Noomah preferred to stay away. For days, he moved downwind of the herd, gradually easing closer, until the scent of one of the mares became so strong that Noomah could no longer stay away. He charged into the herd, identifying the mare that crazed him. He drove her away from the others, and the two-legged made no attempt to stop him. Noomah mounted the mare and felt the ecstasy he craved.

Now he wandered along the edge of the herd, watching the two-legged closely. The two-legged had hair like Noomah's mane. Hair-Like-a-Mane moved among the horses, often touching some of them. One day Noomah came very near this two-legged and heard a strange noise. It sounded as if it came from the throat of the two-legged, and Noomah tossed his head in curiosity, but Hair-Like-a-Mane would not make the sound again.

As Noomah followed, the herd led him far out into the grass where only one watering place existed within a half-day's trot. It lay in the bend of a creek, surrounded by trees. When Noomah became thirsty, he approached this place cautiously with the wind in his nostrils. The other horses were drinking there, but Noomah had learned to fear watering holes as places where meat eaters lurked. Finally satisfying himself that no danger existed at the water hole, he eased his muzzle to the water to drink. He was very thirsty, and his mouth tasted like grass. Noomah drank and drank until his belly felt heavy with water.

Then something strange happened. The two-legged, Hair-Like-a-Mane, appeared riding a horse that rose from the earth. The horse and rider came across the wind, so Noomah had not smelled them. They ran at Noomah, and he tried to flee, but his belly felt as if it would burst. The strange snakelike thing flew at him from the horse and rider and tightened around his neck, terrifying him. He fought against the noose, but Hair-Like-a-Mane slid from his pony and kept Noomah from running. He did not choke Noomah, as the other two-leggeds had done, but he made Noomah stay, and Noomah did not like it.

Noomah lunged against the rope until the sun passed over the treetops of the water hole. All the while, Hair-Like-a-Mane made strange motions. In time, Noomah learned that none of the motions would hurt him. The rope around his neck, though it tightened, never choked him. The two-legged came gradually closer, the rope getting shorter. The two-legged reached, and Noomah shied. But the two-legged reached, and reached, and reached, and finally Noomah let himself be touched.

In the days that followed, Hair-Like-a-Mane touched Noomah all over, and the touching never hurt. Noomah had grass and water. Hair-Like-a-Mane touched him even over his eyes and flanks and ears and testicles. Noomah would strike sometimes, but Hair-Like-a-Mane was wise, and never got kicked or bitten. When he struck, Noomah felt a sharp pain from the rope that now ran around his nose and behind his ears. He learned that the hands of Hair-Like-a-Mane did not hurt him, so he ceased to strike.

In time, Noomah let the two-legged come face-to-face with him. He smelled the breath of this two-legged, and felt Hair-Like-a-Mane take in his own breath. He heard the sound again—the sound that came from the throat of this two-legged. This time, he heard it quite clearly. It said, "Noo-oo-oo-ma-mah."

Something happened. Noomah did not know how to understand it, and did not try. He had become a part of Hair-Like-a-Mane, and Hair-Like-a-Mane had become a part of him.

The two-legged tied a rope to Noomah's foot and taught him not to run away. When he ran away from this wise two-legged, he would trip, so Noomah let Hair-Like-a-Mane approach him whenever he liked. Always, the hands touched him all over and scratched him in places he could not reach without a stick or rock to rub against.

One day, Hair-Like-a-Mane slipped something around Noomah's jaw. It did not hurt, and Noomah did not fight it, but while he was tasting the strange thing, Hair-Like-a-Mane swung silently onto his back. Noomah was startled, and he leapt forward, but the thing tightened around his jaw. Frightened, he tossed his head and kicked, but the two-legged stayed on his back. When he lowered his head to pitch, the thing would hurt his jaw, so Noomah learned not to pitch. He trotted around with Hair-Like-a-Mane on his back.

Now, every day, Hair-Like-a-Mane would come to untie him and ride him. They went faster and faster, and Noomah would sweat, and the sweat would make him cool. He learned to keep his head high, for the thing hurt his jaw when he lowered his head to pitch. Hair-Like-a-Mane would pull his head around to make him turn, and Noomah wanted to please his two-legged in this way, for they had become part of each other. He learned to turn when he felt reins press against his neck or Hair-Like-a-Mane's soft heels press against his ribs. He liked to see his two-legged coming, for he liked to run.

Finally, Hair-Like-a-Mane rode Noomah to a rise on the open plains. They trotted, then loped across the grass. Noomah could see a long way, which pleased him after so many days in the creek bed near the water hole. He heard the good noise of the two-legged on his back, felt the soft heels nudge his ribs. Noomah began to run. He had not run this fast in a long time. Hair-Like-a-Mane stayed with him like a part of him. Noomah ran faster. It seemed he had never run this fast.

Then, he heard something strange. It seized his heart like the jaws of a meat-eater and shot power through his massive muscles. A lion's scream and a wolf's howl and a hawk's cry had come together and burst from the throat of Hair-Like-a-Mane. Realizing this, Noomah's fear turned to sudden joy, and he felt the wind pull at his tail as his heart connected with his rider's. Never had he run this fast. The joyful sound of his two-legged made him lengthen his stride and pound the earth with his hooves. He ran faster than any horse had ever run.

Noomah loved to run.

▲▲▲▲▲
59
January, 1712
Santa Fe, New Mexico
▼▼▼▼▼

Governor Del Bosque opened the door to his *sala* and gaped in disbelief. "*Gracias a Dios!*" he said. "Juan, you look half-dead!" He stepped aside and gestured indoors.

Jean smiled as he entered with his servant. He pointed to a corner in the governor's cozy *sala*. "Throw the burden down there, Paniagua, and that will be all for the night."

The *Tiwa* servant lugged the heavy leather pack saddle pannier to the corner indicated by his employer and dropped it. Without a word, he left the *sala* and entered the night.

The governor's mouth was still open, but now he scrambled for a bottle of wine. Pouring a glass, he looked through the door Paniagua had left open, and shouted across the plaza of the *Casas Reales* toward the kitchen. "We have a guest! Bring something to eat!" He kicked the door shut to close out the evening chill and handed the glass to Jean.

"Thank you," Jean said, sitting near the fire to warm himself. He added another billet of split pine to the flames without seeking permission to do so.

"You look half-starved, my friend. Your face is drawn up like a corpse."

"It was a difficult journey."

Del Bosque glanced at the leather pannier. "That *Indio* servant—Paniagua. Do you trust him?"

"As you would trust me."

"And the bag. Full of gold?"

"Four thousand pesos to put back in the treasury. It is only the first installment. We have many good French guns to sell, my friend. The prices are high. The buyers will come to us." Jean could feel himself beginning to relax, finally, after months of hard travel, hiding, fighting, guarding his goods. He had not let his guard down, even in his sleep, until this moment.

Yet it was Del Bosque who seemed more relieved. He sat down and heaved a huge sigh. He seemed almost ready to weep. "Thank God. I thought you were dead out there. What happened?"

Jean pulled his chair close the governor's and told about Quivira, the stabbings of Night Hunter and Henri Casaubon. "It is strange, but there are rumors out on the plains. Some *Tiwas* at Tachichichi claim they have seen Henri Casaubon leading a party of raiding *Pani*."

"But, you have just told me you stabbed him to death at Quivira."

"I stabbed him good. I thought he was dead. It seems impossible, but perhaps he could have survived."

"He will be looking for you."

Jean chuckled. "I am safe in Santa Fe. If Casaubon survived my blade and desires revenge, he will have to catch me out there some other time."

Jean went on with his tale, describing the Osage battle where he recovered the governor's ill-gotten gold. "The Comanches suffered two dead, and more wounded in the fight. They refused to go on with me, and I do not hold them at fault. I gave them their share of the horses, and went on by myself after we recovered the gold from the Osage thief. I have heard that the Comanche camp on the Rio Napestle was attacked by Battle Scar's band of Apaches in Acaballo's absence. The Comanches have split over the entire escapade. Now there are two bands, and the one under Whip is raiding the settlements in the north for horses."

"Forget the Comanches," Del Bosque said. "The trade, Jean, the trade. How did you do it alone?"

"I never should have attempted it, but I thought that perhaps I could fill the void left by Casaubon before any other *courier de bois* knew he was dead. I traveled mostly at night until I reached Arkansas post, where the Rio Napestle empties into the Messipe. I traded the horses and gold for guns, along with some trade goods, iron, lead, cloth, honey, and other things. I am wanted for treason in Canada, but the potential profits resulting from a trade with New Mexico are worth more to the *couriers de bois* at Arkansas post than the price on my head."

Del Bosque nodded. "How did you get back across the plains?"

Jean shrugged. "I rode."

"You rode alone? All the way from the Messipe to the Rio Grande?"

"Not always alone. I traveled well south of the Rio Napestle to avoid the Osage and the Raccoon-Eyed People. I passed among nations I had encountered with La Salle. The *Tejas*, and the Caddoes. I even met a Frenchman whom I had known. He deserted from La Salle's expedition, many years ago. His name was Mousset, but he did not remember his name, nor me, nor even La Salle. He could not speak French."

Del Bosque frowned. "It is odd how easily white men turn heathen and forget their teachings. Did the savages trouble you?"

"I gave each chief a gun. The Caddoes guided me west of the timbers, but would go no farther for fear of Apaches. I went on from there alone. I came to the base of a great escarpment. Ascending it, I rode west across a vast plain—a high, treeless void—following a river that gradually dwindled as I went west."

"But, you had water all the way?"

"No. The river vanished in a series of draws and dry tributaries. I was completely lost, Antonio. Two of my horses died of thirst, so I had to cache the guns. I knew I had to go west to get back to New Mexico, but I also knew the rivers ran east out there in the land of the cows. So, I went north, hoping to find another stream. I was lucky. The only horse I had left survived until I reached a river I knew by its red water. I found a village of Faroan Apaches whose chief I had traded with before. I traded them six ponies for six guns."

"You only had to give them six guns? I am amazed that the Apaches did not simply kill you for all the guns, my friend."

"I was too smart for them," Jean said, motioning for the governor to fill his empty glass. "When I cached the trade goods, I hid all but six guns in a different place. The Apaches were convinced that I had only six guns. They took the guns and left me to load the other things—the lead and iron bars, the kegs of sulphur for making gun powder, the deerskins filled with honey and tallow. To further assure that they would not kill me, I promised to bring them more guns from the east on my next trip. I camped for two days to make sure they would not return, then loaded the rest of the muskets I had hidden— almost two hundred.

"After seven days, I was out of water again, but God was with me. A party of *Towa* hunters found me out on the *llano* and took me back to Pecos Pueblo. I gave them all the honey and tallow, but I had the guns wrapped in deerskin by pairs, and I convinced the *Towas* that they were stocks for shackling Apache slaves. The *Towas* approved of this idea very much. You know how they have suffered from Apache attacks lately."

"Where are the guns now?" the governor asked.

"Most of them are hidden at my *hacienda*. Some are already in El Paso del Norte. I arranged months ago for a buyer to wait for me in Santa Fe and take them south into New Spain."

"And the profits?"

Jean gulped his wine and grinned. "Sinful. We have perhaps fifteen pesos invested in each gun, so rich are the French in muskets, and hungry for gold and horses. I sold the first shipment of guns to my buyer for two hundred pesos each. He will demand twice that much in New Spain."

"*Gracias a Dios*," Del Bosque whispered. "This is a feat beyond any I have ever heard. From the Messipe to the Rio Grande. Alone, from Arkansas post to Santa Fe! It is a pity that history cannot record your adventure, my friend."

Jean chuckled. "Forget history. We are going to get rich. It is not necessary to go every year, for the inventory will sustain us through two, maybe three years. We do not want to sell our goods too quickly and draw attention to our trade, or bring the prices down. In time, we will supply good French guns to every Spanish officer and *rico* in New Spain. The Crown will benefit from its own ignorance of our secret trade. Even our own colonists will gladly pay a year's wages for the security of a good weapon. I told you long ago, Antonio, that such a trade would make us wealthy partners. New Mexico will become our kingdom."

The door opened and a girl entered with a carved wooden platter stacked with steaming tortillas, sliced goat cheese, sausages, scrambled eggs, peppers, chopped wild onions, and an *olla* filled with butter.

"Teresa!" the governor said. "Why do you behave as a servant?"

Jean stood, realizing that it was the governor's daughter who had brought the food. He had not recognized her at first, for she become a young woman since he had seen her last.

"Forgive me, Father," the girl said. "The servants have gone to bed. I saw *Señor* Archebeque arrive, and decided I should help the cook." She placed the platter in front of Jean and looked up at him. "*Señor*, you look very hungry," she said. She reached for his face and brushed her fingers across the hollowed cheeks and the tattooed chin.

"That will be enough of that," Del Bosque said. "You are too young to consort with a rogue such as the intrepid Archebeque, my dear. Now, run along and play with your dolls."

Teresa fumed and turned away, yet she paused at the door to glance over her shoulder at Jean, the dark pupils hard against the corners of her glistening eyes.

The governor clapped Jean on the shoulder and pushed him into a chair that stood in front of the food. "My daughter has no idea how much embarrassment you have saved her, Juan. Now she will live without care because of you. How will I ever repay you?"

Jean shrugged and reached for a tortilla. He had an idea of how the governor might repay him. Teresa had blossomed in the past year. Though only sixteen, she had already mastered many of the wiles of the provocative *señorita*. Strange to think of it, Jean mused, imagining himself paying court to the governor's young daughter. He had come to this colony a penniless, tattooed traitor. Once, an audience with the governor would have struck fear through his heart. Now, the governor came to him for help in his hour of darkest need.

Perhaps it was only the fact that he had not lain with a woman in months that made his flesh prickle with desire for young Teresa, who was, after all, more than twenty years his junior. Perhaps tomorrow, as he woke in the arms of his favorite harlot, who even now waited for him across the Santa Fe plaza, he would cast off even the most cursory thought of the virginal Teresa. Perhaps.

Still, the image of himself with the *señorita* hinted at certain advantages beyond the possibilities of conjugal pleasure. Across the plains, he might be hanged as a traitor. Here, he was a hero of the colony for defying the edicts of the very crown under whose flag he flourished. The governor poured wine for him. The governor's daughter made eyes at him. Perhaps Jean L'Arch-eveque was, as Horseback had lamented, a man without a nation. On the other hand, he was, perhaps, a nation unto himself, chief among chieftains, the Sovereign of the Southern Plains.

▲▲▲▲▲
60
▼▼▼▼▼

Shaggy Hump's lodge felt cold when he woke before dawn. His heart pounded a hoofbeat in his chest, and sweat covered his body. His breath came like that of a man in battle, rather than a man sleeping peacefully in his lodge. The moon had passed over the mountains, and the lodge was dark as the den of a great bear. For a moment, Shaggy Hump wondered where he lay. Was this the land of humans, or the Land of Shadows? Then he tossed the robe aside and let the cold, dry air of the plains night chill the sweat on his body.

He was alone. Looks Away had slept in her own lodge since River Woman's death, so that Shaggy Hump might concentrate on his grief. Now, he thought of River Woman as though she lay nearby, as she had done many winters ago, in the days before the demons possessed her. "My sits-beside wife," Shaggy Hump said under his breath, thinking of River Woman as she had been in those times of youth. It seemed as if the memories had been made yesterday.

River Woman, do you bear these glorious and terrible dreams I have dreamt? Do you call to me from the Shadow Land? Have you opened the way to the time that comes? I am a warrior. I have lived well. I am ready. I will die bravely.

He lay still for a while, and young River Woman faded farther from his thoughts. For many winters she had served him, aggravated him, amazed him, confused him. Now she was gone. She had possessed mysterious powers. He would not disappoint her. He knew what he must do.

As he listened to the wind fret the smoke flaps above, he began to feel very alone. He groped for the rawhide strap that ran from his lodge to Looks Away's. He found it tied to the lower end of a lodge pole. He pulled on it sharply several times, and faintly heard the noise of the rattles made from deer dewclaws in Looks Away's lodge. She took only a few moments to enter his lodge. She was a good wife. Obedient and willing. She knelt beside him.

"Lie with me," he said.

She pulled her deerskin dress off over her head and lay down next to her husband, gasping when she felt his sweat-soaked body. "My husband," she said, "are you well?"

"Very well. Better than well. I have been dreaming." He pulled the robe back over him, and even this felt clammy with his own sweat. When he felt Looks Away reach between his legs, he caught her hand, and said, "Just lie with me, woman. Make me warm."

"*Hah*," she said, snuggling close to him. "What have you been dreaming about?"

"Times to come." He said nothing for a while. Owls were hooting to each other in the night. "My son's warhorse is beautiful, is it not?"

"*Hah*."

"He knew Medicine-Coat would come. He has good, strong *puha*. Sometimes the spirits tell a good warrior what will happen, so the warrior will know what to do."

Looks Away said nothing. She always listened well and spoke little.

"There is going to be a council. You know our duty is to avenge our dead."

"*Hah*," she said.

"I have dreamed of this vengeance. I am ready. My son has dreamed of a war pony. Medicine-Coat has come. My son is ready. The people in this camp believe in my son again. When Medicine-Coat came, they gasped at the beauty of such a pony."

"That is a beautiful pony," said Looks Away, who rarely spoke in judgement of anything, good or bad. "A spirit-pony."

"You speak well, my wife. Now, listen. I am a warrior. My scars make my medicine coat. I do not wish to die an old man, making arrows and telling stories in the lodges of winter. I do not wish to burden my grandchildren."

"You are strong," she said, gripping his arm. "You will burden no one for many winters to come."

"Listen. I have dreamt. The war with the *Na-vohnuh* comes. I wish to die in battle. My brothers have all gone before me. You will be alone."

She nestled closer to him. "Do not speak of it," she begged.

"Listen, woman. The old ways are changing. Once, a wife would follow her husband to the Shadow Land. She would kill herself over his grave, or the people would kill her. But that was in the old country of poor lands, where a woman could not live alone, or expect another man to take her as a second wife. Here it is different. A man should have many wives. A warrior should wait for his wife in the Shadow Land. She will come along in good time. I will speak of this in council under the sun that comes now beyond the eastern plains. The people will know. When I am dead, you will live. You were born to the *Yuta* people, when the True Humans made war upon the *Yutas*. Now everything has changed. We are at peace with the *Yutas*. When I am gone, you may return to your old people if you wish. Your brother, Bad Camper, will take you into his camp."

"My brother?" she said.

"Yes. I know. I have known for a long time. My sits-beside wife told me. She knew things. When I am gone, you will not be killed over my grave. You may return to the *Yutas* if you wish."

Looks Away lay beside Shaggy Hump a long time in silence. Finally, she spoke, her voice steady and low. "I will stay with the Horseback People. I love my son, Horseback, very much. He is not of my blood, but he is my son. If you die in battle, my husband, I will remain a True Human."

Shaggy Hump rolled toward her and threw his leg over her. Her warmth had beaten the chill of the sweat that had covered him. "You are good, my wife. You are better than good. Now, I am going to sleep beside you. Wake me when the sun comes."

· · · ·

A lively council convened under the following sun. Shaggy Hump spoke first, for he was the elder in the camp of the Horseback People. He told the tales of his exploits in battle, the scalps he had taken, the battle strokes he had counted, the ponies he had stolen. He had survived many raids. He spoke a long time. He said nothing of days to come, except for a vehement insistence that wives should no longer die over the graves of slain husbands.

"No woman is a burden in this land of buffalo," he insisted. "Here, a man needs many women to cure the hides of the animals he kills. If a warrior dies, another must take his widow. I have spoken."

Other seasoned warriors followed Shaggy Hump, relating tales of their many victories. Bear Heart repeated the story of the first visit to the land of the Metal Men and of the return of all five searchers under the leadership of Horseback.

Finally, Horseback's time came to speak, and he rose. Just then, a raven called overhead. It circled the camp and flew to the southeast. Through the southeast side of the council lodge, which had been left uncovered to catch the southern breeze, Horseback watched the raven in silence until it disappeared in the distant sky. Then, he began to speak.

"The time comes for every True Human to decide. Will you live and die in the new country of the buffalo and the pony, or will you go back to the old *Noomah* ways in the land of stinging snow? There the True Humans must hoard pine nuts and pemmican or starve through the cold moons. Here we will hunt buffalo and grow fat, even through the snows of winter. In the old country, the cold days before the moons of spring were called the Time When

Babies Cry for Food. Here, there will be no such time. Here, there is tallow, and meat, and marrow, and pemmican, and fresh brains, and liver, and paunches to cook in, even through the Moon of the Snowblind.

"When I was a boy, our camp lived in terror of attack from the Northern Raiders, and Crow, and Flathead, and *Yuta*. Now the Northern Raiders and Crow and Flathead fear our horse power, and we are far away from their camps where they could not harm us even if they had the courage. The *Yutas* make peace with us, for they know we are powerful.

"The Metal Men do not matter. Only their soldiers fight, and they have few. The Wolf People, and the Osage, and the Raccoon-Eyed People are far away. They will seldom bother us. The *Tiwas* at Tachichichi live under a truce. They attack no one.

"Our true enemies now are *Na-vohnuh*. They have attacked our camp to remind us that we must avenge our ancestors. The *Na-vohnuh* do not know how to ride. They get off their ponies to fight. In the winter they follow the buffalo, but we will find them, take their scalps and ponies, and avenge our dead. In the spring they will go back to their villages. They will be easy to find then. We will hunt buffalo and attack the *Na-vohnuh* camps. They have many more warriors than we have, yet new Horseback People come with every moon from the old country. Our enemies do not know how to possess the power of ponies, as we do. Our enemies do not have the protection of powerful spirits. Yet, the war will last many winters, for our enemies number like pebbles in a riverbed. Our young braves will learn to fight and win glory. When it is over, the land of buffalo will be ours.

"The spirits have summoned us to this good place to bring a nation out of the mist. Yet, they do not give us this land. The spirits say we must avenge our ancestors. We must destroy our ancient enemies. We must *win* the good land. We must *conquer* our new country. Upon all the earth, no land is better. There is much meat. Much meat! Plenty of humps and ribs and backstraps and briskets.

"I have waited for my war pony, and he has come. I will ride Medicine-Coat south and east, the way the raven flies. I will find buffalo to hunt. I will find enemy camps to plunder. I will weave a kingfisher feather into the mane of my pony, and his wounds will heal like the water. When I die, I will die astride my war pony. I am Horseback. I have spoken."

No one spoke against Horseback. Those who did not believe in his power had already gone away with Whip's people. The council agreed to the last man to move into the land of buffalo and seek the *Na-vohnuh* war. The women began to pack things into parfleche bags. With dawn, they would take the lodges down and move.

As the light faded behind the mountains, a large cloud of dust rose in the west. The Horseback People took up weapons and waited, fearing a *Na-vohnuh* attack. Horseback went to scout and came riding back into camp on Medi-cine-Coat.

"The *Yutas!*" he cried. "Our allies! Bad Camper comes with fifty warriors! They come to fight the *Na-vohnuh!*" He galloped all through his camp, shout-ing the news with joy. He saw Looks Away and rode to her, bending low on his pony to speak softly. "Your brother," he said. "Bad Camper comes to fight with us."

The Horseback People cooked all the meat in the camp that night, for they expected to kill many buffalo on the war path. Men, women, and chil-dren feasted until none could swallow another bite.

Speaks Twice came from Tachichichi. He had been summoned by a rider and invited to go with the Comanches. "I will go with you to make talk with your enemies, but I will not fight those you call *Na-vohnuh*. The elders in my *kiva* at Tachichichi forbid it."

Horseback nodded. "Come make talk with us. You will teach me more of the Spanish. No one must fight unless his own spirits tell him to fight."

▲▲▲▲▲
61
▼▼▼▼▼

They began to move southward the next day, Horseback leading on his war pony. He rode east of the Breasts of Mother Earth. From that point, he could see the peaks the Metal Men called the Rat Mountains. One peak had a flat-topped summit that from a distance looked like a *Tiwa* house. This summit overlooked the pass through the Rat Mountains.

Negotiating the pass the next day, Horseback saw a deer sign, and had to ride his war pony carefully for fear of angering his spirit-guide. Yet, he remembered what his father had said. It was not enough to honor Sound-the-Sun-Makes in the sight of men; he must serve his guardian in his heart above all else.

He was relieved to put the deer trails of the Rat Mountains behind him, for over the peaks a beautiful grass-covered valley snaked away to the south-east. Here, antelope darted ahead of the war party, elk loped, and the bulls had rubbed the thin fuzzy skin from antlers that now glinted in the sun. The pole-drags moved easily through this valley, and the Comanches could see the marks of previous pony-drags and dog-drags, surely made by parties of their enemies.

The Rat Mountains dwindled along their left flank after two days of easy moving while, to their right, a few hills rose. Between the hills, Horseback looked across grassy plains that went on to the sky.

On the third day, the Rat Mountains shrank into a series of bluffs. Now

Horseback rode toward a lone mountain on the southeastern horizon, five times as wide as it was high. Horseback named it Five Sleeps, for he arrived there on the fifth day of his journey.

Camping at the base of Five Sleeps, the scouts spotted a few buffalo beyond it. A mounted hunting party eased through the timber that grew on the north face of the wide mountain and charged the buffalo. Horseback rode Medicine-Coat on his war pony's first hunt, expecting his pony would fear the buffalo. To his surprise, Medicine-Coat seemed to crave battle with the horned four-leggeds. He swooped down on them like a coyote after a rabbit, carrying Horseback close enough to shoot an arrow into a large cow, hitting her behind the ribs. When she turned to fight, Medicine-Coat dodged her horns so quickly that Horseback had to grab the pony's mane to stay mounted. The spirits had taught Medicine-Coat how to hunt, giving him courage as well as speed.

Beyond Five Sleeps, another mountain stood on the southeast horizon, even broader than the last mountain. Horseback named it Seven Sleeps. From the slopes of this mountain small herds of buffalo could be seen across the plains and in the valley, which had grown ever broader and more grassy.

The only landmark that stood on the trail ahead now was a double peak that Horseback named Rabbit Ears Mountain, for its twin summits looked like the tips of rabbit ears standing above the grass. All along the trail to Rabbit Ears Mountain, shallow lakes formed at intervals in the valley. Even when the valley began to rise to blend with the plains, the lakes continued to provide water for the ponies and the Horseback People.

On the eighth day of the journey, the True Humans camped at one of these lakes. From this camp, Horseback and several other warriors rode to the flanks of Rabbit Ears Mountain. Upon its slopes they looked toward the southeast, where they expected to encounter enemies and buffalo to kill. They saw no more hills or mountains to guide them. They would have to ride across plains that stretched without end, to the edge of the earth.

"I see a shadow in the sky," Shaggy Hump said.

Horseback looked. The shadow was like a ghost. "*Hah.* What is it?"

"Perhaps the dust of a great herd. Perhaps a flock of ravens and vultures. Perhaps both."

"We will hunt buffalo."

"*Hah.*"

Every day, while the camp moved, scouts rode out in all directions, looking for trails, tracks, signs of game or enemies. Horseback always scouted ahead. On the second day after Rabbit Ears Mountain, he began to see buffalo. He rode into a dry stream bed that would get him closer to the herd so he could judge its number. He saw hopeful signs of a large herd, for wolves prowled everywhere, and many birds circled overhead.

Finally, he rode out of the dry stream bed, to a nearby divide. From there, he knew he would be able to see far across the plains. A few buffalo saw him coming from a distance and trotted away. He did not chase them, for he did not want to alarm the herd. He passed over the divide cautiously, watching carefully, leaning over Medicine-Coat's withers to look like a buffalo.

He made his pony walk as the plains beyond the ridge gradually rose into view. He saw the far prairies first, those near the horizon, and the sight was odd, for the distant parks seemed covered with some strange kind of thick black brush. Then the nearer rolls of the earth fell under his gaze, and Horseback saw that this black brush moved. It lived. It roiled like a reflection of dark clouds that covered half the sky. His breath caught in his lungs, and he tasted dust in his mouth. The sight at once enthralled and terrified him. Not even through the mist of his visions had he seen anything like this.

He wheeled Medicine-Coat and ran his pony all the way back to this band of people, his mouth open, and his eyes wide with wonder. When he approached his band, he waved, and three men rode ahead to meet him. They were Shaggy Hump, Bear Heart, and Speaks Twice.

"What have you found?" Bear Heart asked.

"Buffalo."

"How many?"

Horseback tried to imagine how he would answer. "You will not believe me."

Shaggy Hump smiled. "Tell us. How many?"

Horseback slipped down from his pony. He found a bare spot on the ground and scratched a circle in the earth with his quirt. "My lodge is a circle." He placed a rock in the center of the circle. "I stand in the center of my lodge, here. Now, I throw thick, hairy buffalo robes all over the half of my lodge to the east, and the robes cover the ground."

"*Hah*," said Speaks Twice, practicing his *Noomah* tongue. He smiled, realizing that Horseback had found something these Comanches had never seen. "The robes cover half your lodge."

Horseback nodded. "The sky and the earth meet in a great circle, like ground under a lodge for the spirits. How wide is the circle of the sky, my friends?"

"Three sleeps," Bear Heart said.

"Four," Shaggy Hump countered. "We ride well, but the circle of earth meeting sky is great."

"Perhaps four sleeps," Horseback agreed. "I came over a ridge, not far from here, and I saw half of the great circle of sky meeting earth, covered with buffalo. Nothing but buffalo."

The men stood in silence for a moment, trying to envision such a sight.

"Many small herds, scattered?" said Bear Heart.

"No. You do not understand. They cover the ground like the robes cover the ground under my lodge. It is one herd. The buffalo are thick as bees in a hollow tree. When I saw it the first time, at a great distance, I thought it was some kind of black brush growing like sage in the old country." He looked at the blank stares of the men. "As I said, you do not believe me."

"It is true," Speaks Twice said. "I have seen such herds. They may go on for five sleeps, even six or seven sleeps."

"Then I must see it," Bear Heart said.

"*Hah*," said Horseback. "We will all see it. Now, listen, my friends. Do not tell the other men what I have found. Only the four of us will know. I know a good way to show the others."

The next day, Horseback led many Comanche and *Yuta* warriors to the southeast before dawn. It was a cloudy morning, and in the dark the hunters could not see the dust in the sky. At sunrise, Horseback led the men into a deep draw that ran north and south.

"Stay in this draw, each of you an arrow shot away from the next. I will ride to the east with seven swift riders. We will chase the buffalo into this draw, where the killing will be good."

The hunters agreed, spreading out along the length of the draw. Horseback rode down the draw into the breaks of a big valley. He and his riders leaned over the necks of their mounts to keep from startling the buffalo that filled the valley.

"I have never seen so many buffalo," Shaggy Hump said. "I never knew there were so many on all the earth."

"Wait," Horseback said, smiling. "More stand on the flat lands above this valley. The eyes of those hunters we left in the draw are going to look like the eyes of rabbits caught in a snare when they see the buffalo pouring down on them like the waters of a flooding river."

Coming over the rise of the riverbank, the riders found the buffalo so numerous that they could not even see the ground. Horseback gave his riders a few moments to marvel at the sight, then led a charge into the herd. Medicine-Coat popped his teeth at the cows and calves and they parted, many of them running away to the east, many others running to the west, toward the hunters waiting in the draw. A great rumble of hooves rose into the air, and seemed to make the very earth shake like the surface of a drum. The riders turned in pursuit of the beasts that ran west.

Horseback looked for the finest cows and yearling calves, and Medicine-Coat could sense which animal he wished to close in on. He used his arrows sparingly, killing three buffalo with three arrows. Now he had a robe for each wife to cure, so he angled Medicine-Coat to the south and loosed a battle cry that made his pony burst forward with unbelievable speed. The beautiful pony's head lunged forward with every stride, and his mane rose like the flames of a sacred fire.

As he left the other riders behind, Horseback could see the breaks of the draw where the hunters waited ahead. He had ridden fast enough to see the first buffalo plunge into the draw. In an instant, he saw his fellow warriors fleeing up the east side of the draw before the onslaught of stampeding beasts.

Horseback laughed, and his laughter made Medicine-Coat dart to one side and kick a hind hoof joyfully. The hunters looked like timid rabbits running from coyotes. Now every man who had called him elder sister while he lay wounded would know that he had heard and remembered, and if one let a buffalo catch him and tear the guts from his mount and stomp scars all across his back, he would have no cause to whimper, for a Comanche hunter-warrior must pursue such danger. If he did not, he would not last long with Horseback's band of True Humans.

. . . .

Two days later, the Horseback People made a camp beside a spring of fresh water near a river that ran red. While the women worked on hides and dried meat, Horseback explored farther to the south. Coming out of the breaks of the river he called Red Water, he found himself on a land so flat and treeless that a man could see a day's ride ahead of him, just sitting astraddle of his pony. It was a fearful thing to look at. Even the peaks of Rabbit Ears Mountain had faded far to the northwest, and there was nothing to use as a landmark. Only in his visions had Horseback seen such a land. So flat. So treeless. So covered with good, sweet grass. To wander out upon this land would be dangerous, for water was scarce. Exploration of this country would have to be done gradually. He would watch for flights of birds to find water. He would make maps and remember them. In time, he would know the way to cross that land. From stream to stream. Lake to lake. Spring to spring. It was a land worth mastering, for it teemed with enough buffalo to feed the largest of nations.

But for now, Horseback would hold to the breaks of this valley of the Red Water. There were good springs along this valley. This was the country of the Na-vohnuh. He would encounter his enemies here. He went back to his camp and sent scouts upstream and down. He hoped to find the village of the chief called Battle Scar. There was vengeance to exact which would lead to war. His people were ready to fight.

After seven days of searching, Bear Heart returned to the camp on Red Water. "I have found the village of Battle Scar's people," he said.

"Did you see Battle Scar?"

"Yes. I crept into the village at night. I saw him go into his filthy little lodge. I did not leave any trace behind me. I stole no horses, though I could have taken them all. I did not want his people to know about us here. They will be surprised. They are harvesting their fields by day, dancing by night. They know nothing of our camp."

"How far?" Horseback said.

"Four sleeps downstream."

Horseback smiled. "Let us call our warriors together in council. Let us feast and dance. Let us paint our faces and our ponies, and weave sacred feathers into their tails and manes. It is good to hunt here in this country. It is better to make war."

62

Shaggy Hump reined in his pony and raised his hand, which was barely seen in the pale light before dawn. The other riders stopped behind him. He slid from the bare back of his warhorse, and all his tools of battle went with him as his moccasins hit the ground—his *pogamoggan*, fitted now with an iron point jutting from one side of the club head; his shield painted like the sun, with a stuffed roadrunner *puhahante* tied to the center; his quiver and bow case slung across his back, holding his best bow and twenty good arrows with barbed war points his enemies would not be able to pull out.

He looked back at the faces of the warriors who had agreed to come on this vengeance raid—seventy-two Comanche and *Yuta* fighting men, anxious to kill or die. Their faces looked good all painted with streaks and slashes of black, red, and yellow. As he dropped his reins and walked away from his war pony, he pulled at the strap of his new deerskin sash, the long tail of which was now rolled under his right arm.

Pulling his loin skins aside, Shaggy Hump lifted one leg and urinated on the daggerlike points of a yucca plant, imitating the posture of a male dog marking his domain. This would amuse his fellow warriors, and remind them of his speech. In council, under yesterday's sun, Shaggy Hump had made a long and stirring oration, announcing finally that his dreams had instructed him to start a new warrior society among the Horseback People. The members of the military order would be called the Crazy-Dogs-Wishing-to-Die. He had heard of this society among his old enemies, the Crow, and had long admired the idea. The Crazy-Dogs-Wishing-to-Die would be older warriors, with much experience. In a fight, they would plunge recklessly into battle, then guard the retreat of their war party. They would be known by a long deerskin sash that they would use in guarding the retreat. When unrolled, the sash would drag the ground, and come equipped with an arrow for pinning it to the earth. They would not tie their penises to the ground like Wolf People warriors. They were not that crazy. But each Crazy-Dog would stand his ground against any number of enemy pursuers until a fellow member of the society pulled his arrow from his sash, releasing him. Otherwise he would die staked to his ground. Only another Crazy-Dog-Wishing-to-Die could release a member of the order from the ground he had claimed.

Shaggy Hump knew that his son did not like this idea. It meant that those who guarded the retreat would have to dismount to stake themselves to the ground and give up the power of their ponies. But Horseback was young yet, and did not understand. These Crazy-Dogs-Wishing-to-Die were old veterans. They did not wish to turn gray and grow weak. They wished to die in battle. His dreams had told him to go to war this way. It was good.

He adjusted his medicine bundle next to his penis as he pulled his loin skins up tight between his legs. With the eyes of the younger warriors on him, he swung a leg over his pony's back. It was hard to mount this way at his age, and he remembered how swiftly and smoothly he had once horsed himself, in the old days, when the pony was a new thing sent by the spirits. He drew his bow from the case and strung it.

The enemy village lay around a bend in the valley. Without looking behind him, Shaggy Hump could hear his fellow warriors preparing for the attack. A few of the *Yutas* had guns which caused much clicking and rattling as their owners prepared them to fire. Some men sang softly, bolstering their courage with spirit-music. The ponies could sense the coming of the battle. They snorted and stomped. But Shaggy Hump's eyes remained fixed on the bend in the valley. He realized now that he had seen this place in his dreams— hazy and dim, as it appeared here before sunrise. Bear Heart came to his side, he too wearing the sash of a Crazy-Dog-Wishing-to-Die, the tail of the sash rolled neatly under his right arm.

Then Horseback rode up from the rear, his magnificent spirit-pony tossing its head and rolling its eyes as it pranced. The black and white patches of its handsome coat came together like light against shadows. Horseback's war paint was red on one half of his face, black on the other, running together in a lightning-bolt jag. His chest was marked with a black set of antlers in homage to his spirit-protector and with red crosses that enumerated his kills and battle strokes. Shaggy Hump smiled. Only the spirits could match such a pony with such a rider.

"Hear me," Horseback said. "Our ancient enemies wait around the bend in this valley. They have danced around the scalps of our people. But under the sun which now rises, they will see a new nation ride from the mist. This is not a day to count battle strokes, but to take scalps. We will kill many warriors. We will take women and children for the *rescate* of the Metal Men. We will take all their horses and leave them wailing afoot. Our wounds will heal like the waters."

Shaggy Hump watched his son turn into the valley, and he followed quickly. They held their ponies to a walk until the first lodges of the *Na- vohnuh* came into view. Suddenly, Medicine-Coat leapt forward in a huge bound, and Shaggy Hump felt his heart pound as strength shot all through his body, as if he were a young man again. He followed his son in the charge as hooves rumbled suddenly like thunder.

The *Na-vohnuh* women were just coming out into the bean fields, and they dropped their baskets and trilled a warning back to their village. Now Shaggy Hump felt his war cry burst from his lungs, a scream of some eagle spirit sent to make him powerful in this, his last battle. In a few long strides he, his son, and Bear Heart, had overtaken the fleeing women and charged into the camp to look for warriors.

A man stepped from one of the red-and-white lodges of the enemy. He looked small to Shaggy Hump. He tried to avoid the blow, but Shaggy Hump's *pogamoggan* slammed against his head, the iron point splitting the skull, killing the man as surely as if a great killer stallion had kicked him viciously with a hard hind hoof.

As he rode on by, the iron point of his club head lodged in the skull of the man, and its handle pulled from his hand, the leather wrist strap snapping as it almost yanked him from his mount.

The loss of the weapon made no difference to Shaggy Hump. His bow was ready. He reached for his quiver, all the while galloping through the camp, trusting his pony to choose the way. Halfway through the *Na-vohnuh* village, with screams and battle cries and gunshots mingling behind him, Shaggy Hump peeled away to his right, and those behind him began to swarm like bees. He circled, then reined his pony in. He notched an arrow, drew the bow, found an enemy target, saw his arrow sink into the *Na-vohnuh's* bare chest. He drew another arrow. Made another kill. Horsemen were leaping everywhere before him, dodging and pursuing. Ponies reared and fought the enemies with flailing hooves, the ancient hatreds flowing from the hearts of their riders into their great masses of powerful muscle.

A warrior ran at him with a lance, but Shaggy Hump notched his next arrow with patience. He drew his bowstring as the man threw his lance. He released his arrow, saw it pierce the stomach of the enemy. The enemy spear glanced off the top of Shaggy Hump's shield and struck him in the jaw. Pain shot through his neck and body as hot blood gushed down his chest. He reached for another arrow. His scream rattled with blood that ran down his windpipe, and he knew the lance had wounded him badly. He felt the twitching of severed muscles along the side of his face.

Now, Shaggy Hump felt the recklessness of a Crazy-Dog consume him. It fed on his searing pain, and he charged into the village. He saw Horseback gallop by on Medicine-Coat. He recognized the *Yuta* chief, Bad Camper, clubbing some enemy warrior to the ground. A round of *Na-vohnuh* gunshots began to fire, and one *Yuta* warrior fell from his pony. Another riderless horse thundered by, wild-eyed. The swarm of battle engulfed him as he charged toward the river. Through the dust, he caught a glimpse of the enemy horse herd running across the valley, and knew the Horseback People would have plenty of ponies to ride.

He drew his bow, made a kill. Drew again. Wounded another. A searing pain raked across his back, but when he wheeled, no one stood near enough to have struck him. His fellow horsemen leaped all through the village. Enemy women and children ran and crawled. Blood shot from one man's neck in a stream as he stood, wobbling, singing his death song.

Wheeling again, Shaggy Hump shot another arrow, but missed a man who ducked behind a hide lodge. He saw a young Comanche on his pony, blood covering his hands and face, his eyes wide with terror. The young man was drawing his bow again and again, letting his bowstring go without notching the arrows that waited in his quiver. Shaggy Hump rode to him and tried to speak, but his own jaw would not work, and he only felt blood come out of his mouth. The young warrior looked at him with terror in his eyes, then a wound from an enemy Fire Stick tore his chest open.

Shaggy Hump grabbed the wounded warrior before he could fall from his pony and pulled the boy across his thighs. The boy was already dead, but Shaggy Hump would not leave him to be mutilated by the enemy. As he turned for the valley rim, he looked for enemies to shoot, and took in the glory of the plundered village. He saw *Yutas* and Comanches carrying children and women away. Dead enemy men lay everywhere. Moaning and wailing rose around him.

And Shaggy Hump knew this was only the beginning. The war would drag on. He did not pity the *Na-vohnuh*, for they deserved this. Always it had been told how the horrible ones had tried to rub out the whole *Noomah* nation in the ancient war, but now it was different. Now the True Humans possessed the power of the horse. Not just the power of this animal's speed and strength, but the spirit-magic sent to the *Noomah* in the form of ponies. And his own son, Horseback, was the prophet of all this pony medicine. Shaggy Hump was only now fully realizing this truth as he felt life slipping away from him in the midst of his final fight. Now a new generation of *Noomah* warriors would repeat this horseback raid time and again as village after village of *Na-vohnuh* fell to the great spirit-powers of a new nation. It was good. Glory would rain upon the people like a thunder burst.

The time to retreat had come, and all the horsemen began moving back up the valley, some driving the stolen ponies of the enemy, some struggling with women or children who kicked and screamed against the terrors of captivity, some carrying dead or wounded friends. Shaggy Hump felt weak and dizzy. Looking down, he saw his own blood running over the dead boy he carried, all the way to the tips of his own moccasins, where it dripped off, dotting the ground with a trail.

He came across Bad Camper—the brother of his wife, Looks Away—the *Yuta* warrior he had once waged war against. He could not speak, for he was swallowing his own blood to keep from choking, but he reached for Bad Camper and made signs telling him to take the dead boy who lay across his thighs.

Bad Camper took the corpse, his face grim. He made signs with his right hand: "*You fight well, Snake man.*"

They were at the edge of the enemy village now. The attacking warriors were still trying to gather dead and wounded, for no one would be left behind. Men who had been unhorsed were trying to fight their way out. Here, where the bean fields met the village, the survivors gathered for a mass retreat. Shaggy Hump slipped down from his pony, letting the animal go. He staggered to the edge of the bean field, feeling tired. He prayed for power: one last burst of courage and strength. He placed himself between his own men and the enemy village. He untied his new deerskin sash and cast it with a flourish upon the ground ahead of him. He dropped to one knee, pulled an arrow from his quiver, and stabbed it through the golden deerskin that was now stained with blood. He drove the arrow into the ground with all the strength he could gather, making a ceremony of it. He thought he heard the bellow of a buffalo bull echo through the valley as he drove the stake home. He rose to his feet and looked toward the village.

The last of his warriors were fighting their way out, some dragging friends who could not walk. Behind them came angry *Na-vohnuh* warriors possessed by the reckless fury of men who have seen wives and children carried away. Shaggy Hump found one of these horrible enemy warriors in the strange blur that had begun to fall upon his world, making the moment feel like a nightmare. He had dreamt of this moment. Laboriously, he drew his bow and shot the warrior through. He reached for his quiver, but felt no arrows left jutting from it.

Battling the pain of his face wound and the dizziness that gathered around him, Shaggy Hump swallowed another gulp of his own blood and drew his knife. He saw Horseback and Trotter—his son and his son-in-law—darting into the village, guarding the retreat in their own way, on nimble war ponies. Horseback had four arrows sticking out of his shield. The pride he felt in these young men made Shaggy Hump stand straight and shake the fatigue from his head. He saw enemy warriors break through the rear guard of ponies. They were misty. They moved like dream people. One came ahead of the others. He was older than the rest. He carried a hatchet with an iron head. Shaggy Hump saw his face, recognized him. It was Battle Scar, the worst warrior chief of the whole *Na-vohnuh* nation. He saw the ugly scar across the enemy chief's belly where his daughter-in-law, Teal, had raked her arrow point.

He stepped forward until he felt the sash of the Crazy-Dogs tugging the earth behind him. Battle Scar was running at him. Shaggy Hump called upon his faithful spirit-guides, knowing they offered him no protection, only courage. He forced himself to sing, sending an eerie death song into the air on a spray of blood. Battle Scar came at him like a wolf, fangs bared. Shaggy Hump struck with his knife, but he was weak and Battle Scar was good at fighting. The hatchet hit him on the chest and shoulder, ripped flesh and crushed bones. Shaggy Hump felt the ground slam against his back. Even now, his pain was fading, but he dared not slip away. Horses leapt over him. Something grabbed his hair and he slashed wildly with his knife, mustering every morsel of energy left to him. He kicked and thrust his blade. He would fight to the last breath. He heard the victory cries as the retreat began.

He heard Bear Heart's voice: "I have pulled the stake from the ground for you, Shaggy Hump! Do not cut me as I carry you away."

Shaggy Hump let his knife fall away, somewhere far away. He felt himself lifted. His pain melted like snow under the first warm sun of spring. He heard Horseback:

"Carry my father ahead of me!"

A river of blood flooded into his lungs, and Shaggy Hump felt cool. There was a sudden chill in the air, yet he was too weak to shiver. He saw the bright light of the sun burst into the valley as he floated up. Everything was cold. Everything except the warmth of the pony across which he lay. This was a spirit-pony. Shaggy Hump made himself feel the heart of this animal as he had learned to do in his dreams. He felt warmer. He rose higher. It was good. Everything was good. Better than good. He heard the songs of happy people, songs of feasting, songs of joy. He heard laughter. His spirit-pony bore him away on the warm light of the sun, and Shaggy Hump heard the songs River Woman had sung in the old days. She was young again, and so was he.

63

In the seasons that followed the death of Horseback's father, the *Na-vohnuh* war swelled like a great thundercloud that blossomed in the sky and blotted out the sun. Blood ran like the waters of a rainstorm, and with it the powers of the *Na-vohnuh* slowly leached away to someplace dark and cold.

True Humans continued to come down from the old country. In addition to Horseback's camp, and Whip's people, bands of Comanches emerged with names like the Wanderers, the Antelope People, the Buffalo Eaters, and the Honey Eaters. They came to fight *Na-vohnuh*, and hunt buffalo, and ride horses, and take wives, and trade.

The *Na-vohnuh* villages proved easy to plunder, for they did not understand the power of the horse. They could not fathom how much distance a Comanche war party could cover in one night, and so the horse-warriors would appear without warning when *Na-vohnuh* scouts had found no sign of them anywhere near their villages the day before. When a fight came, the *Na-vohnuh* would stand on the ground to do battle, even if they had ridden to the battleground. They did not understand how to use the war power of a pony. Even if they had, they would not have ridden with the skill of the Comanches.

The *Na-vohnuh* lived along rivers in settled villages throughout the growing season, tending their fields of beans, squash, corn, and pumpkins. Because of this, they were easy to find in large numbers. They became suppliers of ponies for the Comanches. Sometimes Horseback would pass up the chance to raid a *Na-vohnuh* village, saying, "Let us wait until their colts are stronger. Now they are too small to keep up with our retreat."

The Comanches followed herds of buffalo, always moving, hunting, fighting, riding, camping. Some Comanche warriors spent more time on their ponies than off. Some would eat their meals astride their horses, drink by riding their ponies into a stream so they wouldn't have to dismount. Some would not even get down to urinate. Some warriors had their wives build lodges to keep their best hunting ponies and war ponies out of the rain, snow, and hail. Some could sleep astride their ponies. Others coupled with their women on horseback, hoping the children so conceived would know the skill of spirit-riders.

Horseback himself was the most renowned of these such warriors, and he was spoken of throughout the whole nation for his courage, generosity, wisdom, spirit-power, and skill on the back of a pony. His band grew larger than any other, and moved more to keep its huge herd of ponies fed. The herd numbered no fewer than one thousand, and sometimes twice that, as each warrior possessed at least six ponies. Some owned many more. Horseback himself claimed over two hundred, though he gave ponies like other men gave counsel.

His war pony, Medicine-Coat, was the reason for his horse wealth. No matter how many ponies he gave away, his spirit-pony would win more in the horse races that always went along with the great camp-togethers of the True Humans. As a racer, Medicine-Coat was never beaten, nor even seriously challenged. The likes of his speed and strength were beheld in no other pony on earth, for Medicine-Coat had the blood of spirits coursing through his veins. He bred many mares, and the Horseback People were known to possess the finest ponies on the plains because of Medicine-Coat's blood. Many of his foals wore the coat of light and shadows, yet none was quite as beautiful as its father.

As a war pony Medicine-Coat had proven invincible. Bullets went around his magical coat of darkness and light. Arrow and lance wounds closed up like waters behind a kingfisher. As the war dragged on, Medicine-Coat's hide became as a map of many battlefields, and Horseback could stand by his side and point to scars and match them with scars on his own skin, and give the accounts of the making of the wounds. Men would gather around him to hear the tales of his many battle strokes as he fattened Medicine-Coat on bark stripped from *sohoobi* trees.

"See this scar that my wife has tattooed on my thigh," he would say, holding the flap of his loin skins aside to reveal the old wound. "I won this scar in the fight against Battle Scar's people on Red Water. The arrow went through my thigh and into my pony." Here, he would point to the hairless welt on Medicine-Coat's hide. "We have both healed, but the arrow point is still inside my war pony. It does not bother him. Now when we ride, my scar touches his, and we remember the glory of that battle." And he would strip more bark from the *sohoobi* trees to feed to Medicine-Coat as he told the scar stories.

The battles were not all glorious. There were chiefs even among wolves, and each *Na-vohnuh* warrior fought like one of these wolf-chiefs. They protected their women and children to the death, and many young Comanche warriors fell to the sure aim of *Na-vohnuh* marksmen. Yet, the *Na-vohnuh* almost always lost more men dead than the Comanche. And because the Comanche moved around, the *Na-vohnuh* did not attack their camps as often as Comanches attacked *Na-vohnuh* villages. The True Humans lost few women and children to the slave market. The *Na-vohnuh* lost many, making them ever weaker and less able to replace their warriors lost in battle.

Even when the *Na-vohnuh* did make raids on Comanche camps, the Comanche horsemen repelled such attacks with greater success. Comanche warriors learned to keep their best horses staked near their lodges so they could mount in the time a sacred shooting star took to streak across the sky.

Through the many seasons of the war, Horseback spoke often of the revenge he would take on Battle Scar, the *Na-vohnuh* chief who had killed his father. Yet, Battle Scar proved hard to catch. After the first big fight at Battle Scar's village, the old *Na-vohnuh* warrior grew cautious and sly. He made his village on the Red Water a nation of weapons. He traded for many guns, recruited hard-fighting men from all over the *Na-vohnuh* nation, and maintained a constant guard around the village. It was said that he killed a young warrior-guard caught coupling with a woman when he was supposed to be guarding the village. Then he killed the woman, too.

Because of his vigilance, Battle Scar's camp became impossible to attack. Only when his people completed their harvest in the fall and went out to hunt buffalo would Horseback seek battle with him. Then, the fights were short but bloody. Horseback's people would whittle away at Battle Scar's warrior force, riding down the enemy braves and laughing at their attempts to defend themselves when they got down from their mounts to fight.

Every fall, out on the buffalo ranges, Horseback would catch sight of Battle Scar and give chase. Twice his arrows had pierced the flesh of his bitter enemy, yet failed to kill. The old warrior was canny as a fox, quick and clever, and guarded by many warriors.

These *Na-vohnuh* warriors proved so fierce that they were almost never captured, preferring death to captivity. Only once had an enemy warrior been brought back to Horseback's camp, by Trotter. The captive was a young warrior.

"Will it make you powerful to have this boy-warrior tortured to death?" Horseback asked.

Trotter thought a while and replied, "It will only rob me of anger I should use in battle." With that, Trotter tied the young enemy to a tree and let one of the women in camp shoot him with his Fire Stick. The woman did insist on leaving the ramrod in the barrel, however, so that she would have the satisfaction of seeing it sticking out of him like an arrow. This woman had lost both a husband and a son in the war.

But Horseback's band was not the only Comanche camp making war on the *Na-vohnuh*. It was said that Whip's band tortured some captive slowly after every raid. The Horseback People did not make raids with Whip's people, but the stories spread. Whip always chose the oldest captive boy to torture to death as if he were a warrior. The tales of this torture were ghastly. Some people said that Whip would have tortured all the captives had they not been so valuable in trade to the Metal Men.

There were other stories about Whip's band. Disturbing stories. It was said that witches lived among Whip's people, and cast evils spells on people, and even on each other to the point that all the people in the camp had gone crazy. Whip, himself, was said to have made himself a sorcerer and summoned the powers of evil spirits, since the good spirits had never given him a vision. It was even said that brothers and sisters coupled in that camp, and nephews with their aunts, and daughters with their fathers. The tales made Horseback's people shudder with fear, for dabbling with such evil things could cause the spirits to unleash unspeakable punishments.

The only time the Horseback People saw any of Whip's band was when the Metal Men held their trade fairs at the ancient *Tiwa* town called Taos. It was a time of truce among all nations, and even the *Na-vohnuh* and the Comanche would suspend fighting, though they never attended the fair together, one nation waiting for the other to leave Taos before moving in.

Here, the nations would come from the mountains and the plains and the deserts and the valleys to trade things with one another and with the Metal Men, who had items like iron kettles, knives, beads, and looking glasses.

The nations came from the pueblos and the river villages and the wandering camps. They brought hides of buffalo, deer, elk, antelope, beaver, mink, and otter. They brought deerskins filled with honey, tallow, and bear fat. They brought corn, tobacco, lodge poles, salt, pine nuts, and tools of horn and antler. They brought things of beauty like turquoise, and eagle feathers, and shells that looked like rainbows inside, and rich red stone soft enough to carve into fine ceremonial pipes. They brought finely crafted items such as moccasins, winter boots, leggings dyed and quilled, deerskin shirts, tipi covers, fancy cradle boards, baskets, and pots. They brought herbs and medicines. And they brought their human captives—hollow-eyed women and children wrenched violently from their villages by enemies.

The *Tiwa* dwellings at Taos stood in two clusters, one on either side of a fine little river. Horseback had been told that each adobe and rock structure held a hundred families. With the annual fair, the area between the adobe structures filled with goods brought by traders of all the nations. People who spoke as many different tongues as moons of the circle came here to haggle in gestures and broken bits of one another's languages. *Sohoobi* trees made cool shade to lie about in when the sun rose high. Taos was a good place during the trade fairs.

But it was here that Whip began to make trouble with the Spaniards in the year the Metal Men called by the number 1717. Horseback was there the day it started. He saw it happen. The Comanches had been coming to the Taos fairs for six years in a row, without any trouble. Horseback's winters now numbered thirty, and he was known as a warrior-leader in his prime whose wisdom exceeded that of others his age.

The day that Whip began to make trouble, Horseback was watching Crooked Teeth, the former Grasshopper Eater, bargain with a young Spanish trader for a red blanket. The young Spanish trader was the son of Horseback's friend, Raccoon-Eyes. Raccoon-Eyes was at Horseback's side, and they were both smiling at the obstinate traffic of barter-talk between Crooked Teeth and Raccoon-Eyes's son, whose name was Juanito. Behind them rose the adobe walls of Taos, its nooks and corners painted with sunlight and shadow. Beyond the adobe walls stood the high dark slopes of the Sangre de Cristo Mountains, which Horseback knew had been named for the blood of the son of God who walked on earth.

"I must have three buffalo robes for a blanket this fine," Juanito said in a voice yet boyish.

Crooked Teeth fumed and shook his head. He stalked about and looked incredulously up at Father Sun to witness such an absurdity as this boy-trader had offered. "One robe and one skin bag filled with bear fat. That is all!"

Juanito laughed and rolled his eyes. "That would not pay for the shearers who gathered the wool to make the blanket, not to mention the weavers, the makers of the dye, the builder of the loom, the freighters who hauled this blanket here to this remote outpost. Two robes and a skin bag of bear fat. I can do no better."

Crooked Teeth ranted a while in his *Noomah* tongue that he knew the trader would not understand. Then, he said in Spanish, "One robe, one skin of bear fat, and a skin of honey. This is more than the blanket is worth, but I will offer it, for I am wealthy and you look like you need my generosity."

Juanito looked at his father for approval, and Raccoon-Eyes nodded. The young trader frowned at the Comanche as if he were just a little disgusted, then made the deal fast with a handshake. Crooked Teeth turned happily away to collect the goods for his end of the bargain.

"Your son learns well," Horseback said. "I will also be generous with him." He stepped up to Juanito's stacks of goods and said, "I will have three blankets like Crooked Teeth bought. One for each wife. Green for Teal, yellow for Sunshade, and blue for Dipper."

Juanito sighed. "Very well. Since you overheard, I must offer you the same price as Crooked Teeth paid."

Horseback drew back and glared at the boy. He held his chin high and sniffed as if he had smelled something foul.

"Juanito!" Raccoon-Eyes scolded. "Where are your manners? Look who you are speaking to. This is Acaballo, the greatest of the Comanche chiefs, the finest horseman alive. His wealth is twenty times that of Crooked Teeth. It is an insult to treat him like a common warrior."

Juanito seemed astonished and confused. "But, I only . . . He just now heard my bargain with Crooked Teeth. Am I to demand more of Acaballo because he is wealthier?"

"Yes, of course, Juanito. This is not a greedy Spanish miser you are dealing with. Do not treat him as such. This is the great chief of the Comanches. Have I not told you how the noble Comanches hold prestige, wealth, and generosity in the highest veneration?"

Juanito glanced uncertainly again at Horseback. "You mean he *wants* to pay more?"

"He has earned the right to pay more, *hijo*. He is proud of it. His power is strong." Now Raccoon-Eyes glanced around him for Black Robes before saying, "He is guided and protected by powerful spirits who will see that he quickly regains any price you could possibly convince him to pay."

Juanito smirked. "Very well," he said, turning back to his customer. "Ten ponies for each blanket!"

Juanito's face could not contain his surprise when Horseback quickly replied, "*Bueno. Muy bueno!*"

They had shaken hands and Juanito was folding the blankets when a war cry rose across the Taos River. The murmur of voices died all across the trade grounds, and Horseback saw Whip beyond the river. He was mounted and pulling a young Spanish girl onto his lap by her hair. She kicked and screamed, but he muscled her across his thighs and charged past the hands that groped to save the girl.

Horseback and Raccoon-Eyes leapt from stone to stone in crossing the shallow river, arriving at the side of a weeping woman, who was screaming, "My daughter! Save her! Someone help her!"

"What happened?" Raccoon-Eyes asked a Spanish trader who had been standing there.

"The savage wanted to buy the girl. Her parents would not sell her, of course, so he just took her."

From the distance, Whip's war cry pierced the air like a hawk's call, and his pony was seen riding onto a rise that overlooked the pueblo. He was near enough to be seen dismounting, throwing the girl to the ground at the same time.

"Merciful God!" someone cried. "That heathen bastard is going to rape her! Where are the soldiers? Who has a gun?"

Whip's warriors were pouring from the trade grounds now, like bees shaken from a hollow tree. They rode to the rise to protect their leader and to watch him defile the girl.

"They will kill anyone who tries to stop Whip," Raccoon-Eyes said. "And he will probably kill the girl if you go after him with a weapon."

Women screamed and wept, and men shouted for soldiers, as Whip raped the girl in plain view of the trade grounds. Finally, a Taos merchant came running with an old matchlock musket, but had to stop at the edge of the river to load the weapon and get the treated cord lighted. By then Whip was seen dragging the girl back onto his pony.

"He's going to bring her back!" someone cried.

"Do not fire," Jean said, pointing at the man with the matchlock. "He will kill her if you fire. Fire only if he releases her."

Whip came loping boldly back to the pueblo, the weeping girl straddling the pony in front of him. He wore an evil smile on his face and his eyes glinted like those of a lizard-monster. People stood aside for him as he brought the girl back to the same place he had stolen her. Leering, he grabbed her by the hair and said, in Spanish, word by word, "Now . . . she . . . is . . . *good*."

He threw her aside and wheeled his pony. People scattered around him as he galloped toward the rise. Powder flared in the pan of the matchlock as Whip threw himself to the side of his pony. The gun roared and the pony collapsed, the ball having caught it in the back of the neck. Angry Spanish men sprinted toward the downed warrior, but one of Whip's men circled quickly, swung him up behind, and they escaped amid a chorus of victorious yelps.

Instantly, Raccoon-Eyes was pulling Horseback away, as people gathered around the assaulted girl. "The soldiers will be coming," he said to his friend. "You must take your people away."

"I do not like the things Whip does, but I can do nothing to stop him. He has his own band and his own council."

"The soldiers will not understand that. They will come after any band of Comanches they can find. Please, my friend, take your people back onto the plains."

Horseback sensed the anger of the Spaniards gathering around the girl Whip had raped. He knew the way the soldiers thought. Raccoon-Eyes was right. "I will go," he said. He was sure his eyes must show his sorrow. "I will go."

▲▲▲▲▲
64
▼▼▼▼▼

He ducked, but Fray Gabrielle Ugarte could not lean low enough on the back of the big mule to avoid the branch of the juniper. It raked him hard on the nape of his sunburned neck and tore his frock as the mule slid on down the trail that led to the plains, to the country of *los Indios bárbaros*, and to the realm of doomed souls. Quickly, he regained his seat, not even bothering to feel his neck for blood. Below, along a stream called the Cimarron, the ash piles of Comanche campfires dotted the valley. As he trotted to catch up to the soldiers, he found *Capitán* Lorenzo Lujan and the tattooed guide, Juan Archebeque, in the midst of a heated discussion.

"Governor Del Bosque made our mission clear," Archebeque was saying when Fray Ugarte rode into earshot. "We are to seek out the man who raped the girl in Taos, to capture or kill him and as many of his accomplices as we are able."

"I know what our mission is, Frenchman. That is why we are going to follow the trail to the north. It is the largest trail. The rapist stands a greater chance of being among the larger band."

"The trail that leads north was made by Acaballo's people. Whip will not be among them. Whip's band made the trail that leads east, onto the *llano*."

"You have no way of knowing that."

"I know by the size of the bands," Archebeque insisted, his frustration building. "If you will ride two more leagues downstream, I will show you where Whip's band camped. Acaballo and Whip will not camp together, for they have broken off all communication. Acaballo has more people, and many more ponies. The larger trail is obviously his, and the lesser trail, Whip's."

Lujan glared at Archebeque with obvious hatred. "You know too much about our enemies."

"The Comanches are not our enemies. The governor made that clear when he asked me to guide this expedition. What happened in Taos was not an act of war. It was a crime against God and the Crown. Whip is the man we seek. He and his men are criminals. Leave *Acaballo* out of it. He has done nothing."

"He did this," Lujan said. He removed his iron helmet and used his quirt to point to the place on his head where the flesh had grown back together like a hairless battle scar on a fighting dog. "This was his act of war."

"That one little scar on your scalp is nothing compared to the scars on Acaballo's back from the whipping you and Ugarte gave him." He sidled his angry eyes at the friar. "His flesh looks like a map of Spain, and yet he is satisfied with the revenge he took on the export caravan. If you go after him, you will be making a mistake. Whip will get away with his crime, and you will bring war down upon the Kingdom of New Mexico such as you have never dreamed possible. You do not understand the power of the Comanches. They have already caused the Apaches more grief than all the combined efforts of your Spanish military over the last hundred years. Your small force of soldiers will be no match for them."

Lujan's smirk revealed his disdain for his guide's advice. "Fray Ugarte, what do you say?"

The Franciscan mopped sweat from his brow with the sleeve of his heavy robe. "It is God's work to follow in the tracks of the greatest number of heathens, that we may chance to save more souls among them." He knew this would enrage Archebeque. The trader had never appreciated the logic of the Franciscan Order.

Archebeque gathered his reins. "Then, may God go with you, for I will not. The two of you would let a rapist go free in order to carry on your foolish vendetta with *Acaballo*. I wish to take no part in promulgating an unnecessary war."

"The words of a coward," Lujan said.

Archebeque trained his eyes on Lujan like a brace of pistol barrels. "If you are lucky enough to survive your ridiculous quest, *Capitán*, you may choose swords or pistols, for you will have an affair of honor to face upon your return to Santa Fe. I will not be termed a coward." He spun his mount all the way round, piercing Lujan again with a glare that now spoke more of amusement than ire. "However, I suspect that Acaballo will rob me of the pleasure of killing you."

Father Ugarte breathed a sigh of relief as the tattooed Frenchman spurred his horse and headed back up the trail to the pass. The guide had been at odds with Lujan since the very start of this expedition. He was a half-savage heathen himself, his soul blackened as surely as his skin by *Indio* heresy. The expedition was better off without him.

Often, over the years in Santa Fe, Ugarte had been tempted to report Archebeque to Inquisition authorities. Perhaps the trader had the secular authorities fooled, but not the friar. The Frenchman was a good friend of the governor, and a suitor to governor's daughter. As such he represented a danger to the entire Kingdom of New Mexico. He treated with barbarians. It was said that he had participated in heretical ceremonies with shamans and witches.

"Shall we go after him?" a soldier said. "He is deserting."

"Let him go," Lujan growled. "I will look forward to dealing with him upon our return to Santa Fe." He glanced at the friar. "We are going to ride hard, *Padre*. Are you ready?"

"I will not fall far behind. *Vámanos*."

· · · ·

The trail was plain. It led north, then east across the plains. At the end of the day, the soldiers still had not found the next Comanche campground. Instead, an advance scout came galloping back to Lujan's column of twenty soldiers, shouting, "*Capitán! Capitán!* A large body of *Indios* approaches. There must be two hundred!"

Lujan ordered defensive preparations. Men loaded muskets and pistols and took cover in a nearby arroyo. When the savages appeared, Ugarte counted no more than sixty. Still, he understood how they had seemed to number more to the excited scout. Lujan sent a *Tompiro* guide out to speak with them.

"They are Apaches," the *Tompiro* said, when he returned. "Battle Scar is their chief. He wants to help the soldiers fight Acaballo's people."

"Padre Ugarte," Lujan said. "Does this alliance have your blessing?"

Ugarte placed his hand on his chin. If Archebeque's warning about the strength of the Comanches proved half-true, it would not be such a bad idea to have some *Indio* allies along. In addition, this smacked of an opportunity to increase the tally of souls he had ushered to the gates of salvation. "If Battle Scar's warriors agree to be baptized and christened," he said, "they may join our party. We go on together as Christians, or not at all."

The *Tompiro* guide took the decision to the Apaches, and returned. Ugarte and the soldiers could see the glow of the pipe as Battle Scar's warriors passed it and conferred. At dawn, Battle Scar himself came to the Spanish camp and said, in broken Castilian:

"My name . . . Christian name . . . Carlana."

"Very well," Ugarte replied. "You must kneel." He recited a terse version of the Latin liturgy, and then ended, saying, "I christen thee, Carlana."

One by one, the Apaches came forward for Christianization until Padre Ugarte grew weary of reducing them individually, and told the rest to kneel at once. He mumbled the rites, named them all Carlos, and urged Captain Lujan to mount the troops.

The day's ride was a dry one, and the men used all the water in their canteens. The next day, Lujan's force found an abandoned Comanche camp-ground at a lake out on the plains. There was not much water left, but enough for horses to drink and men to cook with.

"They are not far ahead of us," Lujan said to the Franciscan that night at dark. "We will rise three hours before dawn, and be upon them by noon tomorrow."

Noon passed the next day, but Ugarte caught no glimpse of the Coman-ches. Evening came without water or any sighting of the enemy. Drinking the last drops from their canteens the next morning, the Spaniards and Apaches set upon the trail again. They traversed a country of bluffs, dry stream beds, sage, grass, and plains. Their horses were stumbling from exhaustion when they came over a rise and spotted a small lake on the plains where the Comanches had camped.

"How could they have covered the distance between the last lake and this one in a single day?" Ugarte wondered aloud. "They have their women and children with them. We have ridden hard, and still the same ride took us almost two full days."

Lujan licked his dry lips and stared down at the water hole, the sun now glinting invitingly off its surface. "Let them continue to push on this way. Soon, their ponies will be dying. Then, we will have the advantage."

They rode on down the slope to the lake, but found the water muddy and foul.

"They know we are following," Lujan said, bitterly. "The savage bastards made their ponies stand in the water all night. It reeks with filth."

Fray Ugarte recited vespers at a wretched camp beside the stinking water that night. Afterward, he spoke to Lujan as they prepared to sleep.

"I am weary," he said. "I will sleep well."

"Why did you insist on coming along with this expedition, Padre? You might have sent a younger friar as chaplain."

Ugarte shook his head. "It is my duty. I have reason to believe that she is with Acaballo's band."

"Who?" the captain asked.

"The girl."

"What girl?"

"You remember. The raid on the caravan, eleven years ago. A young girl was taken. Her mother was a mestizo prostitute. Her father, unknown."

"Ay, sí. That was a long time ago. Why do you concern yourself now with the daughter of a whore?"

"Every Christian soul lost to paganism concerns me. She must be rescued from the heathens and restored to Christ. I only hope she has not been corrupted beyond salvation."

Lujan snorted and fell almost instantly to sleep.

The next day the trail led to a third lake on the plains, this one made more turbid and foul than the last. As the men strained and boiled water to drink and cook the last of their beans, one of the Apache guards spotted several mounted warriors watching from a distant rise.

"Muskets!" Lujan shouted, jolted suddenly to action.

Fray Ugarte felt his heart pound. He was far from civilization, in the country of savage *Norteños*. He had not seen a tree in three days. Savage warriors were looking down upon him. He had written of this expedition to the bishop, the viceroy, and even to the cardinal. If he did not return, his martyrdom would be well known. Perhaps his penance was at hand. Perhaps Fray Gabrielle Ugarte would finally know peace with God.

As the soldiers primed their weapons and tightened their saddle cinches, Ugarte swung onto his mule bareback.

"Padre!" Captain Lujan shouted. "Wait!"

"I will order them to turn over the rapist, his accomplices, and all white captives," the friar shouted over his shoulder. "Do not concern yourself with my safety. God goes with me."

He flogged the flanks of the mule until she broke into a lope. Approaching the party of Comanches, he recognized Acaballo riding his famous pinto stallion, flanked by half a dozen warriors.

"You are lost, Black Robe," Acaballo said.

"I am not lost. I have come to punish those who sin against God and against Spain. You must turn over the warrior who raped the girl at Taos. Also, any white captives in your camp."

"You have followed the wrong trail. There are no white captives among my people."

Ugarte was somewhat taken aback. He had not stood face-to-face with Acaballo since the day of his flogging. Now, the savage's Spanish was flawless, and the insolence in his voice obvious. "Eleven years ago you stole a girl from the trade caravan. Have you murdered her? Did you sell her as a captive to some other tribe of heathens?"

Acaballo began to chuckle, yet his mouth failed to make a smile. "Eleven winters ago, you and your soldiers captured me, tortured me, and tried to make a slave of me. This is what I remember best. The girl taken in the raid on the carts is now called Sunshade. She is my wife. My third wife. She is a very good wife. She is not a captive."

Ugarte felt his rage rise. It made his jowls tremble. "You must give her back, or the soldiers will attack, and then may God have mercy upon your wretched soul."

"I will ride back to my camp, and ask Sunshade if she wishes to return to the Spaniards. If she does, I will bring her to you myself. If the soldiers attack my camp, they will all die. You are in my country now, Black Robe. You ride with my enemies, the *Na-vohnuh*. Powerful spirits protect me. You are in much danger."

Ugarte reached into his robe and pulled out his silver cross. "Your pagan spirits mean nothing to men of God! Return the girl, or you will taste Toledo steel. You must submit and swear allegiance to the king of Spain, and the Lord, Jesus Christ, or burn in hell forever!" He began to recite the King's decree in Latin—the decree that required allegiance to Spain. But Acaballo merely turned to the northeast, followed by his warriors. Ugarte watched them canter away, awed by the distance they quickly covered, seemingly without the slightest effort by ponies or riders. He thought of himself plodding after them on his mule, and could already feel the exhaustion of the many leagues of pounding travel before him.

"Was that Acaballo?" Captain Lujan asked when the friar returned the soldiers by the lake.

"*Sí.*"

"What did he say?"

"He refused to return any criminals or captives. The girl taken from the caravan is with him. He called her Sunshade, and said he had taken her as his wife. He would not return her. He dared your men to attack."

Lujan smiled.

The next day, the party found a snakelike line of timber winding its way through a broad valley. Riding closer with the soldiers and Apaches, the friar began to see the tops of the hide tents between the trees, like exposed vertebrae along the backbone of a serpent. Through the *Tompiro* translator, Battle Scar identified the stream as the River of Arrowheads, which Ugarte knew to be the Napestle. Seeing no sign of alarm among the Comanches, Lujan's men began preparing to attack. They primed their pistols, donned their leather armor.

"Should we take our horses to water first?" one of the younger soldiers asked. "We could go upstream, out of sight."

"No," Lujan replied. "A bellyful of water will only slow your horses down. If they are thirsty, the smell of the river will make them charge more furiously into the camp. Use your pistols first, then your swords. Do not hesitate to kill any woman who takes up a weapon, for she will kill you. Beware the young boys, as well. Each is anxious to take his first scalp. Father, say the prayers. We must go quickly, before we are discovered."

Fray Ugarte looked at the soldiers. Most were veterans of many such campaigns. They were tough. Their love of fighting and hatred of *Indios* showed in their faces. Some already had twenty or more *Indio* kills to their

credit. Lujan himself had led dozens of such assaults on enemy camps, sometimes slaughtering a hundred hostile *Indios* in a single charge against Pueblos,
Apaches, Navahos. They would stagger the arrogant Acaballo and his heathen
warriors.

"I have already said the prayers for the savages," the friar replied. "The
souls of those killed in the coming battle are prepared for judgement by God.
I will pray for the soldiers as the attack begins."

The men were all mounted now and ready. Lujan led them toward the
brink of the riverbank. The moment the Comanche camp came into view,
the captain drew his sword and shouted, "Santiago!"

The men repeated the familiar cry, their coarse voices bursting into the
valley as their horses charged the Comanche camp. The Apaches followed
close behind, yelping like barking coyotes, spreading across the valley as an
undisciplined rabble. Padre Ugarte fell in after them, their dust gritting his
eyes and teeth. He held his cross in one hand, his reins in the other. His heart
pounded with hope and fear. He had served well, saved so many souls. And
yet, he had sinned. Perhaps it was time to settle with God. He knew the
Almighty would demand severe penance.

They were a long musket shot from the camp when suddenly a shrill cry
rose among the hide tents. Comanche horsemen appeared from nowhere,
some swarming from the camp, some rounding the first bend in the valley,
some bursting from stands of timber that seemed too small to have concealed
them. Lujan's men slowed their mounts to take better aim with their pistols.
The Apaches stopped to dismount, for they preferred to fight afoot. But the
Comanches only rode harder.

The soldiers took aim and waited, but just when the Comanches reached
effective pistol range, they began to swarm, at first in one direction, like the
winds of a tornado, then peeling off like minnows scattering at the shadow
of a bird. One instant they were like bees, making individual attacks on the
soldiers and Apaches, the next moment they became as one, like the waters
of a whirlpool, drawing their enemies deeper into doom. Like hawks, each
striking his own victim. Then like wolves, coming together in little packs to
drag a foe into bloody death.

The pistols fired, and balls whistled everywhere, but Ugarte could not see
that any had hit home. Swords sang from their scabbards as bowstrings
thumped like drumming fingers. A second war cry rose from behind and
Ugarte turned, wide-eyed, to see another hundred Comanches storming down
the riverbank from the rear. Whence they had risen, he could not comprehend.

Swinging his leg over his mule, the friar let his shoes hit the ground as
he clutched his cross and mumbled familiar prayers. He turned to face the
attack from the riverbank, but to his surprise, the warriors parted to go around

him, refusing to even look at him. It seemed they preferred to battle enemy warriors rather than slay a holy man. Ugarte felt relieved, which only made him feel ashamed.

When he turned back to the battleground, he spotted Acaballo, riding his fleet pinto pony into the vortex of the fight. The pony's mane streamed like hellfire, sun glinting on the sheen of the marvelous coat shaped by ripples of muscle. The creature was so nimble, and the rider so fixed up him, that Ugarte had to fight the urge to admire them.

Acaballo struck like a lion with his club, dashing aside an Apache who had dismounted to fight, breaking the arm of a soldier who drew his sword back to strike. And yet, the Comanche failed to finish his victims, paying no more heed to them than a farmer would to a shock of wheat his sickle had left behind. He seemed all the while to be searching for a particular victim. The pinto forever wove among the combatants, the rider swaying with his every turn as if each knew the other's thoughts. The pony seemed in particular to enjoy charging upon the Spaniards, for he would kick a hind foot at a soldier overrun, crane his neck to snap his teeth at a soldier passing by, and once reared to paw a soldier from his very saddle. It had been said that Acaballo's wretched warhorse hated Spaniards.

Now a veteran cavalryman angled in on Acaballo from behind, taking a lethal swipe with a blade that glinted like a diamond. Ugarte's heart swelled with joy—and a morsel of pity he could not suppress—as Acaballo fell to one side of his pony. Then, somehow, the Comanche rose again, unscathed, and bashed his club over the head of the soldier. How he had avoided the blow, remained horsed, and sprung so quickly in retaliation was an unholy mystery.

The soldiers began to fall, and their screams came like cries of heretics in the dungeons of the Inquisition. Ugarte felt his stomach wrench with nausea. He did not know what was holy any more. Where was God? Where was salvation?

Now the Apaches seemed more interested in mounting and gathering their dead and wounded than in fighting. Then the friar understood. Battle Scar's people were preparing to flee. All was lost. The last of the soldiers were trying to fight their way together, but each was swarmed under.

Then Ugarte saw *Capitán* Lorenzo Lujan, still horsed, arrows protruding from his leather armor. The captain broke off a shaft that inhibited his sword arm, and continued to slash with his weapon. His use of the steel and the horse rivaled even the incomprehensible maneuvers of the Comanches, and he swatted them aside like insects.

The Apaches raised a cry, and began to move away from the battle ground. Ugarte located Acaballo. The Comanche chief seemed torn between the two enemy parties, as if he did not know which to fight, for the Apaches and Spaniards were parting ranks. Would he attack the soldiers, who were all but finished anyway? Or would he pursue the Apaches, who were about to escape?

The wind shifted, and Ugarte caught the odors of death—blood mixed with the sweat of horses, the vomitus of dying men, the foul bile of punctured guts. His own stomach seemed to close in on itself, and he bent forward to vomit, yet could not tear his eyes away from the horrible scene.

Acaballo's pinto ascended the riverbank like a soaring bird, closing quickly on the poorer mounts of the Apaches. The warrior screamed and the Apaches parted in fear. Only one turned back to face the Comanche chief, and that one was Battle Scar. The old Apache chief raised a sword he had taken from a Spanish soldier. Just before he clashed with Acaballo, he dropped from his mount. As the beautiful pinto charged upon him, Battle Scar dodged a blow from the war club, rolling in front of the pony. As the pinto leapt over him, Battle Scar wielded the Spanish sword, hacking at the legs that passed overhead.

At first, Ugarte thought the blade had missed. Then the horse stumbled and squealed, landing on his shoulder, spilling Acaballo. A Comanche warrior came to Acaballo's aid. Then another, and another. The pinto kicked, rose, limped piteously, his head nodding with every stride. Battle Scar was back on his war pony in an instant, leaving the field of battle with the rest of his men—even the dead and wounded, who had been fought for beyond reason.

A cry of victory rose from the valley, and Ugarte saw Lujan being dragged from his pony, arrows sticking out of him like banderillas from a bull in the fighting ring. Acaballo gathered the reins of his wounded war pony and handed them to one of his warriors to hold. Mounting another pony, he galloped down the riverbank, charging upon the captive, Lujan. Fray Ugarte himself ran toward the soldier. It was time. The savages would not see him cower.

The warriors stepped away from Lujan, and he fell. Acaballo shouted orders, and the warriors began stripping the leather armor and the clothes from the captain. Elsewhere, across the battleground, Ugarte witnessed the warriors committing ghastly atrocities upon the bodies of dead Spaniards. The women were running from the camp with knives, trilling victory songs, and the friar knew they would hack the bodies of the poor soldiers like butchered swine.

As he reached Lujan, Ugarte could see only one hand moving, the captain seeming to search for his sword. He was naked, facedown. The warriors saw the friar coming. They moved away from him, as if they feared him. Lujan was dying, his blood gathering in rivulets that trickled down the slope of the riverbank. Acaballo had cut a pair of heavy leather reins from the bridle of a dead Spanish horse. His eyes glared first at the friar, then at the captain. Now he descended on the naked body and began lashing it with the reins, the leather popping hideously against the white flesh. Lujan did not even flinch, for he was already dead.

Feeling his fear swarm about him in a dizzy haze, Fray Gabrielle Ugarte removed his robe and began chanting his prayers, standing naked like the crucified Christ, still clutching his silver cross, trying to face his penance with courage, for he had heard much of horrible *Indio* tortures.

Acaballo ceased to lash the dead body with the reins. He spoke to his men. One answered and stepped forward. Acaballo spoke again, and the warrior fell upon the body of Lujan with a knife. The warrior seemed to make a grand ceremony of slashing the scalp and peeling it off.

Victory cries rose and drowned out the singing of the friar. The pinto stallion lay down on the ground where Battle Scar had wounded him. Ugarte felt his voice climb several pitches too high.

"Enough!" Acaballo shouted, raising his hand to silence the friar. "No one will harm you, Black Robe. Save your death song."

Ugarte's throat clenched, killing his song. He felt relief again, and the shame that came with it. "Why do you spare me, Acaballo?"

"I understand the medicine of the Black Robes. I will not make you more powerful by killing you. Instead, you will carry the story of this battle back to the Metal Men. I want war with Battle Scar's people, but not with yours. Tell the governor his soldiers must not attack my people for no reason."

"The soldiers had reason."

"What reason?"

"The girl. The girl! My—"

Acaballo straightened, holding his chin arrogantly high. "I spoke to Sunshade. She does not wish to return to the Spaniards. She told me about you, Black Robe. I know why you have come for her."

"You know nothing, savage."

Acaballo began to pace closer to the friar, still holding the bridle reins in his hand. "The power of the Black Robes is strange. A Comanche warrior who lies with a woman becomes strong, unless the woman is bleeding and unclean. But a Black Robe who lies with a woman becomes weak, and the Great Creator punishes him. You are weak, Black Robe. You wish me to make you strong by torturing you and killing you. You have coupled with a woman. Sunshade is your daughter. She told me."

Ugarte looked at the ground, felt the tears of his shame welling up in his eyes. He gritted his teeth in frustration. "Will you not strike me? Do you forget how I whipped you?"

Acaballo dropped the reins in his hand. "I have taken your daughter as my wife. That is my vengeance."

The Comanche turned and walked away from him, and Ugarte felt foolish, standing there naked. The rest of the warriors went with their leader.

They had wounded to tend to, and perhaps two or three dead to mourn. They disregarded him as if he were nothing more than a dog from an enemy camp. Ugarte had no choice but to pick up his robe, track down his mule, and start the long journey home. His shame was almost more than he could bear. He prayed that perhaps some other savage nation would stumble upon him before he returned to Santa Fe, and duly punish him for his sins.

▲▲▲▲▲
65
▼▼▼▼▼

Jean L'Archeveque winced at the smoke that stung his eyes as he fanned the coals of his cook fire. He wished for an eagle wing but had to settle for the broad, flat brim of his hat. Finally a flame broke through the smoke, and he stacked a few cottonwood branches strategically, to keep the fire flickering until he returned to cook the buffalo meat he had butchered yesterday.

He turned away from the fire and waited for the ghostly images of the flames to melt from his eyesight. When he could again see clearly in the predawn gloom, he began to make his way through the camp of Spanish soldiers, Pueblo scouts, and Apache allies, weaving among smoldering fires, passing Lieutenant-Governor Pedro Villasur's blue tent, and cautiously approaching the horses and mules picketed at the edge of camp. The eastern sky glowed with the promise of another sultry day, as stars clung tenuously to the west. Already, the air felt warm and muggy, as well it should in August on the plains.

He stopped, so as not to spook his mules, for they watched his approach with apprehension, their heads high and ears forward. Jean might have expected them to be gentle as house cats after two months on the trail, but frontier mules could revert to heathenism at the slightest provocation. Perhaps they had snuffed an old lion track or a snake skin down in the tall grass of the river bottoms. They were tied to a picket line stretched between cottonwoods, but Jean knew they were strong enough to set back and break something. Mounted guards were tending most of the expedition's horses and mules up on the grassy river bank, but Jean had tied his animals to facilitate fitting the pack saddles this morning. Soon the guards would be herding the loose animals into the river bottom, breaking the pleasant calm of the sleeping camp.

As he stood still to let the mules settle down, he noticed that the river seemed to be making more noise than it had last night when he retired, and he wondered if rain had fallen upstream, causing a rise. Probably not. Dawn just had a way of amplifying things.

Lieutenant-Governor Villasur and Fray Ugarte had argued last night about what to name the river, for no Spanish party had ever camped upon its banks. Villasur wanted to call it El Rio Del Bosque, in honor of the governor. Ugarte preferred to name it for a saint or a pope. As far as Jean was concerned, the river already had a name. The *Pani* called it Filthy Water, for it was often made rather foul by large herds of buffalo. It ran purer than usual this morning, but Jean could think of other places he would rather be.

The secret trade he had begun with Governor Del Bosque years ago had made him wealthy in land, gold, and influence, but sometimes led to inconveniences like this. He thought perhaps he should have sent his son, Juanito, on this expedition. The young man had become quite an entrepreneur, and had even begun to understand *Indios*, but still knew virtually nothing of the wilderness. It would have been dangerous to have sent him, and so Jean L'Archeveque, a newlywed at forty-nine years of age, had decided to make the trek himself.

His young bride had wept admirably upon his departure, and he had begun to miss the sensation of her flesh upon his almost immediately. Now he had been gone over two months, and was growing weary of camp life. He dreamed constantly of the children he would have with Teresa. He was getting old for this campaigning life. It was time to let Juanito take over the rigors of the trail, and settle back to enjoy his *hacienda* outside Santa Fe. This, he had decided, would be his last trip onto the plains.

He sighed and took a few more casual steps toward the nervous mules. Before the soldiers could break camp, all sixteen beasts would have to be packed with the trade goods he had brought with him at the governor's insistence. Captain Villasur had failed to find or engage the French menace and would begin the return to Santa Fe this morning. Jean was anxious to get started.

Stepping close to a robe, in which Paniagua lay sleeping, he nudged it with his boot and heard his servant's breathing change.

"Hungry?" Jean said.

Paniagua smacked his lips, and his voice came muffled from the robe. "I only want some corn mush."

"No meat?"

"Just some corn mush fried in marrow."

"Good," Jean said. "Start packing the mules. I will cook the corn for you."

He heard Paniagua grumble as he emerged from the robe, but he knew the servant only made this noise to settle the mules. Animals listened to Paniagua.

This expedition had seemed like a good idea two months ago. Jean and the governor had hoped they might make contact with some French *couriers de bois* and trade for more guns, hence the sixteen mules laden with gold, silver, blankets, and other things the French traders wanted. The mules themselves would be much in demand, though half of them would still be needed to carry the guns on the return trip. Yes, two months ago, this had seemed like a fine opportunity to make some money under the protection of forty-two soldiers and sixty or more *Indio* allies, yet the expedition had failed to make contact with anyone but hostile *Panis*.

The fervor that led to this goose chase had begun with Fray Ugarte's return from the disastrous Lujan massacre, three years ago. Jean had sat in on the council of war, and had seen the strange new look of desperation in Ugarte's eyes. He listened intently to the friar's description of the battle, but could only wonder what had really happened out there.

"The Comanches butchered Lujan and his men without mercy," the friar had said, summing up his report.

"They must have taken mercy upon you," Jean had replied, "for you are now sitting among us to tell the tale. Besides, do you expect men to take mercy upon those who attack their wives and children without provocation? Lujan followed the wrong trail. I tried to tell him. I told you, too, *Padre.*"

It was then that Fray Ugarte had blurted out the ridiculous claim that had led to all the trouble. "They had guns," he said. "Acaballo's Comanches had French guns. They have made a treaty with the French, across the plains. If they are not soon dealt with and reduced to Catholicism, they will become the vassals of heretical Huguenots!"

Santa Fe had recently received word of the outbreak of war in Europe between Spain and France, and Fray Ugarte's rash claims had only inflamed fears that the French would make allies of the *Indios*, march across the plains, and attack New Mexico.

"This is nonsense," Jean had argued. "The Comanches care little for guns, especially Acaballo's people. They rely on their horsemanship. Perhaps a few warriors have guns, but they are acquired in raids on the Apaches, not in trade with the French. The Apaches get them from the *Pani*, and the *Pani* from the French." He had turned to implore the governor at this point. "Captain-General Del Bosque, if you please, the nearest French Fort is no closer than the Rio Messipe. Acaballo's people have no contact with them whatsoever."

Antonio Del Bosque had given Jean a knowing look at that moment, there in the war council room of the adobe *Casas Reales*, in the presence of the military and governmental powers of the Northern Frontier. "Yes, but what *about* the *Pani*, *Capitán* Archebeque? Might *they* have had contact with French troops? Their villages lie closer to Fort Creve Coeur than to Santa Fe. We are at war with France. We have never achieved peace with the *Pani*. Might the French be making allies of the *Pani* to mount an invasion of New Mexico? There have been rumors of such an alliance coming out of Tachichichi. Perhaps we should send an expedition to the *Pani* country to investigate."

Jean had understood, and replied, "Yes, by all means. Let us find out for ourselves, once and for all, what is going on out there. But I think the rumors coming out of Tachichichi are designed to convince us that the *rancherías* there need Spanish guns."

After that meeting, the rumors of the French-*Pani* hoard coming to conquer New Mexico began to rival the old stories of gold in Quivira. The governor himself was responsible for many of the rumors, as he hoped they would induce the viceroy to order an expedition. The clergy, particularly Padre Ugarte, spread other fanciful tales, for he longed always to convert souls, even if he had to have soldiers kill the possessors of the souls to send them heavenward. And for three years, the rumors continued.

Jean knew the idea of a French-*Pani* invasion was crazy. Not since La Salle's disastrous experiment with Fort St. Louis had France attempted to enter *Indio* land with a large military force. But he was not surprised when, early in this year of 1720, the order came from the viceroy to mount an expedition to the *Pani* Country. In secret, he and Antonio decided to outfit the pack string of sixteen mules to accompany the expedition. Ostensibly, the string would carry goods needed to treat with nations of *Indios*. In reality, Jean and Antonio hoped to trade the goods to agents of Fort Creve Coeur and increase their traffic in guns and other French goods. They already had a covert market established at Arkansas post, but Fort Creve Coeur was thought by Jean to be much richer. He had spoken to several *couriers de bois* who had been there. Even the mapmaker, Goupil, had told Jean of the place, many years ago. It was connected to the Great Lakes of Canada by a river called the Seignelay, and could transport goods to and from Montreal and Quebec.

And so, seven days before his first anniversary of marriage with young Teresa, Jean had saddled his pony and packed his mules to accompany yet another exploratory expedition onto the plains. Two months of hard riding had brought him to the Rio Jesus Maria, where the Spaniards had encountered a *Pani* village. One of the members of the expedition had a *Pani* slave named Sistaca. Jean wrote a message, in French, on a piece of paper and gave it to Sistaca to carry to the *Pani* town. Sistaca returned with a message that consisted of incomprehensible scribblings.

"Were there any Frenchmen in the village?" Lieutenant-Governor Villasur interrogated.

"I saw only one white man. Maybe he was French. He did not look like a soldier."

Villasur had grown nervous, for Sistaca also said that the *Pani* village proved much larger than at first thought, extending perhaps two leagues down the river. The lieutenant-governor had been commander of some large presidios in Mexico, but knew virtually nothing about plains warfare with *Indios*. Upon the advice of his junior officers, and Jean himself, Villasur had agreed to turn back toward New Mexico.

After a long day's travel, Villasur's party had arrived here at Filthy Water to make camp, having left the *Pani* village a good ten leagues behind. The Spaniards felt confident that the *Pani* would not follow, as no *Pani* war party had ever attacked such a large force of Spaniards. The grass grew so tall here on the Filthy Water that the men had to cut it with swords and run their horses over it to trample it, in order to clear a campground. This action left a ring of tall grass surrounding the camp.

"I do not like this tall grass," Jean said Lieutenant-Governor Villasur. "The *Pani* could sneak through it and get within firing range."

Villasur had sniffed his reply. "I will post extra guards."

Now, as he walked over the trampled grass lining Filthy Water, Jean could hear the large herd of horses and mules being herded back into camp. He looked, but could only see the riders and the heads of the horses above the tall grass. The camp was about to come alive with energy and activity. Approaching Villasur's blue tent, he noticed some commotion going on between the lieutenant-governor and a guard. Jean strode near enough to overhear.

"I saw nothing," the guard was saying, "but . . ."

"But what?" Villasur demanded. "Report!"

"The river, sir," replied the young soldier. "I heard noises. The river seemed to splash more as the night passed. I thought someone was crossing."

Jean raised his brows over his tattooed eyes. He looked around at the tall grass surrounding the camp, but could see nothing out of the ordinary with the coming of dawn. He glanced at his own cook fire and saw that he needed to add more wood.

"Seemed to splash more?" Villasur railed. "Did you investigate?"

"Yes, sir. I found nothing."

"Perhaps the river is on a rise from a rainstorm upstream," Jean said. "I should have marked the water level on the bank last night, but I did not think of it. I, too, thought it was making more noise this morning."

Villasur sighed. "Take an order to the Pueblo scouts," he said the guard. "Have them circle the camp looking for signs of enemies. *Capitán* Archebeque, give the order to break camp. I want to cover no less than twelve leagues today."

Jean looked again at his cook fire and thought of Paniagua's breakfast. But now he would have to give the order first, then tend the fire, then cook. Then he would help Paniagua pack the mules. There was much to do. Much to do.

Suddenly, all the details of the day ceased to matter. The noise of a hundred bowstrings whispered from the grass and arrows came arching into the camp, thick as quills on a porcupine. One of them caught the young corporal in the back, and he cried out as he sank to his knees. A horse screamed. Muskets began to roar in a full circle around the camp, and Jean saw Lieutenant-Governor Villasur gawking stupidly at nothing.

The *Pani* war cry rose and men began to run toward the center of camp, where Villasur's blue tent stood. The lieutenant-governor dove into his tent and reemerged with his sword and pistol. Now Jean forced himself to look around the perimeter of the camp, and he saw the first of the *Pani*—their bodies painted white with fantastic patterns of red dots or stripes. They came wielding war axes, lances, and clubs, French swords and muskets. They charged into camp and overtook the fleeing Spaniards from behind as they tried to gather at Villasur's blue tent. Many of the soldiers had been caught without weapons, and were easily slaughtered.

"Form a circle!" Villasur ordered, but his cry was lost amid shrieks and powder blasts.

Jean picked up the musket dropped by the corporal with the arrow in his back. He poured another measure of powder into the pan, using the soldier's horn, for the prime charge had been shaken out. His eyes swept the fearsome scene. He thought of Teresa, and his sons. He saw a mule running through the timber on the opposite riverbank, and recognized Paniagua on its back. Good! But the *Pani* seemed to number hundreds around the camp, and Jean saw no way out for himself.

Turning, he saw Padre Ugarte kneeling over a dying Pueblo scout, making the sign of the cross. A *Pani* warrior descended on the friar, and Jean leveled the musket. The powder flashed, and the gun bucked as it roared. The *Pani* fell dead at the friar's side, dropping his war axe—a French weapon with an iron head and wooden handle that doubled as a trail pipe. Fray Ugarte glanced back, a smile on his face, to meet the gaze of Jean L'Archeveque. He made the sign of the cross on the painted *Pani*, and continued to mutter his prayers.

A cloud of black smoke passed, and a figure appeared in its place. A grotesque bald head, one eye squinted shut, shoulders burly and muscled. Jean dropped the musket and rushed forward with his knife, too late to save Fray Ugarte. Henri Casaubon brought his cutlass down on the kneeling Franciscan, beheading him before he could have known his murderer stood there.

Jean threw his knife and saw the blade sink into Casaubon's rib cage. The slaver staggered back, but pulled the knife out as if it were a mere thorn. Now he caught sight of Jean. "You cannot kill Henri, traitor."

Jean did not honor him with a reply. He scooped up the battle axe dropped by the *Pani* and advanced on Casaubon. His rage consumed him as he leapt the dead bodies of the Pueblo, the *Pani*, and the friar, the latter's head standing upright in a lake of his own blood. Swinging the axe, Jean backed Casaubon into an iron tripod that stood over a fire. The slaver stumbled over the tripod, giving Jean the opportunity to strike just as an arrow pierced his thigh.

His leg buckled, and he found himself on one knee. He slung the axe back-handed to ward off Casaubon's blow, but the blade of the cutlass sliced through most of his two smallest fingers. Jean roared, sprang to his feet, and remembered the ferocity of the Raccoon-Eyed People he had once seen defending their village from a *Pani* invasion. He passed the axe to his sound hand and made Casaubon duck and roll. Before the slaver could find his feet, Jean crushed one of his ankles with the blade of the axe. All he saw of the cutlass blade was a flash as it got him in the stomach. He humped his back to get away and struck blindly with an overhead blow, feeling the battle axe crush something.

Staggering back, he saw Casaubon fall to his knees, a slack expression on his bloody face. A musket went off nearby, engulfing the slaver in black smoke and fire. The cloud blew quickly away and revealed Casaubon, lying on his back, eyes open, and staring upward.

Jean fell forward, pain shooting through his innards. He turned his head to see the blue tent fall down, Villasur and the few soldiers he had rallied screaming as they fought to the death. Jean knew he would be dead himself in moments, and he found his eyelids hard to hold open, as if the tattoos weighed them down. He looked again at Casaubon. Dead. This time, surely dead. Horseback had not been here to save him again from the slaver, but Jean had fought well and lived the longest.

He was fifty years old now, and had traveled far, conquered much, loved well. And Teresa? Ah, well, she was young and wealthy. *C'est la vie.*

He did not want Casaubon's ugly dead face to be the last thing he beheld in this life of earthly trouble, so he found the strength to roll himself over. Dust and smoke parted overhead, and Jean saw the morning's first rays of sun beaming through the leafy cottonwoods. It was quite beautiful. The sounds of the battle faded as he thought of Paniagua riding away on the big mule. Riding . . . Riding . . . Riding . . .

Jean L'Archeveque thought of meeting the good mapmaker, Goupil. And the Jesuit martyr, Father Membre. And Maria. Especially Maria. Sweet Maria, mother of his sons . . .

▲▲▲▲▲

66

▼▼▼▼▼

Since the strange and painful thing happened to his leg, Noomah had begun to hear the big river speak to him. Like the river of his old home place, this stream possessed terrors in its quicksands and swirling eddies. Yet, the old river had never spoken to him, called his name in gurgles and laughing trickles. He had been too busy running to hear before. Now, Noomah could no longer run, and so he heard things he had missed in other times.

Since the big fight, when the pain lashed his leg and made his hoof flop piteously ahead of him, Noomah had not known the pleasure of speed. Each movement of his wounded leg brought agony. His two-legged, Hair-Like-a-Mane, cared for him, treating his hurt leg with strange-smelling things, but the sorrow of his forced lethargy made Noomah's spirit sink.

And the river called him.

He did not know fear, for Hair-Like-a-Mane kept him near the camp of two-leggeds where the meat-eaters did not venture. He knew neither thirst nor hunger, for his good two-legged brought grass and water to him. He could hobble about and graze. His two-legged would squat on the ground and watch him, speaking to him. Noomah would avoid moving his wounded leg until the last moment. He would leave it in one place on the ground as his other legs shuffled forward and his teeth cropped grass, until he finally had to step forward with the useless leg. Then he would lunge clumsily, keeping his weight off the injured limb.

Noomah could scarcely walk, much less run, and the river called to him.

The two-leggeds brought mares to him. At these times, Noomah would forget his sorrow and think of his loins. The two-leggeds would hold the mares, and he would mount them, rising with a thrust of his good leg. Astride the withers of a hot mare, his legs served him well—even the wounded one, for its hoof did not reach the ground—and Noomah could clench the mare's mane in his teeth and forget his sorrow for a few moments. Then the two-leggeds would lead the mare away, and Noomah would limp about in confusion. Had he not been well for a moment? Had he not felt sound, mounting the mare?

His belly grew round and heavy with grass. His back sagged, and the river called Noomah's name.

Now Hair-Like-a-Mane was scratching his withers, making him feel good. He lunged forward to get another sprig of grass. His two-legged's hand stroked him. Hair-Like-a-Mane made the noise Noomah liked, then turned away to the camp of the two-leggeds. Noomah watched him go. He wanted to follow, but he could not walk even that fast. He was slower than a two-legged. That was slower than slow. A gust of wind came from the river, and Noomah remembered what it had felt like to run. To run! He had so loved to run, his two-legged on his back, screaming the wild sounds, passing the other riders, the buffalo, the bleeding enemies. The gust came again from the river and it carried Noomah's name.

He made a lunge, then another, and another. He stopped to rest. He found the easy trail to the water's edge, and hobbled down. The water smelled good. The stinking rotten things did not bother him today. He smelled fresh water. He felt thirsty. The summer sun beat down on him. The water was cool. He would roll and cool himself. The river called him closer.

His name came louder on this day. The river had grown. It moved fast. Almost as fast as Noomah had once loped. It looked good, gliding by, carrying things that once had made Noomah fear its power. Something large and dark floated by on the frothy surface. It was too far away to strike, so Noomah just watched it. He stood now at the water's edge. The thing moved quickly by him.

He lowered his head, touched his muzzle to the surface. He sucked in a drought and felt it cool his throat as he gulped it. He raised his head, carrying a mouthful of water in which to loll his tongue about as if he were chewing it. The water sweetened the taste of green grass yet in his mouth. For a moment, Noomah forgot, and tried to put his weight on his bad leg. But the pain stabbed him and he had to lunge for balance.

He found himself standing in water up to his hocks and knees. The cool river seemed to soothe his pain as it pulled at him. Noomah had always feared the power, but now the river seemed to be inviting him. Might he ride it? The way his two-legged rode his back?

He pawed with his injured hoof. It did not hurt as much as stepping on it. He let it sink into the mud. It felt good. Noomah let his knees buckle and fell sideways in the water with a splash. The power of the river pushed against his belly. The water was cool on his back. He righted himself and, with a great thrust of his powerful hind legs, propelled himself deeper into the stream. He breathed deep, making himself float. It was like gliding above the ground, for Noomah could still feel the soft bottom under him. He was weightless, and he could use even his bad leg to kick and lift his neck and head out of the water.

He turned his tail to the power, and kicked at it. The river answered with his name, mysteriously babbled among all the rushing-hissing-gurgling-trickling-roaring sounds. He began to move with the water at a speed he had not felt since that bad moment in the big fight. He used his injured leg to bounce off the muddy bottom, while the others kicked at the cool power and drove him forward.

He heaved another breath, as in the old days when he would run. He lunged faster forward. Here, Noomah could use his power. Here, even his big belly did not drag upon his back. He was strong and fast. The riverbank slipped by his side, like timber moving by at a gallop. Then he saw the thing again. He was getting closer. The dark thing that floated in the water. He could catch it. He could.

His legs drove him with a fury, and even the bad leg made no pain, though it would not push the way the others did. Noomah did not care. He felt joy. He was moving! He raced the thing—the big tree in the water. The muddy bottom fell away from him and he floated like a spirit-pony. He swam through patches of light and shadow where the sun shone through the timber on the bank. He found a place where the water moved fast. He would catch the thing in the river ahead. He trained his eyes on it and drove onward as he blasted foam from his nostrils.

The tree was just ahead of him now, and it grew weary, for it sulled suddenly, the water piling up against it. It turned, and rolled, and lodged in the mud below it just long enough for Noomah to dodge around it and pass!

Now there was only flat water ahead of him, and the current gathered him into a place that went still faster. Noomah was tired now, but he did not want to stop. Now he knew why the river had called him. He sank lower as he blasted more hot air from this lungs. His body burned with a good feeling of exertion. As he lunged, he felt water rush into his nostrils, but blasted it away. He liked the speed. He would not go back to the grassy banks, where everything stood still.

He used all his strength, and all the power of the river, and went away— far away from the camp of his good two-legged friend. It felt like running. Yes, it felt almost like running. Noomah loved to run.

67

From where he sat on the bluff, Horseback could see the lodges of his camp. In the distance, to the northwest, he could see the set of rocks where his mother had been buried. He could see the bend in the River of Arrowheads around which Medicine-Coat had disappeared. He could see the beautiful shapes the ponies formed against the vast expanse of grass—large bodies, rounded with muscle and fat, powerful legs tapering to mere arrow points that danced upon the earth, graceful necks lifting noble heads, flowing manes, and tails that twitched with contentment.

He sat, and smoked his pipe, and looked at these things. He saw a shadow on the ground, and heard an eagle scream between the shadow and the sun.

He was weary. With a small party, he had ridden far in search of Battle Scar, in search of vengeance for his war pony, and his father. He had failed to find his enemy, but he had gone farther south than any *Noomah* warrior had ever ridden. He had seen strange new things.

He had discovered a new land. A land of hills and timber and clear running streams. A land of people called Tonkawa. It was the land of the lesser deer, a cousin to the great deer Horseback had always known—the animal to whom he paid homage with his taboos. Yet, this lesser deer was not sacred to Horseback, and he could kill it and eat it. It possessed a tail that flashed a white warning. It was good to eat.

There were bees in the land of hills and timber, and much honey. Trees grew there of a sort Horseback had never seen. One bore acorns, yet had small leaves that it held green through the winter. The lesser bear was abundant there, but the greater humpbacked bear did not exist at all. Horseback had followed a good river to this land, looking for his enemy, Battle Scar. He had found only the strange people called Tonkawas, with whom he had communicated in signs. They had advised Horseback that four sleeps south, a village of strange white men had built a large lodge of stone.

Horseback had gone south—only two day's travel for his mounted warriors—and had found the village of white men. They were Metal Men—Spaniards. He spoke to one of the Black Robes there, who was amazed that Horseback knew Spanish and had seen Santa Fe and Taos. This village of Metal Men was called San Antonio de Bexar.

Horseback and his party of explorers had stayed in the land of hills and timber into the winter, yet never saw snow fall. When he asked the Tonkawas why snow did not fall here, they only laughed. This was a place to spend the winter. He camped on a small stream, near a mound made of bones and burnt rocks that showed the Tonkawas had long considered this a good place to camp. He knew he would bring his people here in winters to come, for the low, timbered hills surrounded this stream like a pair of cupped hands holding water to drink. He had felt good camping there, for he never had to watch for the tracks of the greater deer. Only the lesser deer lived in this country of timber and hills. The Tonkawas would be easy to chase away, for they did not know how to ride and fight like Comanches. It was a good place, and he thought of it now, sitting on his bluff in the country of the River of Arrowheads.

His enemies, the *Na-vohnuhs* claimed all this land between the River of Arrowheads and the country of hills and timber. Yet, the Horseback People crossed this *Na-vohnuh* domain whenever they chose, without fear. One day, this would all be Comanche land. And yet, Horseback was weary of war with the *Na-vohnuh*. For many winters he had carried battle to any band of *Na-vohnuh* he could find, stealing ponies, killing warriors, taking women and children to sell to the Metal Men. He had seen friends and young warriors die. His people spoke constantly of war. War, war, war. In the council lodges, the veteran warriors—the Crazy-Dogs and the Foolish Ones, the Swift Foxes, Ravens, Buffalo Bulls, and Afraid-of-Nothings—they all spoke of annihilation—total destruction of all *Na-vohnuh* people, as the Northern Raiders and Crow and *Yuta* and Wolf People had once sought to destroy the True Humans. As the *Na-vohnuh* themselves, in the time of his grandfathers' grandfathers, had once sought to rub out the *Noomah*, almost succeeding.

Horseback was the greatest warrior in all of his nation. He had led the movement south. He had carried the war against Battle Scar and the *Na-vohnuh*. He had wanted total destruction of his enemies. But now, he was weary, and the spirits were speaking to him of changes. Perhaps his people would not understand him at first—especially the wild young warriors seeking glory—but he would begin a new kind of warfare. He had dreamed of it.

Raccoon-Eyes had come to Horseback in a dream vision during last night's sleep. Horseback had expected this ever since Paniagua rode a mule into his camp and informed him of Raccoon-Eyes's death on the Filthy Water. In his dream vision of last night, Raccoon-Eyes had appeared naked, and showed Horseback the wound Bald Man had given him.

"It is not a bad wound," Raccoon-Eyes had said. "In the Shadow Land, it does not hurt. Nothing hurts in the Shadow Land. There are buffalo and elk to hunt. But these are not things for you to think of yet. You have work to do."

"*Hah*," Horseback had said. "I must destroy my enemies."

Raccoon-Eyes had laughed as Horseback had never seen any man laugh. "The destroyer becomes the destroyed. The mistletoe feeds on the tree and thrives. Then the limbs break off, and the mistletoe dies. The sacred way of things that grow is the way of the spirits. Remember what the Metal Men have said about their sheep. Kill the sheep and skin it once. Let it live, and shear it many times."

"What then is my work?" Horseback asked.

"Think of questions the spirits would ask you. Think of Sound-the-Sun-Makes. Think of the Land of the River of Arrowheads where the grass grows and buffalo number like stars. Think of the Land of Hills and Timber, where the lesser deer lives and honey flows from hollow trees. Think of the life you will leave for your grandchildren's grandchildren. Farewell, my friend. I will keep your pony ready for you."

Raccoon-Eyes had turned and walked into a mist that shrouded the pass to the Shadow Land, and Horseback's dream for the rest of the long night was a dream of this mist.

Now he sat on this bluff and looked over the good Land of the River of Arrowheads. He smoked the last of his tobacco and rose to swing up on his pony, a son of Medicine-Coat. Riding down the gently sloping back side of the bluff, he circled to his camp and staked his pony downwind to keep dust out of the cook fires and lodges. He walked into camp and found his wives tending to a buffalo hide.

They were working the heavy robe through a small wooden circle made of a branch bent and tied into a hoop. The hoop was lashed vertically to a scaffold with rawhide, and the women would pull the hide one way, then the other, through the loop, using all their strength to force it through, for the loop was small and the hide fit tightly through it. This would make the robe soft.

Horseback smiled. They worked well together—Teal, Dipper, and Sunshade—often laughing and calling one another sister. Yet, each had her own special talents that she worked at improving. One wife alone would not have had the time to develop such special talents, but one wife among three did.

Teal had learned better than anyone how to train dogs to pull the pole-drags for babies' cradle boards. Mothers from all over the camp wanted dogs trained by Teal, and she traded these dogs for many good things. She also owned her own ponies that she trained to pull the sturdy pony-drags she built.

Dipper liked to sit quietly and work on things like moccasins and shirts, making exquisite quill work, and a new kind of work with beads obtained from the Metal Men.

Sunshade liked to cook, and made almost all the meals enjoyed by Horseback, his wives, their children, and Horseback's Mother, Looks Away, who always ate with Horseback's family.

In addition to these, each wife possessed her own special talents when wrapped in a robe with her husband at night, but Horseback did not mention these, for fear of making his wives jealous of one another.

He stalked within hearing distance of his wives and said, "Teal. I wish to speak with my sits-beside wife."

Teal left the other two women to work with the hide and followed Horseback to his lodge. He sat inside, and she sat beside him.

"I will call the warriors together in a council lodge. I have had a dream vision. I want you and your sister wives to listen outside the lodge when I speak."

"Will you go to make war?" she asked.

"Listen, woman, and you will know. Now, go."

· · · ·

The seasoned men of the Horseback People gathered in the council lodge and smoked. They all looked at Horseback as he rose. He stood there a long time before he spoke. When he began, he looked northward, as if he could see a long way, though the fine cow hides of the council lodge closed all around him.

"When I was a little boy, in the old country of long winters, I saw the best warriors of the Burnt Meat People die defending their women, their children, and their lodges. These men were brave, but our enemies numbered like flocks of geese, and they carried away our women and babies and burned our lodges. The Northern Raiders, the Crow, the Flathead, the Wolf People, and even the *Yutas*, who are now our allies. When I was a boy, the enemies of my people were powerful.

"Now, the True Humans who have come to this new place are powerful. We use the strength or our ponies. It is good here. We eat until our bellies are full. We carry battle to our enemies. We do not move our camp to get away from them."

He paused to look at the prideful visages of his friends. "Yet, I am weary of war with the *Na-vohnuh*. I see young warriors go to count coups and take scalps, yet come back tied to the backs of their ponies. No man wants to die old. But, no boy should die so young.

"I have had a dream vision. A friend has come to visit me from the Shadow Land. I have thought about this dream. I know what it means. I have avenged my grandfathers' grandfathers. No longer must I carry on the ancient war with the *Na-vohnuh*. The battles I fight with them in days to come will be for reasons of now, not reasons of long-ago. Yes, I will raid their camps and take their ponies. I will strike and kill any who challenge me. I will take swift vengeance on any who violate my peace. But, no longer will I kill *Na-vohnuh* warriors to avenge my ancestors. The spirits tell me that I have killed enough. The ancient war is over."

Horseback paused to give his words the weight of stone. He lifted his arms, and shook the long fringes of buckskin on the beautiful antelope-skin shirt Dipper had made for him. "I have found a good new land—the Land of Hills and Timber—far to the south and east. Our enemies hold this land, but my people will take it. The spirits have told me how. We will camp here in the valley of the River of Arrowheads when the hunting for buffalo is good. We will camp in the Land of Hills and Timber when the winters are cold. We will make a trail between these places, and camp wherever we wish to camp along this trail. If our enemies attack us in our camps, we will rub them out.

"This trail between the River of Arrowheads and the Land of Hills and Timber will divide the *Na-vohnuh* nation. It will drive them apart. Some east, some west. They will fear crossing this trail. These *Na-vohnuh* are weak and foolish. They fight among themselves. They do not know how to rise together, though they number far greater than the True Humans who have come to this country.

"There is only one chief among the *Na-vohnuh* who has the power to harm our people. He has gathered many warriors of many *Na-vohnuh* bands. He is sly and cruel. He skulks like a coyote, yet he is as dangerous as a great bear. He keeps many warriors around him to protect him, for he does not have the courage to act alone.

"I have the courage."

Horseback took the time to look at each man's face. The elders sat with mist in their eyes, remembering their own days of strength and bravery. The veteran warriors appeared rigid and ready to fight, their eyes bright and jaws taut. Among them were Trotter and Bear Heart, who had seen much danger and warfare with Horseback. The younger warriors leaned forward with their heads turned, like eager birds listening for the next sound. Among the youngest was Horseback's son, Sandhill, who had made his first hunt, and was eager for his first fight.

"When I was a boy," Horseback said, "The Northern Raiders killed a great warrior of the Burnt Meat People. This warrior's brother went to avenge the killing. The avenger's spirit-guides told him he must take just one scalp as revenge for his brother's death, and though he wanted to kill the whole Northern Raider nation, he honored his spirits. His shadow made more noise than he did as he crept into the camp of those who had killed his brother. He took one scalp, and left his arrow between the heads of two others who did not wake. This warrior was a great man. Greater than great.

"I am going to kill Battle Scar. I go alone. When Battle Scar is dead, the *Na-vohnuh* will be weaker than weak, and never again will the True Humans think of losing this good country. The old war of our ancestors will be a memory. The new war of now will begin. I am Horseback. I have spoken."

68

He rode the son of Medicine-Coat through the pass in the Rat Mountains, taking care to watch for trails of the sacred deer. The pony traveled at a good smooth walk that matched the trot of lesser mounts. Through the broad valley of antelopes he rode to Five Sleeps Mountain, Seven Sleeps Mountain, and Rabbit Ears Mountain, stopping often to smoke and pray.

At the valley of Red Water, he saw a distant camp and recognized the lodges of Whip's people. He saw some warriors riding toward him so he built a fire and piled on green cedar branches to make smoke. Using his saddle blanket, he collected the smoke and sent the signals into the air. *Noomah. Horseback. I go alone.* The warriors from Whip's camp turned back to their lodges. Horseback felt sad, remembering how he had once smoked out rabbits with Whip, long before Whip's heart went bad.

He turned down the river and rode two sleeps and three smokes, until he knew he was near Battle Scar's village. Then he dismounted and hobbled his horse. "Listen, pony. Stay in the timber where your coat matches the shadows. I leave the power of the Shadow-Dog behind. This night, I will use the courage and stealth of my father. When I return, I will bring you a plump mare to breed, and a fresh scalp to sniff, so you will smell the evil blood of my enemies, and learn to hate them as I do."

He painted his body black and waited for Father Sun to plunge his fiery head beyond the west. Then he felt for the medicine bundle in his loin skins, and walked down the river valley. He went cautiously, staying just under the rim of the river breaks where he could sneak through bushes and timber and stay in the darkest shadows. When the last wisps of twilight had melted from the sky, he had to stop and wait for the moon, for the earth had grown black.

He prayed as he waited, and asked Sound-the-Sun-Makes for courage and *puha*. Horseback knew what happened to men killed at night. The same thing that happened to those who died of drowning or choking. Their souls became trapped in their rotting bodies, never to know the Shadow Land. If he failed tonight, his loneliness and shame would last forever.

When the moon rose, half-full, Horseback continued toward the village of Battle Scar. He crept like a lion, for he knew Battle Scar posted scouts. Soon, he breathed his first whiff of the village. It smelled bad, for the *Na-vohnuh* had to stay in the same place from planting time to harvest time, and the stench of their dogs and horses and their own defecations mounted until it rivaled the smell of a putrid, stinking carcass. He was wrinkling his nose at this smell when he saw the scout.

He might have stumbled upon the young warrior, had the enemy not crouched under a dirt bank to strike a Spanish *chispa*. The sparks flew from it in a flash, and the guard was seen making a small fire which he left burning only long enough to light a short deer antler pipe—but long enough to reveal the musket the warrior cradled.

Horseback smiled. The spirits were with him. Now this foolish young scout had fire ghosts in his eyes and would not see. He was hiding under the dirt bank to conceal his fire and his pipe embers from his own people, so that he would not be punished, never thinking that an enemy warrior might see what he hid from his own village.

Horseback crept down the riverbank, keeping out of sight, making no noise at all except for the passing of his own breath and the slight grind of soil under his moccasins. He came to the edge of the river, and slipped in, causing less sound than the river itself. He crouched in the shallow water until his eyes came just above the surface, and let the current carry him downstream. The stream was cool, but Horseback had learned to swim in icy waters when he was a boy. As he drifted with the current, staying in the shadows of the timber, he could see the orange embers of the young scout's pipe on the riverbank above.

He drifted past the corn fields, to the edge of the village, and crawled gradually out of the river, moving so slowly that his face had dried by the time his feet left the water. Now he studied the lodges. He saw a dog sleeping. He heard a pony stamp a foot, for the *Na-vohnuh* warriors kept a few of their best mounts tied in their village. Looking across the tops of the lodges, Horseback saw one in the middle that stood higher than the others, and knew this was Battle Scar's, for the chief liked to surround himself with warriors, and let no one raise a lodge taller than his own.

A child cried in one of the lodges, and Horseback rose to his feet. He passed a stand of three lances holding shields and quivers, and fought off the urge to urinate on the enemy weapons. He walked on silently, stopping often to crouch in the shadows of a lodge or a lone *sohoobi* sapling or a brush sunshade the *Na-vohnuh* had erected.

He saw someone pass among the lodges ahead, whether man or woman, he could not say. He was only three lodges away from Battle Scar's when a snarl ripped through the silence and a whirlwind of fur rushed upon him with teeth popping. The dog sprang, taking Horseback's forearm in its jaws, but his knife was already in his hand, and he slashed upward, cutting deep through the throat. The dog yelped briefly, and Horseback lifted it, clamping his grip hard around its mouth and nostrils. He held the kicking legs above the ground as the hot blood of the dog bathed him.

A man in the nearest lodge scolded the dog in strange *Na-vohnuh* words, but did not come outside. In the same lodge, a woman mimicked the yelp of the dog and giggled. Horseback held the dog until his muscles burned, for the animal was heavy, and he wanted to make sure it would not move when he put it down. His heart pounded furiously, as the couple in the lodge carried on, murmuring and laughing, and he had to call upon his spirit-protector to keep his legs from trembling.

Finally, the blood ceased to run from the carcass of the dog, and Horse-back let it slowly settle to the dirt. He rested in the shadow of a tree and watched Battle Scar's lodge. He moved closer, walking to the next shadow as if he belonged in this village. He heard noises coming from Battle Scar's lodge and knew the old chief was coupling with a woman. He waited, wondering what to do next. The spirits gave no answers, so he waited longer. He took up a position where he could watch the entry to Battle Scar's lodge, yet could duck behind a deer hide lashed to a scaffold should anyone come out of the lodge. *I will avenge you, sacred deer.* There was also a small wood pile to crouch behind. He would wait here, and watch, and seek his chance.

In time, the noises of the coupling stopped in the lodge. Not long afterward, Battle Scar spoke to the woman, and she quickly appeared at the entry to the lodge. Horseback ducked behind the hide of the sacred deer, which shielded him with its spirit-magic, as the woman went to the next lodge and entered it.

Now Horseback waited. He would let Battle Scar sleep. Then he would watch the moon shadows move across the ground until the sleep of his enemy became the sleep of dark nothingness. He judged the angle of the moonlight and looked at the smoke hole of Battle Scar's lodge. When the moonlight fell upon the floor of the lodge, it would be time to enter.

As he waited, crouched behind a low stack of wood, he heard people occasionally moving through the village. Once, he saw a young warrior and a girl slip away together. They passed near the dog he had killed, but failed to see it in their haste to find a secret place. Watching them go, Horseback remembered his words in council, and thought it well that he no longer sought to kill all Na-vohnuh warriors to avenge ancient crimes. Perhaps that young warrior and the girl would make children, and perhaps they would leave the True Humans alone, and not need killing.

Yet, one thing remained certain. Battle Scar needed killing. He had caused the death of Horseback's mother. He had killed Horseback's father with his own hands. He had attempted to defile Horseback's sits-beside wife. He had ruined the finest war pony Horseback would ever ride. Battle Scar was an evil thing lower than a nonhuman two-legged. Lower than a no-legged. Lower than low.

The moon moved into position, and Horseback crept to the entryway of the squatty enemy lodge. Red and white by day, it now looked black and gray. He found that Battle Scar's woman had simply tossed the wolf-skin cover back over the doorway without pegging it fast. Horseback peeled it back as slowly as if it pained him to move it. When finally he could see the floor of the lodge, he slipped one foot in. He could hear Battle Scar's breath, long and heavy.

He ducked his head into the lodge, and pulled his other leg in, now replacing the wolf-skin cover. He waited for the spirits to give his eyes the power to see in the gloomy lodge. At last, he made out Battle Scar's mouth, his lips hanging slack as he lay on his side. The night was warm. Only Battle Scar's legs were covered.

Horseback drew his knife. It had an iron blade long enough to reach a bear's heart, and a handle of bone that fit his grip like a stick in the talon of an eagle. He remembered his father's story. The story helped him fight the urge to cover the last three steps in a headlong pounce. Instead, he chose each footstep before he took it, at last standing over the sleeping body of his foe.

His crouch settled like a fog, and then a joint in Horseback's knee cracked. The eyes opened. Horseback's palm covered the mouth as Battle Scar flinched. The blade of the knife pierced the bare chest, and he felt Battle Scar's teeth sink into his palm as the hands clawed at him. Horseback withdrew the bloody knife and plunged it in again, trying to keep his weight atop the wild throes of the chief as he choked his own cry of pain in his throat.

Quickly, the body of Battle Scar weakened, his heart pierced. The old warrior's arms fell aside, yet he kept his teeth clenched deep in the flesh of Horseback's palm. The pain made Horseback's stomach wrench, but he called upon his powers and leaned his lips toward Battle Scar's ear. Just when he knew the old chief was almost gone, he whispered, "Acaballo . . . Acaballo . . ."

It came out like a hiss, and he knew Battle Scar would understand his name in Spanish. Still he waited. When the teeth loosened their hold on his palm, he fell back from the horrible bloody corpse and withdrew his knife.

Now Horseback's heart began to beat crazily, and he had to lie back on the floor of his dead enemy's lodge to compose himself. As he lay there, he thought about all the ponies he had seen tied in the village. He remembered exactly where he had seen them, and thought about which ones he would steal first. His hand hurt badly, but he knew he could ignore it. Horseback had often endured more.

Determined now, he rose and drew the single arrow from his quiver. With his good hand, he raised it above his head and stabbed it into the center of the lodge floor. He threw the wolf-skin flap aside and looked out. No one. He stepped into the night and went to the first pony. Grunting in the pony talk he had learned as a boy, he approached the animal and cut the stake rope tied to the forefoot. He moved silently away, knowing the pony would take some time discovering that he had been cut loose.

He crept among the lodges and found the second pony, slicing through its rope with the bloody knife blade. Then he approached the third, and cut it loose as well. He moved like an owl to the fourth, then scanned the village, seeing just one pony left.

He heard the first pony stamp and knew the animal had discovered his freedom. No longer did Horseback creep like a lion. He felt the power of the sacred deer in his heart and made long strides to the fifth and last horse. This horse shied, tripping as it reached the end of its rope, hitting on its shoulder with a thud. Someone grumbled in a nearby lodge. Horseback pulled up on the stake to free it, then pounced on the pony's neck to keep the animal down. He cut the rawhide rope from the animal's forefoot, and doubled it as he let the pony rise. Hooves scrambled all across the ground. Horseback hooked one arm over the pony's neck and made the loop for the war bridle, which he forced into the pony's mouth. As he swung onto the back of the dancing mount, he heard more voices, saw a skin fly aside from the doorway of a lodge.

The pony was well trained, as he had expected from one staked in camp. Horseback raised a shrill cry of victory that burst loose like a trapped animal held in too long. He pounded through the village, gathering the ponies he had cut loose. Cries of men and women rose from the lodges, and many noises rolled together into one big sound.

He pushed the good ponies toward the herd of loose ponies, determined now to have them all, so that he could not be pursued. One of the stolen animals stepped on his own stake rope and tripped, but Horseback knew the ropes would soon break short or fall off. An arrow pierced a lodge cover to one side, and he leaned lower, wishing this enemy pony wore the loop in which he could rest his arm. No choice now but to ride. Ride!

The pony was good, helping him gather the others, and they burst into the bean field as a musket shot erupted from behind. It only made the horses run faster, and they galloped into the herd of loose mounts. Now everything stampeded up the river valley, and Horseback sat upright, his arms raised in triumph. He had only to make it beyond the scouts, and he was free.

He remembered the place where he had seen the young warrior smoking his pipe, and thought perhaps he should have killed this scout to create an escape route. Yet, he felt powerful now, and knew the spirits would shield him. He saw Smoker come out of the timber, the moonlight a dull glint on his musket. He thundered by, a clear target, as the warrior shouldered the weapon. He thought about Trotter, and his gun. How long would it take to latch back the snake-thing and pull the trigger?

The spirits told him how long it would take. Horseback grabbed the mane of the stolen pony, slid off on the side away from the young scout. At a full gallop, he held the mane and let both legs swing forward alongside the churning hooves of the pony. His moccasins hit the dirt as the musket fired. He heard the ball whistle, and the speed of the pony launched his body backward and upward. Holding tight to the mane, his legs spread and he landed behind the withers, solid, like the handshake of Spaniards.

Now he laughed at the useless gunshots from far behind. He was thinking that young Smoker was probably fearing Battle Scar would have him put to death, and this made Horseback laugh harder, for Battle Scar himself was dead. Dead! Killed in his own lodge with the name of Acaballo hissing in his ears! They would tell the story in times to come, around the fires of the storytellers, in the winter lodges of the elders. He had taken all the ponies. All the ponies!

He screamed a war cry—part lion, part stallion, part red-tailed hawk—and felt the spirit of Medicine-Coat possess the pony he now rode. Hooves thundered like the roaring fires of the sun. Ahead of him lay a long journey to the lodges of his people, but that would only give him time to search his heart. He must prepare his talk for the gathering that would celebrate his return.

Already, Horseback knew how to begin. He would look upon the joyful faces of his people and say:

"On the day of my birth, a pony circled my lodge. This was not just any pony, but the very first my people ever saw. The elders told me that it tasted pretty good . . ."